$ 1

The Cumberland Plateau

One God, One King

The Prince

Men have less hesitation about offending one who makes himself loved than one who makes himself feared, for love is held together by a chain of obligation which, because men are sadly wicked, is broken at every opportunity to serve self interest, but fear is maintained by a dread of punishment which never abandons you.

—Niccolò Machiavelli 1513

Un dieu, un roi

D'Arcy

Jane Austen's Pride and Prejudice continues with this modern day sequel. Set in the mountains of Tennessee, **The Cumberland Plateau** is a story of innocence and purity, reckless desire and abandonment, love and betrayal, faith and hope, and family heritage and pride. It is a story of strong men and the women who loved them as they struggle to become the men they were born to be.

Derbyshire, England

The Cumberland Plateau

A Pride and Prejudice Modern Sequel

M. K. Baxley

White Dove Press

The Cumberland Plateau is a work of fiction. Although some of the characters are inspired from historical records, they are used fictitiously. All other characters are either from the author's imagination, or from Jane Austen's novel, **Pride and Prejudice**.

No part of this book may be reproduced without prior permission. If you wish to contact me, please do so at <u>mkbaxley@bellsouth.net</u>

ISBN-10:   1440458561
EAN-13:   9781440458569

© Copyright March 9, 2007 by Mary K. Baxley

All rights are reserved.

First Edition: July 2009

Cover photographs courtesy of Cokie Lewis of the United States and Richard Bird of the United Kingdom.

Cover and internal design © M. K. Baxley 2009

Dedication

This is a book of second chances to

All who have ever loved and lost because…

Sometimes we don't forget.

To

Mary Frances and her Jim

And to

Linda Jane Barnett

We are never too old

A Special Thank You to:

Jennifer Conder for the engraving on the Bennet gravestone, and to my critique partner Naima Bryant. Without Naima, I would have been lost. She kept me on track. Also, I wish to thank my close friend and best selling author, Debra Webb, who constantly reassured me that I could do this, and my best friend Linda B. Haines. Finally, thanks to all the ladies of Jane Austen Fan Fiction, especially Mary Anne Heinz and Debbie Styne for their encouragement, friendship, and most of all, their attempt to make this story readable. Without the above aforementioned, this novel might never have been.

And last, but not least, a special thanks to Richard Bird for his photographs of the Peaks District in Derbyshire, England, and to Cokie Lewis for the photos of The Methodist Church, the old cabin in Cades Cove, Tennessee, and the Old Stone Bridge on Hwy. 90 in Kentucky. All other photographs were taken by me. The old cemetery is from my family home place in Fuga, Tennessee, and the newer one is from a public cemetery in rural Tennessee. The others are of farm lands in Lincoln and Moore Counties of Middle Tennessee.

Longbourn Baptist Church and John Bennet's Cabin

Meg and Ron Bennett

Older Part of Longbourn Cemetery

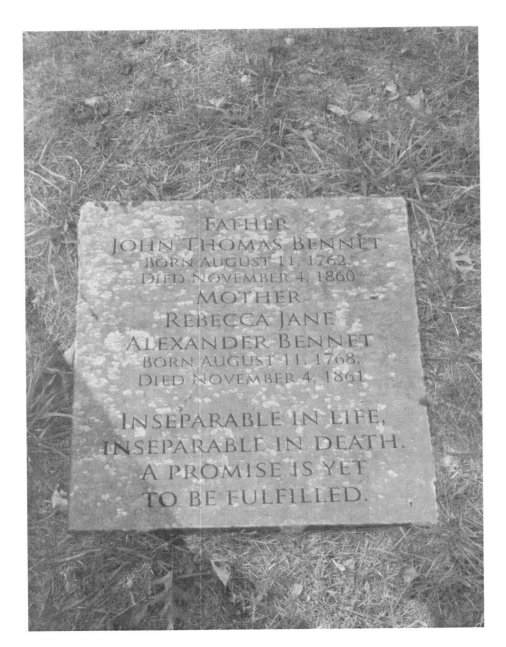

FATHER
JOHN THOMAS BENNET
BORN AUGUST 11, 1762,
DIED NOVEMBER 4, 1860
MOTHER
REBECCA JANE
ALEXANDER BENNET
BORN AUGUST 11, 1768,
DIED NOVEMBER 4, 1861

INSEPARABLE IN LIFE,
INSEPARABLE IN DEATH.
A PROMISE IS YET
TO BE FULFILLED.

John and Rebecca's Grave

Prologue

... we will oncef again be as one ...

6 September 1789

Hertfordshire, England

J ohn Bennet sat on a stone bench in the garden of his ancestral home with his father's words still stinging his ears. *...If you marry her, I cannot support you. You will be disinherited.* He released a heavy breath and rose to his feet. John walked a few steps to the nearest apple tree and plucked one from a low hanging branch. Inhaling deeply, he contemplated his options.

He shook his head and cursed as he took a bite from the apple in his hand. There were none that could satisfy both his father and himself. The thought of sending Rebecca Jane away and placing their child in the house of a stranger was unbearable, and then to discreetly marry the woman he loved off to some man of lesser means tore at his conscience.

John glanced back at the house. Since birth, his father had groomed him to be the Master of Longbourn and that had been his desire. With an income of two to three thousand a year, his life would be set and predictable, but little had he realized that everything would change the day he had laid eyes on Rebecca Jane Alexander—the woman whose clear blue eyes had taken him captive from the first of their acquaintance.

John smiled as he recalled their first meeting. It had been an unusually warm autumn evening. He had been celebrating a prosperous harvest season with drink and fine cigars at his club in London when he and two friends had decided to visit the White House, a brothel in Soho Square for an evening of pleasure. When they entered the establishment, his eyes were immediately drawn to the fair haired woman with the beautiful blue eyes. Eyes that bore little pleasure in what she saw, and yet he felt compelled to know her. He later learned that he was to be her first customer, and since she had to release her virtue to someone, she had told him she was glad it would be to him and not to a hideous older man.

As he leaned against the tree trunk, he recalled how he had felt that night. Somehow, his pursuit of pleasure had dwindled into a desire to know the beautiful woman with the forlorn eyes. They had talked into the early morning hours, and when the dawn came, he was loath to leave her. Miss Alexander told him everything. She had told him of how her father had died, leaving her alone and penniless, and how she had been taken in by a family friend.

As the young ward of a country squire, she had been forced to leave when his eldest son had formed an attachment to her, a dowerless girl with no connections. She had been released to the streets of London with a mere ten shillings and had had to struggle to survive until Madam Kinsley spied her dressed in little more than rags. It appeared no one would help her. No one cared until she had met Victoria Kinsley. The madam had been kinder than most and had invited her to live at White House offering her protection and food and all the luxuries she could desire.

Janey, as he now called her, had been cold and hungry and was soon to face London's workhouse. Consequently, she had reluctantly accepted Madam Kinsley's offer. John remembered well how she had bowed her head in shame as she told him that sometimes beauty can be a curse to a woman, especially if she were poor with no family. John recollected how he had felt upon hearing her words as she laid her head upon his shoulder and placed her hand over his heart.

He shook his head and groaned. He had never considered how a woman with no protector might be forced to live a life not of her own choosing, and he shuddered at the thought of his sisters, especially Elizabeth, so full of life, being forced into such an existence, or gentle Emily, soft and modest, or even the vivacious twins, Emma and Mary. If it were within his power to prevent it, none of his sisters would ever face that grim reality—not while he or Edward drew breath.

It was that night as John lay there holding his Janey, that a tenderness swept over him, and he resolved that no one else but him would have her. Thus, he had made arrangements with Madam Kinsley to set her aside for his personal use. It cost him half his annual income, but she was the only woman he had ever wanted, and if he could not marry her, he would have her anyway he could. He would protect her.

Subsequently their relationship had been sealed, and his love for her deepened with each encounter. He saw her twice a week until a sennight ago when suddenly she had become despondent, refusing to see him. Try as he might, he could not persuade her to tell him the reason for her distress. Therefore, he had been left to wonder—that is, until he had received word from her closest friend, another courtesan, Susan Quentella. Janey was with child and terrified—terrified with the choice of either terminating her confinement or facing London's squalor.

John stared off into the expanse of his family estate. With his back against the tree, he raised the apple and took another bite. As he thought over the situation, he knew he was faced with a choice that would alter the course of his life forever. If he married Janey, his family would be disgraced. They would never be received in polite society again, and his sisters' chances of making a good match would be ruined. His father would never forgive him. And if he did not marry her, her life and that of his child would be destroyed. With either choice he made there were heavy consequences. His only consolation was his brother, Edward, who had promised to remain by his side no matter the cost. But could he really do this to Edward? He shook his head as he tossed the half-eaten apple away. Did he really have a choice? He loved Janey. He had from their first night together, and the thought of her alone with his child was unbearable.

John pushed away from the tree and began to pace about the garden. He would marry her and risk it all, even at the peril of losing his family. Janey and his child were also his family, and as a gentleman, he could do no less than the honorable thing. And if it was necessary, they would leave—possibly to America. Several of his friends, all younger sons with little prospect for living comfortably in England, were leaving. Some had already left and returned with tales of adventure and wealth to be made in the Southern states of Virginia and South Carolina. America was a land of opportunity with the promise of a new life. He had one other person to speak with concerning the venture, and then he would decide. The only problem with his plan was that his allowance was nearly spent. He knew neither how he would obtain the money to leave, nor what fate would await them once they arrived.

John's introspection was interrupted by the sound of fast approaching footsteps. He turned to catch his brother's grim face.

"John, Father wants to see you in his study. He is quite adamant about it. You had best come. He is still rather upset, but I think I might have calmed him a bit. It will work out, Brother. It will."

"I wish I shared your optimism," John said.

"Come to the house," Edward replied as he clapped his brother's back. "I have struck a bargain with Father. I know you wish to leave, and I wish it were not so, but if you are insistent on marrying Miss Alexander, then I fear you have no choice. If that be your decision, then as a wedding present, I will give you one hundred pounds from my allowance for the voyage. I want you to have the best accommodations and a little to spare when you get there."

John turned and gazed upon his younger brother. "You would do that? What about Fanny? You are to be married in a fortnight. Will she approve?"

"It matters not what Fanny thinks. It is my money, and she has no say. In fact, she is to know nothing of the matter."

"I see." John sighed as they solemnly walked. "Then I shall accept your offer."

As they entered the house, they immediately approached Thomas Bennet's library and study. With a knock on the door, the familiar deep voice resounded, causing John to tense once more.

"Enter."

Both brothers quickly did as the voice commanded, taking seats across from their father's dominating desk. Thomas Bennet poured two brandies and pushed them towards his sons.

"I suppose by now your brother has spoken with you. Is that not so?"

"It is." John answered with a curt nod.

"Then you know that I have come to terms with your declarations as of the last few days."

"Yes, sir."

"Well, what you do not know are the terms and conditions of my decision," Thomas Bennet said as he looked between his two sons. "Edward, John, this is what I have determined. As for you, Edward, I am not wholly pleased with your upcoming nuptials to Frances Gardiner. Her connections do not raise the family's standing one iota. In fact, with her being from trade, they lower it. However, I have not denied you since you appear to be a love struck fool hell bent on doing as you please."

He glanced at his older son. "And John, as you know, I cannot give you my blessing. Yet, this is what I shall do. Tomorrow I will leave for London and see my solicitor. The will shall be changed. Edward will become my legal heir, and all that I have will pass to him, but given the direction I see things going, I shall have an entailment placed upon the estate. It shall only pass through the male line of this family. No female shall inherit it, and it shall not be broken apart and sold piecemeal," Thomas said calmly as he glanced to his younger son. "Edward, it shall be up to you to provide the said heir. If not then my cousin, Thaddeus Collins shall inherit it."

Then he turned his eyes towards John. "As for you, I shall give you five thousand pounds in gold. That will be all you shall ever have from me. If you carry on with your foolhardy plans, none of your sons shall have any part of Longbourn. Is that understood?" his father asked with a contrite voice.

"Perfectly."

"Then you are unmoved in your decision?"

M.K. Baxley

"I am."

"Go then, and God bless you. If it were not for your sisters, I might have been more amenable, but you do understand what is at stake here, do you not?"

"I do."

The old man rose from his desk and approached his sons, tears glistening in his eyes. Both sons rose to meet him. "I love you both," he said as he reached and hugged his older son, before turning to walk away.

30 September 1789

On a cold dank morning, two brothers stood on a lonely loading dock at early dawn, waiting for the ship to board. The pitiless cry of seagulls was heard in the distance, and the pungent smell of saltwater and decaying fish permeated the air. The older brother gently wrapped a woolen shawl a little tighter over his wife's shoulders. "Go aboard, my love. I shall join you soon. I would like a few moments of privacy with my brother."

"Of course, I understand. I shall be waiting below. Take what time you need," she said with tenderness reflected in her clear blue eyes.

As Rebecca Jane left them alone on the dock, John turned to his brother. "Edward, this is perhaps the most bittersweet time of my life. I love Janey. You know that, but leaving you and the girls is much more difficult than I ever imagined. You must look after them in my stead and see that all is well with them, and look after Mother, too. She kept to her room and would not see me before I left. I know she is devastated, but assure her of my love. I will write as soon as we reach Virginia. I *shall* keep in touch."

Edward Bennet stepped forward and took his brother's proffered hand as he clapped John's shoulder, giving him an embrace of solidarity. "I shall," Edward said with a solemn nod. "The girls wanted to come and see you off, and you know they would have, had not Father intervened. Elizabeth will marry Mr. Simmons next month, and Mr. Amite has requested to court Emma. Emily will probably remain unmarried. She has professed a desire to serve God, and I fear is considering converting to Catholicism and joining an order of nuns. It would be a good decision for her, as she dearly loves our Lord. She shall do well in whatever choice she makes, but Mary is another matter. God grant a stout measure of mercy to the man who marries her," Edward said with a laugh to break the grimness of the moment.

"Aye, she is quite a rambunctious handful with a sharp tongue to match, but she is a good girl," John returned. "Now, before I go, I must tell you that even though I shall not return, a day will come when Father is gone that I shall send a daughter or a son to you. I know not the hour nor the day or even the year, but this I know, we will once again be as one, and our families will reunite. This, my brother, I solemnly swear to you before God and heaven above. We shall be reunited."

"And I solemnly swear to you, my brother, that I shall name my first son after you and my first daughter after Jane. As I have come to know her, I have come to love her as a sister." Both brothers glanced to the side. All but John had boarded. Edward drew in a deep breath. "Goodbye, John. I shall be waiting. Together we shall join in cutting off the entail as soon as my son is of age, thus allowing for my widow and younger children to be provided for."

"Yes, we shall. An entailment is a dangerous thing. Father will regret it."

With unshed tears, the two brothers embraced before John turned and walked up the ramp to the ship and his new life in America that awaited him.

4

The Legend of the Snow White Mourning Dove

There is an Indian legend told in the mountains far and wide. It is a folklore that is old—very old. The Cherokee say that for every living thing there is a plan and a purpose in the circle of life, and when a soul departs with his purpose unmet, that soul cannot find rest until the matter is set to right. And in the fullness of time, a pair of snow white mourning doves will appear and keep watch over the living until the purpose is accomplished and the circle is once again complete. Only then are the birds set free, and the spirits find their rest.

—Emily Jane Bennett

Longbourn Farm

Chapter One

...he could easily imagine her bareback on a horse, wearing nothing but her hair...

June 2006

Harry Dickens sat at a table in the back of White's Gentlemen's Club. It was a hot hazy summer day in London, and the smog was thick, almost stifling. He sat patiently watching the entrance and occasionally glancing at his watch. He had been here for quite some time, anxious to meet with at least one of his former Oxford classmates. Being well past teatime, he was about to leave when they appeared. He rose to greet them.

"Darcy, Bingley, you're just the two I've been looking for," Dickens said, approaching them with a wide grin.

"Dickens, what are you doing here? I thought you'd taken an academic position somewhere in the States," Fitzwilliam Darcy answered, shaking Harry's offered hand.

"Yes, I have. My wife and I are visiting family, but I have another reason for being here," Dickens said as he shook Bingley's hand next. "I have been thinking about our conversation last autumn. Are you two still interested in teaching positions?"

"Well, that depends on what and where, I suppose. I've been working with my father at Pemberley, but as we've discussed before, teaching is what I've always wanted to do." Darcy wrinkled his brow. "What do you have in mind?"

Suggesting they take a seat, Dickens asked, "How about you, Bingley, are you still interested?"

"It depends, Harry, what are you offering?"

"Well, since you asked, I'll come to the point." Dickens smiled. "I'm the dean of a liberal arts college, which at the present is very small in a moderately-sized engineering university. The Cumberland College of Liberal Arts is wanting, and it's my intention to change that. We now offer a minor in classical studies, but there's an interest in bringing that up to a major." He glanced between his friends with a wide smile. "I'm looking for two professors who can take on that challenge. I need someone who can teach classical Greek and Latin." He turned to face his old friend. "Darcy, if my memory serves me right, that's your field of expertise."

"Yes," Darcy chuckled, "Greek and Latin are two of my favorite subjects, and I'm well versed in them, as well as ancient philosophy and ancient history. Although I do not hold a D.Phil. in either of them, I have studied them extensively."

"Then I'm correct. You're perfect for the position." Glancing at Bingley, he added, "Bingley, your area of proficiency is Classical Literature, is it not?"

"That it is. My D.Phil. is in Classical Languages and Literature, but literature is my preference." Bingley nodded.

"Ah, I thought so," he said, grinning. "Do you two still want a chance to share what you've learnt at Oxford?" he asked, pulling out three cigars, offering one to each of his friends. "You both have the qualifications for the positions, and the pay is reasonable, although I know neither of you need the income. But I believe the experience would be well worth it." He lit his cigar, and then offered them a light.

"Dickens, precisely where is this college located?" Darcy asked, his curiosity now fully engaged.

"I'm glad you asked that, Darcy. It's located on a plateau, the Cumberland Plateau to be exact, in eastern middle Tennessee, surrounded by the Appalachian Mountains.

M.K. Baxley

The natives call it God's country, and I have to agree. It has some of the most beautiful scenery on earth. It'll remind you of both Northern England and Scotland. In fact, the Scotch Irish settled the area some 200 years ago. Quite a few families there are from English descent, too," he added. "I think you'll find it very peaceful and serene."

Handing Darcy and Bingley his business card, he continued. "Look it up online under the university website, and then search for the Cumberland Plateau. See for yourselves. I'm sure you will like what you see, and if you're interested, I'll arrange for a tour. Then if it suits you, at that point we can discuss the particulars. I am at the liberty to offer you both a full professorship. So, what do you say; will you think about it?"

"Dickens, we'll take a look, and let you know," Darcy answered as he and Bingley exchanged glances. "Give me a number where we can reach you whilst you're in England, and we'll be in touch."

"Once you see how grand an opportunity this is," Dickens said with a quick nod, "I'm sure you will."

One Month Later

Driving the long winding road through the Appalachian Mountains of Tennessee, Elizabeth Bennett was on her way home. After eight long years in Boston with rarely a break, she'd finally earned her degrees. It hadn't been easy getting into the Massachusetts Institute of Technology in the first place, but she'd made it all the way, earning her PhD. in mathematics. However, *that* she owed to her parents. They'd worked hard as university professors, struggling to raise six kids on a farm. They had educated them all at home with the benefit of tutors so she and her siblings could receive a classical education, something not available in the rural South, and it had paid off. She, her sister, Jane, and her brother, Joseph, had all been Merit Scholars.

Approaching the town limits, Elizabeth let out a long breath. After all she'd gone through, Walnut Grove wasn't where she had wanted to begin her career. No, she had wanted to teach in Charleston and had considered applying for a position at either Clemson or the Citadel, but a little over two years ago everything changed. Now, after spending most of the summer in Charleston with her former roommate and best friend, Cecilia Lawton, she was returning to help Jane with the farm and to teach at the local university, the very university where her parents had taught.

Rounding the corner onto Elm Street, Elizabeth spied Jane with a concerned look, waiting on the front porch of their Victorian townhouse. No sooner had Elizabeth pulled into the driveway and stopped the car, than Jane flew to meet her.

"Lizzy, you're late—fashionably late, as usual," Jane scolded, hands planted squarely on her hips. "I was so worried that I called Celia to see if you were still there. You still have that annoying habit of turning off your cell phone while driving, I see."

"Jane, you know how I feel about cell phones and driving, and there was no need to worry." Elizabeth hugged her sister. "I stopped in Knoxville to tour the Mountain Flea Market. Here," she reached back into the car for a shopping bag. "I bought you a beaded necklace," she said, pulling the silver and turquoise choker from the sack.

"I also bought one for Kat and a handmade leather wallet for Daniel. And," she said with a wide smile, "I got us all a pair of Indian moccasins, too. Check these out." She pulled a pair of tan fringed leather boots from the bag. "They look just like those elfish boots the elves wore in *The Lord of the Rings*. Now, help me with these bags, and let's get this stuff inside."

Elizabeth handed Jane several more packages and then unloaded her Durango, setting the suitcases on the walkway. Once unloaded, they took everything to the porch, one by one, chatting away as they went.

Walking up the brick walkway with the final load, Jane's expression turned somber. "Still, you should have advised me of your plans, Lizzy. I was really worried. Next time call, young lady! Or keep your phone turned on!"

"Oh, you worry too much! You know perfectly well I do *not* talk on the phone while driving. You know the state motto—Arrive Alive."

"Lizzy, that's *Florida's* state motto." Jane rolled her eyes. "Did you at least check your messages?"

Elizabeth laughed. She knew perfectly well whose state motto it was, but she couldn't help teasing her sister. "Yes, Jane, I did just before shutting the engine off, but I'm here now, so there was no need to call. Besides, Florida is in the South. It's all the same to me."

Jane shook her head as they carried the bags into the house and up the stairs.

Once comfortably settled into the townhouse, Jane suggested they tour the campus. She was already teaching in the English Department, but this term would be Elizabeth's first teaching position, so after the last item was put neatly in its place, they headed towards the university on foot.

Elizabeth inhaled deeply the sweet smells of summer…the scent of fresh cut grass, honeysuckle growing along the fencerow, and the cool earthy smell of the mountains. Years had passed since she had walked the beautiful campus of Cumberland Technological University. Leisurely strolling across campus, she enjoyed the calm of the familiar old stone buildings along with the pleasant sounds of birds chirping and lawnmowers humming—sounds Elizabeth associated with summertime in the mountains. As she walked in silent meditation, Jane's enthusiastic voice interrupted her concentration.

"Lizzy, you're going to like teaching here. I know it's small, but this is home. We have the Bennett townhouse and can go home to Longbourn on weekends."

At the mention of the farm, Elizabeth smiled. It was the one place on earth she could find solace. "How is the farm, Jane? It's been a while since I was last there. As soon as I'm settled in here, I'm heading out."

"You haven't missed a thing. It's the same old place," Jane replied, flashing her sister a beautiful smile. "By the way, speaking of farms, how is Celia? How are her research projects coming along, and who is she dating now? "

Elizabeth laughed. "She's the same as always. She splits her spare time between Carlton and Lawton Hall." Turning to catch Jane's gaze, she continued. "Oh, Jane, you should see the rice at Carlton! It's so pretty poking up through the marshes in waves of green. It's like a carpet of soft emerald velvet blowing in the breeze, and the cotton on St. Helena is gorgeous. This year may very well be the year it pays off, putting Lawton Hall back in business as a real Sea Island Cotton plantation," Elizabeth said with a smile.

"Now, as to who she's dating, well, she's not dating anyone noteworthy. Lawton & Co. and the research projects are keeping her busy during the day. At night, she's either entertaining clients or out with some new guy she's met, but no one in particular." Elizabeth stopped and slapped away a buzzing insect.

Jane's brow creased. "Lizzy, I worry about Celia. She's as kind and good as a person can be, but when it comes to men, she's reckless. It's as if she cannot love them."

Elizabeth frowned. Cecilia worried her, too, and she agreed with Jane's assessment.

M.K. Baxley

Cecilia was not only as kind of a person as you would ever want to meet, but an extremely beautiful person, too. However, with men, she was as cold as she was beautiful.

Elizabeth shook her head. "Celia's been through a lot, Jane. I agree that she's reckless, and I know she can be a user, but it's all she's ever known. And she knows men, too. Most of them are users, as we both well know. But as she says, Celia's nobody's fool. No, with men it's on her terms, not the other way around. But I have a feeling someday things are going to catch up with her when she finally meets a man who's just as shrewd and calculating as she is."

Jane laughed. "I think you're right, Lizzy, and he'll be the one who sweeps her off her feet. She's the kind that will give her heart only once. I just hope the man who captures it is worthy. And I agree, underneath that icy veneer beats the heart of a real woman. The man who wins her love will have to be someone just like her, someone who is every bit as hard-nosed as she is. Any other man wouldn't stand a chance with her in a long term relationship, much less a marriage." Jane gazed at Elizabeth, shaking her head. "She's a modern day Scarlet O'Hara who needs a modern day Rhett Butler. Only I don't know if there are any Rhetts around."

They walked in silence until Elizabeth broached a new subject. "You know, Jane, I had planned on taking a position in Charleston, had I not come here. I wanted to be at Clemson or the Citadel," Elizabeth said, kicking a dandelion seed head.

"I know, Lizzy. But you'll like it here. I feel that I am actually accomplishing something with the English Lit classes I teach, and I love the theatre program we started last year. Dr. Dickens has scheduled me to teach a class in the new classical studies program this fall. It'll be so much fun." Jane laughed as they headed toward the University Center.

Elizabeth gazed fondly upon her sister. "Jane, Jane, you enjoy anything you set your mind to. However, I'm sure you're right, and I will enjoy my students as much as you do yours. I've been looking forward to teaching ever since I graduated, though I do have the first job jitters."

"Lizzy, you'll do just fine. As smart and dedicated as you are to your profession, the students are going to love you and who couldn't? You are the most caring person I know."

They both laughed.

"Thanks, Jane, but you're still going to help me with my Greek grammar, aren't you? I never had the chance to continue my studies while working on my degrees."

"You know I will. We should have the time. Daniel and Kat will be here, but Kat's rarely home. She's busy with study groups and activities, and Daniel will be very busy with his first year in civil engineering. With all of that, we will have time for our own amusements. What classical books we don't have in our own libraries we can get from the school library, or better yet, buy them." Their laughter turned to girlish giggles.

As the two girls walked and talked, an English gentleman observed them from the upstairs window of Morton Hall. He and his friend had arrived several days before as prospective professors for a one week tour of the university and surrounding area.

"I say, Dickens," Bingley inquired, "you sure have some very pretty girls here. Are those two students?"

Dickens walked over to the window and peered out to see who had caught his friend's eye. "I'm not sure about the one with dark hair, but the blonde is Dr. Jane Bennett. She's a third-year associate professor in the English Department, and I've asked her to teach one of the classical studies courses this fall. She has a PhD. in

10

English with a MA in classics from Harvard. She's one of my most dedicated professors," he added. "Umm…Yes, I suppose she is pretty." Dickens grinned as he looked from Dr. Bennett to his old friend.

While the two bantered about, Darcy gazed at the dark haired woman, struck by her simple beauty. He breathed deeply as he watched her walk. A pair of well-fitted jeans with a hole in one knee accentuated her shapely derriere while the simple white tee shirt she wore clung to her ample bosom. She was neither too thin nor too plump, and her long black hair hung in a low ponytail well past her hips almost to her knees. Darcy had never seen such long hair. Bewitching with a captivating smile, she looked as he had always pictured Lúthien Tinúviel, the beautiful dark haired elfish princess from the *Tale of Beren and Lúthien* in Tolkien's **The Silmarillion**. He could easily imagine her bareback on a horse, wearing nothing but her hair, like Lady Godiva. A smile curved his lips as he watched her walk, but thinking she was probably a student, he shook his head, dismissing those thoughts.

"Well, Dickens, if for no other reason, I might just take this job just for a chance to meet this Dr. Bennett," Bingley said, smiling as he watched the beautiful blonde stroll toward the University Center.

"Bingley, your motivation should be the teaching opportunity before you, not the local crumpet," Darcy scolded.

"Darcy, you hold your own counsel," Bingley rebuked with a chuckle. "As for myself, I believe it never hurts to be friendly or to have double motivation."

"Yes, but Bingley, I know how you are! You've never been able to meet a pretty woman without imagining yourself in love."

"And someday I will find myself with a true love, when the right woman comes along," Bingley said with a sly smile.

Darcy didn't bother adding anything to the exchange. He was far too preoccupied with the dark-haired beauty.

Jane had given Elizabeth a brief tour of the university and had taken her to the University Center for a Coke float. Elizabeth had three weeks until she had to officially report to the university to prepare for her classes.

Walking back to the townhouse, Jane asked, "Are you going to spend the next several weeks at the farm, then?"

"Yes, I think I will. Uncle Henry's been complaining about some problems with the summer calves, and I need to spend time with my hounds. It's been over two years since I spent any quality time with them, and even then, it was brief. My Black and Tans are getting old, and I really do miss them."

"Well, give Grace, Aunt Lori, and Uncle Henry my love then, and I'll see you next week. I need to finish up with things here. Then I need to go to my office and look over this term's course of study. It's been forever since I've even looked at *The Medieval Romance of Pagan Antiquity*, and I've never taught it. I've really got my work cut out for me. When that's all done, I'll meet you at the farm. Oh, and stop by the Cut and Curl. Bette and Florence have been asking about you."

"The Barnett gossip hub?" Elizabeth arched a brow.

"Lizzy, that is unkind, and you know it," Jane reprimanded.

"I know, Jane, but you know how I feel about gossip, but I'll stop by to please you."

Jane gave a small smile. "No, Lizzy, do it for momma. It's what she would have wanted. Family is important." With that, Jane waved good-by and turned to walk back into the townhouse.

M.K. Baxley

Elizabeth rolled her eyes and hopped into her Durango. She made her way to the town square and a little shop on a side street where the Cut and Curl, better known as the Walnut Grove gossip shop, was located. After hearing the latest news and paying her respect to her aunts, she was finally free to go.

In her car once again, she tuned the radio to her favorite country station and set out for the farm with Montgomery Gentry for company. The drive to Longbourn Farm didn't take long. It was about twenty miles outside of town, down County Road 52 and off to the right on a dirt road. Bouncing over the bumps in the road, Elizabeth tapped out the beat of *Daddy Won't Sell the Farm* on her steering wheel, thinking of her own family farm.

Longbourn Farm had been in the Bennett family for over two hundred years. They had survived the Civil War, the Great Depression, and the panic of farm foreclosures in the 1980s. Not only had they survived, but they were among the leading families of the Cumberland Plateau.

Proud of her family history, she was pleased that she could trace it back to the 17th century in the South of England. She possessed several journals containing a wealth of information about her family and the history of the Western Expansion, pioneer life, and the rise and fall of the Old South. Yes, she thought to herself, the Bennetts were a hearty people. On the pages of the old journals, it was all recorded: the good, the bad, and the ugly. All things considered, Elizabeth mused as she pulled into the covered parking area of the farm, the Bennett family had been made up of good people carving out a legacy in this new land known as America. As soon as she opened the car door, she saw her younger sister, Kat, waiting on the tire swing under the old oak tree.

"Lizzy! You've come home! I thought you would never get here." Kat shouted, flying to the car and flinging herself into her sister's embrace.

"I got into town about three hours ago, and I've already moved into the townhouse. Jane gave me a tour of the campus, but I had to stop by the Cut and Curl, and you know how Bette and Florence are. They talked a blue streak. However, I'm here now, and I won't leave until the week before fall semester begins."

Kat laughed. "Oh, I know how Bette and Florence are. Of course, they had to fill you in on the latest gossip, and I'm sure you heard all about Liddy and her new boyfriend."

"Yes," Elizabeth laughed, "they filled me in on all the sordid details."

"I would imagine so. It's the hottest topic in town. Everybody's talkin' about it."

"That's what I was afraid of. Liddy is her own worse enemy." Elizabeth sighed.

"Well, I would agree with that, but let's not talk about her." Kat said. "Let's talk about us."

"All right," Elizabeth replied, "Tell me what you and Daniel have been up to?"

"Oh, not much, really. He's out riding with some of his friends, and I've been patiently waiting for you. But Lizzy, why do you have to go back a week early? I want us to spend all the time we can together, especially before school begins."

"Well, I want that, too, but I have things to do before classes start. I've got to see the department head, look over my class schedule, do some course planning, and get my office set up. I could have stayed in town and taken care of all those things, but I chose to come straight home and take care of work details later."

"Well, I'm glad you did! I've been dying to see you, and now that you're here, I want us to ride out together, especially when Jane comes home. We'll go camping and swimming. I cleaned the cabin a few weeks back. It'll be fun."

"Yes, we will. I'm looking forward to going to the cove, and just relaxing. I'd like to get a little bit of a tan before school starts."

Kat laughed. "You always did like to lay in the sun."

Lizzy smiled and then furrowed her brow. "Tell me something, Kat."

"Yes, what do you want to know?"

"Liddy's not serious about Jackie Lee, is she?" Although she wasn't one to pay much heed to gossip, this about their cousin did bother her.

Kat gave her sister a pointed look. "Well, I certainly hope not. The Nunleys are white trash with money. Jackie Lee is nothing but trouble waiting to happen, but let's not waste our breath talking about our cousin. She hasn't a lick of sense, and she's gonna do what she's gonna do," Kat said. "You need to go inside and see Grace and Aunt Lori and Uncle Henry. Grace in particular has been asking about you for hours. Your delay in town was nearly more than she could bear," Kat said as the two sisters walked hand in hand up the graveled walkway.

As they approached the back porch, Kat released Elizabeth's hand. "I'll leave you here, Lizzy. I need to go and see about Callie. She had a new litter of kittens last night. They're as cute as a button. One's a calico like Callie. Would you like to see it? You can come to the tool shed after you've seen everybody. I can wait for you, if you like."

"Umm, maybe later, but not right now. After I've seen Grace and Aunt Lori and Uncle Henry, I want to go see my dogs."

"Okay, Lizzy. I'll see you later, then."

"See you later, Kat," Elizabeth said as she bounded up the back steps to the kitchen door while Kat turned and skipped in the direction of the tool shed.

"Miss Lizzy! Miss Lizzy! It's so good to see you!" exclaimed Grace. The moment Elizabeth stepped through the door the older woman grabbed Elizabeth, kissing her soundly before enveloping her in a tight embrace. Grace had been the Bennett's housekeeper ever since Elizabeth was a child. The memories were fond and lasting.

"Oh, Grace, it's so good to see you. Are you keeping everybody in line?" Elizabeth laughed, giving her a hug back.

"Oh, Kat is fine and Daniel is still a mess, but he'll be fine now with both you and Jane to watch over him. He starts university this fall, you know." The housekeeper beamed. "He's going to be a civil engineer, he says. He wants to build bridges. Kat will be graduating this year and will move away. Whatever will I do? José is at war and Maria dances all over Europe. My niños are growing up and going away," the older woman lamented, raising her hands as tears brimmed in her eyes.

Elizabeth could only smile. Grace, originally from northern Peru, still carried a heavy Spanish accent, though now mixed with Southern inflections.

"Grace, don't cry. Jane and I are here, and we're not going anywhere. Daniel will be here at least four more years, and you know Mary Beth will come home someday to at least visit us," Elizabeth said with a smile. "However, I do worry about Joseph, though. Every time I hear of some explosion or a kidnapping in Iraq, I go crazy. I want this war over soon. I know he's doing what he's always wanted," Elizabeth sighed, "but I just can't help but worry." Elizabeth shook her head and dispelled the thought. "So Grace, tell me how things have gone since I was here last?"

"Oh, things have been good." The old woman nodded. "The chickens are laying well, and the milk cow is still milking, although there have been some problems with the cows. Henry will tell you about it when he and Lori come in from the barn, but there is no need to worry. Yesterday, I saw a pair of white doves. I believe it to be a good sign. God is surely watching over us to have sent them."

"Grace," Elizabeth softly laughed, "I don't believe in old wives' tales. Albino doves are a fluke of nature, nothing more."

"No, Lizzy," Grace said as she tilted her head, "they are a sign from God. He will keep José safe. I am sure God hears an old woman's prayers."

"I'm sure he does." Elizabeth smiled. "Now is there anything else?"

"Well, there is also the problem with Old Dan, but Henry will tell you about that, too."

"Old Dan! Where are Henry and Lori?" Elizabeth's face paled in concern.

"They are in the barn with Old Dan, but please, Lizzy, don't worry..."

Before Grace could finish her statement, Elizabeth was out the back door in a full run to the barn. Dan was one of her Black and Tans that she had raised and trained from a pup, but that was years ago. With the exception of short vacations, she'd been away for eight years, and he and Lady Beth had grown old in her absence. As she reached the barn door, she saw Henry and Lori leaning over Dan's form.

"Henry, what happened? Is he okay? He's not going to die, is he?"

"All these questions, Lizzy," the older man smiled warmly as he and his wife came forward to greet her.

"Lizzy, it's so good to see you," Aunt Lori said, pulling her into a hug.

Elizabeth embraced her aunt, kissing her cheek, and then turned a questioning look to her uncle.

"Lizzy, Dan and Beth got into a fight with a pack of coyotes three nights ago. Coyotes have been attackin' the calves in the far pasture almost every night for, oh, about a month now," Henry said, scratching his chin. "I'd try and sit out there waitin' for 'em to come, but they always knew I was there. I don't know how many of 'em there were, but Old Dan and Lady Beth must have caught their scent and went out on a hunt. You know this breed of dog, Lizzy." He shook head, casting a glance at the Black and Tan lying on a heap of straw. "The Red Bones and Walkers followed, makin' the most God-awfulest racket I've ever heard. I was sittin' in the study readin' the evening paper when the ruckus started. I grabbed a rifle and didn't even have time to saddle a horse, so I went out on bareback with Lori following in the Land Rover."

Placing a hand on the rail, he leaned against the stall. "It must have been Dan and Beth there first from the looks of things when I finally arrived." Henry hesitated. "Lizzy, what I'm about to say ain't easy. Do you really want to hear this?"

Elizabeth cringed and squeezed her eyes shut as she nodded her head.

"All right, then. When I got there, the coyotes were all over him, tearing him apart," Henry said, looking thoughtfully at Dan. "Beth was in trouble, too, but she ain't hurt near as bad as Dan. The other four hounds were there, too. I could see 'em by the light of the moon. It was a clash of force like I ain't never seen before—rippin' and tearin', standin' on hind legs in a vicious fight. The hounds were outnumbered, but coyotes are cowards and hounds will fight to the death. I fired a round, and when the coyotes took off from the hounds, I managed to get in several shots, killin' two of 'em, but Dan lay in a pool of blood and skin. I thought he was dead, but then he looked up at me and whined.

"We wrapped him up in a blanket we keep in the Rover and loaded him and Beth up to bring 'em home. I called Doc Bryant straightaway, and he and his son came out as quick as they could." Henry shook his head. "He's in a bad way, Lizzy."

"Will he live?" she asked, choking back tears.

"I don't know. Doc put him back together as best he could, and he's on antibiotics. That's what I was doin' when you came in—givin' him his medicine. Lizzy, he's old. We need to think about puttin' him down."

Elizabeth gasped. "No, I won't hear of it. I'll stay out here tonight. If he's going to die, then he'll die in my arms. I raised him from a pup. I can't let him go." She swallowed a sob.

"Somehow I figured you'd say that. Doc says if he makes it for a week, he has a real good chance of pullin' through, but he'll never be the same, Lizzy. His back is broken. He'll be a cripple."

"I don't care," Elizabeth said through her tears.

"All right, then. I'm goin' out tonight with some of the neighbors. We ain't the only ones havin' problems. I'll be takin' the high-powered rifle with the night scope. In their prime, Dan and Beth would have whooped those coyotes." He sighed and took Lori's hand before turning to walk toward the barn door, leaving Elizabeth alone with her dogs.

Elizabeth sat in the barn alone with Old Dan for three nights and two days, and on the third day he died. Lady Beth, perhaps sensing that Old Dan was dying, refused to eat, no matter how much the family tried to entice her. Three days after Old Dan passed, she died, too. They were buried together behind the barn on the creek bank that flowed through the farm. Elizabeth planted pansies over the site.

The coyotes didn't return to Longbourn, but instead chose another nearby farm. The neighboring families assembled together and decided the best course of action would be to mix mules and burros within the herds, and though costly to acquire, Elizabeth had located four mules and two burros in Columbia, Tennessee, about 150 miles away. With those necessary arrangements behind her, Elizabeth was ready to begin the fall semester.

Chapter Two

...ten years had passed, and he was still alone...

London, England

One month had passed since Dickens had offered him the chance of his lifetime—the chance to follow his dream. Now, Fitzwilliam Darcy sat in the small sitting room adjoining his bedchamber with a cigar and brandy, contemplating his life and future.

In his undergraduate years, he'd read Greats at Wadham College, Oxford and graduated with the rare distinction of a congratulatory First-Class Honors Degree. He then went on to do a Master of Studies in Greek and Latin Languages before continuing to the D.Phil. program. After that, he applied and was accepted for a fellowship, studying ancient history and philosophy. Fitzwilliam could read and write Latin and classical Greek and spoke four modern languages fluently. Twelve years of his life had been consumed with academia.

At the age of thirty, he'd finally left school, but if he'd had his way, he would have stayed. He wanted to teach, but as the first son and heir to Pemberley, PLC, a multinational conglomerate, that seemed impossible. He took long draw on his cigar.

He, along with his brother David, worked for their father and sat on the board of directors of Pemberley, and since taking control of Pemberley was what his father expected of him, he felt an obligation. Still, he wanted this one last chance to pursue his dream before reality took him. Fitzwilliam sighed heavily as he lifted his glass to his lips.

All things considered, he knew his father would not be pleased with his decision, but that didn't matter. Fitzwilliam had made up his mind. His father had dominated all of his children from birth, making choices for them, even trying to arrange a marriage for him. But this choice Fitzwilliam was determined to make for himself.

He took a sip of brandy then swirled the contents in his glass as his mind turned from his overbearing father to his brother. David, while a good and decent man, did not hold women in high regard, nor did he desire a family of his own, as Fitzwilliam did. He played the field, never dating the same woman on a regular basis. Yet, it wasn't so much the frequency of David's changing partners that concerned Fitzwilliam, but rather the type of women in his brother's life. They were *not* the kind one would bring home to meet the family or marry, and David possessed no real respect for them. He simply used them for his pleasure while they used him for theirs—for an opportunity to be seen on the arm of one of the most sought-after and desired bachelors in all of Britain.

Although Fitzwilliam was certain many of them held aspirations for something more, he knew his brother. The something more would never be a reality for any woman David dated, for when it came to love and affection, David Darcy was as cold as ice. Fitzwilliam sighed and shook his head. Their father was to blame for that, too.

Blowing a ring of smoke, Fitzwilliam contemplated further. He and his brother were diametrically different sides of the same coin—alike, and yet not. David, as touted by the tabloids on an almost daily basis, was flashy, sexy, self-confident, and extremely good looking, with a smile that turned heads. He was also considered outgoing and fun with a reputation of being a good lover and a proclivity to live life on the wild side.

Fitzwilliam, in contrast, was considered shy, reserved, somewhat introverted, and rarely seen in society. And yet in physical appearance, he and his brother were similar. Both were six-foot-two with the same deep, dark brown eyes and dark hair. They were very similar in build and facial features except Fitzwilliam's eyes, or so he'd been told, had a sparkle of intelligence and deep thought, while David's had a twinkle of mischief.

Fitzwilliam took a deep breath and puffed his cigar as his thoughts turned from his brother to his sister, Georgiana—the baby, no longer a girl, but a young woman, and a very beautiful and accomplished woman at that—one of whom he was very proud. She had just completed her BA from Cambridge in music with a classical emphasis and would soon begin touring with the London Philharmonic Orchestra. Always shy, Fitzwilliam could tell she had strength of character awaiting only the space and freedom to flourish. She too, fell under the dominance of their overbearing father.

In fact, George Darcy kept all of his children under his tight regulation, using whatever means he could to control them, but Fitzwilliam Darcy was about to challenge that. His decision was made and his resolve was firm. Tonight after dinner he would talk to his father.

After finishing his cigar and brandy, Fitzwilliam left his bedchamber in a leisurely manner. Dinner was at seven o'clock sharp, and he knew better than to be late.

During the meal, silence reigned as usual with nothing but the sound of clanking silverware scraping against plates and the tinkling of cups returning to their saucers. As they finished the last course, Fitzwilliam took a sobering breath and spoke.

"Father, I would like to have a word with you."

His father met his gaze. "Let us go to my study, then," George said as he rose from his seat and placed his neatly folded napkin on the table.

As they walked the long corridor, Fitzwilliam glanced towards his father, studying him. While some men shriveled with age, George Darcy, at nearly sixty-two, remained distinguished in looks. He stood tall at six-foot-three with coal black hair streaked with silver along the temples. He also shared the same deep chocolate eyes as his sons, except George's eyes were more intense and piercing when he cast his gaze. George was a powerful and dignified man who displayed an air of confidence and strength many found intimidating, and he was a man not to be defied, especially by his sons. Fitzwilliam knew he would have to rise to this challenge as they walked along in silence.

Entering the study, his father closed the door with a resounding click. Fitzwilliam took a seat on the sofa while his father poured two glasses of port. "What can I do for you?" Mr. Darcy asked flatly as he took his seat.

"Father, I've decided to take a position as a classics professor at a university in America—Tennessee to be more specific," he said as he held his father's gaze. "I leave in one week."

George raised an eyebrow. "This is rather sudden, don't you think? I don't believe we've discussed this."

Fitzwilliam ignored his father's last remark. He had no intention of discussing it. "No, actually, it is not. I have thought about it since completing my studies, but I've only recently accepted a position." Never breaking his father's intense stare, he added cautiously, "It's with a five-year contract."

George's gaze bore into his son's, his anger slowly rising, but Fitzwilliam had anticipated this and before his father could speak, he interjected, "Father, I've made up my mind on this. It's very important to me, and if I must, I will leave Pemberley permanently, though that is not my desire." He breathed deeply. "I *do* have my own money. I'm not *entirely* dependent upon you."

"You would give up a fortune of over £4 billion for a mere fifteen million?" George Darcy roared, astonished by his son's defiance. The two had clashed before, but this was the first time Fitzwilliam had directly challenged his father's will.

"If I must, then, yes. I'm willing to honor my family duty, but I want a chance to accomplish my dream of teaching first. Besides, Father, you appear to be in good health, and David is more than qualified for the position. He would make a much better heir than I, and he has the desire."

"That's enough, Fitzwilliam! David is an embarrassment to me, the board on which he sits, and our family. The only way *he* will ever take your place is if you are ***dead***!"

His father rose from his seat and paced back and forth observing his son. From his expression, Fitzwilliam knew what his father was thinking. He'd heard it all before. He probably would give Fitzwilliam the time he wanted to explore his options, sow his wild oats, if need be, as long as Pemberley was not compromised, but in the end, he expected his son to bend to his will. Fitzwilliam drew in a deep steadying breath, preparing himself for the lecture on duty and responsibility that would inevitably follow. He didn't have long to wait.

"Damn it, Fitzwilliam, go if you must! As always with you—your nose stuck in a damn book like some sort of idealistic philosopher." With white-hot anger, George Darcy turned and pinned his son with a piercing gaze. "But when you return, mark… my… ***words***, Fitzwilliam Alexander, I *will* have you married and an heir produced. Do *you* understand me?"

"Perfectly," Fitzwilliam sneered in disgust.

Mr. Darcy stood erect and straightened his clothes as he walked towards the door. Opening it, he stalked through, slamming it shut without so much as a backwards glance.

Fitzwilliam sat alone for a moment in quiet reflection, and then rose to leave the room with a spring in his step and a lightness in his heart. George Darcy embodied the epitome of strength and character, while Fitzwilliam was considered to be meek and reserved, but Fitzwilliam had just proven that character is born while reputation is made. Still waters run deep and a quiet spirit is often misunderstood and underestimated.

Later that evening, his brother David approached him in the upstairs sitting area. "What on earth did you say to the Old Man? I haven't seen him this angry since you refused to marry our step-cousin."

"I told him that I'm taking a teaching position in Tennessee," Fitzwilliam answered flatly as he offered David a cigar before taking one for himself.

"Good for you. I have to admire you," David said with a grin as he lit his cigar and then offered his brother a light.

"I also asked him to let you have my birthright." Fitzwilliam smiled.

"Well," David scoffed as he poured two brandies and handed one to his brother. "First off, I don't want it because then I would be expected to marry Anne. Second, I know how Father feels about me."

"Yes," Fitzwilliam smirked, "that didn't go down very well, and by the way, I will not be marrying Anne. So don't ever mention that to me again."

David laughed aloud. He knew what a sore spot that was with his brother. For the last four years, their father had been trying to arrange a marriage between Fitzwilliam and their mealy-mouthed step-cousin—the sole heiress to Vanderburgh Banking, one of the largest banking systems in Europe. He inwardly smiled as he thought of the heated exchanges between his brother and father. But, if his brother was about to leave him here to face the relentless drumming of their father's lectures alone, the least he could do was join him for an evening out.

"Fitzwilliam, before you go to the States, why don't you come out with me and Benson? I can get you a date."

"No, I don't think so." He laughed. "Are you corrupting Benson now? Uncle Harvey won't like that."

"Benson is his own man. He's twenty-five and decides for himself, as do I," David retorted. "Now, Brother, back to *you*. How long has it been? You could do with some female comfort." David's eyes engaged his brother's from over the rim of his glass. "You know what you need, Fitzwilliam. Monica has a friend who's a real looker. Let me arrange it? It'll be good for you."

"Monica? I thought you were dating Sandra."

"I am," David replied, taking a long slow sip. "I'll see Sandra the day after tomorrow. After all, variety *is* the spice of life, but we're not discussing me. We're discussing *you*. So what about it, Brother? Let me arrange something for you."

"No, David," Fitzwilliam laughed softly, "that's not what I want. I've had my fill of frivolous flings, and I certainly don't need a woman for the night. Thank you very much." Fitzwilliam puffed his cigar. "You go and enjoy your ladies' charms. Just be careful, and don't let some woman trap you."

"Oh, I'm always careful," David said with a broad smile as he chewed on the tip of his cigar. "And I *know* the ways of women. I'm always meticulously careful of the details, but what about you?"

"I've no need to be careful, since I don't take chances, but if I did, I know how to be safe."

"Well, you need to find a wife, then." David winked. "It's one or the other."

"I've no desire or need for a wife, either. I just want to take this teaching opportunity. If I need female comfort, as you call it, I can arrange it for myself." Fitzwilliam smiled, finishing his drink and setting it aside.

"Suit yourself then, but I still think you ought to come out with me. You're way too uptight. I happen to know it's been a long time. Why don't you come along?" David finished his brandy and then poured himself and his brother another.

Fitzwilliam rolled his eyes and smiled as he picked up the offered drink.

"Have it your way," David said, smiling with a simple nod.

As they sat in silence, David cast a quick glance at his brother. He wished Fitzwilliam would take him up on his offer. A night of mindless, passionate sex without the entanglement of emotions would do him good. Tonight it was Monica, tomorrow Leslie, and the next Sandra. David chuckled as he thought of his plans. ...*Ah, yes, a night spent in the arms of a beautiful woman taking his pleasure...Love 'em and forget 'em.* He blew a ring of smoke. *That's what my brother needs. He needs to get laid*

Sipping his drink, David felt an uncomfortable tightness grip his chest as the memory of *that woman* intruded again. His expression turned sober as he took a large gulp. Damn her. Five months ago, he'd had a most unpleasant experience at the hands of a woman—one whom he had greatly underestimated.

They'd met in a boardroom, of all places, where he was attempting to negotiate a contract with her. Her beauty had not escaped him when he had walked into the room that day, but business was business, and he knew better than to mix the two. Yet the attraction was strong, and since when had he had trouble picking up a woman when he wanted one? But this one was different. He blew another ring of smoke, reliving the experience again. She was as shrewd as she was beautiful, and he was all but certain she had wanted him—until she'd rejected him. He bit down on his cigar almost biting it in two.

The impact of her rejection still stung at his ego, and it was not likely he'd forget about it anytime soon. Never had a woman held the upper hand with him, and Cecilia Lawton wouldn't be the first. She was a challenge, a beautiful one at that, and he'd never let a challenge go unmet. This one wouldn't either. It was only a matter of time.

A slight chuckle escaped David's throat, catching his brother's attention. David smiled and nodded at his brother's curious stare. Fitzwilliam probably presumed he was thinking about Monica. He couldn't be further from the truth. David took another sip of brandy. *....Someday, Lawton, you will accompany me. I know you have desires... needs. Every woman does.* He smirked. *Well, Lawton, I've got a few of my own, and I'm going to discover your secrets... I want to know what turns you on. And when I have you, it'll be a night for you to remember. Yes, Lawton, you've met your match.*

Draining his glass, David set it aside and blew another ring of smoke. He put out his cigar and rose to leave giving Fitzwilliam one last chance to join him, which his brother declined.

Later that night, Fitzwilliam poured himself another drink as he sat alone in his room, contemplating his life. Brooding on his upcoming birthday, he keenly felt the effects of his loneliness. Another year had come and gone. Perhaps David was right. He had been alone for so long that it had become an old habit, one which he was rapidly beginning not to care if he ever broke, or if he ever found *her*—the one he was looking for.

As he sat and thought about all he had experienced in the domain of love and sex, his mind drifted back to the cove at Pemberley. The cove had always been special to him since the first time his mother had taken him there. When he grew older, he would go there as often as he could. And the summer before Oxford, he'd even lost his virginity there.

His cousins, William and Benson Darcy, had spent the summer at Pemberley that year, as they did every summer, while the two Harrison sisters had spent their summer with their grandfather on a neighboring estate. The girls would ride out exploring the countryside every day, as would William and Fitzwilliam, until one fateful day when they accidentally met in the area of the cove. From that day forth for the rest of the summer, the two couples met and were inseparable—William with Leah and Fitzwilliam with Rachel.

Fitzwilliam looked back fondly as he thought of the carefree days of his youth. Rachel had taught him much more than he could have ever gleaned from a book. When the summer had ended, they had parted as friends with the intention of seeing each other at Oxford. Somehow, they never did.

He went on to date many women during his first two years at Wadham College, experiencing the university life common among his peers. At first it had been fun and exciting. The women were willing to please, and he'd been more than willing to be pleased by them, but then the excitement began to wane, leaving him feeling empty. He was looking for something and not finding it. He wanted a steady relationship with a woman he could love, one who would love him in return.

He thought he had found what he was looking for near the end of his second year when he'd met Stella Fitzgerald. She'd been lively, witty, and charming. He wouldn't call her beautiful, but she was pretty with long red hair and sparkling green eyes. They had dated for six months when Stella had convinced him that they should live together. Though he had reservations about the idea, he'd consented. But after six months, he'd realized she was not the one, and that he had made a terrible mistake. They had nothing in common beyond the initial attraction. She'd cared nothing for the things he loved—Pemberley lands, books, riding—nothing! All she'd cared for was London society and possessing the Darcy heir, along with his money, which she'd freely spent—sometimes depleting his allowance, causing him to have to approach his father for more money, which in turn, had caused more problems and heated arguments.

Fitzwilliam released a hard breath. Unknown to him at the time, Stella had planned to trap him with an old trick that tested his personal integrity. She had come to know that Fitzwilliam was a man of honor and was always willing to do the right thing, no matter what the cost. An act of Fate or Divine mercy, he wasn't sure which, had saved him from her trap, and he would never forget it, nor would his father let him. And because of it, from that day forward, he'd made a solemn vow. There would be no more one-night stands or casual affairs.

He knew somewhere there had to be a woman for him. But after many years of searching, he had concluded that there was no woman who would love and appreciate the things he loved—Tolkien, Lewis, Medieval and Renaissance literature, Greek plays and philosophies, and Latin histories. No woman who would take the time to understand him. No woman existed whose feelings and emotions ran as deep as his or who could love him for the person he was, not his family name or money.

Ten years had now passed since Stella, and he was still alone. He had caught sight of one such beautiful girl who had piqued his interest while visiting the university, but she was just that, a girl—a student, and that was forbidden. Even if it were permissible, it would be foolish. They were unequal in every way imaginable. It would never work. Therefore, he had made up his mind. He was going to Tennessee to teach and nothing more.

Chapter Three

...I will enjoy sitting here with a cigar and a brandy...

Darcy had just returned from his early morning walk in the hotel courtyard. As he climbed the steps to the second story level, he shook his head, irritated with the current situation. The Plateau Plaza was the only hotel in the sleepy little town of Walnut Grove, and it was a far cry from what he'd been accustomed to on the numerous occasions he'd traveled. For a small town, he supposed, it wasn't bad, but it lacked the excellence in quality he was used to. The sitting room was small, the cable connection ceased to function with every passing rain shower, and the beds were hard. The rooms didn't even have a wireless Internet connection.

Strolling into the room, he found his friend.

"Bingley, I hope that real estate agent we hired comes through soon. I don't think I can take this hotel any longer."

"I hope she does too, Darcy, because I have to say, I'm not pleased with this situation either. By the way, she called while you were out with some prospect she's looking into. She has a few things to check, and if it's available, she'll ring back within the hour."

"Well, let's just hope it's available *and* suitable. I'm more than ready to move. Classes begin in less than a week, and there is so much to do," Darcy said, pacing the floor.

Hearing the phone, he answered on the first ring. "Darcy speaking."

"Mr. Darcy, this is Sylvia Potter. I have fabulous news. I've found a house. Can you see it after lunch?"

"Yes, we'll be ready."

"Good! I'll pick you up at two o'clock. The house is in the Old Town District near the university. I think you will like this one," she said. "A very prominent professor owned the property, but the house has been closed since his death. His son wishes to lease it fully furnished. So, if you find it satisfactory, it's yours."

"Excellent!" Hanging up the phone, Darcy turned to Bingley and smiled. "Let's go to lunch. How about the little diner on Main Street? We have enough time before Mrs. Potter is picking us up. I'm buying. "

"Sounds good to me. You can give me the details on the way."

Promptly at two, Mrs. Potter arrived at the Plateau Plaza. Driving into the historic part of town, Darcy's mood brightened and a smile curled his lips. The entire area was enclosed in a canopy of large oak and maple trees completely covering the road below. It was obvious by the beautiful well kept Victorian houses that the neighborhood was old. As they traveled down Elm Street to Willow, Darcy noticed the beautiful blonde from earlier in the summer sitting on a porch swing reading a book and sipping a beverage. He smiled and glanced at his friend.

"Mrs. Potter, who lives in that house?" Bingley asked, pointing to the house where the young woman sat.

"That's the Bennett townhouse. It belonged to Ron and Meg Bennett, but they were killed two years ago in a tragic car accident out on County Road 52. Their children live there now. That's Jane Bennett on the porch. I believe she teaches English at the university," Mrs. Potter replied.

Bingley smiled. "Yes, I've seen her before."

Mrs. Potter glanced at Bingley and smiled as they turned the corner onto Maple Street. "Her parents taught at the university, too. Meg Bennett was a math professor and Ron taught electrical engineering. It was a great loss for the community when they died. The Bennett family is well respected. They were one of the founding families back in 1803. They also own a large farm in Pleasant Grove. It's very beautiful I hear tell. Many of these homes belong to the upper crust of Plateau County. Jane's a beautiful girl, and I believe she's single. Her sisters are quite pretty, too. The belles of the county from what people say."

"Interesting," Bingley murmured.

"And that's the Harwell house over there, on the corner of Maple and Willow Street," Mrs. Potter said, pulling up to the curb and parking the car out front. "It's a little large, but it is fully furnished. Let's go in and have a look."

Getting out of the car, Darcy looked over the outside of the house, well pleased with what he saw. It sat upon a slight hill, as did all of the houses on Maple and Willow. One had to walk up three steps and follow a brick walkway to the three-story house. It had a wraparound porch with a gazebo on one corner, and the front door was made of very heavy oak.

"Gentlemen, let me tell you about the house," Mrs. Potter enthusiastically spoke while they walked up the walkway. "It was built in 1888 and has been well-maintained, as you can see. Notice the front door. It was hand carved, designed by a craftsman from Naples, Italy. When the house was built, Mr. Randal Harwell had this specific design ordered to be built out of oak. In fact, the entire interior is done in rich yellow and red oak harvested from the family farm out near Pleasant Grove. These houses were the town homes for the wealthy farmers from out in the county. They used them for the season, such as it was." She smiled. "You don't see houses designed like this anymore."

Darcy inspected the door, running a finger along the smooth curve of the wood where the glass was inlayed. ...*Excellent work and very well made...*

When they had finished inspecting the outside, Mrs. Potter unlocked the door and led them into the house. Stepping into a wide vestibule, Darcy noticed a table to the right where a receiving register and a plate for calling cards resided. *Interesting*, he thought. Noticing that it was open, he concluded that it must have been used within the year. He smiled. It had been a tradition long ago in a time when small details were the rule of the day. Perusing the room further, his eyes settled on the large oak staircase that led to the second floor. ...*Beautiful Southern design...* Lost in thought, Mrs. Potter's shrill voice snapped him out of his reverie.

"We'll begin our tour with the upstairs, but first I want you to notice this beautiful bathroom behind the staircase." Taking Bingley and Darcy around the back, she opened the door to a large and spacious room with hardwood floors and oak cabinets. It still had the original claw foot bathtub along with a very large old-fashioned sink.

"This bathroom is in its original condition with only minor updates for comfort and convenience. Very little has been changed throughout the house. Really the only changes to the entire house have been to modernize it with indoor plumbing, electricity, a dishwasher, washer and dryer, and natural gas. But the overall décor of the house is unchanged. Now, let's start our tour."

Both men nodded in agreement. Walking around the staircase to the front and up the stairs, Darcy smiled. ...*The nostalgia of this house is pleasing... I'll have to inspect that registry when we come back down…*

When Darcy arrived at the upstairs landing, he noted six bedrooms and a full bathroom. This would provide more than enough room should his brother or sister decide to visit. Eager to begin inspecting the rooms, he walked to the bathroom first. Glancing inside, he observed that it too had a claw foot bathtub along with an added modern walk-in shower and a full dressing room. A vanity and sink had been added with shelves placed on either side for toiletries and other necessities.

"I like this bathroom. The modern additions have not taken away from the original design but have rather enhanced it. Lovely. Shall we continue on?"

"I agree, Darcy. It's both quite lovely and practical," Bingley said.

As they left the bathroom, Darcy glanced around. The upstairs had a large open area towards the front of the house that had obviously been used as a sitting area. It had floor-to-ceiling book shelves on both sides and two sofas facing each other in the middle. *…This can be our upstairs study…* Another smile crossed his features as he noticed a pair of French doors that opened onto a piazza overlooking the street below. Stepping out onto the balcony, he glanced over the spacious area. *…I will enjoy sitting here with a cigar and a brandy. It appears to be very relaxing and the view is lovely.* The entire house was furnished with historical period furnishings, including the porch furniture. He noted that the floors were oak covered with authentic Persian rugs in bright colors of royal blue, red, and gold. *…It appears to be well-made… tongue and groove… very good.*

Mrs. Potter cleared her throat and once again grabbed their attention. "Well, then, gentlemen if you are ready, we will start with the master bedrooms. In these old houses they had two master suites. One was for the master and the other for the mistress. Strange, but that's the way they did it."

Mrs. Potter led them into the first bedroom. It was furnished in French Provincial cherry with red oak flooring and red and gold Persian rugs. A king sized bed, covered in rich red silk, was flanked on either side by two bedside commode cabinets now used as nightstands. Further scanning the room, Darcy noticed there was a small desk against the back wall and a writing table beside the fireplace while two chaise lounges flanked by lamps sat cozily by the fireside, making it comfortable for reading. Heavy brocade curtains, matching the bedspread, covered a very large bay window which overlooked the street below. Stepping through a connecting door, he discovered the master suite was connected to the mistress' apartment by two large walk-in closets and a large three-quarter bathroom joining the two rooms. *…These rooms will do very nicely.* Touring the other bedrooms, Darcy noted they were similar to the master suites except the regular rooms were somewhat smaller and had queen sized beds.

Concluding their upstairs tour, they returned to the first floor to finish the inspection. Darcy walked immediately to the guest register where he perused the last entries. A pleasing smile crossed his face as he read the names of those who had visited. *…People don't do this sort of thing any longer… pity, really.*

"I see you've noticed Dr. Harwell's registry." Mrs. Potter smiled as she walked over to where Darcy stood. "Dr. Harwell was a stickler for keeping with traditions. Those entries you see are from the last days he spent here. Most of the names are from Hospice."

"Interesting." Darcy ran his fingers over the names, lost in his thoughts.

"Let's begin with the front parlor, if you don't mind."

Leading them into the parlor, just to the right of the registry table, she gestured with her hand. "Gentleman, let me call your attention to the fireplace. The mantelpiece was hand carved by the same Italian artisan who designed and constructed the front door.

This room, like all the others, has tongue and groove oak floors and Persian rugs." With a wave of her hand toward the corner of the room, she announced. "Notice the piano. It is a custom made Bosendorfer 130 CL. Mr. Harwell's daughter was a proficient pianist."

Darcy went over to inspect it, striking a few keys. *...Beautiful! But out of tune...I'll have it tuned after classes begin.*

"You will notice that all of the furniture in this room is also in the French Provincial design," Mrs. Potter said.

Bingley walked over to the sofa against one wall, rubbing his hand over the back of the wooden frame. "I like this style. These older fashions are comfortable and elegant. Beautiful."

They browsed the rest of the room where they observed several tables with lamps or vases and a large bay window overlooking a small flower garden to the side of the house. It wasn't an especially large room, but it was comfortable. There were also two wingback chairs and a divan with a small tea table finishing the room's decor.

"The next rooms, just past the parlor, are two smaller bedrooms and another sitting room. These bedrooms were the servants' quarters in Dr. Harwell's day. They are all simple, yet beautifully furnished," she said, leading them out of the parlor and into the foyer. Strolling over to the rooms, they peered inside, giving them a quick cursory look.

"The library is over there." She pointed. "It's just as the Harwell family left it when Dr. Harwell died. Let's go in."

Guiding them to the first room past the front door to the left, they entered the library, a spacious room with a reading table, various other tables, a large chandelier, and two sofas. In the center of the outside wall was another very large bay window overlooking the front porch, bringing natural light into the room. Floor-to-ceiling oak bookshelves encompassed the remaining walls except for the back where a doorway led to a small study. Darcy ambled to the nearest bookcase and lifted a book from the shelf. *The Chronicles of the Gallic Wars by Julius Caesar...written in Latin...umm...* Smiling, he flipped through the pages, inspecting the book before replacing it.

Mrs. Potter opened the door and motioned for them to follow. "This was Dr. Harwell's study. It still contains his personal books which, I was told, he used in his classes at the university where he taught philosophy. If you wish to have those removed to replace with your own, I can arrange it." As Bingley and Darcy moved into the room, she continued. "Notice the desk. It was also imported from Italy in the late 1880s. It's simply magnificent. Made from mahogany."

"Leave the books," Bingley said, flipping through one of Dr. Harwell's course notebooks. "I see that the late Dr. Harwell and I have similar taste. I'd like to look through his collection."

"Very well then, it's no problem," Mrs. Potter said.

While Bingley inspected the books, Darcy walked over to the desk and ran a finger over the finish. *...Beautiful craftsmanship and well-made, too. It'll do just fine.*

Dr. Harwell's study, though not a large room, had quite an impressive drinks cabinet still filled with Bourbons, wines, and sherry, Darcy observed, strolling over and opening the glass door. "Look, Bingley, Dr. Harwell drank the same sherry as you." Darcy laughed.

"Yes, indeed he did. Very good taste." Both men smiled as Bingley inspected the bottles.

Next on the tour was the informal sitting room, the dining room, followed by the kitchen, and then the breakfast room. "Well, gentleman, what do you think? Is the house suitable for your needs? It is within walking distance to the university."

"Yes, it is a beautiful home. Let us discuss it, and we'll let you know. Give us just a moment," Darcy said as he and Bingley walked over to a corner for privacy.

After talking among themselves, Darcy approached Mrs. Potter. "We'll take the house. It will suit our needs perfectly. I'll need one of the downstairs bedrooms cleared to convert into a business office."

"Anything you want removed will be handled. Give me a list of what you want done. I'll see that it's taken care of," Mrs. Potter replied as she retrieved her notebook from her briefcase. Jotting down their instructions, she continued. "There is one other thing that I must make you aware of. The books and personal items are considered prized family possessions and must be handled with care. The owner stipulates that these things, especially the registry, must be given great care and preserved."

"You can be assured we will treasure them as if they were our own. I have a few more things I'd like to discuss and then we can take care of the lease," Bingley said.

They negotiated further and agreed upon the particulars. The house would be cleaned thoroughly and would be ready by the end of the week. They went to the bank, paid for the first year's lease, had the utilities changed over, and scheduled the phone, cable and Internet service to be made ready per their instructions. Everything necessary would be in place for them to take possession on Saturday. However, there was one other essential thing needed for the two English gentlemen to complete their requirements to move in—a housekeeper. Dr. Dickens had recommended a Mrs. Norris, the sister of the Dickens's family housekeeper. With that last detail taken care of, the two friends prepared to begin their stay in the Cumberland Plateau.

Chapter Four

...she longed for a love of her own...

Fall semester was in full swing with the first week of classes finally over. Elizabeth sat in her office smiling. Her class schedule was perfect with her teaching one course each of Calculus I, Calculus II, and College Algebra. Not too tough and not too easy—it was just right. As she sat at her desk grading the assessment quiz she'd given her Cal I students their first day of class, she paused and leaned back in her chair. It had been a long day, and she was anxious to be done. She released a gentle sigh as she put down her red pen.

Rising from her seat to stretch and take a break, she walked over to the window and gazed out into the courtyard of the math and engineering buildings. Her lips curled in a slight smile as she watched a boy and a girl, obviously a couple, sitting on the ground cross-legged studying. While she gazed at them, she shook her head and thought of her own love life or rather, the absence of one.

When they had all lived in Boston, Jane and Cecilia had often teased her, saying that she preferred math problems to dating. That wasn't exactly true, but as she thought about it, it wasn't too far from the mark either. Most of the guys she had met were full of themselves—always interested in an easy pickup. She shook her head as she continued to stare out the window.

Before she had become so consumed with school work, she had loved to read, especially Gothic literature and mythology. She also loved to discuss history, but the men she'd met seemed to think she was odd, while Elizabeth, in turn, thought they were shallow. Elizabeth sighed heavily as she watched the young couple. She wondered why she couldn't meet a nice guy who was interested in having an intelligent conversation and sharing some of her interests. But no, the ones she'd met were only interested in one thing—and that left her cold. She released another sigh. Although she knew her life was full with school, the farm, and her personal studies, still, she longed for a love of her own, but she had all but given up on meeting a man who held some depth of character. Ordinarily it didn't bother her, but today, as she watched the young couple, she felt the sting of her loneliness acutely as if something very important was missing from her life.

Shrugging her shoulders, she walked back to her desk and took her seat. Picking up her pen, she pulled the next quiz from the stack. As she graded the paper before her, she was determined not to care about her lackluster love life. No, she would not concern herself over it. She would enjoy life just as it came with no thought beyond the present. *...Who needs a man anyway?* The weekend was upon her, and she had better things to do than worry about a man. Grading the last quiz, she cleared her desk and prepared for the walk home.

As she trudged her way across campus, she thought about the upcoming weekend. She, along with the rest of the family, would be meeting Jane's latest interest, one of the new Classical Studies professors from England, a Dr. Bingley. He and Jane had met the first day of school when Jane had clumsily dropped an armful of books while fumbling in her purse for her office key. Seizing the opportunity, he had quickly picked up the books and offered to help Jane into her office. After that, Jane and Dr. Bingley had had several dates for lunch, but since she had yet to bring him home to meet the family, this was indeed an important weekend.

M.K. Baxley

Elizabeth smiled as she thought about it. It was now *Charles this* and *Charles that*. Well, she would take this opportunity to formally *meet* this Dr. Bingley and discern his character for herself. She hoped he was at least better than some Jane had dated, for Jane had been notorious for attracting men who had turned out to be nothing more than disappointments. But Jane, unlike their close friend, Cecilia, was not the kind to have frivolous flings or short term love affairs. So, Elizabeth would carefully observe this English gentleman who appeared to have captured her sister's heart on such short acquaintance.

Walking into the house, she bounded up the stairs, packed a few things, and was out the door at a run, hopping into her Durango and hurrying down County Road 52 to Longbourn Farm. Kat and Daniel were already there, but Jane was staying in town to spend her first weekend with Dr. Bingley before coming out early Monday morning for the Labor Day festivities.

As Charles went about preparing for his day, he was in an excellent mood. Jane had cooked dinner on Friday night, and they had spent Saturday going to the local flea markets. His attraction was growing stronger with each moment they spent together. Humming a lively tune while he prepared his breakfast, Charles glanced up and smiled as his friend appeared in the doorway.

"Do you always have to be in such a good mood so early in the morning?" Darcy asked, ambling into the kitchen. "I've got to have my coffee first."

"Well, Darcy I have a very special date today. I'm going to meet Jane's family. It promises to be an interesting day. Will you not reconsider and come with us? You know Jane would be pleased. The invitation included you as well."

"Bingley, I've got Pemberley business to take care of today," Darcy said with a slight grumble. "It's strange to me that the Americans would take such a holiday, but it's good for me that they do, since I have a lot of work to complete. Besides," Darcy paused, "I would feel like a fifth wheel."

"Oh, Darcy, Jane likes you, and besides, she has a sister who is teaching math this term. You might like her."

"I highly doubt it. Jane is, I grant you, very pretty, but most of the math, physics, and techies I've met are slightly odd, and the girls are plain. If you enjoy talking about simple harmonic motion with maybe a few words thrown in about thermodynamics or the latest article in some engineering publication, then they might have something to say. But try to start a conversation on business, history, the arts, literature, or current affairs, and they're lost, without a clue of anything beyond their own sphere of interest. No, I'm quite sure she would be too singular of interest for me."

"Darcy, you astound me! How can you stereotype people like that? I'm sure she's charming. She is Jane's sister, after all!"

"Charming maybe, but pretty?" He raised a brow with a slight smile. "I highly doubt it, and it does matter. No, you go along and enjoy your lady's smiles," Darcy said as he dismissed his old friend and took his cup of coffee to his office. The only woman he had on his mind was his dark haired Lúthien he'd spied in July. She was ever present in his thoughts. He'd seen her once or twice in the UC, but she always escaped him before he could get a closer look.

After finishing his coffee and breakfast, Bingley set out for the Bennett townhouse. Being a pretty day, he'd decided to walk. As Charles rounded the corner, Jane exited the house with an armful of packages. "Charles, I'm so glad you made it a little early. You can help me load the Tahoe with these things my aunt wanted from town," she said, handing him some of the bags. "I see Dr. Darcy did not change his mind."

"No, he said he has some business matters that need his immediate attention. He doesn't socialize very much."

"That sounds so much like Lizzy. She's lively enough, but very aloof and cautious when it comes to men. I know those two would get along very well if they could only meet. But she's always working, if not on her courses, then on the farm." Jane shrugged. "Lizzy never dated much in college. We always teased her about preferring math problems to men. I really would like to see her get out more. She's such a wonderful person."

"They do seem to be alike then," Bingley said. "Darcy seems to think she wouldn't be interested in anything beyond her profession. What were his words now? Ah, yes. 'The math, physics, and techies I have met are slightly odd and the girls are plain,' or something to that effect. He thinks that she wouldn't want to talk about anything beyond math or physics. I tried to tell him he just might be wrong, but he wouldn't listen." Bingley and Jane both laughed, shaking their heads while continuing to load the Tahoe.

"Well, I can tell you he is very wrong. Lizzy is more than just pretty. She's beautiful. She has the most incredible long black hair you'll ever see and gorgeous green eyes. They sparkle with intelligence when she laughs. As for conversation, he might be surprised about that, too. She's well-read. We both speak two foreign languages, and she reads and writes Latin as well as any scholar. She's an avid history buff, too. He would like her." Jane nodded with a smile. "He doesn't know what he's missing. But you know what, Charles? If I were trying to set Lizzy up, she would probably react the same way. They'll just have to meet on their own, if at all." Jane laughed as she secured the last bag.

Settling into the car and fastening their seatbelts, Jane continued. "Now, I have a surprise for you. This is the first day of dove season, and the men in my family always hunt. Uncle Henry has an extra shotgun. If you're interested, you're welcome to join the men folk. The women will be socializing and arranging the dinner for much of the day."

"Jane, I would like that very much. It's been a long time since I've gone shooting. Darcy and I used to shoot birds on his estate. He'll really be sorry to have missed it, for he loves to shoot as much as I do," Bingley said. "What else should I be looking forward to today?"

Turning onto Clinton Street, she flashed a smile. "Well, it is an old-fashioned smorgasbord that our family hosts each year. There will be roasted chickens, a whole hog, and half a steer, all coming from our farm on an open pit barbeque. My family provides the meat and homemade ice cream while my aunts bring the desserts and side dishes. Most of my aunts, uncles, cousins, and friends will be there, so you will have a chance to meet everybody all at once. And you'll also finally get to meet Lizzy, Kat, and Daniel."

"I'm looking forward to it, and the food sounds delicious. I'll be sampling Southern cooking at its best. Darcy really is missing out!"

"Well, it serves him right, but there will be other days. Only he'll have to wait until next year for our annual Labor Day Dinner on the Grounds."

When Jane and Charles arrived at Longbourn, the atmosphere was hectic. All of the Bennetts and Barnetts, Jane's mother's family, had assembled for the festivities. Three pavilions were set up to accommodate the day's event: one for the smorgasbord tables, one for dining tables, and another for the entertainment.

M.K. Baxley

After setting up the tables and chairs under the larger dining pavilion, the men were busily preparing to leave for the cornfields. And while the older men and those who didn't care to hunt were sitting around whittling and swapping tales, the older ladies were giving orders to the younger ones who scurried around trying to comply. Jane approached the assembled groups of men and women.

"Everyone, I'd like you to meet a friend of mine, Charles Bingley. He's from England and teaches Classical Studies at the university." She smiled and turned to Charles. "Charles, these are my uncles, Henry Simpson, Robert Bennett, Randy Fanning, Johnny Barnett, and Sam Henry Barnett, and my aunts, Lori Simpson, Lydia Fanning, Tana Bennett, Bette Barnett, and Florence Barnett. And this is our housekeeper, Grace Menendez. My cousins, Tammy Sue, Sandy and Lilith Barnett, and Liddy Fanning are over there with my sisters, Elizabeth and Kat, and this is my brother, Daniel."

Daniel tipped his head and smiled while Robert Bennett stepped forward and grabbed Charles's hand. "Robert Bennett, here—Jane's uncle. Glad to meet you."

"The pleasure is all mine," Charles replied, smiling as he pumped Robert's hand, and then proceeded to shake the series of other hands offered.

When the introductions were complete, the men left for the fields and the hunting began while the women went about preparing the food and setting the tables, talking as they worked.

"Jane, I like your Señor Bingley. He seems like a nice man for you," Grace said.

"Yes, he is very nice. He is just what a man ought to be—warm, friendly, and kind. We share many of the same interests, and we always have pleasant conversations. But," she hesitated with a small smile, "he's not *my* Mr. Bingley. I've only known him for a little over a week."

"Well, maybe you have just met, but from the way he looks at you, he soon will be *your* Señor Bingley, and besides, what man could resist you? You are not so beautiful and smart for nothing, you know. All of my girls are smart—and beautiful! Now," Grace said, turning to Elizabeth, "if only our Lizzy could meet someone nice, too?"

"Grace, Grace, please spare me." Elizabeth rolled her eyes. "I have everything I need right here. I have no need of a man. Besides," Elizabeth smiled, "I have a bad habit of attracting shallow men. It will take a very special man to turn my head. No, my life is perfect just as it is, but I *do* admit that Dr. Bingley is very nice and seems just your type, Jane. He's at least a much better sort of man than those you've brought home before. I must say I'm pleasantly surprised and very pleased."

Jane blushed crimson. "Lizzy, I'd like to think I've learned a thing or two over the last few years."

"I know, Jane," she said, giving her sister a hug. "I'm only teasing."

As Jane and Grace walked away, the Bennett siblings' cousin, Liddy Fanning, who had never gotten along with any of the Bennett girls, approached the table where Elizabeth was working. "Oh, Lizzy, you're much too prim and proper for your own good. Always with your high standards," Liddy said with a wave of her hand. "You'll probably marry the only man you ever seriously date, just like Momma says your mother did. You're just like her, you know, with your nose always stuck in a book, never concerning yourself with boys or flirtation, unlike the rest of us." Liddy smirked. "Lizzy, let me give you a piece of advice." Liddy leaned in. "You'll never find a husband traipsin' about the countryside on a horse or readin'. Real men don't like books." Liddy snorted, glancing from one cousin to the next as they all broke out in laughter.

"Well, Liddy, not all of us can get on as well as you do chasing every man between here and the Mississippi," Elizabeth retorted. "I happen to be very content with my life just as it is, but I'll tell you what I'll do. Should I ever meet a man that catches my attention, I'll be sure and let you know about it," Elizabeth said with a smile while she finished arranging the pickles and relishes with the condiments before moving on to help with the desserts.

"You all leave Lizzy alone!" Bette Barnett said as she joined the group. "She'll do just fine on her own. Y'all would be much better off bein' more like Lizzy, considerin' some of the ne'er-do-wells you've dragged in."

"What do you mean, Momma? As far as I know, Lizzy's never even had a boyfriend, and I've had so many." Tammy Sue laughed.

"Yeah, she's a real bore," injected Lilith.

"Well now, Tammy Sue, what about that awful Leroy Wilson you brought home last spring?" Bette Barnett looked pointedly at her blushing daughter. "And how about you, Lilith? What about that Jonathan Montgomery you had clinging to you like some sort of kudzu vine the year before last?" She raised a brow and glanced between her two daughters. "And you, Liddy Fanning, don't exactly have the best track record, either. Girls, if I've told you once, I've told you a hundred times, 'If you lie down with the dogs, you'll get up with the fleas.'"

Liddy simply rolled her eyes and walked off as Bette gave her a look of disapproval.

Tammy Sue tossed her head with a pout. "Well, Momma, how was I supposed to know Leroy was a liar and a cheat?"

"Momma, you know very well how we all thought Jonathan was such a handsome man at the time. How was I supposed to know he wouldn't hit a lick at a snake when it comes to work?" Lilith asked.

"Well, girls, you might try usin' your eyes and ears before latchin' on to some handsome face that comes dancin' your way each and every time. You two haven't got the good sense God gave a nanny goat when it comes to pickin' men! Everybody but you two knew Leroy Wilson and Jon Montgomery were not fit to be seen with. They were the talk of the town."

Both girls murmured, "Whatever!" Clearly not impressed with their mother's assessment of their choices, they left in a huff.

Bette turned an affectionate gaze towards Jane who was helping with the cold drinks two tables over. Turning back to the others, she said, "But, Jane! Now, I am proud of Jane. Why, I'm tickled pink to see her with such a fine lookin' fella as that Englishman. He appears to be an industrious sort as well. And good lookin' too. Here, Lizzy," Bette said as Elizabeth returned, eating a chocolate chip cookie, "put the fried green tomatoes over there with the fried okra and squash, and be sure to keep everything covered up. We don't want flies gettin' on anything. Here, pass this down," Bette said, handing Florence the pickled okra. "Y'all need to try this okra. It's the latest recipe from the July edition of *Farm Journal Country Cooking*.

"Oh and before I forget about it, Lori, did you see those white doves last Sunday?" Bette asked. "They were out by the graveyard in the thicket closest to the old part of the cemetery, perched on a laurel branch. They were sittin' there just as pretty as you please. They shine just like a pig bathed in buttermilk. Odd for these parts don't you think?"

"Umm...yes, I saw them. They were snow white and very beautiful. I hope they stay away from the cornfield today. It would be a sin to kill one of 'em."

"Well, I've already given Sam Henry a good piece of my mind about it. If he comes home with one of those birds in his bag, I'll take that gun away from him and shoot him good. I told him not to harm one feather on those birds' backs. Perhaps they'll have young ones, and we'll see a flock of 'em. Somethin' as rare as that and so pretty, too, it *would* be a sin to kill 'em." Bette turned to her niece and asked, "Sandy, how's that ice cream comin' along?"

"The ice cream is comin' along just fine, Aunt Bette. The strawberry appears to be done, but the peach, vanilla, and chocolate still have a ways to go," Sandy said as she checked the canisters.

"Tana, take the cornbread sticks and the sourdough rolls to the far end of the table, and what did you think of Jane's handsome fella? He sure seems friendly enough, doesn't he?" Bette queried Tana Bennett.

"Well, I don't rightly know. I didn't get a chance to talk with him before Robert and the others snatched him away to the cornfield. He is handsome, though." Shrugging her shoulders, she changed the subject. "Lydia, I want you and Florence to try one of my deviled eggs, and you too, Lori. It's a new recipe Sadie Hopkins put in the church cookbook. Robert thinks they're delicious," Tana said, arranging the table to suit her perfectionist taste.

"Oh, they are good. I made them last Sunday when Pastor Emery and his family came for dinner," Lori said. "What about you, Lydia? You were there, too. What did you think?"

"They were okay, I suppose," Lydia said with a cool tone as she rearranged Tana's table, apparently not very pleased with the setting.

Florence noticed the slight and arched a brow, but she knew it was best to simply ignore it. With a smile she turned to Tana Bennett. "Well, Tana, I'll try your deviled eggs if you'll try my coconut lemon cake. It's Aunt Janey's recipe, and oh, is it so good! She gave it to me last year before she passed on. Speaking of Janey, you know Meg named our Jane after her, don't you? I sure would like to see Meg's children settled well. We'll have to watch that Englishman. He sure seems to like our Jane."

"Florence, I've got to have Janey's recipe," Bette said. "I was meanin' to ask her for it, and then she up and died before I could. You'll have to let me have it. I hope you're right about that Englishman. Oh, and by the way, have you heard the latest about Martha Schrimshire's daughter, Isabelle? You know, the one who was recently married to that Haskell boy. Well now, his sorry no account butt has run off with Jeremiah Handley's daughter, leaving Isabelle pregnant and alone. Isn't that just awful! I don't know what poor Isabelle is gonna do, the poor little thing. She's just devastated, and now her family has to suffer from the likes of that Haskell trash."

Shocked at this news, Florence replied. "I declare, Bette! I had not heard that, and I thought I'd heard everything down at the Cut and Curl."

"Oh, I just heard it this mornin' when I bumped into Sue Ellen Schrimshire down at the Piggly Wiggly. I had to pick up a few things before comin' out here." Bette nodded, picking up the coleslaw and moving it over to where the potato salads were. "But haven't I always told you those Haskells were no good? Why, they come from over there at Slaughter's Holler, and ain't nothin' good ever comes from that holler. It's such a disgrace! But we all knew that Haskell boy was no account. Poor Isabelle!" Bette shook her head. "They say she was in the family way when they married. We'll just all have to keep her in our prayers and help her family through this time of trouble."

"Umm...I hadn't heard that news either," Tana said.

"Nor I, but then I'm not surprised considerin' how naïve that Schrimshire girl is and what trash that Haskell boy is. She'd believe the sky was green and the grass blue if some charmin' boy told her so," Lydia said with little concern evident in her expression.

"Well Lydia," Tana bristled, "I still feel sorry for the poor girl. She comes from a fine family and has always been a good girl. It's our Christian duty to help our neighbors."

"Of course, we'll help, Tana! You know none of us means anything by it, but we all know Isabelle ain't never had a lick of sense. So it is partly her fault for marryin' that trash, and even worse for gettin' pregnant in the first place," Florence said.

"Well, let's look things over. I see the men are coming back," Bette interjected.

As the women continued setting up the tables and chattering on about one thing after another, Elizabeth listened quietly. She could think of nothing worse than to be pregnant and abandoned, unless it was to suffer the pitying stares of gossiping old women. She knew nothing like that would every happen to her, but if it did, she wouldn't stick around to become the latest fodder for her aunts' gossip hub down at the Cut and Curl. It was the only beauty shop in town and the center for the latest *news*.

While the women gossiped, Liddy had the cousins assembled under the old oak tree that stood closest to the house.

"Lilith, what do you think of Lizzy? Don't you think she's strange? And everyone says she's so pretty. Well, what good does it do to be pretty if nobody even notices," Liddy said as she leaned against the tree filing her nails.

"Oh, Liddy! You've always been jealous of Lizzy. She wouldn't look twice at the kind of redneck trash you date, and for that matter, neither would I," Kat scowled.

"And just what's that supposed to mean? Sounds like you're the one that's jealous, Kat Bennett. Besides, Jackie Lee Nunley has a master's degree in organic chemistry and another in botany. They have money, too. So, he's hardly redneck trash," Liddy sneered, her hands on her hips and her belly spilling out over the top of her two-sizes-too-small low rise jeans.

"Oh yeah? Well, you can't make a silk purse out of a sow's ear. Those Nunleys are nothing but white trash. They've always been in trouble with the law, and you damn well know it. His granddaddy did time in the penitentiary for running illegal whiskey up on top of Skyline Mountain, and I've heard tell that Jackie Lee's under surveillance by the DEA for cultivating pot. That's what those degrees in organic chemistry and botany are for. It's just a matter of time before the chickens come home to roost, Liddy. So, you'd better watch your step because Jackie Lee's meaner than a damn snake. And one of these days, you're gonna get bit!"

"Well, I know nothing about that, and just because you've heard tell, don't make it so. I can handle Jackie Lee," Liddy smirked. "You Bennetts are too big for your britches. Momma says so, and I believe it. So, don't you get your drawers in a wad, Kat Bennett!"

"Well, your momma wouldn't say so if my daddy was still alive, and you need to pull the *knot* outa your own drawers, Lydia Louise Fanning." Kat glared. "I don't know why you come to these family gatherings when you clearly don't like us."

"We have just as much right to be here as you do, Katherine Suzanne Bennett, cuz Momma grew up here, too. Just because your daddy was the so-called heir don't make it right. Momma was the oldest. Longbourn shoulda been hers!" Liddy said as she leaned right into Kat's face.

"Go suck eggs!" Kat turned and stomped off, leaving the group of cousins gawking after her.

The men returned from the field tired and hungry. They had been very successful with the hunt. Between Charles and Robert Bennett, they had bagged thirty-six birds, not counting what the other men had shot. After cleaning the birds and putting them in storage, all the hunters went to the mudroom to wash and prepare to eat. Once assembled in the serving line, Robert said the blessing. Everyone took their plates, filled high, to the nearest table under the large pavilion to sit and eat while some of the men played a collection of Blue Grass and country music. The families socialized, ate, and danced late into the evening until it was time to go home.

As they readied themselves to return to town, Jane packed a basket of leftovers for Bingley and Darcy. Charles expressed his thanks several times over to Jane's family, telling them he could not remember ever having spent a more pleasant or enjoyable time.

Arriving back in town, they stopped by the townhouse to unload Jane's things first before proceeding to Bingley and Darcy's house. Darcy, anxious to know how Bingley's day had gone, was waiting up when his friend returned.

"Darcy, I hope you enjoyed your day because I know I surely did mine. I've never seen so much food or such a variety. I believe I must have sampled every Southern dish known to this region." He laughed light heartedly. "They sent a nice variety home for you, too." Bingley said, rummaging through the basket and pulling out paper plates and bowls wrapped in plastic. "Here, we have a little bit of everything—barbecued pork, chicken, steak, homemade bread, a variety of casseroles, a nice selection of salads, relishes, fried okra, fried squash and something they call fried green tomatoes," he said. "It's all simply delicious. And look at these." Bingley reached in once again, bringing out another paper plate piled high. "They call these fried pies. Look, I have chocolate, peach, apple, and cherry."

Bingley continued to talk as he unpacked the basket, spreading everything out on the table while Darcy washed his hands and then picked over the variety of food, inspecting each item.

"Except for a brother serving in Iraq and a sister who lives in New York, I met the whole family—cousins, aunts, uncles, and friends. And I can't tell you when I've had a more enjoyable time."

"Apart from obviously stuffing yourself silly, what else happened?"

"Well then, you might like to know that Jane's uncle took me dove shooting and together we bagged thirty-six birds."

Darcy gave Charles a quick look as he filled a plate. "I see."

Charles continued rattling on as he arranged the table for the two of them to eat. "Oh, and by the way, Jane's sister, Dr. Elizabeth Bennett, is a knock-out, just like her sister. She was the one we saw walking with Jane when we first came here for the tour to look this place over. You remember—the one with the long black hair. Plus," he beamed, "I have it on very good authority that she likes many things beyond math and science." Charles winked at his friend while fixing his plate. "So what do you say to that?" Bingley asked, beaming from ear to ear.

Darcy grinned. "I say the bread smells good and the food looks delicious. Let's heat our plates in the microwave, and I'll take one of those pies."

"Darcy, you're avoiding the question, but the food is too good to miss."

As they ate, Darcy reflected on what his friend had told him and smiled. *So my Lúthien is Dr. Elizabeth Bennett, umm—not a student after all. I'll have to meet her and see if she's as smart as she is beautiful.*

After putting the food away, Darcy sighed in contentment. Everything had been wonderful—including the fried green tomatoes. His favorites, however, were those little fried pies, especially the chocolate. He wondered if his Lúthien had cooked any of it. With that thought, he resolved to discover a way in which to meet this Dr. Elizabeth Bennett without being obvious.

Chapter Five

...I'd love to see her hair down, loose and blowing in the wind...

Dr. Fitzwilliam Darcy stood at the second floor window of Morton Hall and looked out over the parking lot watching a woman walk across campus. Dr. Bennett appeared to shiver against the cool crisp air on this blustery October morning. The chilling wind ruffled her black and white checked skirt around the ankles of her walking boots as she rubbed her palms along the sleeves of a pretty black sweater that appeared to have embroidered beading sparkling along the neckline. The outfit, coupled with her hair swept up in an elegant twist, made her look sophisticated and lovely.

While Fitzwilliam watched her walk, he briefly closed his eyes and breathed deeply. Standing rooted in place, he fixed his gaze upon her graceful figure. *I'd love to see her hair down... loose and free, blowing in the wind.*

Lingering at the window as he propped against the wall, he watched her walk into the UC. A few minutes later, he observed her coming back out with a cup of coffee in her hands gently blowing it and taking a sip as she strolled back across the way to Clemons Hall and disappeared inside the maths building.

She continued in this pattern everyday at the same time, and everyday Dr. Darcy watched, admiring her beauty as she came and went while his curiosity and thoughts concerning her grew. He wondered what she did each day on her coffee break. *...Does she drink her coffee in class or does she sip it in her office. What kind of coffee does she drink, and how does she take it? Would she like to have coffee with me?*

By the fourth day, Darcy could stand it no longer. He decided that he, too, would like coffee. He timed it just right so that he arrived at the coffee shop just as she entered. Opening the door with a smile, they walked in together.

Her lips curled pleasantly. "Thank you, sir."

"You're welcome, madam."

She blushed slightly, heat filling her flushed cheeks. *...British...What a lovely accent! I could get used to that. I wonder if he's Charles's friend...the one Jane keeps telling me about. The one she's been dying to set me up with.*

They both ordered their coffee, but Elizabeth decided to linger instead of following her usual routine. She tried to think of something to say, but nothing came to mind.

Elizabeth noticed the gentleman seemed to be in no hurry, and the way he looked at her, casting a glance every now and then, caused her to smile. Also, from the way he fidgeted, he appeared to be nervous. Perhaps he wanted an introduction as much as she did.

Finally, Elizabeth found her tongue. "Pardon me, but I noticed by your accent that you must be from England. Would you happen to be Dr. Darcy?" she asked with a smile. "My sister, Jane, often speaks of him. I know you are not Dr. Bingley as he visits our house quite a bit these days."

The man's face lit up with a wide grin. "Yes, I am, and you must be Jane's sister, Dr. Elizabeth Bennett, the maths professor. Charles speaks of you often. It is a pleasure to finally meet you."

"I'm sure the pleasure is all mine, Dr. Darcy, and yes, I am Jane's sister," she said, offering her hand.

"Do you need to return to Clemons Hall now or do you have a moment?" he asked as he took her hand and gently shook it.

"Well, I usually take this time of day for a personal study period. Today though, I think I will forgo the lesson."

"Oh? And what subject would a mathematician spend her personal time studying? Some equations in theoretical physics on some research grant?" He gestured with his hand as they took a seat.

"No, nothing like that." She laughed. "Teaching math is enough for me. I've studied it all I want to. Now, I'm pursuing things that I would've liked to have done, but could not for lack of time."

"And what would that be?" he asked with a teasing grin.

"Well, if you must know, I'm trying to relearn Greek grammar. I'm afraid I didn't pay attention when I was first learning it, and now I want to read some original works. So, I need to start all over again." By the look on his face, she knew she'd surprised him.

"When did you first have a course in that subject?"

"In high school. My father hired a tutor for us. But I'm afraid at the time I was not ready for the rigors of the subject. I was more interested in what was going on outside of my window." She chuckled softly. "My mother and father had a great love for learning and desired to pass it on to us, and for the most part, they did." She paused for a sip of coffee. "They believed that history and the works of great men should be read from primary sources. That's why they wanted us to learn Greek and Latin. I loved Latin, and I'm decent with it, but I found Greek to be tedious. I'm afraid I still do." She sighed. "I will admit I'm having a difficult time with it."

"Dr. Bennett, I'm teaching that very subject this semester. I would be more than happy to help you sometime. Your sister often invites me over, but I haven't taken her up on it as I didn't want to be in their way. Two's company and three's a crowd and all that." He flashed a bright smile. "Perhaps sometime I could come over, and we could work on your Greek lesson together."

"Well, perhaps. Jane was supposed to help me, but your friend seems to be occupying most of her time." Puzzled by his offer, but not entirely put off by it, she sipped her coffee as she stared across the table at the tall dark-haired man with the gorgeous chocolate eyes—eyes that with very little effort she knew she could become devoured by. Savoring another sip, she glanced down at her watch, realizing her next class was about to begin. Where had the time gone?

"Umm…this coffee is so good. Peppermint Mocha is my favorite, but I'll have to take it with me. My class begins in fifteen minutes. Thank you for your offer, Dr. Darcy. I'll let you know should I need any help, but it's time for me to head back to Clemons," she said with a warm smile as she rose from her seat. "I've enjoyed our conversation. Perhaps we'll meet again."

"Perhaps." He returned her smile while getting up to see her to the door.

They didn't see each other at the coffee shop on Friday or Monday, therefore Elizabeth seemed pleasantly surprised to find Dr. Darcy there again on Tuesday. He grinned as he approached the counter where she stood waiting to order her coffee.

"Dr. Bennett, it's so pleasant to see you today. I enjoyed our conversation the last time we spoke, and I've looked forward to another, but I've been extremely busy with my classes this term. I'm afraid I'm a little rusty with my Latin. I have a wonderful group of students who keep me on my toes, but my other classes are progressing quite well. How are your Greek lessons coming along?"

"Well enough, I suppose, but the next chapter is going to give me trouble, I can tell." She indicated to the young man behind the counter that she would have her usual.

"And why might that be?" Darcy asked as he paid the boy for his and Dr. Bennett's coffee.

"Infinitives and participles. I'm confused on their usage, and it seems Jane, as usual, is too busy with Dr. Bingley to help me." She smiled. "I'm also confused by the accent marks. They appear to be random. They don't follow any logical rule that I can see," she said, taking her coffee and walking in the direction of a small table for two.

"No, that's not quite right. It actually does follow a rule. You simply have to determine the pattern. The diphthongs appear to be random, but in actuality, they are not." He paused for a moment. "Dr. Bennett, I've told you I would be more than happy to help you with Greek if you'll only ask. I'll help you with the ebb and flow. You'll soon catch on." Darcy set his coffee down and helped her into her seat, catching the scent of her perfume. *Roses... My favorite!*

"Well then, consider yourself asked because I really want to learn this," she said, taking a sip of her coffee as he took his seat.

"In that case, would you like to have dinner with me tonight? Then we could go over the basic structure of the lesson afterwards at your house or mine, whichever you prefer."

"Well, since you're kind enough to offer a poor damsel in distress your services, I'd love to, and my house would be preferable. Is five o'clock too soon?"

"No, five o'clock is perfect. That should give us plenty of time to eat and go over the lesson. The lesson you're having problems with is really not that complicated, but it does need to be explained. I'm sure you'll catch on rather quickly." Darcy thought how incredibly beautiful she was with her dark ringlets framing her face.

"I'm usually very good at figuring things out, but this chapter is not so clear. I really do appreciate your taking the trouble to help me."

"It's no problem at all, I assure you. I don't mind in the least." *...Not in the least.*

They sat and drank their coffee, talking about many things including the Cumberland Plateau and England. He told her about his home county of Derbyshire, and she revealed a little about her home, Longbourn. Before each had realized where the time had gone, their forty-five minutes were up.

Darcy wanted to spend a little more time with her. Summoning his courage, he asked, "Dr. Bennett, I have a two hour block of time starting at noon. When are you free?"

"Please, do call me Elizabeth. May I call you by your given name?" she asked. "And I have the same times lot available. My afternoon class begins at 2:20."

"Elizabeth," he whispered, "such a lovely name. My friends at the university call me William. Since you're free, will you meet me at the UC for lunch?" He beamed, momentarily glancing from her eyes to her lips, wondering what it might be like to kiss her.

"I believe I can arrange it."

He held the door for her as they walked out of the building, each returning to their respective halls.

The fifty-minute long class felt like an eternity as time slowly ground down. When class was finally over and the last student cleared the room, Elizabeth hurriedly dropped her books off at her office and made her way to the UC. Darcy was already waiting when she entered. They ordered their lunch and left for a secluded area, settling in to eat and have a pleasant conversation.

They easily conversed on many subjects, including history, literature, philosophy, and some current affairs. It gave them the opportunity to discover that they liked many of the same things, but her knowledge of the great philosophers was limited. Still, Elizabeth gained much from his insight into philosophy and also realized that they shared a common love for the works of J.R.R. Tolkien.

"Elizabeth, tell me which of Tolkien's works are your favorite?"

"Without a doubt it would be *The Silmarillion* with a close second being *The Children of Hurin* followed by *The Lord of the Rings*. Which are your favorites?"

"Mine are the very same. I just recently finished *The Children of Hurin*. I enjoyed it very much. However, they all mesh together, giving you a complete look into Tolkien's world. That's why I recommend reading them in order," he said with a broad smile. "Did you realize that Tolkien was never able to publish *The Silmarillion* in his lifetime? His son completed the manuscript and published the book after his father's death. It was a difficult go getting his work published."

"Indeed it was. It seemed no one wanted to take the chance. It's all about money, you know," she said matter-of-factly as she lifted her sandwich.

"Yes, but Tolkien pioneered the way for other great authors to be published. I believe, had it not been for him, others might not have been published."

"I agree." She nodded. "But his hard work facilitated the progress for fellow fantasy author C.S. Lewis, and together they paved the way for J.K. Rowling's *Harry Potter* series which will probably go down in the chronicles of literary history as the best creative fiction of the 21st century. She did a fantastic job!" Elizabeth excitedly replied.

"Yes, she did. It is an original concept based on many classical elements. In my opinion, she ranks among Lewis and Tolkien now."

"On that, we both agree. Now, what do you think of Gothic literature?"

"I find the subject very interesting. Do you have a specific author in mind?"

"Yes, I do—William Faulkner. He's considered one of the leading Southern Gothic writers of our time. I have many first editions of his work. You know that his writing is considered difficult to understand because of his heavy use of literary techniques. But I think that is what made his work so exceptional. Consider his short story *A Rose for Emily*. I think that one story has much to say that is relevant to us as readers. What do you think?"

"I think Faulkner was an extraordinary writer, especially in his use of symbolism, allegory, multiple narrators and points of view, as well as deep streams of consciousness." Darcy tilted his head, gazing at her quizzically. "But I'm not sure I catch your meaning with regard to *A Rose for Emily*."

"Well," her lips curled softly, "Faulkner is showing us, through multiple first person points of view, how a controlling father can affect the lives of his children, or in this case, child. Emily was slowly driven insane by a series of events, beginning with a father who controlled every aspect of her life. He drove away all of her suitors. Do you not agree that a controlling father can be detrimental to the health and happiness of his children?"

Darcy pondered her challenge. "Yes, I suppose that could be true," he cautiously responded. "Children do not flourish well under such circumstances, but there does come a time when the child becomes an adult, and then that child is responsible for his or her own choices. Just because one has a difficult childhood doesn't mean that they cannot be a normal adult." Discussing the ramifications of a controlling father on adult children was decidedly *not* something Darcy wanted to pursue.

M.K. Baxley

"Oh, I'm not saying they cannot be *normal*, but only that they have a difficult time overcoming their past. They often hide from the past instead of facing it, or as in Emily's case, eventually become incapable of having normal feelings."

The conversation had taken an uncomfortable turn. "You may very well be right, but that particular story is one I have little interest in. Now, if you don't mind, let's talk of other things. I'd like to know your views on the works of some of the Latin scholars," he said, clearly relieved to be back on more comfortable ground. But nevertheless, *A Rose for Emily* stung as he contemplated its meaning while thinking of himself, David, and Georgiana.

Their two hour lunch break slipped by quickly as they discussed many things. The only subject Elizabeth did not care for was business, especially international business. Darcy figured four out of five wasn't bad, and perhaps it was best she knew so little, or had no interest in that topic. He was not intentionally hiding that part of himself, but he wasn't yet ready to disclose it, either. He wanted to get to know her much better before revealing who he really was. If they were to develop a meaningful relationship, it would have to be based on more than a physical attraction, his legacy as the Darcy heir, or his money. He wanted her to like him, possibly love him, for the person he was, apart from his world of money and high society.

For his part, there was no denying that he was attracted to her, and not only for her looks, but her beautiful mind as well. He was attracted to the entire package as he was beginning to realize that she might possibly be everything he had searched for. She was beautiful, intelligent, and shared many of his interests. She also provided the most stimulating and intelligent conversation on the subjects he loved that he'd had in many years. Everything about her he found enticing and alluring—her smile, her sparkling eyes, her beautiful hair, and her well proportioned figure—especially her figure. Try as he might, he couldn't help from wondering what it might feel like to hold her, to kiss her, to feel her body pressed against his—to lie beneath him. For the first time, in a long time, desire was beginning to stir.

That night they had dinner at the local Italian restaurant where they continued with their lively conversations. After dinner he helped her over her hurdle with Greek. It was only a minor problem which, when explained, enabled her to finish her work. He didn't stay long after the lesson.

Elizabeth walked him to the door, her face slightly upturned. When he placed a chaste kiss on her cheek, she couldn't effectively hide her surprise. He smiled when he realized that she had wanted more, but he would wait until he was sure the time was right. When he really kissed her, he wanted it to be memorable for the both of them, keeping in mind that anticipation made the reward so much sweeter. He intended to take this romance slowly, if there was to be one, for he had learned from past experience to be cautious. Having been burnt once, he didn't intend for it to happen again.

By the middle of November, Elizabeth and Darcy were dating on a regular basis. They spent almost every evening together. He was now helping Elizabeth at least twice a week with her Greek lessons. Darcy was impressed with how quickly she learned and how greatly she improved under his instruction. Even more surprising was how much they shared in common, but he had to be sure of his feelings before he took their relationship further, for he knew that with very little effort, they could become deeply involved. The temptation was great, and yet he still had not kissed her the way he intended, even though it was very much what he wanted.

It was a Wednesday evening. They had just finished a Greek lesson, and he was preparing to leave. Standing at the front door about to say goodbye, he was puzzled. By her fidgeting and worried look he could tell something might be bothering her, but he wasn't sure what. Finally, he asked her.

"Elizabeth, is something wrong?"

She lowered her lashes momentarily and then raised her gaze. "William, we have been dating on a regular basis for almost four weeks. Why haven't you kissed me other than a peck on the lips or cheek?" she demanded, looking at him directly with intense eyes.

He was both relieved and amused and showed it with a wide grin. "Do you want me to kiss you, Elizabeth?"

This direct question startled her, catching her off guard. "Well…I… I thought that perhaps… since we're dating and all... that maybe." Finally she spit it out, flushed with embarrassment. "Yes I do!"

He laughed softly and pulled her into an embrace. "Then, I will. I never disappoint a lady." Releasing a sigh, he reached up and brushed her cheek with his fingers while his thumb lightly stroked her lower lip. Holding her securely, he slipped his hand into her hair and dipped his head, catching her lips in a slow lingering kiss as his tongue slipped in and out of her mouth. Feeling her shiver under his touch served to encourage him, so he angled his head and deepened the kiss. He kissed her repeatedly, his tongue probing, exploring, tasting, breaking away only when they needed to breathe. He was about to kiss her again when he noticed her eyes were still closed with her lips slightly parted in anticipation. He groaned quietly and pulled back, delighted in her response.

Her eyes flew open. "Aren't you going to kiss me again?"

Looking down into her questioning eyes, he was tempted—he wanted to, but… "I think you've been kissed enough for one night, Dr. Bennett." He smiled, tapping her lightly on the nose. "I'll see you Friday night when we have another Greek lesson. We'll see what happens then." He breathed deeply. "I'll see you tomorrow for coffee and then for lunch at our usual times. Good night, Liz." He kissed her with his usual quick kiss and then turned to depart. Glancing over his shoulder once more before leaving, he had to smile. There she stood strangely befuddled, blinking in astonishment as she brushed her fingers over her lips.

Walking briskly back to his house, he took another deep breath. It had taken extreme willpower to draw away from her, leaving him in a painful state of desire. He wanted to do more than kiss her, and in time, he was confident they would. But first he had to be sure she was the one because he wanted far more than a casual love affair. He wanted a lover, someone who would also be his friend and companion, his complement, his soul mate—his wife, and he believed Elizabeth Bennett just might be the very woman he had been waiting for. In time, he would know for certain. The physical attraction was certainly there. He sighed as he turned the corner. *...She has no idea what affect she has on me. The sight of her...the feel of her...the scent of her. I haven't felt like this in years. Sleep tonight will be difficult ...very difficult.*

As she watched him turn the corner onto Maple Street, her frustration piqued along with her disappointment. *...Teasing man! Whatever is wrong with him? The man defies logic!* Elizabeth stomped her foot. She could not comprehend him. Whatever the reasons, his tactic of slowly drawing her in was working. She was falling in love.

Chapter Six

...waiting for the right one...

Friday night, Fitzwilliam picked up Elizabeth for dinner at his house while Charles dined with Jane at the Bennett townhouse on Elm Street. After dinner, he escorted Elizabeth to the library for her Greek lesson where he checked the last assignment he had given her, and finding it satisfactory, he went on to the next lesson. They worked through the next chapter until he was satisfied that she had grasped the concept, and then he gave her another assignment.

Closing the book and putting everything away, Fitzwilliam turned to Elizabeth with a smile. "Now let's have some wine and relax." Rising from the table, he went to his study and returned with a decanter of port.

"Elizabeth, we've dated for nearly four weeks and discussed many things, but I still don't know much about you. Why don't you tell me about your parents, your siblings? I want to learn something of your history—what influenced you, what you did as a child, what were your favorite toys, games, any pets you may have had. Tell me about your horses. I believe you ride. I want to know everything about you." He poured the wine and handed her a glass, then he took a seat at the opposite end of the sofa, facing her.

"Well, I don't really know where to begin. You've asked a lot. But I'll try my best to tell you what you want to know." She paused for a sip of wine. "I think we were like any other family. Mom stayed home when we were little. She baked and cooked and was just always there. She read to us, and we all sang songs together. That's one of the ways we learned to appreciate both music and reading. Then, when Mom needed a break, she would set us all down to watch Public Broadcasting—you know, *Sesame Street, Mr. Rogers Neighborhood, Shining Time Station*. She wanted us to have fun, but she was always looking for educational programs for us as opposed to junk food TV, though we were allowed to watch some of that too—just not a steady diet of it. My favorite show was *My Little Pony*. To this day I still love to watch it," Elizabeth said with a soft laugh.

"As for toys, the girls had baby dolls and the boys had trains and little toy cars. Cherry Merry Muffin and Strawberry Shortcake were some my favorite little dolls, but I also had an American Girl Samantha doll and a Bitty Baby that I loved." She smiled at the memory. "I remember when Kat was born. I carried my Bitty Baby everywhere, pretending that I had a baby too while Mom tofok care of my baby sister. I even pretended to nurse."

Darcy's lips curled while thinking about the Bennett children playing in front of the TV, the girls with their dolls and the boys with trains and little toy cars much like he and David had done. "So you were the nurturing type when you were little."

"To some extent. I wanted to be just like my mom when I was little. She taught math at this university, too. Later, though, I wanted to be like Dad. I didn't think it was fair that he spent so much time with the boys, teaching them about the farm, so eventually, he let me tag along. I learned a great deal about managing a farm, and I suppose it's a good thing now with Joseph overseas."

"Managing a farm or an estate can be very fulfilling," Darcy said, thinking of how much he would have liked to have done just as she had described. Once more he felt the sting of his father's controlling personality, wishing he had been like Mr. Bennett.

"Indeed it is. I think I'll always want to live on a farm. I could never be truly happy on a city lot, stuck in town." She shook her head.

...Nor I, Elizabeth...Nor I.

"Now where was I? Oh yes! Mother would make us cute little dresses, and she would always make one to match for our dolls—especially for my Samantha doll which was my favorite. She smocked and did French hand sewing. We had beautiful clothes. Mom sewed, crocheted, tatted lace, and embroidered as well as many other things. She taught all her girls to do likewise. And soon Jane, Mary Beth and I, and later Kat, were making our own doll clothes. Eventually, we even made our own clothes. Mom taught us to design our wardrobes to suit our individual taste."

"I bet you were very cute." Darcy chuckled.

"Well, I don't know about that."

"Ah, but I believe you were...and still are. Now, carry on. I'm anxious to hear more. Tell me about your dad. What was he like?"

"Dad was special." She nodded as she took a sip of wine. "He was as kind and good as a man could be. Every night he would read to us. He started with simple things such as children's stories, Little Golden Books. Then, as we grew older, he progressed to *The Brothers Grimm* and *Hans Christian Anderson*. Those two are still among my favorites to this very day. He read to us from a series by Walter Fraley about horses, too. That was where my love affair with the horse first began. Dad read all of Charles Dickens and Mark Twain to us as well as many other selections from the classics. He did this until we could read for ourselves, and then continued it at bedtime." She smiled with a twinkle in her eyes. "This opened the world to me, and I became an avid reader. I truly loved to learn and was often found with a book in my hand."

...You're very fortunate. I would like to have had a family like yours. I'm sure you'll make a wonderful mother someday. I hope I'll make a good father. Maybe someday you and I will have a family together.

"How were you educated?" Darcy asked. "You seem to have had an unusual background."

She chuckled. "We were educated at home, but as we grew older, my father hired tutors to teach us Latin, Greek, Spanish, French, and piano, and the girls all took classical ballet, jazz, and ballroom dancing. Mary Beth excelled and was accepted to The American School of Ballet."

...Interesting.

"My younger brother, Joseph, excelled in karate and academics. He was so far ahead of most children that he graduated from high school when he was sixteen and attended this university for one year before he was accepted into the Naval Academy at seventeen." She paused for a sip of wine.

"Now, as to me personally, I was an outdoors type. It was a punishment for me to be kept inside, even in the winter. I would climb trees and hang upside down, which would upset Grandmother Barnett, my mother's mother, to no end, as she would always tell me I would turn my liver over, or that it was disgraceful for a young lady to climb trees. I was a tomboy."

Darcy laughed. "A real hoyden."

"Yes, I suppose so. Much to my grandmother's chagrin."

Darcy shook his head and laughed at the thought of a little girl hanging upside down in a tree. "I loved to play outdoors as a child, too. We would have made good playmates. Continue on. I'm enjoying this," he said.

She slipped off her shoes and curled her feet firmly underneath her as she lifted her glass to her lips. "Well, let's see, what else is there? Oh yes, hounds. My father always kept hounds. We had Black and Tans, Walkers, Redbones, and Bloodhounds. When I was sixteen, my father gave me a pair of Black and Tans, which became my pride and joy. I raised them from pups, and we became inseparable until I left for school."

...Hounds! I like hounds... Better and better. You and I complement one another in that regard.

He nodded as he raised his glass.

"I was also very boisterous. I remember a time when Joseph and I played a prank on Kat. I was ten, Joseph was nine, and Kat was four—well, nearly five, actually. She was dressed in one of her pretty smocked frocks that Mom had made for her. Peach colored, I do believe. It was the Fourth of July, and we were going to have company over for our annual ice cream social and fireworks celebration. It's a very grand affair for our family with all of the aunts, uncles, and cousins coming together for the fun."

"Charles told me all about your last get together. I wish I had foregone my business meeting." *...She grew up in such a close family! My mother would've wanted our lives to have been similar, but Father was rarely there for us.*

"Yes, you should have. We would have met a whole month sooner! And then you could have met my family along with Charles. Anyway, where was I? I seem to have lost track."

"Something concerning Kat, I believe." He sipped his wine as he listened.

"Oh yes, I remember now. Kat had been especially annoying that day. Mom and Dad had tasked us with keeping her entertained. She followed us everywhere, constantly reporting back everything we did, getting us into all sorts of trouble—all because of her tattling. So, we formed a plan for revenge."

"Oh, no! What did you do?"

She snickered. "We convinced Kat to stand very still with her eyes closed near a *very* large and fresh cow-pile in the barnyard. I asked her to count to twenty, since that was as far as she could count at the time. I told her to wait for a very special surprise that Joseph and I had planned *just* for her. She was so trusting...she never suspected a thing!"

Darcy rolled his eyes and grinned, nodding for her to continue as he took another sip of wine.

"We were very naughty, I'm afraid. While Kat counted, we placed firecrackers in the pile and lit them. Then we stood back to watch. When it exploded, Kat was covered from head to toe. Bursting into tears, she ran into the kitchen crying and dripping slimy green manure all over Mom's nice clean floor. Kat's dress was ruined." Elizabeth chuckled. "That day Joseph and I got the worst spanking either of us had ever had, but I got the worst of it because Daddy said I was older and obviously the ring leader. My father never spanked us much, but that one was memorable. Daddy also made me stay inside for the rest of the day with no ice cream and no more fireworks. I had to clean the kitchen floor, too. And Joseph lost his pony privileges."

Darcy shouted with laughter. "Elizabeth, she was a baby—only four years old. That was terrible of you!"

"Well, she was almost five! But you're right. It was terrible. The worse part of it, though, was when we realized what we had done. We were both scared to death, and with good reason, too. We knew we were going to *get it* as my father would say. We never intended it to be the big mess that it was. I kept telling Joseph that three firecrackers were enough, but did he listen to me? No! He used the entire pack!"

"You, Miss Bennett, deserved exactly what you got, and I have no sympathy for you. I would have also smacked your bum, too, had you been my daughter. That was a very wicked thing to do, but to be fair, my brother and I have played our fair share of pranks. Although I don't believe we ever covered anyone in *cow manure*. I can't believe how rambunctious you were—you were awful. A little terror! I'm glad I didn't know back you then. I wouldn't have wanted to be on the receiving end of your revenge then or now," Darcy said, wiping tears of laughter from his eyes.

"Well, I've grown up since then. And I hope I have learned to behave a little better. But Daddy always told me that payback is hell and that someday I will have a little girl just like me. Although, I surely hope not. According to him, Joseph and I were just like him. He often told us we were his penance for all he had done as a child, while Mom said it wasn't fair that she should have to suffer for his sins."

"Well, Miss Bennett, I hope that fate never befalls you or the poor man who marries you. I'm siding with your mother in this instance. However, I must tell you it sounds like there was never a dull moment in your home. I pity your poor parents!"

"No, there was never a dull moment. I can assure you of that. But the rest of my siblings were not like me and Joseph. Jane has always been sweet and kind. She's like Momma, and Mary Beth is like my Grandmother Bennett—refined and always insistent on being proper and ladylike. Kat is a less refined version of me, although more cautious, while Daniel is shy and very reserved. He loves to draw and wants to be a civil engineer. He'll do it, too. We all have a way of determining our future through hard work and sheer force of will. The Bennetts have always been known for that."

"Elizabeth, your family sounds utterly fascinating. I feel as if I'm getting to know them through you. Now tell me about your first horse. What horses do you have now?"

"Well, when I was eleven, Dad bought me my first horse. He was a bluish grey quarter horse gelding named Buck. I learned to ride on him, and I have loved riding ever since. Today we have four mares and two stallions—a black Arabian and a white Lipizzan. Our black stallion, however, is very difficult to handle, and for that reason, I don't ride him. Only Joseph and my father have ever ridden him, but hopefully this spring I can work with him and tame him some. He's very spirited whereas the white stallion is gentle and easy to manage."

His curiosity piqued with this knowledge. Horses were one of his passions. "Elizabeth, Lipizzans are amazing jumpers and climbers, but your Arabian fascinates me more. I would like to see him. I've ridden all my life, and I like spirited animals very much." ...*Spirited women, too.*

"Well, you can try when you come to Longbourn tomorrow. He's quite a handful."

"I'll look forward to it. Now tell me more about your parents. I wish I could have met them."

She dropped her gaze for a split second. "My parents were two of the best people I've ever know, and I miss them dearly. There was never a question that they loved us all unconditionally, even when we disappointed them, like I did when I played that trick on Kat. Mom and Dad were also very much in love. Dad always treated Mom with the utmost of respect. His family was the most important thing in his life, and Mom and his children were always first. We were his world. And Mom was always there whenever I needed to talk. She may not have had the answers, but she always had a cup of hot tea and a listening ear. That's why I miss them so terribly. Mom and Dad could make anything better." She suppressed a sob.

"They were killed in a car wreck nearly three years ago. It was a cold snowy day and they were trying to make it back to the farm before a winter storm set in. They didn't make the curve on County Road 52. Their car jumped the guardrail and tumbled into the ravine below. The state trooper said they were both killed instantly."

Tears filled her eyes.

"Oh, Elizabeth, I'm so sorry. Please don't cry. Someday you'll have a husband and a family like your parents did," he said, as he put his glass aside and slid over to comfort her. "You were truly blessed because not all children have what you had. To know about your childhood helps me to understand you better," Darcy said as he continued to hold and comfort her.

When she'd calmed, she glanced up. "Yes, I was lucky to have had them. But enough about me. I want to hear about your childhood."

"Well, it was not as nice as yours in some ways, but it wasn't bad either," he said as he guided her to where he had been sitting. Leaning back, he pulled her onto his chest and held her close. "I have one brother, David, who is four years my junior, and one sister, Georgiana, who is ten years younger. My mum and dad were not as close as yours. Mum did stay home with us, but my father was rarely there. He was consumed with business, and my mother was often lonely. But she did take an interest in David and me, and later in Georgiana. She taught us to ride and play classical piano. She was a master pianist, educated at Cambridge and later at the Royal Academy of Music. For a short while, we were educated at home, too. Mum organized it, but we were taught by special tutors. Then, when we were old enough, David and I were sent to public school and later to Eton. It's a boarding school of the highest quality. My parents felt very strongly about the educational process." He released a sigh and gathered her closer, planting a kiss on her brow.

"I would say that whilst Mother was alive we were content and even happy, especially when Father came home from London to spend time with us. However, Mum died from complications of a fourth pregnancy when Georgiana was four," he said, sadness resonating in his voice. "The baby, my brother, didn't survive the birth. From that point on, I only remember being lonely. My father was very busy and could rarely spend time with us."

Elizabeth listened quietly, letting him speak.

"Father spent more time with me than David since I'm his heir, but David never appeared to resent it. When Dad was home, he loved to ride as much as I did, so we often rode together. And when at home from school, David and I would ride everywhere on our country estate as often as we could. I would say we were pretty much like other boys, getting into mischief and playing pranks," Darcy said as he gently rubbed her back and planted a kiss in her hair. "We were taught by our parents to be well mannered with all the skills of an English gentleman. Father feels it's very important to be able to handle yourself in society, and so we do. I would say that we were both confident boys. We knew we were loved, even if Father didn't have time to spend with us.

"Georgiana, on the other hand, spent very little time with us since she was so much younger. She stayed in the care of her *au pair* until she was sent to boarding school. The only time we saw each other as a family was when we were all home for the summer or on holiday. It's sad really because I know we should have been closer to her, but circumstances prevented it. However, we are much closer today, and David and I both feel very protective of her."

Elizabeth stroked his arm, and he spoke as he looked down at her.

"Like you, I grew to love books and read as much as I could. I was never alone when I was lost in a book." He laughed softly. "David was more outgoing than me and always enjoyed himself wherever he was. David is very successful in business and helps our father. He's a good man, but he's somewhat of a playboy. He says he will never marry." Darcy sighed. "Father is quite upset with him right now because David likes to date women whom Father feels are potential embarrassments. You see," he paused to snuggle Elizabeth a little closer, "Father is of the old school. He wants his sons to marry what he considers good women. Models and actresses don't qualify in his book, and those are the women David dates."

She turned her head on his shoulder and glanced up at him. "Hmm...I wonder what he would think of me, William."

Elizabeth watched him closely as he appeared to choose his words with great care.

"If he took the time to get to know you, as I have, he would love you. After all, you're not an actress or model." He chuckled.

She gazed at him and breathed deeply as she filed away his words, wondering what he was not telling her or rather what he *was* telling her with carefully chosen words. She had a feeling that Mr. Darcy would not like her or even care to get to know her. She wondered what type of family the Darcys really were.

They sat quietly for a time, just holding one another. Then William sat them upright and reached back to release her hair from the clip, allowing it to tumble down over her shoulders in a cascading blanket. "That's enough talk for now, Liz. Have I told you how much I love your hair?" he asked, breathing in the scent of her long tresses as he ran his fingers through them, planting gentle kisses here and there. "It smells so lovely, like roses."

"It's the rose scented hair oil my mother taught us to make." She sighed, snuggling into his chest.

"Hmm...well, I like it very much," he said softly, moving from her hair, planting kisses down her temple before catching her lips, initiating a soft gentle kiss. With his tongue, he teased her lips, gently parting them. His mouth moved over hers, his tongue slipping in and out in a slow, sensuous kiss. When a soft moan escaped her throat, he leaned in and pressed even deeper, tasting... exploring... coaxing. The sensation rocked her as she shivered in anticipation.

If she thought their first kiss had been pleasurable, this one overwhelmed her. Her pulse raced as her heart pounded. She felt as if she couldn't breathe—that she would faint at any moment. His tongue delved into her mouth as his kiss deepened, growing more passionate. Leaving her lips, he trailed wet, lingering kisses along her jawline to her ear, nibbling and suckling. His warm breath in her ear sent shivers down her back. He then slowly trailed down the curve of her neck to her throat and back up the same path, catching her mouth once again.

Elizabeth didn't know a kiss could make her feel like this—as though her blood had been set on fire. All thought of anything, except him, slowly drained away. Her entire body softened against his as a small tremor coursed through her, leaving her shocked with the feelings he invoked. She whispered against his lips, "Nice men don't kiss like this."

"Yes... Elizabeth...yes, they do. I'm a nice man," he murmured as his mouth closed in on hers once more, kissing her repeatedly, each time more deeply, pulling her into him, tightening their embrace.

When they finally broke apart, he pulled back to gaze into her shimmering eyes ablaze with passion. "You're so beautiful...so very beautiful. Liz, I want you."

He dipped his head once again and caught her lips while his hand slipped under her sweater and cupped her breast in a gentle caress. As his firm body pressed against her, she felt something she had never experienced before—hot desire. And although her body urged her on, telling her yes, her rational mind screamed no. She was not ready.

M.K. Baxley

She was scared.

"William, we have to stop. I've never…I don't…I…"

He pulled back, his brow wrinkled, his eyes questioning.

"Elizabeth, what are you trying to tell me?" he asked tenderly, looking at her in wonder. "Have you never been with a man before?"

"No," she whispered softly, dropping her gaze, flushed with embarrassment.

His fingers curled beneath her chin, tipping it to catch her eyes. "Never?"

"No, I was…well…that is… I am… I'm saving myself… for the right one… for marriage." She hesitated, trailing off into an almost inaudible whisper.

He smiled and seemed to be pleasantly surprised. "Then consider yourself saved." He laughed slightly, hugging her tightly to his chest in a tender embrace. "I didn't know virgins existed past secondary school. Elizabeth, you're truly a remarkable woman, and I admire and respect you for it."

"Then you're not disappointed in me?" she asked, greatly relieved.

"No, Elizabeth, in fact, I'm actually rather pleased. I'm an old fashioned gentleman, and you're clearly an old fashioned lady. I'm simply surprised!" He chuckled softly. "As you can probably tell, it is not the same with me. I am a little more experienced, but believe it or not, getting you into bed is not my primary objective," he said. "Elizabeth, I want more than just a physical relationship with you. That's why I didn't kiss you until a few days ago. I wanted us to get to know one another, to develop feelings." He cupped her face in his hand, stroking her high cheekbone with his thumb. "I'm in no hurry, and my intentions are honorable. I've never trifled with anyone. I'm looking for a long term relationship, not a short term affair. Today, people pop in and out of bed on first acquaintance, without taking the trouble to get to know one another. That's a recipe for disaster. I want more than that, and now that I know you do, too, I'm very pleased. We'll take our time."

He pulled them up to a sitting position. A large smile lightened his features. Taking her hands in his, he said, "We'll have to slow down. I don't want to do anything that you don't want to do, and I'll never take from you what you're not willing to freely give. I'm a man of strong convictions. Now that I know where you stand, I can accept that. I want you, Elizabeth, but on your terms. I'm willing to wait."

Elizabeth released a hesitant breath. "I don't know what to say, since you know what my terms are, but I think I can read between the lines. You say we are both old fashioned. I suppose that means this is, in essentials, an old fashioned courtship like people once did. I can accept that. It means that if all goes well, and we fall in love, then you'll want to marry me."

"How very perceptive of you because, essentially, yes, that is exactly what I'm saying. Now, if you don't mind, tell me how such a beautiful and intelligent young woman like yourself has not already been in love, or have you?"

She blushed and briefly dropped her gaze. "I've never been in love. As I said, I have been waiting for the right man to come along. I dated one boy from the ballet studio when I was seventeen, but there was nothing there. When I was in college, I dated some, but mostly I was too busy, and the men were too immature. None that I met were interested in getting to know me, or to have an intelligent conversation. I want to be loved for the person I am, not to be somebody's good time at my expense. I think you know what they wanted," she said. "I preferred my studies."

"In other words you preferred math problems to sex." He smiled tenderly, stroking the side of her face with the back of his hand.

"I guess that's one way of putting it," she softly said.

"Elizabeth, that's very admirable of you. I, too, want to be loved for the man I am

48

and not for what I have or what my position is. I think we have a lot in common."

"Perhaps. We'll see," she said, relaxing in a contented hug.

They sat on the sofa and held each other for a little while longer, kissing, but this time with restraint. When Charles came home, Darcy drove Elizabeth to her house. Tomorrow they would spend the weekend at Longbourn where he would meet her family and become familiar with the place where she grew up.

When he came home and prepared for bed that night, he thought about what had transpired between them. No other man had touched her. He would be her first and hopefully her last. She was fresh, unspoilt…a virgin, clearly different from most women, but in many ways, Elizabeth was just like him. She complemented him like no other, and he was sure he was falling in love with her.

As he lay there thinking about them and the future, Darcy thought back to Elizabeth's question earlier that evening about his father. No, his father wouldn't like her. She was an American and not from the upper stratum of society. This would be a problem he would have to work out. He would enlist David's help because, if things progressed as he believed they would, he intended to marry Miss Elizabeth Bennett. *…if it's the last thing I do, I will … Sleep would be difficult tonight.*

Chapter Seven

...you were meant to be mine, and I was meant to be yours...

Up at six o'clock, Elizabeth began to prepare for the trip to Longbourn. There was a multitude of things she wanted them to do, and if all went well, she planned to have Dr. Darcy back for the five day Thanksgiving break. She wanted them to ride out over the farm where she would show him the cove...her special place, the site where the first Bennetts had settled. The old log cabin was still there, and was still fully functional. As her thoughts rambled, Elizabeth heard her cell phone's ring tone. *...Damn, the thing's downstairs!*

"Jane, could you get that for me? I don't want to break my neck trying to get to it," she shouted from the upstairs landing.

"Okay." Jane answered. "Lizzy, it's William."

"Tell him I'll be right there," she said, gathering her duffel bag before rushing down the stairs and taking the phone from Jane's hand as she walked towards the kitchen.

"William, are you ready? I'll be over in five minutes."

"Almost. I was wondering if there was anything special you would like for me to bring—some wine perhaps."

"Yes, that would be nice. Uncle Henry keeps other things, but they don't drink wine. However, the rest of us do, so bring two bottles. Oh, and by the way, I almost forgot, bring at least two pairs of jeans with something casual to wear to church. My aunt will insist that we go. Also, we're going to ride out over the farm today. It will probably be muddy since it's rained so much this week. I can wash clothes if we need to, but you'll need extras while I do."

"Excellent. I'm looking forward to seeing your home, and I want to meet this black stallion of yours. What is his name?"

"You're not going to believe this," she laughed, "but it's Black."

"Black? Why on earth did you give him that name?"

"Well, I really loved Walter Fraley's **The Black Stallion**, so when my father bought the horse, he let me name him, and that was what I chose. He's very much like the horse in the book, both in looks and spirit. So I think it fits."

"Well, I want to see him. I've ridden horses all my life. I've even trained a few, and I've never met a horse I couldn't ride. Therefore I'm interested in this one. I also want to see your dogs. I like hounds as well."

She hesitated. "William...my dogs were killed last August. They were very special to me. I'll tell you what happened on the trip down to the farm."

"I'm sorry to hear that. I know how it is to lose something you love."

Not really wishing to talk about this and feeling awkward, she responded, "William, I need to get the Durango loaded. I'll be over soon."

"All right, I'll see you then."

As she slid her phone shut, she turned to her sister. "Jane, I'm leaving now. I'll see you there."

"Okay, Lizzy. Charles and I will be along about dinner time. We have some things we want to do first. You and William have fun." Jane smiled as Elizabeth grabbed her bag and headed out the door.

The trip to Longbourn took about thirty minutes, giving Elizabeth just enough time to tell William about Old Dan and Lady Beth. She told him how she had sat with Old Dan and held him when he died and how she intended to have another pair of Black and Tans someday, however, right now was not the time for that. She was far too busy with school, and to tell the truth, with William. Approaching the farm, she pointed.

"We're now turning into the drive of Longbourn proper. It's about a half-mile to the house. You see that grove of large oaks?" She gestured to the right. "That's where the house is located. It's an old plantation style, but it isn't the original house. The first one was damaged by the Union Army in the War Between the States and much of it had to be rebuilt. I'll tell you the Bennett history while you're here. My ancestors have left a collection of excellent journals, thus I know our history as far back as the 1600s."

"Really? That's fascinating. I would love to have a read sometime, if you don't mind, of course. I love family history and can trace mine back to 1066 to the first D'Arcys who came from Normandy with William the Conqueror."

"Oh, now I have to hear yours as well. I love history. I'm somewhat of an amateur historian. I collect historical period writings—especially old journals."

As a glimpse of a large antebellum house peeked through the trees, she said, "There, that's the house now. We'll just pull around back and park under the covered parking."

As the estate came into sight, Darcy took in all that he saw. It was clear that it had been quite a large plantation in its day. The drive, as you neared the house, was lined with oaks forming a canopy over it, much like the streets in Old Town. Rounding the curve, a large two-story red brick house with white columns in the front and a small balcony on the upstairs level came into full view. He remembered Elizabeth telling him there were ten bedrooms on the top level alone, with four downstairs. The walkway to the house was lined with a small hedge neatly trimmed and well kept. There were also several out buildings scattered along the back. One was obviously a smoke house while the others were an herb and a root building. There looked to be several work sheds and a rather large barn a short walk from the house. The layout of Longbourn was pleasing with the look and feel of a happily situated family homestead.

Grace, Uncle Henry, and Aunt Lori were very pleased to meet Lizzy's William, after having heard so much about him from Kat and Daniel, and Darcy was pleased to meet them as well. They seemed pleasant and friendly, eager to make him feel at home and welcomed. He could see that the Bennett family was not only warm and friendly, but they were genteel with what he had heard called Southern hospitality, and he liked them very much.

Darcy's room was to the left at the top of the stairs. A queen sized, four poster bed covered in a handmade quilt with hand carved pinecones on each post was centered in the room. An antique dresser, chest of drawers, and a Thomas Jefferson style writing desk equipped with writing essentials were all neatly arranged around the room. It was a spacious room with a large walk-in closet and simple furnishings. After unpacking, he met Elizabeth downstairs in the kitchen for some freshly baked bread with homemade butter and strawberry jam served with tea.

"Elizabeth, this is scrumptious. Did your aunt make all of this herself?"

"Yes, she and Grace do this all the time, just like my mother used to. We keep a milk cow and chickens. So everything is fresh and very good. Tonight for supper—they call it supper, not dinner—they're going to fix the doves that Charles and my uncles killed on the first day of dove season. I'm sure Uncle Henry has added more since then," she said. "I believe the menu calls for mashed potatoes with gravy, fried okra, squash casserole, field peas, homemade bread and peach cobbler. All of it comes from the farm. We keep a garden and have an orchard and berry patches."

"It sounds delicious. I believe I could become very accustomed to Southern cuisine," he said as he rubbed his stomach and smiled.

"Well, it's just as well you do, if you plan to hang around me very much," she replied with a teasing grin.

After eating, she led him on a tour of the house showing him the library, the den, the formal living room, the dining room, the breakfast room, the downstairs bathroom, and the parlor where the piano was kept. Elizabeth pointed out that the four bedrooms on either end of the kitchen had been servants' quarters long ago. Darcy followed her upstairs to see all of the bedrooms, where the bathroom was, and the upstairs study. Her parents' bedroom was the largest and most elegantly decorated of all the bedrooms, having French doors which opened onto the balcony he had seen when they first arrived. He thought the house made a cozy home for a growing family.

After touring the inside, they left the house through the kitchen. Stepping out onto the veranda, he noticed the large porch ran along the entire back. It could be accessed from either the kitchen or the den and was furnished with wicker furniture. A round tea table with chairs and a small sofa were at one end and a porch swing with several benches and two rocking chairs were at the other.

Strolling along the back of the house, he observed several gardens. One was a rose garden and the other contained herbs, and also there was one very large garden that must be lovely in spring and summer, he thought. It had flowering shrubs, crape myrtles, mimosas and wisteria trees that climbed an archway leading into an orchard. And there were beds of perennials and annuals which he recognized. In the center of the garden sat a gazebo with benches placed along the sides under the roof, and a table with chairs were placed in the center where one might read the morning paper while taking coffee as they enjoyed the garden.

Walking toward the fence surrounding the barn, he heard the sound of cackling hens and a rooster crowing in the vicinity of a hen house, and he assumed, the milk-cow, mooing. A flock of geese mingled with ducks squawked near the creek. He chuckled at the sight of two barn cats fighting over a captured rat while pigs grunted and rooted in the hog pen. But it was the sight of a flock of strange birds ambling about, calling to one another, which caught his attention.

"Elizabeth, what are those odd looking fowl over there?" he asked, pointing in the direction of the birds.

"Those?" Elizabeth asked as she unlatched the gate leading into the barnyard. "Those are Pearl Guineas. We keep them to control insects. They eat ticks, spiders, garden insects, and just about anything that crawls or flies. They keep the orchard picked clean of yellow jackets, too. Daddy bought them when we were kids because Daniel was highly allergic to insect stings, and the fact that they keep the potato beetles and other highly irritating insects at bay is an added bonus. But we do have to keep them away from the bee hives. They are not selective as to what insects they will eat." She laughed as he shook his head.

"You certainly have a wide variety of farm animals. It must be amusing to watch them in the spring."

"Umm, yes it is. I've always enjoyed spring and summer, watching the new life come forth. I can't think of anything more satisfying than living on a farm. It's always fresh and new, and it's not just the animals either but the gardens and flowers, too. There's nothing like the smell of the countryside in the summertime—the orchards, the honeysuckles, and Momma's gardens—all of it."

As they stepped past the gate, Elizabeth put her arm around his waist, giving him a warm hug. "Umm…and that's another smell I like. Can you smell that? There's nothing like the sweet smell of a barnyard, is there, William?" Elizabeth asked as she raised her nose to sniff the scent of cow manure mixed with straw and fresh feed.

He gently laughed, looking down at the woman beside him. "Only you would think so, Liz, but I must admit it does have its own *unique* smell."

"Oh come on, William, you know it smells good. No true farmer could think otherwise." They both laughed as she latched the gate.

Walking towards the barn, one of the hounds noticed them. The dog rose from his bed and wobbled in their direction, wagging his tail as he came. Darcy reached down to pat the Redbone's lazy head. The other dogs soon followed, delighted to find someone interested in giving them a little attention. Darcy played with them for a little while, rubbing behind their long floppy ears, until the horses noticed them. All six came snorting and tossing their heads, nuzzling Darcy and Elizabeth in search of treats. Elizabeth didn't disappoint them as she pulled some sugar cubes from her pocket.

Darcy was immediately drawn to the large black stallion that approached him eagerly looking for a delicacy, which Darcy just happened to have. "Elizabeth, this is a magnificent animal. He's strong with great conformation and intelligent. I can't wait to ride him," Darcy said, examining Black with a look of intense concentration.

"Let's just see if you can." She gazed at him, clearly amused.

"Oh, don't worry. I'll ride him. He likes me. I can tell."

"Well, for now, let's go back to the house and see if lunch is ready."

"Elizabeth, we just ate."

"Yes, but we've been out here for over an hour. I'm hungry. Come on," she said, motioning for him to follow.

Darcy only smiled. As they walked back towards the house, he bent down, picked a large cream colored chrysanthemum and wove it into the top of Elizabeth's braid.

"There now, you look beautifully natural for this autumn morning." He smiled, pleased with his handiwork.

After lunch, Elizabeth and Darcy returned to the barn and saddled the horses. She took the white Lipizzan, and he took Black. At first, Black would have none of it, and although he didn't try to throw Darcy, he was not willing be controlled. Battling in a war of the wills, Darcy held him firmly while he talked to the horse in hushed tones, gently stroking him until finally, after about a quarter-hour, Black calmed and allowed Darcy to guide him. Ready for a run, Darcy let him go and over the first fence they went.

Elizabeth quickly turned her horse, realizing she was being left behind. She gently kicked her mount and took off after them at a full gallop, clearing the fence and catching up with them in a fast run.

"Let them run and burn off some energy. It doesn't matter where. We have five thousand acres at our disposal," she yelled as her horse pulled up beside Darcy and Black. They ran for twenty minutes before slowing the pace, ending in the east pasture where Elizabeth started her tour.

"This is where we keep the cows in the summer. I think the current number is about nine hundred. We let this pasture rest during the winter. See up over that hill?" She pointed in a northeasterly direction. "That's where they are now. We baled that pasture back in August so they should have enough hay for the winter. Of course, they'll also get grain from the silo. They have plenty to eat without us having to buy anything. In fact, we make so much silage that we sell most of it. Come with me, and I will show you the different fields of corn, wheat, and barley."

They rode fifteen minutes in a southeasterly direction before she finally stopped. "That was the cornfield we cut in late August. It's also where Charles and my uncles shot doves during the first day of dove season. The doves come to glean the field, making themselves readily available for hunting season. In some respects, I hate dove season, although I do love the meat, but doves mate for life. It seems a sin to kill them."

Darcy turned to gaze at her in surprise. He's never considered shooting from that aspect. He smiled at her sentimental ways as she carried on with her tour.

"Look over to your right and you'll see the summer wheat, and over to the right of that is the barley field," she said as she turned her horse to the north. "Now, let's go northwest. I have a special place to show you."

Approaching a densely wooded area, she paused. "Here it is, William. This is the cove. Behind it are about 250 acres of deep woods. I have never explored all of it. Some of it is too dense to make it in on horseback, and I'm not about to walk it. Over there is the first home John Thomas Bennet built upon coming here in 1803," she said, pointing in the direction of a rustic cabin sitting on a slight hill surrounded by large oak and hickory trees. "It's fairly large for a log cabin since it has two rooms with a kitchen through the breezeway. We'll go in and have a look later on, but for now, let's give the horses a drink while we sit and rest," she said, pointing to a large smooth rock in a clearing just above a natural pool.

After the horses drank their fill, Darcy tied them to a low branch under one of the large oaks. Elizabeth took a seat and beckoned him to join her.

Looking around, Darcy observed that the cove was surrounded on two sides by a mountain covered in dense forest with underbrush in places. In the center, a stream tumbled down from the mountain in a cascading waterfall, hiding what looked like a cave behind it. The falls spilled into a small pool of water that flowed into the creek that cut across the fields, and the entire area was surrounded by large oak, walnut, maple, elm, and hickory trees, towering high above the area and covering it in shade. It was a scene that one might see in Tolkien's world of Middle Earth where the elves of Beleriand or Doriath might have lived, the cave being a hidden passageway to Gondolin...Beautiful.

Elizabeth leaned back on her hands and breathed in deeply the sweet scents of autumn. "This is where we came in the summer to play and relax when we were children. We swam in that pool, and then we would sun dry here on this rock. Of all the places on the farm, this is my favorite, and I would often come here to be alone and read. In the summer, we have wild blackberries and gooseberries that grow in the mountain near the edge of the woods. The smell of honeysuckle fills the air, and there is a particular bird I love that nests nearby. It's called the mountain bluebird, otherwise known as the Indigo Bunting. It's the prettiest shade of blue I have ever seen." She gave a wide gesture with her hand as she pointed it all out to him.

"Also, down by the creek bank, mountain mint and watercress grow along the edge of the water. The mint makes the best iced tea you will ever taste. It's steeped in the sun, along with the tea, and the watercress is excellent in a salad."

He caught her genuine smile while receiving all that she told him with pleasure.

"In the summertime, when we were girls, Jane, Celia—one of our friends—and I used to come here and spend the night in the cabin. We would let our hair down, pretending we were elves and dance on this rock in the moonlight, especially on midsummer's eve. That was one of our favorite times." She sighed. "Sometimes there would be a faerie ring by the water's edge, and we would dance in it. We would even skinny dip in the pool until one day, Joseph and some of his friends happened upon us.

They stole our clothes and hid them in the brush, and that put an end to that." She giggled.

As he listened, he thought back to his own boyhood when he, David, Richard, his Winthrop cousin, and William and Benson, his Darcy cousins, had done much the same thing in the cove at Pemberley. They would skinny dip, too, and pretend to be on some quest for the Queen or the elvish lords of Middle Earth.

This place, like the one at Pemberley, was magical, causing his thoughts to turn to how he would like to someday dance in a faerie ring naked or skinny dip in the pool alone with Elizabeth. With that thought, the desire to make love to her returned even stronger. He stifled a moan. *...That, Darcy, is a long way into the future, if at all. You have to win her love first. She is not the kind of woman to be taken. She's to be loved and cherished.*

He realized he was falling deeply in love with her. And he was more certain than ever that Elizabeth was the one—the one he'd been searching for, and it amazed him that he was to find her here, of all places, in a sleepy mountain plateau in Tennessee—what some people would consider the middle of nowhere. Darcy shook his head to clear his mind.

"It's very beautiful and peaceful here. I can see why you would love it. This place reminds me of..."

"Middle Earth?" she interrupted with a smile.

"Yes, exactly," he whispered *...and Pemberley.* "We have a similar place at my home where David and I would go in the summer to swim. I have fond memories of those days. I used to go there and read, too, just like you. It was like stepping into another world. I'll take you there someday."

"Perhaps you will." She smiled. "Now let me tell you our history."

He listened intently as she began by telling him how they were descended from the sixth Earl of Fairington in Hampshire, England. "The Earl of Fairington was born in 1622 and had two sons. My family came from the second son who inherited an estate called Longbourn, in Hertfordshire, England. That son had a son who in turn had a son, Thomas Bennet. It was Thomas Bennet's son, and my ancestor, who had been the problem. He was the oldest with one younger brother and several sisters. He was John Thomas Bennet and the younger son, his brother, was Edward Thomas Bennet. John was to inherit Longbourn, but he fell into a scandal when he married against his father's will."

Darcy wrinkled his brow. "What type of scandal?"

Elizabeth tilted her head and breathed deeply. "It began when a gentleman's daughter became homeless after the death of her parents leaving no relations to take care of her. She was taken in by another family, but for some reason, fell out with them and was cast off. Then she was taken in by a madam of a famous brothel in London. There John met her and soon fell in love. He bought her, as they say, so that no other man could have her, keeping her for his own private use," Elizabeth stated. "She became pregnant and when she was several months along, he married her. This was such a shock and disgrace that his father disowned him, and the estate fell to his younger brother, Edward.

"John's father grieved for his son. He didn't want to disinherit him, but he felt he had little choice. So in order to save his unmarried daughters from the disgrace of their older brother, he gave John five thousand pounds in gold and sent them to America in 1789."

"Elizabeth, that's very sad. What happened next?" Darcy wrinkled his brow and beckoned her to continue, keenly interested in her story. It vaguely reminded him of another Bennet.

"Well, John and Rebecca Jane, his wife, settled in Virginia, but then later, John followed the mountain men on several adventures. When he came through the Cumberland Gap, he fell in love with the land. So when it was opened up for settlement in 1800, he came along with many Scotch-Irish families to stake a claim on the land which he named Longbourn, after the estate he should've had in England. After they cleared the land and built a settlement, John and Rebecca Jane began a new life together. It was very hard in the beginning, and had it not been for the Cherokee Indians, they very well might not have made it. The Indians taught them what was good to eat and what was not. "

Elizabeth went on to tell of the building of the plantation, the crops, slavery, and eventually the Civil War and Reconstruction. She explained the horrors of the war and that which followed—the death, the starvation, and the destruction of not only the land, but of a way of life. The war and Reconstruction had been hard on everyone, but especially those who had not kept their money in gold. Her family had been fortunate in that they'd seen what was coming and had kept their gold, investing it in a bank in England, thus saving the family fortune and the plantation.

"That's basically how we came to be here. There is more, but I'll leave that for another time. Let's just say that we survived. Now, it's your turn to tell me about your family's history."

He smiled and began. "My ancestors came over with William the Conqueror in 1066 and fought for the Duke of Normandy at the Battle of Hastings, securing England for the Normans." Darcy picked up a pebble and tossed it into the stream. "After William became the king, he granted us several thousand acres of land for our service. We went on to serve in the various courts of the Norman kings and later fought with the nobles against King John, eventually forcing him to agree to the Articles of the Barons and sign the Magna Carter in 1215. Then we fought in The Hundred Years' War against France."

"So your family is of Norman decent and was loyal to the king it appears."

"Yes," he said with a smile. "But loyalties were divided in the 15th century with The Wars of the Roses."

"Tell me about it. That's a period in history that I find fascinating." Elizabeth said, tilting her head and catching his gaze.

"Well, since you're interested, I'll give you a brief overview." Darcy drew his knees up and wrapped his arms around them. "The hostilities, as you probably know, spanned a length of one hundred years, but the actual fighting only lasted for thirty-two. The first open fighting broke out in 1455. And as a side note, the name, Wars of the Roses, which was not used during that time, came from the family badges—a red rose for Lancaster and a white one for York."

"Yes, I know what the name means. I've read about it, but it's never been more than an historical event to me. I'm very interested in English history, and this is the first time I've actually known someone who can trace their family history as far back as the Middle Ages. So please continue."

Darcy picked up another small stone and tossed it in the air, catching it with one hand as he began. He explained the acts of treason committed within the English courts and the subsequent consequences, and how family members betrayed one another. His family had been decimated at the Battle of Towton in 1461, leaving only two surviving brothers, Thomas the heir and Richard, the younger. Eventually they were divided through treachery with Thomas killing his brother when Richard betrayed him, and finally how all of his line, except one, Thomas's youngest son, George Darcy, had died at the Battle of Bosworth Fields several years later. Darcy explained the political intrigue and how the various houses had vied for power. They talked for nearly an hour.

"Oh, William, that's terrible! What did they do? How did they survive?"

"Yes, it was…it was very horrible. Blood should never betray blood." Darcy shook his head. "George learned a very hard lesson, and as a result, he had become shrewd. He was offered the title, Earl of Derby, in 1485 but refused. He preferred to remain part of the landed gentry. There'd been too much bloodshed, and I suppose he was leery, though he never stayed completely outside of things. He eventually married Mary of Wiltshire and had two sons. It was through the Wiltshire alliance that he recouped our losses, and eventually his sons and grandsons became ministers in the courts of King Henry VIII and Queen Elizabeth I. It was in the Queen's court that my ancestor, George Darcy's grandson, William Darcy, met and fell in love with Elizabeth of Salisbury."

"Did they continue at court, or did they leave? And did things improve?"

Darcy nodded as he picked up another pebble and tossed it. "Yes, I would say things did improve. They married and retired to Pemberley in Derbyshire, and through that alliance, our estate grew and prospered into one of the wealthiest in the kingdom. And like your family," he said with a wide smile, "each consecutive generation has added to both the house and the improvement of the property. We had numerous tenants and farmed it for many years. We still have horses, and there are some sheep and cattle, but we don't really work the land anymore. Pemberley, like Longbourn is to you, is very dear to me. It's my home, and I'm to inherit it someday, although my brother and sister will have a lifetime right to live there. There's a lot more to the story which is contained in the many volumes of our family journals, but essentially, my ancestral grandfather took what he inherited and built an empire."

"Your family has had a violent past, hasn't it? I have no records that far back, so I don't know if we were involved. Does the violence of your forbearers disturb you?"

"Not in the least." He released his legs and stretched. "There comes a time when a man has to take a stand. The secret is knowing when to fight and when not. Besides, I'm a medieval type of guy, and I understand my family's history perfectly."

"Well, William," she said as she arched her back, "I'm captivated by your family's history. Next time, I want to hear about The Hundred Years' War and what your family did during the English Civil War."

"Ah, yes, the Hundred Years' War and the British Civil Wars or Wars of the Three Kingdoms as it's now called. My family was especially involved in the latter, and there is a great deal written about it. Our family's role in the conflict is recorded in the annals of our family history by my ancestor, Henry Darcy." Darcy chuckled softly as glanced across the pasture. "Henry was a well-connected barrister in London. He and a friend, Sir John Gell, raised an army in his local district for the defense of Derbyshire and Staffordshire against the Royalists—the supporters of King Charles I."

"Your family sided with the Parliamentarians," Elizabeth said with a gentle smile.

"Yes," Darcy nodded. "Henry declared himself to be a Parliamentarian, but I think in his heart, Henry was really a Royalist. Our family had always been devoted to the king, and I know he was torn by divided loyalties. On the one hand, as a member of the landed gentry, he identified with those opposed to the king, and yet, as he rode with Oliver Cromwell on various campaigns, he was appalled by Oliver's cruelty. Henry was also disgusted by the outcome of the war and the subsequent trial and execution of Charles I. When asked, he refused to have any part in it."

"From what I've read, Cromwell was no better than the king, was he?"

"No, in fact, he was worse. Oliver Cromwell declared himself the Lord Protector of England in 1649, and, until his death in 1658, he made life miserable, especially for the Irish. He was excessively brutal to them and made it his task to bring them under control. He sent an army there, and despite promising those who surrendered to him that he would treat them well, he slaughtered all who surrender to his forces, using terror to bring them under his control. The Irish people hated him. He sent their children to the West Indies to work as slaves in the sugar plantations. He knew many would die out there, but his reasoning was that dead children could not grow up to make more Irish Catholics, and I suppose he was successful in that regard."

"That's horrible. I never knew this to that detail. Did he really do all of that?"

"Elizabeth, he did all that I've told you and more, and all in the name of God. The man was insane. He even banned mincemeat pie."

"Mincemeat pie? Why?"

Darcy laughed and shook his head. "Oliver Cromwell and the Puritans detested Christmas as a pagan holiday—one that promoted gluttony, drunkenness, and debauchery, therefore on December 22, 1657, Cromwell and his Puritan Council banned it altogether. Christmas decorations such as holly and ivy were forbidden, and soldiers were ordered to roam the streets and if necessary, take by force food being cooked for Christmas festivities. The smell of a goose cooking could condemn you. And Cromwell considered pies especially to be a sinful, forbidden pleasure, thus mincemeat pie was banned. That was but one example of his insanity which eventually led to the return of the king. The people hated him. They had had enough, and thusly when Charles II ascended the throne in 1660, he restored Christmas."

Darcy sighed and glanced at Elizabeth. "My ancestor felt the atrocities that occurred were something that must be remembered, and so he chronicled the events of that time period in absorbingly meticulous detail: the political and religious intrigues and upheavals, the alliances and confrontations, the betrayals and acts of loyalties, and the triumphs and tragedies of the era are all documented. To kill a king is a travesty," Darcy whispered.

"Yes, yes, it is. Your family's history is truly fascinating. I'd like to read those journals someday."

"Well, someday I'll show you mine, if you'll show me yours." He flashed a wicked grin, giving her a teasing wink.

She laughed, shaking her head at the double entendre. "Show and tell, eh?"

"Perhaps, but seriously, I would like to see them."

"Sure, we can do that, if you really want to."

His brow furrowed. He tossed another pebble into the pool as he slowly contemplated Elizabeth tale of her history. Finally, he asked, "Elizabeth, you said your family originated from an estate in Hertfordshire. Do you happen to know what became of Edward Bennet?"

"No, I don't think we ever did hear. The connection was severed several years after we came to America. Why do you ask?"

"Because the first Fitzwilliam Darcy married an Elizabeth Bennet from Longbourn in Hertfordshire, and I think there's a possible connection. Perhaps a distant cousin of yours married an ancestral grandfather of mine, making her my ancestral grandmother."

"I suppose it's possible. My family is from Hertfordshire. If it is, it would be a strange coincidence." Elizabeth tilted her head slightly. "Fitzwilliam Darcy," she whispered, "Hmm...you said the first. Who else is called by that name?"

"I am. That's my full name, Fitzwilliam Alexander Darcy."

"Fitzwilliam..." her lips curled softly. "I like how that sounds...different and distinguished! I think I'll call you Fitzwilliam if you don't mind."

"If you like, you may. My family, as well as some of my friends, calls me by that name. But many call me William. However, since I do have a first cousin by that given name, it does get confusing sometimes."

"Then I shall call you Fitzwilliam," she said. "Now, Fitzwilliam, come with me. I want to show you the cabin."

Elizabeth stood up and stretched and then offered Darcy her hand, beckoning him to follow her. She led him around the pool and up a rise to the cabin and, with a little bit of effort, entered the slab door.

"This is it," she said. "Kat cleaned it last when she and I and Jane stayed here this past summer, but it needs to be re-done. Anyway, this room was the main living area."

As they stood in the center of the cabin, Darcy noted a large bed up against the wall and a sofa made from saplings covered with cushions.

Moving through the room, Elizabeth directed his attention to a large bench style table. "This was the kitchen table which was used for more than eating. It was the family gathering place." Pointing to a rack over the bed, she said, "The gun hung there for easy access in case there was trouble in the night, and that large fireplace was for heating and some cooking. It has a hook for a stew kettle." She stepped towards another door and opened it. "In this room, is another bed, but I'm not sure why it was that way. Perhaps it was a guest room because over there," she pointed, "the ladder leads to the loft where the children slept, and through this breezeway is the kitchen. It was separate from the house because in summer, it was unbearably hot."

"Even though it appears rustic and quaint, I see that it can still be a fully functional place to live," Darcy said, inspecting each space and piece of furniture carefully.

"Yes, I always thought it was romantic, too. I used to pretend to be a pioneer like Laura Ingalls when I was little."

At that, Darcy laughed. "Come here, you little minx," he said, gathering her into his embrace. As they kissed, his thoughts wandered to how nice it would be to spend a night here with her and how much he wanted to make her his wife. She quickened him in a way he had forgotten existed, kindling a fire he'd long since thought extinguished. The warmth of her kiss and the feel of her soft body against his stirred his blood. He whispered softly against her lips, "Elizabeth Bennett, someday...I'm going to marry you."

"You're very sure of yourself...aren't you?" she murmured, catching his lips once more as she tightened her arms around his neck and relaxed against his body. He invoked feelings in her she had no idea even existed. *...We hardly know each other...but I can't help myself...I want him...I need him.*

"Yes, Elizabeth, I am...I'm very sure. What do you feel?" he asked as he trailed kisses down her neck.

She tilted her head. "I hardly know," she whispered as she felt her conscious thoughts fading into oblivion. Just as she was about to completely let go, the wind blew a low hanging branch against the windowpane. Abruptly, reality struck. Elizabeth shuddered as she broke their embrace. With a slight smile, she said, "I think we need to return before they send out a search party. It'll be dark soon."

"As you wish. I'm at your command," he said softly as he stepped aside and took a deep breath.

Elizabeth gave him a quick kiss on the lips and then pulled him through the cabin door, shutting it firmly behind them. They mounted their horses and rode off at a full gallop, jumping fences as they went, until finally entering the barnyard. After the horses were put away, they walked towards the house where Aunt Lori greeted them, "It's almost supper time, Lizzy. Come in and wash up, you two. Charles and Jane have just arrived; we'll be eating shortly."

The meal was excellent. Charles and Darcy thanked the ladies and declared themselves full, unable to eat any dessert, which was a pity because both could tell it was very good. As they left the table, Uncle Henry invited the gentlemen to the library for some Evan Williams.

While the men went to enjoy their bourbon and Jane sat and talked with Lori and Grace, Elizabeth slipped outside to the porch swing to sit and think as the sounds of the night echoed through the darkness.

...Fitzwilliam is very confident in himself. I don't know what to make of him. I strongly believe, by the things he keeps saying and by the way he acts, that he loves me. He told me as much in the cabin. He wants to marry me, but what do I want? Is this love? I do feel something for him, but I'm not sure it's enough to make a marriage. A marriage is more than passion... isn't it?

When I marry, I want it to last. I have to keep my wits about me. How do I know his love is true? I can't make a decision based on feelings and emotions alone. I have to be able trust him. I have to use logic!

"Elizabeth?"

Her thoughts were interrupted by a soft familiar voice.

"Hmm...yes."

"What are you doing out here all alone?"

"Oh, just thinking... and enjoying the night sounds. Do you hear them—the whippoorwill, the barn owl, the crickets, the call of the coyote? And, if you listen closely, you can hear the cry of a bobcat off in the distance."

"Yes, it is rather peaceful. Do you mind if I join you?"

"No, come right ahead. You can even share my blanket if you're cold." She patted the seat next to her.

"That's all right. I have a jacket," he said, taking a seat on the swing, resting his arm over the back of it. For a few minutes, they said nothing as they swung gently back and forth, listening to the night sounds. Finally, he asked, "Elizabeth, what were you thinking about?"

"Oh, just things ...things about us ...you and me. The things we discussed earlier and how I feel about them."

"And how do you feel about those things we've talked about?" he asked softly.

"I'm not sure, really. That's what I'm trying to decide. I'll try to be open and honest with you. When you told me that you want to marry me someday," she hesitated for a moment, "I mean, you did say that. I was thinking and wondering why?" She dropped her gaze momentarily before glancing in his direction. "This seems awfully sudden to me. How can you talk about marriage so quickly? I have to wonder what you're basing your feelings on. Do you really love me or is this just lust?" she asked. "I think you know me well enough to know that I have no intention of giving myself to someone only to discover it was wrong," she said with conviction. "Fitzwilliam, when I marry, I want it to last forever. I want a love and affection rooted in respect and trust. Passion is wonderful, but when the fires burn low, what's left? Now, don't misunderstand me. I like you very much, but—"

He cut her off before she could continue. "Elizabeth, I think I understand what you're telling me. These are deep thoughts indeed. Let me try to explain as best I can. First, although it may seem so, this is not sudden for me. I was attracted to you when I first saw you as far back as the last week in July. That was when Charles and I came to inspect the university and surrounding area." He paused, looking out into the night with a slight smile, as if reflecting on that day.

Turning to face her, he caught her eyes. "That day, we were standing by a window on the second story of Morton Hall. Charles saw Jane first, and I think his attraction was formed at that very moment. He pointed her out, remarking to Dickens and me something about the beautiful women in this place, but when I looked out the window, my eyes were drawn to you, not Jane. You were wearing your faded blue jeans with the torn knee and a white tee shirt, and your hair was caught back in a low ponytail. It was so strikingly beautiful, hanging down your back almost to your knees. I remember thinking you looked like my mental picture of Lúthien Tinuviel. But then, thinking you were a student, I dismissed you almost immediately from my mind." Hesitating for a moment, he looked her directly in the eye. "Elizabeth, I didn't know who you were then, but your image was indelibly imprinted on my mind. I thought of you many times even before I had the opportunity to meet you," he said. "It was a whole month later before I learned who you really were. And I must confess that I secretly watched you on campus until one day I finally decided that I had to meet you. Elizabeth, it was no accident that I was in the coffee shop that day because I knew you came there at that time each day." He took her hand in his, giving it a gentle squeeze before releasing it.

"I never realized you had seen me back in July. That must have been the day I arrived in Walnut Grove. And you had been watching me?" She smiled.

"Yes, Elizabeth, I was watching, and the more I watched, the more I was drawn to you. You were so lovely, and I suppose it was infatuation at that point. However, it was when we began to talk that I realized you are not only beautiful, but intelligent as well. I already desired you, but as I have gotten to know you better, I have fallen in love with you. The more we talked, the more I realized how much we are alike and how many things we have in common. I admired your independent spirit. You do as you like with no thought as to please or conform to others. I believe you are a confident individual. Elizabeth, I have never met anyone quite like you. I not only admire you, but I'm very much in love with who you are!"

Feeling encouraged, he took her small hand in his and caressed it gently as he gazed intently into her fine eyes. "So you see, it's not so sudden for me. You've been in my thoughts for some time, though I didn't intend to reveal my feelings to you so soon. I didn't realize that you were not as experienced in the world as most people your age are, but I should have suspected it from your demeanor. Anyway, it came out, and I'm not sorry for it. My feelings are genuine and real, and I'm not ashamed of them," he said. "I believe you do feel something for me. I can sense it when we kiss and the way you embrace me. Could you love me, Elizabeth?"

"I think I can…maybe… maybe I already do. I know I feel something for you." She sighed as she fixed her eyes on his. "When we kiss, I become so weak that my logical mind shuts down. I don't think at that point. I only feel. That's what worries me, Fitzwilliam." Her eyes were intense, almost worried. "In a moment of weakness I could slip, and then I would have a lifetime of regret if this isn't real. It's a razor's edge, and I'm just not sure."

"Elizabeth, you can trust me. I don't say things that I don't mean. If I'm anything at all, I'm a man of my word. And I want the very things out of life that you do. I want a marriage where there is mutual respect, love, and trust. I want to have children. And most of all, I want to be part of their lives from birth through adulthood. I want my children to experience what I never had—a home where their parents are united in one accord, creating an environment of love, security, and comfort for them to grow and develop in. I want to be there for everything that involves my family, but most of all, I want my wife to always have first place in my heart. Elizabeth, I will cherish you always."

She looked at him tenderly, tilting her head slightly, but before she could answer, he continued.

"I didn't come to the Cumberland Plateau looking for a wife. It was the last thing on my mind last July. You have to believe me when I tell you I had no intention for our love affair to catch fire as it has. I wanted to take things slowly. I've been burnt before, but I've also been alone for a very long time," he said as he looked off into the distance. "You took me by surprise. I wasn't expecting you to be a virgin. I was expecting, well, what couples normally do, but when I discovered that you were untouched, that changed everything. Elizabeth, I'm thirty-two years old. I'm not a foolhardy adolescent. I'm a man, and I know what I'm about. How old are you— twenty-six—twenty-seven? I believe you're old enough, too."

"I'm twenty-five, and I am old enough to know what I want. I just want to make sure it's right."

"Elizabeth, this is right," he pleaded. "When the fires burn down, we'll have a love that is rooted in mutual trust and respect. We will be forever," he softly said, once again taking her hand in his.

"Well, you certainly have self confidence and go after what you want. I suppose you're used to getting it, too," she said with a teasing smile.

"Yes, I do believe in pursuing what I want." He paused for a second, contemplating his thoughts. The momentum was set. It wouldn't do to hesitate. He had to ask. "Elizabeth, is it too soon? I'm not asking you to live with me or to have a casual affair. I want something more. Elizabeth, will you marry me?"

Elizabeth sighed. "Fitzwilliam, I was trained to think in terms of logic, and my rational mind tells me that I don't know you well enough to be thinking in terms of marriage."

He could tell by the look in her eyes that she was deeply involved in an internal struggle, therefore he challenged her. "And what of your heart? What is your heart telling you, Liz?"

"My hearts tells me that I want you. I don't know if it's love I feel, but I do know it's desire."

He shook his head and released an exasperated sigh. "The problem with mathematicians is that they think too much. Feel, Elizabeth, feel! Trust your instincts. I know what you're feeling. I feel it, too. Elizabeth, I'm promising you my love. I don't have to think about it. I know it!" Fitzwilliam swallowed hard as he waited for her response.

She paused, gazing at him quizzically, and then looked away. Finally, as if coming out of deep thought, she answered.

"I do trust you, and I believe you're an honorable man." She paused briefly. "If you truly mean everything you say, then yes, I will. I will marry you, Fitzwilliam."

Overjoyed, he pulled her into his lap and cradled her tightly against his chest. "Elizabeth Bennett, I love you."

He bent down and kissed her with a heartfelt exhilaration. She was vibrant and alive, and she made him feel just as alive. He felt her surrender to his will as she curled her arms around his neck and slipped her fingers into his thick curls.

"I didn't know there could be this much pleasure in a kiss," she whispered against his lips.

"Do you enjoy it, Elizabeth?" he asked in-between kisses.

"Yes...very much."

Pleased, he murmured, "Good! I want you to enjoy it. There's so much more to be had than a kiss, and in time, you will know that pleasure, too. You were meant to be mine, and I was meant to be yours. We were meant for this," he whispered as he pulled her close to his body, kissing her again and again, delving deeper and deeper while his hand lightly brushed the side of her breast.

She thought she would die. His mouth was warm and sensual and his kiss left her weak and breathless. Her toes curled and her body went limp. She was no longer thinking, but only feeling—feeling the pleasure he gave with a simple kiss.

When he finally broke the kiss, they sat there on the swing gently swaying back and forth, caught up in the moment. As Elizabeth lay there in his arms with her head resting upon his shoulder, she realized that for the first time in her life, she wanted to give herself to a man—to the man that now held her close.

Suspending the comfortable silence, Fitzwilliam reassured her. "I love you, Liz. I am a man of convictions if I'm anything. I'll never hurt you. You'll have no cause to repine. There's no need to worry. I have to go to England after the semester ends, so tomorrow we'll talk. I have much to tell you."

Chapter Eight

...the winds of troubles brew...

The next morning Fitzwilliam couldn't have been in a better mood as he sat down to eat with Elizabeth's family. Surveying the table, a pleasant smile curved his lips. Grace and Aunt Lori had made a big breakfast, and conversation around the table was lively.

"Lori, pass the gravy and eggs to Charles." Henry turned to Fitzwilliam. "William, is it William or Fitzwilliam? Lizzy's been calling you Fitzwilliam, so which is it?" Henry asked.

Fitzwilliam laughed. "Either, actually. My full name is Fitzwilliam Darcy, but you may call me whatever you wish."

"Well, in that case, I'll call you by your given name. Here," Uncle Henry smiled, "have some grits," he said as he passed the bowl down Darcy's way.

"You know," Uncle Henry continued, "after puttin' those mules and burros out amongst the cattle, we haven't had a single coyote come back after that first week when I found three dead. Why, we ain't seen none in a week of Sundays, have we, Lori?"

"No, I don't reckon we have. Here, Jane, pass the gravy down," Lori said, sending the bowl around.

"Pass the bacon this way, Fitzwilliam. Won't you have some more biscuits and gravy, Lizzy?" Uncle Henry inquired, not missing a beat.

"Oh, by the way," Henry said as he passed the sorghum. "I near clean forgot. You haven't heard the family news yet, so let me fill you in. I'm sure you've heard the local news, but just in case, I'll start with that. Jackie Lee Nunley's been busted for growin' marijuana down in Owl Holler. You know where it is—over yonder down around Coldwater Creek." He paused long enough to stab a piece of ham as it came around. "It seems the DEA's been watchin' him for some time now, and the day before yesterday they descended on a well-hidden cove where he was growin' it. They say it's the biggest drug bust in the State of Tennessee's history."

"Yes, Uncle, we heard about it, but what does it have to do with any of us? We're not involved, are we?"

"Well now, Lizzy let me tell it. I'm fixin' to get to it," Henry said. "You see, it's your cousin, Liddy. She's been seein' Jackie Lee for some time now."

Jane and Elizabeth both put down their knives and forks and looked up, giving their uncle their full attention. Fitzwilliam looked up, too, mildly curious at this bit of news, wondering what ties it had to the Bennett family.

"Liddy Fanning ain't been nothin' but trouble since she was knee high to a grasshopper. Daniel, won't you pass the biscuits please," he said, snatching one from the plate as it came around. "Well, as it turns out, she's three months pregnant, and Lydia and Randy are beside themselves 'cause there ain't no coverin' this up. This is the first big scandal to hit this family in pert near two hundred years." He paused for a moment. "Well, if you don't count the moonshinin', that is. But it's not so bad that she's pregnant as it is to who the father is."

Jane gasped. "Uncle, you're telling us that Liddy is pregnant with Jackie Lee Nunley's baby, aren't you?"

"That's exactly what I'm sayin', Jane, but the worst part of this sorry mess is that Jackie Lee is denying he's the father. Can you believe that? They've been datin' since summer and now he's saying Liddy's as loose as a spring goose and that anyone could be the father. He even roughed her up when she told him about her condition. He ordered her to have an abortion, or he'd beat the hell out of her. That should've been a real eye opener, but one has to wonder where Liddy's concerned," he said as he paused for a sip of coffee. "Why, she's still fully expectin' to marry him, of all things!" Henry set his cup down and picked up a fork full of eggs.

Elizabeth visibly stiffened as she shoved her plate aside. Glancing over at Darcy, she quickly averted her eyes.

Sensing her concern, he gently caressed her knee, attempting to reassure her.

"Well, it's not wholly unexpected," Kat said. "I told her that Jackie Lee was meaner than a snake, and that she was gonna get bit if she kept hanging around him. So, it's no surprise that he would threaten her or slander her name. The chickens have come home to roost. I told her as much back two months ago. If she's too stupid to see it, then she deserves exactly what she gets," Kat stated matter of factly as she buttered her biscuit.

"You've hit the nail on the head, Kat, but, of course, none of that matters anyhow, 'cause he's on his way up the river to the big house, followin' in the family tradition, just like his granddaddy did for bootleggin' back in the 50s." Henry paused for another bite of eggs. "But Randy and Lydia? Well, now they're another kettle of fish altogether. They ain't been doing nothin' but fightin' and arguin' ever since all of this has come to light. Each blaming the other for Liddy's wild behavior," Uncle Henry said.

"They will have to deal with it, but we'll all help as much as we can," Aunt Lori said. "Liddy will have the baby, and we'll all accept it. The child's innocent of its parents' sins." Lori turned to Elizabeth. "Here, Lizzy, have another cup of coffee."

Elizabeth whispered her thanks while she poured herself another cup. Looking up, she said, "Yes, Aunt, I understand what you are saying, but people will whisper and stare. I know they will not overtly be unkind, but they will think less of us just the same. I know how people are in this Sunday-go-to-meetin' farming community. I feel awful for poor Isabelle Haskell. I've seen the pitying stares and heard the quiet whispers that she has to endure—and through no fault of her own, I might add. I personally could not stand to be the object of their well-meaning pity. Isabelle would have been better off if she had simply left the community to stay with her older sister. At least Knoxville is big enough that people won't care about her circumstances.

"But now Liddy is a different matter altogether. She's either too stupid or too indifferent to care about what people think. " Lizzy paused for a sip of coffee. "I don't know which it is, but the damage is done just the same. She's put fodder into the mouths of fools to spread gossip. Why does she always pick the lowest common dominator to become involved with? A drug dealer of all things! And not a small time dealer, either. When Bette and Florence told me she was seeing him, I dismissed it as a passing dalliance. I shouldn't have."

"Well, Lizzy, let's not speak of this any more. It won't help solve things. Everybody knows Liddy Fanning is as wild as a March hare, so I'm sure you're wrong. What Liddy has done will not affect this family as you might think. Let's hush this talk," Aunt Lori declared, her word stated as final, giving Henry a sharp look.

As if taking her cue, Uncle Henry moved on. "That reminds me." He snapped his fingers. "I've got to have me two more hounds. I'll have to go to Dog Days on first Monday and pick up another pair of pups. I guess I'll get another pair of Black and

Tans. There're about the best hounds around when it comes to trackin' big game—well, them and Redbones," he added. "What do you say, Lizzy? You want to go with me?"

It appeared that as soon as the words slipped from his mouth, Henry remembered. "Oh hell, you can't go. I forget you have a regular job now." Uncle Henry laughed, shaking his head as he poured white gravy over the top of another serving of eggs and grits. "I'll just have to go by myself. Pass the ham and red-eye gravy Lori."

As she passed the ham and gravy to her husband, Lori turned to Lizzy. "What's the matter, child? You seemed to have lost your appetite."

"I'm fine," she whispered. "I'll help you clear away the dishes, and then I think Fitzwilliam and I will go for a walk." Shoving away from the table, she collected their plates and moved towards the dishwasher.

After breakfast, Elizabeth and Darcy left for a stroll in the garden. It was a crisp, beautiful, autumn morning as they sauntered leisurely hand in hand, enjoying in the sights. The pansies and chrysanthemums were in full bloom with beautiful bright colors while the trees were now mostly bare, and pecans and black walnuts were falling. The smell of the fireplace and wood burning stove from the house filled the air. All this combined to create a quiet reflective mood.

Darcy could see that she was clearly upset, and not only from the news of her cousin, he suspected, but from the mention of her dogs as well. He remembered that Elizabeth had meant to show him the graves, but she had obviously forgotten. As they walked in the garden, Darcy broached the subject.

"Elizabeth, are you all right? I noticed you seemed a little upset with the news of your cousin."

She glanced up at him. "That would be an understatement." She heaved a heavy sigh. "Liddy's behavior is no surprise at all. It was bound to happen sooner or later. Aunt Lydia has spoiled her all of her life. I'm just so embarrassed you heard it; that's all."

"Elizabeth, don't worry about that. It's not important, but don't you feel a bit sorry for your cousin's parents? I mean, things must be terrible for them right now."

Elizabeth's face softened. "I do feel sorry for my aunt and uncle, but Aunt Lydia has never been close with any of us. There was always tension between my aunt and my father," Elizabeth said, shaking her head. "And there has always been this undercurrent between my aunt's family and us. The rest of the family ignores it, sloughing it off as 'that's just Lydia.' Uncle Robert and Aunt Tana laugh about it. But it irks me, and Liddy is just like her, except my aunt is not so crude and reckless. She does give some consideration to what people think, and family reputation is important to her, so I imagine this is tough for her to take."

Darcy puzzled a bit and then finally asked, "Help me to keep things straight. Who are Robert and Tana?"

"Oh, sorry about that. Robert is my father's younger brother. He's a lawyer in town, and Tana owns Bennett Florist downtown across from Watson and Moore's Funeral Home." She smiled, looking up at him. "There's also Sam Henry and Johnny, my mother's brothers, and their wives Bette and Florence."

"I see. Now, back to what you were saying about Liddy's situation."

She sighed in exasperation. "Liddy doesn't directly affect this branch of the Bennetts, but we are a close family, so we will come together as one and support her no matter what the cost to the family. That's what bothers me."

She kicked a pile of leaves as they walked. "We care. Liddy doesn't. Whereas I, or any of the rest of us, would make a sacrifice for the good of the family, Liddy would not. She's selfish." She stooped and picked up a magnolia fruit as they walked along, shucking the red seeds from the cone as they went. "Another thing that upsets me is the whispers and the pity of well-meaning neighbors, but let's not dwell on my cousin's stupidity."

"It's just talk, Elizabeth. It'll pass quickly, and then they'll go on to the next topic soon enough." He paused to squeeze her shoulder. "There's an English saying— Today's news is tomorrow's fish and chips wrapper."

"Yes, I know, and I choose to think nothing more about it," Elizabeth said, tossing the cone aside before intertwining her hand with Darcy's once again.

As they followed the garden path in silence, Fitzwilliam sensed her continued disquiet. "Elizabeth, something is still bothering you. Is it the dogs?"

She put her arm around Darcy's waist and leaned against his strong frame. "Yes, it is. I wanted you to see the place where we buried them. Before we leave today, we'll visit the gravesite. I planted a bed of pansies there. They should be beautiful by now. Another thing that bothers me is the thought of replacing Old Dan and Lady Beth. The new pups won't be mine. They'll be Henry's."

Fitzwilliam hugged her while placing a quick kiss in her hair, inhaling the sweet rose scent he loved so much. "If you would like a pair of new pups, we can get some. Though, of course, it might be better to wait until we know where we are going to live."

"Someday, that would be nice. However, I want to have the time to handle and train them myself, and now is not the time. I already have a full plate." Embracing him, Elizabeth thanked Darcy for his kindness as they turned to walk back into the house to prepare for church.

Church was at eleven a.m., and as Elizabeth had predicted, they were all expected to go. The sermon was about the importance of the Christian home and raising children as God would have you to do. Pastor Emery quoted scripture on how the husband was to love the wife as Christ loved the Church and how the woman was to be the keeper of the home where both parents were to love, nurture, and protect the children. Elizabeth thought it was fitting with regard to what they had discussed the night before. Darcy took her hand in his, gently squeezing it as if he had thought the same.

When church was over, they all walked towards the door to shake the pastor's hand. Everyone was friendly and kind, but as Elizabeth had predicted, the whispers had already begun. A group of ladies had gathered in a far corner quietly talking while shaking their heads and looking in the direction of the Bennetts. Lizzy only smiled politely.

After returning from church, they ate a light meal and prepared to return to town. Elizabeth packed a few boxes and set them, along with their bags, on the back porch while Fitzwilliam patiently packed her car.

"Elizabeth, the Durango's loaded. Are you ready?"

"Almost. Here, help me put this in the car."

"What's in here?" He frowned. "It weighs a ton."

"Two dozen eggs, two gallons of milk, two quarts of cream, and some bacon and ham left over from the pigs we killed last year. Don't worry. It's not all for me. I'm taking some of it back for you and Charles. I want real cream in my tea when I'm at your house."

He chuckled as he put the cooler in the back of the car.

"Now, let's go to where I buried my dogs. I want to see where they're resting."

She took his hand in hers and led him around to the back of the barn near the creek

M.K. Baxley

bank. There they found the two graves covered in rich colors of yellow, purple, red and white. Bending down quietly, she said a few words to her dogs as if they could hear her.

After several minutes, Fitzwilliam stooped and gently helped her up, slipping his arm around her shoulder. She leaned against him. "Someday I will let you give me another set of pups."

As they wound their way through the gardens and across the lawn towards the car, she said, "When we come back at Thanksgiving, I want to visit my parents' graves. I have not been there since the funeral," she said softly. "It has been too painful." She glanced up at him with questioning eyes. "Will you come with me?"

"Of course, darling, we shall go together," he answered, giving her a tender squeeze. Her eyes were the sweetest eyes he'd ever seen.

The ride back to town gave them the time to begin discussing their plans for the future. "Elizabeth, there is something very important I must tell you." He paused, glancing in her direction. "First of all, I'm not exactly who I appear to be," he hesitated. "What I mean is, I'm from a very old family, as I've told you, in the North of England. We just happen to be...ah...well...we are quite wealthy—old money if you will. Have you ever heard of Pemberley, PLC?"

"No, I can't say that I have." She wrinkled her brow.

"Well then, I suppose you don't read the *Financial Times* or listen to the business news because we're the largest corporation in the United Kingdom. Our stock is traded on all the global exchanges. I personally have a net worth of £15 million right now, which is almost $30 million, and it may even be more than that as I haven't checked my investments lately." He drew a deep breath, not certain how she would react to what he had to say next. With trepidation, he trudged on. "When I inherit my fortune upon my father's death, I'll be worth over £4 billion and the business itself, which is somewhere in the neighborhood of £400 billion, but control of that I will share with my brother David."

Fitzwilliam studied her cautiously, trying to appraise her thoughts after revealing his news. From the shocked look on her face, he thought it was a good thing she had let him drive because he could tell she was having trouble absorbing what he had just told her.

He nervously laughed aloud. "Hard to believe, isn't it? It sounds like Monopoly money. However, there is a catch of which I must make you aware." He cringed, but he knew he had to tell her.

Elizabeth eyes shot in his direction, and then she tore her gaze away. Looking out the window, she released a tense breath. "I'm afraid to ask, but please continue."

Glancing at her with apprehension, he flatly stated, "I hate to tell you this, darling, but my father may not approve of my choice. He wants me to marry an English girl."

Her jaw went slack. She gawked at him in shock.

Sensing her distress, he pleaded. "Elizabeth, please try to understand. My father is of the old school, wanting me, and, of course, David, but especially me to marry in the first circles of London society, which both of us have refused to do, but for different reasons. I insist that I will marry for love, whilst David simply wishes not to marry at all. Although I hope he will if he ever meets someone as wonderful as I have. David's a bit of a playboy, but that's neither here nor there." He slipped his hand across the seat, catching hers in his, giving it an affectionate squeeze. Inhaling deeply, he continued. "As for me, well, Father has even gone as far as to attempt to arrange a marriage for me, but I flatly refused to cooperate. He's told me if I ever marry someone he doesn't approve of, he will cut me off. I'm not afraid of that, as I already have enough money, and if invested properly, we will never be poor."

Elizabeth gaped at him in astonishment. He could tell this was not being received very well. He quickly tried to recover. "But I don't believe he will actually do that for two reasons. One, he likes David's playboy lifestyle less than he will disapprove of my choice. And two, he really does love me.

"Anyway, up until now, David and I have been confirmed bachelors," he said. "My father deplores our choices in life. He is desperate for us to do what he thinks is the right thing, and part of that is by marrying well and producing the next generation of Darcys. So, if I marry and produce the much wanted grandchild, preferably a boy, I think that he may forgive us."

Elizabeth seemed momentarily speechless, but he felt sure she would soon find her tongue if the fury gathering on her face was any indication. Fitzwilliam braced himself.

"Forgive us!" she gasped, eyes flashing as the blood drained from her face. "Fitzwilliam, I don't like the sound of this one bit. Are you telling me that the only way your father will accept me is if I squeeze out a child right after we are married? That I have to do that in order to appease your family?! That's insane." Elizabeth fumed.

"It's not exactly like that. David and Georgiana will love you because I love you. My cousins will, too. My Uncle Harvey and Aunt Susan will be pleased for me. It really is only my father and well, maybe my Aunt Hilda who are stuck in the dark ages. As for having a child, is that really so bad? You know I want children—at least two if we can. Would it really be so bad to have them earlier rather than later? Elizabeth, I'm thirty-two and you're twenty-five. I don't feel we have a lot of time to wait."

"Fitzwilliam, I just finished my doctorate. I had hoped to work a little longer before even thinking about marriage much less having children. Other than working as a grad assistant, this is my first real teaching job. My mother had Jane almost one year after marriage, and then the rest of us came nearly every two years. It was a long time before she could teach again. And as to our ages, men can father children up into their eighties, and twenty-five is not that old." She cut him a sharp look.

Tension building in his chest, he breathed deeply. "I know that twenty-five is not old and that you have time. And I have no doubts about my own virility, but I want to be young enough to enjoy my children in all stages of their lives. That includes playing football and teaching them to ride a horse. When I reach my forties, I may not feel like I do now." He paused and took another quick breath. "You mentioned your mother's circumstances. Didn't she have a choice in the matter? I mean, she did have six children. Was your mother unhappy with so many children?"

"No, of course not," Elizabeth shot back. "Dad and her children were very important to her. My mother had other things which she did besides rearing us." Throwing her hands up in the air, she burst out, "Oh, Fitzwilliam, you must give me some time to think. I'll need to sort through my feelings about all of this. I might be able to teach part time if I have a child right away, but right now, I don't know how I really feel about what you've shared with me concerning your father's expectations and your financial status. I'm not sure I want a child right now either. I don't know when I'll be ready for motherhood. How could you spring this on me all at once? I wish you had told me this before you proposed."

"Elizabeth, I'm sorry for unloading on you like this. It's just that I had to be sure it was me you wanted—not who I am in terms of money and status."

Her eyes widened. "If anything, Fitzwilliam, your money and status would be a turn off. I've been around people with money, and I generally find them not worth the trouble of knowing. I probably wouldn't have given you a second look had I known, or at the very least, it would have been harder to have taken you seriously."

"So, you would have refused me then?" he asked, a little worried.

"I might back out now."

"Oh no, you won't."

"And how can you be so sure of that?" She cut her eyes at him.

"Because you love me, and you can't resist my charms." He cautiously smiled. Hopefully she was accepting things and still accepting him.

"You're very confident in yourself, aren't you?" She clasped her hands in her lap and stared out the window, calmer now, having finally come to grips with all that he had told her but still clearly upset.

"I always get what I want, and I want you!" Reaching over, he took her hand in his once again, giving it another gentle squeeze as he flashed a wide smile.

"Well, what other bombshells do you have to drop on me?"

"No, no more bombshells. I'll just tell you my plan," he said with a smile. "When I go to London in December, I'll recruit David's support to get my father's blessing. I think Father will relent, especially if I promise him a grandchild sometime before he dies. Now, will that do?"

"Oh Fitzwilliam...what can I say? I guess if I'm going to marry you it'll have to do. But, if and *when* I have a child, it will be because it is what you and I want, *not* what your father wants."

"Elizabeth, let me make this *clear*. I want a child because it *is* what I want. Yes, it will soften my father, but having a child is between you and me, not him and me."

"Well, I'm glad to at least hear that." She gave him another sharp look.

Desiring very much to change the subject, he said, "Splendid, now Elizabeth, tell me, what type of ring do you want?" Patting her knee, he gave her a devilish smile he hoped would dispel the tension.

"A ring...hmm...yes, I suppose I must have a ring." Elizabeth mused, "Nothing too big or vulgar, please." She raised a brow. "Nothing over one or two carats at the most, and I'd like either white gold or platinum. Also, I prefer a plain band."

"Well, then, it will be two carats in platinum with a plain wedding band for now. But, eventually, you will have at least one of the heirloom sets when I inherit the estate. Shall we announce our engagement to your family at Thanksgiving? We can tell Jane and Charles tonight."

"Yes, that'll be fine." She sighed, her voice trailing off.

After a moment of quiet, Elizabeth spoke. "Fitzwilliam, with all that you have told me, there is one other thing I don't understand. Why are you here taking a teaching position when you could be in London attending to your family's business? And don't you dare tell me it was to find me."

"That's a fair question. I guess you could say I'm pursuing my dream." He sighed. "I'm still very active in Pemberley, even though I'm not presently in England. I teleconference with David and my cousin, Richard, once a week so that I can keep up with all business details, and when I go to London in the summers, I'll be attending board meetings and conferences. David acts on my behalf, representing me on the board as well as himself when I'm not there, therefore the company isn't neglected. I'm very much in the loop with what is happening in the family business.

"But, my dream has always been to teach. I'd like to follow in the steps of three Oxford Dons that I admire greatly. Two are dead and one still lives. Actually, I wanted to become an Oxford Fellow, but those positions are hard to come by. So, when our good friend, Dr. Dickens, approached Charles and I in London and asked us to come here, we decided we couldn't turn down such an excellent opportunity," Darcy said with a broad smile. "And I enjoy both the subjects I teach and being part of the academic world."

"I see," Elizabeth said, listening intently.

"Eventually, I will become the CEO of Pemberley, PLC. Once that happens, I doubt I'll be able to teach anymore. And since that's inevitable, I'm doing what I want to do whilst I have the opportunity."

"Well, we're almost to the townhouse," Elizabeth announced. "Fitzwilliam, I'm not through discussing this. We have several hours before the others arrive back in town, and I need some answers. I want to know more about your father and what he expects, and I want to know just what type of lady he wants you to marry. Who is this mystery woman he found for you, and what is she like?" Elizabeth said as they pulled onto Elm Street.

Darcy inwardly groaned. Perhaps she was not as accepting as he had previously thought.

After they arrived at the Bennett townhouse and unloaded the Durango, they settled into the front sitting room. Fitzwilliam tensed as he felt the inquisition was about to begin anew.

Taking a seat, Elizabeth resumed. "Now, I want to know why your father would not accept me as his daughter-in-law, and what exactly is it that he does expect from someone who would marry one of his sons?" She folded her arms across her chest.

With his hand against the window frame, he looked at her from across the room, meeting her penetrating gaze. He released a tense breath. "I don't exactly know how to tell you this in a way that will make you understand and at the same time convey what I feel deep inside, but I'll try by being as truthful as I can."

Stepping away from the window, he raked his fingers through his hair. "In England there are certain expectations from members of the upper levels of society, especially if you are descended from the aristocracy, which I am—and I might add, so are you, although it is now far removed." He paced the floor, glancing at the ceiling, and then back at her, sitting there, arms folded, eyes inquisitively waiting for him to continue.

"Typically, we marry within our own circle, or at least from families who are closely related in circumstances to our own. For example, my mother was descended from the aristocracy, and her father owned a very profitable publishing company which she inherited from him. And she was educated at Cambridge, so my mother was within those guidelines. She was also sophisticated and beautiful, another thing my father finds important."

Elizabeth rolled her eyes, anger once again creeping over her features.

...*Oh God, she doesn't understand*..."Elizabeth, please. Don't look at me that way. I am trying to be forthright with you."

"All right, I'm sorry. Do continue," she said, releasing a long sharp breath.

"You fit all those criteria, except you're not British, and you're not fabulously wealthy. But that doesn't matter to me. I have enough money. Enough for both of us and any children we would have. I don't think like my father. Many in Britain don't these days. Even Prince William is dating a beautiful girl whose family doesn't quite measure up by those old standards." He gazed down into her silent, solemn face and shook his head.

"What about this woman your father has chosen for you? What is she like? Is she pretty and sophisticated and fabulously wealthy?" Elizabeth asked, her eyes piercing.

He turned and faced her. This was not easy. Speaking in a quiet voice he replied,

M.K. Baxley

"Yes...yes, she is. She's all of those things, and she's set to inherit her father's banking and financial empire worth billions. She's also my Aunt Hilda's step-daughter on my mother's side. We're not blood related, but we did grow up together. And yes, she's beautiful, sophisticated, and fashionable. She's impeccable in all ways imaginable, except one. The most important one—I don't love her."

He paused for a second, attempting to gauge Elizabeth's reaction, but it was unreadable. He shook his head while continuing to pace. "I dated her for two months, trying to feel something for her. We barely kissed, and when we did, her response was, well, uninterested. She cares nothing for me, or for anything I would want. She's only concerned with social functions, society, fashion, and money. To her, what is important is to receive the right invitations to the right events, who will attend the Queen's Garden Party, and what she can gain from being seen at those places."

...It's time to lay my feeling open. She'll have to take them at face value or leave them. I want her to love me for me. If I can't have her love, I've got nothing... He sighed heavily. "Elizabeth, I can't live like that. I want to love and to be loved like any other ordinary man. You've told me about your mother and father and the life you had growing up. Well, that's what I want. I want to love a woman like your father loved your mother, and I want to be loved by that same woman as your mother loved your father. Is that too much to ask in life?"

Elizabeth's lashes lowered momentarily. "No. No, it's not, and that's what I wanted to hear." She raised her eyes to his and for the first time since they'd left the farm, a genuine smile crossed her face. "Of course I want to be accepted by your family. Only a fool wouldn't care about that. If I am to enter your family on the terms you've lain out, I have to have a good enough reason to do so. If you really love me enough to go against your father and you truly desire the things you've told me, then I will accept you just as you are."

He was instantly at her side, pulling her into his arms, hugging her close. Cupping her face in his hands, he said, "I do love you, Liz, and I mean every word I've told you." He bent low to kiss her.

When they separated, he dropped down on the loveseat and gathered her into his lap. Holding her close, he said, "In spite of what you must think of my father, I want you to know that my mother was nothing like him. She was kind and loving and good. She taught me to be that way as well. In fact, not just me, but my brother, too. And my sister, who was only four when Mum died, is very much like me. David, despite his bravado, is very much like Georgiana and me as well. He *is* a good man. They will accept you as my mother would have, had she lived." He kissed her once more, contented in finally having all of this behind them.

Almost as soon as they had finished their discussion, Jane and Charles pulled into the driveway, along with Kat and Daniel. Elizabeth and Darcy went to door to greet them.

"Hey you two, come in. Here, let me help you with those," Darcy said, taking a package from Jane. "Are there any more packages? I'll be glad to get those for you."

Jane smiled. "Yes, there are a few more in the back of the Tahoe."

"I'll get them. You make yourself comfortable," Darcy insisted, heading out the door.

Darcy wore a contented smile, happier than he'd been in years as he and Charles fetched the last two packages from the car. Once they were settled in the house, Darcy and Elizabeth, arms around each other, approached Jane and Charles.

"We have an announcement to make," Darcy said, beaming and holding her close. "Elizabeth and I have decided to marry."

Jane immediately pulled away from Charles and crossed the room to Elizabeth, giving her sister a big hug.

"Lizzy, I am so happy for you. I told Charles you two would be perfect for one another. We just had to get you together, but it looks like Fate took care of that for us. Didn't it, Charles?"

"I'll say it did," Bingley said as he grabbed his friend's hand. "Congratulations, old man." He glanced at Jane. "Congratulations are in order here, too. Janey and I also have an announcement to make." He turned around for Jane's hand. "Jane and I are to be married, too."

The couples hugged each other so happily excited that Kat and Daniel rushed downstairs to see what was happening.

"What's going on down here?" Kat asked. "I can hear you all the way upstairs."

Jane took Kat's hands in hers and told her the happy news.

"Oh, Jane! That's wonderful. I'm so happy for you both. Let me give you a hug." Kat embraced first Jane and then Lizzy, while Daniel shook hands with Darcy and Bingley.

"I guess now I can call you two by your first names, except at school, of course. When are you all getting married?" Daniel asked.

"Daniel, you may call me whatever you like. As to the other, we haven't discussed it yet, but it won't be until after I return from England, probably in the summer." Darcy turned to his friend. "What about you, Bingley?"

"It's the same with us. Maybe we could have a double wedding. What do you two think?" Charles asked, glancing between Darcy and Elizabeth.

"I think it's a splendid idea. We must all get together when we come back from England. Perhaps we will have a June wedding." Darcy gave Elizabeth an affectionate kiss on her cheek while Jane nodded in agreement, looking at Charles and smiling.

"Well, it's getting late. I think we need to leave for home, Charles," Darcy said.

Bingley glanced at Jane, but before he could speak, Elizabeth spoke. "Jane, will you help me in the kitchen. I need to repackage some of these things for Fitzwilliam and Charles."

Elizabeth and Jane put together a basket for the men to take back to their house. As the two gentlemen were about to leave, Darcy pulled Elizabeth aside and kissed her. "Are you happy, Elizabeth?" he asked.

"Extremely. I didn't think I could ever be so happy." Looking up at him, love sparkled in her expressive emerald eyes. "I wasn't quite sure before, but now I am. I love you, Fitzwilliam."

Upon hearing her words, he pulled her into a tight embrace. "You don't know what that means to me. I love you so very much. I look forward to the day when you truly are mine." He tightened his embrace and gave her a lingering kiss, his heart overcome with joy. For the first time in his life, he felt he had a real purpose and meaning in being alive.

"I wish you could come home with me now."

"As much as I would like to, you know I cannot do that. I have to prepare for tomorrow. We have a short vacation coming in two days. We'll spend the five day break together when we go to Longbourn for Thanksgiving. I'll call you tomorrow, and we'll have lunch on campus. Oh, and don't let me forget—I need to tell you some details about me and my own financial situation. I'm not penniless. I have an inheritance, too. Though not as large as yours, the Bennetts are not exactly poor."

Chapter Nine

...A promise is yet to be fulfilled...

The day dawned cold and miserable with a biting wind coming down off the mountain and settling into the plateau. Having driven down to the farm the night before for the Thanksgiving holiday, Darcy and Bingley were up at the crack of dawn, preparing for the morning's shooting party with Elizabeth's uncles. Darcy had been looking forward to this all week as they were going to shoot wild turkey, Canadian geese, and Mallard ducks. Pulling on his boots and donning his camouflage jacket, he was more than prepared to meet the challenging elements when Henry peered around the corner into the mudroom.

"Fitzwilliam, let's get a move on. Charles and Robert are waitin' on us. I'd like to get at least two turkeys. A couple of geese would be nice, too, and perhaps two ducks."

Darcy cast a wide grin. "I'd like that, too. Let me grab the shotgun and several boxes of shells, and I'll be right out."

Exiting through the back door and stepping out into the garden, he met up with the others where Henry made the introduction to Elizabeth's father's brother of whom he'd heard so much about. Robert Bennett, a tall lean man in his mid forties with clear blue eyes and sandy blonde hair, had just arrived for the morning's event. Darcy could see the family resemblance. He looked very much like the picture of Elizabeth's father that hung in the family gallery.

Grabbing the offered hand, Bennett had a hardy handshake and a firm grip. "Darcy, I'm pleased to meet you. I've heard so much about you that I feel as if we're already friends, especially since you're soon to be family. Congratulations on your upcoming marriage to one of my favorite nieces." The man flashed a wide grin.

"I'm pleased to meet you, Mr. Bennett," Darcy replied with a smile.

"Darcy, we're to be family, so there's none of that Mr. Bennett stuff," Bennett insisted. "Like I told Charles here, it's either Robert or Bennett, but emphatically ***not*** Mr. Bennett. That's reserved for my secretary and the office staff." He let out a hardy laugh. "Now, let's get goin', or those turkeys will leave for higher ground. They're in the rye fields now, but they'll quickly move if they sense us comin'. These are wild turkeys—not those domestic birds with undersized brains. They're smart and cunning, so we'll have to be one up on 'em."

"Bennett, you'll do splendid for an uncle. I already sense camaraderie. Are these your dogs?" Darcy asked, gazing at the two black labs poised at Bennett's heels.

"Yeah," he answered with a lilting laughter. "That's Ruff and Ready, and they are just that—rough and ready, two of the best retrievin' dogs in the county. They'll pick up anything we shoot," he said, rubbing the male dog behind the ears. "Let's head out." Glancing at the sky, he added, "It looks like snow, so we'd better get a move on."

Darcy and Bingley exchanged grins. They both knew this was going to be a quite an adventure. Turning up their collars and pulling their fur lined hunting hats down over their ears, the four braced against the cold as they moved in the direction of the winter rye fields where, just as Robert had predicted, a flock of wild turkeys took to the air. Not just any turkeys, either. They were some of the biggest, plumpest birds Darcy had ever seen. All four men fired at once and four birds fell. Ruff and Ready sprang into action, and Robert gingerly snatched the retrieved birds, placing them in the burlap sack.

After the rye fields, they left for the cow pond which Darcy thought more resembled a small lake than a pond, but then, no, it had to be a pond with all of the cat tails and marsh reeds springing forth out of the water. As they approached, a flock of ducks and geese flew up. Once again the boom of shots rang out, and two geese and four ducks fell. At the sound of the first shot, Ruff and Ready were in the water, paddling out to the center of the pond, bringing the birds back one at a time. Their bags full, the men walked back to the house, declaring the trip a success. Tomorrow there would be turkey and a goose on the table to complement the ham from this year's spring pigs.

With the hunt behind them, Darcy looked forward to spending time with Elizabeth. As they approached the house, Robert called out, "Darcy, Henry and I'll clean these birds, and when Daniel gets up, he can help. You and Charles are guests, and I suppose you want to spend every spare minute you can with my nieces, so y'all head out to wherever you wanna go. Tana and the others will take care of the cookin'. We'll be fine." Robert shot him a smile that indicated he understood what it was like to be in love and to want to be alone at every chance.

"Thanks, Bennett. I believe we'll ride out after breakfast." Gazing upward, Darcy said, "You may be right. It looks like rain or snow, so this may be the only chance we'll have."

"Well, there's always the barn loft, but you didn't hear that from me. You either, Bingley." He tossed a look over his shoulder to Charles who was bringing up the rear. "Tana would kill me, but truth be known, we spent quite a few hours there ourselves when we were datin'." He winked.

Darcy laughed aloud. "Bennett, now I *know* I like you."

"I quite agree with Darcy," Bingley added.

"Well, I suppose a young college professor's not much different from a young lawyer, and as long as your intentions are honorable, I see no harm with stealing away whenever you can. Besides, it'll give you somethin' to look back on when you're middle-aged like me. Now go on...and remember, you didn't hear it from me." He winked.

All three laughed.

After the birds and guns were deposited in the mudroom, Darcy went to find Elizabeth. Searching the various rooms he finally found her ensconced in the library, drawn up in the bench seat of the bay window with a book.

"What are you reading, darling?"

"Hmm? This?" she replied, marking her page as she closed the book. "It's Sarah Morgan's journal, *The Civil War Diary of a Southern Woman*. It's an account of what it was like to have been sixteen when The War Between the States began. Sarah lived on a sugar plantation in Louisiana. I've almost finished it."

"Is it good?"

"Yes, I'd say it is. It's informative, but not very much different from what it was like around here from 1861 through Reconstruction. It reinforces what I already know. The sorrow and misery was everywhere. I'm nearly to the part where she marries her handsome beau and moves to Charleston," she said on a grin. "She was a girl much like me. It's a history that's heartfelt and heart shared as she reveals what they suffered. I'll tell you about it sometime," she said, setting the book aside. "Let's have some coffee and scones, and then we'll go for a ride."

"Handsome beau, huh...." He smiled.

"Yes," she said, returning his smile. "Now help me up, and let's go. Oh, and by the way, I have a handsome beau, too."

He reached out his hand, taking hers as they walked hand in hand to the kitchen.

Once they'd finished eating, they saddled up and headed in the direction of the cove. The temperature had dropped and was still falling when they made it to the cabin. Elizabeth was chilled to the bone and shivering, so Darcy started a blazing fire in the fireplace.

"Come here, love. You're cold. I'll hold you and warm you up."

"Fitzwilliam, it may not have been such a good idea coming out here. With the way the temperature has dropped, it could possibly mean snow. The weather forecaster is not always right when he calls for rain. Occasionally they miss it."

"Well, if it does, we'll live with it. But for right now, let's get you warmed up. Your cheeks are chapped and your hands are frozen."

As the fire burned bright and cozy, he held her close while they sat on the bed. Unable to resist, she pulled him to her for an innocent kiss, but when their lips touched, she lost all conscience thought. As the kiss deepened, he began to caress her, stroking her arms and sides, and then her breasts, gently massaging them through her soft flannel shirt.

Caught up in the moment, she fell backwards onto the bed, without breaking their kiss, taking him with her. Soon he was lying with her in an intimate embrace, kissing, touching, caressing, and stroking her inner thigh ever so gently. Elizabeth knew they should stop, and yet she didn't want to. The more Fitzwilliam kissed her, the more he touched her, the more she burned with an insatiable ache.

His fingers hovered at her neckline for a moment, and then he gently began to unbutton her shirt. Pushing the flannel aside, he freed one breast from her bra and cupped her flesh as he palmed it. The feel of his cool hands against her hot skin sent pleasurable sensations coursing through her body, pooling in a hot desire she'd never expected to experience. Pulling him on top of her, she instinctively parted her legs, allowing him to settle between them. Fitzwilliam arched against her, and soon they writhed against one another. Elizabeth had never felt such desire…such need. She wanted him and she wondered if she could wait until her wedding night or if she even cared.

Fitzwilliam felt the strain on his self control snapping as her soft body pressed against his. His mind and body conflicted with one another. His body wanted her now, but his mind was determined to respect her wishes. Lying there together, reality finally slipped back into play, and he abruptly pulled away.

"Elizabeth, we shouldn't be here like this. If we continue, we won't be able to stop, and I know that is not what you want." His heart pounded as his pulse raced in time with his throbbing body. It would have to be her call, not his, no matter what the cost to him. Releasing a long breath, his control held firm even as his body ached in pain.

"I know, Fitzwilliam…I know. It's just that I have never felt this way before. It's all so new to me. I love you, and I want you…but…" She looked down and then cut her eyes over to the corner of the room. Chewing on her lower lip, she said nothing.

He looked at her with longing, his eyes searching, waiting to see how she would respond, waiting for her to ask. He had told her he would not take anything from her unless she freely gave it. He wondered if she realized how much he needed her, how much he wanted her.

He waited, but she never asked. Releasing a tightly held breath, he figured it was best if they left temptation behind. "Come Liz, we need to go." He pulled her up and buttoned her blouse, straightening their appearance before extinguishing the fire in the fireplace as well as the one in his soul.

The following day was Thanksgiving, and the house hummed with the hustle and bustle of the day's preparations. The smell of delicious food cooking permeated the air. Casseroles already baked, cornbread dressing and mashed potatoes and gravy sat on the side table while field peas and corn on the cob simmered on the stove. A goose was in one oven and a turkey in the other. Cooked ham cooled on the counter and pies, cakes, and bread, baked fresh earlier that morning filled the baker's rack. The table was spread with a white damask cloth and set in Old Country Rose china. Cranberry relish and spiced blueberries lay about the table in crystal dishes, and goblets filled with iced tea were alongside each person's place.

A soft chuckle emanated from Darcy's throat. This was nothing like a formal dinner at his house where servants took care of these seemingly meaningless tasks. Seemingly meaningless, and yet not.

The difference was that this house was filled with love while his house was filled with order and careful routine. How he almost envied Elizabeth and her family. They were the picture of family life he'd often dreamt of—the American Norman Rockwell, and God help him, he loved her for every bit of it. This, his first Thanksgiving with the Bennetts, would be a day for him to remember. Not since his mother's death could he recall a better one. With the ladies scurrying about, neatly placing dishes on the table, the feast was about to begin.

The tinkling of his fork against Henry's tea glass called the family together as they all took their seats around the table. Except for Mary Beth and Joseph, they were all here—Robert and Tana, Jane, Elizabeth, Kat, Daniel, Grace, Henry and Lori, and he and Charles.

Clearing his throat, Henry began. "Let us give thanks for this bountiful meal before us. As you know, most of it has come from the farm this year, even the turkey and goose, which Charles and Fitzwilliam helped to provide," Henry said with a twinkle in his eye. "Yes, we have much to be thankful for. The crops were better than expected, the cattle bred well with no problems, aside from the coyotes that is. But the best news of all is that there are to be two new additions in our family circle. Jane and Charles… Elizabeth and Fitzwilliam, congratulations! Now Jane, would you give thanks?"

Linked together, holding hands, Jane returned thanks for all the blessings bestowed upon the family as another year had come and gone. When she finished, they all said in unison, "Amen."

Robert broke out in a big smile. "Now let's eat. Pass the food!"

The next day proved to be tedious. A steady downpour of rain mixed with sleet and snow had fallen all day, leaving everyone confined to the house. Jane and Charles spent the day in the upstairs sitting room watching movies while Fitzwilliam spent the day with Elizabeth in the library reading.

Poring over a volume of Gibeon's *The Rise and Fall of the Roman Empire,* Darcy's mind was anywhere but on Gibeon. Thursday had been much like today, wet and dreary. There had been ample opportunity for them to be alone, but he had steadfastly resisted it. After what had happened, or nearly happened, in the cabin two days ago, he was afraid to be alone with Elizabeth because, unlike her, he knew what those feelings…those stirrings were. He also knew that with very little effort, he could take her virginity, and in fact, almost had. It had taken a sheer force of will to break away, and next time, he might not be able to do so.

She was an innocent. He was not, but he wasn't the player his brother was either. He wouldn't take her. They would wait. There would be no more passionate kissing, no more caresses, and no more close embraces, no matter how badly he wanted it. No, he told himself, he would sequester his emotions, keeping them under lock and key—under tight regulation until their wedding night. He sighed as he watched her engrossed in her tome of *Chaucer*. It would be difficult, but he could do it. Yes, he was a man of principle, and he would remain firm. Returning his thoughts to his book, he heard her sigh. He smiled and turned the page.

As Elizabeth attempted for the third time to concentrate on her book, the veil of her lashes hid her eyes as they once again cut across the room to Darcy. He seemed deep in thought, probably engrossed in his book as she should be. Still, she couldn't help but think of the cabin and what had almost happened as the memory of two days ago flashed inside her mind. She'd come within a hair's breadth of letting him have her. If he hadn't stopped, she wouldn't have resisted him. But he had stopped, letting the dog sleep at her doorstep, leaving the decision up to her. It was obvious he would not take the initiative unless she gave him leave to do so.

She softly sighed... *I'm acting more like a teenager than a grown woman. This is ridiculous. We're engaged, for Pete's sake! Will we be able to continue on like this until June? Will he? Will I?*

Once again her eyes drifted in Darcy's direction. He'd just turned the page and smiled. *I'd best return to my book,* she thought. She smiled and turned her page.

Darcy set his book aside and looked up. "Elizabeth, do you think I might have a look at your family journals," he asked, "and could we have some wine?"

"Sure, I'll get some." Pouring two glasses, she handed one to him then walked over to the bookcase and pulled the first volume from the shelf in the family history section.

Taking the volume from her hands, he reverently brushed over the soft leather cover with his fingers before opening the book to the first page. Taking a deep breath, he began to read out loud as they sipped their wine.

25 September 1789

As I sit in the Carriage Inn, I pen this entry. Today, I went to the White House to collect Rebecca Jane to become my wife. She is now several months with child. Though she protests, I will marry her. It is no fault of her own that she resides with Madam Kinsley, but rather due to our cruel rules of society. She was in tears when I proposed, wondering why I would take her, a poor prostitute with no money, to be my wife. She is convinced that, had we met when she was under different circumstances, I would not have sought her out, being that she was then a poor dowerless girl, but she could not be more wrong, for I have loved her from our first acquaintance. I have no doubt I would have loved her then, had I found her before misfortune did.

I paid Madam Kinsley three hundred pounds for Rebecca's freedom, and then we were off to Gretna Green. Father has disowned me, but I, as a gentleman, could allow neither my child nor the woman I love to suffer. I will protect them.

30 September 1789

Today we boarded the Southern Star bound for America. We shall make a new life for ourselves and our children. Father has given me five thousand pounds in gold. I know he loves me and is doing what he must for Edward and my sisters. I bear him no ill will, but I can never return to England. Leaving my brother and sisters has been the most difficult thing I have ever done, especially leaving Edward. It grieves me that I shall never see him again on this side of life, though I have promised Edward that our lines shall cross again. Someday my son or perhaps my grandson shall marry his daughter or granddaughter, or the reverse. I know not when, but I feel certain that our lives will intersect.

Darcy filed that last entry away as he pondered its meaning. "Elizabeth, how tragic this is! He must have loved Rebecca very much to have given up his inheritance for her. That was not an easy thing to do in the 18th century. Had he stayed in England, I believe the entire family would have fallen into disgrace, and Mr. Bennet's daughters would not have been able to marry or be received in society. His father had no choice really," Darcy said with a sigh. He knew from his own family history how brutal society and class censure had been.

"I believe you're probably correct, but I do think it happened for the best. John Bennet recovered everything he lost, and his brother benefited, too. If you read on, you will see that they were very close, though, unfortunately, world events separated the families, and it didn't help matters that Edward's wife, Frances, did not like Rebecca at all and had made her sentiments very much known within the family. There are a few letters that survived the years, and that's all the knowledge we have."

"Elizabeth, if it is as I think, then I know it was for the best. My Darcy ancestor, Fitzwilliam, married an Elizabeth Bennet from Longbourn, and if things are as I suspect, then you and I are distantly related. If that is the case and your ancestral grandfather had inherited Longbourn in Hertfordshire, then my ancestral grandfather would not have been able to marry his Elizabeth, as they most likely would not have met. I would not be here and neither would you, so things happened as they should have. When I go to London during the holidays, I'll check the records. I've never been to Longbourn in Hertfordshire. I suspect the house has been given up for progress, but the parish church should still be there."

"Do check it out. I've heard so much about Longbourn in England from my grandparents and great aunts and uncles. We've passed so many tales down through the generations that I feel as if I know the place. I'd dearly love to know what happened to everything."

"I'll find out what I can."

They continued reading for several hours with Darcy rapidly skimming over the journals, going from one generation to another, conferring with Elizabeth and gleaning as much historical information as he could. By the time they had finished, Darcy had a full picture of the Bennett family. Now, he would look in his own family history for the rest of the story, determined to see if his hunch was correct, and he was very sure it was.

Before returning to town, Elizabeth took Fitzwilliam to the family cemetery at Longbourn Baptist Church. It was a quiet spot under several large pine, cedar, and oak trees, now barren of leaves.

"Elizabeth, before seeing your parents' graves, I'd like to see your ancestors' graves, particularly John Bennet's."

"Yes, we can do that. It's over here in the older part of the cemetery."

They walked for a bit until they came to a very old flat stone, eroded from the weather, but still remarkably readable. Darcy stooped down and brushed the dirt and leaves from the granite so that he could read the inscriptions. He traced his fingers gently over the words *Father John Thomas Bennet Born August 11, 1762, Died November 4, 1860. Mother Rebecca Jane Alexander Bennet Born August 11, 1768, Died November 4, 1861. Inseparable in life, inseparable in death. A promise is yet to be fulfilled.* Darcy stood and took his personal digital assistant from his coat and recorded the names and dates.

"Elizabeth what is meant by a promise is yet to be fulfilled?"

"Umm…I think it's recorded in some of the old letters we have that he made a solemn oath and had intended to send one of his sons back to England to marry one of Edward's daughters, only it never happened. I know Edward, his first son, was supposed to go to Hertfordshire in 1812, but with the war, that was put off. He found someone else instead and married her. I don't think he was ever keen on marrying a stranger in the first place. Then Nathanial, John's second son, was to go in 1819, but with the Panic of 1819 and the first American depression that followed, well, several things got in the way, and he never did go either. After that, it seemed not to be so important, and as the generations continued on, none paid it much mind. I guess the desire to return was lost. It's kind of sad, isn't it?"

"Yes…yes, it is." Taking a few steps to his left, Darcy asked, "Are these his sons?"

"Yes, that's my great-great-great grandfather Edward Samuel and his wife Mary Alice Prophet, and next to him is Nathanial Bedford and Martha Tripp, his wife. John Newton, Robert Lawrence, and two of the girls are buried elsewhere with their families."

"Tell me again, what were the girls' names?" Darcy asked as he studied the gravestones.

"Let's see, there was Emily Jane Bennet Sanders, whom my sister Jane is named for, and Mary Bethany Bennet Snow, whom Mary Beth is named for, and then there are Barshaba Nan, Cassandra Elizabeth, and Margaret Inella. They were known as the three spinster aunts: Aunt Barshie, Aunt Cassie, and Aunt Maggie Nell. They're buried on the other side of Nathanial and Martha. And there were several others that died in infancy. They are to the right of John and Rebecca. William Thomas lived two months, Ella Catherine lived nine months, and Daniel Clifton only lived one week. That's all the children there were. Anything else you'd like to see or know?" Elizabeth asked.

"No, I'm just a little curious at the dates on these stones," he said as he walked back to John and Rebecca's headstone. "I'm going to check them against some dates in England to see what I come up with."

"You do that. Now let's go visit Mom and Dad."

"Lead on," he said as he placed his PDA back in his pocket.

They walked a bit around the back of the church to the newest part of the churchyard to where the larger and more elaborate gravestones resided.

"This is it," she said. "It's so sad because they were so young. Mother was only fifty-three and my father fifty-four. They never had the chance to see any of us marry or live long enough to see their grandchildren. Grace always tells me they are in a better place. I like to think that they are allowed to look down and see us." Elizabeth slowly knelt down to place some fall flowers on the grave.

"From what you've told me, your parents loved all of you very much, and I know from what I've seen that they did an excellent job rearing you and your siblings. I can only hope we follow in their stead and do as well with our own family."

When Elizabeth heard him say this, she immediately rose to embrace Darcy. Holding her, he continued to reassure her of his desires for their future happiness.

"Liz, I also want to believe that your parents can look down upon us. I want them to know that I love their daughter very much, and that I will always cherish you. I hope they can see that you and our children will be forever dear to me. I know that it's not the same as it once was a hundred or even fifty years ago, but to the best of my ability, I will see that you are happy and don't want for anything, either materially or emotionally."

Elizabeth was struck by how Darcy looked up to the sky as if he were telling her parents not to worry about their daughter's future. She gave him a gentle hug while thanking him for his kindness. Leaving the cemetery, they walked to the car hand in hand. Just as they were about to enter the Durango, a pair of snow white mourning doves flew by, headed in the direction of the older part of the church cemetery. Fitzwilliam and Elizabeth glanced at the birds. "Those must be the doves I've been hearing about. They're unusual," Elizabeth said.

"They're just white pigeons. What's so unusual about them?"

"No, they are not pigeons. They're mourning doves, and it's only once in a blue moon that a pair of albino doves appear. There's some sort of superstition associated with them because they are so rare."

Fitzwilliam smiled and shook his head as he helped her into the car.

Later that night—The midnight call

The phone rang and rang, going to voice mail and then ringing again. David reached across the redhead in his bed, fumbling to find his mobile.

...Damn it, who's calling me at this hour? Surely not Father...

He checked the caller ID. "Fitzwilliam, why on earth are you calling me at this Godforsaken hour? Do you know what time it is?"

"Yes, it's precisely 12:06 in the morning USA central standard time, and it should be 6:06 your time." Fitzwilliam softly laughed, clearly in a good mood.

"Has something happened? What the bloody hell is wrong that you have to get me out of bed at this hour?"

Another voice interrupted. "David, who is it? Who are you talking to?" asked the woman lying next to him.

"Hush love, it's my brother, and I need to find out what's wrong. Fitzwilliam, now why are you calling?"

"Who are you in bed with this time—the redhead, the blonde, or the brunette? Oh never mind. I don't really want to know. I'm calling to tell you that I'm getting married, and I need your help."

"What the...? Fitzwilliam, did I hear you correctly? You're getting married?" he asked in shock, finally becoming awake. "You've only been there four months!"

Fitzwilliam laughed. "Yes, I know it's been a short time, but when you find the right one, you know it. And she's the most wonderful woman in the world. She's a maths professor here at the university where I teach, but before you get too wound up, let me tell you a little about her. Her name is Elizabeth Bennett, and she comes from a very good family, educated in one of the best schools in the Northeast—MIT to be exact. There's so much more to tell, but I'll save that for when I see you in December. My problem is going to be telling Father. He's not going to like this. I'll need your help in convincing him to accept my choice. I'm afraid he may disown me."

David, now fully awake, sat up in bed and propped against his pillow, smiling as he rolled his eyes at the impulsive behavior of his otherwise reserved brother. "You don't do things by half, do you, Brother? Father's going to be furious. But don't worry. I'll support you all the way." David chuckled. "I can't believe you're actually getting married or have even found that perfect woman you've always talked about. I'll be in Charleston in a few days. Do you want me to come up and meet her?"

"No, not this time. We're going to be extremely busy with the semester ending. Elizabeth and I won't be spending much time together over the next few days because of our schedules. I'll see you in London. When will you be there?"

"I have an appointment with Lawton & Co. for that blasted coffee contract Father wants, and then I'll leave for London either that night or the next day. I'll be home by December 5th."

"Good, I'll see you on December 12th then."

"Fitzwilliam, congratulations! I'm in shock. She must be an amazing woman, and I want to know all about her when I see you. And I mean all the details."

Fitzwilliam chortled. "Maybe not *all* the details, David! But I will tell you everything you need to know. Oh, and David, did your Lamborghini arrive?"

"No, I was in Sant'Agata Bolognese last week to have the seats fitted. Fitzwilliam, it's a dream. They allowed me to drive the prototype. I'm in love! It's to be delivered after the New Year."

"Ha! I can't wait to drive it. I'm sorry it won't be there for Christmas. Keep me informed. I'll see you when I get home. Good night or rather good morning."

David chuckled. "Good night to you, too, and I'll see you in December."

David slid his mobile shut and fell back on his pillow.

"What was that about?" Cybil asked.

"That was my brother, and as you heard, he's getting married."

David put the mobile down and folded his hands behind his head, trying to absorb the information he had just received.

"That's wonderful. I'm so happy for Fitzwilliam. Many of us wondered if he'd ever meet anyone that would suit him." The woman laughed. "He's so stuffy and reserved. Nothing like you, darling. You know, I think I would like to marry someday." She giggled and reached over to kiss him.

He jerked away, staring at her in disbelief. "As long as you don't have any delusions about marrying me, I think marriage would be a good thing for you, but I would hate to lose you."

"David, don't you ever want to marry?"

"I've told you before I'm not the marrying kind. I've not given any indications to the contrary. All of society knows how I feel on that subject, and I'm not about to change my mind for you or anyone else." David gave her a poignant look. "You don't have a gold-plated pussy, love. You can be replaced."

She threw back her head and cackled. "I understand our arrangement, but even if I do marry, we can still see each other."

"No, love, that's one thing I don't do, and I won't make an exception for even you, not withstanding that you are one of the best shags I've ever had. If you marry, it's over, darling. Adultery is not on my agenda."

He thought of his parents when he spoke.

"Well then, I'll have to stay single, won't I?" She laughed

He smiled and caressed her bare shoulder. "Yes, single is my preference—it suites you much better and suits me as well."

Chapter Ten

...has anyone ever told you how desirable you are when you're angry...?

December 4

David Darcy sat in the lobby of the Lawton Executive Complex waiting for his appointment with Cecilia Lawton, President of Lawton & Co. He was there to renegotiate his contract for Lawton's South American coffee, believed by many to be the best premium coffee in the world. This was his third business meeting with her. As he sat waiting his turn, his mind drifted back to this time last year, and the subsequent events that had followed.

One year ago

David had been bargaining with Ms. Lawton for close to two hours, leaving him on the edge of his restraint. It had been a brutally exhausting experience, and had it not been for the fact that his father had told him not to come home without a contract in hand, he would have walked out on the negotiations. In fact, he almost did. She had the upper hand since she either owned the plantations outright or the rights to them. No other coffee in the world competed with what Cecilia Lawton owned.

After two hours of wrangling back and forth, David jumped out of his seat in angry frustration and leaned into her face. "Enough, Lawton! I've made you a reasonable offer, and if you don't like it, then the negotiations are at an end."

She, too, leapt to her feet. They stood there in total silence, nose to nose, staring each other down from across the table. A spark of hot violet-blue fire flashed in her eyes, sending a sharp quiver coursing through him. He wanted to call her a bitch or tell her what she could do with her bloody coffee one bean at a time, but the fierce blaze in her eyes tantalized him. He wondered who would blink first.

Electricity crackled and popped as their gaze slowly dropped downward to each other's lips, leaving him with an incredible urge to kiss her senseless. As he watched her lick her lower lip, he swallowed hard. He could almost taste her. She had come within inches of his mouth, and as her hot breath brushed over his lips, he was all but certain she would kiss him, but it was Cecilia who blinked.

She smiled and then laughed, backing away. "You win, Darcy. It's yours. Now, have dinner with me tonight, and we'll discuss the shipment." She tossed her long blonde hair. "I've spent entirely too much time with you. I do have other appointments, you know."

He stared at her, blinking in stunned disbelief.

"Don't look so ridiculous, Darcy. We have to finish this, and I can't attend to it now. See Ashley out front for directions. Pick me up at six, and don't be late. I hate it when people are late." She smiled, dismissing him with a flippant wave of her hand. After gathering the loose papers scattered about the table, she filled in a few numbers, signed the contract, and then threw it across the table at him.

He snatched it up and looked at her in astonishment, still fuming. Turning to leave, he looked back over his shoulder. "I'll be there, Lawton." His voice dripped sarcasm.

Stopping outside just long enough to get the required directions, he left the building in a hurry nearly running over an older man as he made his way to the lift and out the door to his parked car. Once inside the car, he paused, letting out an aggravated breath.

M.K. Baxley

...What the bloody hell just happened in there? I thought she was going to kiss me. I know she was! I got the contract and at the price I wanted. But why? Is she propositioning me? She's known to do that...but to me? What's your game, Lawton? Well, I guess I'll have dinner with her and see what happens. I know her reputation.

Making sure not to be late, he arrived promptly at her door on South Battery Street. Cecilia's maid met him and escorted him to the front parlor. While he waited, he took notice of the room's elegant décor. The Persian rugs and Queen Anne furnishings gave the room an air of a different time—one that was pleasant and restful. He walked to the back of the room and brushed his fingers over the fine linens covering the side tables where dishes were on display. Picking up a tea cup, he noted the bottom *Fine bone china, England 1758...Hmm...old.* As he gently returned the cup to its place, something else caught his attention.

Moving over to the piano, he studied the old photographs on display, examining them closely. He picked the first one up. It was of a little girl secured on a man's shoulders as they walked through a pergola of vibrant blue wisteria. He smiled. She looked very pretty, he thought, with her long blonde ponytail and girlish smile. Setting it down, he picked up the second one of the little girl sitting in front of the same man seated on a white stallion. She was turned around, gazing upward at the man who smiled tenderly upon the child. Placing the picture in its original spot, David thought of how the man must have loved the little girl. Little girls had always held a tender spot in his heart, too, reminding him of his sister and a time when life hadn't been so complicated.

Just as he put the photograph down, Cecilia entered the room. "That was me when I was three with my father," Cecilia said softly, her lips curved in a gentle smile.

Startled, David looked up. "You were a very pretty child," he said, touching the frame reverently.

"Some have said that. My father often said so."

David turned, squarely facing her. Wanting to bring the focus back to where it belonged, he pushed away whatever tender thoughts the photographs might have inspired. "Miss Lawton, if you're ready, I think it's best if we go."

Cecilia grabbed her coat, and they were out the door. She had made reservations at an exclusive French restaurant where they sat and enjoyed their dinner, sipping wine as they went over the shipping arrangements.

"The coffee will ship via cargo flight out of Columbia as soon as it can be processed after the harvest. You're getting my best product and at a damn good price, too. You are aware that I gave you a better deal than I did Emerson Foods, aren't you?"

"It was a fair price," David said as he lifted his glass, looking her straight in the eye, not willing to give an inch. If she wanted a boot licking fool to grovel at her feet, she'd get no such satisfaction from him.

"Well, if you want it even cheaper, I can arrange to have it shipped ocean cargo via Taylor Shipping. If that's the case, it may take two weeks longer," she shrugged, "but it is a few hundred dollars less, and that's with a discount. It's your call, Darcy." Cecilia scribbled out a few more numbers, running quick calculations in her head.

"Air cargo will do." He observed her closely while she finished filling in numbers, wondering why she was being so agreeable and if there was a hidden agenda.

"Okay, that about does it. Sign here, authorizing a bank draft for this amount, and it's all taken care of." She smiled as she handed him the final contract.

"You'll have your payment by the first of next week, Lawton," he said, very pleased with himself as he signed the document.

She leaned back in her chair relaxing a bit, studying David. There was a moment of silence as they sipped their wine. Finally, she asked, "Darcy, has anyone ever told you what a cute dimple you have when you smile?"

His head darted up. He gazed at her with curious amusement. "What a question, Lawton. We're right in the middle of a business negotiation." He laughed wryly. "Just as I assume your adversaries don't tell you how sexy you look when you're angry, I'm not about to bite on that." Narrowing his eyes, he looked at her suspiciously. "Though I'm sure you have received plenty of compliments."

She laughed and tossed her head. "Am I fishing for a compliment? Would you give me one if I were?" She arched her eyebrow, giving him a sexy smile.

"Lawton, you know perfectly well you're a beautiful and desirable woman, and I imagine that you're very used to getting precisely what you want. Trouble is, I'm not exactly sure what it is you *do* want." His eyes held hers for a long moment until she broke the contact.

Returning her eyes to his, she inquired, "What if I want you?"

His mind faltered for a split second but his gaze did not. "Is that a personal or a business proposition?"

"Perhaps a little of both," she chuckled, "but it's getting late, and I need to return to my penthouse. Would you mind seeing me to my door? It's at the Lawton Hotel. It's been a long day, and I'm tired." She rose to her feet, preparing to leave.

"Of course. I've had a long and exasperating day too, thanks to you. You really know how to put someone through the wringer, don't you?" He smirked. "They don't call you the Dragon Lady for nothing. I'll give you that."

She smiled as they headed towards the door. Escorting her back to her hotel suite, he fully intended to return to his hotel, but when they came to her door, things suddenly changed.

The atmosphere snapped as Cecilia reached up and curled her arms around his neck, pulling him into her. She kissed him deeply, taking him totally by surprise. Well, maybe not completely, he thought, as he deepened the kiss, enjoying the sensation until she broke their contact.

"Darcy, why don't you come inside and have a glass of wine? We can continue our conversation." Before he could answer, she pulled him through the door as though it never occurred to her that he wouldn't want to join her.

David eyed her guardedly. Once again he felt the tension crackle and pop between them, causing his guard to go up. He knew of the talk in the business world concerning her. She slept with men at her leisure and threw them away like yesterday's newspaper when she grew tired of them. Men were to her what cars were to men—toys. David knew he shouldn't be here even as he contemplated what he would do.

Going over to her wine cabinet, she removed two long stem crystal goblets and a decanter of wine. Filling the glasses, she handed one to him and then took a seat on the sofa, beckoning him to join her as she kicked off her shoes and propped up her feet.

He shrugged. Deciding that he could control the situation, he settled beside her and leaned back as he took a sip of wine. "Umm...a very good wine, Lawton. The star of Versailles—the King's wine. You have excellent taste."

They sat quietly savoring the wine for a few minutes before she spoke again. "Yes, Château Lafite Rothschild Pauillac is a very good wine. I'm glad you like it." Sliding her bare foot over the top of his shoe, she inched her toes up his pants leg.

...Lawton, you're very sly...and seductive! The wine, in addition to the ones he had at dinner, was already having an effect on him as he put his arm across the back of the sofa, leaning in a little closer, breathing in her exotic scent of jasmine mingled with

sweet oranges. He nuzzled into her hair, and then took another sip of wine.

Her foot made its way up his leg, her knee caressing his crotch, titillating his growing erection. She set her wine glass down and then turned to take his empty glass, placing it alongside hers. Turning back, she cupped his face with her hand, guiding his mouth to hers. Catching his lips in a deep lingering kiss, her leg brushed against him as she gently pulled him down on top of her.

For a moment, just a moment, he almost considered giving her what she wanted. *...I could become lost in her kiss. It's tempting...Those violet-blue eyes...those lush lips...that look...No, Darcy. You know better than this.*

David sat up. "Miss Lawton, I don't think this is in either of our best interests. I negotiated with you, and I'll not have you or anyone else say I slept with you to finalize our deal. I got a good price...a fair price, which I happen to know is better than anyone else gets, Emerson aside. I won't have people think I slept with you as a negotiating tactic—sex to seal the deal."

If her composure was shaken, he couldn't tell. She appeared cool, calm, and collected.

"So you never mix business with pleasure?" she asked as her eyebrow shot high.

"In a more level playing field, perhaps. You're an enchanting and beautiful woman as *you* well know, but not worth the price my business reputation would pay for one night spent with you." He rose from the sofa, straightening his clothes. "I need to go. Good evening, Miss Lawton." Moving away, he didn't miss the very evident look of shock on her pretty face which quickly darkened with anger. She was furious.

He paused. "Miss Lawton, what would you expect me to think? If you want to behave like a tart, by all means proceed, I'm willing to enjoy the show," he grinned, amused by her shocked expression, "but don't expect me to be your boy."

"How dare you, Darcy! How dare you say I would use sex to manipulate business!" Violet-blue fire flew from her eyes as she picked up a vase and hurled it at his head.

He ducked just in time as it smashed against the door.

David almost laughed as he watched her fury trumped by the sting of rejection. Pausing for a moment, he said, "Lawton, has anyone ever told you just how incredibly desirable you are when you're angry?" He chuckled. "You are *indeed* captivating and beautiful, and I bet you're every bit as good in bed as you are in the boardroom. You almost make me want to reconsider, but business is business. Good night, Miss Lawton." Flashing a roguish grin, he opened the door and walked through it.

David lay awake that night contemplating what it might have been like to take her to bed. He'd never met anyone quite like her. Miss Lawton was stubborn, strong willed, intelligent, and cunning. He was sure all of that would translate into a passionately hot lover, and he'd just passed on it. *...I'll give her some time to recover from her disappointment, and then I'll give her what we both want. ...She could do with a good shag...and one from someone who knows what he's doing...* He chuckled to himself as he finally found sleep.

Chapter Eleven

...I'm nobody's fool...

Four months later

As they were preparing to leave Ottawa for New York, David approached his pilot. "Jenkins, we need to stop in Charleston for a day, possibly two, before flying into Atlanta. Make the arrangements. I want to be there by two o'clock tomorrow afternoon."

"I'll take care of it, Mr. Darcy."

Cecilia had called David's London office with some additional information concerning the execution of their recent contract. There was a problem regarding the scheduled shipments with the current crop. David knew it could have been taken care of with a PDF via email or a fax, but since he was to be in the general area, he decided on the spur of the moment to attend to the matter in person. That was the stated reason, but the real reason was that he wanted to see her again. He knew it was unorthodox to stop in without an appointment, but it was a risk he was willing to take.

Since that night in November, he could think of nothing but her. Although it was against his better judgment to become involved with a business associate, enough time had passed where he felt one encounter with Cecilia would not impede his professional reputation. It was a calculated risk which he had decided to take. If all went as he wished, he intended to fulfill her desire as well as his own.

They touched down in Charleston right on schedule. He had just enough time to get through customs, pick up a rental car, check into the hotel, and make himself presentable before he saw Cecilia. As he cleared all hurdles and made his way to the BMW he had rented, he thought of her.

...Lawton, I think I'll make your dreams come true. A one night stand is all you're getting from me, and you should count yourself lucky I'm even giving you that. I'm not your toy, Cecilia, so don't think you can play me. It is I who will play with you. Yes, Lawton, I intend to explore your passionate nature. I'm going to rock your world. He laughed out loud as he pulled into the entrance of the Planter's Inn.

Once he settled into his room, he quickly put his things away and threw a grey suit along with a pale blue shirt and coordinating tie on the bed. He took a quick shower, dressed and was out the door heading for the Lawton Executive Complex.

David entered the vacant lobby at 3:30 in the afternoon. He had called once he was in town, telling her he'd be stopping by. He was not surprised in the least when she had agreed to work him into her schedule, sparing him what time she could. He hoped for fifteen minutes. That was all he needed. Fifteen minutes.

David paced back and forth in the lobby waiting for his appointment, when an older man in his late fifties approached him.

"Ah, Mr. David Darcy, I presume. I'm Daniel Russell. I see you've returned to see Ms. Lawton," the gentleman said as he offered his hand, along with a warm smile.

"Yes, yes I have. We have some unfinished business concerning our contract agreement." David looked at the man quizzically while shaking his hand.

"Yes, I know all about it. I'm the one who noticed the oversight, but I believe it only needed a signature and a few places filled in. Why did you not attend to the details and send it back instead of making a personal appearance?"

"I beg your pardon, sir, but who are you?" David asked, raising his brow.

"I've already told you my name, but my position is Senior Vice President of Lawton & Co., and I'm Cecilia's godfather." The older man's expression grew poignant. "That said, I'd like to see you in my office briefly before your appointed time with Ms. Lawton."

Glancing back over his shoulder at the busy receptionist, Mr. Russell instructed, "Ashley, when Ms. Lawton is ready to see Mr. Darcy, he can be found in my office if he has not yet returned to the lobby."

"Yes, Mr. Russell, I'll call for him there if he's not here."

"Thank you, Ashley."

Walking towards a large executive office to the right of the lift, they entered the VP suite, shutting the door behind them. Once inside, Daniel turned and faced Darcy. "Now, why did you come all this way when you and I both know it could have been handled just as easily, if not easier, via a fax or PDF?"

Not expecting an interrogation, David tensed under Mr. Russell's questioning stare. "Well," David said, giving the man before him a challenging look. "If you must know, I will tell you. It's no secret. I was in Ottawa when Ms. Lawton contacted me concerning the needed adjustment. Since I am on my way to Atlanta, I thought I would attend to this matter in person."

Daniel eyed David closely. "Perhaps it is as you say. However, I'm the man you bowled over when you bolted from her office, clearly upset four months previous." Daniel arched an eyebrow as David coughed while embarrassment colored his features.

"I am sorry. I didn't realize it was you I had run into. As you say, I was upset, but I should not have displayed it as I did."

The older man looked upon David fondly with a twinkle in his eye. "Let me give you a piece of advice, Darcy. Celia is tough as nails, and some people have referred to her as cold-hearted, but it is not true. She's had a difficult time, and I'm afraid it has made her a bit hard. Nevertheless, she is a warm, generous, and caring woman if someone will take the time to figure her out."

"What do you mean, Mr. Russell? Why are you telling me this?" David wrinkled his brow.

Daniel smiled. "I have my reasons, Darcy," he stated flatly. "But I will tell you this much. I can tell she frustrates you as I witnessed your last exchange. I have spoken with her concerning the matter, and now I'm speaking with you. I hate for people to think poorly of her. There is a reason for everything, Mr. Darcy, so before you judge her, perhaps maybe you should try to understand her."

"I apologize, sir, if my conduct appeared a bit unprofessional. As we've already discussed, I was frustrated that day."

"Perhaps I've overstated then. If that is the case," he shrugged, "I apologize. Cecilia's father was a very close friend of mine. Consequently, as her surrogate father, I feel a responsibility where she is concerned. Cecilia's mother died when she was young. James did the best he could as a single father. However, good intentions don't always go as one would wish."

David tilted his head. "I've heard of Mr. Lawton. I believe everyone knows of his business reputation, but is there more?"

"All I will say is that Celia grew up in a difficult situation. Keep that in mind when you deal with her. She's a tough businesswoman. If you want more information," he said, "I'm sure you will find out whatever you want to know. That's all I have to say on the matter. Now, I'll let you keep your appointment. I know how Celia feels about being late for anything."

David smiled as the older man led him to the lobby. As he watched the man depart, a frown furrowed his brow ...*I wonder what he means?* Before he could contemplate any further, the receptionist approached him.

"Mr. Darcy, Ms. Lawton is ready to see you now."

David turned at the sound of his name. "Thank you, Ashley."

One corner of his lips curled upward as he walked into Cecilia's office, wondering how she would receive him, especially after his conversation with her godfather. He knew his excuse for being here was flimsy at best, but he would adlib if he had to.

Cecilia rose to greet him. "David, I'm surprised to see you. You know this could have been taken care of via fax or PDF?"

"So I've been told." His satisfied gaze fell on her.

She smiled and gave a casual shrug. "Well, since you are here, if you'll just read over these revisions and sign where I've marked, we'll be good to go." Handing him the papers, she sank back into her seat.

Intrigued, he took the offered document and dropped into the seat by her desk. Reading over it, he placed his signature on the line indicated, initialed a few places and looked up, returning her smile. Her composure was all business as if their last exchange had never occurred. Shuffling the papers, he inquired, "Now, Lawton, where are we going?"

Glancing up, she met his self-assured penetrating gaze. "Going? I beg your pardon."

"Yes, going. You didn't think I came all this way just to sign this, did you? I'm asking you to dinner, so where do you want to go?" He smiled, confident in himself. It never crossed his mind she would refuse him.

"Well, I tell you what," she said in a clipped tone. "Since you *did* come all this way, I'll take *you* to dinner. We'll go to a bar called O'Malley's up by the beach on Folly Island. It's one of my favorite haunts." Tapping her lower lip with her pencil eraser, she continued. "Wear something casual. It's a private club with dinner and dancing. Come prepared to dance. Pick me up at my penthouse at six o'clock sharp, and don't be late. I—"

"Yes, I know. You hate it when people are late." His lips twisted in a wry grin. "I'll see you at six." Taking back the contract, her fingers brushed his while her eyes focused on him with an unsettling stare. He shuddered. ...*Darcy, you're playing with fire. This woman is enticing ...alluring...even tormenting ...different from others you've known. Don't let your guard down...*

Arriving at her penthouse promptly at six o'clock, David was cool and self-assured as the maid let him in. However, that changed as soon as Cecilia stepped into the room. His jaw dropped. She was dressed in a simple sapphire blue spaghetti strap dress that fitted her like a glove. It was so short he was sure her knickers would show if she bent over just right. Drawing in an unsteady breath, he eyed her from head to toe—waist length blonde hair, long slender legs, and shapely breasts. *Lovely!*

"David, you look nice tonight," she said with a smile. "Stone Dockers and a blue polo...hmm...our outfits coordinate...it's as if we planned it." She laughed, flashing him a smile that made his heart skip. "Now, I think you will enjoy this place. They play music from the 70s up to the present. I especially love Nickleback and Jet, but I also like the 70s and 80s sound, Boston being among my favorites. How about you? What do you like?"

"The same as you. I like The Cure from the 80s, and Foreigner. Oh, and ah...you look very good yourself," he said, his voice slightly hoarse.

M.K. Baxley

"Thank you, but we'd better get going. You know how I am about being late. We have reservations for a table at seven. I'm driving since I know where we're going," she said, satisfaction gleaming in her bright velvet eyes.

As he followed her to her car, his lips gently curled. She looked damned good, and he intended to enjoy every minute of her company. Once inside, they sat in relative silence while she drove. And in spite of his best efforts, he kept staring at her legs. He was right, the dress was short, coming nearly all the way up, almost exposing the mystery. Another smile tugged at the corners of his mouth. This was going to be a night he would file away for a long time to come as he imagined what they might share. If reality was half as good as his musings, it was going to be one hot, passionate, lust-filled night. He grinned as he cut his eyes across at the woman sitting beside him.

When they arrived at the private club, they were greeted at the door and escorted to their table. Cecilia ordered lobster with hazelnut mushroom pilaf and asparagus in a rich cream sauce for the both of them. They enjoyed their meal while making small talk. As he listened to her voice, he watched her closely. ...*She has a pretty face to go along with that stunning body! In this lighting, her eyes are almost a bluish amethyst. Beautiful and alluring like a siren—be careful Darcy.*

"David?"

"I'm sorry. What did you say?"

"You're distracted." She laughed.

"Only a little." His lips curved slightly. "Now, what were you saying?"

"I asked you how you liked the rice and asparagus." She shook her head in a mirthful chuckle.

"It was very good. How did you know I liked asparagus?"

"You mentioned it once." She tossed her hair. "I pay attention, Darcy. Do you?" An eyebrow shot up.

"I'm quite observant, and right now, I'm paying very close attention to *you*." He flashed a sexy smile.

"That you are." Cecilia returned his smile, picking up the gauntlet he had clearly thrown down. Choosing her strategy closely, she ordered one large chocolate mousse for two.

"The chocolate mousse is to die for, Darcy. Here, let me give you a taste." She picked up her spoon, scooped out a generous bite, and fed it to him purposefully smudging a little on the corner of his mouth. "Oh, how careless of me! Let me get that." She reached over and kissed him, licking the chocolate from his mouth. Tension crackled and snapped between them like an electrical surge as a small groan rumbled deep in his chest.

All distractions faded into the background as David picked up his spoon and fed her one luscious bite, followed by another. She followed suit, feeding him as he fed her. As they continued, Cecilia slipped off her shoes and began to play under the table with his foot, watching him closely. He only smiled. Encouraged, she began tracing a path up his leg. A smile crossed her face when she noticed his breath catching in his throat.

While they fed each other one decadent spoonful at a time, her toes tickled his shin, but he didn't flinch. Her foot traveled up his leg in a slow sensual exploration, and yet, he still didn't flinch. He continued to feed her. But when her toes began to play with the erection she had inspired, he flinched.

"Lawton, what do you think you're doing?"

"I'm playing," she said in a sly, seductive voice, running her foot over his length in a tantalizingly slow stroke.

"I see." ...*Two can play at this game, Lawton.*

Slipping his hand under the table, he took her foot into the palm of his hand and began to gently stroke the inside of her arch as he continued to feed her in sinful delight, one bite followed by the next. Like him, she didn't flinch. He slid his hand up her leg, cupping her calf, sliding back and forth, gently caressing, and brushing his fingers ever so slightly in the bend of her knee. Finally, she flinched and quickly drew away.

Biting down on her lower lip, she said, "They're playing our song, Darcy. Let's dance."

"I wasn't aware we had a song," he said, clearly amused.

"Well, you are now." She grabbed his hand, dragging him to the dance floor. The song, *Waiting for a Girl Like You,* played as she pulled him into a slow dance, curling her arms around his neck while his went instinctively around her waist, encircling her in a natural embrace.

...Umm...she feels so good... He caressed her back and ran his fingers through her long blonde hair as she snuggled closer. The scent of her perfume and the feel of her in his arms were intoxicating. As he pressed against her body, she reached up and caught his lips in a long, slow, lingering kiss. He deepened the kiss and pressed into her all the more. His desire increased as her fingers sank into the thick curls at the base of his neck while she wiggled even closer, playing ever so gently, relaxing him all the more. He lost all conscience thought of anything else in the room, except her.

Breaking the kiss, he tucked her head under his chin, gently caressing her back and bottom. They slow danced with not a thing on his mind except her and this moment in time as they swayed to the music. While he held her close, she lifted her head once again, taking his lips with hers. David was pleasantly surprised and very pleased in her willingness. He broke the kiss and proceeded to trace light, sensual kisses down the length of her neck while she continued to play in his hair. He released a sigh, enjoying her touch *...I'm as hot-blooded as any man, and you know how to turn up the heat. Just as I imagined, you know how to please a man. This is our night, Lawton...yours and mine. It will be a night to remember...*

While lingering in his thoughts, the music changed to *Party Like a Rock Star.* Cecilia immediately fell into step. Stunned by her boldness, David followed her lead. A smile slowly crossed his features. Cecilia was an excellent dancer, and David could barely keep up. The suggestive movements of the dance stimulated him even more as they moved against one another, their bodies rubbing and grinding together.

When that song ended, *Midnight Special* followed where they laughed and danced swing as if they were the only two on the dance floor. David was impressed at how much they complemented each other, laughing, smiling, and having a good time. He was surprised at how much he enjoyed Cecilia's company. He hadn't had this much fun in a long time.

They finished the night as they had started, in a slow dance as the song *Wonderful Tonight* played while they danced. Once again, he held her close and enjoyed her warmth while kissing her deeply, thinking *Tonight, Lawton, tonight's our night...*

The entire drive back to her penthouse, David played out the scenario in his mind of how they were going to end the night. First, they would have a glass of wine and relax, possibly sitting on the sofa where he would slowly caress her body and snog before moving to her bed. He intended to undress her slowly, tasting every inch of her body with his eyes. Then he would pleasure her over and over again until she writhed beneath his touch and begged for more. They would make love all night long until both were exhausted. He would fall asleep with her in his arms.

No woman had ever been able to resist his charm, and Cecilia Lawton would not be the first. He smirked as he glanced over at her. He liked her, and because he liked her, he'd take extra special care to please her. Unfortunately though, because of their business relationship, this would be their only night. He sighed. Well, he would make this good. He would take his pleasure, satisfying his lust, and leave her. Too bad. He was sure she'd probably make a good long-term lover, but he couldn't afford the emotional attachment such an affair would entail. Once again, he cast a wry glance in Cecilia's direction, caressing her with his eyes, desire for the night welling up inside of him. He smiled and turned away, looking out the window.

Arriving back at the Lawton Hotel, Cecilia tossed her keys to the valet as they exited the car and entered the lobby arm in arm, laughing and smiling, thoroughly enjoying each other's company. When they approached the lift, she punched the button and turned, throwing her arms around his neck, pulling him into a deep kiss as they waited. The door opened, and they entered.

"Darcy, did you enjoy the evening?" she asked, sinking her fingers into his hair, drawing him into another embrace as the door closed.

The sly look in her eyes invited him...or did it warn him. Her intent left him unsure, but he was certain of his abilities. She wanted him, and he knew it. He bent down to kiss her, tightening his embrace. "Hmm...very much," he whispered against her neck.

She pressed into him, rubbing against his full erection, caressing it, driving him even further towards the edge. Fully aroused, he cupped her bottom, pressing her into the back of the lift, kissing her deeply. Rubbing and grinding, David was drunk with desire, certain there would be a payoff. She was hot, willing, and eager—his for the taking. Lust completely inflamed him.

The lift door opened and they exited, arms around each other, as he escorted her to her door, confident that he would be spending the night. Once at her door, she gave him a slow lingering kiss, once again pressing her body into his. When she finally broke the kiss, she looked him straight in the eye.

"I'm sorry, Darcy." Her eyes swept downward and then snapped back, catching his gaze. "I'm just not in the mood this evening." She released a deep sigh. "All that dancing has made me rather tired."

He tensed. His jaw went slack. She had to be toying with him again. "What?! Not in the mood... but, Lawton..."

She cut him off, eyes blazing, "You think you can show up here unannounced whenever you *damn well please* and trifle with me, playing with my feelings just like that." She snapped her fingers. "Well, you've got another *think* coming. I'm nobody's fool, especially not yours. And I am damn sure **_not_** your *whore*."

She arched her eyebrow and gave him a devastatingly sexy smile, "It's you and your hand tonight, Darcy." She laughed. "Payback is hell...and all's fair in love and war. *Business* is *business*." She reached up and pecked his very shocked lips, and then opened the door and walked through, slamming it shut in his face before he could gather his wits to respond.

Stunned, he stood there, blinking at the closed door. Then he shook his head and laughed out loud. "Damn you, Lawton. If you think this is goodbye, you had better think again," he said with a sly smile. "This is **war**, Lawton, and I will indeed have *you*!"

Damn it! I will... With that, he spun sharply on his heel and left. Whatever her game was, he loved it, and he would play. He would take the challenge, and seeing her bid, he would raise the stakes. Their day was coming. It was only a matter of time.

Chapter Twelve

...I can't love her...she can never love me...

The Present

David lips curled into a smile. It had indeed been a night to remember—one he would never forget. He was still lost in his thoughts when he heard his name called. "Mr. Darcy, Ms. Lawton is ready to see you now." Snapping out of his daydream, he responded, "Thank you, Ashley."

He gathered his things and entered the Dragon Lady's office.

Sitting in his office, Mr. Russell was acutely aware David Darcy was meeting with his goddaughter. He felt sure they shared a mutual attraction, but as he contemplated the situation, he wondered what, if anything, he should do about it. Daniel tapped his pencil on a notepad and let out an exasperated sigh as he shook his head. His concern for Cecilia bothered him excessively.

James Lawton, Cecilia's father, had been Daniel's best friend since their days at the University of South Carolina and even before then when they had been boys in grammar school. He'd also been the best man at James's wedding, and unfortunately, he'd had the displeasure of watching Cecilia grow up in that sorry excuse of a marriage he had tried to prevent his friend from entering. The misfortune continued as he watched James attempt to raise his daughter like a son after her mother's death. As Daniel sat there, tapping on his note pad, his mind drifted back thirty years...

"Daniel, what do you think of Emmaline Bouchard? She's beautiful, don't you think? She's the talk of Savannah, and she's even known in Charleston. I saw her with Taylor at the Magnolia Festival last spring. I've never seen a more beautiful woman. Those violet blue eyes are enchanting set against that long black hair. She's divine. I intend to have her. What do you think?"

"James, you have got to be kidding. A beautiful face does not translate into a beautiful woman. As your mother would say, 'Beauty is only skin deep.' Emmaline fits that description perfectly and you damn well know it. She's a flirt, James! She's all over Taylor and Garrison. I'm sure she would like nothing more than to catch the heir to Taylor Shipping or Garrison Industries—either one would do. It's all the same to her. Leave her alone, James! She's mercenary."

"Perhaps she is, but then aren't all women to some degree? Come on, Daniel, she's the most beautiful woman in the South. She won the Miss South Carolina title, was third runner up in the Miss America Pageant, graduated cum laude, and she's modeled in New York. You know I'm far richer than Taylor or Garrison. And I've never had a problem picking up women. Emma's no different. I didn't say I was going to marry her, only that I intend to have her."

"James, I am telling you the truth! That woman is dangerous. You may not intend to marry her, but once she finds out what you're worth, she'll be intent on marrying you. And you're just fool enough to do it!"

Daniel raised his eyes from his notepad and leaned back in his chair as he recalled their conversation. He thought about what could have been...what should have been, had James not made that one fatal mistake so many years ago. James, well known in

M.K. Baxley

both the business world and the prestigious historical societies in the upper classes of the South, had much to offer and so much more to lose.

James, James...my old friend...why, James, why...you were rich, coming from a family with old money, and one of the most handsome men in both Charleston and Savannah...You had it all... my friend...six feet three inches tall with sandy blonde hair and those clear blue eyes no woman could resist...How many times did I see the girls swoon over you... Together we were skirt chasers in our day... the world was in our hands, but you always knew you needed to marry and produce an heir... Daniel sighed as his mind wondered on. *...You were the last of the Lawtons—the last of a long line from one of the most prestigious and influential founding fathers in Charleston's history. You could have done better, James...so much better...*

As Daniel had predicted, Emmaline was instantly attracted to him when she realized who he was and had set her mind to marry him, but not because she loved him or even respected him. Her love was for something much more material—his money and social standing in both Charleston and Savannah. And as Daniel had warned, after three months in her company, James was totally besotted with her, taking every opportunity he could to be in her presence. But as much as he tried, she would not let him touch her—not without a wedding ring on her finger, and James could resist neither the challenge nor the beautiful face. So James Lawton fell to the beauty and charms of Emmaline Bouchard, and the wedding of the decade was announced.

It was one of the most outlandish and celebrated weddings of its time. Everybody who was anybody was invited, including the governors of both Georgia and South Carolina. Emmaline's father went to great lengths to provide his only child with a society wedding, for which James paid for. But a large and expensive wedding could not guarantee a happy marriage. And it was not too long afterwards that James discovered the reality of another old saying—charms are deceitful, and beauty is fleeting.

"Daniel, you were right. I've made a terrible mistake. She's as cold as ice, and now that she's pregnant, Emmaline won't even let me touch her. What am I going to do? I don't believe in cheating. Once you're married, that's over. What am I to do?"

"Damn it, James, divorce her! Find someone else. You're young, good looking, and as you used to say, you can have any woman you want. This time pick one who will love you for you, not for what you have."

"I can't leave her. She's carrying my child. You know how badly I want that child, and I'm afraid the mother comes along with him. Besides, I love her. I'll simply have to find a way to win her love for the sake of my child. You know how important it is to me to have a family."

Daniel put down his pencil and rose from his desk to get another cup of coffee. After pouring a cup, he strolled over to the large window overlooking Meeting Street and gazed down. A slight smile lightened his features. A child with long blonde pigtails laughed and danced along as her mother pulled her into one of the stores. He shook his head, his mind once again recalling the past...

Since the War Between the States, Carlton House had not known the joy or laughter of children. Throughout the generations, people had whispered that a curse had been placed on the family. The supposed curse began when Samuel Lawton lost all of his sons in the war, save one. The pattern continued to the present day, but James had never believed in old wives' tales, and he fully intended to break the long standing occurrence. However, after the birth of Cecilia, Mrs. Lawton not only refused to give him anymore children, she had also taken a separate bedroom, locking him out. Society functions and flirtations, along with James's money, were all she cared for.

Yet, in spite of it all, Emmaline had become pregnant once more when Cecilia was seven. She was not pleased at first, but Daniel later thought she had accepted it. And then the accident occurred, causing her early delivery of a stillborn son. James was devastated, and from that day forth, they never spoke again.

Emmaline died in an accident a year later with James blaming himself and taking on the guilt for both deaths. Daniel remembered the mess he walked into when he went to pay a visit six months later.

"James, what the hell do you think you're doing, lying around drunk? Women in and out of the house like some sort of downtown brothel. Pull yourself together, man! You've got a daughter to raise. You cannot bring your whores into the house with an eight-year-old little girl living with you. You need to marry and give Celia a mother. She needs a woman's touch."

"Daniel, I have no intentions of marrying. I will not go through that hell ever again."

"What about an heir, James—a son? You need a son!"

"Cecilia will be my heir. I'll teach her everything she needs to know. I'll teach her how to run Lawton, how to handle herself in society, and the importance of our heritage. She'll have it all, and I'll teach her how to handle men, too. She'll be nobody's fool. But you are right about one thing. The whores need to go. I'll take a mistress."

"James, once again, let me warn you, this is foolish...You need a wife, and Celia needs a mother!"

James did take a mistress, many of them, in fact, but there was one who stood out among the rest—Anna Carrington, a well-bred lady from Atlanta whom he called Annie. She'd loved him with a deep abiding love, but sadly, unable to commit, James had let her slip away.

Daniel rubbed his brow as a small tear escaped his eye. A headache was forming. *I tried to warn you, James, I tried...* His memory continued on...

After Anna left, James grew even harder, taking Cecilia everywhere he went—to his gambling haunts, private drinking parties, the race track, and eventually allowing his mistresses to live with them. While other young girls were enjoying dolls, games, and childhood friendships, Cecilia was learning how to run a corporation and manage a historical society. She was also caring for a father who'd often had too much to drink. Many was the time when Cecilia had had to put her father to bed with the help of a servant and then care for his hangover the next morning.

As the young Cecilia grew older, the colder she became. She witnessed not only how her father treated his mistresses, but how, while in high school and later college, other young men treated their girlfriends. Only those in her closest circle knew the true side of her—that she did have a heart, and she could care. But she was very cautious, never allowing herself the opportunity to be used as she saw others used.

Instead, Cecilia, led by her father's example, learned to use men like they used women. Only once had she considered caring for a young man, and that had not gone well. Afterwards, Cecilia's emotions and heart were not easily touched. In fact, they were never touched. The few men who'd made the mistake of falling in love with her had been left brokenhearted when she discarded them. She didn't care how much they pleaded, how much they begged. Their anguish left her as cold as stone.

Daniel sighed once more as he recalled the last, and perhaps most painful, of all his memories—the death of his boyhood friend. James Lawton had recognized his mistakes too late to affect any significant change in his daughter, and so, on his deathbed, he'd asked Daniel to watch over her. Daniel thought back to that day as

M.K. Baxley

James lay there dying in the CCU...

"Daniel, I worry for Cecilia after I'm gone. She's not right—too much like me."

"James, Celia will be fine. You've given her everything—love, money, education."

"Everything except a normal home life! You were right, I should have married... I should have married Annie. She loved me...and I cared for her, but my pride would not allow me to go after her when she left...I wanted to... I almost did... I was a fool."

He'd drawn a labored breath as he pressed his last request. Daniel remembered it well. *"Promise me you will watch over Cecilia...I've made such a mess of things. Promise me, Daniel. Promise me you will take care of my baby...See to it that she marries a man who will respect and love her. She's the only good thing I've ever had... The only one, except for maybe Annie, who loved me in spite of myself."*

"I'll take care of her, James...I promise...

So after James's death, Daniel took the promotion to senior vice president in his friend's company. He wanted to retire, but he stayed on to watch over Cecilia. Daniel took his commitment to James very seriously, intending to fulfill the promise he'd made to his old friend to the best of his ability. But there was a problem. Although he knew the softer side of her, Cecilia's attitude towards men worried him excessively. He, like her father, wanted her to find happiness in marriage since she had never known it as a child. But he also knew that she was the last in the line of the Lawtons. If she did not marry well and produce a child, the Lawton family would die with her.

Daniel reached across his desk and picked up a picture of a chubby little girl about three years old with blonde pigtails sitting on a Shetland pony. He sighed, placing the picture back in its place. Shaking his head once more, he lifted his pencil and jotted down another note.

Daniel wanted Cecilia to marry for love. But he understood, probably better than she did, that she must marry someone who comprehended the importance of her family heritage, her position in Charleston's society, and most importantly, someone who would love her for her and not for her money. She needed a man with wealth and social position all of his own, apart from her but equal, so therefore, he had formed a plan to help her along in that direction.

He had taken notice of a certain gentleman, David Darcy, from England who came from time to time on business. Daniel sensed Darcy's attraction to his goddaughter, and had also sensed that she was not unaffected by it. Whenever he mentioned Darcy's name, she would overreact. He also knew of the Darcy legacy and family linage and had gone to the trouble of discovering David's character through both talking with him and research.

Through his contacts in London, he had learned not only of the younger Darcy's reputation, which was much like James's had been, but also of the family situation. Realizing that Darcy and Cecilia were very much alike, he felt that with a little encouragement there might be a possibility of something developing between the two of them. It would take a man like Darcy to handle her—perhaps even make her happy. Mulling it over one more time, he had now firmly decided to go ahead and take matters into his own hands. That was why he was canceling his long standing duty to escort Cecilia to tonight's gala.

Daniel knew it was a gamble, but it was one he felt compelled to take. Now to set his plan into motion. Picking up the phone, he made his interoffice call.

"Celia."

"Daniel?"

"I hate to disappoint you darlin', but I cannot make tonight's function."

"What? What do you mean you can't make it?!"

"I'm sorry, Celia. I know how important this is, but I'm just not feeling well and would be poor company."

"Daniel, you can't do this!"

"Celia, it cannot be helped. Hopefully, with a little rest, I'll be recovered in a few days."

"But Daniel! Just *what* am I supposed to do? The dinner is in four hours! I can't find another escort on such a short notice."

"Why don't you ask that English dandy sitting in your office? You've gone to dinner with him before. In fact, were you not out with him a few months ago? I'm sure he would be more than pleased to escort you. I'll call you later on. I'm leaving for home now as I *am* feelin' very poorly."

With a sly smile, he hung up the phone. Daniel knew he had unnerved her. He could hear it in her voice. He had disturbed her equilibrium and set the stage for what he hoped would follow. In this mind, Darcy was the man for his goddaughter. Having done his part, the rest would be up to them. He smiled to himself. *...Yes, James, he's just like you. He cannot resist a pretty face any more than you could. And Celia? She's like Emma. She's got what it takes, and she knows how to use it.* Chuckling, Daniel picked up his briefcase and headed for the house.

David and Cecilia were almost finished with the negotiations, which were not going as well as he would have liked, when David noticed Cecilia's annoyance. He mildly wondered what had affected her. When she hung up the phone, she turned and looked him straight in the eye.

"David, I have a special request. A favor, more like it." She released a sharp breath. "My escort for tonight's dinner party has had to cancel, and I have no one to escort me. This is very important to me as I'm hosting the event. In short, I need a date. Would you consider?" she coaxed. "It's a black tie affair."

David could clearly see she was flustered by the change in plans, and by the pretty red blush spread across her features, he suspected she was flushed with embarrassment at having to ask him for a date. But he also recognized an opportunity when he saw one, and he fully intended to take advantage of the one that'd so eloquently dropped into his lap.

A roguish grin split his countenance as he caught her gaze and held it. "Yes, I will, on two conditions. One, you give me another five percent on the deal we've been negotiating, and two," his gaze deepened as he pressed his advantage, "you won't tell me you're **not** in the mood ...*not again*...not tonight."

She inhaled sharply. "David, that's not fair. You know I'm in a lurch." She paused for another breath. "But I'll tell you what I will do. I'll give you three percent and," she said with a wry grin, "we'll see about your other stipulation. Pick me up at 6:30."

"You drive a hard bargain, Lawton, but I'll take your odds. And," he paused to drive his point home, "all's fair in love and war, Miss Lawton." He winked. "And you don't have to remind me. I won't be late." *...So, now we play, Cecilia...now we play. I won't take **no** for an answer this time. I, too, have a way of getting what I want...and love, what I want is **you**!*

David left her office whistling Dixie. With the coffee deal in hand and a smile on his face, he was looking forward to tonight's dinner engagement. Normally he didn't enjoy formal society, but tonight held a promise. He'd been thinking about Cecilia ever since that night one year ago when she had flung that vase at him. His last attempt at getting what he wanted still stung, but his resolve was firm. She taunted and teased, denying him what he wanted, driving him to distraction, but he was determined to have her, and have her he would.

When he entered his hotel room, David threw the folder with the coffee contract on the table and went to the closet. He had several sets of clothes with him as he never knew just what he might need. Perusing through his dinner suits, he picked out his attire for the evening and tossed it on the bed. Smiling, he went for a quick shower and shave. "Tonight's the night, Darcy," he spoke aloud.

Dressing for the event, his thoughts turned to Cecilia. For some strange reason that he didn't quite understand, he found himself determined to please her. He took extra care with his preparations to look his best, planning to play the part of her escort to the very best of his gentlemanly ability. He wanted to please her in her own society, and *if* he got the chance, he would take the extra trouble to please her even more. He smiled. *...She's one of the most beautiful and fascinating women I've ever met. Yes, I'm looking forward to this night, Cecilia. I wonder what you're like in bed. Hopefully, I'm about to find out. You won't tell me **no** this time. ...No, **not** this time.* He laughed out loud.

David arrived at the Lawton Hotel promptly at 6:30. Entering the lobby was like stepping back in time. It was a five star luxury Inn with uniquely fashioned antebellum rooms in a prettily restored historic building. The atmosphere of elegance far exceeded that of most hotels where David had stayed, and he rather liked its style and refinement, thinking it reflected well on its owner. As he glanced around, he resolved that next time he would stay here. There was something nostalgic about this place.

He took the lift up to her eighth floor suite. The door opened. A few more steps and he would be there. He wondered how she'd look tonight. Probably stunning.

After the maid let him in, he waited. When Cecilia entered the room, he was not disappointed. His breath stilled as his eyes slowly canvassed her figure, desire welling up inside of him. She was drop...dead...gorgeous in a deep plum strapless evening gown, hugging her shape, accenting her every sensual curve to its best advantage. Her amethyst and diamond choker served to bring out the shimmering hue in her violet-blue eyes. *...Oh, yes, she's beautiful!*

"Good evening, Cecilia. You're looking lovely tonight," David whispered, reining in his emotions as his eyes once again swept over her body.

Cecilia smiled warmly. "Thank you, David. You look very handsome yourself. We have a few minutes. Would you like a glass of wine?"

"Yes, that'll be fine." David spoke softly, suddenly finding it difficult to breath as the sly glance from beneath her lashes jolted his senses, causing his blood to run hot and quick. Filling two goblets, she handed one to him and moved to the sofa. David took a chair opposite to her, where he watched her over the rim of his glass.

As they sat sipping their wine in quiet solitude, Cecilia noticed he was staring. She shuddered. His dark intensive gaze unnerved her, as if perhaps he might like to taste something other than the wine. She inhaled sharply, attempting to recover the composure he had so eloquently disrupted.

She wondered what he was thinking, but then from his look, she could easily guess. She had to smile. He wanted her. She knew the physical attraction between them was strong, but there was something more. He was different from anyone she'd known before, but in what way, she couldn't exactly say. Glancing at the clock, she was relieved. It was time to go. After finishing their wine, she took the glasses to the kitchen, and they left for the Lawton Blue Room.

Upon entering, several of Cecilia's friends came to greet her. Mrs. Appleton approached first, taking Cecilia's hands in hers while reaching over to kiss her cheek. "Celia, darlin', we were so worried when we heard poor Daniel was ill. I hope it's nothin' serious, dear."

"I'm sure it isn't. I think he has the flu. However, I did manage to find an escort for the evening," Cecilia said, slipping her arm around David. "Mrs. Appleton, I'd like you to meet my friend and business associate, Mr. David Darcy. David, this is my good friend, Mrs. Tabitha Appleton," Cecilia introduced, gesturing between the two. "Tabitha, David's from London. He's new to our society, so please make him feel welcome." She flashed David a brilliant smile.

Mrs. Appleton presented her hand, avid curiosity gleaming in her blue gaze, curious about the unknown man escorting Cecilia.

"Mrs. Appleton, the pleasure is mine," David said, offering a charming smile as he took her hand in his and pressed a kiss to the thin skin on the back of her fingers.

"Mr. Darcy, how very pleased I am to meet you," Mrs. Appleton drawled with a careful calculating look. "And what a lovely accent," she added with a gentle smile.

Cecilia barely managed to prevent her eyes from rolling towards the ceiling at the older woman's inquisitive stare. She could hear it now. Who is this man Cecilia's with...I hope it lasts...she needs a man in her life. Oh, well, she shrugged. It was part of the price she paid for being in the probing eye of society. Everyone wonders who you're with and what you're doing. She refused to let it ruin her evening.

David and Cecilia moved to the bar where they each ordered a glass of port. While casually sipping their wine, several more people came by for introductions, and before long, David had met nearly everyone in the room. As they talked and mingled, Cecilia was called aside to speak with Mrs. Robinson, the society's treasurer, about tonight's event.

"David, I hate to leave you here alone like this, but I really must attend to this matter. It involves tonight's speech. I'll only be a few minutes as we're about to start."

"Take your time. Don't worry about me. I'll have another glass of port wine whilst I wait. I'll be fine."

While he sipped his wine, David watched her as she mixed and mingled so naturally among her peers, smiling and laughing. Cecilia was so different from the hard-nosed woman he was accustomed to seeing at the negotiating table. There was a softness about her features he'd never noticed before. Curiously, she was not like the women he'd previously dated, not even those from among his own sphere. But what was different? He didn't know. There was an elegance and grace in her movement, but that wasn't it. It was something else. She appeared to care about her duties and the people here in this room. The curve of her lips when she smiled was gentle and relaxed. She was perfectly at ease in society. He took another sip of wine, settling in to watch her closely.

While he was watching Cecilia, another man watched him. A man in his late fifties or early sixties approached and ordered a glass of Gentleman Jack.

"She's a lovely lady, don't you think, Darcy?"

David turned to face the man. "Yes, yes, she is."

The man extended his hand. "I believe we met a little while ago."

"Yes, we did. I believe you are Mr. Robert Russell, owner of the Ford and Mercedes Benz dealership here in Charleston, and Daniel Russell's brother," David said with a friendly smile as they shook hands.

"Correct again on both accounts. And yes, my family has been in that business since after the Second World War." Mr. Russell followed David's eyes to where Cecilia stood.

"I see Celia is talking with Jenny. She's the current president of the South Carolina Chapter of the United Daughters of the Confederacy. I believe Celia is running for that office come this January. She's very dedicated to her work here at the historical society."

"What exactly does she do?" David asked, as he continued to watch Cecilia.

"Oh, mostly she oversees the projects, making sure they're managed properly. There are several volunteers who travel throughout the South lookin' for old historical journals to publish and sell in the little bookshops around town. She buys property in the historical district to renovate, turning them into historical museums or homes for neglected children. She also collects artifacts from estate sales to display, lectures here and there about the Old South, the War Between the States, and the settling of Charles Towne. And she's been known to act in several Civil War Reenactments, too. But probably the most important thing would be her father's cotton and rice research projects. She's attemptin' to finish his work and reintroduce the Sea Island Cotton and Carolina Gold Rice back into production in South Carolina's agricultural economy."

The corners of David's mouth arched upward as he listened.

Russell smiled as he sipped his drink. "She's also very active in our community, personally supportin' projects for the less fortunate such as our homeless shelters and Hannah's House, a home for battered women, and I might add, one of her favorite charities," Robert drawled in his strong Lowcountry accent. "That's somethin' that is very important to Celia. Nothin' gets her ire up quicker than to see a woman or a child abused by those who are supposed to love and protect them."

"I would have never guessed she was involved in such endeavors," David said, raising his glass to his lips, his eyes steady on their target.

"Yes, it's not readily obvious, I know." Robert chuckled. "And I also know what people say, but that's not true. She's as good as gold to those around her who suffer, 'cause you see, Darcy, she's suffered, too. Just because you're rich doesn't mean you're immune to pain. Celia's quite a lady, Mr. Darcy, and she's greatly loved and admired by the people of Charleston, especially those among the oldest families—the ones who keep this town grounded in its roots." Sipping his drink he pressed on. "But then again, there are those among us from that blue blooded crowd that holds her in contempt because of her father. They were jealous of him, too," he said matter-of-factly. "But James did as he damn well pleased. He didn't care, and in that regard, she's just like him. But the rest of us 'blue bloods' keep them in check. And Celia couldn't give a rat's ass about them anyway."

"I didn't realize she was so active in her community." David's gaze locked on Cecilia, staring as if seeing her for the first time. The ruthless business woman in the boardroom was a far cry from the concerned activist Robert described.

"Yes, there's a lot to people that often gets overlooked, and that's especially true of Celia. She keeps a low profile when it comes to her personal life. Her life growing up was not easy. We've all been protective of her."

David tilted his head, his attention completely focused on Robert. This was the second time someone had mentioned her early life. David's curiosity was piqued. "What was her life like?"

"Well, her mother and father, I'm sorry to say, didn't get along none too well." Robert looked away for moment and then caught David's gaze and held it. "They fought like cats and dogs, and when Celia was eight years old, her mother tragically died." Robert paused again to clear his throat and have another drink. "Now for some reason, of which I know little of, James felt guilty for Emmaline's death, taking it very hard. He fell into reckless living, and all I will say on that matter is that Celia saw more than a young girl should *ever* see."

David's eyes widened as he sipped his wine.

"Now don't get me wrong, Darcy," Robert reassured, noticing David's countenance. "James loved her. It's just that he couldn't handle his personal life's crises, but Celia was always the center of his world. He loved her very much, and Celia was loyal to him. She went everywhere with him, and when he died, she took it very hard. Some say she has become just like him, cold and indifferent, but I don't think so. I remember the sweet little girl who used to ride ponies and sing songs. How you see her tonight is how she really is—the girl I remember." He paused as he spied a portly woman waving. "Well, if you will excuse me, I believe my wife is callin'. I bid you a good evenin', Mr. Darcy." Mr. Russell shook David's hand once again before taking his leave.

Meanwhile, another man closely observed Cecilia and David's movements. "Keeler, who's that Brit Celia's seein'? She never brings a date here, and she's been seen with him before. I was told they had an unusually good time at O'Malley's."

"Why do you care, Cameron? You dumped her years ago for Amelia, remember?"

"Yeah, and what a mistake that turned out to be. I traded brains for a bitch." Cameron smirked, "I intend to win her back, and I don't need some damned Englishman gettin' in my way." Cameron nursed his whiskey while he watched Robert speaking with the Brit.

As Robert walked away, David frowned ...*That was a completely different side to her ...So she had a difficult time as a child...not unlike me...hmm...*

While David was lost in his thoughts, Cecilia approached him. "David, I think we should take our seats. It's about to begin."

Cecilia guided him to their table where they ate and talked with those around them until the time arrived for Cecilia to give the annual report to the Charleston Historical Counsel Board. She rose from her seat, papers in hand, and walked to the podium.

"Ladies and gentlemen," she smiled, "I open this meeting with the reading of the minutes of the last meeting. Margaret, will you please do the honors."

A tall thin woman in her mid-thirties stood up and read the minutes. When she concluded, Cecilia inquired. "Are there any questions?"

No reply.

"All right, since there are no questions, I will proceed with our annual report." Cecilia paused for a sip of water, and then she read the report. "Sullivan House has been purchased for just under two million dollars and plans for its restoration are well underway. Also twenty-five journals dating from 1795 to 1947 were located and are now published and for sale in the historical bookstores. And lastly, the Charleston Heritage Cookbook, sponsored by the Junior League, is entering its fifteenth printing." She continued on with the report of the sales in the historical shops which had exceeded expectations. Concluding the business section of the report, she moved on to a personal project that was very dear to her heart.

"That brings me to a point of new business. Since we are a nonprofit organization, I would like to take some of the extra money we have and donate it to Hannah's House, but no decision is to be made on that point tonight. We will take it up at our next scheduled meeting."

Stopping for a brief moment, she leaned onto the podium and surveyed the audience. "I must temporary halt here to say something that distresses me to no end. I read just the other day in *The Charleston News Courier* that there were far more battered and abused women this year than in the previous. I want you to know that I am appalled and ashamed that such a thing still exists here in Charleston." Cecilia paused. "There should be **no** battered or abused women in Charleston or anywhere else, for that matter. I want us as a group to do all within our power to help women overcome their co-dependency on these men, or dare I say animals, who abuse them. This wretched behavior is unforgivable."

The room broke out in applause. When the clapping calmed, she continued. "Moving on to the next item, we are renovating Choler House on East Battery for the new Children's Advocacy Home. Battered and abused children will be given a home there where they will be allowed to heal and grow. That project will be finished next week with the center hopefully opening before Christmas. I've promised the children a Christmas party when it finally opens," she said with a smile. "I would like to see all of us come and read a book, play, or share some time with the children in whatever way we can. They need to know that people care. I'm also sponsoring an Angel Tree Program. I have a list of what each child needs and wants for Christmas, so if you would like to participate, see me after the meeting. Let's give these children a good Christmas." Another round of applause erupted.

"Before I conclude this report, are there any questions?"

There was no answer.

"No one?"

She nodded, accepting the silence as the society's acquiescence. "Well, since there are no questions, that concludes my report. I now turn the floor over to Cameron Taylor. Cameron." Cecilia smiled as she handed the microphone to the gentleman, who upon taking it, gave her an affectionate kiss on the cheek.

She glared in warning.

Not missing Cameron's kiss and Cecilia's reaction, David smiled, amused, thinking of his own experiences. At least she had been affectionate with him, even if he had failed to seduce her.

The dinner was a great success, with almost everyone taking a child's name to sponsor for a Christmas gift. Even David took one, leaving Cecilia with enough money to purchase the gifts for the older boy he had selected. Besides the Lego Technic/Expert Builder Kit and Ipod Nano the child wanted, David insisted the child be given a collection of **The Chronicles of Narnia** which he had loved as a boy.

When all the names were taken, David and Cecilia mixed and mingled among the crowd. One by one, the guests came to talk with David.

"Mr. Darcy, it's good to meet you. We always enjoy new and varying company in our society, and you seem interestin' to talk with. It's not often that I find someone who enjoys a fast horse or a fast woman, and I believe you enjoy both." Solomon Abercrombie winked as he eyed Cecilia across the room.

"Well yes, Mr. Abercrombie, I do admire a fast horse and own several Arabians, but as to women, I never discuss that." David paused and changed the subject. "I understand your South Carolina thoroughbreds are among the best. Did I hear you tell Mr. Russell that your horse, Southern Diamond, won the Preakness Stakes?"

"Why yes, Darcy, she did, and the Belmont Stakes, too. And she came within a nose hair at Churchill Downs, puttin' me one race shy of the Triple Crown. But there is always next year with a filly I own that's lookin' pretty promisin'." Solomon's brow arched. "Say, Darcy, you keep up with horse racin' do you?"

"As a matter of fact, I do. My white Arabian stallion has potential, but unfortunately I lack the time to explore it." David smiled as Abercrombie's curiosity piqued into an area David felt comfortable discussing.

"Oh? Tell me about him. What's his name and who sired him?"

"His name is Sea Crest, and he's from the royal line in Saudi Arabia. He was a gift from the King—one of his prize stallions, bred for speed across the desert."

"Umm, I see. I'll have to look him up." Solomon frowned, staring at David with newfound respect.

"You do that. I'm sure you'll like what you find." David chuckled, clearly amused.

"Now, what kinda car do you drive?" Abercrombie asked, eyeing David closely.

"Hmm…well, I have several, actually. I own a black Jag XK, a red Romeo 8C Competizione, and a few sport utility vehicles. I also have a Blue Hera Lamborghini LP640 Murciélago Coupé on order."

"A Murciélago you say? Umm…quite impressive, Darcy. Six hundred and thirty-one horse power. Zero to sixty in less than 3.5 seconds from a dead stop with a top speed of 222 mph. It's one of the fastest cars on the road. I saw the Roadster version at the Los Angeles Auto Show last month. At over $320,000, the LP640 is quite a car. Your other cars aren't half bad either. Hmm… fast cars, fast horses, and fast women. Some like it hot," Abercrombie said on a soft chuckle, sipping his whiskey while he glanced between David and Cecilia. "On horses and cars, you appear to be a man of knowledge with some good sense and understandin', but Darcy," he grinned widely, "when it comes to the woman, I'm afraid you're in for a real challenge. Cecilia is quite a little filly herself and hot to trot from what I hear, but what I wonder is…are you the right stud?" Solomon's eyebrow shot up as he nodded with a dry grin. "Remember, Darcy, women are a lot like horses. They have to be broken in and trained." Mr. Abercrombie winked as he moved along.

David's eyes flashed in amusement. *…Broken in and trained indeed! I have a feeling nobody breaks or trains Cecilia…and I wouldn't want to be the man who attempted it!*

While David went on to talk with another gentleman, Cameron approached Cecilia. "Who's the Brit you've been seein'?"

"Why do you want to know?" she inquired in a frosted tone. "Are you seeking an introduction?"

"Hardly," he snarled, "I want to know why you're seein' him, and why you took him to O'Malley's—the place we used to go." Cameron's eyes narrowed.

"Look Cameron, we haven't dated in years. I owe you no explanations as to who I see or what I do. Is that understood? Now leave me alone and go back to Amelia. The two of you deserve each other." Giving him a scornful look, she walked away to join a group of ladies near the refreshment table.

Cameron's eyes followed her as he sipped his whiskey. *…Celia, you will be mine, and no damned Englishman is gonna interfere.*

As Cecilia approached the assembled ladies, Glenna Cunningham reached for her hands, taking them in a gentle squeeze. "Celia, darlin', your Mr. Darcy is such a charmin' young man, and he has excellent manners, too, so polite and thoughtful. Maybelle, Jenny, Tabitha, and I have all been talkin' to him, and we just love him, darlin'. Don't we, girls?" she said as she looked to the other ladies present.

"Oh, yes, indeed we do," Maybelle said with the others agreeing in unison as they nodded among themselves.

"I hope you'll bring him to more of our functions. He has really impressed my husband with his knowledge of huntin' hounds." Jenny added, "Apparently, he and his brother keep a variety of dogs, and they hunt. Did you know they have a large estate in

England?" Her eyes danced with mirth. "Oh, and they raise horses, too. I heard him and Mr. Abercrombie talkin' about race horses. Your Mr. Darcy sure knows a lot about em', suga."

"No, Jen, I didn't know," Cecilia's voice faded into a whisper, surprised at the more human side of David Darcy. "You all appear to know him better than I do. I only know him through our business association. ...*He raises hounds and horses does he? Interesting... Daddy raised hounds and horses...I like both ...*

"Well, honey, a good lookin' man like that? You need to get to know him, darlin'. The way he looks at *you* tells me he'd like to get to know you better." Tabitha said.

"Everybody's talkin' about him, honey, and Celia, they *like* him. Look how he laughs and converses with the men—so at ease as if he's known 'em forever." Mrs. Cunningham raised her hands in praise while glancing in David's direction.

Cecilia cut her eyes across to where David stood talking with several gentlemen. "I suppose you're right. He seems to mix and mingle as if he belongs here," Cecilia said with a slight frown. "Somehow I didn't expect that."

"Well, Celia darlin', I don't know why not. He's a perfect gentleman, and if I were you, I wouldn't let that one slip away. You need to snatch him up. We all know you can do it, if you only will." Mrs. Appleton smiled while everyone present mumbled in agreement.

"Perhaps. Excuse me, ladies. I think I'll join him."

The ladies only smiled while gently nodding.

Cecilia strolled across the room and approached David, slipping her arm into his while she looked up at him admiringly. "David, let's have another glass of wine."

David turned and smiled. "If you wish," he said before turning back to the gentleman he'd been talking with. "Excuse us, Mr. Smith. My date has reclaimed me. You take very good care of that English Setter. She sounds like a good dog. I think my male might be what you're looking for in a stud. Perhaps someday I can see her, and we can discuss breeding in more detail, and give my regards to Mrs. Smith," David said, shaking Asa Smith's hand.

"Louise will be please you thought of her," Asa said.

David and Cecilia walked together to the bar where she ordered two glasses of port. "It seems everyone has occupied your attention but me."

"Oh, I wouldn't say that." His eyes swept downward before lifting and holding her gaze. "You've occupied my thoughts for months."

Smiling up at him, she sipped her wine as they engaged one another in quiet conversation until the hour approached eleven and people began to leave. Cecilia once again slipped her arm into his. "David, we need to go. Would you escort me to my suite?"

"Let's go," he said with a warm smile.

Approaching the lobby, he told her, "Cecilia, I had a very interesting evening. The people were warm and friendly. I don't usually enjoy being in society, so that's a compliment to you. You see, I can give an admiring comment, when one's warranted."

She smiled affectionately as they walked towards the lift. "With those I saw talking with you, I can only imagine what they had to say about me. Not all of them like me, but that's all right. The feeling's mutual."

"It wasn't bad at all. They had nothing but good things to say."

Escorting her back to her penthouse, uneasiness settled in over David. He felt as nervous as a first year university student as he contemplated the close of the evening. It was not like him at all. His mind was in turmoil.

When they came to her door, he reached over to kiss her goodnight, deciding it was probably best to simply leave. Somehow the things he had desired seemed hollow, and he was not entirely sure what would happen if he should stay, considering their past. But when she returned his kiss with such desire, such fervor, his uncertainty gave way to his desire to stay. If he had ever felt this much passion while kissing a woman before, he couldn't remember it, not even with her. He felt her draw and pull on him, and without realizing what he was doing, he was in her suite, kissing and caressing her.

"This is the second half of your bargain, David," she whispered softly against his lips. "I just happen to be in the mood tonight." Her lips caught his once more in a deep lingering kiss. Breaking free, she looked him directly in the eye. "But, before we continue, one thing must be made crystal clear, Darcy. Just because I screw you, it does not mean that I love you, or that I ever will. Understand that, and we'll get along just fine."

David swallowed hard, taken aback by her boldness, for that had always been his line. Although he had never considered the possibility of loving her, he was stunned just the same that she would echo his own words, the very words he had spoken many times, and disappointed that she had.

Composing himself, he gazed deeply into her passion filled eyes. "That's all right, Cecilia. I'm not the marrying kind." Even as the familiar words fell from his mouth he wondered if they were true. For the first time that phrase sounded empty and false.

"Then we understand one another?"

"Perfectly," he whispered.

His gaze held hers while a mixture of uncertain feelings washed over him. He could sense that she might possibly hold a power over him, and he wondered if this night was such a good idea after all. David momentarily thought of leaving, but the chemistry between them and the intensity of built-up desire, coupled with need, was incredible. Even if he had wanted to, he couldn't have resisted her. She was captivating and beautiful—and he wanted her.

His breath caught in his throat. David looked at her with uninhibited longing before taking her into his arms and kissing her with a wet, ravenous kiss, his tongue devouring hers. He was determined to have her. If her words had meant anything to him, they were quickly forgotten the moment his lips touched hers.

Cecilia broke their embrace and took him by the hand, leading him into her bedroom where they silently undressed, and for a brief moment, stood there gazing at one another. David drew in a deep breath as his eyes traced over every inch of her beautiful body. The gentle curve of her neck begged to be kissed. He followed the line of her throat flowing into her ample breasts, imagining his lips grazing them as well. Traversing downward, he focused on her flat, well-toned stomach, and then the curve of her waist into her well rounded hips. Perfect! Then there were her long shapely legs—a leggy blonde, his particular weakness.

Given his experience, he wouldn't have thought anything or anyone could have stirred his sensibilities to this degree, but he was wrong. She was more beautiful than any woman he'd ever seen, and yet it wasn't her physical beauty that attracted him to this level. It was something else entirely. Something he couldn't quite fathom—an enigma better left to another day to comprehend.

She stood, tall and erect, watching him observe her. She smiled, her lashes sweeping downward. Then she turned and gathered back the coverlet and slid into bed.

"Come," she said.

He obeyed. Not even in his wildest dreams had he imagined what it would be like to take her to bed or how strong his attraction had become. His pulse quickened. The violet-hue in her shimmering eyes flashed with desire. She wanted him, and he wanted her. As he settled in beside her, she pulled him into her arms, kissing him, touching him, tasting him, savoring him. And David welcomed her embrace, tenderly returning her kiss while he caressed her as if she were a treasured possession.

"Beautiful…you're so beautiful," he whispered inaudibly against her neck, inhaling her exotic scent—jasmine mingled with gardenia and sandalwood. He handled her with more tenderness than he was aware he even possessed. It was suddenly important that this night become special for the *both* of them.

Just as he made every effort to please her, she made every effort to please him, and please him she did. Her hair teased his skin as she bent low, running kisses interspersed with light traces of her tongue as she ever so lightly caressed his body, working her way down to his arousal and taking him in, sending shivers coursing through his body. When she retraced the path she'd descended, he moaned softly. She had discovered the tender spot on the nape of his neck that many of his lovers overlooked. The sensual feel of her warm breath against his skin unleashed a torrent of feelings he was unaware he possessed, driving him to places he'd never been. He caressed her, tenderly memorizing her every curve with the tips of his fingers.

They made love on pure raw instinct—taking, giving, consuming. It was different—she was different. When he entered her, she tightened around him, flooding him with a euphoric feeling he could not remember ever experiencing. The ferocity of his desire overwhelmed him as they rhythmically rocked and swelled as one upon the silken sheets. When they reached their completion, he withdrew and fell back, pulling her into the curve of his body. Holding her close to his heart, he lovingly stroked her hair and back, tenderly caressing her every curve all over again.

His mind was a tempest, and he could tell from the way she trembled that she had felt it, too. Every kiss, every touch, evoked feelings that he'd never felt with anyone, and while he laid there holding her in his arms, David Darcy felt for the first time in his life that he wanted to tell a woman he loved her.

…How can this be? I can't love her. I don't even know her…And she could never love me. Darcy, did you not hear her words? It's just sex. I wonder who's using who.

No, I must be rational—this is only one night. I leave for London in the morning. Even if…NO! She is not the kind of woman who would commit. She said so herself, and you have heard the rumors about her.

No, tonight I'll love her and hold her, but tomorrow I must leave. I cannot allow my feelings to become engaged—especially not by her. I will not be her plaything. I can't let her know how much she has affected me. I'm not in too deep…not yet.

He'd been with countless women, had known their passion and enjoyed their charms, but none had stirred his senses like the woman he now held in his arms. He had intended to please her for his own selfish purposes, but instead, he pleased her because he wanted to. He'd have to shake this feeling before he saw his brother in a few days. He couldn't hide much from him. *Fitzwilliam read me like a book.*

Cecilia took a deep breath. Although she would never admit it, David had moved her like no other, throwing her emotions into chaos as she lay there trembling in his arms. He was the best lover she had ever experienced. He had truly rocked her world. She reached up and kissed his cheek as she snuggled closer. And there was another thing that she had not expected—the softer, genteel side of David Darcy. With what she had seen tonight, Cecilia had garnered a newfound respect for him.

Chapter Thirteen

...I love him...I truly love him...

Elizabeth stood at her upstairs bedroom window, staring out at a vortex of twirling leaves playing in the street below. It was the eleventh of December, and the fall semester had finally come to a close. With final exams, scoring papers, and submitting grades, there had been little opportunity for her and Fitzwilliam to spend time together. She sighed.

Tonight was Fitzwilliam's last night in town before leaving for London. With all of the activity, she had not had a chance to really talk with him since Thanksgiving. She needed to tell him about her trust fund. It had been on her list of things to talk about, but for some reason, they had never gotten around to the subject. Tonight she had to do it, but something else occupied her mind as well.

Every day since the Thanksgiving break, Elizabeth had been thinking about *this* night. She walked back from the window and flopped down on her bed, gazing at her scattered collection of CDs. Shuffling through them one by one, her mind was lost in careful thought as she listened to the song *Tonight's the Night* and thought of Fitzwilliam. Even with their limited time together, they had not really *been* together. Having reverted back to his behavior before they'd shared their first real kiss, he had not so much as touched her, in spite of the desire and longing she saw reflected in his dark brown eyes. Wanting each other, desiring each other, and yet, not having each other—she shook her head. "This will not do," she softly said to herself."

Getting up, she went to her closet and surveyed her wardrobe, wanting to pick an outfit that was both sexy and elegant. Finally deciding on a blue and black plaid long skirt, she took it from the rack. Then she selected a black cashmere sweater with a neckline low enough to reveal a bit of cleavage—enough to be sexy, yet feminine.

Once she had her outfit selected, Elizabeth decided a bubble bath with the rose scented gift set Jane had given her for graduation was in order. Remembering that Fitzwilliam liked this fragrance, she combined it with her mother's rose scented hair oil as she dried her hair. Once dressed, she put the final touch to her hair, pinning it up in a chic figure eight twist with a Ficcare clip that matched the blue in her skirt perfectly. With another quick look in the mirror, she grabbed her CD and purse and was out the door for Willow Street.

Fitzwilliam hummed a light melody as he went about setting the table. Charles was spending the evening with Jane, and having given Mrs. Norris time off to spend Christmas with her son in Ohio, he and Elizabeth would have the house to themselves. Since he knew she enjoyed Italian food, he'd made a simple pasta dish and salad. Handel's *Messiah* played in the background as he put the finishing touches on the table. Just as he lit the last candle, the doorbell rang. Elizabeth... he smiled.

Upon entering, he helped her with her cape as he leaned in and kissed her cheek, catching the scent of roses. He stepped back and froze. Inhaling sharply, his gaze dropped. Eying her slowly from head to toe, his eyes rested on her low neckline. Something was different. She was unusually beautiful tonight. Her sweater clung, flattering her well shaped breasts, and his pulse quickened as he remembered how her bare breast had felt in his hand. He groaned silently as his body automatically stiffened into an almost painful arousal. If this kept up, they would have to marry before June.

107

She smiled coyly, sniffing the air. "What's for dinner? It smells wonderful."

As if coming out of a dense fog, he replied, "Right this way, Elizabeth," he gestured. "I hope you like fettuccini. I also made a salad, and bought some Italian wine."

"I love it! I can't wait to try it. Let's eat."

He hung her cape on the coat rack and took her by the hand, leading her to the small dining room. All through dinner, he couldn't take his eyes off of her while he tried to pay attention to their conversation, finding it more difficult as time passed.

As she began discussing her trust fund, telling him something about mutual funds and the stock market, his mind tuned out, more agreeably engaged on her physical form. Her eyes were intense, but her expression and mannerisms were casual; the contradiction confusing him.

"Fitzwilliam, are you listening to me?"

"Oh, I'm sorry, Elizabeth. What were you saying?"

"I was telling you about my trust fund. I will have access to it when we marry. The stipulation was either when I married or on my thirtieth birthday. Since I will be married first, I will have access to it then as opposed to later."

Slightly blushing, Fitzwilliam responded, "I'm sorry, Elizabeth, my mind is distracted. I don't believe I heard you. Is it substantial?"

"I said the principal is three million dollars. It has earned between ten and fifteen percent annually for the past two years, and should do the same this year if the economy remains stable. Fitzwilliam, you're still not paying attention to me," she scolded playfully.

His body tensed as his eyes drifted to her slender neck, following the graceful curve to her cleavage. Glancing up to meet her eyes, he said, "Liz, I assure you I *am* paying perfect attention to you."

He stood up to clear the table, automatically prompting Elizabeth to help. When the kitchen and dining room were cleaned to their satisfaction, Fitzwilliam said, "Let's go to the library where we can talk or listen to music."

Once they reached the library, Elizabeth retrieved her CD from her purse and handed it to him. "Fitzwilliam, play this. I'm in the mood for Rod Stewart. It's our last night together for three weeks, and I want you to hold me while we dance."

He tensed. The contents of the CD and her provocative suggestion unnerved him. His eyes searched hers carefully as he placed the disc in the player. Pulling her into his embrace, he held her close, swaying to the slow melody. The scent of her perfume and the sensation of her body next to his, along with the soft music, all combined to awaken the slow burn he had tried very hard to control. He pulled back and gazed into her eyes, attempting to read her thoughts.

And then he saw it...desire. The same desire that he'd seen in the cabin at Longbourn, the same desire that ached within him—the desire he'd fought so hard to suppress. Suddenly, his body burst into flames. On impulse, he reached back and removed her clip, dropping it to the floor and freeing her long flowing hair, letting it cascade over her shoulders and down her back.

She reached up and cupped his face in her hands, pulling him down, taking his mouth in a fiercely possessive kiss. The sensation hit him like a blow to the chest. He groaned and pulled her tighter into his arms, the desire to make love to her overriding his senses as he kissed her again and again while the music played.

Breaking the kiss, he stepped back and whispered, "I love you, Liz...I love you, but I'm only a man. You're making this very hard for me to keep our agreement. I don't think you understand what a woman can do to a man who is in love with her."

"Oh, I think I do," she murmured. "Just kiss me…hold me."

She melted into his body and pulled him closer while her fingers sank into his thick dark curls. Helpless to do anything but obey, his arms slipped around her, gathering her to him as one hand encircled her waist while the other tangled in her hair.

"Elizabeth… my Elizabeth …I love you," he softly said, skimming her lips with his before capturing them in a deep kiss, kissing her over and over again.

Breaking away, he dusted light kisses all over her face and then trailing down the curve of her neck to the space between her ear and shoulder where he suckled and kissed. Running his tongue over her pulse, he felt it throb in perfect time to the ache throbbing in him. His tongue stroked the valley between her breasts, licking and kissing, softly whispering words of love before retracing the path to catch her lips once again. He both heard and felt the small whimper that escaped her throat as her mouth eagerly engaged his, returning his passion with equal fervor and need. Fully aroused, he pressed and stroked against her, causing them both to burn.

The next thing he knew, they were on the sofa, and his hand was under her sweater. Reaching back, he unhooked her bra and cupped her bare breast, moaning softly at the feel of her silky skin against his hand. His palm lightly grazed her firm nipple before taking her breast in a gentle caress, massaging it with a slow deliberate movement. The song *Tonight's the Night* played and the words, the mood, and the feel her body, all ignited a blaze within him like liquid fire coursing through his veins. She was seducing him, and he knew it, but he was too weak to resist or even care.

"What are you doing to me?" he pleaded on a ragged breath. "Have you any idea what you're doing?" He kissed her again with uninhibited passion, pulling her into his body, pressing hard against her.

Elizabeth gazed into his eyes. "Yes, I do," she murmured softly. "I know exactly what I'm doing. *Tonight's the night.*"

"Elizabeth, are you sure…absolutely sure? Once we start down this road, there is no going back. And, as I've told you before, I won't take anything from you that you don't freely give."

"I know, and…yes, I am." She nodded. "I'm very sure…I can't wait until June."

That was all he needed to hear. Fitzwilliam took Elizabeth's hand and led her up the stairs to his bedroom. He cupped her face and caressed her high cheekbones with his thumbs as if she were the most precious thing he'd ever beheld. Taking in a steadying breath, he dipped his head and kissed her tenderly, his tongue exploring… tasting… savoring. When they broke the kiss, he lit a candle.

After undressing, they stood facing one another. His eyes moved over her body, tracing her every sensual line. Elizabeth was more beautiful than he ever imagined. Stretching forth his hand, Fitzwilliam brushed the tips of his fingers over her face, tracing her jaw line to her chin, hovering there for a moment, and then continuing down the hollow of her throat and over her collarbone. His nimble fingers edged downward, clutching her firm, round breast. He held it in the palm of his hand as he brushed his thumb over her nipple, watching it harden. She closed her eyes and gently swallowed—the pleasure of his touch written across her face as she inhaled deeply. Releasing her breast, he stroked down her side, pausing in the arc of her waist. It was small and her hips nicely curved. Her hair covered her like Lady Godiva, and he was sure, more than ever, that she looked like an elvish princess.

He ran his fingers through her hair, spreading it over her shoulders like a cloak. She glanced up, catching his gaze and holding it, her eyes shining. It humbled him to know that she was pure, that she had saved herself for him, her husband. He would treasure her always as he made her his.

As she reached up and grazed his face with her small hand, he turned and kissed her palm. Her hand gently caressed downward over the strong planes of his chest, running her fingers through the tuft of hair over his heart, pausing to feel its steady beat.

Breathing erratically, he closed his eyes, relishing the feel of her hand exploring his body as she continued slowly over his abdomen in light feathery touches with the back of her fingers, traveling lower until she caught him in the palm of her hand. He opened his eyes, and their gaze locked.

"Will it fit?" she asked.

"It'll fit," he reassured.

She dropped her hand to her side. "We need a towel for the bed," she whispered softly as he turned and pulled back the bedcovers.

He presumed she didn't want to leave the evidence of her innocence behind for Mrs. Norris to find, so he quickly did as she had asked. After turning on the sound system, he picked her up and gently laid her on the towel. Then he climbed into bed beside her.

Her eyes, filled with desire and love, burned into his while the song *Feels so Right* softly played in the background.

"Elizabeth, as far as I'm concerned, this is our wedding night. Your virtue is kept and honored with me. I intend to make you my wife."

"Fitzwilliam, I am not worried about it. I trust you...I love you. It's better to love than to burn."

"And better to marry than wait."

She nodded.

The look in her beautiful eyes spoke to him from the depths of her heart. He would take their lovemaking slowly, easing her as gently as he could into the consummation of their union.

"I love you, Liz. You have no idea how much. I won't hurt you...not if I can help it."

"I know."

Drawing in a tattered breath, he lowered his mouth to hers, catching her lips, exploring her mouth as one hand followed the curve of her body while the other held her close. He kissed her face, licking her lips, suckling them before devouring her mouth.

She kissed him back with equal passion, threading her fingers into his hair, fiercely taking his mouth in challenge, kissing him like she'd never kissed him before. He was pleased by her response—no, more than pleased—he was elated. His mouth found its way with hot, wet kisses to her neck and shoulder, working his way to her breast. Taking it in his hand, he gently caressed it before gently running his tongue over her firm tip, grazing it with his teeth, nipping and flicking it with his tongue before suckling it.

His hand descended over her well-toned, muscled stomach, gently stroking her silken hair. She arched into his hand, writhing at his touch. Pleased with her reaction, his hand found its way to her center, touching and caressing her as she trembled and softly moaned his name. His mouth covered hers to suppress a cry as his hand continued stroking her.

She shook violently when his fingers slid inside where he found her fully aroused and more than ready for him. He sighed softly, parting her legs with his knee, settling between her thighs, and adjusted himself.

"I don't want to cause you pain, my love, but I'm afraid I may not be able to help it.

If it's too much for you, then tell me, and I'll stop. I love you so very much."

"No. Please don't stop. I...I want you." Her voice quivered.

With one last look into her beautiful eyes, he drew in a sharp breath and entered her with one hard thrust, breaking through her virginal barrier, and settling himself inside of her. But when she cried out in pain, he stopped.

"Liz, are you all right? Do you want me to stop? I think I still can." His voice strained, struggling for control.

"No, please don't," she pleaded. "I want this very much. Fitzwilliam, I love you. Please love me...please, please don't stop."

Gathering her into his arms, he held her close.

"Liz, try to relax," he reassured her. "If you relax, the pain will ease, and all you'll feel is pleasure. Trust me."

"I do." She breathed softly as she ran her fingers into his hair and kissed him.

Slowly and tenderly he kissed her until he felt her unwind. As her body gave in to his, she raised her legs and wrapped them around him.

"That's right, Liz. Just let yourself go and let me love you, darling...let me love you..." his voice trailed off as his lips reclaimed hers in a warm tender kiss before his mind closed down completely and pure instinct took over as he made love to her.

He collapsed on top of her, spent with pleasure and exhaustion, both of them trembling. They embraced each other tightly as he feverishly kissed her, finally achieving his long held desire. Rolling over, he took her with him and held her firm against his body, stroking her every curve as he whispered words of endearment.

"Liz...Liz, I love you...now and forever...I love you," he said softly, kissing her face and hair. "It'll be better next time, my love. I promise. I hope I didn't hurt you too badly."

"The pain was fleeting. It quickly passed." She released a sigh. "So this is what it's like to be loved. I always wondered." She softly laughed as her fingers played in the damp curls on his chest.

He chuckled. "It gets better. You'll learn to enjoy it even more than you can imagine."

Elizabeth nestled close with her head on his shoulder. "Fitzwilliam, I love you. I can't imagine it being better, but if it is, I'm very much looking forward to it."

They drifted off to sleep for a little while before awakening to make love again. They continued throughout the night until the early morning hours. With each encounter, Elizabeth became a little more relaxed.

He was amazed that she appeared to enjoy their lovemaking as much as he did. He had always heard that was not the case for a woman's first time. He also knew she was passionately in love with him, or she would never have decided to trust him.

As he held her close, securely tucked in the curve of his body, he softly said, "Liz, I hate to do this, but we must get up and shower. I have to pick Charles up at your house at six."

"I know. It's been planned. I knew you'd have to leave this morning."

"I don't want to leave you, especially now. In fact, all I want to do is stay right here making love to you over and over again, but I must go. When I get back, we'll make plans about getting married. After last night, I can't bear to be parted from you ever again."

"Fitzwilliam, I hate to see you go. I'm going to miss you," she said, clinging to him as she kissed his cheek.

"I know, Liz. I know. But I have to go. I'll ring you up every day. Expect my call around five p.m. your time," he said as they lay there holding one another.

M.K. Baxley

A few minutes more and they rose to shower and then quickly dressed to return to the Bennett townhouse. Jane and Charles had risen earlier, and Jane had breakfast waiting when they entered the house. Since the car Fitzwilliam and Charles were taking to the airport had been packed the day before, after breakfast the men said their goodbyes, leaving the ladies teary-eyed on the front porch as the first rays of morning light peered over the mountain and split the eastern sky.

Chapter Fourteen

...she's the one...the one I've searched for...

Fitzwilliam found the flight to London long and tedious, with rest eluding him. Twisting in his seat in an attempt to find a comfortable position, he glanced at Charles resting next to him and smiled. Apparently Charles had no such problem. He was sound asleep and snoring gently.

Finally finding a comfortable position, Fitzwilliam picked up the book in his lap and retrieved the photographs he'd placed there before leaving Tennessee. They were pictures of him and Elizabeth on the farm. He held them in his hand, slowly shuffling through them one-by-one, grinning as he savored the sweet memories. Placing them back in the book, he yawned as he closed his eyes.

...Elizabeth... He smiled a contented smile, almost able to smell the scent of her perfume as he thought about their impending future. He wanted to spend a lifetime with her—to have a family. A family like she'd had growing up. To sit and work together, to do course preparations and mark papers, to take her to bed each night after the work was done and make love to her, and then to wake up in the morning with her in his arms and love her all over again. He wanted her as his wife. And the mere thought of her bearing his child thrilled and overwhelmed him. But...Father. He moaned, his features contorting into a grimace.

He knew his father would object. Elizabeth would not be worthy of the Darcy name. She would hurt the family standing in both the business world and London society. Of course, none of this was true, but his father would spew it forth just the same. It didn't matter.

Fitzwilliam drifted in and out of thought and sleep for the entire flight, only to become fully awake as the plane circled Heathrow, waiting for permission to land. Once they were on the ground, Fitzwilliam wasted no time exiting the plane and going through customs. Since David had arrived earlier, he was there to meet them.

"Brother, Bingley, how was your flight?" David asked with a big smile, slapping them both on the back.

"It was long and wearisome," Fitzwilliam replied as they began to walk. "We had a security problem leaving out of Nashville, causing the delay we experienced. So, I'm more than ready to get home. Let's get out of here."

"In a hurry to see Father, I see." David laughed, shaking his head. "Well, come along then."

"No, David, I am not in a hurry to see Father. I merely want to find a place to relax, have a brandy and maybe a cigar."

"Bingley, how about you?" David turned to greet his friend. "Do you want to come with us? We can unload your things at your townhouse."

"No, but thank you, David. I need to get home. I have several things to do, and I want to ring Jane."

"Jane? Who's Jane?"

"Jane Bennett." Bingley laughed. "She's the most wonderful woman I know and soon to be my wife. She's an angel. We'll go to White's one day next week, and I'll tell you everything."

David chuckled. "I'm all ears. I have to hear all about her. And your Elizabeth, too, Fitzwilliam!" he said, turning to his brother. "You've certainly piqued my curiosity—the both of you. The Cumberland Plateau sounds like a place I need to stay away from, after seeing what it's done to you two."

"David, don't you want to find someone and settle down someday?" Bingley asked.

"No, I'll leave that to you and Fitzwilliam. I am *not* the marrying kind."

Fitzwilliam looked at his brother in amusement. "You will be, when the right one comes along."

David smiled and shook his head. "I highly doubt it, but one never knows." He chortled. "Now, Fitzwilliam, you'll have to check in at home and see the Old Man. He's requested our presence, and you know what that means. It is *he* who *must be obeyed*," David said with a laugh. He clapped his brother on the back once more as they exited the main door out into the crisp December air.

"I have every intention of seeing him. He is our father, after all, and I owe him due respect. Besides, I want to see him."

Upon entering Darcy House, they were greeted by the butler. "Master Fitzwilliam, it's so very good to see you home again and you, too, Master David." The old butler smiled warmly. "Let me take your coats."

"Thank you, Sammons," Fitzwilliam returned cheerfully.

In a good mood, Fitzwilliam took the stairs two at a time, humming to himself as he walked to his room. In some ways, it was good to be home. His valet, Watson, was already laying out clothes for the evening. For once, Fitzwilliam was looking forward to dinner as he prepared to greet his father.

While Fitzwilliam showered, shaved, and dressed for the evening, he contemplated how he would approach his father. He would first speak with his brother, and then he would gauge his father's mood. When the time was right, they would see him together. Lost in thought, he glanced up as Watson approached him.

"Sir, David asked me to inform you he would wait for you in the upstairs foyer before descending."

"Thank you, Watson. I'll go directly," Fitzwilliam said, turning to face his valet. "Oh and see to it that I have some brandy and a box of Cuaba Generosos in my sitting room for tonight. That'll be all."

"Yes, sir."

With that done, Fitzwilliam went to meet his brother. Approaching the stairs, he inquired, "Have you any idea what he wants?"

"Oh, I have a very good idea. He's not happy in the least that you've gone to America. You're going to hear about it, so prepare yourself. Also, he's been in an unusually foul mood of late. He wants us married, so prepare yourself for that, too," David turned to his brother with a sly grin, "and I don't think he will be very receptive of an American as your choice, either. He and Aunt Hilda have been talking."

"Oh, God, not *that* again." Fitzwilliam rolled his eyes as they descended the stairs. "Well, my mind is made up, and there is no chance in hell I'm going to change it. I intend to marry Elizabeth and no one else."

"I hear you, Brother," David said sympathetically. "I'll do all I can."

When they approached the study, they found their father pacing the entrance in a somber mood.

"Ah, there you are. Come in and take a seat. It's good to have you home, Fitzwilliam." Eyeing his son closely, Mr. Darcy remarked, "I see you haven't been overeating. Would you like a glass of port or brandy?" He glanced between the two as they entered.

"Neither, thank you," they both replied.

Ignoring them, he poured three brandies. "I want you to drink with me." He pushed two in their direction. "I have several things we need to discuss. I'll set the agenda. After dinner, we'll begin our discussion in earnest."

Mr. Darcy took his place behind his large, imposing desk as he motioned for his sons to have a seat. Clearing his throat, he took a rather large sip of brandy. "I don't have time for idle chit chat, therefore I'll come straight to the point. We need to discuss your future and what I expect from you. First of all, there is the business. Both of you currently sit on the board of directors and are my second and third in command." He paused for another sip of brandy, and then turned his attention towards his oldest son. "Fitzwilliam, I wish you had not gone on sabbatical. The press has noticed your absence, and there is speculation. I've calmed it for now, but I need you home." Moving his attention to his younger son, he asked, "By the way, David, what about the coffee deal? Tell me about it."

David took a deep breath. "I returned with it last week. It should have reached your desk by now."

"Yes, I saw it." Mr. Darcy frowned. "That's the problem. I'm concerned about the price. Explain!"

David shifted uncomfortably in his seat. "I got the contract, just not at the price you wanted. However, I did get a better price than our competitors. Ms. Lawton is—"

"Damn it, David! That's not what I asked." He released an exasperated breath. "I know Lawton is a bitch and a rather forthright and shrewd businesswoman, but couldn't you use some of your charm on that Southern Belle? You don't mind using it on women who do not matter." George Darcy rubbed his temple in irritation.

Fitzwilliam glanced at David with a quizzical brow.

David simply rolled his eyes and cursed under his breath.

"The material point, Sons, is this. I want tighter controls on efficiency with more detail paid to profit margins. Since the markets are highly competitive, we need to get more of the share." Shifting his gaze back to David, Mr. Darcy didn't miss a beat. "I'll have to look over that coffee contract and get back with you on it."

George leaned back in his chair with a weary sigh. "Now, more importantly, to corporate business. As you know, I will be sixty-three in August, and since I would like to take some time for myself, I will soon be turning everything over to the two of you." He lifted his glass for another drink. "Fitzwilliam, you are to be Chairman of the Board and CEO over all of it, and David, you are to be president and vice chairman, unless something should happen to your brother, in which case you will become CEO and chairman." With a brief hesitation, he looked from one to the other. "I'm tired, boys. I want to retire. Therefore, I would like to begin the process of turning the business over to the two of you when Fitzwilliam comes back from America this summer.

"And that leads me to the next point I wish to discuss—family business," he paused, "or rather, duty and responsibility. Boys, I want to see the next generation of Darcys. I want a grandson, and I want one before I am too old to care." Turning to Fitzwilliam, he continued. "Fitzwilliam, you are thirty-two years old. I want you married within the coming year, but absolutely *not* to some jumped up strumpet from lower society, or God forbid, an American. You have a duty to fulfill." His eyes briefly locked with his oldest son before proceeding to his younger. "And David, that includes you as well. I want you married. Is that understood?!"

David glared. "Father, I have no prospects for marriage, and I don't see any in the

M.K. Baxley

foreseeable future. Quite frankly, I'm not at all interested."

Completely ignoring David's comment, George affirmed, "David, at twenty-eight, you have time yet, but I *will* have you married and a child produced—and I don't want any bastards." His father's eyes narrowed sharply. "Do you understand me?!"

David held his father's piercing gaze. "There will be no *bastards!*"

"Well then," Mr. Darcy raised his glass. "I'm glad we understand one another."

Returning his attention to his older son, he retorted, "And I take it there will be none from you, either. I trust you have learnt your lesson."

Fitzwilliam's features darkened as he stared back at his father. ...*He never forgets, does he... nor will he let me.*

Ignoring his son's contemptuous look, George pressed on. "Now, Fitzwilliam, I would like to announce your engagement to Anne this month. Hilda and I have discussed it, Anne has agreed, and I think it is a wise move. It will unite our business interest with Vanderburgh Banking, making us unstoppable in the global economy. You can marry when you return to England this summer," he stated mater-of-factly.

The color drained from Fitzwilliam's face as he leaned forward. "Wait a minute, Father. I'm not engaged to Anne, nor do I have any plans to be. When I marry, my wife will be of my own choosing—someone whom I love. You *do* understand that don't you?"

George glowered. "Damn it, Fitzwilliam! What the bloody hell does love have to do with it? We're talking about an international business concerning billions."

"Father, you did *love* Mother, didn't you? I know she loved you. I mean, you *do* understand don't you?" Fitzwilliam bit back.

Mr. Darcy paused for a moment, blinking, as if taken by complete surprise at the mention of his wife.

David squirmed in his seat, glancing between his brother and the floor. He wondered how his older brother could be so naïve at times not to know how things worked in this family. Though no one had ever told him, David knew how things had been with his mother and father. David's jaw tightened as he caught the look in his father's eye.

"Fitzwilliam, I married your mother for reasons that are my own. Love is a state of mind. It is something you decide to do. You can decide to love Anne, and if you do not, well, you know what to do about it. I didn't neglect your education that much, did I?" His eyes narrowed. "Or do I need to take my thirty-two-year old son aside for further education?"

"No, Father you *didn't* neglect my education," Fitzwilliam replied in a deliberately cool tone, holding his temper in check, "but I will not marry Anne."

George slammed his glass down. "We'll talk about this later. I will see you at dinner, seven o'clock sharp. Off you go." Mr. Darcy rubbed his brow with one hand, dismissing his sons with the other.

Fitzwilliam shot from his seat and left the study in a fury, followed close behind by his brother. They briskly walked towards the library vaguely aware of servants scampering out of their way. Fitzwilliam was highly incensed. David was used to it. As they entered the room and closed the door, David twisted the lock and turned to his brother.

"I'm sorry about that little experience with Father. I can't imagine being married to that social climbing step-cousin of ours. Anne doesn't even have a sweet disposition." David shuddered, pouring them both a stiff drink. "Later tonight, I want you to tell me all about Elizabeth, but first we need to discuss *Father*," he said, taking a rather large drink of his Scotch. "I'm also sorry you had to hear about Mother in that insulting manner. I figured it out years ago that there was not much, if any, love between them. Their marriage was a sham—a business contract on his part, a means for him to acquire Winthrop Publishing." David gave his brother a pointed look. "Although I think she did love him, and I know she loved us. Mother was the only good thing we ever had."

David's jaw hardened as he looked away. He would never reveal it to anyone, but the memories of his mother's tragic life haunted him, and the pain of it bothered him to this very day. The only good memories he had were of his times together with his brother and, to some extent, his sister, Georgiana. His mother had tried, for the sake of her children, to hide her pain, but David had seen it.

Restless, David began to walk the floor. "Fitzwilliam," he glanced at his brother, "do you remember when we were boys back at Pemberley? How we used to play and horse around all over the countryside? Those were the good years, but then Mum died, and we had to go away to school. You seemed to be absorbed in your books and learning, whilst I found other amusements. It wasn't that I didn't enjoy books and such. It's just that you were the romantic, whilst I was the practical one." Turning to his brother, his eyes locked with Fitzwilliam's. "How does it feel to know that we were the products of a business contract—an heir and a spare?" he smirked, his words ripe with sarcasm. "The whole process sickens me. Father kept mistresses, you know? I've even met a few. I actually liked one of them, but all they ever were to him was something for his enjoyment. And Fitzwilliam," he hesitated, "he even kept them when Mother was alive. Why do you think she stayed at Pemberley while he stayed here in London? It was because she knew." David's lips twisted in a bitter smile.

Fitzwilliam leaned against the chimneypiece, his back to David. "And you think I didn't know?" He spun around. "Of course I knew! Just because I never discussed it with you doesn't mean I didn't know. I have ears that heard and eyes that saw. I used to stand outside her bedroom door when I was a child, listening to her muffled cries. Sometimes I would slip inside and run to her. She would pull me up onto her bed, and we would talk. She would tell me that she was just being silly, and that I shouldn't worry. Sometimes I would ring for tea because a good cup of tea comforted her whilst we talked. I remember one time in particular that was rather painful." Fitzwilliam stiffened. "After Father had left from visiting one holiday, I asked her why he didn't live with us. I'll never forget the expression on her face as her smile faded away, replaced by pain. I never asked again." Fitzwilliam gulped his drink and paced the room, his mood now dark and raw.

Glancing at his brother, he continued. "Remember the time when Mum was pregnant with Georgiana? You were almost six, and I was ten. Mother was in her eighth month, and it was mine and Father's birthday. We had all come to London to surprise him. Mother wanted us to celebrate together. Do you remember?"

David cringed. "I remember."

Fitzwilliam walked over to the window and propped his shoulder against the frame, glancing out as if in a daze. The muscles in his jaw hardened and a grim smile overcame his countenance. "Mrs. Beasley took you to your room whilst Mum and I went to his chamber to find him. There was a woman's laughter coming from his room, so Mum immediately sent me away, only I didn't go. I hid in the servants' hall to watch. She opened the door to find Father in bed with his mistress, celebrating his birthday. Mother was devastated. She gathered us up, and we returned to Pemberley immediately." Fitzwilliam scornfully laughed. "It should have been a clue to her when the servants tried to keep us from the family wing, and perhaps it was. I don't know. All I know is that I was so angry I wanted to kill him!" Fitzwilliam balled his fists and pushed away from the window, turning sharp on his heel. "So don't tell me I don't know. The difference between us is that I wish to forget it. If I don't, I will never be able to forgive him."

Breathing deeply, he glanced at his brother and asked, "But what about us? What kind of men will we be? I, for one, will not be anything like him. I intend to cherish my wife and children. It's my way of making it up to Mother." He looked his brother directly in the eye and pressed the issue. "What about *you*? What choices will *you* make?"

David folded his hands behind his back and began to pace anew, glancing between his brother and the vast breadth of the room as he walked. What did he think? He smirked. Trouble was, he didn't. He only existed from day to day, his ability to love and care—dead, stone cold long ago. Cold as a winter's chill on a warm summer's day. It had died a slow, lingering death while watching his mother and father in his formative years. David laughed silently. ...*It died the day my mother died.* He took a deep breath and squared his shoulders.

"Choices? Oh, I know I'm no better than him. That's why everyone I've ever been involved with knew where they stood up front. And if I even suspect anyone is coming close to forming an attachment, I drop them, just like that." He snapped his fingers with a loud click. "Unlike you, I have no desire for love or marriage, and I make *that* very clear. If I wasn't absolutely in love with a woman, I couldn't remain faithful. That's why a marriage is out of the question for me. I can't commit any more than Father could, but the difference is I don't want to hurt anyone—especially children. That's why I have chosen to remain single and childless. I'm just like him in every respect, except one—*I* am no adulterer." David paused and sipped his drink.

"So you see, Brother, whilst you were off gaining more degrees and expanding your mind with higher education, I've been here learning from the best in the business," he laughed ironically, "but what I won't do is enter into a loveless marriage that would condemn one or more children to the loneliness we've had to endure ever since we were old enough to understand. That's the choice I've made," David said, meeting his brother's stare with a sharp nod.

"David, I'm not as idealistic as you think. I've had my share of women, even if it hasn't been for a while, but to me it was cold and empty after what—ten seconds of ephemeral pleasure. No," he shook his head. "I don't want a mistress, a live-in, or an arranged marriage. If I can't have what I want, then I'll take nothing. That's why I am determined to marry Elizabeth, even if I lose everything because of it. If Edward could give up the crown for Wallis Simpson, then I can give up my inheritance for Elizabeth," he said, looking directly at his brother. "David, don't give up totally on marriage. There is a woman out there somewhere for you, and when you find her, you'll find that everything you currently think will change."

David laughed. "No, you misunderstand me. I don't want a woman, or at least not a wife. As I've told you, I probably wouldn't be any better of a husband than Father was. It would take one bloody hell of a woman to turn my head. She would have to be just like me to survive, and I don't think anyone like that exists," he smirked. "Someday, I might take a mistress, but certainly *not* a wife."

Pulling in a deep breath, he changed the subject. "Now, as far as your inheritance, I don't think it will come to that. After all, he'd have to leave it all to me, and we both know how he feels about that." They both laughed. "I'm just like him, only since I don't hide it, it disgusts him. You see, he can't stand to see himself in the light of day. I'm a shrewd business negotiator, I drive a hard bargain, and I can be as cold-hearted and ruthless as I need to be—just like him. Nothing gets to me. I am what I am, and I don't hide it, nor do I give a damn what some society twit thinks of me. I have enough money that I don't have to court their good opinion."

"Well," Fitzwilliam shrugged as he pushed away from the window, "be that as it may. However, I do think Father has a heart somewhere. I remember times when he seemed happy with Mother and us, too. There was once tenderness there, but then something changed. I don't remember him being at Pemberley much when I was little, but when he was there, he would play with me. And you may not remember it, but he played with you, too. Mother would laugh, and so would he. The way he would look at her, I could have sworn there was affection there, but then he would always leave, and she would become sad again. Then later, when we were older, all of that changed. I don't understand what happened between the two of them. But when he came, they would fight. Those are the times you remember, but David, it wasn't always that way."

"That may very well be, but except for the summer before Mother died, I never saw any of what you've just described. Perhaps the change, as you call it, had to do with his mistress. That'll do it every time," David said with a sharp nod. "The man is incapable of love. Much like me I'm afraid."

"Well, nevertheless, I have a Plan B. I will evaluate my finances to see exactly what I'm worth. Currently, I think I have £15 million—probably more." He sighed as he rubbed his forehead. "Father has a way of draining a person. The flight was tiresome, and I need some rest. I'm going upstairs. I'll see you at dinner."

"All right. I think I'll stay here and read."

"What? You read a book? Since when?"

"Since J.K. Rowling. I'm trying to finish the latest book." David laughed. "You go and rest. I'll see you at seven."

That evening dinner was quiet and solemn. George Darcy sat at his usual place at the head of the table with Fitzwilliam to his right and David to his left. As they sat eating in silence, George studied his sons, analyzing them carefully. He shook his head. David possessed the ability and business savvy to run Pemberley all on his own, but he lacked the moral fortitude. David was a loose cannon with no regard for discretion.

George took a sip of wine and turned his eyes upon his older son. Fitzwilliam was soft, lacking in drive and ambition, or so it outwardly appeared. But was he really? No, George didn't think so. Fitzwilliam possessed a keen intellect with a sharp, well-honed, calculating mind, able to think and respond with speed and accuracy. He didn't often show it, but George had seen it when they'd crossed intellectual swords.

George sighed, his burdens weighing heavily on him. With speculation running rampant in the press concerning his sons, he wondered how long he would be able to hold everything together. He had always been very careful with his public perception. Glancing between the two seated beside him, it bothered him that they were not.

While Fitzwilliam was obstinate in his reluctance to court the media, David had no problem with making a spectacle of himself at every opportunity. Neither gave a damn about their public image. Well, he would make his point crystal clear with them tonight. His time was nearly at an end. Theirs was at hand. If he could just get through to them, together they would be a formable team that would carry this company forward to the next generation. If it was the last thing he did, he would make sure the legacy was passed on—*intact*. If only…

After dinner, the boys followed their father back to his study. "Sit," he commanded pouring them a brandy and handing it to them without even asking. When he was through with them, they'd *need* it, and more. Cutting through to the chase, he came directly to the point.

"David," he pinned his son with a stare, "you know I am most unhappy with your public image."

"Yes, sir," David stiffened, "I am aware of it."

"Have you seen this?" His father handed him a copy of the latest tabloid.

David looked at the front cover. Staring at the image of him in a compromising position with one of England's most famous triple X actresses, his muscles twitched. The caption read *"Billionaire Darcy Heir in love with Porn Star Sandra Hamilton."* David's jaw clenched as he shook his head in disgust while he skimmed the article. Glancing up, he threw the paper back at his father in revulsion. "I don't read this rubbish."

"Well," George stormed, "most of Britain does! Damn it David, the *Star* is reporting a speculative engagement between you and Miss Hamilton. And let me make it *very* clear, there had better be *no* such engagement, or I will cut you off completely. Do you understand me, David Jamison? I'll not have it!"

"Clearly!" David said coolly though his eyes were set with fire.

George Darcy cleared his throat and leaned into his second son. "You needn't be saucy with me, David Darcy. I know you, and I know what's best. And you can rest assured I *will* demand it. Which brings me back to point. I have more complaints than this supposed engagement. It's being reported in the other scandal sheets that you have dipped your nib in half the sullied ink wells in the Kingdom. David, they're reporting you as one of the worse libertines in all of England, the worst since the Prince Regent, and I don't like it—any of it!"

David took a rather large gulp of brandy and breathed deeply. ...*Well, I wonder where I learnt it!*

George followed with a large sip of his own before laying into his son. "I want you to know, David Jamison, that *this* is the kind of thing that embarrasses both the board and me. *You* are a member of Pemberley's board of directors and in line for the Chairman of the Board and CEO. How do you think this looks?" he angrily demanded. "People are talking! They say you have slept with almost every actress or model in London. And what's worse, you do it openly for the whole world to see. Your behavior is appalling! Pemberley has certain standards, and disrespect for the position you hold is *unacceptable*. The board expects better of you. *I* expect better of you," George shouted. "I expect the both of you to remain on the cutting edge of both integrity and dedication to your purpose. By your behavior, you are not *fit* for your position. Neither of you!"

"Father," David snapped, "my activities are grossly exaggerated, and the board need only look at their own sons before scrutinizing mine." David knew how this was going to be received, but it was the absolute truth. One only had to look at his cousins for confirmation of this fact. Many frequented sex clubs, had been responsible for several unplanned pregnancies, and were known to have an affinity for cocaine—all of it kept quietly out of the public eye, covered up with family money.

Mr. Darcy's fury unleashed. "Their sons do not sit on Pemberley's Board of Directors, nor do they get their pictures in the tabloids. Damn it, David! Their sons have the decency to be discreet. Is that too much to ask of you? You do *not* behave this way in public where pictures can be taken! David, public opinion is paramount. Negative publicity hurts Pemberley, lowers your standing with the shareholders, and affects how the board views you. I'll not have a son of mine behaving in this manner!" Pounding his fist, he sent papers flying. "You are viewed as irresponsible and reckless, not possessing the ability to take Pemberley forward. Negative behavior translates into a lack of dedication, and *that* translates into a lack of confidence. Whilst some in our social class can get away with it, damn it David, *you* cannot!"

Mr. Darcy steadied himself and looked directly into David's eyes, reining in his anger. "This is *non-negotiable*. I want you married and settled down. I'm already making arrangements to have you introduced to some suitable girls. I want you to choose one by this summer. That is if I can convince their fathers to overlook your sullied reputation. Fathers today want their daughters treated well."

"Like you treated Mother?" David shot back hotly.

Taken aback, Mr Darcy drew in a deep breath. "What is it with you and your brother? Your mother understood, apparently better than either of you. She knew her place!"

"No, Father, I don't think she did," David ground out bitterly.

"You will **do** as I say, David Jamison Darcy. My brother has two sons who could take your place, and do not *ever* mention your mother to me again! You don't know what you're talking about. Do you understand me?"

"Perfectly!"

George turned to his older son and lit into him. "Now *you*, Fitzwilliam Alexander, your public image is only marginally better than your brother's. Stories are circulating that you are not fit to head Pemberley, either. The financial editorial pages say that *if* your heritage was important, you would be here, taking an active role in the family business. Look at this!" He flung a newspaper in his son's direction with a caption reading "*Danger in the Darcy Family.*"

"There is talk that you plan to leave the family business entirely. No one knows where you are, so they speculate, and I don't like it one damn bit!" George barked. "You are to come home after this year. Is that clearly understood?!"

Fitzwilliam released an exasperated sigh, tossing back a large swallow of brandy. The air hung thick with tension as father and son stared each other down. After a long uncomfortable moment, George spoke, his voice somber and cool as he broke the deafening silence.

"Fitzwilliam, pay close attention to me." George leaned forward. "This obstinacy of yours must come to an end. I want you married! And I want it to be Anne. I have promised Hilda we will have a merger. Anne will be a big asset to you since she will double, if not triple, our income—"

"Father, how much money do we need," Fitzwilliam interrupted, "and why do you let Hilda dominate you so? She's a thorn in our side. I've already told you I don't love Anne, and I never will!"

"Enough, Fitzwilliam! A merger with Hilda is not only prudent, it's smart. Her power and influence carries a great deal of weight. Money is power and Hilda Vanderburgh *is* money. If she's your enemy, she can break you. If she's your friend, nobody can touch you. Hilda is never to be underestimated. Can the two of you not see how things are?" He stressed. "We have to please the board, the shareholders, and those in power in the global economy. All I'm trying to do is preserve Pemberley for the future and to insure that it stays in Darcy hands. I am simply asking you to do your duty."

"Father, I can't do this." Fitzwilliam jumped to his feet and began pacing the floor. "All I have ever wanted is a simple life with a woman that loves me for *me*. I want to teach. I know that someday I'll have to give that up. I understand my responsibilities, but I thought I could follow my own desires for a little while—at least whilst you're still active within the company." He turned, catching his father's severe look.

"Fitzwilliam, take your seat!"

Staring at his father, he turned and dropped into his chair.

George Darcy shook his head and placed his hands on the sleek mahogany finish of his desk as he pressed forward. "Fitzwilliam, you and David are Darcys. You can't have the luxuries of other men. You were born to a different sphere. The two of you, especially you, Fitzwilliam, were born for a reason and a purpose. It's best if you come to terms with that fact," he said. "Both of you must understand that whoever runs this company *is* this company. You *are* Pemberley's image. It was built over the generations, piece by piece, with the blood, sweat, and tears of dedicated men—Darcy men, and I will *not* have the two of you destroy everything this family has sacrificed to build! If the board hears of this conversation, they will *remove* you—both of **you**!"

Fitzwilliam took a deep, steadying breath before emptying the contents of his glass. "That isn't the way it's always been. I've read **The Masters of Pemberley**, and I *know*, starting with the first Fitzwilliam, it was different for at least a hundred and fifty years. He married for love and did quite well. In fact, we owe much of our fortune to him and his son, Alexander, also married the woman he loved as did all of Fitzwilliam's sons."

"I am aware of our history, Fitzwilliam." George said. "His family didn't approve, and neither would have I, had I been there. His uncle, Lord Matlock and his aunt Lady Catherine both broke from him publicly. Lady Catherine never spoke to him again. He was simply lucky. Drive, determination, ambition, and desire are what it takes. The bottom line is…can you deliver the *goods*? Can you turn a profit for the shareholders? You've **got** to have that fire in your belly—the fire that burns hot when under the gun, and I'm beginning to wonder if either of you has what it takes to run this company. As it stands currently, neither of you do!"

He paused, looking from one to the other, and held up his hand. "Do you see this ring?"

The brothers nodded.

"For five hundred years the man who sat at the helm, keeping watch over the keep, has worn it. It is a ring that signifies power and the family name. I wear it. My father wore it, his father before him wore it, Fitzwilliam wore it, and Alexander wore it. And *you*, Fitzwilliam, will one day wear it, but will you be worthy?" George solemnly shook his head. Glancing between his two sons, he cleared his throat. "Like my forefathers before me, I understand what it takes to run this company, but do either of you?" He threw up his hands in acquiescence before taking his drink and downing it. "We will continue this at another time," Mr. Darcy said, dismissing them with a wave of his hand.

Later that night, David planned to meet his brother in his private sitting room. As he paced about his own sitting room, many things were coursing through his mind. This evening's family meeting had shaken him badly. And as a result of it, one thing had become crystal clear to him. He would have to break off his public trysts with his longtime girlfriend, Sandra Hamilton in lieu of a more *private* affair. He wondered how Sandra would take the news when he told her, but if she wished to continue seeing him, she would have to abide by his wishes. If not, he would drop her. He had warned her about the tabloids, and she understood perfectly his concerns. She might be his favorite girlfriend, but she was *not* indispensable.

His own private life neatly tucked away, his mind shifted to his brother. He and Fitzwilliam had discussed his brother's situation at length after they had left their father's study and decided to put everything aside for now. However, in light of what had transpired, David had considered it further. If he was going to help his brother defy their father, he had to know everything there was to know about this Elizabeth Bennett. He knew how much Fitzwilliam wanted a wife and a family, and he also knew that his brother had already had one failed relationship ten years ago with hardly anything in-between. The fact that this Elizabeth was an American and that his brother had only known her for four months, weighed heavily on his mind. He had to make sure his brother was not being drawn in once again by some fortune hunter. Only then would he feel confident enough to take a stand against their father. Passing his hand over his face, he exited his room in route to his brother's.

David entered Fitzwilliam's sitting room to find him with a bottle of brandy and a box of cigars. Fitzwilliam poured two glasses and motioned for his brother to take a cigar. "Do you know how long it's been since I've had a fine cigar?" He blew a ring of smoke. "You can't buy these in America, and the liquor there is not as fine as we have here. They drink Jack Daniels and Kentucky Bourbon." He grimaced. "They're an acquired taste." Fitzwilliam leaned back in his chair and stretched out his long legs, enjoying his Cuaba Generosos and drink.

David took a sip of brandy and then lit his cigar. "So, Fitzwilliam, tell me about this American woman who has bewitched you. Is it really love or something else? It's been many years since you've been with a woman."

"You come straight to the point, don't you? Well," Fitzwilliam chuckled, "it's a little of both. I do love her, and it is time for me to settle down. And I do need her in the way you're insinuating, but there's so much more to it than the physical aspect. She's the best woman I have ever had the pleasure of knowing—very intelligent, and beautiful, too. She can hold her own with almost any subject we choose to discuss, and sometimes she even gets the better of me. There's nothing like an intellectual challenge, and she's certainly that. Let me tell you the story from the beginning."

Fitzwilliam related the entire story to his brother, starting with the latter part of July up until his departure to London, omitting the finer details of his last night in Tennessee. He revealed to David about the coffee shop, how they met, her love for horses and hounds, and finally her family farm and his suspicion of a family connection to which David listened to with keen interest, asking several questions before nodding for him to continue. Lastly, he told him about their lively discussion on history, literature, and current events and then how he proposed to her.

"So she didn't know who you were before you proposed? You say she was hesitant at first concerning marriage?"

"Yes, she was," he said. "I know our love developed rather quickly, but I pushed much more than she pulled. And she is willing to marry me with or without the Darcy conglomerate. She's not poor by American standards, but it's nothing compared to our wealth. And, David...I love her." His lips twisted into a sly grin. "She completes me in every way and brings out the best in me. I want you to know her. You'll love her like a sister." He reached for the book resting on the side cabinet. "Here, look at these pictures. This one," he pointed, "is of her on her white Lipizzan stallion with her hair down her back covering her like I've always pictured the heroine from Tolkien's *The Tale of Beren and Lúthien*. And here, look at this. She's wearing those blue jeans with a hole in the knee and the white tee shirt I first saw her in."

"Hmm... She's got a great body. I can appreciate that." David softly laughed. "She is beautiful."

"Yes, I would definitely say she is at that. Look at this one. She's sitting on the same horse, and see how beautiful she is with her hair blowing in the wind."

"Ah, I like this one of you in the swing with her in your lap," David laughed, shuffling through the pictures. "Her smile is evident in each picture, but it's your smile in this last picture that stands out to me. I don't ever remember seeing you this happy."

"I am very happy. She's the one—the one I've searched for, and to think I found her hidden away in a small, sleepy little town in the middle of nowhere."

David's lips pleasantly curled, perusing the pictures once more. "Hmm very well, I get your point. I do want to meet her someday. I can see that you clearly love her, and if she loves you half as much, I'll be very happy for the both of you. It looks like you'll marry a cousin after all," David said with a smile as he handed the pictures back to his brother.

Fitzwilliam chuckled. "Yes, it does at that, doesn't it?"

"Now," David said, turning with a smile, "we have to get past Father. He may remove you from the board, but I doubt he'll disinherit you, at least not completely."

"Well, if he does, I'm prepared for that. We'll make a living on what we have, if we must."

David shook his head and shrugged. "I really don't think you will have to worry about that, and I'll tell you why. With all of our talk about Father, I'll grant you one concession. He does love you as much as he knows how to love anyone. Of that, I'm certain."

Fitzwilliam rolled his eyes and laughed. "I hope you're correct." Taking another puff on his cigar, he asked, "Do you happen to know what he was alluding to with the board of directors?"

"Yes," David sipped his drink with a nod, "it seems that Uncle Dashwood, Stanley, and Wesley don't think you or I live up to the image of Pemberley, PLC. They would like to replace me with one of our Darcy cousins and *you* with Artimus Dashwood. In fact, there are several of the cousins that have long since despised us. They think I'm a pampered playboy, and that you're not dedicated enough to the company. Father fears that they may act to take the company away from the long line of first sons. That's why he's insisting that I behave and you marry well. With Anne's money, they wouldn't dare touch you."

Fitzwilliam frowned. "Which Darcy cousins?"

"The usual suspects. Edward, Charles, Edmund, Henry, Sebastian, and several others who're afraid to show their animosity publicly. They'll make a move if they think they can win."

"What about Uncle Harvey, and William and Benson?"

"Uncle Harvey stays out of it. He and Father have never gotten on very well. As for William and Benson, they support us. You know we have always been close with them."

"Well, let's just hope it doesn't come to a fight. I won't compromise my convictions, but I am a Darcy. If it ever comes to a showdown, you know where I stand. I won't let our legacy fall into ruin," Fitzwilliam said, downing his drink.

"I agree. I'm not looking forward to that fight, either."

"David, we'll cross that bridge when we come to it, if indeed it ever happens." Placing his pictures safely back in the book, he closed the volume and set it aside. "Now, one day this week I want you to come with me to pick out the rings. I already have in mind what I'm going to give her. Elizabeth doesn't want anything bigger than one or two carats with either white gold or platinum. I prefer platinum."

"Well, she could have asked for something more. You can certainly afford it."

"Yes, but that's not her. She prefers simple things."

"I'll see you tomorrow then, and I'll be glad to accompany you when you go shopping." David smiled as he left his brother's sitting room. Confident that it was the right thing to do, he would stand with his brother.

That night in his room David thoughts turned to his recent business trip to Charleston. His frustration was mounting. ...*What are these feelings I have, and more importantly, why do I feel anything at all. She's not right for me, and I'm certainly not right for her. We're too much alike...and yet... I can't get her out of my mind. ...Cecilia Lawton, what are you doing to me?*

Chapter Fifteen

...he caught a glimpse of a white bird...

Fitzwilliam frowned as he looked out over the garden from his bedroom window, unable to see a thing, as a dense fog covered the ground. It was the Winter Solstice, four days before Christmas, and he hadn't yet had the opportunity to visit Garrard's. Meetings with Pemberley's executive group, a meeting of the board, and many excruciating hours spent with his father poring over spreadsheets and financial reports had precluded any time for shopping, but today he had no engagements.

He sighed. The fog wouldn't be burnt off for another two hours, but there was a bright side to things. After ten minutes spent with his solicitor, he'd discovered that he was now worth £22 million as opposed to fifteen. With this unexpected revelation, he could afford to splurge on what he planned to buy for Elizabeth. With a smile, he jerked the curtains shut and turned to leave in search of his brother.

Finding David in his sitting room, he approached him and clapped his shoulder. "David, let's go to White's for lunch. The fog should be lifted by then," he said, moving to the window and looking out again. "We'll be meeting Bingley there. I also want to stop by Garrard's and look at rings for Elizabeth," he glanced back at David and smiled. "I want to find the perfect ring. Roger will drive us."

"Sounds good to me." David shrugged. "However, have you already spoken with Singleton? I thought he was busy this morning."

"He is," Fitzwilliam grinned, "with us."

"Ah, you have me on that one. Just give me fifteen minutes, and I'll be ready. I need to ring Cybil. I'm going out tonight."

"You go ahead. I'll meet you downstairs for coffee, but we won't leave for another two hours." With that, Fitzwilliam left his brother and hurried down the stairs.

For the first several minutes of the short drive, the brothers sat in silence before David finally asked, "I don't suppose you want to go out tonight, do you? We're going to the Embassy. You could come along for dinner, but you'd have to find a way home after that. I'm spending the night with Cybil."

"No, David," Fitzwilliam chuckled, "I don't. I've got things to do at home, and then I want to ring Elizabeth. I don't suppose you and Cybil could come by the house for a few minutes—no, don't answer that." Fitzwilliam held up his hand. "I was only joking. But seriously, why don't you consider dating someone you *could* bring home?"

"Because if I did that, not only would Father get ideas, but the press would never leave me alone until I had a ring on my finger." David shifted in his seat, his lips curving into a mischievous grin. "And you *know* they will find out where we're going today."

"Yes, I know. Let them speculate all they want. It doesn't matter to me. I suppose we could pay the sales clerk to deny everything." A wide grin spread across his features. "But then, that would never work. I'll take my chances."

"I'll cover for you so you can have the privacy you deserve. I can only imagine what it might be like otherwise. Well, here we are," David said as Singleton pulled in front of the store.

Getting out of the car, Fitzwilliam gave instructions. "Roger, pick us up in one hour, and then we're going to White's."

"As you wish, sir."

Strolling through the door of Garrard's, the Darcy brothers were recognized immediately. "Gentlemen, what a pleasure it is to see you today!" The manager extended his hand, greeting both brothers. "What might I assist you in?"

"I'd like to see your selection of platinum engagement rings ...and," Fitzwilliam whispered, "if you will, please keep it confidential."

"Mr. Darcy, you can be assured of that. We serve the most exclusive clientele in Britain," he smiled, "and we *are* discreet." He directed them to a sales associate in a small private viewing room with instructions to provide whatever the gentlemen wanted and to keep it quiet.

Even though Garrard's possessed one of the largest selections of rings available anywhere, Fitzwilliam found nothing suitable. "None of these are what I have in mind." He shook his head. "She's a very traditional lady whom, I believe, would prefer a solitaire, about one to two carats in size, and I want a blue diamond. Her taste runs along the lines of the mystical. Tolkien and Lewis are among two of her favorite authors."

The associate nodded. "Ah, I have just the ring, Mr. Darcy. It's the most expensive ring we carry and of the highest quality. It's a round, two and a quarter carat eternal cut solitaire—and it *is* a blue diamond."

"Fabulous!" Fitzwilliam beamed, "I would like to see it. It sounds like what I have in mind."

The associate gathered the cases and took them to the back, returning with the most beautiful ring Fitzwilliam had ever seen. He reverently lifted it from its case, sending shards of pale blue color dancing through the room as he held it up to the light, turning it ever so slightly in his fingers. It was an ocean blue solitaire on a delicate band etched with vines and leaves interspersed with tiny channel set white diamonds. The set was complete with a matching wedding band. It looked as he had always pictured the Silmaril from the world of Middle Earth would look, and it reminded him specifically of Lothlorien.

"I'll take it!" he eagerly declared. "She'll love it, and I'll take a matching band for her and one for me, along with a plain one for her. I want them engraved with the inscription *Elizabeth & Fitzwilliam*. They are to be resized to a size five for her and a size eleven for me."

The sales clerk hastily scribbled all of Fitzwilliam's instructions. When she had finished writing, she glanced up with a pleasant smile. "We can have those ready to be picked up by Wednesday of next week, if that suits you. Will there be anything else, Mr. Darcy?"

"Yes, I'll take these as well." Fitzwilliam pointed to an emerald pendant he wanted for a wedding gift and a beautiful pair of ebony bone hair sticks adorned with rubies for Christmas. "That'll be all." He gave the clerk a satisfied smile along with his credit card.

Once in the car, David eyed his brother closely, reflecting on the particular attention he'd displayed when selecting his purchases. He could see his brother was completely besotted and violently in love. David rolled his eyes. *...I hope I never act like that over a woman. But I'll do whatever it takes to help him. He's happier than I've ever seen him, and he deserves it. I wonder what she...? Darcy, you've got to shake this...* He released a heavy sigh. *...This is getting damned irritating. When I least expect it, she invades my thoughts, be it day or night...But not tonight... Tonight I'm* *going out ...Cybil has a way of making me forget everything... including you, Cecilia...*

Finally arriving at White's, they exited the car with special instructions for Singleton to pick them up within ninety minutes. Meandering through the crowd to their usual table, they found Charles waiting. "Bingley, how very good to see you," David said as he grabbed Bingley's hand. "Tell me, are you as taken with your Miss Bennett as my brother is with his?"

"Oh, indeed I am. I miss Jane terribly."

"Well then," David laughed as he took his seat, "I have to hear about *this* Miss Bennett, too. You're both acting like complete love-struck fools." Directing his gaze at his friend, he asked, "Charles, have you ordered yet?"

"Yes, I ordered what we usually have. Fitzwilliam told me he didn't have much time. I hope that's all right with you," Bingley said as the waiter approached with their order.

"That's fine. I'm in a bit of a hurry myself. I have to pick Cybil up at five."

"Still seeing Cybil, I see," Bingley chuckled, as the waiter set his sandwich, soup, and salad in front of him.

"Yes, when I'm in town, and she's not working."

After dismissing the server, Bingley leaned forward and asked, "David, why don't you date a nice girl? Surely you know more than show girls from strip clubs."

David laughed aloud, flashing a wide grin as he picked up his salad fork. "You already know the answer to that, so let's not talk about me. I want to hear about you and what you're doing. Tell me about this Jane Bennett."

As they began to eat, Charles related his story in full, explaining how he and Jane had met and how their relationship developed. Concluding, he stated, "David, I don't know when I've enjoyed life more. The school is small enough to form a personal relationship with other faculty members, as well as the more serious students, and yet, it's large enough to experience the full academic life."

"Bingley, it looks like you and Fitzwilliam have found your calling. It sounds laid back, sort of like your personality, and the people seem friendly enough, according to my brother."

"Oh, they are," Bingley replied while stirring his soup. "I enjoy the society very much, but I don't think you would. The night life is rather dull, unless you're interested in whatever is taking place on campus."

"Well, if catching a husband is the current rage, you're right, I wouldn't be interested." David lifted his sandwich.

"Oh, I wouldn't say catching a husband is the rage." Bingley laughed. "But they are people like you'll find anywhere else. You will come to wedding, won't you, and bring Georgiana?"

"I wouldn't miss it, and neither would Georgiana, but getting around Father will be the sticking point. He's not going to approve, and you know it," David said, casting a cautious glance at his brother.

Fitzwilliam nervously picked at his salad. "I know, David, believe me I know, especially after our last talk—or rather his last talk at us, but I'm going to persist in speaking with him. He may surprise me."

"I highly doubt it, but we'll see," David said, raising his glass to his lips.

"Darcy, you mean you haven't told your father?" Bingley frowned. "I guess that's the advantage I have over you. My money is in trust, the business is run independent of me, and my father is dead. But I honestly don't think he would have been as narrow minded as your father. I do feel for you."

"Well, I'll find out soon enough," Fitzwilliam said calmly, "but it doesn't matter. I'm over thirty, and I will do as I damn well please." Picking up his spoon to taste his soup, Fitzwilliam added, "Now let's find something else to talk about."

All agreed. They sat and talked for over an hour until Bingley finally looked at his watch. "We'd better finish up. I have to be at my solicitor's office in one hour. Belington needs to go over my personal finances with me before we return next week. I don't suppose I will see you again until we go back on the 30th?"

"No, I don't think so, unless you call 'round. With Pemberley complex officially closed for the Christmas holidays, I'm taking a trip to Hertfordshire tomorrow, and then to Pemberley. Ring me up after Christmas so that we can make plans for the return flight."

"Will do," Bingley said, getting up to collect his things. "I'll see the two of you later."

Chapter Sixteen

...Elizabeth belonged here... with him...in his life and in his bed...

Up bright and early the next day, Fitzwilliam prepared for his trip. As he packed enough clothes for one day, he thought about all he'd learned concerning Elizabeth's family. He was anxious to be on his way to gather the evidence he was looking for. He also wanted to go to Pemberley to see the old paintings in the family gallery and take a closer look at his own family history. He had many questions. Snapping the bag shut, he walked downstairs to his waiting Jag where he set out on the short scenic drive to Meryton and then on to Longbourn village.

He'd never had a reason to visit Hertfordshire, therefore he had no idea of what to expect. Glancing around as he entered the village, he suspected the house had once been on the corner of Longbourn Street and Church where a local pub now stood. He sighed as he continued on his quest. Once he reached his destination, it was not too difficult to check the records. First, he went to the Longbourn Parish Churchyard.

Reverently brushing away the dirt and debris from an old stone in a secluded area, he found what he had come to see—the grave of Thomas Nathanial Bennet. Thomas was buried next to Mary Elizabeth Beauford Bennet, and next to them were Edward Thomas Bennet and Frances Emily Gardiner Bennet. He pulled out his PDA. The record matched the name and dates Elizabeth had given him, and, as he already knew, Thomas Nathanial Bennet and his son, Edward, were his ancestral grandfathers.

As Darcy left the family cemetery, he thought he caught a glimpse of a white bird, but when he turned to catch the sight more fully, it was gone. He wrinkled his brow and looked about, but there was no bird. He shrugged it off and walked in the direction of the church. The rector was more than agreeable, and after checking the parish records he had provided, Darcy found what he was looking for—the birth confirmation of John Thomas Bennet, matching the exact date recorded on the gravestone in the Cumberland Plateau. It was the same family; therefore, John Thomas Bennet was indeed his distant uncle. As he closed the book, he wondered about the inscription on John Bennet's headstone. Was John Bennet speaking of him and Elizabeth? He needed to know more before he could make that judgment.

Having learned all that could be learned here, he left for Pemberley, taking the longer drive, savoring the scenic beauty of the English countryside. It had been so long since he had been to Pemberley that Fitzwilliam had almost forgotten the beauty of his boyhood home. As he pulled into the long drive to Pemberley House, a strange euphoria came over him.

"Pemberley," he whispered to himself. This was where he belonged...where his family belonged, and that included his brother and sister. The house was more than big enough for three families. He sighed gently as he rounded the curve to the Great Elizabethan Hall. *...I have grown apart from Georgiana. I need to rectify that. I love her, and I want her close to me... Family is important...at least to me.* Finally, when he pulled up to the house, two servants came out to meet him.

Dorothy Reynolds's beaming face greeted him as his Jag rolled to a stop. She had been in the Darcy family's employ for many years. In fact, for generations, her ancestors had worked for the Darcys. She was like a mother to him, and Fitzwilliam loved her very much.

"Master Fitzwilliam! It's so good to see you. I cannot tell you how glad I was to hear from you when you called yesterday."

"Dorothy, how have you been?" he asked, giving the older woman an affectionate hug while he kissed her cheek.

"I've been well, but I'm even better now, seeing you here at Pemberley. I've made the master suite ready as you requested and will have a light meal prepared for you immediately."

"Thank you. I want to change first and go for a ride. I'll eat when I get back. I especially came to see the family gallery. I feel like a trip down through the past."

As soon as he entered the house, he took the stairs two at a time and turned to the left once he reached the landing. Heading towards the gallery, Fitzwilliam reflected on his lineage while he contemplated the future. The gallery was old, holding images of five hundred years of Darcys as well as his own family. Walking the hall, he looked over the generations, observing how they all seemed to favor each other in appearance. While he studied each one, he remembered stories that he'd either read or had been told.

Finally, he reached the portraits he was looking for—Fitzwilliam Alexander Darcy and his wife, Elizabeth Rose Bennet Darcy. Staring at the portrait, he frowned. Why had he never noticed it before? He looked almost identical to his ancestor, and since David looked enough like him to be his twin, they both did. Then, he focused on the image of Elizabeth Darcy. He was amazed at how strongly she resembled his Elizabeth. Their hair and eyes were the same color with that same unmistakable sparkle, and their smiles pleased in the same manner. He marveled. Perhaps the past was going to meet the future. ...*Well, I dare say if we can be as happy as you were, then we shall be quite happy indeed.* He continued for several more minutes looking over the portraits, before turning to leave.

Once he had changed, Fitzwilliam walked to the stable, saddled his chestnut stallion, and headed out. Riding over the estate gave him a certain satisfaction as he explored places he and David had ridden as boys. A sudden peacefulness filled his heart, and he smiled as a herd of red deer bolted and thundered into the woods. *This is where I belong...My strength is renewed here...this is home.*

Fitzwilliam breathed deeply, taking in the crisp, clean, fresh air of the cool December afternoon. As he rode over the fields, he had one place in mind—the cove, his boyhood secret place where he and David had spent most of their time in the summer.

The cove was nestled back amongst a grove of ancient Spanish oaks that towered high over the earth. And in the heart of the cove was a large waterfall, roaring down out of the side of a steep hill, tumbling into a natural pool where they'd swam as boys. Beside the pool, there was a moss-covered spot of ground where they would lay, staring up at the sky with nothing in particular on their minds, except maybe contemplating their futures or solving world problems. As he galloped across the fields, he remembered the carefree days of his youth, of laughter and fun, and of summers gone by. Then, he thought of the future, his wife, and another set of children who would play here one day. His heart was light and filled with joy as he rode.

Entering the grove of trees, he slowed his horse. It was a little barren this time of year he thought as he glanced around, but it was still as he remembered it. Riding on into the heart of the cove, he stopped and dismounted and tied the horse to a low hanging branch. Walking over to the thickly carpeted mossy floor near the waterfall, he paused, thinking that someday he would bring Elizabeth here as his wife and make love to her right here on this very spot in the wilds of the outdoors. This would be their place—a special place for them alone. Gazing at the waterfall, he closed his eyes, imagining them swimming naked in the pool. Fitzwilliam smiled, amused with where his thoughts had taken him. Someday, he promised himself, he would return, and perhaps he would build her a replica of the cabin at Longbourn on the higher ground near the falls.

Returning to the house, he hurried to the kitchen. It was late in the afternoon, well past tea time, and all the activity of the day had left him famished. Hot soup and a sandwich, along with a cup of hot chocolate, were just the things he needed. After eating, he went to the library and selected the first volume of his ancestral grandfather's works, **The Masters of Pemberley Vol. I**, which contained a summary of the journals and writings of Fitzwilliam Alexander Darcy 1806—1866. He had read it, along with the others that went with it, several years ago, but he felt the need to read it again. Signing the register, indicating he had the book, he took it to his room.

Making himself comfortable, he settled in to read. Hours passed as he turned the pages. *...Hmm, it's just as I remember...He felt the obligation and sense of duty thrust upon him deeply and at such an early age, too.* Fitzwilliam laughed softly. *He was proud—like me in some respects. Pride under good regulation is never a bad thing.* He shrugged. *...He weighed his decisions carefully, as I do... What time is it?* He glanced at the clock upon the chimneypiece. *...It's time.* Pulling out his mobile, he keyed in her number.

"Elizabeth, love, how was your day?"

"Oh, well enough, I suppose. I'm getting ready for Christmas. We've been baking cakes, pies, and cookies. Kat made some fudge."

"What kind did she make?"

"Umm...French vanilla with candied cherries and triple chocolate with pecans and raisins—my absolute favorite." She giggled. "If I don't stay out of it, I'm going to get fat."

"I doubt you'll become fat," he laughed, "but just in case, you need to exercise."

"Well, I asked for that one didn't I? So tell me, how are you doing, and what are you up to?"

"I'm here at Pemberley looking over the estate and reading family history. And I'm up to six foot two." He chuckled as her peal of laughter echoed in his ear.

"Fitzwilliam, you know perfectly well what I meant. But I can see what you're up to. It seems you are reminiscing about old times, as I often do."

"You know me well. That's exactly what I'm doing—that and dreaming of you. I'd like to share my home with you someday."

"I'd love to see it." She sighed. "I love you, you know."

"Yes, I do know. I love you, too, and I can't wait to see you again."

"And I you," she whispered softly. "I suppose we should go. I know it's late there."

"Yes, it is, but before we say goodnight, I have one more thing to tell you. I stopped by Longbourn Parish today before coming up to Pemberley, and my hunch is correct. John Bennet *is* the brother to my ancestral grandfather, Edward, so we are distantly related. The church is still intact, but I'm afraid the house is gone."

"Somehow that doesn't surprise me on either account, given what we've already discussed. Nor am I surprised with your discovery, given what we have discovered here on my side of the family, although I am glad to have it confirmed. We are indeed cousins." She laughed. "Is there anything else?"

"Yes, I plan to go through the records I have here and discover what I can about the English Bennets. I'll do that tomorrow before I leave for London."

"Good. I'd really like to know about them."

"Elizabeth," Fitzwilliam hesitated, "do you suppose we are the fulfillment of the promise John Bennet made to my grandfather all those years ago? Do you think it *could* be us?"

"I don't know. I've never thought much about it, but I suppose it could be. To me it's just an interesting coincidence, and it's something to draw us closer, but I don't think there's anything to it more than that. Do you? I mean you don't really believe in such things as Fate or Divine Providence do you?"

"I don't know. It doesn't really matter I suppose. All that truly matters is that I love you, and I want you for my wife. That's all I care about."

"I love you, too, but Fitzwilliam, it is late, and I need to go. We'll talk about this when you come back."

"All right, darling. I'll ring you tomorrow. I love you."

"I love you, too. Goodnight."

As he hung up the phone, Darcy sighed heavily. Every night after talking to her, he felt the gnawing separation. He couldn't wait to see her again, to hold her, to make love to her. Glancing around the room, he breathed deeply as he turned down the bed and crawled between the covers. Someday this would be their room. Three hundred and fifty years of Darcy men had brought their brides to this room and over forty children had been conceived in this very bed. Elizabeth belonged here... with him...in his life and in his bed. He smiled. His day was coming. He hadn't written in one for years, but tomorrow he would begin a new journal...one to record his new life.

Chapter Seventeen

...he'd once married for love and look what had come of it...

Christmas came with all the Darcys home for the holidays. Georgiana had just arrived and was anxiously awaiting her brothers' return from their shopping outing. She smiled in contentment as she put her presents under the tree. The house was beautifully decorated with two large silk trees, one downstairs in the music room, and one upstairs in the formal sitting area, both adorned with fine hand-blown glass German ornaments and antique handmade silk roses. The stairwells were decked with silk boughs of holly mingled with pinecone laden fir, and there were elegant handmade candle arrangements in every room. The servants and professional decorators had garnished the house like a scene from a Victorian Christmas painting. All of it was lovely.

She sighed as she cast a cursory look at the grandfather clock. Where could they be? Walking over to the window and gazing out, she saw David's red Alfa Romeo come to a stop in front of the house. *David!* As soon as she heard David's rich laughter, she ran to greet her brothers. "Fitzwilliam! David! I'm so very glad to see you both." She flew into David's arms, hugging him tightly.

David lifted her off the floor and swung her around. "Georgie, you're home!" He kissed her cheek and hugged her tight. Releasing him, she grabbed Fitzwilliam next.

"Georgie," he said as he kissed her cheek.

"I've missed you both terribly. Come," she said, taking them by the hand, "let's go for a chat. It's been ages since we've talked."

All three walked, smiling and laughing, arm in arm to the drawing room where Georgiana called for tea. They talked for hours, catching up on everyone's news, with Fitzwilliam telling her about Elizabeth, mentioning that he was to be married, and that Bingley was to marry Elizabeth's sister.

"Fitzwilliam, I want to come to the wedding. I have to meet these ladies. Any woman who can capture my oldest brother's heart must indeed be special, for I know how long it's been since you've seriously dated, and I was beginning to worry about you." She clasped his hand and gently squeezed it. "I couldn't be happier. I know I will love her."

Georgiana turned and cast a loving smile towards her brother David. "I haven't lost hope in you, either. Someday a beautiful woman is going to turn your world upside down when you're least expecting it."

David chuckled. "Don't get your hopes up. Marriage is not for me. I want to stay single and spoil yours and Fitzwilliam's children rotten."

"I hear what you say, David, but I can still have my dreams for you," she said, as she reached for his hand. "You will take me with you to the wedding, won't you?"

"Georgie, you know I will. I could never deny you anything, except perhaps a sister-in-law." He winked and laughed.

"You cheeky devil, but I shall tell you what we will do. Whilst I'm here, I want us all to go to the theatre. *The Phantom of the Opera* is playing, and I so want to see it. We never spend any time together," she pouted, "and I want us to do so this Christmas, just the three of us. That's what I want for Christmas—some of your time." Georgiana released David's hand and turned back to Fitzwilliam.

"We'll go then," Fitzwilliam agreed. "You're right, we don't spend quality time together, and I want that to change. I want you to come and spend the summer with me. You will love Elizabeth and her family, and they will love you," he said with a smile. "The farm is beautiful, and I can only imagine how much more so it is in the summer with the fields planted in corn and wheat and the animals with their little ones."

"But won't you have to be here with Father?" Georgiana asked.

"Yes, I will, but we can still have a few weeks to ourselves. I want you to see Longbourn Farm. Then we will all come back to England together."

"Well," she smiled warmly, "I'd love to see it. Now come, we need to prepare for dinner. You know how Father is, and he's in an even fouler mood than usual. I thought he'd be glad to see me, but he barely acknowledged me," Georgiana whispered, hurt evident in her features.

"Don't worry," Fitzwilliam reassured her. "It has to do with David and me, not you, but let's not talk about it. Instead, let's enjoy the holidays," he said, giving his sister an affectionate hug as they walked towards the stairs.

Dinner was quiet, stiff, and formal as per usual with no one speaking. George noticed the tension and assumed he had created it, but it was Georgiana who took the initiative and broke the stifling silence.

"Father, would you like for me to play for you? It's been ages since we all had a night together. Would you like that?"

George Darcy put down his knife and fork and looked at his daughter. "Georgiana, that sounds lovely. The grand piano hasn't been played since you were here last spring, and it's Christmas Eve. Perhaps it would be pleasant."

So that night after dinner, Georgiana led the family party to the music room where she sat and played a variety of Christmas carols while she and her brothers sang. Mr. Darcy sat for the event, watching his grown children, regret slowly passing over him as he observed them.

...She plays like you, Anne, and she looks like you, too. I never noticed that before. Anne... Anne, what have we done? I barely know them, especially my daughter. He sighed deeply. "Georgiana, you play very well."

"Thank you, Father. Since you're rarely complimentary, I'll take it as a great compliment," Georgiana said tenderly, her eyes fixed upon her father.

"Georgiana, it is a heartfelt compliment, and I should give them more often." Mr. Darcy smiled. "Now if you will excuse me, I'm tired."

"But Father, aren't you going to open presents with us?" Georgiana asked.

"No, dear, I am not. I will see you in the morning."

Mr. Darcy wearily got up and walked towards the stairs. When he left the room, Georgiana turned to her brother. "What is wrong with Father? He looks so tired."

"As far as I know, it's nothing physical. He has been disappointed in us, but other than that, I have no idea," David replied, rather perplexed.

"Why would he be disappointed in you?" Georgiana glanced between her brothers. "Both of you are excellent men."

"Well, it seems we're not living up to the Darcy image and name. He wants us both married—and to women he picks, not to whom we would want." Fitzwilliam paused for a moment, furrowing his brow. "He doesn't know about my plans yet, so if you would, please let me tell him."

"Of course, I wouldn't want to cause problems."

Fitzwilliam rose from his seat and strolled across the room to the tree. "Georgiana, you could never cause problems. You're far too sweet for that. Even if it did slip, it would not be your fault. But just the same, let's keep it quiet until I'm ready to tell him. Now, let's exchange gifts, have some wine, and continue to play and sing. David, you or I will play next."

David laughed. "I haven't practiced since last year. But if that's what you want, then that's what we'll do."

They opened presents, laughing and playing. Fitzwilliam played and sang while Georgiana and David danced. Then David sang and played while Fitzwilliam and Georgiana danced. And on it continued until the hour grew very late. But before retiring for the night, Fitzwilliam proposed a Christmas toast. "To the future. May we find what is important and have the courage to embrace it. Let us be together this time next year with our family intact."

Touching their glasses, David added, "To the Darcys, may we be happy in the New Year to come."

That night while lying in bed, Fitzwilliam thought about what next year might bring. If all went as he intended, he would have his wife with him and perhaps there might be someone else, too. Maybe they would all be together at Pemberley. He smiled and released a long sigh at the pleasant thought. ...*Christmas... Christmas is for children...maybe...just perhaps. Hmm, I think I'll ring Elizabeth.* He picked up his mobile and made the call.

"Merry Christmas."

"Fitzwilliam! Merry Christmas to you, too. I so hoped you would call. I miss you. I wish we could have been together for the holidays. It snowed, and all I could think about was you—and us playing in the snow."

"I miss you, too, my darling, and I would love to play in the snow with you, but our time will come. I'll be home New Year's Eve. I can't wait to see you, Liz."

"Home?" Elizabeth laughed. "I thought England was your home."

Elizabeth may have laughed, but Fitzwilliam did not. "Elizabeth, home is wherever you are. And next Christmas, I want us to spend it together. You know, I've thought about our last night together. It's possible that we could have an addition to our family by next Christmas."

"Is that what you would really want?" she softly asked. "I mean, we're not even married."

"Yes, it is what I would want. Or at the very least, I wouldn't mind, and we will be married soon. We'll talk about it when I get there. If you aren't, then that will be okay, but if you are, I will be very happy."

"Well," she hesitated, "I hate to disappoint you, but I'm not pregnant."

"I see, but we still have time. However, that's not why I called." He paused for a second, hiding his disappointment so that his voice would not betray him. "I want to hear all about your day. Tell me, darling, how is your Christmas holiday?" he asked with a smile on his face as he propped back on his bed for the long, but welcomed, dissertation which he knew she would give.

"Well, let me see. I've already told you we had a major snow storm. The power was off for three days. We got twelve inches out here on the farm, and I believe they got eight in town. It began to snow while we were out searching for the perfect trees, but fortunately, the storm didn't hit until we had finally found what we were looking for."

"Perfect trees? You mean you cut your own Christmas trees—two trees?"

"Yes, two trees. A cedar for me in the upstairs sitting room, and a Scotch pine for Jane downstairs in the formal den."

"How fascinating that must have been, picking out your own trees," he muttered.

"Well, Daniel didn't think so. He was exasperated with my insistence that it be perfect with no holes."

"I can see him now." Fitzwilliam softly laughed. "He probably wanted to cut the first one he saw, thinking it was good enough."

"Exactly, but I wouldn't have it. However, when I saw the storm clouds moving in, I knew we had to hurry, or we could find ourselves up the creek without a paddle very quickly. But since we were in the cove, we would've had shelter if it had come to that. Anyway, we made it back just in time before the sky opened up."

He smiled. *...I can think of nothing better than being snowbound with you in that cabin.*

"Of course, we were worried about the snow, or at least I was because my sister Mary Beth was coming home for Christmas with her fiancé, André. He dances with my sister in New York, but anyway, back to what I was saying. I was worried."

"Did they arrive safely?" he asked with a slight frown.

"Yes, they did, but I am getting ahead of myself, so let me get back on track. When we came back to the house, Daniel set the trees up in their appropriate places. He strung the lights while Jane, Kat, and I decorated them. We have some antique glass ornaments, but more special are the ones which Mom and Dad helped us make over the years. We keep them in shoeboxes in the attic, one box for each of us, and bring them out every Christmas for the main tree downstairs. I'm going to email you some pictures of the trees and of Mary Beth and André, too. Our tree is not as pretty as some of the designer trees, but it is very special, representing a lifetime of memories."

"I bet it is." *...The kind of memories I want to build with you and our children.*

"When we were just about finished, Grace brought us some Christmas tea along with teacakes made from an old family recipe."

"What are they like?"

"Well, they are not a cookie per se, but almost like a biscuit, and they're delicious. These particular teacakes were made with crushed black walnuts from the cove."

"Hmm...black walnuts? I've never heard of them."

"Well that's because they're native to America." She giggled.

"That could be it." He returned her laughter.

"They grow wild all over these mountains, and the tea is something we only have during the holidays. It is made from dried orange peel and cloves. It's another one of Grandmother Bennett's recipes. I'll fix you some when you get here."

"That sounds lovely. I'll look forward to it," he said with a genuine smile, propped up in bed listening to the melodious sound of her voice.

"How is your father? Have you told him about us yet?"

"No," he hesitated, "I've not had the chance. Father is ...well ... very burdened down with business. We've had two lengthy talks, but it didn't come up. I plan on speaking with him in the next day or two. I'll tell you all about it when I come home."

"Home... I'm very touched that you think of Tennessee as home when you've only been here for less than five months."

"Elizabeth, I think of *you* as home, be it here in England, or there in Tennessee. Wherever you are *is* home."

"And that is why I love you. I'm very touched that you would feel that way about me."

"I feel that way and more. And next Christmas we *will* be together. I promise."

"Yes, we will. I know that. Fitzwilliam, it's getting very late. It must be close to daybreak there. It's two a.m. here. We need to go. I love you, and I look forward to seeing you. Daniel and Kat will remain at Longbourn until classes begin on the tenth, so we will have some privacy. Come home soon. I miss you."

"I miss you, too, Liz. I'll be home New Year's Eve. I love you, and I will see you then. Goodnight, my love."

"Goodnight or rather good morning, and I hope your Christmas Day is all that it should be."

Fitzwilliam slid his mobile shut and sat in quiet reflection. *...How differently we celebrate the holidays! Ours is cold and formal, except for the little bit Georgiana, David, and I share, whilst hers is warm and loving. She's everything I've ever wanted. Mum would have loved her.*

After hanging up the phone, Elizabeth lay awake, thinking about their conversation. *...Why do I get the feeling his Christmas is not as good as mine? He seemed lonely, out of sorts. I wonder if things are all right with his dad. Why has he not yet spoken to him? I wonder if his father will approve of me. Fitzwilliam says it doesn't matter to him, so I suppose it shouldn't matter to me either. Oh well, I trust him. That's all I can do.*

Elizabeth snuggled into her bed and fell into a restless sleep, disturbed, but not sure why.

The next morning, Christmas Day dawned bright and beautiful and very cold. Elizabeth quickly jumped out of bed and ran downstairs in her flannel nightgown and bare feet, her long braid trailing behind her. "Merry Christmas," she greeted her sister Mary Beth as she flew into the kitchen. The sound of church bells from Longbourn Church pealed through the air, and the smell of fresh apple-cinnamon scones and hazelnut cream coffee permeated the room.

"Good morning to you, too, and Merry Christmas." Mary Beth turned to greet her sister. "Lizzy, look! Look how beautiful and fresh the world looks this Christmas morning. It's magical."

Elizabeth came to stand beside her sister, gazing out the large window by the kitchen door. How beautiful indeed the world seemed, Elizabeth thought. Icicles dripped from the barren trees, and snow covered the ground, glistening in the brilliant sunshine like a blanket of diamonds. It formed a beautiful contrast to the deer off in the distance, foraging for what little food there was. And bright red cardinals enjoyed their Christmas feast of millet and suet in the winter feeders while fat bunnies ran hurriedly through what remained of the vegetable garden.

"Look, Mary Beth, aren't they beautiful? I mean the birds and the deer, and look at the rabbits."

"Umm, yes, Lizzy, they are. You know, I really miss the farm. It was the perfect place to grow up. We had such a good childhood, didn't we?"

"Yes... yes we did. I only hope we can pass on what Mom and Dad taught us."

"We will, Lizzy," Kat said as she lazily walked into the room to join her sisters. "I have no doubt of that, and you before me."

"Umm, that coffee smells wonderful. Pour me a cup—cream and sugar, please. And your day will come, Kat," Jane said, coming into the room.

"I know it will, but I'm in no hurry. I have my career ahead of me, which I am very much looking forward to," Kat answered, handing her sister a cup of coffee in their mother's best Christmas china.

As the girls enjoyed the scene from the large picture window, Daniel appeared all excited. "Joseph's on the phone, and he wants to talk with each of you. It's Christmas morning in Iraq, too, I think—or is it Christmas afternoon? Hmm... Oh never mind.

Come to the phone. Hurry!"

Fitzwilliam paced his bedroom floor and raked his hand through his hair as he glanced at the calendar on his desk. Two days remained before his return trip to the States, and yet he hadn't spoken with his father. He sighed heavily... *well the time is now.*

Leaving his room, he went in search of his brother, finding him in the library. "David, it's time. I've got to face him."

David closed his book and rose from his seat. "Well, let's go and get it over with."

Together they walked the long hallway, neither saying a word, silence and dread weighing heavily on them both. When they arrived, Fitzwilliam knocked on the doorframe.

Their father glanced up and put his pen down as he raised a brow in curiosity and bid them to enter with a slight wave of his hand.

"Father, I need to have a word with you."

"Would you like something to drink?" he asked, eyeing them both closely.

"No, thank you," they both answered in unison.

"Well then, out with it. What do you want?" he asked as he poured himself a brandy.

Fitzwilliam squared his shoulders and glanced between his brother and father. "I want to tell you. Well, that is, I need to tell you...that...that I have decided to marry."

"Is that so?" His father folded his hands and leaned back in his seat. "Why don't you tell me about it?"

Glancing at David, Fitzwilliam breathed deeply. "I'm marrying a wonderful woman from the university where I work." He paused briefly. "Her name is Elizabeth Bennett. She's an associate professor of mathematics, and I'm very much in love with her. She's beautiful, intelligent, and the most wonderful woman I've ever known. I hope to have your blessing, Father." Fitzwilliam stepped back.

The room was cloaked in hushed stillness for a full minute.

"Well, it seems that both of my sons are to disappoint me I see. First David, with his licentious lifestyle, and now *you*. You know I cannot give you my blessing. Our position in society and business interests forbids it. You are the grandson of an Earl. We belong to the highest stratum of society which this American will never reach, not even as your wife. I am certain she is a wonderful woman, as you say. I trust you in that much, but she is not of our sphere." Mr. Darcy hesitated and cocked his head. "Fitzwilliam, do you really think you can ask a modern woman—especially an American woman, to change for you simply because you claim to love one another." He paused once again, looking first at one and then the other. "I have sacrificed everything for this company. Apparently, I did not instill the same drive or force of determination in my sons for the same thing." He cast his gaze upon David. "I suppose you are here to lend support to your brother?"

David nodded in agreement.

"Father, it is not as you think. She's a wonderful young lady whom I'm certain will not disgrace the family, and you know nothing about her position in society. She was educated in one of the top schools in America. Her family was part of the gentry of the Old South and still remains prominent to this day. She is the descendant of an English Earl from the 17th century, and also from the same Bennet line from which we descend. I verified this when I visited Hertfordshire before Christmas. Her ancestor was the brother of Edward Bennet, our ancestral grandfather. She will not impede my position in this family. Father," he leaned down, placing both hands on Mr Darcy's desk. "I intend to claim my place in the Darcy legacy and carry this company and family into the future. I have been reading the journals of my namesake, and it seems he survived a similar family situation admirably. I know I can do the same. And Father, I will not ask her to change. I love her the way she is, and just as importantly, she loves *me* for who I am, not for what I am or what I have. Father, we love each other."

At this point, George interrupted. "I hear what you're saying, Fitzwilliam, and even if it's all true, what *was,* is *not* what is. The Old South is dead and a bloodline three, or even two hundred years into the past, is irrelevant," he said, holding his son's steady gaze. "I want you to know, I do understand what you are saying regarding your feelings, but as I've told you before, *you* are different. You have a duty and an obligation, and you need a woman who will understand that. Americans tend not only to miscomprehend duty and responsibility, but they have a flagrant disregard for the things we hold dear. If it ever comes to a place where you must take a stand and sacrifice for the company, she will falter and crumble like a two day-old biscuit. She will not understand. It is a cultural difference, Fitzwilliam. It would be like the Prince marrying beneath himself. It's just not done."

Fitzwilliam stood erect. "Father, things are changing both here and abroad—"

Mr. Darcy's eyes narrowed. "Not in this family, **not** as long as *I* am in charge. *That* will be understood. As for Fitzwilliam, your namesake, yes, he did do as you intend on doing, but if I'd been his father, I would have forbidden it. But since he was his own master, he did as he wished. As to the present, I cannot risk David as Chairman and CEO, therefore I have no choice, but if I had a son on whom I could depend, I would disinherit you *both*. Believe me when I tell you I have seriously considered it to the point of looking at my nephews, but in the end, I could not do that."

Fitzwilliam clenched his jaw in anger as he stalked the floor. "Father, I am going to marry her, and there's not a thing you can do about it. As I have already stated, I have my own money. I *am* my own master."

Mr. Darcy looked his oldest son directly in the eye. "If you marry her, Fitzwilliam, from that day forward we will be estranged. You will not be accepted back into this house as long as I shall live." Mr. Darcy glared at his younger son, and then back to Fitzwilliam. "You will, however, continue on the board. As I have already stated, I cannot trust your brother. So in that, you are spared my full wrath. That is all. You may be excused, the both of you." He dropped his gaze and picked up his pen.

"Father, you are making a mistake. David and I both love you, but we're not you, and you are wrong about David."

Once again putting his pen aside, he slowly raised his eyes to meet his son head on. "Fitzwilliam, you have a duty, both to your family and to Pemberley. I have already told you where that duty lies—"

Fitzwilliam cut him off, his anger flashed. "Father, you astound me! You have the audaciousness to speak to me of duty and responsibility to family, yet *you* neglected your most important duty and responsibility of all—your duty to *us*. What irony. What audacity you have to speak to *me* of duty and responsibility! What about your duty and responsibility to your *wife* and *children*. You think I don't know what went on between you and Mum? Well, I *do*…I've known for years."

Mr. Darcy dropped his gaze, staring down into his empty glass as his son continued.

"I was there, and I saw what you did to her. Remember your fortieth birthday? Well, I remember it *very* well," he scoffed as he looked from David to his father. "Do you remember how Mum found you when we all came up to see you? Mum sent me away, only I didn't go. I stood in the servants' entrance and watched. So don't talk to me about family duty and responsibility. I've seen quite enough, and I've been sick of it for years."

His father raised his eyes and with a cold, calm, collected voice he responded, "Fitzwilliam, if you marry this woman, I will not give you the time of day."

"Father, do you even know the time of day? Have you ever known?!"

An uncomfortable silence filled the room until George Darcy finally broke the still ambience. "Leave me, Fitzwilliam. Leave me, David." Picking up his pen once more, he resumed his writing.

"Is that all the answer I'm to receive?"

George glanced up. "I believe we've said quite enough, don't you? Now, if you will excuse me, I have a letter to write."

Fitzwilliam stormed out of his father's study, slamming the door behind him as he and David cleared the threshold, fury coursing through his veins. He would do everything he could to be faithful to both himself and his family obligations, but his father's words stung at his heart and sensibilities.

While he watched his sons leave, George Darcy placed his pen aside, staring at the closed door as he stroked the signet ring on his right hand. Sitting alone in his study, he poured himself another brandy. He felt tired and old...very old. He remembered a woman he'd once thought of as beautiful and intelligent. She, too, had been the most wonderful woman he'd ever known. Yes, he'd once married for love, and look what had come of it. It had wrecked his life and cost him everything he'd held dear, including his children. He wiped a tear from his cheek.

...Fitzwilliam will marry his American woman and there is nothing I can do about it. He shook his head as he sipped his drink. *... but I must keep this marriage as quiet as possible. ...Anne, Anne, I never realized our marriage would affect them as deeply as it has. But I have to do what I have to do ...for Pemberley...for them. I have to protect them and their heritage. Everything I do now is for my sons...*

Walking down the long hallway towards the front of the house, David smiled. "Fitzwilliam, I'm sorry, but it's not as bad as it could have been. I told you he would not disinherit you. Marry your elvish princess and let the next generation of Darcys be happy." David slapped Fitzwilliam on the back, feeling rather proud of his big brother.

"David, when it's our turn to run things, we're going to do it differently. I want both you and Georgiana to share Pemberley House with Elizabeth and me. We can make a home for our families like Mother would have wanted. I will never, and I mean *never*, treat my wife and family the way Father has treated us. He infuriates me!"

"Fitz, you're a good man." David chuckled. "We'll see."

As they turned the corner and headed to the outside, David's mind wandered ...*I wonder what she's doing tonight... NO! I don't need to be thinking about her.*

Before Fitzwilliam's plane landed in Nashville, reports were circulating around Britain that he and David had been seen entering Garrard's, and that both brothers had bought engagement rings for two mysterious ladies. George Darcy denied everything, immediately contacting his public relations coordinator to circumvent the rumors, while David only smiled with a *no comment*. Fitzwilliam was unavailable to make a statement, his father claiming he was on a business assignment. David laughed at the absurdity of it all.

Chapter Eighteen

...the woman he'd always wanted...

Jane paced back and forth in front of the picture window, parting the curtains every now and then, peering out into the front lawn. "Elizabeth, will you check the pot roast? It should be about done. The green beans are ready, and the potato casserole is about there." Jane casually spoke as she turned from the window. "I think another five minutes will do it. We need to get those rolls in the oven, and how are you doing with the lemon cream pie?"

Elizabeth rolled her eyes. "Jane, everything is set. One would think you were anxious. I mean it's only been, what, twenty days? But who's counting?"

Jane giggled. "You're right, Lizzy. I am anxious, but they will be here when they get her. Let's talk of something else. Ever since our last talk, I've been thinking. You know there has been a pair of albino doves seen in the vicinity of Longbourn church—especially in the old graveyard. Do you think they are linked to the old Cherokee Legend?"

"Jane, not you, too. Grace has mentioned those doves as some sort of sign from God. Surely you don't hold to superstition. You know better than that. You're an educated woman, for Pete's sake."

"Yes, but still, Lizzy, there are some things that cannot be explained, such as Blackberry Winter or why sauerkraut ruins if a woman is on her period when she's making it. Not everything can be explained with logic or science," Jane said. "Lizzy, we're not just of English descent. We're Scots Irish, too. And the Scottish have second sight. We have the ability to know things. Edward Bennet's wife, our great-great-great grandmother, Mary Alice Prophet, was Scottish, and their only daughter, Cordelia had the sight, and—"

"Yes, I know. You think you have it, too. We've discussed this before."

"Lizzy, listen to me. Don't pass me off as someone who has lost her mind just because I am different from you. I think there is something to all of this. Aunt Cordy gave a foretelling about the legend. Cordelia Bennet Cole lived to be a hundred years old, Lizzy, and on her death bed she spoke a prophecy. She saw a vision of a dark haired man and woman. She said the fulfillment would come through the line of first sons. Except for the Scottish line, we were all blonde. And there was one other salient thing." Jane took a deep breath and looked her sister directly in the eye. "She said that someday a dark haired man would come from England and the Bennetts would reunite, but the course of true love would not run smooth. She said our destiny is fixed by Fate. The family talked about it for years. Lizzy, I have a strong feeling about this. You told me over Christmas that Fitzwilliam is distantly related to us through the English Bennets. What if the doves mean something? What if it's true?"

"It's not. It's merely a coincidence. Jane, I can't believe we're having this conversation. I don't believe in Scottish folklore, second sight, Indian legends, or white doves. Let's not talk of this anymore. It unnerves me. The next thing you will be telling me is that something bad is going to happen. I won't have it. I'm too happy to even consider it. We've got better things to occupy our time rather than prattling on about superstition. Charles and Fitzwilliam are due here any minute. Let's think about them."

"All right," Jane said as she breathed deeply and rolled her eyes with a smile. Her sister, who had a keen intellect and a sharp mind, was as stubborn as mule and blind as a bat when it came to things that defied logic, and Jane was well aware of the difference that existed between them. She also knew her sister well enough to know where the line was and when to stop, so the subject was quickly dropped.

While the sisters continued to talk of other things, the doorbell rang. Jane hurried to the door. "Charles, Charles, I'm so glad to see you," she squealed, throwing her arms around his neck.

Elizabeth stood back and looked on with an amused smile, watching Jane make a display. But her amusement quickly faded when Fitzwilliam came through the door. Darcy moved with a slow deliberate walk—a walk filled with great confidence and pride. When he reached her, her arms instinctively curled around his neck as he pulled her into a tight embrace, kissing her again and again. Stepping back, he reached and brushed an errant curl from her face.

"I've missed you, Liz." He smacked her bottom playfully. "Now, what's for dinner? It smells good and I'm hungry." He smiled seductively, the heat in his dark eyes leaving her in no doubt of his unguarded double entendre.

"Come this way," she breathed out. "It's almost done. Let me take your coat."

After they finished their meal, the men loaded the dishwasher while the ladies put the food away. When the kitchen was clean, they took the pie and coffee to the front parlor where they all nestled in for conversation.

"Our brother, Joseph, has been in contact. Things are rather slow right now, so he will be coming home next week for one month," Jane said, serving Charles a slice of lemon pie. "It's the first leave he's had in almost three years. His birthday is in three days. He'll be twenty-five."

Fitzwilliam turned to Elizabeth. "You and your brother are that close in age? It escaped me before."

"Yes, we're eleven months apart and very close."

"I gathered as much from all of your escapades. Especially the exploding cow piles."

"Exploding cow piles?"

"Don't ask, Charles. I'll explain later." Jane rolled her eyes.

"She's right. You don't want to know," Fitzwilliam said, affectionately squeezing Elizabeth's knee.

Elizabeth put her cup back in its saucer. "Oh, forget about that." Elizabeth smiled tightly. "It's nothing really. I was about to tell you about Daniel and Kat."

Fitzwilliam's lips curled. "Carry on then."

Elizabeth took a slight breath and began. "Daniel wants to move into the civil engineering frat house, and Kat has decided to move in with Marion Henley and Sandy Burns. Since she already spends all of her time at their apartment, studying, moving in with them would be a good option for her."

"That sounds well and good for Kat, but don't you think Daniel is a little young to be on his own?" Darcy asked.

"No, not really. Our older cousin, James Barnett, is the house advisor. He'll watch after him. Besides, Daniel needs his freedom and space."

"Well, if you say so, then I'm sure he'll do fine." Darcy smiled. "Is there anything else? You look as if there's something else on your mind."

Elizabeth hesitated. This next news she'd just as soon not tell. "Well, yes...there is one other thing," Elizabeth dropped her eyes. "It's our cousin, Liddy. She says she's going to marry Jackie Lee Nunley...the drug dealer you heard about at Thanksgiving." Elizabeth cringed. The worried look on Fitzwilliam's face did not miss her notice. She looked to Jane who took the subtle hint and picked up the conversation.

"I'm afraid our cousin Liddy is the talk of the town right now, and Elizabeth and I are both embarrassed. We get questions and looks, and it's...well...it's uncomfortable. Walnut Grove is just a sleepy little Southern town made up of mostly farmers and local merchants. Since nothing ever happens around here, it was quite a shock to discover we were supplying most of the pot and cocaine for the Southeastern Hub." Jane paused for a sip of coffee and cleared her throat. "It has been discovered that Jackie Lee was growing the largest and most potent marijuana in this country." She cast an uneasy glance between her sister and Charles. "It's also come to light that he has connections to a drug lord in Colombia, South America. He was importing cocaine into the United States and selling it out of Knoxville. He had quite an operation in place. And rumor has it that his empire may have reached as far as Canada. Anyway, the Canadians are interested in the investigation."

"The U.S. Attorney's office wants him to give up his contact for a reduced sentence or possibly no sentence," Elizabeth interjected as she poured herself another cup of coffee. "If they can catch a bigger fish, they would be even happier, or so I've heard. Also, of all things, his attorneys intend to play the family card should he and Liddy marry."

"Elizabeth, that sounds terrible. Would they really give him such a light sentence or let him off? I don't think that's likely." Fitzwilliam put his cup down, leaning back to catch her every word.

"That's what Uncle Randy says, but I doubt it, too. My uncle is trying to cover for his daughter who is hell bent on disgracing us all."

"Lizzy, we'll get through this like our family always has, by sticking together and supporting one another. Nobody is going to blame us, and I don't see how they could blame poor Liddy, either. She's young—only twenty-one. Girls that age make mistakes all the time," Jane said as she tried to set her sister's mind at ease.

Charles nodded in agreement.

"For God's sake, Jane, she's pregnant! This isn't a small mistake," Elizabeth railed. "She will take everyone down with her to get what she wants. And what kind of life will that child have? Lydia and Randy will have to raise it. They have no money. We will have to help them. It will be expected." Elizabeth picked up a napkin, twisting it nervously.

"Lizzy, if they need us, it's our Christian duty to help. After all, Lydia is Daddy's sister. He would take care of her and her family if he was here, and you know it. He loved her. We owe it to Daddy to help them if they need it."

"Well, I don't know why he cared so much. She only used him for what she could get from us. She squandered her inheritance and then wanted more. Our cousin is no different. She hasn't got a lick of sense and takes every opportunity to goad us. You know that. Besides, Jane, Liddy thinks things are owed to her."

"Lizzy, please, they are family. It will all be forgotten in time."

"Perhaps. It's just that I expect people to be responsible and honorable, and the Nunleys and our cousin are neither. Don't get me wrong. I do feel for Liddy, if for no other reason than she's too damned stupid to come in out of the rain. And blind, too." Elizabeth fidgeted with her napkin, ripping it in shreds.

"Elizabeth, it will pass, and as you have said, she is your cousin, not your sister." Fitzwilliam took the napkin out of her hands then took her small hand in his, patting it gently.

"I know. It's not that." She shook her head. "We're a close family. When one of us hurts, we all hurt." She looked poignantly at Fitzwilliam. "This is going to make the national news, and I will be so embarrassed. No, I'm already embarrassed. I'm mortified. The local networks out of Knoxville, Chattanooga and Nashville, the major three, and CNN and Fox News will all be here during the trial, swarming like bees in a honey hive. They will be all over us looking for a story. I don't like it one bit. Our whole family will be scrutinized, and Liddy will make a fool of herself while Uncle Randy and Aunt Lydia will be helpless to stop her. I know I am coming across as cold and unfeeling, but I can't help it." She looked directly at her sister. "I'm so angry. Liddy may be our cousin, but she is one of the most vain, self-centered persons I have ever known." Elizabeth glanced between Charles and Fitzwilliam. "While it is true just as Jane says, I have never understood it. Father always overlooked everything where Lydia and Liddy were concerned. I know he loved his sister, but that doesn't excuse it. I'm so embarrassed that the two of you will be exposed to this," she said, casting a fleeting look between Charles and Fitzwilliam.

"Elizabeth, please," Jane begged. "You are making a mountain out of a molehill."

"Jane's right." Charles glanced at Fitzwilliam. "You needn't worry about us. Darcy and I will stand by you and Jane. It isn't going to change how we feel, is it, Darcy?"

"No, not in the least. Elizabeth, don't concern yourself. It doesn't matter. Let's not talk of it any longer." Fitzwilliam pulled Elizabeth into a reassuring hug, but he was anything but sure himself as his thoughts drifted to his father. Although the thought of publicity of this kind connected to him, and eventually his family, bothered him, he chose to push it aside. He would consider it at a later date.

As the evening wore on, Fitzwilliam pulled Charles aside for a private talk. "Charles, how are we going to manage this? I want time alone with Elizabeth, and I know you feel the same way about Jane. What do you suggest we do?"

"Well, Jane and I are going to watch a movie. You can join us if you like, and then…" Charles paused for a second, rubbing his chin. "Do you think Elizabeth would stay with you at our house tonight, and perhaps I could stay here since Kat and Daniel are still at Longbourn? I don't know where your relationship is in that regard, but I suspect it's the same as ours."

"I think she would, and since that's agreeable with you, I'll ask her. I'm not interested in a movie. You and Jane go ahead. I want to talk with Liz. We'll go to the library and listen to music whilst we talk."

"Sounds good to me." Charles grinned.

When the men returned to the ladies, Fitzwilliam and Elizabeth left for the library. As soon as they were alone, Fitzwilliam gathered Elizabeth into his arms, murmuring between kisses, "Liz, stay with me tonight. In fact, stay with me this week whilst Kat and Daniel are at Longbourn."

"What about Charles?" she whispered.

"Charles won't mind. I've already spoken with him. He's staying here with Jane. I need you tonight. Come home with me…stay with me," he urged. His voice deepened as he continued to trail kisses gently down the side of her neck.

Quivering from the rush of warmth rising in her, Elizabeth closed her eyes. "You certainly have a way of convincing a girl, don't you?"

"I'm a man set to his purpose," he answered in hushed tones, "and my purpose is *you*."

"All right," she said quietly. "I don't think Jane will mind. I'll speak to her privately once the film is finished. Let's pick out some music. Then we can just sit and talk. I want to hear all about your trip to Hertfordshire and what you found out."

"Not tonight, Liz. I have other things on my mind. When the time is right, I'll tell you everything. Right now all I want to do is hold you."

After selecting a few CDs, they took a seat on the sofa where he pulled her into an embrace as they lay down together, snuggling close. "Liz, you don't know how much I have missed you. I've thought about you day and night, especially at night."

She smiled, lifting her head from his shoulder, "I've missed you, too. My days have been busy, but my nights have been lonely. Hold me." She rested her head in the curve of his neck and slipped her arms around him.

With a contented sigh, he said, "Next time I go to England I will take you with me as my wife." He squeezed her gently. "We have much to discuss, but it'll wait until we get home—to our house. Elizabeth, we belong together," he whispered, brushing his lips against hers before catching her mouth with his as he pressed their bodies together. They listened to the music, one CD after the other playing while they held one another, occasionally kissing, as the night closed in around them.

Finally fatigue from the long trans-Atlantic flight began to set in. But tired as he was, sleep was not what Darcy had on his mind. "Elizabeth, it's eleven o'clock, and if we stay here much longer, I am going to drift off. Let's collect your things and go home before we both fall asleep. I have much I want to tell you, and I have some things I bought for you. Two of them are a surprise, but as you can guess, I have your engagement ring. Let's go home."

"You really do think of us as a couple, don't you?" She laughed softly. "Do you realize you have said 'home' two times now?"

"As I've told you before, home is wherever you are, and I never exaggerate." Chuckling, he tapped the tip of her nose. "I'll explain later. Come on. Let's go." Pulling her up from the sofa, they walked into the den only to find Jane and Charles cuddled up on the chaise lounge fast asleep. As they quietly slipped from the room, Elizabeth quickly ran upstairs and packed her bag while Fitzwilliam waited near the front door.

Entering the Harwell House, Fitzwilliam turned on the lights. "Liz, let's put your things in the adjoining room to mine. It was the mistress's suite in its day. When you're ready, meet me in the upstairs sitting room. Here," he said, picking up her overnight bag, "I'll help you with this." Taking both his and her luggage, they walked up the stairs.

After putting away her things, Elizabeth took a small box from her bag and placed it on the dressing table. Then she changed into a long white low-cut silk nightgown, fitted at the bust with a drawstring. It held her full bosom securely, displaying her cleavage pleasingly. She brushed her finger over the delicate Brazilian embroidery gracing the bust line of her gown, and sighed. ...*This was supposed to be for my wedding night. It was part of Mom's trousseau—white for purity and delicate pink roses for femininity. Well, this is close enough. We will be married soon.* Quickly wrapping herself in the long white matching robe and taking one quick look in the gilded mirror, she grabbed the box from her dressing table and went straight to the upstairs sitting room to wait for him.

Darcy appeared shortly in a pair of silk pajamas wrapped in a thick cotton terry robe. He placed a small gift bag beside the sofa as he took a seat next to her. They sat silently, lost in their thoughts with too many emotions stirring within them. After a moment, Fitzwilliam broke the quiet.

"Elizabeth, I think I know you well enough to understand how you feel about some things, and I know how I feel, so I'll come to the point. I'm in love with you," he said softly as he placed her hand in his and gently stroked her fingers while he gazed into her eyes. "I want us to marry soon. I'm not the kind of man to do things by half. Now that we are a couple I don't think I can wait until summer, or rather, I don't want to. What do you say about a wedding in three weeks?"

She looked at him thoughtfully. "Fitzwilliam, we won't be able get away for a honeymoon. Once school starts, it will be hard to spend time together, especially with the heavy load we both have, and after being with you, I don't think I can be without you, especially at night. Therefore, a wedding in three weeks is fine with me. But what about Charles and Jane?"

Fitzwilliam flashed Elizabeth a big smile. "It's all taken care of. I've talked with Charles on the flight back, and he is just as eager to marry as I am. How do you think Jane will feel?"

"I happen to know she won't mind." Elizabeth grinned. "While Mary Beth was here, the three of us made our wedding gowns. Mary Beth's wedding is set for February 6th in Nova Scotia, and I was secretly hoping you and I would marry sooner than summer." Elizabeth raised her hand and gently stroked his face. "I can think of nothing I would like better than to come home to you in the afternoon."

"Nor I." He released a contented sigh and turned his head to kiss her soft palm as he pressed his own against it.

She glanced at him and then momentarily looked away. "However, there is another matter of concern that I wish to share with you."

Sensing the weightiness behind her words, Fitzwilliam nodded, bracing himself.

"I don't wish to start a family right away. Fitzwilliam, I hope you can understand. I really do want to teach a little longer before I become a mother. I also want more time to be alone with you. I'll be twenty-six on February 25th. We have time." She paused a moment. "I saw a doctor while you were gone, and I'm on the pill."

He flinched involuntarily as he looked away, disappointed that she'd made this decision without consulting him, but he quickly recovered, hiding his regret, knowing that if they could not agree, it would be best to wait.

He turned back with a warm smile. "If that is what you wish, then that is how it will be, but I can think of nothing I would rather have than a little girl with long dark hair and green eyes or a little boy with deep brown eyes and dark curls." He took her hand in his and gently caressed it. "You will have beautiful children, and I know you'll be a wonderful mother."

He dropped his gaze for a moment and then glanced at her again. "We need to get the license this week and make the arrangements. I want my brother and sister to come. My father will not come, as he is not pleased with our pending marriage. But I don't want you to worry about that because he *will* accept it. I'll not lose anything as a result of it, either, but even if I did, it wouldn't change my mind. I love you, and nothing will ever change that."

"I love you, too, but why does your father not approve? What did he say?"

Taking a long breath, he lifted her hand and enclosed it in his, stroking it gently. "He wants me to marry an English girl. Someone from our own social circle, but Elizabeth," he quickly added, "please don't despair. I've explained everything to him clearly. He knows that you are my equal in all ways that matter. He also knows how much I love you. I told him as much. He will accept it in time, so don't worry, my love, and please don't let it hurt you."

"I hope you're right. This does make me feel uneasy, but I love you…I trust you."

Fitzwilliam looked at her tenderly. The momentary flash of hurt in her eyes did not go unnoticed, and it grieved him to see it. He wished he didn't have to tell her, but he firmly believed in being forthright. If his father would give them a chance, he knew he would see how wonderful she was and how happy she made him. He pulled her a little closer. "Don't worry, Liz. It will all work out." He held her, comforting her as best he could. "Now, come. I have something for you."

He leaned over to retrieve the small gift bag he'd placed by the side of the sofa. Taking three packages from the bag, he handed one to her. "Open this one first," he said with a gentle smile.

Opening the box, she gasped at the sight of the ring. "Oh, Fitzwilliam! It's a blue diamond, deep blue like the ocean and so very beautiful. I love it." Tears flooded her eyes, as she took the ring from the box.

He took it from her and reverently placed it on her finger while he gently gave her a kiss. Then he took the wedding bands out and showed her the inscription. *Fitzwilliam & Elizabeth.*

"Fitzwilliam, they're beautiful. I will cherish them always, and once the band is placed upon my finger, it will never leave."

He wiped the tears from her eyes with his finger before pulling her to him for another kiss. "Now open the next one." He handed her the second box. "This is your engagement present."

She opened the box slowly and was immediately overcome with emotion once again. "Oh, Fitzwilliam, you should not have done this… It's gorgeous!" she gasped. "It's a replica of Arwen-Undomiel's necklace from **The Lord of the Rings**, except it's an emerald instead of a diamond." She gently lifted it from the box. "This is the most beautiful pendent I have ever seen, and I have certainly never owned anything like this. It and the ring must have cost you a fortune." She hugged him tight and kissed his cheek.

He softly laughed. "Whatever it cost, you are worth every penny. Arwen was the great granddaughter of Lúthien and said to be the most beautiful of all living beings in Middle Earth, and you, my darling, are the most beautiful woman I've ever seen. If anyone ever looked like Arwen or Lúthien, it is *you*." He smiled as he picked up the third and final box. "Here, I saw these and had to have them for you. It was meant as a Christmas gift, so it's a little late."

She opened the third box. "Oh, Fitzwilliam!" she exclaimed, taking the ebony and ruby hair sticks from the box. "These are lovely. I can't wait to wear them. Fitzwilliam, thank you so much." She threw her arms around his neck and gave him a kiss that nearly knocked him over.

"Hold on, Miss Bennett." He laughed as he grabbed her to keep them both from falling. "I do appreciate your enthusiasm."

Settling back down, she reached and retrieved the small box she'd brought with her. "I have something for you, too. It isn't much compared to what you have given me, but I hope you will like it just the same."

He took the offered box and slowly opened it to find inside a dozen fine Irish linen handkerchiefs embroidered with his initials covered in an intricate pattern of English ivy mingled with morning glories.

"Elizabeth, these are beautiful." His fingers reverently grazed the delicate needlework. "This is very fine craftsmanship. Where did you find handkerchiefs made like this?"

"I know of a shop in Charleston which imports the finest fabrics from all over the world, so I ordered the cloth from there. I made the handkerchiefs myself and then stitched the designs. They reminded me of Middle Earth, and since you love Tolkien as much as I do, I thought you would like them." She softly laughed. "It seems we understand each other very well. Both of us thought of Middle Earth when we selected our gifts."

"You made them yourself?"

She nodded with a gentle smile.

"Elizabeth, I love them, and I'll cherish them always because they came from your heart. Thank you." Laying the handkerchiefs aside, he stood up and pulled Elizabeth to her feet. "Now come and let me show you how much I appreciate you…how much I love you."

She closed her eyes as he lowered his head, catching her lips in a slow, possessive kiss while his hands cupped her face. Stepping closer, her fingers clenched his robe, and she pulled him towards her. Breaking the kiss, he scooped her up into his arms and took her to his bedroom, dusting her face with tender kisses as he walked.

Carrying her past the threshold, he gently set her down and took her in his arms once again, kissing her deeply as he slipped her robe from her shoulders, letting it gently fall at her feet. Steadying himself, he broke the kiss and stepped back. He reached up and brushed the contour of her ample bosom as his fingers traced over the intricate embroidery of her gown. Moving down to the strings that held her breasts captive, he took them in his hands, and diligently untying them, he freed her breasts. His fingertips gently slid over her collarbone and slipped the straps of her gown off her shoulders, letting it join her robe on the floor.

His breath caught sharply as she stood before him naked in the dimly lit room. Reaching forth his hand, he stroked the curve of her throat before working his way down to her bare breast. He ever so lightly caressed her firm nipple with his thumb, feeling it harden under his touch. Unable to wait any longer, he turned back the bedcovers and stripped off his clothes. Then he swept her up in his arms again and gently placed her on their bed before climbing in beside her. Ever conscious of her needs and desires, he intended to love her slowly, determined that she receive as much pleasure as he could give her as he leisurely made love to her, savoring every touch…every kiss…every feeling. It was only when he felt her body shudder that he allowed himself to let go. Folding her in his arms, he rolled over and gathered her against his chest. Satisfied and contented, they finally fell fast asleep embracing one another.

Chapter Nineteen

...a peace he'd made long ago...

The next day Fitzwilliam awoke to the bright morning sunshine streaking across his bed through the parted curtains. He glanced to his side. There lay Elizabeth asleep on the pillow next to him with her hands folded peacefully under her cheek, looking beautiful and serene. He had to smile at the sight of her. She looked so natural, and it felt so right to have her in his bed. He lightly traced the gentle curve of her lips with his forefinger.

"Umm...Fitzwilliam." She snuggled closer and slipped into his embrace.

"Wake up, love. It's morning. We need to shower and meet with Charles and your sister," he said, gently tapping her lips. "We have plans to make."

"Hmm...not yet...not yet, darling." She pulled him on top of her. "Make love to me."

A large smile graced his face. Fifteen minutes later, shower water was running.

Upon entering the Bennett townhouse, the smell of ham cooking and fresh coffee greeted them.

"I'm so hungry I could eat the house. Let's go to the kitchen to see what Jane is cooking. I can't wait to show her my ring."

Fitzwilliam laughed. "Yes, I'm sure you are, especially after last night and this morning. Let's go and see. I'm sure your sister will want to show you her ring, too." He grinned as they walked into the kitchen.

"Jane, come here. Look, look at what Fitzwilliam gave me. Isn't it beautiful?" Elizabeth asked as she presented her left hand.

"Oh, Lizzy, a blue diamond. It *is* beautiful." Jane squealed in delight as she took her sister's hand, admiring the ring and giving Elizabeth a hug. "I'm so happy for you."

"Yes, and I notice you're wearing something *new*, too. Let me see it."

Jane sheepishly held out her hand for her sister to see. "Charles gave it to me after you all left for the night."

"Oh, Jane, it's lovely! A white diamond in yellow gold—it's what you've always wanted. And it has a circlet of blue stones! Are they diamonds, too?"

"Yes, light blue diamonds. I had mentioned that my favorite stone was a blue topaz, and Charles remembered. He says they match my eyes."

"Well, it's very beautiful, and it'll go well with that pale blue nail polish you're always wearing," Elizabeth said, turning to take Fitzwilliam's hand. "Now, Jane, what do you have for breakfast? While we've been having all the fun, poor Fitzwilliam has been starving."

Fitzwilliam chuckled. "Oh, who's been starving? I seem to remember it being the other way around."

"We're both hungry," Elizabeth said as she gave his hand a squeeze, "so what do you have?"

"Well, let's see," Jane said with a smile. "We have ham, bacon, biscuits, eggs, and strawberry jam with some of your favorite scones." Smiling, Jane cast a quick glance at the men, "And, of course, grits and coffee for Charles and Fitzwilliam."

"Oh...I guess we're getting used to grits by now," Bingley said with a smile.

"Charles, don't complain. It's not so bad," Fitzwilliam said.

As they sat down to breakfast, Fitzwilliam addressed Charles. "So, what did you two decide about an early wedding?"

"How about in two weeks?" Jane answered.

"Two weeks!" Both Elizabeth and Fitzwilliam responded simultaneously.

"Is that not soon enough?" Jane looked at them quizzically.

"We were thinking a little longer. I don't think we can arrange everything in two weeks," Elizabeth replied.

"Well, we'll have to move quickly to have everything done. I want my brother and sister to come, but I think Elizabeth is right. Two weeks is pushing it. As much as I would like it, I don't think we can."

Upon further discussion, it was agreed that they would marry in three weeks. They would get the license this week, preferably tomorrow, and Elizabeth and Jane would go to Longbourn Baptist Church to speak with Pastor Emery about January 23rd as a possible wedding date. They would also have to speak with Aunt Tana about the flower arrangements, and then there was the reception to be planned.

Elizabeth and Jane quickly made out their guest list to include their aunts, uncles, cousins, and close friends. Since there was so little time, they made phone calls as well as mailed invitations. Cecilia Lawton, the Bennett girls' childhood friend, and there sister Mary Beth were the only ones unable to come on short notice. Mary Beth was in Europe and Cecilia was in South America.

After speaking with their aunts, it was agreed that they would handle the wedding and reception with the help of the church ladies, but then the church, as a whole, would have to be invited. Both couples reluctantly agreed.

Joseph would be home next Friday, and it was decided that he would give his sisters away as the current Master of Longbourn. As such, Joseph wanted a private conference with each prospective husband.

David informed Fitzwilliam that he and Georgiana would schedule a month's time for the event, and they would arrive on Friday as well. Georgiana wanted to spend time getting to know her new sister-in-law as well as seeing some of the sites in the area. David, though, claimed he had business matters in South Carolina arranged for the week following the wedding.

Several days before the guests were expected to arrive, a phone call came from Mrs. Norris's son, informing them his mother had become ill, and therefore, would not be returning. He requested that her things be packed and sent to his address in Ohio. After discussing the matter, Elizabeth and Fitzwilliam agreed it would not be necessary to hire a new housekeeper. She would assume those duties with his help.

During the daytime, they took care of the wedding preparations. In the evening, they used their time to prepare for the upcoming semester. Both worked together in the study side by side, helping one another as needed. When nighttime came, they took care of their other needs. Elizabeth was everything he knew she would be. Her sensual nature came alive under his tutelage. She was a hot passionate lover—eager to learn and eager to please. Their desire for one another was nearly insatiable as he made love to her until they were both utterly spent. By the end of the week, they were more deeply in love than either could have ever imagined.

On Friday the guests began to arrive. David and Georgiana flew into Nashville on Pemberley Two and rented a BMW to drive to the Cumberland Plateau. Georgiana flushed with excitement at all the sights she saw as they drove East on I-40 up into the Great Smoky Mountains. David chuckled while watching his sister's reaction. Looking about, he understood why the mountains were known by that name. They reminded him of what the Misty Mountains of Middle Earth might have looked like. This time of year the trees were barren, but the rocks, hills, and evergreens cast against the snow-capped mountains shrouded in thick clouds stole his sister's breath away. And the sight of an occasional deer running alongside the path in an open field thrilled her even more as she pointed everything out to him.

While he listened to his sister chatter away as they drove across the landscape steadily climbing upwards into the plateau, David secretly meditated about a certain lady in South Carolina. Alternating between Cecilia and his brother's future wife, he silently made it his primary goal to make sure Elizabeth truly loved his brother. Once he was convinced of that, he intended to go to South Carolina.

He'd had more women than he dared to count, but none had stirred him like Cecilia Lawton had that night in Charleston. No matter what he did, he was unable to forget it...or to forget her. He had to go back. As they entered the town limits, David snapped out of his daydream, paying close attention to the BMW's navigation system as he found their way into Old Town.

With the exception of Mary Beth, the entire Bennett clan gathered together, waiting for Joseph when the doorbell rang just before it opened.

"Joseph!" Lizzy squealed, running to him, wrapping her arms around his neck before he could fully come through the door. Kat and Jane were just a few steps behind, with Daniel standing off to the side, grinning like a kid at Christmas.

"It's good to be missed and even better to be home!" Laughing, he grabbed all three sisters in a bear hug, lifting them off the ground and swinging them around.

Daniel finally got in between his sisters and slapped his older brother on the back. "Welcome home, Brother. I've missed you."

"And I have missed you!" Joseph exclaimed, giving his brother the same bear hug. "Keeping the girls in line, eh?"

"As much as can be," Daniel grinned. "With Jane and Lizzy conveniently occupied, it's just me and Kat now."

Joseph laughed, looking over his shoulder to his two older sisters standing beside two strange men. Clapping Daniel's shoulder, he stepped aside to walk in their direction. "Hi, I'm Joseph Bennett."

Each man shook his hand.

"Charles Bingley. I'm glad to finally meet you."

"Fitzwilliam Darcy. It is a pleasure to meet the brother I've heard so many tales about. Your sister has told me quite a lot about you."

Glancing over at Elizabeth, Joseph grinned. "Well, I hope it was all good."

"Oh, nothing more than many of your escapades with cow manure." Elizabeth laughed.

"Well, since those stories involve *you*, too, I'm sure he is fully aware of what he is getting himself into." Joseph flashed Fitzwilliam a wide grin.

Releasing a playful giggle, she smiled. "I'm sure he does."

"Oh, I'm sure I don't, but I'm more than willing to find out."

They all laughed.

Joseph glanced to the side. "Robert!"

"It's about time you noticed! I thought I'd never get a word in edgewise." Robert Bennett stepped forward and shook Joseph's hand as he slapped his shoulder. "It's good to have you back, Joseph."

"Well, what can I say? You know how the girls are." He winked over his shoulder at his three sisters. "How have you been, Uncle?"

"It's been better, but tonight is not the night for any of that," Robert said in a somber tone. "We'll talk soon."

"Is something wrong?"

Robert smiled. "We'll talk later."

All of the aunts and uncles, and finally Grace greeted Joseph. Elizabeth introduced David and Georgiana and before long they all made their way into the dining room. As they sat and ate while laughing and talking, Joseph couldn't help but notice Georgiana Darcy stealing glances his way every now and then. Once when he smiled and nodded, he was pleasantly surprised to see her blush crimson.

After dinner, Joseph called his two older sisters into the library for a private conversation. "Jane, Lizzy, I am so happy to see you. So much has changed since we were last together. We have all grown up, haven't we?"

"Yes," Jane said softly as she and Lizzy took a seat by the fireplace. "We're grown now and will soon have families of our own. There's no need to worry about us. In fact, dear brother, it is you whom we worry about."

"Oh, there's no need to worry about me. I'm doing very well. I have two more years until I have completed my service obligation, and then I'm coming home. I just want to make sure you and Lizzy are happy."

"We'll be fine," Jane said, "but there is something on your mind."

"Ah, Jane, you are always the elder responsible one and very perceptive. From what I have observed already in this short time, I believe your fiancés do love you. But you are right. I do have something to tell you. We can talk about it now, and then we won't mention it again."

The three siblings pulled their chairs around, settling close together. Joseph took the hand of each sister and drew a deep breath while squeezing their fingers. Looking from one to the other, it grieved him to tell them the things he had to say, but he had a job to do, and that required he squash every emotion. He didn't want to scare them, but he also had to make them aware of his situation.

With a cool head, he began. "I am here because our unit is about to go out on our most dangerous mission so far. They have let the entire team take a month's leave before we begin training for the largest, most important, and perhaps most daring assault yet. I must prepare you for the inevitability that some of us won't come back."

Jane and Elizabeth both began to argue, but Joseph stopped them with a shake of his head. "Let me finish with as much detail as I am allowed to reveal. I leave here in one month for Camp Pendleton. Then from there, I go to Twentynine Palms to train for my part. I will then meet up with the rest of the group in an undisclosed location for further training. When we are ready, we will proceed to check point alpha. It's critical to the war effort, and top secret. This is all that I can tell you. You must not say anything about what I've told you. I won't be able to contact anyone after I leave Twentynine Palms, but I could not go without telling you just in case…I don't return," he quietly stated. "I wanted the two of you to be especially prepared. That is what I needed to tell you both."

By now both sisters were crying and hugging their brother.

"Jane, Lizzy, please don't cry." Oh God, this was hard enough. He didn't need their tears. Once again, he attempted to reassure them. "I'm not afraid. It's my job, and I'm trained to do it. If I should die, I want you to know that I am ready for that." Pausing for a moment, he glanced between the two of them and stressed, "This information is for you alone. You can tell your husbands that I'm going on special assignment, but please don't mention it to anyone else. I know both of you understand this, and I trust you." He smiled gently. "Now dry your eyes and compose yourselves so we can return to the others."

"Joseph, do you not have a choice in this?"

"No, Jane, you know the answer to that." He shook his head with a dry smile. "That choice was made when I entered the Naval Academy eight years ago. It's my duty to go. I have been well trained, so don't fear. I'm at peace—a peace I made a long time ago."

Jane was by far the most tender hearted of them all, and the most sensible. Although both in age and temperaments he was closest to Lizzy, he knew it was Jane whom he could count on to take care of things should anything happen to him.

With a deep sigh, he addressed his oldest sister. "Jane, you must look after the others and always watch over Daniel. I regret that I did not spend more time with him. If anything happens to me, he will be the Master of Longbourn. I am glad Daniel is prepared should it come to that since Father spent his time equally between the two of us." Joseph lips curved upwards. "However, cheer up. I intend to return. I'm highly trained in survival skills, but nine tenths of it is sheer will and determination, and I definitely possess that."

After several minutes, they returned to the others, putting on cheery faces, laughing, talking, and socializing for the rest of the evening as if nothing was amiss.

Chapter Twenty

...one love...one lifetime...

Longbourn

"Hurry Jane. Hurry Lizzy. We need to be at the church by eight o'clock. Have you got the four items I arranged for you?"

"Aunt, calm down. We're the ones getting married—not you," Elizabeth teased as she picked up her mother's embroidered slip, Fitzwilliam's emerald pendant, Tana's linen handkerchief, and the blue silk garter Bette had given her—something old, something new, something borrowed, something blue. "Jane already has her things in her bag, and now I have mine. The dresses are in the Tahoe, so we're ready to go."

"Well, let's leave then. Your other aunts are already there. Your uncles are in town helpin' your fiancés, but if you're not careful, they will arrive at the church before you do. You don't want to be late for your own weddin', do you?"

Jane and Elizabeth both rolled their eyes. "By all means," Jane said, "let's go."

The church was a flurry of activity when Tana Bennett walked into the fellowship hall. Grace and Lori were supervising the church ladies as they decorated the room for the reception, and the organist was practicing her part while the music minister was setting up the sound system. Tana looked around and frowned. She asked about Bette and Florence and was told they were busy in the dressing room arranging the hair styling and makeup center. Tana smiled and complimented the ladies before taking the girls to where they belonged. As soon as Tana entered with the brides-to-be, they were rushed over to the dressing table where Bette and Florence took over while Tana went to help Lydia with the flowers.

"Lizzy, how would you like baby's breath woven into the top of this Grecian style?" Bette asked as she handed Elizabeth a styling booklet. "I can clip tiny blue roses to the ringlets down your back? I've done hair like that before, and it turned out beautifully. I think it will complement your gown very well." Bette stood back observing Elizabeth's face and hair while Elizabeth looked over the picture.

"Umm...I'd love it, if you don't overdo it on the roses." Elizabeth placed the booklet aside and picked up the tiny rosebuds, examining them closely. "The blue matches the embroidered roses on my neckline perfectly. Where did you ever find them?"

"I have my connections, darlin'. I've been doin' this a long time, well before you were born." Bette pulled out a long section of hair and wrapped it around a curling iron. "In fact, Florence and I opened The Cut and Curl back in the 70s just after we married your mother's brothers in our double weddin', and we've been stylin' hair and doin' makeup ever since, haven't we, Florence?"

"Umm, yes, I guess we have. Doesn't seem like it's been that long, though, but it sure enough has—and think of all the *news* we've heard over the years." Florence giggled as she combed and styled Jane's blonde locks one twist at a time.

"Oh lord, yes." Bette stepped around to the other side of Elizabeth, wrapping another strand. "And that reminds me. Martha Schrimshire was in the other day. She says Isabelle lost the baby. Poor little thing! And have you girls heard the latest news?

If not, let us fill you in, but we don't repeat gossip, so you'd better listen close the first time." Bette and Florence both cackled.

Lydia's eyes darted away as she carelessly dropped one of the flowers she was working on. Tana glanced at her as Florence and Bette began repeating all of last week's gossip. Lydia's gaze fell. Tana only shook her head as she watched.

Finally giving the latest topic of interest a rest, Florence picked up Jane's French comb and turned it over in her hand. "What a beautiful comb...hmm... mother of pearl with encrusted stones. It's lovely. Are they real?" she asked while attaching the comb in place.

"Yes, they're pink diamonds. It was a Christmas gift from Charles." Jane smiled, turning from side to side, staring at her image in the mirror.

"Well, it's absolutely beautiful," Florence replied. "Now, Jane dear, these ringlets look so lovely framin' your face like this. I'll place a few delicate pink rosebuds here and there, and that will set it off," she said as she turned to Lydia. "What do you think? Doesn't she look stunnin'?"

"I think it looks very lovely, very lovely indeed. Your mother would be proud of you, Jane." A tear slipped from Lydia's eye and slid her down cheek. "She would be proud of you both."

"Lydia, darlin'," Tana said. "Come with me. I need your help in the sanctuary. Bette and Florence seem to be doin' quite well without our interference." Tana smiled, gently guiding Lydia out the door.

Once in the sanctuary, Lydia turned to Tana. "You don't need any help. Things look beautiful as they are."

"No, I don't, but you do. I caught the look in your eyes when Florence mentioned her *news*. I know how you must feel. Would you like to talk about it?"

Lydia burst into tears. "Tana, how can you be so kind?" She sniffled.

Tana handed Lydia a tissue. "There, there, Lydia. It's all right...it's all right," Tana said as she patted Lydia's back.

"No, it's not... it's not all right. I've cut myself off from everyone. I have no real friends."

"That's not true, Lydia. We're your friends...we're your family."

"Oh, Tana, how can you say such a thing? I've been unkind at the very least and downright mean at the worst." She wiped another rush of tears. "I've looked down on you, Meg, Bette, Florence, and Lori."

"Lydia, please don't bring all of that up. You can't change the past, but you can do somethin' about the here and now. It's a new day. It's Jane and Lizzy's weddin' day."

"You're so right." Lydia wiped her eyes. "I need all of you now. Can you forgive me? Can they?"

"Lydia, there is nothin' to forgive. You've never actually been mean...I mean not really. I'm sure the others, as well as myself, have thought nothin' of it. It's just your personality. I would worry if you *were* overtly friendly. But, if you want to be a little closer with us, we'd gladly welcome you." Tana laughed and gave Lydia a brief hug.

"Tana Bennett, don't you lie to me! I know what I am and who I am." Lydia glanced up through tear-laden lashes. "However, I want us to be friends, especially now. But what about Liddy? I can't do a thing with her."

"Oh, Lydia, Liddy will be fine. She'll mature in time and see the pain she's causin', not only to you and Randy, but to herself as well."

"No, I'm afraid she won't. Liddy's out of control—resentful and hateful, and it's all my fault. She's my only child. I have never refused her anything. I was always givin' in, showerin' her with things, encouragin' her in her selfishness."

Not knowing what to say, Tana simply held her sister-in-law and let her cry on her shoulder. As they stood there, Tana remembered something she'd overheard in the floral shop the day before yesterday. The district attorney's wife had come in to order a funeral arrangement. While she was making her selection, Tana had heard her tell her companion that the DA's office was investigating another party in connection with the Nunley case—a woman. She had thought of Liddy at the time and had meant to speak to Robert about it, but with six funerals in one week and then the wedding, it had completely slipped her mind, and she hadn't thought a thing about it until now as it hit her full force.

Gently broaching the subject, she asked, "Lydia, Liddy's in trouble, isn't she?"

"Yes," she breathed out through a new rush of tears. "We've been warned she's under investigation. Apparently, Jackie Lee used her in his drug ring. She didn't understand the consequences. I know she didn't! And if they indict her, I don't know what we'll do. We don't have the money to defend her, and she's pregnant with Jackie Lee's baby, and I'm so afraid she will marry him. Only Ron's family has enough money to help us, and I can't ask Lizzy or Jane, let alone Joseph with the war and all."

Tana held her tight. "It's all right, Lydia. We'll find a way. Let's get through this weddin', and then we'll talk about it. Now, come on. Let's go downstairs to the bathroom and get you cleaned up. You can't let people see you like this."

Tana shuddered with genuine fear. Robert had to have known Liddy was under investigation, and yet he hadn't told her. She knew her husband would mortgage everything they owned for his sister. With Ron gone, Robert was the senior Bennett, and there was no way he'd let his sister down. The two ladies walked toward the basement stairs with Lydia still crying.

Returning to the dressing room, Lydia felt much better now that she had finally unloaded her burden and confessed her concerns. She was determined to make amends, knowing she faced a very uncertain future. She needed her family, especially her brother, Ronald, whom she had always depended on. Her chest tightened. In spite of all the mean things she'd done to him, he had always been there for her, but now, with him dead, she felt truly helpless. She let a heavy sigh escape her breast. Perhaps her little brother would be there for her. She didn't know. She'd never paid him much mind. He was twelve years younger and had been of little consequence to her. How ironic!

Walking towards her nieces, she smiled. "Come here, girls, and let me see you. We don't have much time." Lydia directed the brides to the outside dressing area. "Here, stand in front of this full length mirror, and let's have a look. Now, don't you both look lovely?" She turned to the other aunts. "Flo, you and Bette did a wonderful job. I've never seen their hair look better. I've half a mind to let you style mine." Lydia smiled as she straightened their hems and smoothed their skirts.

"Flo? Did a nice job? You've never called me Flo…and you want us to fix your hair? Lydia Fanning, what's wrong with you? Have you lost your mind?" Florence asked.

"No, I haven't," Lydia said with a soft smile. "I've finally found it." She glanced between the brides and the others. "This is a day of celebration, and I intend this to be a very special day for my brother's two oldest daughters." Her genuine smile told all in the room that something was different. She looked peaceful in spite of the storm brewing about her.

Lydia noticed everyone's shocked expression and smiled all the more. "I owe all of you an apology for my behavior over the years, don't I?" She swallowed against the lump in her throat, tears brimming in her eyes once again. "Seein' Jane and Elizabeth here has reminded me of it." She turned to face her nieces. "Girls, in spite of my actions, I want you to know I really loved your father. Oh, yes, I know." She nodded. "We may have fussed and fought all those years, but we always knew we loved one another."

As Lydia embraced each and every one, Bette looked at her and blinked in shock. "But, Lydia..."

"Let's let sleeping dogs lie. We'll talk about it another day. This day is not the day for hashing out differences. It's our nieces' day," Tana said as she stepped forward and gave Lydia a hug. The others followed. When they had recovered, Lydia turned to Jane and Elizabeth.

"Now, let's look at our girls. Oh, Jane, you are so beautiful. Meg taught you to embroider, didn't she? I love your design. Those delicate pink rosettes with the pale green filigree and glass beadin' are stunnin'. And you, Lizzy," Lydia turned and brushed her fingertips over Elizabeth's dress, "pale blue rosebuds with intertwining green stems and leaves. I don't recall ever seein' that style of needlework. What is it? And the two of you didn't make your dresses yourself, did you?"

"It's called Brazilian embroidery. Grace taught me, and yes, we did make our gowns, well, mostly. Jane and Mary Beth had Grace and Lori do much of their work, but I made mine entirely."

Lydia's hand flew to her mouth. "Oh Lizzy! It's bad luck to make your own gown. Don't you know that?"

"Oh, don't be ridiculous." Elizabeth laughed and rolled her eyes. "I don't subscribe to superstitions."

"Yes, you're probably right." Lydia paused a moment. "Mama wasn't right about everything. Now, let's take one last look."

While Lydia fussed with the girls' appearances, Florence spoke. "I don't suppose either of you need any advice about tonight, do you?"

Jane stiffened, flushed with embarrassment, while Elizabeth snickered. "I hardly think now is the time for that. Besides, we might have a thing or two to teach you. You never know." Elizabeth winked.

They all erupted in laughter.

"I guess our girls really have grown up," Florence said.

"I'd say they have," Bette agreed.

"Well, I hear Sadie playin' the organ. We're about to begin," Lydia said, scrutinizing the girls one last time. Releasing a sigh, she opened the door and looked out. "It's time to go. Joseph's waitin'."

223 Willow Street

Pacing the floor of his bedroom, Fitzwilliam cursed under his breath. His jaw hardened in frustration and anger. He felt hurt and betrayed. Turning to face his brother, he stormed, "David, why did you wait until now to tell me this? Why on earth did you not tell me last week, preferably when you first came into town?"

David drew in a measured breath. "Fitzwilliam, with all the guests arriving at the same time as Georgiana and me, and with you spending all of your time with Elizabeth, I never had the opportunity. Besides, I didn't want to throw a spanner in the works."

"Oh, so you choose my wedding day to throw the spanner? Great!" Fitzwilliam passed his hand over his face as he leaned against the wall. "Well, I know it's not your fault. I guess the rift between Father and me really is irreparable, isn't it?" He shook his head and pushed away from the wall. "How am I going to tell Elizabeth? It will break her heart. I don't know what to do, but I'm not telling her today." He cut his eyes across at David. "This is our wedding day, and it will be a good day!"

"Fitzwilliam, think of it this way. Since Father is in denial about your wedding, at least the paparazzi will not be here. Father's deliberate squashing of any news about you and your marital status can work to your advantage," David asserted. "If the press had any idea of what was happening here today, they would be crawling all around the place, and you wouldn't have any privacy. In a way, Father is doing you a favor."

Fitzwilliam looked at his brother is astonishment. "Doing **me** a *favor*? **David**, he is denying that I'm marrying! He's parading me about England as if I am still an available bachelor, telling the press and all of London that I'm on assignment with Brit Am in the oil fields of Saudi Arabia. How dare he! I'm so angry right now that I could tell him where to go in no uncertain terms."

"No, think about it—do you really want the press here, especially with what I'm picking up about Elizabeth's family? It may only be her cousin, but I can already tell her family is a close knit one. Elizabeth, and therefore *you*, will be dragged into whatever is happening."

Fitzwilliam turned a careful eye to his brother. "You're talking about that drug dealer her cousin is involved with, aren't you? Well, I don't think it's a real problem for us. I mean how can we talk about anyone when we have our own—"

"Listen to me, Fitzwilliam, and listen carefully." David leaned forward, his voice deadly serious. "Whatever goes on in our family is well concealed. Except for me, we don't parade our sins for the world to see. No one knows about Edward's cocaine addiction or Artimus's aborted offspring. It's all neatly hidden away," he stared at his brother, flexing his jaw, "but Elizabeth's unfortunate circumstances cannot be hidden even if they had the money to do so, which they don't." Sitting back and rubbing his chin he continued. "It's amazing what you can learn at a bachelor party, especially when everyone is drinking."

"David, it's not that bad. Liddy is not married to the bastard, not yet anyway. I don't think it's as serious as you think. I mean she's not under investigation and—"

David jumped out of his seat, nose to nose with his brother. "Fitzwilliam, pay careful attention to me and listen *closely* to what I have to say. Joseph and I have been talking. The girl's father fears his daughter *is* going to be indicted, and he doesn't have the money for her defense if she is—and *you* had better not pay it for him. If the money is traced back to you, it will be disastrous." David broke the contact, shaking his head as he walked towards the center of the room and turned back. "This will pull them all into the fray. To make matters even more complicated, she's five months pregnant. Father will be furious should he find out, and rest assured," David bore down, "he *will* find out, though I intend to do all that I can to delay the discovery." His hard gaze held his brother's as Fitzwilliam froze where he stood.

"Okay, David, I get your point," Fitzwilliam said as he bit his lower lip. "You're right. It would not be good for the paparazzi to be here taking pictures. I've never been the lightning rod for controversy that you've been. And this is not the way I would want my wedding covered in the press. We will have to roll with it and see what happens." Fitzwilliam ran his fingers through his hair as he paced the floor. Releasing a hard breath, he turned to face David as if to speak, but David spoke first.

"You've got to tell Elizabeth and the sooner the better. She needs to understand how Father feels about this marriage."

Fitzwilliam closed his eyes and shook his head. "I'll tell her sometime over the next

M.K. Baxley

four days whilst we're in Gatlinburg. That is if I can bring myself to do it. She's not like us, David. It will hurt her. She won't understand. She and Americans in general, believe that a person should be judged on his or her own merit. Surely it's not as bad as it seems." Fitzwilliam plopped down in a nearby chair, perplexed.

"Oh, I have a general idea of how Americans look at things, but Elizabeth is marrying into an aristocratic British family, one with high connections and old money, so even if this cousin is not indicted, it *is* as bad as it seems. The girl is carrying that man's child, and she plans to *marry* him. She'll be viewed as a strumpet, and people will sneer at your wife's family." David sighed and glanced away. "I'm glad you and Elizabeth love each other, although I wish she didn't have such an obnoxious connection. Let's drop it for now." David went to his brother's dresser and poured them both a glass of claret. Fitzwilliam took the offered drink and gulped it down.

"Come now. Get up." David looked at his brother sympathetically. "You have a wedding to attend. I'm going to get Bennett, and we're going to get you ready. I think one of the uncles wants to help, too. The others are helping Charles." David walked over to the closet and opened the door. "What are you wearing today?"

Determined to make this the day he intended, Fitzwilliam pushed all concerns aside and leapt to his feet. Strolling over to his wardrobe, he said, "I'm wearing the only morning dress I have here with me. It's the one I had made last year from Anderson & Sheppard for the AIDS Foundation charity dinner we hosted." He pulled out the garment-bag, shirt, and shoes.

"Yes, I remember. It looked very nice. It was the charcoal-grey woolen with the silk lapels and pinstriped trousers, wasn't it? I had one made, too. What else, a waistcoat?"

"Yes, the matching lighter grey waistcoat, white French cut shirt, and a burgundy cravat." Fitzwilliam paused and cocked his head. "You think you might be able to help me tie it? I've never tied one before, and Watson isn't here to do it for me." Fitzwilliam took his suit out of the bag and laid it across the bed, and then went to gather his cufflinks.

"I suppose I can." David shrugged. "I've only done it a few times myself, but we'll get it done."

While Fitzwilliam laid out his things, there was a knock at the door. David walked across the room and opened it. "Mr. Bennett, Joseph, come in. I was about to come and get you. Nice to see you again," David said, reaching for Joseph's hand and then Robert's.

"Good to see you, too, but do call me Robert, and I'll call you David, or maybe Darcy when your brother's not around to confuse things." He laughed. "There's no need for formality."

Turning to the groom, Robert said, "Fitzwilliam, my wife insists that you have these. I know it's only supposed to be for the bride, but Tana insists. And I learned a long time ago not to argue with her over trivial things. So here, I have somethin' old, somethin' new, somethin' borrowed, somethin' blue. Oh and don't worry. Charles got a similar collection. Here," he said as he handed the items to Fitzwilliam. "I have a pair of black suspenders, a pair of new black shoestrings, one of my own white linen handkerchiefs, and a white rose tinted in blue."

Fitzwilliam laughed. "Thank you, sir, and thank your wife. I'll use your 'suspenders' as opposed to mine."

"I appreciate it, for Tana will surely be lookin' to make sure I did as she asked. Now, let's get you dressed and ready to go."

David's face twisted into a smirk as he laughed out loud. "Let me see you in those.

160

How are you going to hold your socks up with those 'suspenders'?"

"David, don't be ridiculous! Excuse us, Robert," Fitzwilliam chuckled as he turned to Robert with an amused grin, "but in England these are referred to as braces and suspenders are used to hold one's socks up. My brother likes to see the humor in almost everything you Americans do that differs from how we would do it."

Robert and Joseph both laughed, shaking their heads. "I've heard them referred to as braces before, but it never occurred to me to call them anything other than suspenders. I know of no one who wears garters, as we would call them," Robert said.

"Oh, I beg to differ," Joseph interrupted. "We still do in the Armed Forces. I don't, but the soldiers who guard the Tomb of the Unknown Soldier do."

"Well, the culture differences are fun to explore, but we really do need to get ready," Robert said, glancing at the clock on the wall.

Fitzwilliam took the cue and went into his dressing room. When he came back, David and Robert were waiting with the cravat, 'suspenders,' and waistcoat. When Fitzwilliam was ready, David placed the tie around his brother's neck and proceeded to tie it. "Hold still. I'm no valet, and this is not easy," he fussed. "How is it you never learnt to do this for yourself?"

"I hate these blasted things, and besides, Watson has always been there to do it for me should I have to wear one. Someday I'll learn, but today is *not* that day. Watch it!" he scowled. "You're choking me."

David frowned. "There, I have it."

Robert stepped forward. "Okay, let me just fasten this in," Robert said, securing the rose in place. "Yeah, that's got it. It looks good enough. At least I won't sleep on the couch tonight." Robert chuckled as he glanced at Fitzwilliam. "Let me give you a piece of advice, and remember it *well*. Lizzy is always right, even if she's wrong. Follow that advice, and you'll get along just fine. Unless it's something big, it's not worth arguin' over. The couch can be a very lonely place, especially on a cold winter's night."

Everyone laughed.

Joseph looked on the situation and smiled. "Charles told me he and Jane are going to Chattanooga for four days. Do you and Lizzy have a trip planned, too?"

"Yes, Elizabeth wants to go to Gatlinburg for the skiing. She's made reservations at a resort for a cabin in the woods. Some place called Cherokee Lodge," Fitzwilliam said, pulling and fumbling with his cravat. "David, it's too tight. What were you trying to do, choke me?"

David rolled his eyes. "In the future, you tie your own."

"Joseph, have you ever been to this place Elizabeth has arranged for?"

"As a matter of fact, I have. We used to ski there over the holidays when my parents were with us. It's very tranquil, and they have plenty of snow, so if you're like Lizzy, you'll like it."

"Well, I like to ski, so I probably will."

"Let's take a look at you. Umm…it looks like you're ready. Are you nervous, Brother?" David asked teasingly with a twinkle in his eye. "You don't need any advice for tonight, do you?"

Fitzwilliam erupted, "No, you cheeky bugger! Save your advice for someone who might actually *need* it."

David chuckled. "Are you sure about that?"

Fitzwilliam frowned with a sharp look.

Joseph laughed out loud. "You two amuse me. I kind of wanted to hear his advice."

"You might not, once you've heard it. My brother thinks he has the corner on women. But one of these days, some woman is going to teach *him* otherwise."

Fitzwilliam glanced at his brother and winked.

"I don't know about that. I've been told I'm pretty damned good."

Fitzwilliam rolled his eyes, suppressing a laugh as Joseph adjusted the silk rose, getting it just right.

"A real Casanova, huh?" Joseph said while Robert laughed. "Well, now that the groom is ready, I think the rest of us should get dressed. We need to leave in an hour and a half. I'm going down the hall to check in on Charles. He seemed rather nervous when I left him." Joseph glanced over at David and chuckled. "He might be able to use some of your advice."

"Yes, Charles probably could." David laughed. "I'll go with you to see how he's doing."

"He's probably all right. My uncles and brother are with him. They were having a whiskey when I left. I had better make sure they haven't had too much. I want him to feel relaxed, but still be able to stand up, at least long enough to get married." Joseph chuckled. "Jane would kill me if he couldn't."

"Fitzwilliam, you look cool and calm for a man about to lose his freedom. As the sayin' goes, a man isn't complete until he's married…and then he's finished."

They all laughed.

"But on a serious note," Robert continued with a wink, "there's nothing like having a good woman to warm your bed on a cold winter's night."

With that said, they all turned and one by one they left the room.

When he had finished dressing, David found Robert Bennett alone smoking a cigar on the upstairs piazza. David lit his own and made small conversation. Finally working up his courage, David broached the subject foremost on his mind. "Robert, would you mind discussing something with me concerning what I heard last night about one of your nieces?"

"Perhaps. What do you want to know?"

"How serious is this affair with Miss Fanning?"

"Oh, *that*. Well, I'm not a trial lawyer, and I don't know the specifics. But I'll tell you what I do know. Grady Abernathy is an ambitious district attorney. He wants to be the next governor of this state, and one of the ways to get free publicity for his campaign is to be seen as being aggressive on crime, especially drug crime. He thinks he has the evidence to indict my niece on state charges, and he's workin' with the federal prosecutor on the federal level. As to what evidence he's got, I don't rightly know. But what I do know, based on how things work around here, is that he most likely will indict her. Of that I feel certain," Robert said as he took a long draw off his cigar and stared off into the distance. "You see, Darcy, when you're an ambitious public figure, it's all about perception.

"And though my brother-in-law clamors on about his daughter's innocence, he is worried and rightly so. Anytime you're under investigation for drug trafficking, it's serious—very serious." Robert glanced at David. "Liddy runs with a wild crowd. Always has. And if you lie down with the dogs, you'll get up with the fleas." Robert narrowed his eyes. "If she is indicted, we will be out a large sum of money for her defense, 'cause as I said, I am no trial lawyer. I can't handle the case. However, I do know a few, and they are *not* cheap." Robert paused. "It's no secret that Lydia and Randy are in debt up to their eyeballs. They've squandered every dime they've ever had, and as we say around here, they don't have a pot to piss in. But Lydia is my sister, and as such, I'll do whatever I can to help her."

"What do you mean by that?"

"I mean I will have to mortgage my farm to come up with the money." Robert clenched his jaw.

"No, you won't." Joseph said, walking out onto the balcony, lighting a cigar. "I have $30 million at my disposal, and I'm going to make arrangements for you to have access to two million of it for Liddy's defense, should it come to that."

"Joseph!" Robert turned to meet his nephew. "Are you sure? That's the money my brother left you—"

"And Father would do the same if he were here. Now fill me in on the details."

"There's not much that you don't already know by now," Robert shrugged, stepping aside to allow Joseph to join them. "Jackie Lee has been indicted. The next grand jury convenes in March. If they arrest Liddy, it will be between now and then. If she's indicted, as I feel certain she will be, we'll know more at that time."

"What happens if she and this individual should marry?" David asked as he puffed his cigar. He intended to learn all he could. His brother's interests were his utmost concern, not that he cared what his father or anyone else would think, but he didn't want to see his brother's name dragged through the scandal sheets.

Joseph nodded, indicating he wanted to know, too.

"If they marry, it would keep Liddy from being forced to testify against Jackie Lee, and of course, he would not testify against her, either. So it would be in both their best interests to marry for legal reasons, but that's all. And that's only if the prosecution's case against Jackie Lee is weak, which I know it isn't. Nunley has the most to lose if they don't marry. But then Jackie Lee has another option, if he's willin' to take it. The federal prosecutor wants the name of his Colombian connection. They'll be willing to cut him a deal if he turns state's evidence."

"I see." David said.

"What Colombian connection?" Joseph pressed as he blew out a stream of smoke.

Robert shook his head. "I'll elaborate on that later. Today is Jane and Elizabeth's weddin' day, not a day for this sordid mess."

Joseph released an exasperated sigh as he shook his head, his brow etched in either worry or concentration. David wasn't sure which.

The Wedding

Fitzwilliam and Charles stood at the altar waiting for Jane and Elizabeth while Peter, Paul, and Mary's version of *The Wedding Song* played softly in the background. David stood nearby.

"Darcy, are you nervous?" Bingley asked.

"Anxious maybe, but not nervous. You?"

"More nervous than I've ever been in my life, but I'll manage. It must be time. The music has stopped and the organist has taken her seat."

At about that time, the wedding march began. Fitzwilliam and Charles both turned to see Joseph Bennett in his dress blues flanked on either side by his two sisters. Fitzwilliam had never seen Elizabeth look lovelier as Joseph escorted his sisters to the front of the church, placing each one beside her intended husband. He then took a position beside Charles while David stepped in line beside his brother.

Pastor Emery began with the standard address concerning the sanctity of marriage and the responsibilities of a husband to his wife and a wife to her husband. Each couple repeated their vows. Fitzwilliam and Elizabeth had made special arrangements with Pastor Emery to crown their vows with a special ending they had written together. At the indicated time, Elizabeth reverently picked up Fitzwilliam's ring from the plate, and spoke her personal vows.

"With this ring, I pledge to you, Fitzwilliam Alexander Darcy, one love, one life, and one lifetime. I will share each day and each night with you, following you wherever you go. With this ring, I take you as my husband, pledging myself to you always." She placed the ring on his finger, her eyes never leaving his.

When it was his turn, Fitzwilliam picked Elizabeth's ring up, and began his promise. "With this ring, I pledge to you, Elizabeth Rose Bennett, to be your shelter and your light, to be a safe haven from life's storms. I will share with you one love, one life, and one lifetime. I will be with you always, anywhere you are, and anywhere you go. With this ring, I take you as my wife, pledging myself to you always." When Fitzwilliam slipped the ring on Elizabeth's finger, the smile on his face said all that he felt. Completing the ceremony, Pastor Emery pronounced each couple man and wife.

Chapter Twenty-one

...she beckoned him with an outstretched hand...

S ince the women had planned a cookout for the day following the wedding, Joseph had thought this was the ideal time to call a family meeting. All the men were present, including his mother's brothers.

While Henry offered a drink or a cold beer to the men as they settled on the sofa and chairs, Joseph surveyed the room, reflecting on his father. Ronald Bennett had been a man of integrity, grounded in deeply-rooted principles of honesty and the importance of family. He had taught his sons that the quality of a man's character is measured in how he treats his fellow man. A man lived by his word, but was judged by his walk. As Joseph reflected on his father's teachings, he asked himself *...what would my dad do, and how would he handle this situation?*

Joseph knew his father had been adamant about family coming together in times of trouble and had taught all of his children the value of close family ties. Therefore, the decision was easy. He would do whatever he could to help his Aunt Lydia and Uncle Randy, even though he knew Liddy was trouble with a capital T and always had been. But first, the problem needed to be discussed because, before Liddy's situation could be assessed, he would have to know all the available information. He turned and stared at his uncle.

"Robert, I'd like to know everything you know about this sordid business with Jackie Lee, and then I want to know how it ties in with Liddy. I assume you still hear everything that happens downtown at the courthouse."

Robert stepped forward. "Yes, it's the talk of the town. There isn't a person around who isn't talkin' about it. The leaks I hear comin' out of the DA's office are that the Feds want Jackie Lee to give up his Colombian connection."

"Colombian connection. You mentioned that yesterday. Tell me more, and I want to know *everything* you know." Joseph's brow creased as his quizzical gaze settled on his uncle.

Robert walked back and forth, glancing from those gathered on the sofa back to his nephew. "Well, there's more and plenty of it. Apparently, Jackie Lee was not only growin' marijuana, but he had others throughout these mountains farmin' crops, too. They were supplyin' most of the Southeast. He also had a botanist in his employ whose job was to increase the THC levels through genetic manipulation. Jackie Lee personally managed the entire operation. It was a very well put together organization, producing millions in unreported revenue, but since Jackie Lee didn't live too high on the hog, he didn't stand out. So you see, he's in trouble with the IRS as well as the DEA."

Joseph continued to walk the floor, twisting his academy ring in deep thought, digesting all that he heard. "I see." He drew in a sharp breath. "Tell me more."

"Well, not only was he involved in the marijuana growin' business, but he managed the cocaine connection for the southeastern United States and Midwest, possibly extending into Canada. Every so often, he met down in Miami with men from Colombia—men who work for the Cali Cartel." Robert paused, as if gauging Joseph's reaction.

Joseph shook his head, and then signaled for his uncle to carry on.

Robert nodded. "The cocaine was being brought into the United States usin' low flyin' planes with night drops east of Knoxville. Packages of cocaine would be parachuted to predetermined locations identified with GPS. At times, a man with kilos of cocaine strapped to his body would parachute into the selected location and then meet with others at an agreed upon rendezvous point where it was collected and transported to Coldwater Hollow. From there, it was distributed across the Southeast and Midwest."

"How strong is their case? Are the Feds going to cut him a deal?" Joseph asked.

"From what I've heard, it's rock solid. They caught one of his minions a while back who confessed to everything, namin' names and givin' locations. That's how they caught Jackie Lee. As to cutting him a deal, of course, they will. They want to break the back of the Cali Cartel. What they want from Jackie, as I said before, is the name of his Colombian contact which I know he won't give up." He stopped and reflected. "He'd be a fool if he did. They'll kill him, and they may anyway."

"Thank you, Robert," Joseph said. "Now, how does Liddy fit into this equation?" He turned to his uncle seated on the sofa. "Randy, why don't you inform us as to how things stand in that regard."

Robert nodded and took a seat next to Randy who nervously crossed his legs as he studied the room. "I think all of you know it's pretty serious. We have Liddy stayin' in Nashville with my sister. I thought it best to remove her from both the situation and, of course, from Jackie Lee." Randy paused for a sip of whiskey. "Apparently Liddy has been drivin' across state lines, using her car to deliver packages for Jackie Lee, but she swears she had no idea what was in those packages. They were delivered to sweet little ole ladies whom Liddy believed to be relatives. After all, he called them aunt so and so."

"So she had no idea those packages contained marijuana?" Robert asked, narrowing his eyes.

"That's what she says, and I believe her. Hell, she's scared to death. So much so that I think we have about convinced her that marryin' Jackie Lee would be a grave mistake." Randy said, getting up to pace the room, worry lines etched across his face.

"What does Jackie Lee say about it?" Uncle Henry asked.

"Humph!" Randy turned to face the others. "That lying son-of-a-bitch is sayin' Liddy was his accomplice all along. Oh, he admitted to me privately that Liddy didn't know a thing about it, but it's my word against his, and since I'm her father, I'm afraid the DEA believes him over me," Randy retorted. "He's doin' this because Liddy's balkin' at gettin' married."

Johnny Barnett spoke up. "That's not good...not good at all, Randy. You need to get yourself one of them there high dollar lawyers from out in L.A. or someplace like that. I don't know what you're gonna to do, but you'd better do somethin', and do it quick before they formally charge her."

"I agree with Johnny. You need to get a lawyer and get one soon. I don't know what you're gonna to do either," Henry Simpson said.

"I'll tell you what he's gonna to do." Robert suddenly interrupted. "I have a call in to my Navy buddy, Sam Armstrong in Baltimore, Maryland. He's one of the best defense attorneys in the country." Robert got up and again walked over to the window and gazed out.

Henry took a swallow of beer. "I've heard the talk down at the pool hall. The county D.A. has been boasting how the Nunley case has dropped in his lap just in time for the summer primary."

Sam Henry Barnett shook his fist in disgust. "Abernathy! I see why that ole cuss thinks he has a case now. He thinks he's gonna be this state's next governor."

"Well, Abernathy will never get my vote, even if it wasn't for this whole sorry mess with Liddy," scoffed Johnny.

"Let's get back to the subject at hand here," Randy said, pouring another whiskey before returning to his seat. "Robert, what do you know about him, this Armstrong fellow, I mean, and why do you think he can help?"

Leaning against the window jamb, seemingly lost in thought, Robert turned to face the others. "I'll tell you what I know about him. He was a JAG and one of the best men I've ever known. They call him the *junkyard dog* and for good reason. He doesn't let up until he has what he's after. He's been known to rip the prosecution's case apart. When he's makin' a cross examination, he meticulously dismantles the prosecution's witness piece by piece, and his specialty is pickin' apart law enforcement. Sam rarely loses."

Joseph perked up at this intelligence. "How did you meet him? You weren't in the JAG."

Robert pushed away from the window frame and strolled over to where Henry stood. "No, but we went to the Citadel together. He was brilliant and instrumental in pulling me through my freshman year, and then later in law school, we were inseparable. " Robert grabbed a beer and popped the top. "When I came into some trouble in Baghdad back in '91, he was there for me. It cost me my naval career, but at least I was acquitted." Robert took a sip of beer and glanced off to the side.

"I remember that now. I was nine years old. You were in command of a SEAL squad during Desert Storm when one of your petty officers mistook a group of Shiites for insurgents and fired on them. You weren't even there, and yet they charged you with the offense." Joseph narrowed his gaze and clenched his jaw. He understood only too well the consequences of having someone in his command make a mistake.

"Yes, that's what happened," Robert said. "We were court-martialed, and had it been any other JAG representin' me and Luttrell, we would've both been convicted. He'd have been sent to prison, and I would've had to resign in disgrace. But as it was, Ervin was discharged, and I was asked to resign. Anyway, Sam will call me on Monday."

"That's the man you need, Randy." Henry voiced his opinion. "I think you ought to hire him straightaway."

Sam Henry and Johnny affirmed Henry's opinion.

"Robert, how are Lydia and I going to afford Armstrong? He won't be cheap. All of our money is wrapped up in that house your sister had to have, and I can't afford to mortgage it. My income is not sufficient to make the payments," Randy asked hesitantly, his voice filled with apprehensive.

"You're not to be concerned about that. I'll pay the cost." Joseph said, returning to the group from the fireplace where he had been listening. "Robert and I are making arrangements this week."

"Joseph!" Randy looked up sharply. "I appreciate your help, but you must know I cannot repay you."

"I know, and it doesn't matter. As long as I'm able, I intend to help my family, so don't worry about it."

Randy stood and approached his nephew. "Joseph, you are a man like your father. You don't have to do this, but I want you to know how much I greatly appreciate it." Randy offered his hand.

Joseph surveyed the room for any other comments or questions. When none were forthcoming, he said, "Well, it looks like we have about beaten this horse to death. I think we should adjourn until further notice. Robert will act in my absence when I return to my duty station. Lizzy and Jane have power of attorney to settle the bills."

As everyone exited the door, Joseph and Robert lingered. "Robert, is this really as serious as it seems? I mean, this is Liddy's first offence. She is barely twenty-one and five months pregnant. Surely the D.A. will take that into consideration."

Robert put his hand on Joseph's shoulder. "She will most likely receive indictments on both federal and state charges, so it is serious. Serious in that Jackie Lee claims she worked for him, though there is no payment record. Randy forgot to mention that, but I've talked with my contacts in Abernathy's office. Consequently I know a little more than Randy has disclosed. Also, the U.S. Attorney's office will try and cut a deal with Liddy. The Feds need her to testify against Jackie Lee to nail the prosecution's case shut. Liddy's balkin' on that. That's why she needs a damn good criminal lawyer. Liddy may or may not have realized what she was doin', though I doubt it. The Feds suspect she knows a lot more than she's tellin', and frankly, so do I. I'm not buyin' Randy's assertion that she's an innocent bystander. Liddy knew, or at least suspected, what was in those packages."

As they walked through the door and into the foyer, Robert clapped his nephew on the back. "Joseph, you and I will meet together in my office tomorrow, but I don't want you to become distracted by all of this. You're at war. You need to keep *that* as your primary focus. I know only too well what you face, so don't let the home front cloud your thoughts. We'll handle this situation. Is that not right?" Robert asked, glancing around at the others.

All nodded, mumbling their agreements. A few moments later, Daniel came to inform them lunch was ready.

After lunch, Joseph decided to saddle a horse and ride out over the farm since it had been almost three years since he had last been home. As he was going to the barn, he noticed Georgiana Darcy playing with the hound puppies. He watched her for several minutes until she noticed him. She gave him such a large and friendly smile that he could not resist walking over to where she stood.

"Good afternoon, Miss Darcy. You're looking very nice."

She blushed. "Thank you, Mr. Bennett, but please call me Georgiana or Georgie, as I'm sometimes called."

"Georgiana it will be, then," he said with a smile. "I like the sound of your name. Call me Joseph. Do you often play with hounds?" he cheerfully asked. *...She is quite pretty with her long blonde hair.*

"No, not often, but my family has always kept hounds at Pemberley. I have grown fond of them over the years. Hounds are quite pretty and playful when they are puppies." She smiled. "I see you also keep horses. We have several horses at Pemberley as well."

"Do you ride, then?"

"Yes, I do, quite well, actually. But it has been some time since I've had the opportunity. I've been busy in the last few years."

...Hmm...better and better, Joseph thought.

"Well, I'm about to saddle one of the stallions. Would you like to join me?"

"I would like that very much, thank you."

"Then I'll saddle Lizzy's appaloosa mare for you. Her name is Apple. She's not too spirited or too tame."

He saddled two horses and brought the appaloosa mare to Georgiana, who assured him that she could jump. After mounting their horses, they left the barnyard in a full run, jumping fences as they went, riding out into the open fields of the farm.

Joseph showed Georgiana the various fields, the woods where he had played as a child, and finally, coming to the cove, they dismounted.

"Here, let me take her reins. I'll tie the horses to this low hanging branch. They can forage, and we can rest on that rock," he said, pointing to the rock on the rising hill.

"This feels strangely familiar. It reminds me of a place we have at Pemberley." Her lips gently curled. "It's my brothers' favorite place. The only difference is that we don't have a cabin in our cove." She laughed.

Removing the clip that held her hair, she tossed her head, shaking her long blonde tresses loose.

"Really? You have a place similar to this?" He smiled. "And here I thought I would be showing a London girl something unusual. Are you familiar with the countryside, then?"

"Oh yes! Pemberley is my family's country estate. We have several thousand acres of land with cattle and sheep and horses. There are deep woods as well as open fields. Don't you remember, I told you we kept horses and hounds?"

"Ah, that you did. I guess it didn't fully register." He grinned.

"Pay attention, Joseph. I might say something extraordinary, and you wouldn't want to miss it." The sound of her gay laughter rang through the air. "Now tell me why you have a cabin here in the woods. Did your family build it for a getaway or for when you go shooting? My father has a hunting lodge. It was the original manor house of Pemberley."

"Really?" he said, amused by her gleeful air. "What a strange coincidence. Our cabin is similar, though I don't use it for a hunting lodge. It is the original home place of the first Bennett family who settled this land in 1803. We have kept it in its original state to preserve our family history."

"Fascinating! Tell me about it. I love to hear family histories. I have a few of my own."

He smiled warmly and chuckled while resisting the incredible urge to put his arm around her. "I'll tell you if you promise to share yours as well."

"It's a promise—so tell."

Joseph began the long tale from beginning to end, telling her about the scandal, the discovery of the Cumberland Gap, the Westward Expansion, the settling of the land, the War Between the States, and on and on until the present day. He held her interest through the entire story, and when he finished, she told her own family history. He felt very relaxed and at ease in her company. How long had it been since he had been with a girl? He had to wonder. It had not been since he was at Annapolis, and then that had been infrequent. Her smile and animated hand gestures reminded him of his sisters. She had Lizzy's liveliness when she spoke, but Jane's quiet, soft features when she listened, and Kat's forthrightness with Mary Beth's gentle smile. However, there was nothing sisterly about the feelings she invoked in him.

That presented a whole new problem. It was a good thing she would be returning to town soon, because he knew if he spent very much time in her presence, it would make it all the harder when he had to leave for Camp Pendleton in a few weeks. As much as he'd like to get to know her better, he knew it was in their mutual best interests that he not do so, especially considering the uncertainty of his future.

Joseph and Georgiana returned three hours later, laughing and talking. Georgiana actually flirted with the young officer, and he seemed to enjoy it. All of this did not go unnoticed by David, who had been walking around the farm, getting a feel for the place. He only smiled as he watched them go into the house. It was about time Georgiana showed an interest in a man, and Bennett appeared to be a rather nice sort of chap. David thought they would suit each other quite well.

Turning back to his purpose, he walked through the gardens and into the barnyard to find all the horses there. Uncle Henry had told him it would be all right for him to saddle a horse and ride out over the farm. He'd even gone so far as to suggest which horse might suit him. Of all the horses Henry had described, David thought he would prefer the black stallion, but since Joseph had just ridden him, David would have to select another.

Carefully watching so as to not step in a cow-pie or a horse-apple, he ambled towards the mares grazing at the feed trough. David examined each horse meticulously, finding them all to be well-kept and healthy with great conformation, but the only spirited one amongst them appeared to be the black stallion snorting and stomping in the yard. Yet, upon closer inspection, he determined that the chestnut mare held more spirit than any of the others available, so he chose her.

"Come on, milady," he said, taking her by the bridle and leading her into the barn where he found saddles and a bit laid over a rail. Saddling the horse, he thought of the cove Joseph had described. He desperately needed some place of solace to sit and think—some place quiet and peaceful where he could sort out what he was discovering about Fitzwilliam's new family. And then there was the woman who continued to invade his thoughts and haunt his dreams. He'd think about her, too.

As David mounted the horse, he bent low and stroked her neck while he whispered in her ear. "Lady, take me away to some place where I can hear myself think." He gently caressed her mane. "You're a good girl, so let's find the cove."

The mare snorted and tossed her head as if she understood and was off like a bullet when David gently set his heel to her flank. He didn't know the horse's name, so to him, she was 'Lady' for she held herself well and gaited with a smooth grace, having characteristics he could only assign to a sophisticated lady of noble birth. When she took the first fence, her jump was made with ease, as fluid and effortlessly as any horse he'd ever sat.

It was not hard to find the cove with the instructions he had received, and the horse seemed to instinctively know where to take him. Slowing down to a canter, David smiled as he leaned forward to rub her neck once more. He had a way of making a connection with mares, and Lady was no different. He slowed the horse down even more and trotted into the heart of the cove where he came to a stop by the stream and dismounted, tying the mare to a nearby tree branch. Lady shook her head, whinnying and pawing the ground as her master walked over to the flat rock and took a seat.

Sitting there, he felt the peaceful, easy feeling this place had to offer. It was very much like his favorite place in his boyhood home in Derbyshire where he would steal away anytime he needed quiet relaxation. The fresh aromas of cedar and pine from the woods, mixed with the smell of a recent rain, soothed his spirits while the steady rush of water and the crash of the falls tumbling into the pool relaxed his body, setting the mood for deep concentration.

...Fitzwilliam may not agree, but it would be best if no one in England learns of his marriage and consequently, this sordid affair with Elizabeth's family. They're all involved with it...as is to be expected, I suppose. The stupid girl has to be protected, even if it is mostly from herself. If it were reversed and one of our cousins was involved, Fitzwilliam would do all that he could to help, whilst Father would try and distance himself from it. What would I do? I don't know. What will I do now?

He mulled it over, trying to decide. *...I'll protect my brother, that's what I will do.*

I'll help Father to keep Fitzwilliam's marriage a secret, and I will try and keep this information about the Bennett family away from my father, even if it puts me between the two of them. Elizabeth makes Fitzwilliam happy, and anyone that makes my brother happy is important to me, therefore, I will protect her, too. Father must not discover any of this.

That finally decided, his mind drifted to the woman…the woman who wouldn't leave him alone. No matter what he did, he could not squash those thoughts or repress those feelings—feelings he was unsure of, feelings he had never felt before. For whatever foolish or perhaps impulsive reason, he'd bought Cecilia a gift. Except for his sister, he'd never given any girl or woman a gift, and even now, he wasn't sure he would actually go through with it. He struggled. *…I'm only a few hundred miles away…I want to see her. I have to see her. I have to know what it is I'm feeling. I know it's not what they call love. I don't have the tender disposition Fitzwilliam has. I never have. I'm not romantic.*

I've got to get hold of myself. I'll go to Charleston, see Cecilia, give her the gift, and then I will have it out of my system. Yes, that's what I will do. I'll spend two days with her. She can be a lot of fun, and I do enjoy her company, so what does it matter? I'm not in love. It's just a fantasy—one we can both enjoy for two days, and then I can go back to London to Cybil or Sandra, or whoever else I choose. I will take what I want and leave when I want.

He smiled, content in finally having come to an understanding with himself. Lying back on the rock, he closed his eyes, allowing visions of Cecilia standing there before him naked and dancing in the light of a harvest moon to take his mind captive. She was beckoning him with an outstretched hand to join her. In his mind's eye, he stripped off his clothing and danced with her before they both dove into the pool. He could feel her soft wet hand stroking the side of his face. Hear the muffled sound of her gentle voice. It was so real—too real. He woke up to find one of the farm hounds whining and licking the side of his face. Shocked, he jumped up, glaring at the Redbone who apparently thought she had found a buddy. Unable to resist, he reached over and rubbed her head, scratching behind her ears. Pushing himself up, he promptly went to the pool to wash his face and hair.

When he felt sufficiently clean, David stood erect and walked back to the hound, patting her once more. "Come on, Lassie. Let's return. Would you like to run? Well, let's see if you can keep up." David grinned, ruffling her ears before turning to walk in the direction of the mare. With one smooth fluid motion he mounted the horse and tore out of the cove in a full gallop. To his amazement, the hound kept pace quite well, even clearing the fences with ease. Back in the barnyard, he unsaddled the horse, rubbed her down, and gave her a scoop of grain, and then gave the dog a biscuit from the dog tin by the barn door. Once the horse and dog were attended to, he left for the farmhouse.

With a light step, he walked towards the house, intending to rest on the porch swing, but as he approached, he noticed it was occupied by his sister and Joseph. Springing up the steps, he greeted them. "Bennett, you have some very fine animals. I rode your chestnut mare. She has a fine gait and a strong run. Jumps very well, too. How old is she? Two…three years?" he asked. "And what is her name? I called her Lady," David laughed, "and she seemed to respond quite well."

"Well, that's because she is Lady Macbeth. She thought you knew her." Joseph chuckled. "I believe she's three and a half. She was a foal the last time I saw her, and yes, I think she is a fine animal. She's the lead mare. I noticed Sally Mae coming back with you. She appears to be taken with you, too."

"So that's her name. Yes, I think she does like me. She woke me up with her kisses when I napped after my ride," David smirked. "Not exactly the way I'd like to be awakened, but it served its purpose. Had it not been for her, I might very well still be out there. Does she usually travel that far out from the house?"

"All the time. She loves to track and often goes to the woods. Sometimes she's gone for days, so I'm glad you brought her home. Like I said, she likes you, or she wouldn't have approached you like she did. I guess she's like all the rest of the ladies. She can't resist your charm either." Joseph laughed.

"Well, Sally Mae's kisses are one lady's affections I think I could very well do without." David grinned as he walked over to the wicker bench and took a seat. "Tell me, Bennett, how much longer are you going to be here before you leave for your next duty station?"

"It was supposed to be a full month, but I received a call a few hours ago. The general wants us all back at Camp Pendleton in two weeks. I've been cut short a week. How about y'all? How much longer will you be staying?"

"We should probably leave at about the same time. I have a lot of work to do when we return to London. That reminds me," David said, turning to his sister. "Georgiana, I am leaving in the morning for South Carolina. I have some things there I need to attend to. Do you think you will be all right at the townhouse by yourself?"

At about that time Lori and Tana walked out onto the porch. "Heavens, no, she won't. Georgiana, dear, you are invited to stay here with us while your brother is away. In fact, just stay for the next two weeks," Aunt Lori said.

David smiled, catching the gleam in the ladies' eyes and the embarrassment on Bennett's face while Georgiana's lit up.

"I'd love to stay, Mrs. Simpson." Georgiana rose from the swing to greet the Aunts. "Mrs. Bennett, will you be here, too?"

"Yes, I'll come out for some of the time, but it will have to be after five. That's when I close the flower shop. Miss Darcy, if you would like, you can visit me in town at the shop."

"Oh, I'd like that, but do call me Georgiana. Miss Darcy sounds a bit stuffy."

"Georgiana it is then, and you can call me Tana." Turning to Joseph, she said, "Do bring Georgiana to town while you attend to whatever business you have with Robert tomorrow. We'll all have lunch together down at Loony's Diner."

"I'd love that," Georgiana replied. "So you own a floral shop?"

"Yes, I do. I'll show it to you when you come in, then we can meet the men for lunch." Tana clutched Georgiana's hands as the two women laughed.

"How about you, Mr. Darcy, would you like to stay with us?" Lori asked.

"Ah, no, I thank you. I'm going to South Carolina in the morning, and I plan to be gone for a couple of days. When I come back, I will stay with my brother and have a look around town. I'd like to get a feel for the small rural atmosphere of a Southern town."

"Well, you're most welcome to stay with us when you return if you change your mind."

"Oh, and do drop in on us while you're in town," Tana interjected. "Usually we're at our farm, but this month we're stayin' at our townhouse on Vine Street. It's just down from Willow and Elm. Elizabeth and Fitzwilliam can give you the directions."

"Thank you, Mrs. Bennett, I would love to." Turning to Lori, he continued. "And thank you, Mrs. Simpson for your kind offer. I'll consider it. Now, if you will excuse me, I think Georgiana and I should be on our way back to town. I will drop her off early in the morning on my way to South Carolina."

Lori spoke up in alarm. "Oh, but you cannot leave. You must stay for supper. I can't bear the thought of you two havin' to eat cold leftovers or goin' out. You must stay. It's already fixed. I just need to set it on the table."

"Yes, you both must stay. We have all this food here. It would be a shame to let it go to waste," Tana pleaded.

The aunts were so insistent that David felt compelled to comply.

Chapter Twenty-two

...I will never forget anything about you...

Cecilia paced back and forth in her executive office, exasperated. "Cameron, what do you want from me? I've agreed to co-sponsor the Camellia Festival with you. I've even gone so far as to foot the bill for most of the preparations. I'm even hosting the ball in the Lawton Ballroom. Is that not enough?"

Cameron Taylor let out a sigh as he sat down and crossed his legs. "No, Celia. No, it's not. If you are gonna co-sponsor the event with me, then we need to attend together...as a *couple*. It's less than two weeks away. We need to settle this now. If we appear as a couple, it will generate more publicity, and consequently, more donations for the Charleston Arts Foundation. You *do* care about that, don't you?"

She strolled across the floor to the window and looked out at the busy street below, her hands held behind her back as she rubbed them together in frustration. "I care," she gently nodded, "but that's not the point. I just don't want or need a date. I would much rather watch this year than dance, and if you and I are there as a couple, I won't be allowed to stay in the background. Besides," she softly said, glancing over her shoulder, "people will view us as an item and begin talking."

Folding his arms across his chest, he rolled his eyes to the ceiling. "Since when do you give a damn about what people think or say?" He gave her a pointed look. "But I know what you are alludin' to. Don't worry yourself darlin'. I have no intention of announcin' an engagement. *Not* yet anyway."

She turned sharply on her heel and shot him a warning glare.

"Come on, Cecilia, you know it's expected of us, and we were once very close. We can be so again. It's time both of us thought about our futures. We have our families' heritages to think about." He got up from his chair and walked over to where she stood, placing his hand on her shoulder and leaning in close. "The merger of Lawton & Co. with Taylor Shippin' would be a wise and very profitable move," he hesitated just a moment, pursing his lips, "on both our parts. It's time we grew up and thought about our responsibilities to more than just ourselves."

Refusing to face him, she jerked out of his grasp, snapping her head away from his feverish breath burning down the side of her neck. "No! I won't do it. We're not even dating, and you are already planning our future. What makes you think I would marry you? You're still seeing Amelia. Why would I be so foolish as to align myself with you in any manner, let alone in matrimony?"

He smirked at her reaction. "Because you need to secure your future, and you need a man who knows how to manage not only a business, but a home and a family, too." He reached out and grabbed her arm. "You need a family. We both do. As for Amelia, I've already told you she means nothin' to me, and as soon as you are back where you belong, I'll drop her. But remember, a man has needs. You don't expect me to be without while I wait for you to come around do you? After all, you're not—"

She cut him off and jerked out of his grasp. "What the hell is that supposed to mean?" She felt as if a large hand had just grabbed her middle section and squeezed hard.

"You're seein' that Brit, and I know it." He cast a feigned nonchalant look, retreating back to the other side of the room.

"A man has needs, huh? And I guess you can't temper your needs to suit the situation? Not much different than last time. Well, let me clue you in on something, Taylor." Her eyes locked with his in a deadly stare. "A woman has needs, too, and they are not necessarily *all* in the bedroom, either."

"Oh, and I suppose your Englishman understands those needs, does he?" Cameron narrowed his gaze.

"He knows how to treat a lady, unlike you," she mocked. *...At least he's a quick learner, which you are not!*

"A lady, huh. I seem to remember you being a little less than a lady, but then that was a long time ago." He chuckled, running his fingers across the back of the chair he'd sat in earlier.

Cecilia's chest tightened. Her eyes flashed a warning for him to drop it.

"We'll not discuss this subject any further for the time being." Cameron stood, focusing intently on her. "Back to the Camellia Festival, are you goin' with me or not?"

She looked at him, shaking her head while wringing her hands as she stepped away to pace the floor, choosing to ignore his last comments. Cameron was right. She knew it—and hated it. *...Why did my brother have to die? If he had only lived, then I would not carry this heavy responsibility. I would be free to do as I please.*

Anxiety gripped her. She chewed on her lower lip, contemplating the situation. She threw up her hands.

"Okay, I'll attend with you, but it will mean nothing. That is, nothing more than that I've agreed to host the function with you and to be your date for the evening, but that's *all*. Nothing more," she firmly stated. "I want you to understand that. I am not the girl I once was, nor do I harbor any tender feelings for you, and I doubt that I *ever* will."

"You once did." He laughed with a glint in his eyes. "You will again. I'm not the fool I was seven years ago, as you are not the naive girl. I'll pick you up at your penthouse at six, and I won't be late, so *you* be ready. Now, how about dinner tonight?"

"No, not tonight. I'm very tired. I just got in from Peru late Sunday, and I've had a busy day. I'm going to call it an early evening and get some much needed rest. Call me in a day or two, and we'll talk more." Cecilia dipped her head, rubbing her temples, trying to suppress the terrible headache threatening to erupt.

"Suit yourself. I'll call you by the weekend, and we'll have dinner. Remember, I'd rather be with you than anyone else." He crossed the room to where she stood and pulled her into an embrace, kissing her brow, and then he moved towards the door.

Finally alone, Cecilia grabbed a couple of aspirin from her desk drawer, downed them with what remained of the bottled water beside her phone, and collapsed onto the small couch in her office. She threw her head back and closed her eyes. She must have sat there for over an hour thinking over the events of the afternoon. "How did I get myself into this mess?" she asked out loud, releasing a long breath.

"And what mess would that be?" a man asked in a distinctly British accent as he walked through her open door.

"David!" Cecilia jerked, startled, but pleasantly surprised. "What are you doing here?" She jumped up and ran to him, throwing her arms around his waist and giving him a hug.

He chuckled as he looked down at the woman in his arms. "Well, I'm glad you're at least happy to see me."

She released him and stepped back. "You don't know the half of it. I've had a

M.K. Baxley

difficult day, but I am surprised to see you. It's unexpected." She creased her brow. "I know we don't have an appointment."

"No, I don't have an appointment. I'm visiting in the area, and since I happen to have some time on my hands, I decided to stop by to invite you to dinner. That is, if you don't already have plans. I tried calling all afternoon, but Ashley said you were busy." He hesitated a moment and smiled. "I decided, on the spur of the moment, to take a chance and see if you were free. When I arrived at the front desk, Ashley told me you were alone and to go right in. So here I am."

His smile was warm and friendly and inviting, and God only knew how much she needed a diversion, especially such a handsome one as David Darcy provided.

"As a matter of fact," she tilted her head with a genuine smile, "I am free tonight, and I would *love* to have dinner with you." She felt her body finally releasing some of the tension Cameron had created. "Where are you staying?"

"I'm staying at the Lawton, and I have made reservations at the Woodlands. I walked over. Shall I walk you back to the hotel?"

"Yes, I would appreciate that. I'll get my coat, and we can be off."

They walked the short distance from the Lawton Executive Complex to the Lawton Hotel where David escorted her to her suite before returning to his room to prepare for their evening. He told her he had two days in the area before having to rejoin his party in Tennessee. They agreed to have dinner that night and the next. They would have lunch the next day at a little sidewalk café she preferred on Queen Street.

They also agreed to meet in the lobby of the hotel before leaving for the Woodlands. Within thirty minutes, David was ready to go. When he walked into the entryway from the lift, Cecilia was waiting.

"David, do you want me to drive, or would you prefer to do so this time?"

"I'll drive since I know where we're going," he said, placing his hand on the small of her back as he led her out the door to the parking lot where they settled into his car.

When they arrived at the Woodlands, the hostess took their coats and then directed them to the waiting maître d'. After David told the gentleman his name, the stoic man observed them closely and smiled. "Table for two in the private dining room, just as you requested, Mr. Darcy. Come this way." The man escorted them past the main dining room and into a room illuminated with candles and decorated with fresh camellias on the table. Cecilia smiled, evidently pleased as she took in the sight of the room.

"Do you like the flowers?" David asked as he helped her into her seat before he took his own. Pleasantly amused by the look on her face, he smiled as he watched her fingers delicately brush the curve of the vase.

"Yes, they are beautiful," she said. "Crystal seahorse...my very favorite. I've always admired this vase, but never bought it. This is a Waterford."

"Yes, yes, it is, and it's for you, along with the flowers. I'm glad you like it. I know it can't replace the one you broke when you threw it at me, but I thought I would make the attempt just the same."

"Oh, David, you didn't have to do that." She looked up at him in wonder. "I'd just as soon forget that night."

He loved the way her violet eyes twinkled and sparkled in the candlelight. Her look was priceless.

"I know I didn't have to, but I wanted to. And I will never forget that night, Cecilia," he gently said. *...I will never forget anything about you. This time we have will be with me always.*

"Well, it is very thoughtful of you, and I do appreciate it. Thank you."

176

Changing the subject, he picked up the menu and began to scan over the selections. "Now, shall I choose for you since you chose for me last time?"

"Make a suggestion. I'll tell you if I like it." She took a sip of water, eyeing him closely as the corners of her mouth lifted.

"All right. What do you think about filet mignon stuffed with roasted peppers, spinach, and goat cheese in port wine sauce?"

"That sounds delicious, but let me choose the sides. I want a garden salad with olive oil and red wine vinegar, and some brown rice served with wild mushroom sauce. You choose the wine." She closed the menu and set it aside.

He smiled, very pleased by her relaxed expression. Placing his menu aside, he picked up the wine menu and scanned over the selections, finding one that piqued his interest. "We'll have Chateau La Fleur Petrus, 1980 for the year you were born." He glanced first at her and then at the sommelier before folding his menu and placing it, along with the main menu, atop hers.

"That's so sweet of you, Darcy."

The wine steward soon returned and presented the bottle to David for his approval. After sampling the wine, David smiled and nodded, whereupon the man poured each of them a glass.

When their dinner was served, they ate with quiet conversation. David listened, not having much to say, as Cecilia went on and on about first one thing and then another. He tried to pay attention to the details about the Camellia Festival or was it the Magnolia? He couldn't remember. She'd talked about both, but it didn't interest him, and the more he tried to listen, the more his mind drifted. He hoped she didn't notice his disinterest in the conversation, or the way his eyes surely glazed over from fatigue. He shook his head, trying to dispatch the mental fog while he continued to cut his meat, but evidently Cecilia did notice.

"David, I'm not wearing any panties."

He froze. Almost choking on his last bite of food, tears filed his eyes. Recovering, he put down his knife and fork and looked up as he reached for his napkin. "Excuse me, but did you just say you're not wearing any knickers?"

"I see I now have your full attention," she said, continuing to eat as if nothing out of the ordinary had transpired. "I guess you're not interested in the Magnolia Festival," she shrugged. "And yes, I did." She glanced up with piercing eyes before returning to her meat.

"I'm sorry, Cecilia. No, I wasn't listening."

"That's good of you to admit it! Now pay attention to me when I'm talking to you. I might have something interesting to say." She glanced at him and raised one eyebrow, giving him a sensuous smile.

"Yes, well, ah…what were you saying?" …*Interesting indeed!*

"I was saying that I would like to invite you to escort me to the Magnolia Festival in April, if you would be interested."

He hesitated for a moment, wrinkling his brow. "I'll have to get back with you on that. I'm not sure of my schedule for April. Write down the date, and I will ring you up to let you know if my schedule permits."

Cecilia pulled out a business card, quickly jotted down the event and date along with her cell phone number and handed it to him. He took it and placed it in his breast pocket, smiling at her, still enthralled with thoughts of her missing knickers.

Picking up his knife and fork, he said, "Lawton, I never know what to expect from you. One minute you're a professional businesswoman and then just like that you change, and you're just a woman." …*No, not just a woman…but an irresistible woman.*

Staring at him from across the table, she responded with a salacious grin, "David, there are many facets to a woman. It's up to you to figure them out."

He laughed, shaking his head. "No, Cecilia, you're one woman I shall *never* figure out."

Cecilia prattled on for the good part of an hour before they decided it was time to leave. She gathered the vase of flowers and they headed toward the front to collect their coats.

David shook his head while wearing what he thought must be a silly grin as they walked to the car. Although he gave the appearance of paying careful attention to her every word, his mind was pleasantly engaged elsewhere.

Upon arriving back at the Lawton Hotel, a steady, pouring rain had begun to fall. Pulling under the canopied entrance, he said, "Cecilia, the valet seems to not be on duty. You get out here. I'm going to park. I'll be in shortly."

"David, you'll get soaked! Do you have an umbrella?"

"No, but I'll be all right. Perhaps it will lighten. Either way, I'll join you in the lobby." He let her out just as lightning streaked across the sky followed by a loud clap of thunder.

Cecilia paced in the lobby as she watched the door. ...*Damn, it's too bad David didn't arrive sooner. I could have asked him to the Camellia Festival, and then I wouldn't have to go with Cameron. Well, Cameron Taylor, I've beat you to the draw this next time. Oh yes I have. There's no way in hell I'm going to the Magnolia Festival with **you**, and you can forget about a future between the two of us. I'd just as soon marry Darcy.* She laughed at the wily turn of her thoughts. ...*And I sure as hell won't marry him either, even if he were the marrying kind.*

Turning to glance at the door once more, she saw David enter, pausing to shake the dripping water from his coat. Spotting her from across the lobby, he smiled and headed in her direction, his coat flapping about him and water dripping on the floor as he walked.

A shiver coursed through her body as her eyes fixed upon his tall frame. David Darcy walked the way he made love—slow, easy, deliberate, and with great confidence. Her body tightened as he approached. When he stood next to her, he bent down and kissed her cheek. She blinked twice and shuddered.

...*Daddy! He reminds me of my daddy—powerful and full of confidence. A man like Daddy. Oh, you must be careful, Cecilia...very careful!*

"Come on, let's go. I need to get out of these wet clothes. We'll stop by my room so I can change, then if you want, we can go to the bar for a drink or have coffee. Anything you like." He put his arm around her, escorting her to the lift.

As they stepped through the door, she slipped her arm under his coat and around his waist, nestling into his chest. "I'll think about it and let you know when we get to your room. You know, I haven't been in one of my own hotel suites in years. I'll have to see what it looks like." She looked up at him with an irresistible smile, and he, in return, couldn't resist bending down and tapping the tip of her nose just as the lift door opened.

Opening the door to his room, they stepped inside. "Well, what do you think? Does it meet with your approval?"

Her eyes swept over the Jefferson Davis Suite, well pleased with what she saw. This was the most luxurious suite the Lawton had to offer next to her own. It was a spacious two-room suite with a handcrafted cherry four poster king sized bed, fitted with a handmade quilt. It had a large marble bath with gold-plated fixtures and a separate sitting room with an elegant fireplace, and all fashioned, from the paintings to the furnishings, in authentic pieces from the antebellum period. She smiled and turned to David.

"Hmm…it looks like my decorators did a decent job last year. But the question is, how do *you* like it?"

"It's very comfortable… and beautiful… as you are beautiful. Let me change, and we'll make our plans for the evening."

He nudged her chin upward with his forefinger and gave her a quick kiss before departing into the bedroom.

After David changed, he approached Cecilia in the sitting area. "So, Miss Lawton, what would you like to do for the rest of the evening?"

…If you only knew. "Oh, I don't know." She tossed her hair over her shoulder. "I'm not in the mood to sit in the bar. What would you say to coming back to my suite for coffee and maybe watching a movie or a little TV, or perhaps we could just sit and talk? I promise I won't attack you or throw anything. I've had a very tough day. I need to unwind and relax, so what do you think? Would any of that be agreeable to you?" She smiled innocently, knowing exactly what she desired, but considering their history, she wasn't sure she wanted to make the first move. She'd play it by ear.

"That's fine with me. But I'm rather disappointed that you aren't going to attack me. I must be losing my charm." He closed the distance between them and gathered her into his arms. Looking deep into her mischievous eyes, he asked, "Tell me, Lawton, are you really not wearing any knickers?" He nuzzled her hair as kissed her temple. His hand brushed the side of her cheek and trailed down her neck to her shoulder.

She lifted her head as his lips found their way to hers, while his fingers sank into the back of her hair. Breaking the kiss, she whispered softly against his lips, "Come upstairs and find out."

He flashed a sexy smile with a devilish look in his eyes. Again Cecilia shuddered. He was just what she needed tonight.

Once in her suite, she placed the vase on the buffet and went to the kitchen to make a pot of fresh coffee while David settled on the sofa. Shortly, she returned with two steaming cups and sank down next to him. David took a few sips before setting his aside.

"What would you like to watch? I don't have any movies here with me, but there should be something on TV or pay for view."

She perused the channels, but the look in his eyes told her TV was not what he had in mind.

"The only movie I want to watch is the one we make together," he said as he pulled her to him and snuggled into her hair, inhaling deeply.

Snuggling a little closer, she reached up and gently kissed his jaw while placing her hand on his cheek, guiding his mouth to hers.

David groaned, his arms encircling her as he laid them both down gently, deepening the kiss.

Cecilia broke away and whispered in-between kisses, "Stay with me tonight."

"If that's what you want, I'll stay."

"That's what I want." Desperate for his touch, she claimed his lips once more. Her tongue slipped into his mouth as his met hers, battling for dominance.

His hand slid down her body, caressing her every curve as he made his way to the hem of her dress. Sliding his hand underneath and traversing upwards, he broke their kiss and pulled back. Looking into her teasing eyes, he released a deep throated laugh.

"Lawton, what are you doing to me?" He nuzzled her nose. "You really aren't wearing any knickers, are you?"

Smiling back at him, she shook her head and answered, "I never lay down a wager I can't back up, especially about such things as that…and especially not with you."

He chuckled. "Lawton, you little imp. You're full of surprises, and you never cease to amaze me." He smacked her tantalizing bottom and grabbed a handful, but when his eyes met hers, he grew silent, his breath coming quick and erratic.

Rolling him over on his back, she firmly settled on top, sinking her fingers deep into his dark curls, aggressively kissing him—touching, caressing, and stroking. His hands massaged her bare bottom as they kissed while his mind relaxed, giving into the pleasure she gave as his body hardened in response to the woman finally in his arms—the woman who had haunted his dreams for nearly two months, tantalizing and teasing him.

Releasing his lips, she summoned him. "Come with me." Getting up, she stretched forth her hand, and without a word, he took it and followed her.

They quietly undressed, each carefully studying the other. She pulled back the coverlet and slipped between the sheets, beckoning him by the intense expression in her eyes. Closing out all thoughts of work, society functions, and family responsibilities, Cecilia surrendered her body to him as he gathered her into his arms.

As they made love, he showered her with more tenderness than she had ever known with anyone. He worshiped her with his body, cupping her breasts gently, his lips hotly brushing over her skin while his hands stroked her every curve. She felt cherished, loved, and desired as she savored his every touch… his every caress… his every kiss, and she made it her goal to return as much as she had been given. David Darcy was the only man who had ever taken the time, or put forth the effort to love her with his body. It was another night to equal their first. Satiated, Cecilia's thoughts drifted as she rested her head on the shoulder of her lover while her hand lay over his heart, feeling its steady beat.

…What am I going to do? I can't love him… I don't even want to love him… I have to be logical. It will never work—he's not the marrying kind and someday I must marry. I have a responsibility. Cameron says he loves me, and I could possibly learn to love him, couldn't I? The merger of Lawton with Taylor Shipping is the logical thing to do, and clearly for the best. We'll have a couple of kids, and life will go on.

David is too much like my father. He will never love anyone. I probably won't, either…But what about passion? What about what we share?

She drifted off into a contented sleep only to be awoken within the hour by his soft lips on her throat. He made love to her repeatedly throughout the night, their desire nearly insatiable, until they both collapsed, completely spent from sheer exhaustion.

The next day Cecilia called her office, asking Daniel to cover her early morning appointments. She had breakfast sent to her suite where they ate, talked, and made love most of the morning. Later, beneath the protection of her umbrella, they walked around the corner and down the street where Cecilia and David had lunch inside the sunroom at a little sidewalk café on Queen Street.

Had it not been for the drizzling, intermittent rain all morning mixed with a cold biting wind coming in off the ocean, she would have preferred they take their lunch outside under the pergola covered in grapevines and blue wisteria. In late summer, it was beautiful with the grapes falling down between the beams, and in her mind's eye, she could see them sitting there together, sipping iced tea, talking and laughing while they ate. But for today, they had hot tea and ate their sandwiches with very little conversation. She mildly wondered what was on his mind as he seemed to be in the midst of a mental struggle. Was he feeling as awkward as she was about what they had shared?

When lunch was concluded, David set his napkin aside and called for the bill. Hesitating, he finally spoke the words she dreaded. "Cecilia, I'm afraid my plans have changed. I'll be returning to Tennessee today." His eyes traced her face as if he were searching for her reaction.

She was greatly disappointed. She'd been looking forward to another evening with him, but she'd be damned before she would allow him to see it.

"I see," she said coolly, slipping back into her aloof mask of disinterest. "Let me thank you for dinner and the lovely evening, then. I enjoyed it," she said with a clipped tone, "Oh, and thank you for the vase of flowers. It was truly a lovely thought." Her smile was more forced than an indication of true pleasure. But it was all right. She had learned a long time ago not to expect too much. Last night, David had given her what she needed most, tenderness and a night of hot passionate sex, and with that, she would be content.

He walked her back to the Lawton Executive Complex and dropped her off in the main lobby. After kissing her goodbye, he left. Cecilia closed her eyes and shook her head as she reached up and wiped away a single solitary tear. It had stung when he had told her he was leaving, but she knew to hold on loosely. That way she would never be hurt like the women who had loved her father—a strong and powerful man who had been unable to love anyone but her. She understood that. And after all, had she not told Darcy not to expect anything from her? So why should she expect anything from him? They had an agreement. She would be content with whatever he gave her and would ask for nothing more.

Feeling more satisfied than she had felt in a long time, Cecilia took the elevator to the second floor. A smile graced her face as she entered her office, but no sooner had she stepped over the threshold, than the smile faded from her face.

Chapter Twenty-three

... More than a Feeling...

Taken aback by the unexpected appearance, Cecilia halted abruptly in mid-step. "Cameron! What are you doing here?"

"Surprised to see me, I see, or is it just plain *shocked*," he sneered. "I thought you were too tired to go to dinner last night!"

Cecilia closed the door behind her and strode over to her desk, glaring at him every step of the way. Going through the motion of looking over the afternoon schedule, her mind was in turmoil and on anything but her upcoming appointments. She looked up and caught Cameron's narrowing gaze. "I recovered," she said coolly.

He paced in front of her, a pointed look first at the clock on the wall and then at her. "Tell me, did you sleep with him?"

"It's none of your business."

Ignoring the warning bite in her voice, Cameron probed, "Do you love him?"

"Have I ever loved anyone?"

"Oh, I'd like to think you loved me once. We were *close*, as I recall."

"Don't flatter yourself, Taylor. It was an infatuation—sex—nothing more than that."

"Just sex? I don't think so. I was there, too, or did you forget?"

Tapping her fingers on her desk, she glanced up. "You're hopeless, Cameron. I wish I'd taken the day off."

"Hopeless?" He laughed. "No, not hopeless. I remember how you trembled in my arms when we made love and how you would laugh and sport around with me when we rode together on my daddy's plantation. You cared, and you loved me." He walked over to the large window and looked out.

Listening to him recall their past did nothing for her as she paused to think about it. Had she loved him? No, she knew she hadn't, because when she found him with someone else, she hadn't even cared as she presumed a woman in love surely would. Instead, an icy hardness had frozen her heart, reminding her of how foolish she'd been to have trusted him in the first place—a mistake she'd vowed never to make again. No man would ever own her heart. The cost was too high.

Cameron turned from the window, watching her, becoming increasingly irritated with her lack of response. Finally he burst forth. "Celia, I insist on an answer. Do you love him?!"

"I don't owe you any answers, nor am I accountable to you—"

"Cut the crap, Celia. Just tell me. Do you love him?!" Fire flew from his steel blue eyes as he shouted from across the room.

"No, he's just a friend. Are you satisfied?!" She raised an eyebrow, appearing cool and in complete control, though her mind was in a state of turbulence.

Cameron breathed a breath of relief and walked over to where Cecilia stood, taking her hand in his. "I'm sorry, babe. I know I hurt you," he said as he rubbed the back of her hand. "I was only twenty years old. We were young—too young for what we were gettin' into. You don't know how many times I have regretted it. We'd be married today, if not for that one little indiscretion."

"One little indiscretion?" she shot back, withdrawing her hand. "After all these years, you still don't have a clue, do you? Well, allow *me* to clue you in. I was your girlfriend for nearly three years! And yes, we were young, but I was old enough to know that you don't cheat on someone you're talking marriage with." Cecilia recoiled and turned away as tears of anger stung her eyes.

Cameron grabbed her shoulder and spun her around. "I meant it back then, and I mean it today! We were meant for one another. It's just that I was young and stupid. If I could take it back, I would!"

His penetrating stare appeared to search for a truce or perhaps a trace of those old feelings. She didn't know which, but she felt none of it. She remained unmoved. "I don't know what you meant back then. All I know is that we were together as a couple. You were the first man I'd ever been with in any way, and yet, after three years, I wasn't enough for you." She stepped back. "You had to screw around on me, and not with just anyone, either, but with the *one* person who loathes me and always has! *That's* what I cannot overcome or forgive, so let's just drop it!" Cecilia slammed her appointment book shut as she dropped into her seat, giving him a cold stare.

"You'll have dinner with me tonight. I'll pick you up at six." He turned to walk in the direction of the door, stopping long enough to pick up his overcoat draped over a chair back before turning back to face her. "Cecilia, we were meant for one another, and no damned Englishman can prevent it. I intend to make everything up to you. I'll begin tonight."

"Don't bother, Cameron. I'm working late to make up for this morning. Call me by the weekend. Perhaps I'll reconsider and we'll talk, but that's all we'll be doing."

"You have to eat, so if we don't do anything more than just sit here in your office with Chinese takeout, we'll have dinner together. *Tonight!* Everybody has to eat." He wavered, dropping his gaze momentarily. "I really am sorry, Celia, but I mean it. I love you, babe. We can be as good as we ever were."

Cameron turned to open the door, but before he had time to walk through it, she called out to him. "Cameron, don't bother to bring anything." Cecilia rose from her desk and walked over to where he stood. "If you really want to make things up to me, then respect my wishes. Call me in a day or two, and we'll talk about dinner. Now, if you will excuse me, I really *do* have a lot of work to do."

"I'll call you tomorrow," he said, hesitating, his eyes searching hers as he pressed his hand to her face, gently stroking it. He then turned and drifted into the executive lobby toward the elevator.

As she watched him go, Cecilia noted that he had none of the confidence in his walk that David possessed. She had also seen the sorrow and longing in Cameron's eyes, but she remained untouched. If he cared as he claimed he did, it was not her concern. Whatever he felt for her, she didn't care. It wasn't reciprocated. It was gone...scattered like the fluff of a dandelion dispersed by a summer breeze. Her heart of flesh had been replaced a long time ago with a heart of stone.

As for David Darcy, she smirked, she didn't love him either, and she had no intentions of giving herself the opportunity to discover if she could. If he wanted to see her, she would see him and enjoy his attentions with no expectations of anything else. After all, had he not told her he would stay and take her to dinner tonight and then for some unexplained reason left? She knew there was an attraction between them, but he was either unable or unwilling to develop it. She didn't know which, nor did she care. Perhaps they shared the same reservations. A tear slid down her cheek. She brushed it away and moved back to her desk, taking her seat to await her first appointment.

David left the Lawton Executive Complex more disturbed than ever before. If this was supposed to have settled things for him, it hadn't. Listening to the radio as he drove back from Charleston, his mind drifted. He hadn't anticipated leaving a day early, but after their night together and following morning, he knew he couldn't stay—not after what that excursion had cost him in terms of his feelings and emotions. He intuitively knew Cecilia's grip on him would tighten to an intolerable level if he spent another hour with her, let alone another night. He didn't understand what was happening to him, but whatever it was, he was sure he didn't like it.

Why had he come, he asked himself? The answer was quite simple. He couldn't get her off his mind. He had to see her, if for no other reason than to assure himself that he could spend time with her, romance her, and then turn and walk away as he had done a thousand times before. They had an agreement they'd established their first night, one he made with every woman he dated, but if this trip had been to prove that she was just like any other woman, it had failed miserably.

What David hadn't counted on was her enthusiasm when he surprised her in her office. In fact, he'd been pleasantly shocked. A smile graced his lips at the thought of it.

...She hugged me. How could I have anticipated what a simple hug would mean to me? How it would affect me? She said she'd had a rough day, but she was clearly glad to see me, and I was touched by what appeared to be a show of affection.

She said something about a mess—must be an American term for some sort of trouble or an unwanted situation. I don't know, but she was definitely glad to see me. And her reaction to dinner was more than I expected. For a moment, I thought I almost saw something there. Could she? Could I? Could we?

Then she had to tell me about her lack of knickers. He laughed out loud. *I never know what to expect from her. I guess I expect the unexpected. I don't know what I'll do about whatever it is that she has invited me to in April—some sort of ball, I think. She gave me her mobile number, so she expects, and probably wants, me to ring her. I guess I'll have to in order to tell her whatever I decide about that. What did she call it? Magnolia Festival—ha! How could I forget it when I nearly choked to death because of it ... that and her lack of knickers?*

Their evening together had been pleasant, even fun. He thought of it fondly, smiling uncharacteristically in reflection, and then his memory of their night came into focus. She was everything he had imagined she would be: impulsive, witty, intelligent, and an intense lover. They complemented one another perfectly in bed, and as he thought about it, everywhere else from the bedroom to the boardroom and probably to the ballroom. She knew how to give as well as she received, and he had felt the desire to give more than the need to take. *I see why men fall for her. She's beautiful... charming... provocative, and a good lover...and ... I ... I...*

Just as quickly as his thoughts had slipped into reflections of the multifaceted attraction they shared, his rational mind shoved them aside. *No! This was a bad idea. Seeing her again has only made the attraction stronger. She may have been glad to see me, but she was certainly not disappointed to see me leave... not in the least. I looked carefully, searching for some sign of regret in her features, some emotion in reaction to my change of plans, but there was none. All I saw was her usual cool, unaffected demeanor. She'd had a hard day, and I relieved her stress. That's all it was—sex, nothing more. And even if there were, I'm not sure I would want it. She is a challenge which I have conquered ... or have I? If it's just sex, why am I even thinking about her? Sex has never been difficult for me to find. No, it's not just sex. The more I'm with her, the more I want to be with her. I need to dismiss this and get past it. I will conquer this! I will!*

Static interfered with the music on the fading radio station. David went through the selections and picked up a classic rock station from Spartanburg, South Carolina. That would do just fine since he was in the mood for that. The next song they played was from Boston. *...Hmm...didn't Cecilia say they were among her favorite groups from the 80s? I'll turn it up.*

Reaching to turn up the volume, he suddenly stiffened as the words from *More than a Feeling* drifted through the speakers, catching his total attention. Listening closely, his mind focused on the lady who held his thoughts and imagination captive. Did he really want to simply walk away—walk away without knowing what, if anything, would come from it? The problem was that she upset his equilibrium, and his deep-seated fear of an emotional attachment stopped him cold. However, the thought of fleeing from the unexplored and uncertain contrasted sharply with his history of not letting a challenge go unmet. He struggled with a mixture of feelings, some of which were antipodal...feelings he'd never experienced before. She was beginning to mean more to him than a romp in the sack, and it distressed him. He fully understood their respective personalities, but vacillated as to whether or not there could be a shared future for them.

Finally, as if snapping out of a brain fog, David turned the radio off. He had no intentions of falling for her. In due time, he would ring her up and inform her he would not be attending the Magnolia function, or whatever it was. He'd make up some oblique excuse about a business engagement he couldn't miss, or whatever he could think of and make it sound believable. She wouldn't care anyway, no more than she had cared when he'd left a day early.

Suddenly a computerized voice interrupted his thoughts, bringing his mind back into focus on the task at hand—returning to Tennessee. His impending exit was coming up.

Chapter Twenty-four

...friends don't kiss like that...

When his aunt had invited Georgiana Darcy to stay on the farm over the next two weeks, Joseph was annoyed. Ordinarily, he would not have minded a guest at the farm. This, however, was no ordinary guest. It was a beautiful young lady whom he happened to find very attractive, much to his consternation. He knew she would be a distraction, and that was not what he wanted or needed.

The first day, he tried to ignore her, saying no more than was necessary when they drove into town to meet with his Uncle Robert. Georgiana had visited his Aunt Tana at the flower shop while he'd spent the morning in Robert's office setting up the transfer of money into a special account, as well as solidifying their plans for Liddy's defense, should it become necessary. When their business was concluded, they all had lunch together. Joseph noticed how well Georgiana and his aunt got along, laughing and cutting up as if they were old friends. That, too, was a bit annoying, for now surely Tana would tease him.

The drive back to the farm was most uncomfortable as they sat beside one another in dead silence until he switched on the radio and found some New Age station out of Nashville, which she appeared to enjoy. Of all the situations for his time at home, why did he have to spend it with a beautiful blue-eyed blonde who spoke in the most adorable accent he'd ever heard? If he could, he intended to avoid her over the next two weeks, but glancing sideways at the girl beside him, he somehow knew that would not be easy.

Once they were back from town, he managed to pass the remainder of the first day out of sight, toiling on a broken fence in the far pasture. The second day he worked in the barn stacking hay bales in the loft, cleaning stalls, and laying fresh hay for the horses and milk cow, but by the third day, he accidentally kept running into her.

That morning he'd headed towards the gazebo, anticipating reading the morning paper with a cup of hot coffee. But there she was with a book, and he presumed, coffee of her own. He'd then backed away and gone to the porch instead. By late morning, he thought he'd walk to the barn to play with the hounds, but she was already there frolicking with them. He turned and retreated to the house. After lunch, he'd journeyed to the creek for solitude, and there she was again, throwing rocks in the stream. From the confused expression on her face, he could tell she wondered what was wrong. He withdrew again and went to the tool shed to collect a ladder and bow-saw. He'd noticed the fruit trees needed to be pruned, and not knowing what else to do, he figured now was as good a time as any to do the job. He had thought surely she would not come to the orchard, but he was wrong again. There she was, walking towards him, looking rather disturbed.

"Joseph, have I done something to offend or upset you?" she asked. "You have been avoiding me. I realize that being strangers divided by a common language may cause difficulties, but I must assure you I would never intentionally insult anyone."

He climbed down from the ladder and put the bow-saw aside. He then turned to catch her intense, questioning eyes. "Georgiana, it's not that. It's not that at all." Glancing away for a moment, he turned and fixed his gaze upon her. "I'll be truthful with you. I'm not trying to avoid you for anything you have done. And it's not that I don't wish to be in your company—it's just that…well…to be honest …it's quite the opposite."

Georgiana's mouth flew open.

He silently cursed under his breath. Now he'd done it! He had just confessed to something he had sworn he wouldn't do. Well, he had better explain, for he suspected she would not leave without clarification. Taking a deep breath, he began. "Miss Darcy…in a few days, I'll be gone, and I don't know when, or even if, I will return." He paused to wipe the sweat from his brow. "We're at war, Georgiana, and I'm often in the heat of the battle. It's bad enough that my family has to endure the uncertainties that situation presents. And…" He hesitated while twisting his ring. "I can't afford to make friendships."

"Joseph, I understand that your country is at war, which means that people will die, but that shouldn't stop you from making new friends. I would like very much to become your friend, and if I'm not being too bold, perhaps to be a pen pal as well."

He didn't know what to say. He couldn't tell her he was not an ordinary Marine. Ordinary Marines would like letters from home from anyone who would write, but he didn't know if he would even get her letters or his family's for that matter. Finally, after a long moment, he said, "I'm not in a position to receive regular mail, but if you'll give me your email address, I'll try to contact you when I'm able; then you will have my email address. As of now, I don't even have one."

"I would like that very much. Then, if you do write to me, I will reply."

She had one of the sweetest smiles he'd seen in a long time. How could he resist?

"Well, I have exactly eleven days before I have to fly to San Diego, so I suppose spending a little time with a new friend won't hurt." His mouth turned up in a sly, teasing grin. *…At least I dearly hope a new friendship won't hurt me…or her.*

"Georgiana, if you would like to help me with my job here, why don't you hold the ladder? When I'm finish with this tree, I'll be done for the day. We'll drag the limbs over to that pile I've started and burn them. After that, I'd like some tea and scones. How about you? Or would you prefer hot chocolate? Grace makes wonderful Peruvian hot cocoa."

"I'd like that very much." She reached to stabilize the ladder while he climbed and began to cut the dead limb he'd started before she'd interrupted him. After the twigs and limbs were all burned, they put away the tools and walked back to the farmhouse for refreshments.

Over the next few days, they spent every day together. Georgiana and Joseph often walked out across the lawn and toured the winter gardens. The pansies had seen better days, but the crocus and grape hyacinths were beginning to peek through the frost-covered ground.

Georgiana surprised Joseph at how quickly she took to farm life. She was always finding ways to make herself useful. He would accompany her to the hen house where she gathered eggs. The look of wonder in her eyes when the hens cackled, announcing their great achievement—their *magnum opus*, an egg for the day, was priceless. And several times he'd had to rescue her from an aggressively territorial Bantam rooster, who, after the third offense, became chicken and dumplings for Sunday dinner.

In-between spending time with Joseph, Georgiana spent her days in the kitchen. Aunt Lori and Grace taught her how to make butter and sour cream and how to bake bread. She would often help with the meal preparation, which she appeared to enjoy. Grace taught her to crochet, and when not in the kitchen or out on long walks or rides with Joseph, she could be found by the fireside, working on a little lace doily. By the end of the week, it was finished. She showed it to Joseph with great pride. He laughed, telling her how pretty it was.

In the evenings, they would sit and watch movies or read to one another from the vast collection of books available for their pleasure, including the history journals. In fact, they spent many long hours ensconced in the library with tea or hot chocolate and a blazing fire in the fireplace.

Always the perfect gentleman, Joseph showed her the utmost respect. He didn't even kiss her. Hence on his last day, while strolling in the garden, Georgiana did the unthinkable. She reached up and kissed him. Shocked at first, Joseph didn't know what to do, but then he did what any red-blooded American guy would do—he kissed her back.

Drawing away from each other, Joseph spoke first. "We shouldn't have done that, Georgiana. Friends don't kiss like that. Perhaps…if I were not in the midst of a war, but I…" His voice trailed, full of sorrow and regret. It would be hard to leave in the morning.

"Well, Joseph, I understand your position now, and it doesn't matter to me. Please, do write. And yes, I know, *friends* don't kiss like that." She smiled warmly.

Chapter Twenty-five

… I'm no fool…

Davidid had returned from South Carolina the previous week, feeling no better than when he'd left. He and Georgiana were to spend a few more days with the newly married Darcys before flying back to England. Sitting on the veranda, sipping a cold drink, his mind was alerted to his sister's return from the farm.

As Georgiana pulled into the drive in Elizabeth's car, David rose from his seat and approached his sister.

"Let me carry those for you," he said, bending down to pick up her bags.

"Thank you, David," she said as they walked up the walkway. "So, how was your time in South Carolina?"

"Quite good, actually. I attended to some business and did a little shopping whilst I enjoyed the pleasant scenery." *…Pleasant scenery indeed!*

"Well, I'm glad you enjoyed your time away. I had a lovely time on the farm. We baked bread and made butter. I helped gather eggs, cook meals, and took lots of long walks over the grounds." She chuckled merrily as she glanced up. "I even learnt to crochet. I'll have to show you the cute little doily I made." She paused for a moment as David looked on. "You know, David, I think I might enjoy living on a farm someday."

"I'm glad you enjoyed yourself. Long walks and fresh country air are very good for you. I believe your complexion is a little rosier," David teased, knowing full well what his sister had meant.

"You look better, too. Much more content and relaxed. Your week in South Carolina did you good as well." She opened the door for him as they walked into the house.

David drew in a sharp breath. He didn't want to tell his sister he hadn't actually spent the entire week in South Carolina. She would ask questions—questions he didn't want to answer. Sighing inwardly, he wished he could be more like his sister and brother. He envied the warmth they demonstrated and wished he could feel the same.

Elizabeth, having heard part of the conversation between the two, excitedly added, "Oh, yes, South Carolina is wonderful, especially Charleston. That is my favorite city in the entire South. I especially like downtown Charleston, and I love the food." Turning to catch her husband's hand as he approached, she continued. "Fitzwilliam, I must take you there sometime. You will love the charm of the old city."

…I see Elizabeth shares my view of things. If she only knew…umm…charm…yes, charming is one way of looking at her. Charleston is not a subject I want to discuss.

"Yes," David interjected, "I quite agree. Now, do you have any plans for dinner, or would you like to dine out? I noticed there is a nice little Mexican restaurant just outside of town. What do you say? It looks like it might be good, and we need to give the newlyweds a break from cooking." David turned to Elizabeth. "How would that be?"

"I think it's an excellent idea since we had already decided to go out tonight. Mexican food sounds great!"

"Then it's settled," Fitzwilliam asserted.

M.K. Baxley

David hoped this restaurant was at least better than the others he'd tried in this small town. Elizabeth had warned him that the South was known for its 'greasy spoons,' and after eating at Chester's Barb-B-Que, Daisy's Country Diner, and Catfish Corner, he believed it.

After dinner, they returned to the townhouse. Elizabeth and Georgiana settled on one of the sofas in the front parlor while David went with Fitzwilliam to his study for a brandy and a cigar and then out to the back porch to sit and talk. Lighting his cigar, Fitzwilliam asked in a light hearted manner.

"You've not had the chance to tell me about your Lamborghini. How do you like it?"

"I love it!" David beamed. "I picked it up in Germany just before coming here and took it out on the Autobahn. It's a dream to drive. She's exotic. Sleek, fast, and luxurious. Perfect. Tight on the turns with steady handling."

"That good, huh?" Fitzwilliam chuckled, watching his brother's animated features.

"That good and more," David gloated. "The Murciélago's manners are peerless. It meets all of my expectations and more. It's incredible. True to the specs, it *will* hit zero to sixty in 3.4 seconds. It's the fastest car I've ever driven, brutally powerful! I got a top speed of 225 mph with an occasional blue flame coming from the twin tailpipes."

"Hmm…next time I'm in England, I want to drive it. If she's as good as you say, I may have to have one."

"Oh, I know you will. At 225 mph you can barely feel the road. In my opinion it's the best car ever made. When I'm behind the wheel, I'm in complete control. She purrs like a satisfied woman." David chuckled as he lifted his drink to his lips.

Fitzwilliam laughed in return. "Ah yes, a satisfied woman. There's nothing like a fast car or a beautiful woman." Fitzwilliam looked at his brother and tilted his head. "Speaking of women, David, you really should reconsider the married state. Find a woman to love and marry her. I highly recommend it. I don't know when I've been happier or more content as I am at the present. Even my work is more fulfilling."

David smiled while he lit his cigar. "Yes, I can tell you're happy by that foolish grin you wear, but I don't think I could find your contentment in marriage. I haven't your good nature. I'm too hard-nosed, too cynical. Most women bore me to death when they open their mouths and speak. Although I am getting somewhat tired of playing around. When the first thrill is over, I just want to get up and leave. If I ever do find a woman who is my equal, as you have, I might consider it, but so far there has hardly been anyone who stimulates my mind long enough for me to stay interested for a long term relationship," David said, and then added, inaudibly, "Except for maybe one."

Fitzwilliam looked up sharply. "What did you say, David?"

"Nothing, I was talking to myself, that's all." David puffed his cigar, looking off into the expanse of his brother's garden.

"I could have sworn you said something about possibly one."

"No," David smiled, "you misunderstood."

"Well, I thought I heard you say something, but it doesn't matter." Fitzwilliam shook his head, smiling at his brother as he took a sip of brandy. "Anyway, David, let me give you a piece of advice. Your problem is that you're looking in the wrong places. You don't find the kind of woman to marry and settle down with in the places you go. Stop looking for the quick pick up. Look for someone who has a little more significance than a one or two night affair. Surely, you have met someone who is more intriguing, captivating, or mentally stimulating."

"Well actually, there *is* someone that I have seen more than a few times, but I don't think it will go anywhere. I'm too much the unsettled type, and she's too much the shrew."

"Oh?" Fitzwilliam raised a brow. "Who is this woman and where exactly did you meet her?"

David laughed softly. "Her name is Cecilia Lawton of Lawton & Co., and I met her in a boardroom of all places. I had to negotiate with her for that blasted coffee contract Father wants so much. You remember—the one he lashed me over at Christmas."

Fitzwilliam smirked, "How could I forget it. He ranted over it for days."

"Well, he wants it, and for good reason. It's the best coffee in the world, organically grown and certified by the Rainforest Commission, and Lawton either owns the coffee plantations outright or at least the rights to them. Nobody gets a contract arrangement to their advantage with her. Father should be grateful. I'm the only one to have ever broken even." He cast his brother a mischievous grin. "I think it's because she might like me."

...Hmm...I wonder about this. "Tell me about her," Fitzwilliam said. "She sounds interesting."

David paused for a moment, staring into his brandy. "You might not think so when I tell you."

"Why's that?"

David's jaw hardened as he peered out into the night. "She's known as the 'cold hard bitch,'" he said in a whisper as he took a large gulp of his drink. "She's a stunner with long blonde hair, beautiful violet-blue eyes, and long shapely legs, among other things, but she goes through men like a fish glides through water."

...Oh...I don't like the sound of this. She sounds too much like you.

"I got the coffee deal because I wouldn't play her game. I told her what I would pay, and I meant it. She smiled and agreed, and then she asked me to dinner." David paused for a puff on his cigar. "I later escorted her to her private penthouse suite at the Lawton Hotel," he glanced at his brother, "a five star hotel which she also owns."

"What happened next?"

David chuckled. "She invited me in for a glass of wine. I could tell she wanted me to stay, but I had no intentions of a one night stand with her."

"David, since when did you not want a one night stand with a pretty girl?" Fitzwilliam asked, very much amused in this subtle change in his playboy brother who, to the best of his knowledge, had never turned down a pretty woman.

"Since I met someone who's more of a shark than I am," David said with a smile. "The thought of being used by her is more than I want to think about."

Fitzwilliam laughed again, shaking his head. "Well, continue your story. I'm intrigued by this woman and your reaction to her. Tell me more." *...David just may have met his equal.*

David softly laughed as he took another sip of brandy. "I told her I don't have affairs with business acquaintances. I said that it was very unprofessional of her to even suggest it." He glanced at his brother and smirked. "It must have shocked her, making her furious, because she threw what looked to be an antique vase at me as I was preparing to leave, barely missing my head whilst I was about to open the door."

Fitzwilliam leaned in towards David. "I'm afraid to ask, but what happened next?"

"Well, I smiled, bowed politely and told her goodnight. Then I walked out." He shrugged. "That incident occurred a little over one year ago, and, as you know, Father wants that coffee contract renewed every year, so I must renegotiate annually." Blowing a ring of smoke into the night air, David continued. "But after one year, I've gotten to know her a little better. She's not as bad as I first assumed. In fact, I found out the reason why she's so cold-hearted."

"Why's that? Tell me about it, I'm keenly interested."

"Well, from what I've heard, her father took his little girl everywhere with him, to his card games, the horse tracks, even to parties. He even kept mistresses, and kept them with his little girl, all living in the same house. She grew up loyal to him, but cold to everyone else. And when he died, she inherited it all. Mr. Lawton was much like our father, except he was a little more open about it. And I do think his daughter was more important to him than we are to Father."

"Where was her mother when all of this was taking place?" Fitzwilliam took a sip of brandy, intense curiosity creasing his brow. "What was their relationship like to have allowed such behavior?"

David sighed. "I was told her parents fought bitterly, and when Cecilia was seven or eight, her mother died."

"That is indeed sad, and I can see how it might have a profound impact on a little girl, but you say you know this person a little better. What exactly do you mean? I hope you're not being pulled into this woman's snare?"

David chuckled and shook his head. "I do know her better, but I'm no fool! God help any man foolish enough to fall for her. Like her father, the preservation of Southern history and tradition are important to her, although she couldn't care less what the top circles of society thinks. And I have to admit that she not only stimulates my mind, but she entices me in a carnal sense as well."

"Oh, David, this doesn't sound good. Should I be worried? I don't think you need this type of entanglement."

"No, Fitzwilliam, I am a man, but as I said, I'm no fool."

"Be careful, Brother...be *very* careful. Your pride and your inability to resist a pretty face will be your downfall. I can tell she turns heads. Just don't let it be yours, and I mean that in more ways than *one*."

Fitzwilliam only shook his head as he looked at his younger brother. David was holding something back. Fitzwilliam suspected this Southern Belle did more than stimulate and entice him. She drew him in like a moth to a flame. David had always been driven by his lower passions rather than his good sense when it came to beautiful women, and Fitzwilliam suspected this incident was no different. Snuffing out their cigars, they rose from their seats and walked back into the house to join the ladies.

That night, while trying to find sleep, David's mind drifted back to the woman he'd left behind in South Carolina. As he lay there reliving their most recent encounter, he wondered if he would have the strength to ever pull completely away.

As much as he tried to suppress it, the look on Cecilia's face when he had surprised her in her office kept resurfacing in his thoughts, haunting him. He knew what he should do, but as *More than a Feeling* played through his mind, he knew he had yet to decide. A small struggle had taken form in his heart the morning he'd left Charleston. No, that wasn't true. It had taken form from the first time he'd gone out with her over a year ago, and like a match set to a dry, parched land, it threatened to erupt into a raging fire.

Chapter Twenty-six

...we are fulfilling some sort of Divine Providence...

As things settled into a routine, Fitzwilliam remembered the journal he had brought from the library at Pemberley. After they had finished dinner and cleaned the kitchen, he approached his wife.

"Elizabeth, come here. I have something to show you."

"What is it?" she asked.

He took her by the hand. "It's a chronicle of the history of Pemberley, our estate in Derbyshire, whilst under the care of my ancestor, the first Fitzwilliam Darcy. I want us to read it together. Also, I want to tell you what I discovered concerning the English Bennets. We've yet to talk about it in any detail. Come, let's go upstairs. I'll tell you about it and then I'll read to you. I told you that I checked the information you had given me," he said as they climbed the stairs.

"Yes, you told about it. What else did you discover?"

"Well, I remembered you telling me you didn't know whatever became of Edward."

"Yes, that's correct. It's recorded that he had three daughters. Other than that, I don't know what happened. But I presume you do?" she asked.

"Yes," he said with a smile, "as a matter of fact, I do. Edward had five daughters— not three, and there were no sons. Longbourn was passed to a distant cousin, since neither John nor his sons were entitled to inherit it. Four of the daughters, as it turns out, had almost the same names as you and your sisters and the fifth was named *Lydia*. Isn't that strange?" he asked, gently putting his hand to the small of her back as they reached the landing.

A small laugh escaped her throat. "Yes and no. Our family names are generational. They have been passed down and reused throughout our family's history. It's not recorded in anything we have as to what the names of Edward's children were, let alone that he even had more than the three daughters I mentioned, so that part is news to me."

She paused in reflection. "From what you're telling me am I to assume that Edward had a daughter named Elizabeth, and there is a story associated with his Lydia?"

"Yes, on both accounts. And as to Lydia, there is most certainly a story there, but we shall explore it together as it unfolds in the book." He gently squeezed her hand. "Let's just say that the apple doesn't fall too far from the tree, and I can assure you we will *not* have a Lydia," he said. "There seems to be a bad omen associated with that name."

Elizabeth laughed as they reached the bedroom door. "From what I know about John's sisters, none were like my Aunt Lydia or cousin Liddy, so I had assumed that it must have come from Rebecca Jane's side of the family, but now you're telling me that Edward had one, too. And since I now know it runs on both sides of the family, you can rest assured there will be *no* Lydia Darcy. The name stops with Liddy."

"Good. I'm glad to hear it, but Lydia is not the topic of tonight's discussion. I want to discuss something more akin to us. Now," he said while picking up the book from the side table, "This volume contains the story of the courtship and love affair of Elizabeth Bennet and Fitzwilliam Darcy, and I can tell you, from what I have read, that in the beginning, it didn't run smoothly. In fact, they had a very rough go before finally coming to an understanding. Then, even at that, they almost didn't." He placed the book on the nightstand while they undressed and prepared for bed.

Propped up in the bed with Elizabeth's head resting on his shoulder and his arm secured around her, he continued. "The first Fitzwilliam appears to have been a mixture of David and me. From what I've read, I think we share many of his traits. It's like looking back into the past and seeing yourself. I think you'll enjoy learning about it."

As they settled in, he read of the first Fitzwilliam childhood, his sister's birth, the consequent death of their mother, and of his struggles as a young man with a childhood friend, George Wickham, whom his father favored enough to treat as a second son. He read of Fitzwilliam's Eton days, Cambridge days, his love of classical studies, his friendship with Charles Bingley and of the young man's struggle after his father's death, leaving him with the massive undertaking of caring for his young sister and the estate. Fitzwilliam Darcy was often lonely with the weight of the world on his shoulders. He read of George Wickham's near seduction of Fitzwilliam's sister and how devastated Fitzwilliam was by it. Had it not been for his impulse to visit her at Ramsgate, she would have been lost forever.

Darcy continued reading for another hour, reciting about Charles Bingley's taking the house at Netherfield, three miles from Longbourn. He read about the Meryton Assembly, Jane Bennet's illness and her consequent sojourn at Netherfield, and Elizabeth's trek through the mud to care for her sister. Darcy stopped after the entry where his ancestor had recorded his viewpoint of the Bennet girls and their mother. The entry was filled with a bitter barrage of his thoughts and feelings concerning Mrs. Bennet, a woman whom he found to be abhorrent, and though he was strongly attracted to her daughter, he could not come to terms with such a mother—a mother who would risk her daughter's health, making it known in no uncertain terms that she fully expected her eldest daughter to snatch a rich husband thereby throwing her other daughters into the paths of other rich men, and the thought that she might have designs on *him* as one of those rich men was especially revolting. And yet, knowing what he knew, Fitzwilliam struggled with his feelings, especially at night while alone in his room.

"Hmm, he had a difficult time, didn't he?" Elizabeth frowned. "I feel sorry for him. There appears to have been little joy in his life," she said, snuggling closer to her husband, reading some of the text for herself.

"His early life was much like mine and David's, but I wouldn't say that either his or ours were without happiness." Fitzwilliam glanced at his wife and nodded. "Yes, there was a lot of sorrow there, but he did grow up at Pemberley, and that does not allow for complete unhappiness. Still, his struggles are what shaped his personality and character as you'll see later on. Do you not see the similarities?"

"Yes, I do. One thing you have in common is your love of studies. He liked the very things you enjoy," she paused, studying her husband. "And he was somewhat reserved as you are."

"Yes," Fitzwilliam chuckled, "and believe it or not, we share a strict moral code. You'll see it more and more. He also had an unshakeable loyalty to family which David and I both share. We are very protective of those we love. Later we'll read more." He carefully marked his place and closed the book, dropping it onto his lap before leaning over to kiss his wife.

"You know," Elizabeth said as she tilted her head. "From the things you've read and what little I already knew, I'm getting a better understanding of things. Edward's wife was so very unlike Rebecca Jane. Fanny was more like a frivolous airhead whereas John's wife was thoughtful and kind. I feel sorry for Edward, and I can understand why your great-great-great grandfather disliked his future mother-in-law. Frances Bennet was vulgar and crass. I would have been embarrassed to death to have had such a mother. With this new insight into her personality, I think I now know what might have come between John and Edward and why they didn't continue writing. Fanny hated Rebecca, and John knew that. John was prosperous. He had money and could have helped Edward, given the entailment and all, but as you say, John's sons were not entitled to inherit Longbourn. Nevertheless, John still wanted one of his sons to marry one of Edward's daughters. And had Edward had a son, well, John fully intended to reunite the house. Longbourn in Hertfordshire was very dear to him."

"Well, that's probably right. From what I've read and now know about John, the brothers were close at one time. Although, as far as I know, Edward did not keep a journal, and there are no surviving letters to my knowledge, so we will never know how Edward felt about things. However, from what I do know of him, he didn't have a resentful temper. He was a jolly man known for his keen sense of humor and sharp wit. I suppose it was necessary in order to live with Fanny all those years, and yet Fanny was not wholly bad. They were simply a mismatched couple."

"That very well may be. Who knows? I still say that when you compare the two, John made the better match, but enough about them. I'm curious about something else. Tell me, who is this Charles Bingley your ancestor speaks of? Is he related to Jane's husband?" Elizabeth asked.

"Yes, Charles is. The Bingley family and the Darcy family go back over two hundred years. Later, you'll find that he too married a Jane Bennet."

"Really? You're kidding."

"No, I'm quite serious."

"That's very strange, almost unbelievable."

"Yes, it's all very extraordinarily coincidental. I'll grant you that," he agreed. "But as you said, your family uses family names generationally. Well, old families in England do the same thing. But what is even *stranger* is that two Fitzwilliam Darcys and two Charles Bingleys would marry sisters, Elizabeth and Jane Bennett, respectively." He pulled her close and kissed the tip of her nose.

"Okay, you've got my full attention. I want to know more about my English family. Were you able to discover anything about them?"

"Yes, I did some more checking, and this is what I know. John and Edward's sisters all married well, except for Emily. She remained unmarried and served in the Church. Elizabeth *Rose* Bennet—yes, another Elizabeth Rose, married a Frank Simmons and had three daughters. Emma Felicity married a widowed solicitor, James Toppan, who had three daughters and one son. They had no children of their own to survive beyond childhood. Mary Allison married a Samuel Hayes, and I found no record of their children, so I assume there were none.

"Of Edward's children, you already know about Rebecca Jane and Elizabeth Rose. Mary Frances, the next oldest, never married. She cared for her aging parents until their death and then came to live with my ancestor. Catherine Fiona married a clergyman in Hampshire and had two sons and five daughters. I don't know what became of them. And sadly, Lydia Anne died in childbirth as did her son. That's what became of the Bennets. Charles and I are the only viable line from that family. We are your English relatives," he said as he patted the volume in his lap.

"On the Darcy side of the family, there are over one thousand years of family history and heritage to be held up, and when my time comes, I will rise to the challenge even more so now that I have you. My heritage is something I must protect and preserve to someday pass down to our children." Releasing a sigh, he gathered her in his arms.

She smiled and reached up to kiss his cheek. "It will be our history together. Our children will have a rich heritage on both sides."

"Yes, they will, and next time we're at Longbourn, I want to read more of John Bennet's writings. I want to thoroughly go through them, and I'd like to see those old letters you have. I'm beginning to get an odd sort of feeling about things—as if our destiny is governed by Divine Providence. I'm also very curious about my American relations. I want to come to know them as well as I know my Darcy lineage. When I think of Edward, Nathanial, John Newton, Robert Lawrence, or the girls, I want to feel the same connection I feel when I think of my namesake's progeny."

"All right, everything you want to see is kept in the library. Remind me, and I'll get them for you. But Fitzwilliam," she laughed and shook her head, "I'm not sure I buy into Fate and superstitions. I think it more a coincidence than anything else. And Jane keeps mentioning Indian Legends and white doves. I don't believe any of that. The supernatural can always be explained," Elizabeth said with a pointed look. "I prefer to think of you as my kissing cousin. This reminds me too much of the X-Files." She giggled.

"I don't know about that, Liz. Some things cannot be explained away with logic. I think there are forces out there that watch over us."

"Perhaps. I do believe in God, I'm just not sure I believe that he concerns himself with the affairs of men. We control our own destiny through choices we make. I don't think our lives are governed by unseen forces. The unknown can always be explained. But, to change the subject, there is one other thing I'm curious about."

"Yes, and what might that be?"

"I want to know how your family made their fortune. I realize that there was old money with land passed down through the generations, but how did your family transition from old money into the multibillion dollar conglomerate you have today?"

"Oh, that. Well, that's easy enough." He chuckled. "Although we were never part of the peerage directly, we did marry into it throughout the Middle Ages and into the Renaissance, thereby increasing our wealth substantially. Where the transition came, though, was in the Industrial Age. Even though the term paradigm shift wasn't coined in his day, my namesake understood the philosophy behind it very well. He saw the coming demise of the agrarian society and began to invest in trade through friends he'd made whilst at Cambridge. He invested in shipping and commodities from the Orient, mainly the East India Company, and from the Southern U.S. and West Indies. The Darcys imported cotton, silk, indigo dye, saltpeter, tea, sugar, rice, and opium. We owned a mercantile business in Liverpool and a cotton mill in Lancashire. Fitzwilliam Darcy also invested heavily in the steam engine and locomotive travel, but the biggest investment of all came through his great-grandson, William. He founded what is today Brit Am, the British American Petroleum Company."

"So your family owns Brit Am. Somehow I had missed that," Elizabeth softly said, "and opium...hmm."

"Liz, before you say a word, opium was legal in the 18th and 19th centuries."

She raised her hand and smiled. "I wasn't about to say a thing. Not really, I mean, how could I, considering that my own family was heavily involved in moonshine whiskey throughout that same time period?"

He laughed and shook his head. "Well then, I guess both of us have our dark shadows, don't we?"

"Yes, we do," she said with a smile.

Placing the book on the night table, he turned back to his wife. "Now come here. I am in need of a different kind of lesson."

Chapter Twenty-seven

... If there is more, I shall surely die...

Thick moisture hung in the air, and it was cold, dreary, and dark. Fitzwilliam strolled to the window and peered out. Glancing at his watch, he noted it was merely four o'clock. He frowned. If he didn't know better, he would have sworn a winter storm was moving in, but the early morning forecast had made no mention of foul weather. He shrugged it off, dismissing the thought as he turned and left for the library. It didn't matter. Inside was cozy and warm and his mood was light and happy.

After pulling a CD with soft romantic songs from the shelf, he walked back to the dining room and put it in the sound system. In celebration of Elizabeth's twenty-sixth birthday, he had come home from the university early, canceling his weekly student gathering for *The Society of Ancient Languages* in order to cook dinner for her, setting the mood with candles, flowers, and soft music. With great effort and not a little expense, he'd found an out-of-print book he knew she wanted. He had also learned from the journal, that each year in celebration of their anniversary and his wife's birthday, his ancestral grandfather had given his grandmother jewels from Garrard's in London. Fitzwilliam had thought much about it and decided to restore the custom, so in keeping with that established tradition, he'd ordered a pair of amethyst earrings with a matching pendant. At the sound of his wife's car in the driveway, he smiled and left for the foyer.

"Burr...it's blustery cold outside, damp and unpleasant. If I didn't know any better, I'd say it was going to snow," Elizabeth said as she walked through the door, shivering.

"I don't think so. The morning forecast said the temperature would be dropping throughout the day, but there was no mention of anything else."

"Well, the weatherman isn't always right. Once in a while he misses it. Here, help me with these things, and what's that smell?" she asked, sniffing the air as she handed him her book bag.

"That, my darling, is your birthday dinner, if I haven't burnt it," he said. "We are supposed to be enjoying Beef Wellington with potatoes, asparagus in crème sauce, and a garden salad with Madeira wine." He greeted her with a kiss as he helped her out of her coat. "I had a raspberry torte prepared at Hudson's Bakery, as I don't think I could accomplish that on my own."

"And we have no lights?" she teasingly asked. "It's very dark in here."

"I thought you might like an old fashioned evening with candlelight," he said. The twinkle in her fine eyes caused the corners of his mouth to lift.

"Very romantic, I see. I love it when the lights are low. By the way, I noticed the music. I love you, Fitzwilliam." She lifted her gaze to his with a smile that thrilled him.

They sat and ate their meal while listening to the music and enjoying the mood. When the meal was over, he insisted that she not help him clean the kitchen, but rather have her tea while waiting until he had finished.

Once finished, he escorted her to the informal sitting room where the wrapped gifts waited on the tea table.

"These are for you." He grinned.

"What are they?"

"Open them and see." He motioned to the larger package first.

"Fitzwilliam, you should not have gone to so much trouble." She opened the book with a smile, recognizing the title immediately. "**The Allegory of Love** first edition by C.S. Lewis. Where did you find it? I have looked for this book for years." She glanced up. "I absolutely love it! This is the book that launched C.S. Lewis's career as a leading expert in the critical analysis of medieval and renaissance literature. Oh, Fitzwilliam, thank you." She looked up with teary eyes.

"Wait just a minute. You still have one more." He handed her the second package and sat back to watch.

"I'm almost afraid to open this. I don't know how you can surpass the book." Opening the box, she gasped at the amethyst jewelry it contained. "Oh, now I know you should not have! These are beautiful!" She jumped up from her seat and embraced him.

"Well, if this is the response I get, then I shall do this more often, and yes, I should have."

Taking the box from her hand, he set it aside. "Now, take down your hair, Mrs. Darcy."

She did as he said and shook her head, her loose tresses falling freely about her shoulders and down her back. It wasn't long before more than her hair was loosened. He removed the CD and blew out the candles, except for the one he took to their bedchamber, leaving their discarded clothes on the sitting room floor.

"No flannel gown tonight, Elizabeth. I know what you say, but I hate them. When we are old, I might relent, but for now, I want you naked in our bed with your hair down. No braid."

He lit the candles in their room and put the CD in the sound system, the song *Kiss You All Over* playing softly in the background. Taking her hand in his, he led her to the bed. Her sparkling eyes shimmered in the candle light, and her dark hair covered her like an ebony cloak of silk. No matter how often he saw her like this, the effect was always the same. Involuntarily his body would tighten into a knot only to be released by losing himself inside of her. Breathing deeply, he pulled her into his arms and began to kiss her in that sensual spot between her ear and shoulder—the spot he knew caused her to lose all conscious thought. Her arms instinctively curled around his neck as her hands found their way into his hair, caressing and playing with his curls, driving him wild with desire.

Placing her onto the bed, he climbed in beside her and began to stroke her waist, gliding down along her hips to her inner thigh, caressing her in a way he knew she loved. While she softly moaned his name, his other hand captured the back of her head and shoulders, supporting her while his mouth found its way with soft, gentle, kisses from her lips, to her neck, and finally to her breasts.

She drew in a sharp quick breath. She was losing control quickly, and it was not long before she pulled him onto her, kissing whatever she could. He sensed his caresses were exactly what she wanted…exactly what she needed. Skin against skin—hot with desire.

"Fitzwilliam, now… Please…I need you…" she pleaded, urgently tugging at him, but he would not let her take him just yet.

"Just a little more, Liz.…Just a little more," he whispered against her throat.

"If there is more, I shall surely die."

"No, my love, you won't die, but you shall enjoy it."

He continued to kiss, caress, and stroke until finally, his need reaching an apex, he gently laid her onto her back and rolled on top of her as she parted her legs naturally and raised them to encircle his body. Her pleasure always drove his, and feeling her tighten and convulse, he began to fall over the edge, taking her with him. He kissed her neck, face, hair, any part of her he could as he called her name softly, collapsing on top of her. When they regained some composure, he rolled over, backing away slightly to gaze deep into her beautiful eyes.

"Happy Birthday, Mrs. Darcy." He smiled. "Are you happy, Liz?"

"Very!" She snuggled closer. "I don't know when I have ever been so happy. I love you, Fitzwilliam, and I always will—now and forever." Completely satisfied, she gently stroked his face with her hand.

"I shall always love and cherish you. Never forget that, my love... never." His look, he was sure, matched hers as he caressed her face one more time with his lips.

While he lay there holding her, he could finally go no longer without expressing what had been on his mind since yesterday.

"Elizabeth, there is something I want to ask you." He hesitated as he gently stroked her arm. "Yesterday, in the bakery, a man was there with his little girl. She must have been two or perhaps a little older. She was bouncing around the shop with her little curls dancing about her shoulders as she called for her dad. She was so wide-eyed and innocent. When I looked down at her as she held her arms out for her father to take her, I saw our child holding her arms up to me." He paused and took her hand in his. "Would you...would you please reconsider and agree to have a child later this year?" he asked. "It would mean the world to me. I will be thirty-three in August. Darling, I would really love to have a child with you. Would you reconsider waiting?" He released the long breath he was holding and pulled her a little closer, kissing her forehead. "Elizabeth, please darling...could we?"

She paused for what seemed like an eternity. "Fitzwilliam, I know how important this is to you. I have thought about it, too. I will agree, but we must wait until summer to start. I also want to teach, and I don't know how I am going to do both."

"Elizabeth, if you want to teach, then we will find a way. We can afford tutors, nursemaids, and an *au pair.* Georgiana had one for years. You will make me happier than I could ever imagine if we have a child."

"Well then, in May, I'll go off the pill, and we will see what happens. However, you must agree to help me with everything, and that includes getting up at night, changing diapers, and feeding. I want to continue teaching, and you know how exhausting that alone can be."

"Elizabeth, I have already told you I want you to teach. That is not a problem. And as for helping you, that won't be a problem, either. It'll be a joy. If I weren't obligated to the university, I would stay home myself."

She smiled and kissed his cheek. "How can I ever refuse you anything? I love you so much."

He grinned and pulled her close, kissing her brow. "I love you, too. You will make a beautiful mother. I hope our first child is a daughter who looks just like you." He tapped the tip of her nose.

"Well, I hope it's a boy who has those same adorable eyes and impish grin his father has."

He pulled her into his chest, resting her head on his shoulder as they both drifted off to sleep in each other's arms.

Chapter Twenty-eight

...There's nothing like having a woman to warm your bed on a cold winter's night...

The next morning Fitzwilliam and Elizabeth woke to a cold house. The Cumberland Plateau, known for its harsh wet winters, occasionally experienced a winter storm that broke power lines with ice and deep snow, shutting down everything. This was such a storm.

Elizabeth shivered as she glanced at the blank alarm clock. "Oh, no! It looks like the power is off. We must have had a winter storm in the night. It did look like snow. We should have listened to the ten o'clock news," Elizabeth said, pulling the covers up and snuggling closer to her husband. "It's cold in here. It almost makes me wish I had my gown."

"You don't need flannel, Liz. I'll keep you warm, but I do want to look outside and see what happened during the night." He kissed her forehead and tumbled out of bed. Grabbing his robe from the bench at the foot of the bed, he wrapped it tightly around him and walked over to the window and pulled back the drapes.

"It looks as if you're right." He grinned over his shoulder. "The grounds and street are covered in white. It must be at least six inches. Umm... it's beautiful. Would you like to come and take a look?"

"No," she quickly responded. "It's cold. Come back to bed, or I'm getting up to find my gown."

"I don't think so." He strolled back to the bed and dropped his robe before rejoining her under the thick covers. "Come here, darling," he said as he folded her into his arms, "I'll keep you warm."

His heated caresses traced her silky skin until with a soft moan, Elizabeth pulled him on top of her, and they were once again making love.

Lying there in his arms, feeling completely satiated, Elizabeth murmured, "Fitzwilliam, we need to get up. We're not prepared for a winter emergency like this, but Jane is. If the hot water is still available, let's take a quick shower and then go over to Charles and Jane's. They will have an ample supply of wood for the wood burning stove, and there's a generator with plenty of gasoline."

"What about cooking? Will we be able to cook?"

"Yes, she has a gas stove, and if that doesn't work, we can always cook on the woodstove. But we do need to pack enough clothes and things for a few days. If it's as I suspect, the power will be off at least three days."

"Well, then, as far as I'm concerned, let it snow. I, for one, will enjoy a few days off, and I'm sure the students will as well. Let's get up. I'll light the gas log." He threw back the covers and rolled out of bed, followed by his wife. After the log was lit, they made their way to the shower. Thankfully, hot water was still available, so after a speedy shower, they dressed, packed two duffel bags, and then carefully made the bed.

As Elizabeth sat at her dressing table, Fitzwilliam sat behind her by the fire and gently combed her hair. When it was sufficiently dry, he fashioned it in a long French braid to wear down her back, admiring it as he plaited.

"Elizabeth, have I ever told you how much I love your hair?"

"Umm...yes, you tell me every time you brush it."

"Yes, I suppose I do at that." He softly laughed while putting the final touches on her braid. "I hope you never cut it."

"I have no plans to ever cut it. I've always had long hair. As Grandmother Barnett would say, it's my crowning glory. Her hair was so long, it touched the floor, but of course, she was only five feet tall, and I'm five eight. I don't think I will let mine get *that* long." She smiled as she turned her head from side to side, admiring her husband's handiwork.

"Oh, I don't know. I don't think I would mind if you did. Just don't cut it short. Your hair is one of the things that makes you uniquely *you*. Now come on, we need to get going." He pulled her up from her vanity seat and smacked her bottom.

"Fitzwilliam! You keep that up and we'll be back in bed!" she playfully said as she reached up and kissed his chin.

"If we had the time, I wouldn't say no. But we really should go. Tonight, we'll play in your old bed at your sister's house."

She placed her arm around his waist and leaned into his tall frame. "You impish man. Don't you ever get enough?"

"Not when I have an *impish* princess to please." He grinned and kissed her cheek as he nudged her towards the door.

They made their way downstairs, stopping long enough to straighten the house and pick up their clothes from the sitting room and put them in the laundry chute. Elizabeth packed her birthday presents in her duffel bag, and when everything was in place, they bundled up to set out for their trip around the corner.

As they trod through the snow, Fitzwilliam made note of his wife's good humor. Her features were bright and cheerful, like that of a child, but she was certainly not a child. She took him places he hadn't been in years. In fact, she had taken him places he'd never been before, and she had a way of bringing out the playful side of him that he had long forgotten existed. His wife could light up his world with a simple smile, and he loved her more than he'd ever imagined he would. He smiled as they turned the corner onto Elm Street.

As they trudged through the snow, she reached her arm around his waist and laid her head on his shoulder, shivering, but he suspected she was not cold in the least. They seemed to have that effect on one another. After walking up the steps of the Bennett townhouse, they shook the snow from their boots and were about to knock when Jane and Charles came out with shovels in hand.

"Oh, Lizzy, I'm so glad you have come. We were just about to clear the walkway, but we can do that later. Come inside and warm yourselves. I have coffee, hot chocolate, and some fresh blueberry scones."

They entered the foyer and peeled off the layers of clothing while the sisters laughed and planned the day. "That sounds wonderful, Jane. Umm... I can smell those scones now! I can't wait to eat." Elizabeth laughed. "I'm in such a good mood today. Let's cook chicken and dumplings, and I want to bake a sweet potato pie and potato sourdough bread. Do you think we can get the gas oven lit, and do you still have some Christmas tea?" she asked. "Since Charles and Fitzwilliam were not here for Christmas, perhaps we can have a cup of tea and sit by the fire like we would at Christmas."

"Yes, there's plenty left, and that sounds like a good idea. Let the men take care of shoveling away the snow. Let's cook and put in an Alabama CD—the red one over there. Ultimate Alabama," she pointed. "I'll put on the kettle for the tea."

"Good, that sounds great, and later we'll play in the snow."

Fitzwilliam glanced at Charles with a broad smile. "Charles, I think we've been relegated to the cleanup crew. Let's get the shovels. Did you get the generator going, or do you need help?"

"Yes, the generator is running. We have plenty of gasoline, but we do need to bring in some more firewood."

By the time the men came in the house from clearing the walkway, the girls were giggling and singing as *Song of the South* played. Elizabeth ran up at Fitzwilliam. "I love you, Fitzwilliam. Have I told you lately?"

"Yes, I believe you have, but I love to hear it, so continue telling me whenever the mood strikes," he said, smiling down at his Liz in his arms. "Now, Charles and I will get the wood, and when you ladies are ready, we'll go outside and play," Fitzwilliam said as he turned to Bingley.

"The wood is in the mudroom. Come, Darcy, we'll get it," Charles said.

The men gathered the wood, put some of it in the stove, and then loaded the fireplace and stoked the fire. When they finished their tasks, they went to the library for brandy and cigars while they waited for their wives to finish in the kitchen.

"Darcy, I don't think I have ever been happier than I am at this moment. I'm certainly glad we went to White's that day. It was Providence or Fate, I don't know which, but I'm glad Dickens found us." Bingley sighed, contented as he sipped his brandy and puffed his cigar.

"As we talked the day before yesterday, Charles, I think Divine Providence had everything to do with it. We were meant to be here. John Bennet is the lost branch of the family your great-great Aunt Tessie spoke of."

"Hum, well, she was certainly old enough to remember stories and rumors. She lived well into her nineties and had a rabid curiosity about the family ancestry. Unfortunately, none of us cared enough to listen, but now that you and I have talked, and Jane has filled me in, I'm keenly interested, and like you, I've been reading the Bennet journals. Jane is certain that we are indeed the fulfillment of her ancestor's promise and that somehow our ancestor's spirits brought me and you here. She believes in Providence. She even told me of an old Indian legend. Something about white doves and unfinished business. She thinks they have everything to do with us." Bingley paused to puff his cigar. "Also there is one other curious point. Jane had an aunt, Cordelia Bennet Cole, who gave a prophecy on her death bed, and Darcy, this is spooky, but it was the very oracle Aunt Tessie pronounced on *her* death bed except that the man and woman were fair-haired and she said nothing about troubles."

"Troubles?"

"Yes, Jane says their aunt predicted that the couple would endure hardships. This is what she said." Bingley went on to relay all that Jane had told him. When he finished his tale, he looked up. "Jane claims to have the second sight—a Scottish folklore. She says Lizzy has it, too, but won't admit to it. What do you think Darcy?"

"Oh, I don't know. She could be right, but Elizabeth doesn't subscribe to superstitions, and will hear none of it. However, I do believe in Fate, but as to an Indian legend, that I'm unsure of. And as far as Scottish folklore goes, I don't subscribe to that either. Dear Aunt Tessie was a sweet old lady, but she was a bit eccentric. I never put much stock in what she had to say, especially her gibberish about your Scottish lineage and second sight."

"Well, nonetheless we're here, and I'm grateful for whatever it was that brought us here. What do you say about having a marker placed by the graveside to commemorate the fulfillment of the promise?"

"I think it a splendid idea. When do your propose we accomplish it?"

"I'd say we should wait until late spring or early summer when the weather is better."

"Then come May, after the term is over and our paperwork completed, we shall do just that."

"Indeed we shall," Charles said as he sipped his drink. "I owe a debt of gratitude to John and Rebecca Jane. Without their choice to marry, I wouldn't have *my* Janie. She makes life worth the living."

"Yes, I quite agree." Fitzwilliam looked at Charles as he blew a ring of smoke. "I've never been happier myself, and a child would be the icing on the cake. If things go as we wish and luck prevails, I hope to have that come next year."

"Luck has little to do with it. I think you know what to do, don't you?" Charles winked.

"That I do." Fitzwilliam laughed.

Jane watched Lizzy in quiet amusement as they finished up in the kitchen. She had never seen her sister so happy and content. She had known it all along. Dr. Darcy was just what Lizzy needed. He had been so good for her. Now if her sister would only listen to her about the legend. Jane shook her head and sighed. With a slight smile she put away the final dish and turned to Elizabeth. "Lizzy, I believe we're finished for now. Let's collect our husbands and go outside."

"Yes, let's, but first I want to show you what Fitzwilliam gave me for my birthday." Elizabeth left to retrieve her gifts. Retuning, she said, "Look, Jane, aren't they beautiful?" Elizabeth pulled the book and jewel case from her bag, handing the case to her sister.

"Oh, Lizzy, they are beautiful, and it's your birthstone! They will look very lovely with that deep purple outfit you never wear. You know, the beautiful silk noil Victorian style suit Grace made for you last fall," Jane reminded.

Returning the jewel case to Elizabeth, she then took the book and opened it to the title page. "Lizzy this is wonderful! You have been looking for a copy of this work for years. Fitzwilliam must have sent all the way to London for it. I have not seen it for sale in the States for several years, and when I did, it was well over three hundred dollars."

"Hmm, I never thought of London, but I suppose he must have. I have searched everywhere—even the Internet. I suppose he must have spent a small fortune for it. He never thinks of what something costs—unlike me. As to the jewelry, yes, it *will* match my purple outfit perfectly. I don't know why I haven't worn it more often. I guess I was waiting for my birthday present." She giggled. "Well, let's get our things and go. The men are waiting," Elizabeth said as she retrieved her presents and took them back upstairs.

Recalling her earlier thoughts as Jane watched her sister depart, she breathed deeply. Jane was all but certain that she and Elizabeth were part of the promise. But something loomed on the horizon, and she had not a clue as to what it was. Perhaps it was Liddy. That was another thing that pressed on her—that and the promise. However, Jane knew better than to bring either of them up again with her sister. They had agreed to disagree, and she would leave it at that. She sighed deeply.

The girls met their husbands in the hallway where they donned their coats, scarves, winter hats, and gloves. Once outside, Elizabeth and Jane picked up handfuls of snow and began to pelt Fitzwilliam and Charles as they ran, but the men soon caught up with them. They fought for several minutes until Jane and Elizabeth finally fell in a large drift of snow, laughing.

"Enough! You two are too much," Elizabeth relented, panting for breath. "You're supposed to let us win. Didn't they teach you that at your boys' school?"

"No, I think we missed that one." Charles laughed, pulling Jane into a hug.

"It was under 'How to be a gentleman and win your lady,'" Jane said.

Elizabeth got up and dusted herself off. Then she picked up a handful of snow and the fight was on again until both couples collapsed in a mound of white fluff, exhausted and out of breath.

"I truly give up this time. Let's stop this and make a snow couple," Jane said.

"Okay," Elizabeth joined in, "Fitzwilliam, you start by rolling the first ball, and Jane, you go in and bring us what we need."

Jane scurried into the house. When she returned, the men had already begun in earnest while Elizabeth stood back watching and giving directions. In fact, Charles and Fitzwilliam did all the work while Elizabeth and Jane critiqued. They spent hours laughing and frolicking, making two snow-people—one snowman and one snowwoman. Jane made them complete with carrot noses, scarves, hats, and two buttons for eyes. When finished, both couples stepped back and admired their work.

"So what do you think, Lizzy?"

"Jane, I think they're wonderful. We did a good job."

"Oh, *who* did a good job?" Both men said at once.

The girls giggled.

"We all did a good job, but it's getting colder, and I'm tired. Come, Charles," Jane said as she reached for her husband's hand, "let's go in and have a cup of coffee. How about you two?" Jane called back over her shoulder as she and Charles walked up the steps.

"We'll be there soon," Elizabeth returned. "You two go along, and fix another pot of tea. We'll be in shortly."

As Jane and Charles entered the house, Fitzwilliam turned to Elizabeth. "Don't you want to go inside, Liz? You look chilled, love."

"No, not yet. It's not often that we get this much snow. This is our second one this season, and it'll most likely be our last, so I want to enjoy it just a little while longer."

"Well, then come here. You're cold. Let me warm you," Darcy said as he put his face next to hers.

At about that time a car full of college kids slid by, whistling at the couple as they called out, "Dr. Darcy! Carpe diem—seize the day."

Fitzwilliam glanced up just in time to catch the sight of some of his second term Latin students. Smiling, they gave him a thumbs up. He smiled back and waved as he folded Elizabeth into his arms. He had always gotten along well with his students, but since his marriage, the relationship was even better. He knew he smiled more and was much less reserved than he had been when he first came to the plateau. He sighed in pleasure. His wife definitely had a positive effect on him.

Finally, Elizabeth agreed to going inside to warm up. As they sat together on the loveseat in front of the fire savoring their tea, Fitzwilliam gave thanks for the little things in life, such as a heavy snow in late February and a woman to warm his bed. He heaved a sigh and smiled as Elizabeth's uncle's words on their wedding day came to mind ...*There's nothing like having a woman to share your bed on a cold winter's night.*

Chapter Twenty-nine

...storm clouds gathering...

Robert walked over to his desk and threw down the legal papers he'd just received an hour earlier. Meandering over to the large second-story office window of Bennett and Bakersfield, Attorneys at Law, he glanced down at the courthouse square. It was the first week of March. The snow from the winter storm still clung to the grass and buildings where they were shaded from the sun. He had a call in to his long-time friend, Sam Armstrong. Deep in thought, he almost didn't hear his legal assistant standing at the door, rapping gently against the glass pane. Robert turned and grimly motioned for her to enter.

"Mr. Armstrong is on line one."

"Thanks, Andrea. I'll take the call now. If you don't mind, bring me a cup of coffee, and then close the door. I am *not* to be disturbed."

"As you wish, Mr. Bennett," she curtly nodded. "I'll be right back with that coffee."

Andrea left and quickly returned with the coffee. "I'll hold all calls. Let me know if you need anything else." She stepped outside and quietly closed the door behind her.

Robert sat the coffee down, plopped into his oversized chair, and picked up the phone. "Sam, it's good to hear your voice."

"Robert, what's up? No problems with the case, are there? I assume the arrest warrant has been issued."

"Yes, I've just been notified. I'm to present her to the county jail the day after tomorrow by noon. The feds are going to take jurisdiction over the case. They want Jackie Lee, and Liddy is their chosen tool to nail him with—if she'll cooperate." Robert thumbed through the documents on his desk.

"What are they charging her with, and when is she to be arraigned?"

"She'll be arraigned within five days at the federal courthouse in Nashville. They're chargin' her with felony drug trafficking, conspiracy to possess with intent to distribute marijuana, and conspiracy to possess with intent to distribute cocaine. There is a little more to it, but that's the summation of the arrest charges." He paused for a moment and wiped his weary brow. "Sam, she's facin' thirty years to life with a fine of nearly a million dollars."

"I see. And how is Miss Fanning taking this upcoming event? What is her state of mind?"

"She's scared to death. Her baby is due in two months, and she's afraid she's gonna have the child in jail while awaitin' trial." Robert blew on his coffee to cool it before taking a sip.

"Okay, I'll catch a plane to Knoxville this afternoon. My legal assistant will call within the next hour with my travel plans. It's time I met with Miss Fanning, the D.A., and the federal prosecutors. I don't want any surprises, and I don't want her saying a thing unless I'm with her. Keep that girl's mouth shut. From all we've discussed, she reminds me of another high profile case which I lost."

"You lost a case? When and where?"

Sam hesitated. "Seven years ago. It was the Carrie Anne Nelson case, one of my greatest defeats, not to mention my most tragic. She was an accomplice in a murder case with James Alvin Monroe, a man whom she fancied herself to be hopelessly in love with. I had her defense locked solid, and then she did something very stupid. She wrote a series of secret love letters to him, denying her defense."

It was evident to Robert by Sam's strained voice that this was a painful memory, yet Robert was intrigued and wanted to know more. "I seem to recall a short blurb about a case that sounds a lot like what you are describin'. I caught it on the evenin' news about the time you said—seven years ago. What happened?" Robert propped his feet up on his desk and took another sip of coffee.

Sam blew a frustrated breath. "The jury was so outraged that they not only found her guilty, they recommended the death penalty, which the judge agreed to, sentencing her to death in Alabama's electric chair, yellow mama. The ironic thing about it was that the man who actually committed the murders got life in prison. I'm still working on the appeals for that case. It happened in DeKalb County, Alabama. The murder Carrie Anne was standing trial for had a witness that swore it was James Alvin who'd pulled the trigger, but the jury totally disregarded his testimony when those letters came out in court. The poor girl was seventeen and pregnant. She'd run away from home at the age of sixteen with a twenty-seven year-old man. They kidnapped and murdered six young girls from Georgia to Alabama before they were apprehended in Pinedale, Alabama. She was pregnant throughout the whole crime spree and delivered a baby girl while in jail."

Robert shook his head. He could see Liddy being just as naive and just as foolish as that young girl had been. "Yes, I do recall the event. It happened about a hundred miles from here as the crow flies. We've got some serious talkin' to do, Sam. I'll pick you up in Knoxville. You can stay with Tana and me. This town doesn't have a decent hotel. Bring Angie along, if you want to. That way she and Tana can visit. We'll meet with Liddy tomorrow afternoon. I've already arranged for bail."

"My assistant will get back to you with the arrival time. I'll see if Angie wants to come. With Sam Jr. off at UCLA, she might want a diversion." Sam chuckled. "I'm bringing some old newspapers from the Carrie Anne trial. I don't intend to be blindsided again. And don't worry, Robert. I'll go down to the county jail with you when you take your niece in to be processed. We'll get through this."

As Robert hung up the phone, he leaned back in his chair and took a long sip of coffee. He needed to call Lizzy. They would need Sam's retainer released shortly after he arrived, and he needed Lizzy's signature for Liddy's bail.

The Next Day

Fitzwilliam sat at his desk, busily preparing for his 2:20 Latin class when his mobile rang. It was his wife.

"Fitzwilliam, I'll be late coming home tonight. Andrea, Robert's legal assistant, just called. I have to stop by my uncle's law office and sign some papers and write a check. Liddy's defense attorney needs his advance, plus they have some other expenses. Liddy has to turn herself in tomorrow."

Fitzwilliam hesitated. "Elizabeth, must you be the one to sign? I mean, can't Jane sign or someone else?"

"Jane has the flu, and the papers need to be signed today. The only way anyone can sign in my place is if I give them power of attorney. Fitzwilliam, do you have a problem with this?"

He sighed, tapping his fingers on his desk. He was treading on thin ice, and he knew it. "Yes, Elizabeth... yes, I do. It's not only your name going down on paper. It's mine, too. You are my wife, and if you sign that document, it's as if I have signed it, and I don't want my family name connected with it in any way."

"Well, you had better explain this to me because I'm not getting it. This is my family, and I owe them my allegiance."

Fitzwilliam could feel the ice crack beneath his feet as her rising annoyance coupled with anger came through the phone clearly. Getting up from his desk, he walked over to the cooler for a cup of water as he listened. Finding middle ground was not going to be easy. "Elizabeth, I don't want this scandal attached to my family name. I've always been low key–kept a low profile if you will. I don't want my association with this sordid affair picked up in the press. So far, no one from the U.K. knows I'm here. Should I be connected to this, it will make the London news. It will *be* news—big news. I can see the headlines now. *Darcy Heir's Defense of Drug Smugglers*. It will not be good for my family, and my father—"

"*Your* family!" Elizabeth interrupted. "Fitzwilliam, we're talking about *my* family here! My father's sister and her daughter—my cousin. I'm sorry, but that's where my concerns lie."

He drew in a long measured breath and closed his eyes, slowly shaking his head. She was clearly angry, and the last thing he wanted was a disagreement with his wife. "It will be all right. Hopefully no one will notice. Just keep a low profile for my sake, Elizabeth…please."

"I'll see what I can do. I won't go out of my way to advertise your name, but I *will* take care of my family."

"Elizabeth, you're not going downtown alone," he quickly added. "I'll meet you in your office after class, and we'll go together." He paced his office floor, running his hand through his hair. The situation was serious, and he couldn't lose total control of it. There was too much at stake.

"Suit yourself. You are more than welcome to accompany me. In fact, I would like that," she said. "I've got to go. My Cal I class starts in ten minutes. I'll see you after class. Bye."

He slid his mobile shut and groaned. "If Father hears of this, he very well may disinherit me. Scandal is the one thing Father will not tolerate. He's going to be furious," he said out loud. Walking over to his desk, he picked up his copy of Wheelock's Latin, along with the class notes he'd composed and headed for his next class.

Late that afternoon, Robert and Sam Armstrong sat in the legal conference room in heavy concentration, poring over legal documents with an occasional question directed at an obviously bored and very pregnant young lady sitting across the table from them. When Sam had asked Liddy a question, she answered with a smart retort.

Fire flew from Armstrong's eyes. He was *not* a man to be disrespected, especially by the dim-witted girl he was trying to help. Getting up out of his seat he walked around the end of the table and grabbed the young woman by her hand, pulling her out of her chair. "Come with me, Miss Fanning." He dragged her over to the window and pointed to a very large tree standing in the courtyard of the county courthouse.

"You see that tree? Take a good look at it. Do you know its history?"

Liddy glanced out the window and then drew her eyes back to Sam. She shook her head.

"Up until 1913, that tree there was where they hung people. It's known as *The Hanging Tree*. Now, if I lose this case, they won't be hanging you, nor will you face the electric chair like the last young lady I represented. But like you, that young woman didn't understand the seriousness of the charges leveled against her. She chose to protect a man who had murdered six young girls, and *that* landed her on death row in Alabama. Unlike her, you're *not* facing the death sentence, but you *are* facing thirty years to life at a maximum security prison for women. Do you know what they do to little girls in prison?"

She stood there like a deaf mute.

Sam pressed on, intent on making his point. "You will be exposed to the worst dregs of society. There's a pecking order in prison, and *you,* being young and pretty, will be at the mercy of an older woman who will do with you as she pleases." Sam pinned her to the wall with his intense and piercing gaze. Liddy swallowed hard.

"These charges are serious, and I need your full cooperation in order to defend you. Do you understand that, Miss Lydia Fanning?"

The fear was evident in her eyes as she nodded.

"Good, now let's start over. Tell me how you came to be a courier for Jackie Lee?"

Liddy waddled back over to the conference table and flopped down. Dropping her head into her hands, she shook and cried. "I swear I didn't know what he was doin'. Not at first, anyways. Yes, I had heard the rumors, but I didn't believe them. I loved Jackie Lee, and he was good to me… in the beginning, at least."

Robert pushed a bottle of soda in her direction. Liddy twisted the cap and took a long drink before setting it back down.

"One night, when they thought I was asleep, I overheard them talkin' about a drop east of Knoxville in Cocke County. It's high up in the mountains near Thunder Road. Jackie was talkin' about kilos of cocaine, and about killin' someone who knew too much. I kept very still, strainin' to hear every word they said. My name was mentioned, and I heard Jackie Lee say that there was no need to worry about me because I was now involved.

"Later, I asked him about what I'd heard. He slapped me, sending me sprawling across the floor, and then he picked me up and shoved me up against the wall. He told me I was lucky he didn't kill me for listenin' to his conversations. I cried hard. I was scared to death. No one had ever struck me, not even Momma or Daddy. I guess the cryin' must've bothered him, 'cause he left." Liddy paused for another long drink from her soda bottle. Wiping her mouth with the back of her hand, she continued.

"He came back later and held me. He told me he was protectin' me, and that this was not his operation alone. That's when he told me that the packages I had taken to Aunt Wilma in Kentucky contained pot and cocaine. He said that if I ever thought about talkin', that I would go to jail, too, or worse. And I didn't have to ask him what he was talkin' about, because I knew. I knew they'd kill me." Liddy paused and reached for the soda, gulping it down. She was clearly shattered. "They'll kill me. So many have died already. Please, Mr. Armstrong. They'll kill me." She burst into tears.

Robert rose from his seat and came to his niece's side, giving her a hug. "Liddy, nobody is gonna kill you. We can get you protection. Whatever plea bargain the prosecution offers, you need to take it if Sam thinks it's in your best interest. It looks to me as if you fell into this before you knew what you were into, and now you're in deep."

"Who are *they,* and who has been killed, Miss Fanning?" Sam inquired, never looking up. Notepad and pencil in hand, he scribbled as she talked.

"I don't know who *they* are. Possibly the Colombians, but I don't know."

"Could you identify the men you heard that night," Sam asked, still not looking up from the pad where he continued to write.

"Yes, I can identify them. I know them. They work for Jackie Lee, and I recognized their voices."

"Very good, now who has been killed?" Robert asked, searching Liddy's face.

"I don't know, exactly. I heard Gunther and Lenny talkin' with some other men about it. One was a game warden. That's the only one I actually saw. It was late at night—well past midnight. I couldn't sleep. It was around Halloween." She paused for another drink. "No, it was Halloween night. I remember it now. I woke up and stumbled over to the window for some fresh air. The smell of pot was so thick in the air, and I was nauseated. The moon was shinin' bright, and I looked down from my upstairs window." Liddy shook her head, tears streaming down her cheeks.

Robert reached over to a box of tissues he kept in the room. Pulling one from the box, he handed it to Liddy.

"Liddy, do you think you can continue now?" Robert asked.

She nodded and swallowed hard. "It was then that I saw it—a man wrapped in a blanket. They, Slim and Jimmy, were carryin' him to the truck. I heard Jackie Lee yellin' at Gunther for bringin' the body back to the house in the first place. I heard them, that is Slim and Jimmy, say that the game warden had been found nosin' around up in the holler. That's where they killed him, and that's where they took him back to... back to the holler. He's buried somewhere up there in Coldwater Holler, but I don't know his name or exactly where they buried him. He'd accidentally stumbled into one of the coves where they grow the pot. One of Jackie's men shot him and brought him down to the house, and then that night they took him back up there—back up to the holler and buried him."

Liddy wiped a few tears, shaking her head. "I don't know nothin' about the rest, only that there are others. It was a week or so later when I couldn't sleep again. And again it was around midnight. I heard a man with a heavy Spanish accent sayin' that the body-count would get higher if there was a double cross, but I don't know what he meant. Now I figure they want me to be part of that body-count." Liddy burst into a new rush of sobs as Robert held her.

"Liddy, did you get a good look at the man with the Spanish accent?" Robert tenderly asked.

"I've seen him once before. He's known as 'The Colombian.' That's all I know, but yes, I could identify him," Liddy said in between shed tears.

"It's all right, Liddy. It's gonna be all right."

Sam, who'd been rapidly jotting down notes, glanced up at the door. Two people were standing in the doorway. He stared at them, wondering how much they'd heard.

"Lizzy? Fitzwilliam?" Robert called out.

"Uncle, I signed the document you had for me and wrote the check. I left them with Andrea." Elizabeth's face was white, while Fitzwilliam's jaw was clenched hard.

"How long have you been standin' there?" Robert asked, getting up from his chair to approach Fitzwilliam with his hand extended.

"Long enough to hear how serious this is," Fitzwilliam flatly answered, taking the offered hand.

"Well then, you know this must be kept in confidence...for Liddy's sake."

"Yes, we realize that." Fitzwilliam walked into the room, followed by his wife. "I have my own reasons for wanting it kept as quiet as possible and my wife's name kept out of it."

"I'm sorry, Fitzwilliam, but it's too late for that. We're all in this hip deep," Robert said, motioning for Andrea, who'd also just come to the door.

"Andrea, have Marsha take Liddy home, and then get my sister on the phone. Liddy's emotionally distraught. Her mother may need to call her doctor."

"Yes, sir, I'll take care of it."

"Thank you, Andrea." Robert turned around to face Fitzwilliam's cold stare. "Mr. Darcy, none of us want to be a part of this nightmare, but Lizzy is part of this family, and as such, she or Jane has to write the checks to pay the expenses or sign whatever papers are required to release money for this case. I'm puttin' some of my own money up front, but Lizzy's brother is payin' the bulk of it."

"I know, Robert, and it's Fitzwilliam. My father is Mr. Darcy. You must understand. I am trying to protect my family, and Elizabeth is part of that family. If news of this reaches Britain, the tabloid press will milk it for all they can, which in turn, will have an undesirable effect on my family. My relationship with my father is tenuous at best, and this will only worsen the situation." Fitzwilliam twisted his wedding band, his face etched with anxiety while Liddy sat in her chair, bawling. Robert moved to her side, again attempting to comfort her.

"I'm sorry, Fitzwilliam. We're all doin' the best we can. I hope it doesn't cause problems for you and Lizzy with your father," Robert said as he continued to rub Liddy's back.

"I hope not, too. Things are complicated enough as they are. Whatever ramifications fall from this, I'll deal with them. It's just that I wish to avoid publicity whenever possible." Fitzwilliam drew in a deep breath, obviously worried that the situation was spinning out of his control. "I can see you have a lot of work to do, and I don't want to get in your way. Liz and I must go now. We have a lot of work of our own to do at home." Fitzwilliam glanced over in Elizabeth's direction, motioning for her to come.

"Well, before you leave, I want you to meet my old friend Sam Armstrong. Sam, this is my niece, Elizabeth Darcy, and her husband, Fitzwilliam." Robert gestured to Sam, who placed his pencil down.

Rising to walk in their direction, Armstrong offered his hand. "Pleased to meet you, Mr. and Mrs. Darcy."

"It's a pleasure to meet you, too, sir," they both said as they shook hands.

"I wish we could have met under more pleasant circumstances," Fitzwilliam said, a strained smile tightening his lips.

"As do I, Fitzwilliam, as do I."

Fitzwilliam turned to Robert. "Robert, we really must go. You are busy, and we need to eat. I have over fifty papers to mark by morning. Ring us up, and we'll have dinner."

"I'll speak with Tana, and we'll call. Let me escort you out."

Robert saw Fitzwilliam and Lizzy to the door where the stairs led to the first floor and said goodbye, kissing Lizzy's cheek and shaking Fitzwilliam's hand. He let out a long breath in a whispering whistle as he traversed back into the conference room.

Sam, who had been rather quiet up until now, began rummaging through his briefcase. Locating what he was looking for, he pulled it out and stood up, sliding back his chair. He went around the table to where Liddy sat and handed her the bundle. "Miss Fanning, this package is for you. It contains a selection of old newspapers and my personal report on the last case I handled that was similar to yours. I want you to read everything in this file. Do you understand me?" He hooked her chin with his forefinger to insure he had eye contact.

"Yes, sir," she said weakly.

"Good. A test will follow the next time we meet." He turned on his heel and walked back to take his seat where he picked up his pencil and once again began to scribble.

Andrea entered the conference room and took Liddy by the hand, escorting her outside to the other assistant who would drive her home. Once Liddy was securely in Marsha's care, Andrea picked up the phone and dialed Mrs. Fanning's number. When Lydia was on the line, Andrea peeked into the room. "Mr. Bennett, your sister is on line one."

"Thanks, Andrea. It's after five. You can go home now." Robert wiped his brow wearily as he reached for the phone.

"Lydia."

"Robert, how is my baby? Where is she?"

"Calm down, Lydia. Liddy is fine. Marsha is drivin' her home as we speak. They should be there in twenty minutes. Liddy's very upset. If you need to, call her doctor to see if he can give her somethin'. That is if you think it's needed. I have more to discuss with Sam. From what Liddy has told us, I think we have somethin' to go on. It looks promisin'. I'll tell you more when it's settled." He sat on the conference table and rubbed his brow, trying to relieve the stress, knowing there were hours of consultation yet to come.

"Thanks, Robert. I don't know what I would do without you. It's been a long time in coming, but I want you to know that I love you and appreciate all you are doing for Liddy."

"I love you, too, Sis. Everything will be all right. Trust me, Lydia. I need to go now."

"I do, and Robert…"

"Yeah?"

"Ron would be proud of you if he could see you."

"Thanks, Sis. Now don't you worry about a thing. This is all gonna work out." Robert hung the phone up, hoping he spoke the truth.

Once the room was cleared of all but Sam and Robert, Sam put down his pencil. "Well, we have our strategy. Liddy was a witness to a murder. Once we dig a little, no pun intended, we're going to find a body." Picking his pencil back up, he tapped it against the table. "I'm bringing in my investigating team. I'm going to put feet to the pavement. The first order of business will be to contact Fish and Wildlife and find out who's missing from among their ranks. Then I want a warrant and a pair of cadaver dogs to find that grave and any others. I suspect we may find a graveyard full of bodies. Nunley's charges are about to include at least one murder charge—maybe more. When I have all of my strategy planned out, I'll approach the prosecutors for a deal. Liddy can identify the culprits, including the Colombian."

Throwing down the pencil, Sam stretched back in his chair and folded his hands behind his head. "Nunley's looking at a capital murder charge in a drug related crime—and that, my friend, as you well know, carries the death penalty in a federal case. We'll know more when Miss Fanning is formally charged, but I'm hoping to cut a deal with the prosecuting attorney for immunity. I feel certain I can get the state charges dropped," he said with a smile. "It's the feds I'm concerned with. It all depends on how strong their case is, but if we do go to trial, I'm going to use a similar defense to the one I used in the Nelson case. Liddy is a victim—a victim of an unscrupulous man. If your niece doesn't blow my strategy, we'll succeed."

Getting up from his seat and walking over to where Robert stood, Sam put his hand on Robert's shoulder. "It's going to work out, my friend," he said with a twinkle in his eye. "Do you still own Jack and Jill?"

Robert met his friend's stare, a smile crossing his features. "No, and even if I did, they would be too old. However, the Plateau County Sheriff's Department owns their descendants. They have the best K-9 division in the state, and that includes the bloodhound cadaver dogs."

Sam slapped his old friend on the back. "Tomorrow, I go to work. As I said before, the first order of business is a little talk with the Fish and Wildlife Agency. Have Andrea find me a house close to the town square, if possible. I want to be within walking distance to the courthouse, the sheriff's office, and your office. Let's get some supper and come back here. We need to roll up our sleeves and burn the midnight oil."

Chapter Thirty

... I promised your parents ...I would protect you... and protect you I shall...

Taking their seats at Tucker's All You Can Eat Buffet, Elizabeth and Fitzwilliam settled in, though neither was hungry.

"Fitzwilliam, you're upset. You haven't said two words since we left my uncle's office. Won't you talk to me?"

He glanced up from his plate. "Upset is *not* the word for it. You Americans appall me. You still execute people—how barbaric!"

"Fitzwilliam, I think you misunderstood. No one is going to be executed. Sam Armstrong was simply trying to make a point with my dense cousin. She doesn't exactly have a corner on the market when it comes to good sense. You have to use sensationalism to garner her attention. That's all."

"No, I distinctly heard Mr. Armstrong say that one of his clients was on death row in Alabama. While you were busy with your uncle's legal assistant, I heard him say those very words. You may not have heard him, but I certainly did."

"Fitzwilliam, calm down! I did hear him say that, and you and I should not have been listening. Furthermore, you shouldn't have gone to the door like you did."

"Enough, Elizabeth. I was so shocked by what I heard that I was drawn to that door like a magnet to steel, and it's my belief that this entire situation is rotten to the core."

Elizabeth closed her eyes and shook her head. She knew what really concerned her husband, and it wasn't the death penalty in Alabama. Opening her eyes, she released a deep breath. "Fitzwilliam, look at me."

He raised his eyes from his plate where his food sat barely touched.

"You're worried, aren't you?"

"Worried?" He raised a brow. "Whatever makes you think that?! Of course I'm worried. I don't know how this can be contained, and my family—or should I say *our* families will suffer greatly because of it. I just hope my father will not cast me aside. In spite of what I've said, I do love him, and I can't bear to see him suffer because of—"

"Me." Putting her knife and fork down, she placed both hands on the table. "I'm sorry... I'm really sorry my family will cause you pain—that they are such an embarrassment," she retorted. "Liddy is an embarrassment to me, too. Do you think it's easy for me to endure the stares and whispers I get every day? I want to fall through the cracks in the floor. I've told you before that Liddy doesn't have enough sense to be ashamed for herself." Tears filled Elizabeth's eyes. "I'm holding up for my family's sake, but I am deeply mortified by all that we now know, knowing that soon—very soon, everything will be exposed."

He reached across the table and took Elizabeth's hand in his. "Elizabeth, don't worry. We'll bear this together. It's just that I worry about my father. He's always been robust and vigorous. He's sixty-two and in a constant state of agitation, especially with me of late, and I've begun to worry about his health. The last time I saw him he looked pale and sickly. It's not like him at all."

Elizabeth's eyes widened. "You've never voiced that concern before. Is there something wrong with him?"

"No, not that I know of, but I can't help but worry. He looked thinner, more drawn, and much older than he did last summer." He stopped short. He didn't want to talk or think about his father any longer. If anything happened to him, he knew he'd feel responsible, even if he wasn't. He cleared his throat and changed the subject. "Come on. Let's go. Neither of us appears to be very hungry. You have a test to prepare for your Cal II students, and I have a pile of papers to mark." He threw down a generous tip and helped Elizabeth with her coat.

That night after all their work was completed, Fitzwilliam decided to forgo the scheduled reading from his family journal. Somehow he just didn't feel like reading. As he'd done every night since their wedding, he held Elizabeth close after making love, but instead of tender thoughts, his mind was a thousand miles away across the ocean.

...My dad is going to be furious. Well, I did say I would be willing to give up my inheritance for her, and I suppose it will come to that, now. But what about my dad? I'm really worried about him. What would become of the family if something were to happen to him? He has always depended on me. He looked down at Elizabeth asleep in his arms. *I worry about her, too. She really doesn't handle stress very well at all. I'll have to protect her as best I can. I love you, Elizabeth. I promised your parents at their graveside that I would protect you, and protect you I shall. Good night, my Liz.*

He gently rolled her out of his arms and snuggled close behind her back. Pulling her in an embrace, his hand cupped her breast. Soon they were both fast asleep.

London England

Sitting around the conference table in a plush corporate suite, Harry Dashwood scanned the room, examining the faces of all present. Edmund and Henry Darcy, second cousins to George's sons, were there. The brothers hated Fitzwilliam and David—envious of their status in London and the fact that they enjoyed a privileged lifestyle to which Edmund and Henry felt was denied to them. Yes, they would be willing to help and more than willing to sink their teeth into their more affluent cousins. Dashwood smirked.

Also present was Edward Darcy, another second cousin, with an inflated ego and an overrated sense of his own self importance. Looking and waiting to exact his revenge, Edward managed the L.A. office of Darcy Technologies, but believed his real worth would be in a position on the board of directors, which George had denied him. Yes, he was a very useful fool indeed!

Dashwood moved on as he scrutinized the room. Ah, Charles Wilson! Yes, Charles, married to Lora Darcy, a third cousin, managed the New York office of Darcy & Winthrop Publishing. He also coveted a position on the board. He would be more than willing to help. Lastly, there was Sean Ashton, overseer of the Ottawa office in Canada, another second cousin by marriage with a reputation for insatiable avarice and greed. Any form of vice could be useful.

Glancing to his left, he spied Jonathan Stanley, Executive Director of Management in charge of Darcy & Winthrop Publishing, International, and Jason Wesley likewise of Darcy Technologies. And then there was himself. Harry had married Samantha Darcy, the sister of George and Harvey, shortly after graduating from Christ Church, Oxford. It had been a convenient step-up into the most powerful family in the United Kingdom. Harry smiled to himself. All three had been contemporaries of George Darcy, and all had attended university together. When George had inherited Pemberley, he had taken them on as business associates. Harry, because of his marriage to Samantha, had quickly risen up the corporate ladder to Executive Director in charge of management operations for British American Petroleum, the heart of Pemberley, PLC. The other two had moved up a little slower.

Because of their positions on the board and their close friendship with George, he had taken them into his confidence, and they, as part of his team of advisors, were privy to privileged information—information they could use to their advantage. Yes, they knew of George's struggles and worries, of his weaknesses and declining health. And they knew of Fitzwilliam's marriage, now cloaked in secrecy. And most importantly, they had a plan. Harry Dashwood smiled as he poured his friends a drink.

"As you know," Dashwood began, "I have convened this meeting to discuss Pemberley's corporate stability. You have seen the latest reports, so it's no news to you that profits are down for another straight quarter in a row, an accumulated 63.5 percent drop over the last five years. Things are likely to go even further into decline if we don't do something about it." He eyed each man closely before proceeding. "George is out of touch with the business, completely oblivious to the current economic climate. He's too embroiled in a dispute with his sons, thus the reason for the decline in revenue.

"This is our opportunity—the one we have been waiting for. Whilst George is distracted, we'll move to gain control. Our strategy is as follows: George and his sons own 39.5 percent of the publicly-traded stock, but between us and those I've been able to convince to support us so far, we own an amount nearly equal to theirs. That puts us on equal footing with them and within striking distance of a serious challenge. And, if I spin things just right, I believe I can convince some of the other major shareholders to join us. With their support, we should be able to pick up another ten percent, giving us about fifty percent. Then we will only need another two percent, which we'll need to purchase. With those things accomplished, we'll have gained the controlling interest with a little to spare," he said with a smile. "As we speak, I have a team of solicitors working on the formalities. Once everything is in place, we'll have an iron-clad coalition, one George and his sons won't be able to stop." Dashwood chuckled as he surveyed the room. From the response he'd received from those present, and some who weren't, his confidence soared.

"George has made the critical mistake of loaning me a considerable amount of money. I've secured other loans as well. If all goes as planned, we'll have the money we need within a month, and we'll have control of Pemberley before George or his sons are even aware of what has happened."

"Yes, but Dashwood, that loan exposes you to unnecessary risk. Your own solicitor advised you against it. It has a six months' duration clause. Surely you are aware of that danger?" queried Stanley.

"Of course, I am. It's a gamble, but I have all the confidence in the world that we can achieve everything we need to accomplish within six months. I will be able to repay George in full and gain control over Pemberley, too."

Edward lit up a cigarette and listened quietly while closely watching all those present. "Harry, what are you planning to do about Fitzwilliam and David? They won't just let us take control. You must know that?"

"They are of no consequence. Fitzwilliam is far too soft. He doesn't have the fire in his belly for a fight. Pemberley has never been high on his list of priorities. He will take his money and leave, probably settling in America with his American wife at some university. David, on the other hand, might present a challenge, but he doesn't have the intestinal fortitude, either. Besides, Samantha has informed me that he's held in contempt by the majority of the family. Now Harvey may prove a little difficult, but it's no secret that he and George barely speak. It's well known within the family that the brothers hate each other. He won't stop us, either. However, I would like his support just the same."

"I don't know, Dashwood. If Fitzwilliam and David present a challenge and win, we stand to lose substantially."

A large smile crossed Harry Dashwood's face. "Wesley, don't even think about it. I know they won't present any serious difficulties. I've watched them grow up. They don't have the stomach for it. We have nothing to worry about." The room reverberated with Dashwood's proud and hearty laugh.

Wesley, still a little worried, posed one last question. "What about Hilda Vanderburgh?"

"Hilda follows the money. She'll support us when the time comes."

Edward Darcy focused on his fellow cousins. "We'd better plan carefully. I don't think it wise to underestimate Fitzwilliam. He *is* co-chief executive officer and vice-chairman of the board. Although my cousin and I don't get along, I know him well enough to know that he has a deep-seated regard for the family legacy." Edward smirked. "He actually reads those dusty journals. He will fight, if for no other reason than that."

"Edward's right. We'd be unwise to count Fitzwilliam out," Edmund said, with the other Darcys nodding in agreement.

"Pish, I tell you Fitzwilliam is not prepared to fight dirty. He is too forthright and honorable. And even if he does attempt to rise to the challenge, we don't play by the same rules. Fitzwilliam's Achilles' heel is his wife. If I have to, I will get to him through her. I'll dredge up everything I can find on that family. I'm investigating them as we speak. Perception is everything. I know how to handle Fitzwilliam."

"Now, all we have to do is solicit a little more support from the Darcy family and a few of George's closest friends, whom I should add, have no respect whatsoever for either of George's sons. And by the time I'm through, they'll have even less. We'll assume control before George or his sons have a chance to react." Dashwood scrutinized all those sitting around the table, looking from one to the other.

Henry Darcy, who had been silent until now, spoke up. "What exactly *do* you plan to do, Dashwood?"

"I'm glad you finally asked. First of all, I intend to alert the media as to where Fitzwilliam really is and what he is doing…that he's in America, *not* Saudi Arabia as George has claimed. That alone will unleash the press to investigate matters as they see fit. Next, my strategy is to mysteriously release a few carefully planned news stories with juicy tidbits about David. With both brothers under scrutiny, family members and close friends will give anonymous interviews about how the company is suffering due to lack of leadership. Last year's annual report to the shareholders speaks for itself and is in our favor. Profits were flat. This will draw George's focus to the news media." He grinned. "That will give me the chance I need to begin enticing the Pemberley Five, the five most prominent shareholders outside of the family, away from George and to us. I'll convince them that George is too engrossed in family struggles. How can a man run a corporation when he cannot manage his own house? I'll sadly emphasize that Fitzwilliam is ill-disposed and unwilling to lead such a large corporation. It is no secret where his true interests lie. And David," he heartily laughed, "he's far too busy with his pleasurable pursuits. He has become obsessed with fast cars, fast women, and a profligate lifestyle of debauchery, lost in a world of mediocrity. They are both unsuitable for their positions. Pemberley is nothing more than a means for sustaining their way of life."

"A house divided cannot stand." Jason Wesley interjected with a sneer.

"Exactly." Dashwood reaffirmed. "That is our pretext—"

"Whilst our real motivation is control," finished Edmund Darcy, nodding in understanding. "Ha! I love it! I think we can pull off that line of reasoning. What do the rest of you think?"

"I say we should go ahead and do it," Henry Darcy said.

"Yes!" said the other Darcy cousins in unison.

Dashwood smiled and lifted his glass to his lips. "With the major shareholders' support and the stock we're buying, George won't be able to stop us." Dashwood laughed deeply followed by most of the others. Only Sean Ashton and Charles Wilson remained unconvinced. Not being blood related, they had the most to lose.

Chapter Thirty-one

... Jacta alea est—the die is cast... you keep your friends close and your enemies even closer...

Things in London were in a state of turmoil. Harvey Darcy hadn't spoken to his brother George in years, but he had heard the gossip, and along with some of their cousins, was concerned.

Rumors and innuendo were spreading among the family that George Darcy had come into bitter conflict with his two sons and had even disowned Fitzwilliam over a supposed marriage to an American. No one outside the inner circles knew the particulars since George kept everything effectively concealed, and though Harvey knew the marriage had occurred, he could only speculate as to George's thoughts and motives for his actions.

George must be slipping. He usually held a firm control over everything, or had George set the stage, planning to use this as a device against his sons? Harvey didn't know, but if he had, Harvey was very sure George had no idea he was being double-crossed, and that things were more serious than he realized. Thus, given the seriousness of the situation, Harvey would have to break his estrangement from his brother and contact him.

They hadn't spoken in years, but it hadn't always been like that. In fact, they had once been close, but a woman had divided them. Consequently, it was with a heavy heart that Harvey made the call he dreaded.

"George, it's Harvey. I have to see you, and it has to be today. It's urgent."

"Of course, Harvey. I'm at home and have some time. To what do I owe this honor after all these years?" George's voice showed no emotion.

"I'll explain everything when I get there."

Harvey realized that a battle of the wills was inevitable. Little had changed. It would take Harvey about thirty minutes to make his way through London traffic at this hour in the afternoon, giving him time to reflect on their past. The last time Harvey had come to Darcy House was when he had spoken with his brother about Anne. It had been a bitter confrontation on which both brothers parted never to speak to one another again, until now.

...Anne, he sighed. The memory grieved him. No, the truth was that it more than grieved him. It broke his heart. He had once loved her, and they had been engaged before her marriage to George. Harvey shook his head. How she had managed two more pregnancies after David was still a mystery to him. After all, she had given George his due—his two sons. The other two, he supposed, must have been Anne's doing. When they'd been engaged, she had often talked about her desire for a large family. So he deduced that his brother had granted her wish on those rare occasions when he came home to Pemberley.

As Harvey weaved in and out of the London traffic, his thoughts ventured back to thirty-nine years earlier. Both he and his brother had been strikingly handsome in their prime, and many a heart had wilted at a mere glance from either of them. They resembled one another closely in looks, but in personalities, they were polar opposites. Harvey was soft, tender-hearted, and easy going, while George was dark, serious, and brooding. And though their temperaments differed, they were linked by a close bond—that is until the beautiful Anne Winthrop separated them.

Harvey swallowed against the lump in his throat. His and Anne's story had been tragic—one in which youthful foolishness had cruelly intervened. One summer in the sun spent in the South of France had changed everything. Harvey shook his head.

When he came to the massive gates that led to Darcy House, Harvey's thoughts dissipated as he pulled onto the yellow brick drive. Rolling to a stop, he exited his car and walked the familiar path to the front door where a friendly face met him.

"Master Harvey!" greeted the old butler as he took his coat. "It is a pleasure to see you again. It has been so long!"

"Sammons, it's very good to see you, too. How have you been?"

"Very well, sir. Very well indeed. Now, if I may, I shall show you to the study. Master George is expecting you."

Sammons escorted him down a long hallway—one he knew well. As he entered, George rose to greet him with a handshake and a thin smile.

"Come in, Harvey. Sit down and have a drink." George poured two brandies.

"Thank you, George. I believe I will."

"Now, Harvey, come to the point. You never visit me, so what do you want?" George asked flatly.

Harvey suppressed a smirk. This was the George he remembered—always to the point, always forthright. Harvey picked up the gauntlet. "Simply this," he shifted in his seat, "you have to end this disagreement with Fitzwilliam. If I've heard the rumors, then you must have heard them."

"Still covering my back I see. Well relax, Harvey." George smiled dryly. "Everything is under control. There's no need to worry."

"No need to worry? George, look at what you're doing. You're tearing Pemberley apart. You have to reconcile with Fitzwilliam and accept his wife. Announce the marriage. David and Georgiana speak well of her, and if Benson or William found a woman like her, I would be honored to have her as a daughter. Fitzwilliam loves her! You must accept that. She *is* a Darcy now. And David, you have to make amends with him, too."

George leaned back with a contemptuous smirk on his face. "Harvey, what business is it of yours concerning me and my sons?"

"Enough, George! I'll be blunt with you. Our brother-in-law is undermining you. He plans to take control of Pemberley, using our cousins as pawns along with your arrogant pride as the weapon to sway the board. If you care anything about Fitzwilliam and David, you will make this right!"

"Harvey, I will *never* accept that marriage or David's flagrant disregard for propriety. But you know full well, short of disinheriting them, there is nothing I can do about it. However, if I had my way, I'd have Fitzwilliam's marriage dissolved and a proper English wife found, and I'd—"

"You'd what?" Harvey interrupted. "Oh, let me guess. You're hoping his marriage will fail, aren't you? That's why it hasn't been announced. George, you have to let the boys go. They are men now. If you don't, you will lose them forever. You cannot continue to control them." Harvey was up and out of his seat, pacing back and forth.

He leaned on his brother's desk. "Your vocal disapproval of the boys has set the stage for your enemies to take control. They're using your very words to say your sons are unfit to run Pemberley. You've been so preoccupied with David and Fitzwilliam that you can't see what's happening right under your very nose. If you don't rectify things and present a solid unified front, you'll leave our heritage in shambles, and the boys may not be able to protect it. George, you had better think about it!"

"You take an eager interest in my sons. What are they to you—your bastards? I know Anne loved you," George sneered through clenched teeth.

Taken aback, Harvey's anger deepened. "I won't have you insult Anne's memory like that. You know she was always faithful to you, and as for the other, I would know nothing about it. If she pined for me perhaps it was because you weren't the husband you should have been."

George's eyes grew dark as he pushed back in his chair—tears of anger glistening in his gaze. "If she was unhappy, it was her own doing."

"How can you say that? I know Anne tried to love you."

"You know no such thing!"

"Do I not? Sadly, I think I do." Harvey held George's cold stare with one of his own as they verbally crossed swords. "She told me so when I begged her to leave you before *your* first son was born. I wasn't married yet, but Anne wouldn't hurt *you*. Even later, for her sake and the sake of her children, she wouldn't leave. She told me that she was committed to her marriage. She may not have loved you at first, but later, she *did* love you."

"You know so much about it, and yet you know nothing—"

"I know you withdrew from her, and that you wouldn't talk to her. I know that she pleaded with you to come home, but you refused. I know how much she cried over you." Harvey walked the room, glaring at his brother. "George, why wouldn't you talk to her? Why didn't you try to work things out? Why didn't you love her? It's all she ever wanted, George—just to be loved. Why didn't you come when she was dying? Why, George!? Didn't you know that she kept asking for you—asking when you would come?"

"Loved! It wasn't me she loved. It was you, Harvey—you that she loved, not me! You were ever present in our marriage and in our bed. It was *you* who was there when I made love to her. It was your name she cried out—not mine! When she held me, it was *you* she was holding. I would come to home Pemberley to see my boys, hoping that Anne and I could somehow resolve our differences—come to some sort of agreement. But no matter what I did, I could never get *you* out of her heart, so I stopped caring and found consolation elsewhere. If she loved me later on—it was too late! By the time she wanted to talk, I no longer gave a damn. I am ***not*** a man who is ruled by his emotions. *That* is a sign of weakness, and *I* am anything but weak. As to why I was not there when she died?" George's eyes flashed. "Why should've I come? *You* were there in my stead." George threw himself back in his chair, his face contorted in anger and pain.

Harvey's heart was heavy at the sound of his brother's words. His face also twisted in pain. "When did we become such men, George?" he calmly asked. "You and I both hurt her when all she ever wanted was to be loved... and to have a family."

George wiped the sweat from his brow and shook his head wearily. "I know she wasn't unfaithful, at least not with her body, but her heart was another matter. However, Anne and our love triangle is not why you are here. My sons are my responsibility, not yours. They are all I have left. I have a duty and an obligation to Pemberley, and I must have them do their duty to the business and the family legacy. I know business-wise they know what to do, but there is more to it than a spreadsheet." He held his brother's gaze. "I must do what I must do in order to assure the future is secure."

Harvey looked at his brother with great pity. Choices had been made long ago. The die had been cast. "No, we have failed each other. I am sorry, Brother, but if you continue in this path, you will lose it all, except perhaps your money. What's important to you, George? You had better think about it. Think about what you are doing before it's too late. *Jacta alea est.* The die was cast, but it does not have to be cast a second time," he said with great sorrow as he moved to leave.

When he reached for the door, George called out to him, "Harvey, when or if the time comes, I will have your support, won't I?"

"Yes, George, you'll have my support, or I would not have come. Your back is covered." He put his hand on the doorknob and looked back one last time. "Goodbye, George."

Harvey's mind was full when he left Darcy House. *...So, it was Anne's memory of me that separated her from my brother, and here I thought it was his indifference, his inability to love.* He moaned in agony. *...That I should learn of this after all of these years! If only I could take that summer back, Anne...if only. I never thought my actions would affect anyone but me...but I was wrong.*

After Harvey left, George sat and reflected on his brother's words as he stroked his signet ring. *...Harvey, I wanted to be there with Anne, but you were there—you were always there. If I had believed that she loved me, nothing would have kept me from her. I would have moved heaven and earth, but it was you, Harvey, not me, she loved. You, the idealistic fool much like Fitzwilliam has become.* A silent tear slid down the old man's cheek.

As to his brother's other concern, George knew about that, too. He'd always known every beat of Pemberley's heart, and he'd already taken measures to stop his 'old friend'. He would give him enough rope to hang himself.

George was gambling that the effort of the conspirators would last past the six month due date on the loan he had advanced his brother-in-law and that he would be able to manipulate the stock prices into a temporary fall, forcing Harry to sell at a loss, thus financially ruining him. Harry had not a clue that George was watching him. Five hundred years of family history had taught George Darcy that you keep your friends close and your enemies even closer.

George glanced to the side. He felt a strange presence and thought he had caught a glimpse of something out of the corner of his eye. A woman's silhouette? It was white and fleeting...strange. He winced in pain and slipped a pill under his tongue.

Chapter Thirty-two

...a woman's mind is never very far from...

A fter a grueling five week-long tour of business and contract negotiation, David Darcy was finally back in London. Walking into the large executive complex of Pemberley, he wiped his brow. His father had left him a voice mail on his mobile, demanding his presence in his office as soon as he arrived. Fatigue from the long flights and laborious negotiations were beginning to take its toll. *...I'm exhausted. I wonder why Father is so adamant to see me. He wouldn't even allow me to return home first. Well, I'll shower in my executive flat and get to him as quickly as I can. From the sound of his voice, it must be urgent.*

As soon as he could, he headed directly for his father's office. "Good afternoon, Betty. I understand my father wants to see me. Is he available now?"

"I believe he is," she said in a terse tone. "He's been like a bear with a sore paw all morning. I have no idea what it's about, but I have to tell you he is not in a good mood. I'd be careful if I were you." She picked up the interoffice phone to inform Mr. Darcy that David was waiting outside.

"Send him in!" barked George Darcy.

"Good grief! I wonder what I've done now." David rolled his eyes and shook his head.

"I don't know, but you'd better go in and face your inquisition. I'm sure it's not as bad as you think."

"You want to bet?" David smiled as he strolled towards the door. He entered cautiously to find his father pacing back and forth, chewing on a cigar.

"Well, don't just stand there, looking like an arse. Come in! We've got to talk—and I want answers—not excuses." Mr. Darcy walked back to his desk and took his seat.

David followed and took the one across from his father.

"So what is the problem that has you all up in arms?"

"The problem?" Mr. Darcy asked, throwing a copy of *The Nashville Tennessean*, *The Knoxville Sentinel*, and *The Atlanta Journal and Constitution* across his desk. "How long have you known about this?"

David picked up the papers, closely examining each one. *The Tennessean* showed a very pregnant Liddy Fanning being escorted into the U.S. Federal Courthouse in Nashville, Tennessee by her uncle, Robert Bennett, and a man David had never seen before. *The Atlanta Journal and Constitution* had the headline caption *Largest Drug Ring in the Southeast Found in Plateau County, Tennessee* and *The Knoxville Sentinel*'s headline read *Jackie Lee Nunley Now Indicted on Murder Charges*.

Perusing the articles, David noted an assortment of quotes from various townspeople and family members concerning Miss Fanning and the Bennett family in general, and then he saw *it*. Fitzwilliam's name was mentioned alongside Elizabeth's. He released a heavy sigh and folded the papers, placing them back on his father's desk.

Mr. Darcy pinned his son to his chair as he asked once again. "How long have you known?"

David dropped his gaze and then glanced off to the side. His body was racked with fatigue, but he had to find the strength to face his father. "Since before the wedding."

"And you didn't bother tell me! You allowed me to find out through the newspapers and Blakely?"

223

David could only look at him. He knew that he had no answer that would satisfy his father.

His father nodded. "Yes, I've had my top public relations man in America since January. Did you really think I would simply let your brother go without taking measures to find out what he was getting himself into and to protect him, should it come to that?"

David sat there, his jaw clenched hard as stone, staring at his father, unsure of what, if anything, to say. He knew he was in trouble.

Mr. Darcy leaned over his desk. "Your loyalty lies with your brother, doesn't it? Well, that's very admirable of you. It serves you both well, but it's time the two of you got on board and put your loyalty where it really belongs—with this family and Pemberley! The article on the fourth page of the Atlanta paper has a nice journalistic portrait of the Bennett family, complete with mention of the *new* Mrs. Darcy and her marriage to your brother... *The heir to the Pemberley Conglomerate based in London, England.*"

David closed his eyes and shook his head. He was physically exhausted, and now he was mentally shattered. "Father, I don't know what to say. I had hoped it wouldn't come to this."

"Wouldn't come to this, you say? I warned your brother. These people are not polished. They have no regard for decorum or civilized behavior. Look at that strumpet! Pregnant by the worst sort of rubbish."

"Father, she's only a cousin. I can assure you that the Bennetts are good people. Every family has a black sheep. We've certainly had ours. Bloody hell, I'm a black sheep—"

"Not like them!" Mr. Darcy growled. "I've had this family under investigation for months. It was about time I took a more direct interest in the private lives of my sons. Would you like to know what I have found out?"

David remained silent, glaring at his father.

"I can see that you still wish to defy me. Well, I'm going to tell you anyway. This Robert Bennett appears to be a small town country lawyer, a country nobody, but don't be fooled by that illusion. He is a graduate of the Citadel, class of 1981, along with his good friend here," George said as he stabbed the picture on the cover of the *Tennessean* with his forefinger. "Samuel Mason Armstrong, who, I might add, is the man representing that tart—their cousin. They later attended Harvard Law School together and then joined the American Navy."

Mr. Darcy reached in his desk and pulled out a folder. He scanned down a written synopsis before resuming. "Bennett became an officer in the Navy SEALs whilst Armstrong was accepted into the Judge Advocate General's Corp. Armstrong was instrumental in pulling Bennett's arse out of a scandal in 1991 when he was charged with being negligent in duty concerning his command. It seems that one of his officers snapped under pressure, opening fire on friendly forces he mistook for the enemy. His excuse was the death of two of his comrades the day before."

Seizing the opportunity, David quickly responded, "Father, that was beyond his control—"

"Beyond his control! He was derelict in duty. It was his job and responsibility to see that his men were properly trained and did not *snap* under stress. The Navy SEALs are supposed to be one of the elite forces of the American military. They don't *crack* under pressure!" His father paused, studying his son. "David, in war, as in business, if someone under your authority makes a mistake, it is *you* who is ultimately responsible. *You* must answer to the board of directors—not the minion under you who failed or made a mistake in judgment. Mistakes cost money and in this case, lives. That's what I am trying to get through to you and your brother—responsibility, obligation, and duty!" He pounded his fist with each word.

David swallowed hard. Would his father's never-ending barrage ever let up? Apparently not!

Putting on his glasses, George picked up the report and traced his finger down, looking for a particular item. "Ah, here it is. Fitzwilliam was correct on both accounts. They are related to us, though distantly, and they did descend from an English earl, but their family has been riddled with scandal from the 18th century to the present. The Bennet who left England was much like you and Fitzwilliam—a renegade." George flipped the page and picked up where he left off. "During the 19th century, the Bennetts were involved in the distilling of illegal whiskey on their plantation. They were also involved in the first court case in Plateau County. Seems as if one of them was caught up in a land swindling scheme." George glanced up and cleared his throat. Adjusting his glasses, he continued. "In the 20th century one of their relations was caught smuggling illegal whiskey in meat carcasses into Alabama and Georgia during the American Prohibition. That particular Bennett's sons now operate a prosperous distillery in Southern Kentucky, not more than fifty miles from the family farm. They evaded scandal for the rest of the 20th century, but they have more than made up for it in the twenty-first."

David was stunned at the lengths his father had gone to.

"But, that's not all I have been investigating. I've been investigating *you*, as well."

David sat up straight. How dare his father invade his privacy!

"Don't look so taken aback, David Jamison. Did you really think I would not keep up with you as well as your brother? Well, I happen to know what you've been doing both here in London and abroad. And if you think that I don't know about your affair with James Lawton's daughter, you can think again." A wide grin spread across Mr. Darcy's face. "At least you have discriminating taste for once, or perhaps you took my advice about using your charm. All I can say is that in this instance, I don't disapprove. You have shown proper judgment in both the lady and in being circumspect. I knew her father. You and Ms. Lawton are two of a kind. Marry her if it pleases you."

"Well, I'm glad I meet with your approval and have your blessing, Father, but why are you investigating me? I am *not* your chosen heir." David's voice dripped with malice indignation.

"David, don't get saucy with me and drop that derisive tone from your voice. I have every right to know what my sons are doing—including you. I employ the best PR staff in the business, and they are paid well for what they do. They are on top of things, putting out more fires than you will ever know of, always one step ahead of the press, suppressing what I don't want known and releasing what I do."

David marveled in disbelief. "Father, no matter what you do or who you pay, this story cannot be contained. These papers are merely days old. In a matter of days this will explode in Britain. The paparazzi will be all over Tennessee and will cause uproar at the university and within the community where Fitzwilliam lives."

David rose to his feet and stormed out of his father's office, slamming the door in anger—anger at his father for probing into his personal life and anger with what he knew was to come in the following weeks. He rubbed his brow as pressure built in his chest. He needed to see Sandra tonight. He needed sex—sex with no strings attached and no nagging feelings of doubt. He released a hard breath. He also needed to ring Cecilia concerning their pending date.

M.K. Baxley

The cigar abandoned, Mr. Darcy slumped back in his chair and poured himself a stiff drink, speaking out loud to someone only he could see.

"Anne…Anne, what am I going to do? They won't listen to me. I'm only trying to protect them—them and Pemberley. It's for them, Anne. Can they not see that? I love them—they are all I have left… all I have left…" He finished his drink, sitting there staring off into nothing, looking at a woman visible only to him.

As David appeared, Mrs. Foulkes glanced up. "I guess it was that *bad* after all."

"You have no idea," he retorted, storming past her desk towards the lift. Tonight, he would not be going home, and he just might bring Sandra back here to his flat right under his father's nose. He'd be discreet all right, just as his father demanded, but he would take what he wanted, from whomever he wanted, whenever he wanted it, his father be damned!

His first order of business was to ring Sandra, and then he would make a quick call to Cecilia, but right now, Cecilia was the last thing he wanted on his mind. He also needed to call his brother and alert him to what was happening, but that he would take care of tomorrow. Stepping out of the lift, he moved towards the entry of his flat as he glanced at his watch. *…Four thirty in the afternoon. This should give me ample time to take care of my personal business and possibly take a nap.*

Once inside, he eyed the bed in the middle of the room. It looked tempting, but before he could rest, he had business to take care of. Pulling himself together, he staggered over to the bed and plopped down. Taking out his mobile, he quickly located Sandra's number.

"David?"

"Sandra, how have you been, love?"

"I've been fine, but it's been a while since I heard from you. January I believe. Where have you been?"

"I've been busy with business affairs in Asia and Eastern Europe. I just got back into London today." He paused for a second, frowning. He knew he must be very tired as he was having trouble concentrating. "Sandra, love, could you see me tonight? It's been a long time… and I've had a rough day… I really need to see you… *tonight.*" It was the only time he could recall when he appeared to beg, but he really did need her or somebody.

"Sure, David. I'm working until midnight. Do you want to meet me at my flat?"

"No, I'll pick you up. You're coming here tonight—to *my* flat. Where are you working?"

"At the Pink Palace. David, are you sure? That's right under your Father's nose. Do you think it wise?"

"Why not? Besides, I don't care. It will be late, and I'll be discreet" *…just like him.* David sneered, "I'll pick you up at half past midnight. Look for my Alfa Romeo outside. I may have to pull around a few times, but look for me."

"Ooh David, the red Spider 8c! Won't all my friends think I'm cool?"

David rolled his eyes. "No! Don't tell anyone. I don't need the paparazzi following us. If you want to continue seeing me, you'll have to be circumspect. I can't afford to take chances anymore."

"Okay, love. I'll be good, and I'll see you after work. And David…I've missed you, too."

Sliding his phone shut, he fell back on his bed and wearily closed his eyes, pushing his unsettling thoughts deep into the back of his mind. Exhausted from his long flight and all that had happened between himself and his father, he drifted off to sleep.

It was nine o'clock when David finally woke up, reality slowly creeping back into focus. He needed to make his call and then get something to eat before picking up Sandra. Rummaging through his wallet, he located Cecilia's card. He turned it over and looked at her elegant penmanship. He smiled. Her handwriting was beautiful—just like her.

Picking up his mobile, he slid it open and then hesitated. He'd been struggling with his feelings for several weeks now. There had been numerous times he'd picked up his mobile to call but hadn't. The Magnolia Festival was in just over a week. He couldn't wait any longer. He had to call, but he was still struggling with whether or not he would attend. Thinking about what he would say, he reflected on what he was afraid of.

His answer was complex. He was afraid of a feeling he'd never experienced before and afraid that he might possibly be falling in love with her. Cecilia was so different from Sandra. Both were beautiful, but with Sandra, he had no concerns, yet with Cecilia, he had every concern. She was gorgeous, intelligent, and kept him on his guard every minute he was with her. She was the female version of himself—sharp and cunning! He knew he shouldn't keep seeing her. If he did, he wasn't sure he'd be able to pull away.

He sighed. He probably wouldn't even care in the short term, but in the long term? No, he couldn't go. It would be best if he not attend. He'd think of something to say. Teetering on the edge of what that might be, he keyed in her number.

"David, how nice to hear your voice. I thought you might have lost my number."

"No, it isn't that. I've simply been busy. In fact, I'm very busy during the month of April. Cecilia, concerning the event you invited me to. I—"

"David, if you don't want to come, don't worry yourself about it. I was looking forward to seeing you, but I do understand how busy you are. After all, I run a corporation, too, so I *do* understand. It's just that...well, I really *would* like to see you again," she murmured softly.

Sensing the evident disappointment in her voice caused his resolve to falter and his heart to leap. "It's not that I don't *want* to come." That statement was the absolute truth. He wanted to see her.

He hesitated. The silence on the other end was deafening. His desire to see her overrode his resolve. Reasoning that one more weekend together wouldn't hurt, he acquiesced. "I suppose I can rearrange my schedule. You wrote down the first weekend in April. I'll be there. Email me at DDarcy@Pemberley.co.uk with the details, and I'll come." He released the breath he'd been holding, uncertainty creasing his brow, realizing he'd just agreed to do the very thing only a moment ago he'd decided he wouldn't.

"You know you don't have to come if you don't want to. But if you do, I'd be very pleased to see you."

"Then I'm looking forward to it. And..." Again he hesitated, but quickly pushed his doubts aside. "Now that you have my mobile number, feel free to ring me should you ever wish to talk, or if you need me for anything. It's always with me. That is unless I'm asleep, or in a meeting, or—"

"In somebody's bed?"

"Perhaps," he mused. "Lawton, is your mind never very far from the bedroom?" She never failed to catch him off guard with a zinger when he least expected it—as if she understood him. That was a frightening concept. "I'm going to have to remember to expect the unexpected from you."

She laughed. "My mind is in a lot of different places at a lot of different times. You figure it out. And David, with you, my mind is always especially focused. Remember what Queen Elizabeth I said?"

"And what did she say?" He chuckled.

"She said a woman's mind is never very far from... You fill in the rest."

"...From her—oh no you don't, Lawton. I'm not going there."

"Well, David I could say something, but I'll keep my powder dry," she said wryly.

"Ha! You do that. Now if you don't mind, I do have a meeting to attend early tomorrow morning, so I need to go. If I don't hear from you between now and then, I'll assume everything is still as planned. Oh, and I'm not in anybody's bed but my own—yet."

He heard her peal of laughter, and couldn't resist one more flirting tease. "Have a good evening and *don't* misbehave."

She laughed again. "Never, Darcy... never. But if I do, I'll name it after you?"

Closing his mobile, David chuckled to himself. ...*I know why men find her attractive. She has a way of drawing you in, of stirring your very soul. If you're not careful, you'll be caught in her web, Darcy. Sandra's safe—Cecilia's not!*

Chapter Thirty-three

...After all these years it's just like me to fall in love with a woman who is untouchable...

After a long, difficult week, David finally boarded Pemberley Two for South Carolina. He had left a message with his personal assistant informing her where he would be, but since his father had chosen to investigate him, he'd let him find out on his own.

David leaned back in his seat and thought about the two prominent women in his life. Sandra had always been his favorite girlfriend. He liked her a little more than any of the others he had dated, but of late, she held little interest beyond the sexual attraction they shared. And after the last three nights together, he was ready for her to go. When the sex was over, so was his interest. All he wanted to do was to roll over and go to sleep at the best of times, and at the worst, he wanted to get up and leave. Sandra would do for short term gratification, but in the long run, she left him empty and dissatisfied. There was no danger of an emotional attachment there—ever.

Cecilia, however, fascinated him from the boardroom to the bedroom and everywhere in-between. Her sharp mind, her indomitable spirit, and her gorgeous body occupied his thoughts every time his mind was idle and sometimes when it wasn't. She held a lethal attraction on his sensibilities and presented a threat to his emotions. With her, he knew he was in danger of losing his heart.

David sighed and stretched out his long legs as he threw back his head and closed his eyes. He'd be with Cecilia in a little over ten hours. He'd worry about the consequences of time spent with her another day. This weekend he intended to enjoy himself—and her.

David arrived in Charleston at five o'clock in the afternoon. Since he would be with Cecilia all weekend long, he'd decided against renting a car and took a taxi to the Lawton Hotel. He gave the bellhop a generous tip and had his things sent to Cecilia's penthouse suite. Once he was settled, he gave her a call.

"Cecilia, love, I'm here at your penthouse."

"Oh, good. I'm on my way out the door. I'm walking to the hotel. Would you like to meet me at the sidewalk café on Queen Street? I'm not much for a formal dinner tonight. How about you?"

"That sounds fine, but wait there at your office, and I'll walk over. Then we can go to Queen Street from there."

"Sounds good to me. I'll see you when you get here."

David slid his mobile shut and was soon out the door headed in the direction of the Lawton Executive Complex. When he walked through her office door, she rose from behind her desk and approached him, greeting him with a kiss.

"Cecilia, you look lovely as usual," he said, his eyes twinkling with a sheepish grin.

She laughed. "And you, Mr. Darcy, are just as handsome and debonair as always, but let's get out of here before my phone rings again. It's been a busy day." She strolled over to the cabinet and grabbed her purse.

"By all means," he said, standing aside. "After you, madam."

Cecilia extended her hand as she walked by which he gladly took, and the two stepped through the door and moved towards the lift.

M.K. Baxley

Strolling down Queen Street, David couldn't help but take in the smells, colors, and beautiful warmth of the late afternoon spring day in Charleston. Tulips, azaleas, and spring flowers were everywhere in the sidewalk gardens, and the aroma of food cooking filled the air. The weather was warmer than he was used to, so soon his coat had to come off.

"Is this typical weather for Charleston this time of year?" he asked as they approached the café.

"Umm… yes, pretty much. Sometimes it's a little warmer, but this is typical. I did tell you to bring short sleeves, didn't I? The temperature will reach into the eighties tomorrow."

"Yes, you did, but I didn't own any, so I had to buy some. I'm glad I deferred to your judgment instead of my own, or I would be in trouble. Well, here we are. Pick a table." He gestured with his hand as they walked around the back to the outdoor tables.

"This one over here, David, under the pergola. I absolutely love pergolas, especially when they are in full leaf and bloom. We have a wisteria pergola at my home up the Ashley River. We'll go there someday."

David chuckled. "I'd like that, but let's order. I'm starving."

Glancing over the menu, he decided on a hamburger with extra chips while Cecilia ordered a ham and cheese sandwich with none. After their food and iced tea arrived, they dined and talked.

"Cecilia, what is a Magnolia Festival? I'm very unfamiliar with such things."

"Well, it's like a street festival or a Renaissance fair. Are you familiar with either of those?"

"Vaguely. I've heard of them, but I don't think I've ever attended one. Tell me a little more." He took a sip of tea as he studied her.

"Well, there will be vendors of various kinds where people sell things they make— pottery, crafts, flower arrangements, things like that. There are also booths where girls and ladies can have their hair fashioned in styles from the 17th though 19th centuries." She paused for a bite of her sandwich. "There are stages set up with live music. We have everything from classic rock to country to bluegrass. This year Foreigner, Creedence Clearwater Revisited, and a few others will be there. Oh—and the food! Yes, I could not forget the food. There are funnel cakes to die for, and Alligator on a Stick, and hotdogs, grilled shrimp, seafood Carolina style, crawfish, and so much more. You will love it!"

David shook his head. "I'm not so sure about Alligator on a Stick." He frowned. "That doesn't sound good to me at all."

"No, no… it's really very good. You must try it. And then there is the Belle and Beau contest. I won Belle of the Ball when I was sixteen. The Belle and Beau will open the Magnolia Festival Ball Saturday night. It will be held in the ballroom of the Lawton this year. You and I will be attending as host and hostess."

"I'm looking forward to it," he laughed quietly, "but tell me, who was your beau the year you won and what was he like?"

She dropped her gaze to her half-eaten sandwich, murmuring, "He was of no consequence." She glanced up and caught the look in David eyes. "I barely remember him." She glanced over at David's plate and then down at hers. He'd eaten all of his food, but hers was barely touched.

"David, I'm not really hungry. Let's go. I want to go home, take a shower, and put on something more comfortable. I hate stuffy business suits."

"As you wish, milady." David rose from his seat and helped Cecilia out of hers. He laid down the tip, paid the bill, and escorted her back to the Lawton.

Once they were inside her suite, she reached up and gave him a quick kiss. "I'll only be a minute. Make yourself at home. The bar is fully stocked, and I bought some brandy especially for you. Help yourself to whatever you want. I'll be back shortly." She turned and quickly disappeared into her bedroom.

After she left, he leisurely walked over to the cabinet and perused the selections. Deciding upon the brandy, he poured a glass of the amber liquid and strolled back to the sofa to take a seat. The music playing from her sound system in the bedroom mixed with the sound of the shower running gave him a feeling of contentment. As he sat sipping his drink, his mind shifted to the sidewalk café. *...I wonder why she wouldn't tell me who had been her beau. Why would she keep that from me?*

"David, did you find everything you needed?" Cecilia inquired while walking into the room with her hair wrapped in a towel.

"Huh? Yes… yes, I did. Hmm… you look nice!" A smile slowly tugged at the corners of his mouth. She was wearing a pair of soft blue yoga pants cut a little lower than usual and a well-fitted midriff top.

"These old things?" She glanced down and ran her hands over her pants. "I wore them at Harvard. They're out of style now, but they're comfortable." She took her hair out of the towel and stood in front of the fireplace, leaning over to comb it out by the blaze of the gas log. "Why don't you shower, and then we can watch TV or listen to music. It really doesn't matter to me." She grinned, gesturing with her head toward the bedroom. "I cleaned the hair out of the drain for you, and I would appreciate it if you did the same."

He laughed out loud. "Now that's the first time I've been asked to do that, but I'm your guest, so clean the shower I will, but wouldn't your maid take care of it in the morning?"

"Yes, she would, but I'm not a slob for my maids. My father always made me pick up after myself, and I still do. Besides, when I was in college, I didn't have a maid. I shared an apartment with two other people, and we had to fend for ourselves. It's a habit now."

He quickly went in the direction of her room and promptly showered. Afterwards he returned wearing nothing but a pair of pajama pants and a smile. He noticed the room was lit only by jasmine scented candles with soft music, possibly from the 40s, playing in the background. Except for the few flickering candles and the light from the gas log, the room was dark.

As he took a seat next to Cecilia, she asked him, "What would you like to do?"

"Let's just listen to music and watch the fire. We'll sit on that sheepskin rug, and I'll comb your hair dry for you. I used to do that for my sister when I was a boy."

Rising from the sofa, he pulled her up and guided her to the rug where they sat down. He took the comb from her hand and began to comb through her thick mane. Her long strands were almost waist length and stick straight. As he sat there cross-legged, combing her hair with one hand while smoothing the length with the other, a familiar feeling he hadn't felt in years—one of domestic contentment, swept over him, but he quickly snapped out of his thoughts when Cecilia suddenly peeled off her top and tossed it aside as she turned around.

"David, make love to me—here—in front of the fire."

Gazing into her passion filled eyes, he dropped the comb and cupped her face, kissing her slowly as he laid them both down on the rug. He broke the kiss long enough to remove their clothes, and then gathering her into his arms again, he slowly began to traverse her familiar curves with his hand while hers slid over the planes of his back urging him on. He could feel the heat of the fire enflaming him, or was it the slow stroke of her hand across his back and down his hips as she dug her fingers into his muscles. He didn't know. He didn't care.

She was a lover with an easy touch who slowly took him where no one had ever taken him before. By now she had discovered every sensitive spot on his body, and she knew what to do with them.

With Cecilia, he was never in a rush. He wanted to savor every touch…every kiss…every caress. For the first time in his life, he cared for nothing except for her and this moment in time. They made love as they always did—slowly, deliberately, and passionately with great care to please one another.

Afterwards, he lay there with her comfortably resting against his chest, satiated and contented, his hunger over the long months finally filled. He held her close, gently stroking the curves between her waist and hips as she rested her head on his shoulder. This felt so right. How was he to know that a woman like her would come into his life?

Smiling, he tenderly looked down. She was sound asleep wearing a slight smile as her warm breath tickled the hair on his chest. Realizing they couldn't stay here for the night, he gently rolled her onto the rug and rose up to go to the bedroom and turn down the covers. Returning for Cecilia, he scooped her up in his arms and took her to bed, tucking her in before climbing in beside her and pulling her close. He kissed her cheek and drifted off to sleep with her snuggled into the curve of his body, her back against his chest.

The next morning Cecilia awoke more relaxed than she had been in months. She stretched out in her bed like a lazy cat waking up from a long nap. Suddenly she realized she was not alone. Confused at first, she finally remembered that David was spending the weekend with her. She smiled as she looked over to where he lay, still sound asleep. They had made love by the fire. That was all she remembered. She rose up on one elbow, propping her head in her hand as she watched the gentle rise and fall of his chest, his breathing calm and relaxed. He was so beautiful. Could a man be beautiful? She didn't know, but he certainly was, and the way he kissed her. She'd never been kissed like that before. Her heart might not be easily touched, but her body was another matter entirely. His kiss burned like fire, and her body trembled when his lips trailed down the curve of her neck. She had never known a man could kiss the way he kissed or could make her feel the things he'd made her feel when he made love to her. She breathed in deeply the scent of his masculine smell…woody tones of sandalwood, cedar, and spices. …*Umm…if we had the time, I'd wake him just so we could make love all over again.* She sighed.

Shaking her head, she tumbled out of bed, found a nightgown, and then went to the kitchen to prepare breakfast. Since they had a busy day ahead, there was no time to waste lounging in bed.

The toast was buttered, the bacon crisp, and the coffee was brewing. As she stood there scrambling eggs, suddenly a pair of strong arms encircled her waist while a pair of soft lips caressed her neck.

"Good morning, love. Did you sleep well?"

"Umm… very well, and you?" she asked, reaching up for a quick kiss.

"Yes, but the smell of bacon and hot coffee brought me here. I had no idea you could cook?"

"It's a useful thing to know, especially when you're away at school. I learned a lot of things besides what's taught in a book. Have you had your shower yet?"

"Yes, and now I'm ready to eat. When will the eggs be ready?"

"They're ready now," she said, taking them out of the pan and fixing two plates. "Get the orange juice out of the refrigerator and help me take these things to the table.

The glasses are in the cabinet to the right of the sink and the flatware is in the drawer to the left of the dishwasher. Help yourself to the coffee. I'll get mine when I'm finish here."

After they ate and cleaned the kitchen, she showered and dressed, and they left for Magnolia Springs Garden. Crossing the bridge over the small duck pond, they entered the heart of the festival. The outer rim of the park was bordered by thousands of blooming azaleas in colorful hues of white, purple, pink, and red. Vendors were scattered about, and the smell of food being prepared by local restaurant owners permeated the air. Huge magnolia trees in full bloom graced the park with pink and white blossoms, and the live oaks draped in thick blankets of Spanish moss finished the scene as they walked hand in hand into the center of activity.

"David, let's stop here. We must have a funnel cake. Get the large one, and we'll share it."

David smiled and stepped forward to place his order. He couldn't help but catch the flush of peaches in her creamy complexion. She was beautiful in her mint green sundress and white wide-brim floppy hat.

She took the cake from him and broke off a piece to feed him. "What do you think?"

"Umm… it's delicious. I don't think I've ever had this before."

"That's the fun of it—trying new things. Funnel cakes are a Southern specialty." She broke off a few more pieces and gave them to him, but she ate most of it herself.

She pulled him along to almost every food vender there, trying Gator on a Stick, shrimp, and many other selections, but he drew the line when she offered crawfish.

"David, won't you at least try it? You might like them."

"First of all, they are bottom feeders, and I don't eat them. In Britain, they are called crayfish, and they are an endangered species. You have them if you like, but to me, there is just something wrong with eating such a thing."

"Well, we have plenty of them here, so Britain is welcome to some of ours." She looked down at her plate and picked one up. "If you don't want any, then that leaves more for me."

He smiled and shook his head. "Lawton, if you keep eating like this, you're going to get fat, and then I'll have to trade you in for another Carolina Belle who doesn't eat as much."

She licked her fingers and wiped them on her napkin and then playfully smacked his arm. "Trade me in, indeed! I'm not yours to trade. And besides, I don't eat like this every day. In fact, it's probably only once a year that I do."

David chuckled. "Perhaps you're not mine to trade, but you are mine for the weekend, just the same."

He smacked her bum as they walked towards the classic rock stage where Foreigner was playing. Stepping back, he watched as Cecilia swayed to the beat of the music. While he listened to the songs, his mind focused on the woman before him. He realized that with very little effort she could make him reconsider his dedication to bachelorhood. ...*Cecilia Lawton*, he inwardly groaned ...*What are you doing to me?* He sighed as he reached to put his arm around her. Pulling her a little closer, he wondered if she could ever love a man like him.

How long they stood there, he couldn't tell. Foreigner had finished and Creedence was wrapping up when Cecilia grabbed his attention once more.

"David, it's time for the Belle and Beau Contest. Let's go over to the pageant stage and see whose competing this year." She smiled, tugging him along, talking as they went. "They have three categories. The first is for girls and boys ages six to eight. The second is for ages nine to thirteen, and the last is from fourteen to eighteen. Come on, or we'll miss the first category. Look," she pointed toward the platform. "Do you see that little girl on stage with the long blonde ringlets? She looks like I did when I was her age. My mother entered me in the pageant when I was six. I was mortified."

David laughed. "Why? I'm sure you were beautiful. I've seen your baby pictures. Remember?"

"I was three in those pictures, but that's beside the point. I was a tomboy, and my mother was always trying to make a little lady out of me. She fixed my hair like that little girl's, except I had this huge purple bow attached to the back of my head, and she had me dressed in a purple silk dress with a cancan slip. I felt so humiliated. My father even laughed. He called me a grape lollipop. But later he told me that I was his little lollipop. Needless to say I didn't win, but the next time, when I was older, I did."

David laughed out loud. "A grape lollipop. That has interesting possibilities."

"David Darcy, you get your mind out of the gutter. This is a beauty contest, not a porn show."

"How do you know what I'm thinking? Besides, when I'm with you, you're the only thing on my mind."

He hooked her chin and lifted her head to give her an affectionate kiss as she closed her eyes and gently kissed him back. They stayed for all three contests before returning to the Lawton to prepare for the ball. Cecilia complained that the girl who won the third contest wasn't the most beautiful, but David hadn't noticed. To him, Cecilia was the best looking of them all.

When she was dressed, she came out and asked, "David, how do I look?"

His eyes traversed her figure from her hair to her toes and back. "Do you even have to ask? You'll be the prettiest belle of the ball." It was the absolute truth. Her white gown trimmed in black hugged her figure to the waist and then flared to an elegant floor length drape, falling gracefully about her hips. David wore black trousers and a white dinner jacket with a black silk bow tie and matching cummerbund. Together he thought they made a striking couple.

Walking into the ballroom, Cecilia complimented her staff. The arrangements were lovely. The food was beautifully laid out on tables lining the near wall. Tastefully arranged among the food items were pink magnolia blossoms floating in crystal dishes, interspersed with sweetly scented candles. Garlands of pink and white flowers woven together with glossy magnolia leaves hung above the platform where an orchestra sat warming up. As she canvassed the room, well pleased with all that she saw, she didn't notice the man standing in the corner sulking.

"Keeler, go over to Cecilia and tell her I want to see her, immediately."

"What about Amelia? She'll be furious if you approach Cecilia while you're with her. Do you want to start a hell-cat fight? You know how those two are!"

"I don't give a damn. I've about had enough of her naggin'. Fetch Cecilia."

Cameron knew Cecilia had a date for the Magnolia Festival, but he had not thought it would be the Englishman she sometimes dated. It never occurred to him someone would come all the way from England to be with Cecilia. He snarled and breathed noisily. That Brit was beginning to annoy him.

"All right, but I don't think this is smart," Keeler said as he turned to walk in the direction of Cecilia and her date. When he approached them, he said, "Cecilia, I am sorry to disturb you, but I've been sent to escort you to someone who wishes to see you."

"Who?" She raised one brow and cocked her head.

He motioned in Cameron's direction. Cecilia's eyes burned white hot. "Excuse me,

David. I'll only be a minute," she calmly said as she stomped across the floor to where Cameron stood.

"What the hell do you want?!"

"What the hell do you *think* I want? What are you doin' inviting *him* to our society functions?!" He pointed in David's direction.

"He's my friend, and I'll invite whomever I damn well please. Look, Cameron, I've about had enough of you, and if you don't want a scene, you'll leave me alone."

"You never were afraid of makin' an ass out of yourself—"

"And you sure as hell don't mind showing yours now, do you?! I don't have to put up with this, and I'm not going to." She turned on her heel to leave, but he grabbed her arm and spun her around.

"Just don't forget who you'll be spendin' the rest of your life with—and it's *not* with *him*."

"Let go of me!" The warning in her voice was clear as she jerked loose from his grip.

David carefully observed the far end of the room, wondering if he should intervene when he saw Cecilia jerk away. If the man hadn't let go of her at that instant, David was sure there would have been a fight because he wouldn't stand for a man treating Cecilia that way.

When she reached him, he asked, "Who was that? I don't like the way he handled you."

"He's nobody. Just a bad dream, that's all."

"No, Cecilia, he's somebody, and I want to know who he is."

Cecilia was about to speak when the master of ceremonies interrupted to announce that the ball would be opened by this year's Belles and Beaus *and* by all Belles and Beaus from the preceding years, something that had never been done before, but was a special request from a former Beau. David saw the burning anger in Cecilia's eyes as the man from across the room approached to claim his dance. All David could do was stand back and watch.

While David watched the dance floor, a beautiful blonde in a red strapless gown approached.

"Care to dance, Brit?" she scowled.

"Who are you?"

"His date. Come on," she said, dragging David onto the dance floor.

As a slow song played, David found himself in the tight embrace of a woman he'd never seen before while Cecilia looked on clearly distressed. To David's utter shock, the woman reached behind and pulled him against her as she pressed a hot kiss upon his very shocked lips. It was too much. He broke the embrace and stalked across the dance floor, snatching Cecilia out of Cameron's arms.

"Cecilia, come with me. I need to talk to you."

"Who do you think you are, Brit?"

David turned a formidable Darcy gaze upon Cameron and spoke coldly. "I have a name. It's David Darcy, and **Miss Lawton** is *my* date." He looked down at Cecilia, and then gestured with his head at the lady in red. "That over there is *yours*. I suggest you reclaim her—and don't push me, or you'll have a nice crimson stain on your pristine white tux to match your date's dress." David warned as Cameron backed away.

"Come on," David commanded, taking Cecilia by the hand and leading her off the dance floor.

"David, I can't believe he did this to me. He paid the MC to arrange that dance. Please, take me upstairs. I need a minute to get myself together. I'm so humiliated."

M.K. Baxley

"I certainly will **not**. You are hosting this ball with me as your guest, and we're staying. I've never given a damn what people think of me in London society, and I sure as bloody hell don't here!"

Looking up at him, she nodded her head and slowly grinned. "You're right. I don't give a damn, either. You're my kind of man, Darcy." She took him by the hand and escorted him back to the center of the dance floor. Turning, she circled her arms around his neck. "If we're going to cause a scene, let's give them something to really talk about—something that will amaze the whole room," she said, pulling him into a deep kiss while everyone stared, including Cameron. Breaking the kiss, she nuzzled his nose. "Let's dance, Darcy."

David laughed and gathered her in his arms for the waltz while the orchestra played on. "Lawton, you're my kind of woman." He tipped her chin, "and we're too much alike for our own good. Let's dance." Neither cared who stared, nor did they acknowledge the looks people gave them—some approving and some not, but most behaved as if nothing out of the ordinary had happened.

Later that night, after making love, David held her close and asked, "Are you going to tell me what that was all about in the ballroom? I want to know who that bloke is, and why he treated you the way he did."

"I'd rather not. I'm very tired. Let's just go to sleep."

"And I would rather you did. Who is he, Cecilia?" David hooked her chin, bringing her eyes to his.

She released a heavy sigh. "David, I don't want him to come between us." She glanced down for a second and then met his intense gaze. "He's someone I used to date a long time ago. We've begun dating again recently, and I ... I thought maybe we could ... David, there are things about me you can't understand—things about our culture and my responsibilities. All I know at this moment is that, for now, I have you, and I want to cherish this moment we have together. I like you."

"Why don't you tell me, and let me judge for myself as to whether or not I can understand?"

She tenderly stroked his face, gazing into his questioning eyes. "All right then. David, we've always been honest with one another, but this is complicated." She dropped her gaze and gently shook her head, her voice laden with sadness. "Someday, I have to marry. I have no brothers or sisters, no cousins, and no aunts or uncles. I am the last of my family line. Cameron Taylor, that's his name, wants to marry me. He owns Taylor Shipping, and a marriage between us would be a prudent merger. I have to consider that. I don't have the freedom you or others have." She buried her face in the curve of his neck.

David sighed, tightness constricting his chest. "Cecilia, I do understand." He caught her chin once more, raising her eyes to meet his. "I face the same thing with my family—only I have an older brother and a younger sister, as well as many cousins, but my father has expectations, too. Are you going to marry him? I have to know."

"I don't know," she softly said.

He drew in a long steady breath. "Do you love him?"

"No, that much I *do* know." She shook her head. "David, I don't know what love is. I know what I've read and what people say it is, but I've never experienced it. My father never found it. My mother didn't love him, and it killed him." She hesitated. "Please, David, I can't talk about this anymore. I just can't." She began to cry.

He gently wiped the tears from her cheeks. "Don't cry, love. Shh...don't cry. It's all right. I do understand."

He pulled her closer and kissed her brow as she snuggled into his embrace. The thought of her marrying the man he'd met tonight sickened him. He knew that man would break her spirit, leaving her a shell of the person he'd come to know…and love. Did he just think that? He sighed and gently shook his head. There was no denying it anymore. He instinctively knew what this feeling was. He loved her.

David had been thinking about it all day. He could offer her another choice. He wasn't sure he was ready for marriage, but the thought of Cecilia married to someone else tore at his heart. After a long silence, David summoned the courage to speak again. "What if you had another choice?"

"Umm… what do you mean… another choice?" She blinked her tears away.

"I mean, what if you could choose between him and someone else?"

She thought about it a moment. "I'd analyze my choices and choose, just as I do with any decision." She stretched out and snuggled a little closer. "I don't want to think about it anymore. Let's go to sleep, David. I'm exhausted."

He reached over and pecked her lips. "All right, love. Goodnight."

He inwardly groaned. Analyze and choose. That was not the answer he wanted to hear. If she was willing to marry one man without love, would she marry another? Was marriage nothing more than a business contract—a merger of two empires? Would she choose the highest bidder? Did he even have anything to offer her other than himself? Pemberley was Fitzwilliam's inheritance, not his. He came from one of the wealthiest families in the United Kingdom and was featured in tabloids everywhere as one of the most eligible men in Britain, and yet, none of that mattered. He pulled her a little closer.

He felt a strange urge to protect her, and he knew why. It was obvious. He was in love with her, but after growing up in a home where there was unrequited love, he was not willing to enter such an arrangement of his own making. Apparently, her parents had not shared reciprocated love, either.

Again, he faced a calculated risk. The choice before him now was would he risk his heart and try to win her love, or let it go? This he would consider. Marriage was a frightening prospect in the best of times, and there was no way he would even consider it without her love. Until he heard her utter those three words he now longed to hear, he would neither give her his heart nor declare his love—not until he was sure of hers. That much he knew with certainty.

He reached over and gently kissed the top of her head. She wiggled and clung to him a little tighter, softly breathing and sleeping soundly. Looking down at the woman by his side with tenderness, he thought …*after all these years it's just like me to fall in love with a woman who is untouchable.*

She would never know it, but her words had cut him like a knife. This would be the last time he would sleep with her—the last time he would make love to her. He was already in over his head. One more encounter, and she would hold the advantage. As it stood now, he felt he could still walk away if he had to. It would be painful, but he could do it.

He swallowed hard against the lump in his throat. Tomorrow he had to leave for a global marketing convention in Atlanta. He'd think about it then. Gathering her close one last time, he held her until he too, fell asleep.

Chapter Thirty-four

...when a man loves a woman, he gives her the power to bring him down ...

As Fitzwilliam sat in on a meeting with the department head for the History and Classical Studies Department, he felt his mobile vibrate. Unable to take the call, he reached into his pocket and switched it off. Since Elizabeth had not been feeling well, he hoped it was her informing him she had decided to see a doctor that afternoon.

Once he was free of the meeting, he pulled out his phone and chuckled as he checked the message. It was from his wife. *"Fitzwilliam, you win. I have an appointment with Dr. Griffin this afternoon. I need to get some relief from this pollen. If I'm not back before you, go ahead and start dinner. I left a casserole in the refrigerator to put in the oven. Set it for 350°. I'll see you when I get there."*

A wide smile crossed his face as he sent her a text message, telling her he had gotten her message and that dinner would be ready when she came home.

Annoyed, Elizabeth exited the doctor's office. Spending two hours sitting in a lobby listening to crying babies and watching the Jerry Springer show was not her idea of a good way to spend an afternoon. Looking at her watch, she realized Fitzwilliam had been home for over an hour. She shook her head as she headed towards her car. Pulling out her cell phone, she quickly located his number. "Fitzwilliam, I'm sorry I'm running late. It took longer than I had anticipated. It seems that a lot of people are sick. How is dinner coming along?"

"Don't worry about that, darling. Everything is taken care of. How are you? What did the doctor say?"

"I've had a severe reaction to this year's pollen."

"That bad, huh?"

"Yes, Dr. Griffin's nurse says it's one of the worst years on record. And I also have the beginnings of a sinus infection, so he gave me an antibiotic and some prescription grade antihistamines. I'm on my way to Blue Front Drugs right now. Then I'm stopping in at the Cut and Curl to see my aunts and to pick up some shampoo and conditioner. I'll be home shortly."

"Take care, love, and don't worry about a thing."

She smiled as she slid her cell phone shut.

Fitzwilliam had the table set and the food arranged when Elizabeth came through the door. "How were Bette and Florence? Is everything all right? You look a little perturbed," he said, taking her coat and hanging it on the rack.

"They're just as fine as they can be. It's not them," she said, following him into the dining room. "When I walked into the shop, they had Fox News on, complete with the latest happenings in the courtroom today. It seems that Liddy gave some damning testimony and apparently the defense tore her apart," Elizabeth sighed as he helped her into her seat. "They are making her out to be a low class whore who used Jackie Lee for his money. They practically called her a prostitute. Can you believe that? The gall of that man," she said, shaking her head. "And then there was an older woman who didn't realize who I was before she opened her mouth. She spoke her true feelings about my family, or I should say about Aunt Lydia, since she knows my aunt from their school days. She was quite embarrassed when my aunts introduced me. She apologized profusely, but I told her not to worry about it."

"What did this woman say?" Fitzwilliam frowned as he took his seat.

"Well, she went on and on about how high and mighty we've always been, and about how Lydia was such an arrogant snob which, I might add, there is some justification for that position, but she painted us all with the same brush. You see, one of my distant cousins owns a distillery in Fugie, Kentucky which was in operation as a moonshine still when making whiskey was illegal. It was somewhat of a scandal back then. She had to mention that in conjunction with what is going on now. Anyway, she said it was about time we were exposed for what we are with vice always surrounding us. Apparently, from what the old biddy says, my aunt was quite wild in her younger days." Elizabeth shrugged. "I learned she ran away in the 60s and was a drug addict."

"And you knew nothing of this?"

"Well, I had heard things. I knew that she and some man she dated hitchhiked to Woodstock in 1969 and that my grandfather had to track her down. And I knew she was the only one of my father's siblings who flunked out of college. She and my father never got along." Elizabeth unfolded her napkin and began to eat. "She made fun of him because he was always studying or helping my grandfather around the farm while she was busy being popular. She never did any work. Grandmother Bennett doted on her because she was their only daughter. But whenever she was in trouble, it was my father who came to her rescue, and now it's Robert's turn to salvage things."

"I'm sorry." Fitzwilliam shook his head. "Was there anything else said?"

"No, except my aunts told me while I was checking out that we are the talk of the town. Liddy's known all over the county as loose trash. Her name is associated with some of the worse sorts in this community." Elizabeth picked up her fork. "Bette told me that Maybelle Perkins stopped by yesterday and announced that Jane and I will not be asked to join the Ladies Home Gardening Club this spring, and that our applications for the Plateau County Historical Society have been rejected." Elizabeth glanced at Fitzwilliam from across the table. "I told Bette to tell her 'That's all right. Neither Jane nor I were interested in being a part of their snob society anyway,'" she said, taking a bite of salad. "It's awful. Just awful. How am I going to continue to hold my head up in this town? I just don't know."

Fitzwilliam reached over and gave her hand a gentle squeeze. "It'll be all right, darling. You wouldn't have time for their clubs at any rate. If all goes well, you'll be with me in England this summer. Anything else?"

"No, not really, but I need to stay clear of the Cut and Curl for a while. It's the gossip hub of Walnut Grove, and right now I don't want to hear it."

"And how did your aunts react to what's being said?"

"They made light of it, and that's what I intend to do. Ten years from now no one will even care."

"That's my girl. Let's put this out of mind and not let it dampen our evening. After we eat and mark papers, I want to finish reading to you. We've had to put it off for long enough; tonight I want to finish the first volume."

"That sounds good to me. I'd rather not think about the trial, Liddy, or my aunt."

After dinner, the couple settled into bed. Reaching for **The Masters of Pemberley**, Fitzwilliam opened it to the place he had marked, and began to read, picking up with Elizabeth Bennet visiting Pemberley with her aunt and Uncle Gardiner. Divine Providence had intervened. Of all places, that was the last one where Darcy would have expected to find her. At first, he thought it was but a dream, but there she was in the flesh, looking more beautiful than he remembered. This time he was determined to win her love and assumed nothing where she was concerned.

He made every effort to show her that he had attended to her rightful assessments of his flawed character. All was going well, and by her smiles and pleasant conversation, he was almost certain she returned his affection. His intention was to propose once more as he rode out to meet her at the inn in Lambton, only to once again be upstaged by his boyhood *friend*. George Wickham had eloped with Lydia.

"Oh my gosh!" Elizabeth interjected. "It's just like Liddy. Did Lydia not realize what she had done? A man could get away with such a thing, but *not* a young lady— not back then. That girl was impulsive and reckless, and stupid."

"Oh, she was all of that and more."

"Well, read on. I want to know what happened next."

Elizabeth snuggled closer while he continued. He read of George Wickham's seduction of Elizabeth's youngest sister which his ancestor was sure had been meant to thwart him. Regardless, his ancestor felt the impact of such an act keenly, blaming himself for the deed because his pride had prevented him from exposing George for the worthless man that he was. And so, as the woman he loved left for Longbourn, Fitzwilliam Darcy left for London, determined to right his perceived wrong. No matter the cost, he would save his love's family's reputation. After many days of searching, he discovered the couple in the seediest part of town.

As his wife clung to his every word, Fitzwilliam read of George and Lydia's forced marriage, of Lady Catherine de Bourgh's, visit to Longbourn, and finally of his ancestor's second proposal to Elizabeth Bennet which she finally accepted. Then there was the courtship, the wedding, the honeymoon, and Fitzwilliam's reflections on his wedding night, and the subsequent conception of their first child, Alexander Bennet Darcy, born nine months later. Thus, Volume I ended. Fitzwilliam closed the book and dropped it in his lap.

"Fitzwilliam, this story is fascinating. Poor Fitzwilliam. Poor Elizabeth! Their story was gut-wrenching." Elizabeth said. "They did work through their problems at least, and it looks like they went on to live a very happy life."

"Yes, they did, but it wasn't without its trials and tribulations. When we go to England, we'll learn more about those in Volume II. But let's suffice to say the road to happily ever after was rocky. Elizabeth Darcy never was fully accepted by London society and her husband paid a heavy price for his choice in terms of his family. His Aunt Catherine never spoke to him and Lord Matlock only begrudgingly did," Darcy said. "Now, tell me, did you notice any resemblance between your cousin Liddy and my ancestral grandmother's sister Lydia?"

"I couldn't miss it. It was so obvious. I understand from my father and Uncle Robert that Aunt Lydia was quite the attention seeker when she was younger, and you know what I told you earlier. However, she has improved with age, especially since our marriage."

"Yes," Fitzwilliam chuckled, "I think she must have. She's not so bad to be around, but that cousin of yours I could easily do without. She's a little more reserved since her arrest, but before, I don't think I had ever met a more obnoxious, spoilt brat."

He pulled his arm out from under Elizabeth and stretched it to relieve the ache. Throwing his head back on his pillow, he glanced over at his wife who was looking mischievous and attempting to suppress a giggle.

"What are you thinking?"

She shook her head and smirked. "I'm thinking about your namesake. The nerve of that man! He deserved the set down he got. I would have given him a good piece of my mind, too, and probably sooner rather than later. I'm very proud of my cousin. I would have liked her very much. She had the infamous Bennett spunk."

"Bennett spunk, huh? More like cheeky impertinence to rival his pride."

"Whatever it was, she was his equal when it came to a strong will and self-confidence."

"Then I suppose it was a good match, because *that*, love, was the famous Darcy pride on exhibit at its very best. Our family has a strong tendency towards a superiority complex, but a few of us have learnt from history to keep it in check."

"You will get no argument from me in that regard."

He kissed her cheek. "There is nothing wrong with family pride when it's kept under good regulation, or when there is a true superiority of mind, as he told her. I'm a lot like him in many respects." He picked up the book and placed it back on his nightstand before gathering his wife in his arms.

"Well," she laughed quietly, "I don't think you were ever quite as bad as he was, though you do have a good measure of self confidence. I'll give you that."

"Perhaps not as bad, but I do have some of the same problems he had when it comes to mingling with people I'm unfamiliar with, and self confident or not, I did have a problem meeting you that first time. It took all of the courage I had to come to the coffee shop that day."

"I never knew that." She looked at him in wonder. "You always seemed so sure of yourself."

"Well, it's true. I didn't come with Charles to your house after I discovered who you were because I didn't want to appear too obvious. I wanted our meeting to seem accidental, even though I planned it. If you remember, I didn't come back to the coffee shop for two days."

"Yes, I did wonder about that. I was expecting, or rather hoping, you would. Why didn't you?"

He chuckled. "A man never really knows how to read a woman's mind, and you appeared hesitant at first, but with our next encounter, I felt I at least had a chance."

"Fitzwilliam," she gazed at him intently, "I'm truly surprised. I never thought you to be shy."

"Images aren't necessarily reality, but I have a tendency to rise to the occasion when need be, just like my ancestor. That's another thing we have in common. We both sought out what we wanted in life and pursued the women we loved once we had made up our mind, and for him, that took quite a lot of courage. You have to understand, it was unsuitable during Regency times for a gentleman, especially one of his station in life, to marry a woman not in his social sphere, but I'm glad he did. He had to struggle to overcome his own pride and propose a second time. The odds were against them, but they made it."

"He must have really loved her then, because I do understand what it was like from my own family journals. Fitzwilliam risked his heart and his position in society for Elizabeth which proved to be a loss for him in some respects."

"But he also gained. They had a full, rich life together. You will see that even though they were snubbed in London, Derbyshire's society more than made up for it. Mrs. Darcy was greatly loved by all who knew her." He paused for a moment. "Elizabeth, when a man truly loves a woman, he gives her the power to bring him down or build him up."

"Well, it's the same for a woman. When she opens her heart, she gives a man the power to wound her. I guess the one who loves the most is also the most vulnerable.

Now, tell me, which of the four Darcy sons are you descended from?"

"The first son," he beamed, "Alexander Bennet Darcy, and if we are fortunate enough to have a son, it is my desire that he is named Alexander Bennet Darcy as well. It was a tradition in the Darcy family for the first son to have the mother's maiden name. I was one of the few exceptions to that, but if you agree, we will return to the tradition. Sometimes all the children had the mother's maiden name as part of their name. When the time comes, we'll consider it as well, and we'll spell it with one 't' as our ancestors did."

"I think I might be agreeable to that. We've never done it in my family, but it sounds like a nice gesture of respect. Besides, I love old family customs. Family means a great deal to me, and I'm a stickler for holding to family traditions."

Fitzwilliam stroked his wife's arm. "You know, Elizabeth, with all of our exploring of our family histories, I've thought a lot about the inscription on John Bennet's headstone. Charles and I both are descended through Edward Bennet and you and Jane through John. I believe the hand of Providence reached out and brought us to this place to fulfill a destiny. When I came here, I had no idea I would find a wife—and not just a wife, but a lost branch of my family that I didn't even know existed. Together all four of us fulfilled an ancestor's promise. Our marriages reunite the house."

Elizabeth furrowed her brow. "I don't know. I still don't believe in the supernatural...myths or superstitions, but I will admit that in the abstract sense, you are correct. However, I don't think it was us or Jane and Charles that John had in mind. I imagine he was thinking about the family in his own time. But whatever the method, in a roundabout way, our marriages *do* complete John's promise to his brother, no matter how coincidental, don't they?"

"Yes," Fitzwilliam laughed, "they do at that. In fact, they do more than just that— they complete the promise on both continents. Someday I must return to England, but Charles has no such obligations, and I do believe he will be staying here. As you see, my love, John and Edward have the best of both outcomes. Their family is united both here and in England. And Liz, I'm not so sure about the paranormal elements of it. I think they do know. Call it a feeling, but I believe they are aware of who we are."

"Then, if that be the case, I'm sure they both must be happy wherever they are, but Jane's notion of white doves is out of the question. That I don't buy, and I won't even listen to it. We are the makers of our own destiny, not doves and spirits. You and Charles are here because Dr. Dickens made you an offer and you accepted it. There is no other explanation but that. No spirit had anything to do with it."

"Well, as to the doves, I might agree with you. I'm still unsure. And as for John and Edward, I don't know if they're happy, but I'm delighted. Charles and I have discussed it, and when this term is over, we are going to have a stone marker made for the cemetery, commemorating the date the promise was fulfilled—our wedding date. What do you think?"

"Whatever you want to do, darling. Now let's go to sleep. Tomorrow is going to be a busy day. We're going to Longbourn to help my uncle with the spring calves."

"All right, love."

He scooped her into his arms and after making love, they drifted off, content in one another's embrace.

Chapter Thirty-five

...I love you, Liz. I hope you know that...

Elizabeth called shortly after Fitzwilliam's last class had let out, telling him they needed a loaf of bread and a gallon of orange juice. After Elizabeth's call, he dropped his Latin text off at his office and picked up a stack of essays from his Classical Philosophy class he needed to mark. Placing them in his briefcase, he left for the day. As he walked past the student lounge in Morton Hall, he glanced in. The television was on and various staff members and students were gathered around watching TRU TV. Fitzwilliam shook his head and walked on by. Everywhere he went the blasted television was on with the town members glued to the set. It was the biggest thing since the OJ trial, and it was the most significant thing to have ever happened in this sleepy little town. If Fitzwilliam had heard it once, he'd heard it a thousand times: Walnut Grove was finally on the map. Even the Piggly Wiggly had a set tuned to the trial. Was there no escaping it? Apparently not.

As he drove home from the market, his mobile rang. He reached over and picked it up. It was David.

"David, I wasn't expecting to hear from you so soon, is there a problem?"

"Yes, there's a problem. Are you watching the news?"

Fitzwilliam released an exasperated breath. "How can I escape it? It's everywhere I go."

"It's the same here. I'm in Atlanta for a marketing convention, and no matter where I go the sets are tuned in to that blasted trial. It seems all of America is watching this. Everyone is talking about it—it and that woman. She just had to wear a red dress to court. They're calling her the lady in red, and I'm afraid the conversation is not flattering. Fitzwilliam, this is worse than I would have imagined. I don't care how her defense attorney tries to spin it. People don't see her as a victim at all."

"Well, it's even worse here." Fitzwilliam laughed sarcastically. "Every dirty little secret about Liddy and the family is being brought to light. The Bennett family seems to be the talk of the town at the moment. The local television stations from Knoxville, Chattanooga, and Nashville are here, interviewing town folks and prying and digging, trying to catch the next bit of breaking news. The whole town is talking about it from the clerk at the drugstore to the men at Murphy's Pool Hall. Even the faculty members are discussing it. I can't tell you how many times the room hushes when I walk in for a meeting."

"Well, be forewarned. It's only a matter of time before this story breaks in London. I mean, the *real* story—that you are not on assignment for Brit Am, but that you are in Tennessee and involved. As I told you last week, your name has popped up in a few of the American papers. I'm doing as much damage control as I can, and so is Father. I'll be in London the day after tomorrow. I'll let you know something later."

"Thanks, David...and how is Father? Is he all right?"

"As far as I can tell he is, but as I told you last time we talked, he's furious. We've been at loggerheads ever since his interview with me last week."

"Yes, I know, and I appreciate all you're doing. Well, I just pulled up to the house. I'll talk with you later."

"Take care, Brother…and I do mean take care. These are perilous times."

Fitzwilliam slid his mobile shut and grabbed his briefcase and the bag of groceries. Walking up the back steps to the kitchen door, he could hear the television set. He entered the kitchen and dropped his briefcase on the counter, giving Elizabeth a quick kiss as he passed by.

Retrieving the orange juice from the bag, he walked over to the refrigerator and placed it on the shelf, grabbing a beer and twisting the top before he closed the door. As he took a long slow drink, his eyes caught the image on the set. CNN was broadcasting the latest developments.

"Miss Lydia Fanning collapsed in the court room today under the intense cross examination from Nunley's defense attorney, Lawrence Braswell. It appears that Mr. Braswell's attempt to connect Miss Fanning to the murder of Michael Spears, the Fish and Wildlife agent Jackie Lee Nunley is accused of murdering, may have backfired. Miss Fanning became emotionally distraught and stood up, screaming just before she fainted. With the tactics displayed today, many around the courthouse are saying that public sympathy will surely begin to shift in favor of Miss Fanning who is eight months pregnant.

This is Tom Weatherly reporting from the Federal Courthouse in Nashville, Tennessee. And now back to you, Jeff. What are they saying on the streets of Nashville?"

"Well, Tom, you are right. With the defense calling Miss Fanning a woman of loose moral character from a family with a long history of vice, Braswell is perceived as…"

Fitzwilliam walked over and clicked off the set. Casting a sharp glance at his wife, he asked, "Is it necessary to bring this claptrap into our house?"

Elizabeth turned from the stove. "Fitzwilliam, is that anyway to greet your wife?" She paused for a moment. "I have it on because Jane, Bette, and Lori have all called in the last fifteen minutes, telling me to turn on the TV. My family is clearly worried about Liddy. Apparently she's in the hospital having a nervous breakdown."

"I don't care. I don't want this on in my house. It's bad enough that I have to see it everywhere I go, but to have it in my own home? I won't have it, Elizabeth."

Elizabeth set aside the spoon she was using to stir the Chinese vegetables and walked over to her husband. Putting her arms around his waist, she gave him a hug. "Believe me, I do understand. This is wearing thin on all of us." She sighed. "It's your father, isn't it? You're worried about how he's taking this."

He set the beer down and pulled her tightly against his chest, tucking her head in the curve of his neck. "Yes. Since that call from David last week, I have worried about him. He's not well. I sense it, and he will not speak to me. I called him this morning before my first class, and he wouldn't even take the call. Mrs. Foulkes told me he was busy, but I knew he wasn't. I could hear it in her voice. Betty never was a good liar. But she did tell me that my dad does not look well and that he's drinking far too much."

Darcy pulled back and looked Elizabeth directly in the eye. "If something should happen to him, I would feel responsible."

Elizabeth bristled and pushed away. "Feel responsible? Why—because you married me?"

"No, Liz, it's not that, and you know it. I love you, and about that I have no regrets. What I would feel responsible for is that he and I could never see eye to eye on anything. I want what any son would want. I want my father to love me for me. I want him to accept me for who I am." He turned away and ran his hands through his hair.

Elizabeth picked up her spoon and began to stir the vegetables again. "It's almost ready. If you will set the table, I'll have this served in five minutes. And no, Fitzwilliam, I do not completely understand. It is I who has come between you and your father, but you are the one who made the choice. I didn't force you. And it is me and my family who have to suffer the disgrace brought upon us by Liddy. I know people are talking. Let them. The old busy bodies! As long as they are talking about us, they're giving someone else a rest. That's what Aunt Barshaba used to say, and I think it's true. Aunt Ida used to say that those who know us know that we are good people, and all will be forgotten in time."

As he set the plates and flatware on the table, he looked up and said, "Darling, let's not talk about this any longer. I'm sorry for snapping at you. I didn't mean to. It's just that everywhere we go, it's in our faces, and yes, I know it will pass. I'm the one who's been telling you that, remember?"

"Yes, I remember. Now get the iced tea, and let's eat. I have fifty papers to grade, and you have those essays. Tomorrow we go to the farm—away from all this madness. Uncle Henry wants you to help him band the pigs, and I'm going to help Lori with the garden."

"All right, Liz, let's eat," he said as he took the pitcher of tea from the counter.

"I'm going off the pill next month," she said as she followed him into the dining room, "so let's forget about this and enjoy ourselves with more pleasant diversions like practicing for that baby you want—after we've finished our paper work, of course."

"I agree," he said with a warm smile as he helped her into her chair before taking his own.

One Week Later

Sunday morning at approximately three a.m. CST, the phone rang.

"Fitzwilliam."

"David, do you know what time it is here?"

"It can't be helped. Father has had a serious heart attack. The doctors don't think he will live. You need to get here right away. I've made reservations for you to fly British Airways out of Atlanta at ten a.m. EST. You'll have to hurry. According to my calculations, it's a four hour drive to Atlanta from where you are," David paused for a moment. "Fitzwilliam, there's one other thing I have to tell you. There's a problem with Pemberley as well."

Fitzwilliam sat up straight. "What is it, David?"

David exhaled into the phone. "There is an attempt by some on the board of directors to take control away from the Darcy family, or I should say away from you and me. Three, maybe more, board members have begun buying stock to get the controlling shares. They are moving to secure a coalition against us. We have to move quickly to get that stock before they do. I can't do this alone. You are now the acting CEO and Chairman of the Board. Fitzwilliam, you and I are now in charge."

"I'm on my way. I'll ring Bingley and have him and Jane cover for me at the university. Elizabeth will ring the Maths Department Head—"

"*No*, don't bring Elizabeth. If she comes, it will only make matters worse. It seems that some on the board are dissatisfied with us over our willful disobedience to Father's wishes, or at least, that's what they're saying."

"David, what are you talking about? She's my wife!"

"You know what I am talking about. They're dissatisfied with you on several fronts—your marriage aside. There have been several news leaks from within Pemberley about you and me—our loyalty to the family, your disinterest in the company, and my immoral lifestyle. They think you should have been here. Apparently, they think that Father has been distracted by us and has not managed things as they think he should have. They don't like it that you married against Father's wishes. They say it shows a flagrant display of irresponsibility and disrespect. They also think you should have remained among our social class, but you knew how they felt before you married. Some within the family and company say we have shown a lack of concern for the family and the company. And there is one other thing."

"What more can there possibly be?"

"The story broke yesterday in London concerning your connections with that drug trial in Tennessee, but that's not all. It was quite a shock for London's society to find out that you were not working for Pemberley and that you had married. No one outside the family and Father's close circle knew of your marriage since he had kept it a close secret. As you can guess, the tabloid press is eating you and your wife alive. She has become your Yoko Ono."

"I see." He released a heavy sigh and closed his eyes, shaking his head. He could only imagine the chaos breaking in London. Releasing another deep breath, he continued. "I'll be there as soon as I can. I'll have to explain it all to Elizabeth."

He hung up the phone and fell back on the bed, clearly upset.

"Fitzwilliam, what's wrong?"

"My dad has had a heart attack. I have to go to London right away. Ring Charles. I'll need him to drive me to the airport, and I'll need you to ring Dr. Dickens at a reasonable hour," he said, getting out of bed.

"What about me? Am I not coming?"

"Not this time, sweetheart. There are some very big problems. It seems that some on the board of directors are using this as a time to attempt a corporate takeover via a proxy fight."

"Proxy fight? What's that?"

"It's a way of gaining enough leverage to effectively reorganize the board of directors in order to remove certain members—namely David and me." He looked pointedly at her while pulling on a pair of jeans. "Elizabeth, they are using you, our marriage, and Liddy's scandal as a weapon against me. My business integrity is being called into question. I don't have time to explain it all right now. Trust me. I need you to stay here until I send for you." He walked over to the closet, retrieved his suitcase and began throwing his things into it.

She fought back tears. "All right… I will do as you say. I'll take care of business at the university. Jane can cover your Classical Philosophy class. I might be able to cover the Latin I class since I have helped you with it, and I know where you are and what you are doing. Could Charles cover the Latin II and Greek?"

"Yes, he can. If not, I know Jane can help him. She's almost as well versed as I am. I know she can handle it. Besides, Dickens has others who can help. We have that grad assistant, Shockley. I think he can handle it." Jerking another shirt from the closet rack, he glanced over at Elizabeth and emphatically said, "They'll manage. My class schedule is the least of my worries." He stuffed the last of his items into the large case before grabbing **The Masters of Pemberley** and gently placing it on top of his clothes.

Zipping the case shut, he turned to Elizabeth. "I'll ring you as soon as I arrive. This means we'll have to postpone our honeymoon. We'll also have to give up our teaching positions. Elizabeth, I'm so sorry. I know what teaching means to you, but once we are settled, you can secure a position in England."

Suppressing a sob, she replied, "It's all right. I am your wife and a Darcy. I will do whatever is needed for the preservation of our family."

"Elizabeth, I'm so relieved you understand. You don't know what that means to me. I love you so very much. Even without Pemberley, we are still quite wealthy. It's not the money. This empire began with Fitzwilliam Alexander Darcy and has been passed down through the line to me, Fitzwilliam Alexander Darcy II. I can't fail my family or my heritage. I take my responsibility very seriously in spite of what some may think. I will do whatever is necessary. David and I must carry the day. Make plans to close up the house and pack for the move to London. I will send for you when this is over. Charles will help you." He stopped what he was doing and took her in his arms. "I love you, Liz. I hope you know that. I will call."

"Fitzwilliam, I may not be able to go to London with you, but I'm driving you to the airport—not Charles. Since it may be some time before I see you again, I'm spending these last few hours with you." She was at the point of tears.

Compassion overcame him. "You're right. I wasn't thinking. I'm afraid I've shifted gears into business mode. I have so much on my mind."

With his things loaded in the car, they set out for Atlanta. He brought her to the gate leading to his plane. Elizabeth looked up at him with tears in her eyes as he cupped her face for one final kiss, and then he was gone. Elizabeth had a foreboding feeling that this was much more serious than the little information Fitzwilliam had revealed to her.

Chapter Thirty-six

...Death? The last sleep? No, death is the final awakening...
-Sir Walter Scott

The tedious flight to London gave Fitzwilliam time to think. He oscillated between worrying about his father and trying to fully understand the situation in London from the limited information David had given him. One thing he knew for certain. When he did take up his post as CEO, he was going to make a clean sweep of the board and dismiss many of the corporate executives.

Deep in thought, he tried to prioritize his concerns. His primary interest was his father, then he had to protect his wife, and finally he had to secure Pemberley. In a little over four weeks, the semester would end, and although he longed to have Elizabeth by his side when he faced the trials that were certain to come, he knew for her own welfare she should remain where she was. There he was certain she would be safe from the firestorm of publicity the tabloid press would create. As for Pemberley, he would evaluate the situation once he was sure of his father's state of health. Wiping his brow, exhausted from worry, he pushed his thoughts aside and leaned back in his seat, drifting off into uneasy sleep.

The plane touched down at Heathrow in the early morning hours. His brother and cousin, Richard Winthrop, were there to receive him. David looked anxious and utterly exhausted as he came forward and hugged his brother.

"Fitzwilliam, thank God you are here."

"David, when did it happen? Where is Father? Can we see him?" he asked as he quickly moved to claim his luggage.

"Hold on! Let's get your bags, and then I'll explain everything I know."

After retrieving his luggage, they raced through the airport, loaded the car, and once on their way, David explained, "Wallace found him at about six a.m. yesterday. When he noticed Father was late in calling for him, he went to find out why, and that's when he found him still in bed unconscious. Wallace called me right away. I rang 999, and they rushed him to the CCU at St. Thomas'. He's alive, but the doctors say his heart is severely damaged. Apparently this wasn't his first heart attack. He was keeping it from us. I suppose that's why he kept pressing us to marry and produce an heir. Whenever he regains consciousness, he asks for you."

"Have you seen him yet?"

"No, he wants to see us together. He's spent what little time he's been awake with Georgiana, Harvey, and Samantha."

"Samantha? She came?"

"Yes, she did. Father is her brother, after all. Hopefully, they've made up."

"I do hope so." Fitzwilliam sighed, "Now, give me the up-shot on Pemberley."

"Well, three of the board members are leading the drive to have us removed from the board. They are buying up shares to gain the majority holding needed to call an EGM. They're intent on drumming up enough proxy votes to pass a resolution to reorganize the board. Richard, tell him what you know."

"An EGM... extraordinary general meeting ...I see," Fitzwilliam breathed out.

"Fitz, as David said, it involves three members, Harry Dashwood, Jonathan Stanley, and Jason Wesley. Then there are your Darcy cousins, Edward, Henry, Edmund, and Charles Wilson and Sean Ashton as well as several other Darcys who aren't brave enough to come out into the open but who appear to support the opposition. It would seem that several of them don't approve of your American wife, especially now that they've heard the news about the drug trial in Tennessee—or that's what they're saying. Then there's the issue of David's indiscretions." Richard glanced sharply in David's direction. "You didn't expect them to ever forgive you for dating those strippers and porn stars, did you? I'm afraid Sandra has been quite the topic of conversation. And your father has made it abundantly clear how he feels about it, too."

"Well, let them take their best shot. When the time comes, we'll meet them with an equal force, but for right now, Father comes first. I'll deal with the rest later," Fitzwilliam added while rapidly trying to process strategies to overcome these pressing issues.

The brothers arrived at the hospital and immediately made their way to the CCU. Georgiana, together with Harvey and his sons, William and Benson, and Samantha Dashwood were already present.

"Are you Mr. Fitzwilliam Darcy?" asked the CCU ward sister.

"Yes. Yes, I am."

"Your father is asking for you. Please come with me. He's right this way."

When Fitzwilliam entered, he was startled by what he saw. Before him lay a shell of a man, not the giant he had known as his father. This man was fragile, with the look of impending death upon him. Fear gripped Fitzwilliam.

"Fitzwilliam, you have come," George Darcy whispered weakly.

Fitzwilliam walked over to George's bedside and gently took his father's hand.

"Yes, Dad, I've come. I'm here. You're going to be all right. All will be well," he said, swallowing against the lump forming in his throat.

"No, Fitzwilliam all will not be well. I'm dying, and I know it." The old man paused for breath. "You and I have rarely seen eye to eye of late, but I do want you to know that I love you... I always have... you and David and Georgiana," he said, glancing towards his younger son and daughter.

Fitzwilliam nodded, pressing his father's hand as he looked back in time and saw the man he once was—the man who used to pick him up when he was a little boy—the man who loved him when he was a child.

"My doctor tells me that ninety-five percent of my heart has been destroyed. I don't have long to live, but there are a few things I needed to put right. Seeing the parish vicar was the first, telling you... your brother... and sister that I love you is second, and Pemberley the third." He paused. "I have a living will, giving you control over everything. See Metcalf tomorrow. As my solicitor, he'll know what to do." George paused again for breath. "I know what Dashwood is up to, and I hope to ensnare him. Metcalf and Blakely have been fully briefed about everything. They will fill you in, if I cannot."

Mr. Darcy paused to rest. When he was able, he continued. "You... and David... must stop Dashwood. You must!" Glancing down, George stopped and slipped the Darcy ring from his finger. He took Fitzwilliam's hand and pressed it into his palm, folding it closed. "I am handing the torch over to you. You are now keeper of the keep. You must, Fitzwilliam... become the man you were born to be." Then George placed his hand over his son's, sealing the transfer of power as he drew in another ragged breath.

He motioned for David to come closer. "David… I must see David."

"I'm here, Father." David stepped forward and took his father's other hand.

"You too, must become the man who you were meant to be… a man of principle… a man of honor. You have the strength of character that makes you a Darcy, but you lack discipline. That's my fault, and I'm sorry that… that I neglected you. If I could, I'd make up for it, but if I don't live long enough to tell you everything you need to know, you'll find the answers in my journals. Mrs. Foulkes is having them printed and bound. I've written about my life with your mother." Almost physically spent, he painfully gasped. "Harvey has agreed to answer all your questions. We've made our peace." George was now wheezing, but he grasped his sons' hands as firmly as he could and made another valiant effort to speak." Promise me, David… Promise me, Fitzwilliam," he said, looking from one brother to the other, "Promise me that you will rise to the occasion and *stop* your uncle. Do whatever it takes…whatever you have to, but stop him! Promise me!"

Both nodded in affirmation as George tried once more to speak. His final words were a frail whisper. "And remember, my children, I love you…" he said, his voice trailing off.

"Dad, please don't talk. We'll do whatever it takes. Everything will be fine. David, Georgiana, and I are all here." Fitzwilliam could see his father fading. "We won't let you down. We love you, Dad… Dad. Know that." Fitzwilliam squeezed his father's hand as tears pooled in his eyes.

He glanced over at David and saw the tears glistening in his brother's eyes, too, though he had the same cold, stoic expression that he had always worn when standing before their father.

David's appearance unnerved him, but seeing Georgiana standing at the foot of the bed softly crying, was more than he could take as they all watched George fade into unconsciousness.

"Dad. Dad!" Tears spilled from Fitzwilliam's eyes as he shook his head and began to weep.

A firm, but gentle, hand fell on his shoulder. "Mr. Darcy, I'm Dr. Matthews, your father's cardiologist. He's slipped into unconsciousness. He does that off and on. Soon he will not be able to come out of it."

Fitzwilliam turned to meet the doctor. "How bad is he? How long does he have to live?" Fitzwilliam choked.

"A day, maybe a few more… not much longer. His heart is tired. Your father has been under a great deal of stress for the many years I've known him. I am not only your father's doctor, but I am his friend as well. He'll need to rest for the remainder of the day. I suggest that you not press him any longer should he awaken today."

"What about tomorrow? Can we see him tomorrow?"

"Probably. As I said, he slips in and out. He's very tired."

"He wants to speak to my sister. I'm sure his brother would like to spend some time with him, too."

"He spent the better part of yesterday with Harvey and Samantha, and he's already had time with Georgiana. Come back tomorrow, and we'll see. He needs to rest now."

Dr. Matthews walked the siblings to the door. As they were about to leave, he said, "Fitzwilliam, there is one other thing you may like to know. I've never known your father to be a religious man, but he did ask to speak with his vicar. They spent about thirty minutes together, and I saw them praying. I believe he's has made his peace with God, and now he wants to do likewise with his family. As his friend, I can assure you that he does love you, and he's been very concerned about your future."

"Thank you, Dr. Matthews," Fitzwilliam said, shaking his hand.

As Fitzwilliam stepped out of the room, all those present rose to greet him, asking questions.

Harvey came forward and put his arm around Fitzwilliam and David's shoulders. "I'm sorry. If there's anything we can do, please feel free to call us. Samantha and I have put aside our differences and spent time with George. We've made amends," he said, looking towards his sister.

Samantha Dashwood reached out and took Fitzwilliam and David by the hand. "I want you to know that I don't approve of my husband's actions, but I am powerless to do anything to stop him. George knows that, and he's forgiven me. I hope you'll forgive me, too. Harry's my husband. I may not approve of what he does, but I do have to stand by him, especially when everything comes crashing down on him, as I'm sure it will."

"There's nothing to forgive," Fitzwilliam said stoically as he withdrew his hand and walked away, while David lingered on.

"Aunt Samantha, who can tell what the outcome of all of this will be, but I certainly don't blame you." He released her hand and joined his brother who had pulled a sobbing Georgiana into his arms. Together, the three Darcys held one another and wept.

George Darcy drifted in and out of a restless sleep, dreaming of images he could only vaguely recall. Anne was standing before him illuminated in white, wearing a gold crown encrusted with brightly colored jewels. Her golden hair brushed the floor as she glided across the room to his bed. He opened his weary eyes as she stood before him. It was not a dream.

"Anne, you are here?" he whispered.

"Yes, George I'm here. I've been allowed to come for you. I've been with you for several months now, watching and waiting."

"When… where…where have you been? I haven't seen you?"

"Oh, but you have. Remember? I was there when you saw David in the executive office at Pemberley, but only now am I allowed to speak to you."

"Yes, I remember. You were standing in the corner by the book case, but I thought it was a vision."

"It was." She smiled. "I was also there at Christmas, and then when Harvey came."

"Why are you here now, speaking to me? Why speak only now and not then?"

"Your time was not yet full, so I wasn't allowed to speak. As to why I'm here?" She laughed softly. "I was sent to guide you because we have issues that are unresolved. I forgave you long ago, and I want you to know that I love you," she gently said, her voice like a sweet melody of classical music. "What Harvey said is true. I didn't love you when I married you, but I did love you later, and I love you now."

"Am I dead? Is this the last sleep?"

"Death? The last sleep? No," she laughed merrily, "*death* is the final awakening. Come George."

She stretched out her ivory hand. George reached to take it. When their hands touched, his body fell back against the bed while his spirit clasped the proffered hand, and he stepped out of his body. Clothed in white with a golden crown of his own, he stood in front of his wife.

"They'll be here soon," she said, caressing a red rose she held in her hand.

"Where did the rose come from? It looks like one you used to tend in the garden at Pemberley."

She laughed again. "It's from the Celestial Garden in the City on the Hill where we shall soon be going. The Master said I could bring it. It's 'A Rose for Fitzwilliam.' It will give him comfort."

"Comfort, yes, our son will need that in the days to come," George said.

"But he will rise to the occasion, just as you've taught him, my love. He will overcome."

"And what about his wife… what of her?"

"Their world hangs in the balance by a thread, controlled by the hands of Providence. Many trials await them."

The couple grew silent as a nurse, followed by the doctor on call and a team of medical personnel, came rushing through the door in response to the alarm sounding at the nurses' desk. The lifeline was flat. While the doctor and the medical assistants checked the monitors, the ward sister gazed on the inert form lying on the bed. Mr. Darcy seemed to be staring blankly with a serene smile upon his face. "Doctor, look," she commented. "He looks so peaceful. He must have died in his sleep."

"Umm… Yes, I suppose he did," said the doctor as he closed George's eyes. "You'll have to ring the family."

"I'll take care of it." She paused to glance around. "Doctor, do you think it's unusually bright in this room?"

The doctor surveyed the room with a frown. "Nothing seems out of the ordinary to me. It's late, and you've probably not had enough coffee."

"Hmm… I just had a strange feeling we weren't alone," she shrugged, "but I suppose you're right. I'll go and make that call."

Fitzwilliam tossed and turned in a restless sleep, dreaming of his mother and father in the rose garden at Pemberley, when he heard his mobile ring. Thinking it must be the hospital, he reached over to the night table, fumbling for his phone.

"Fitzwilliam Darcy."

"Mr. Darcy, this is Sister Williamson at St. Thomas'. I'm sorry to inform you, but your father died peacefully in his sleep around three o'clock this morning."

Fitzwilliam let out a hard breath, "Thank you. We'll be there as soon as we can."

Sliding his phone shut, he scrambled out of bed and dressed quickly. A few doors down, he woke David first, rapping on the door until his brother answered.

"Fitzwilliam? It's Father, isn't it?"

"Yes, he's gone. Get dressed. We're going to the hospital. I'm going to break the news to Georgiana."

The three Darcys entered the CCU room an hour later to find their father with a look of serene peacefulness upon his face, just as the nurse had found him. Georgiana ran across the room, flinging herself at him, crying as, unbeknown to her, two beings illuminated in white watched from the corner of the room.

"Anne, I must go to her."

"No, George, you can't.

"Why not?"

"The time for that has passed. She cannot see or hear you. Only when a soul's time is near can they see into our world, and hers is not for many years to come."

"Have I really gone through life with my eyes shut so often that I never saw how much they needed me? Can grace not be imparted to an old man one last time?"

The melodious tinkle of Anne's voice filled the air. "You're no longer an old man, George. You're young again and just as handsome as you ever were."

He looked down at his hands and noticed that they were no longer wrinkled. Frowning, he asked, "Cannot I even touch them—embrace them just one last time?"

"No, only in life could you do that. You shall not see them again until it is their time. But your time has come. The tunnel has opened and we must go." She took him by the hand as they stepped into the gateway through the bright light and into eternity. Just before the light closed behind them, Anne dropped the rose.

Fitzwilliam swallowed hard as tears stung his eyes. He gently put his hand on his sister's shoulder. "Georgiana, we need to go. There are arrangements to be made. Come." Prying her away from the body, he pulled her and David into his embrace, and wept.

As they moved in the direction of the door, Fitzwilliam noticed a solitary red rose lying on the floor. Puzzled, he reached down and picked it up. Its sweet smell reminded him of his boyhood and his mother's rose garden. Remembering his dream, he swept the room with a furrowed brow. ...*Mother?* He tilted his head. No, it couldn't have been. It must be a coincidence. The nurse must have dropped it. He sighed wearily. ...*It evokes peace, and I need that. I'll keep it. I must ring home and tell Elizabeth what's happened.*

He clutched the rose as he and Georgiana left the room, followed by David.

Back in his father's study, he poured himself a whiskey, something he rarely drank, but today, it was what he needed to soothe the heavy ache in his chest. Glancing down at the ring on his finger, he shook his head and swallowed back his pain.

...*How am I going to cope without him? Pemberley...I can't go on alone. It's too difficult for me. How am I going to manage this? I know I've got David and Georgiana, but this is a heavy burden to bear. Elizabeth! I need Elizabeth.* He picked up the phone and keyed her number.

"Fitzwilliam?"

"Elizabeth, it's good to hear your voice," he said, repressing a sob.

"He's dead, isn't he?"

"Yes... I didn't have a chance to say my final goodbyes. He died during the night in his sleep, but at least I got to see him beforehand. Oh God, Elizabeth, it's so hard. He's left me with a gargantuan task, and he's not here to help me. How am I going to cope without him?"

"It's hard. I know. I've been there, remember. Fitzwilliam, there is a time and a season for everything. A time to live and a time to die." She paused. "Go ahead and cry. It's okay for a man to cry."

He broke down, sobbing into the phone. "Elizabeth, he had the most tranquil look on his face that I've ever seen. He made his peace with everyone before he died. For that, I'm thankful." Fitzwilliam drew in a sharp breath, steadying himself. "We've made arrangements for him to be taken to Pemberley Estate and to be buried in the family cemetery in three days. I meant to talk to him about us, but I didn't get the opportunity. I so regret that."

He hesitated, knowing it was not in her best interests, but unable to resist, he asked anyway. "Elizabeth, I need you. I wish you'd come. Elizabeth, do you think you could? Maybe for a few days?"

He could hear the remorse in her voice. "No, Fitzwilliam, I can't. It's two weeks before finals, and there's no one to sub for me. Both my grad assistants are sick. It seems everyone is sick, and I've been under the weather, too. There never is a good time for a funeral, is there, and this is certainly not."

"No, there never is," he whispered. "But I do understand. After all, I'm a lecturer, too."

"Fitzwilliam, I hate to cut you off, especially now, but my morning class is about to begin. I'm standing in the doorway now. Call me tonight."

"Yes, I will. I love you," he sighed. ...*I wish she could have been late for class... just this one time.*

"I love you, too."

After hanging up the phone, he sank back into the oversized chair and downed the contents of his glass. The task that lay before him was overwhelming, but hearing Elizabeth's voice had comforted him and had also spurred him on to finish the job he was certain had taken his father's life. He didn't know how he was going to do it, but he would not only finish the job, he would also get even. He fixed his gaze upon the ring and made a solemn vow. He would get them all—every last one of them—uncle, cousin, it made no difference. They *would* pay!

Later that night, numbed by the events of the last few days, David sat alone in his room nursing a glass of brandy. His father's last words reverberated in his mind. ...*What's in those journals, and what does Harvey have to do with it? Do I want to know? Yes, I have to know. I'll get hold of them as soon as I can and read them in the privacy of my flat. That way I'll be alone.*

As he sat brooding, his mind drifted to Cecilia. ...*I wonder what she's doing and who she's with. I need her, but will she even think about me? I know she's heard the news. It's been all over the international media.* His reverie was broken by the ring tone of his mobile. Reaching over to retrieve it, his mouth curved into a smile.

"Cecilia!"

"Yes, it's me. David, I was in South America when I got the news. I'm so sorry. I know as well as anyone what it is like to lose a parent—especially when it's your remaining parent," she breathed softly. "Fortunately, you have family to comfort you. How are you, darling?"

His smile broadened. It must have taken a great deal of effort for her to call him 'darling.' Perhaps she did feel something after all. "I'm fine, love. It's been awful, but I'm getting my feelings under control. Although right now, I'm numb. I don't think I've completely accepted the fact that he's no longer here. I still expect to be called into his office or study at any moment. I'm sure my feelings will settle down soon."

"Yes, they will. I felt the same way when my father died. David, if there is anything I can do, let me know."

He paused. Yes, there was something she could do. "Could you come to London? I... I could do with your company."

"Unfortunately, I cannot, but if I could, I would come. I have many business meetings to attend to. In fact, I have to leave for a meeting in twenty minutes. I just wanted to call and let you know I'm thinking of you and that I care."

Disappointed, he responded, "I'm glad you called. It means a lot to me." ...*You have no idea how much.*

"I'm glad to know that. I need to go now. I'll call you soon. Take care."

He slid his phone shut. "Take care, Cecilia," he murmured to himself. "Take care." He closed his eyes and sipped his brandy. He needed her, and not just physically. He thought briefly about Sandra. She had rung as well, but he hadn't taken her call. He knew what she wanted, apart from giving her condolences, and for once, he wanted none of it. He wondered if he would ever want her again.

The funeral took place three days later at Pemberley Chapel in Derbyshire. The day was cold and miserable as George Andrew Darcy was buried in the chapel cemetery beside his wife, Anne Margaret Winthrop Darcy. Family members and close friends stood in a circle under umbrellas while the vicar concluded the sermon with the final proclamation as the casket was prepared to be lowered into the ground. "George Andrew Darcy is laid to rest with his fathers. He now belongs to the ages."

Fitzwilliam wiped a tear from his eye.

Just as the casket was being let down, a pair of white doves flew up from a nearby bush. A small budded rose fell from the beak of one of the birds onto the casket when the doves flew over. Fitzwilliam looked up in astonishment as the pair flew in the direction of the cove. ...*Mum? Dad?* Watching them go, he wondered what it meant.

After the service, Fitzwilliam called his wife. "Elizabeth, it's over. We've just buried Father in the family cemetery. I must say it was a fitting day for a funeral. There was a cold drizzling rain to match our mood." He choked as he fought back tears.

"I'm sorry, Fitzwilliam. This is about the same time of year we buried my parents three years ago, and it was raining then, too. I know how you feel. I should have been there with you."

"I wanted you here, but darling, hearing your voice makes it easier, and I know it was best not to interrupt your classes. By the way, are mine being covered?"

"Yes, everything is fine. I took your Latin I class, Charles took the Latin II and Greek, and Jane took the Classical Philosophy class. My classes are fine, too. The semester ends in three weeks."

"How is your family—Robert and Tana and, of course, Liddy. How are they all holding up?"

"As well as can be expected, I suppose. You do know the jury came back yesterday afternoon with a guilty verdict for Jackie Lee, don't you?"

"No, I hadn't heard."

"Yes, they did. The judge will formally impose the sentence in two weeks. He was spared the death penalty on a plea bargain."

"What about Liddy?"

"She's doing as well as can be expected. She goes before the federal judge to plead guilty sometime in the month of June. It's just a formality." Elizabeth sighed. "Mr. Armstrong could not get full immunity, and we had to pay five hundred thousand dollars in fines. Liddy has to serve one year in a minimum security prison, and then she will be out on parole. Aunt Lydia, of course, is devastated by it all, but it could have been much worse."

"Yes, it could have. Mr. Armstrong was right. Had they married, they very well both could be serving life sentences, or worse, as I understand American law. Public opinion was so strongly formed against your cousin, and sad to say, women are sentenced to death in your country. This way is better." He paused for a moment, his chest restricting his breathing as he quietly asked, "Elizabeth...you didn't sign that check, did you? I mean you didn't sign it as Elizabeth Darcy?"

"Well, how else would I have signed it? I mean, that is who I am, isn't it? But for the amount that had to be paid, both Jane and my signatures were required. That's the way the bank account was set up."

"Yes...it's just that I want to keep things as low key as possible. I'm very glad this is nearly over. What else is there with Liddy—anything I should know about?"

"Nothing except that she will also have to testify in the capital trial of the Colombian, Carlos Sanchez. Jackie Lee turned state's evidence on him. And I am keeping everything as low key as I possibly can." Elizabeth hesitated. "Fitzwilliam, you seem nervous about all of this. Is something the matter? Is this being covered very much in the U.K.?"

"Well…it's a big story. Consequently it is in the news, but it's nothing for you to be concerned with." He couldn't bear to hurt her, and he knew the truth would do just that because it was being covered, but not in a way she would care to know about. Every scandal sheet in Britain was running a story about him, his wife, and her family—and it wasn't flattering, but so far the mainstream media had had very little to say on the matter. He glanced up to see that his family was returning to the car.

"Listen Elizabeth, I don't have much time. We're getting ready to go back to London, but I need to tell you that things are about to become very intense here. For that reason, I may not be able to call you for a while. After the will is read, I'll have to work late, meeting all the advisors, solicitors, and faithful executives. Until this has been settled one way or the other, I have to fully concentrate on the task at hand. I'm determined not to lose control over Pemberley no matter what I have to do. This is of the utmost importance to me as Pemberley is my legacy. I'm in the fight of my life. I made a promise to my father, and I intend to keep it."

"Fitzwilliam, do you want me to join you in London when the semester ends?"

"No, I think you had better stay where you are. A lot of things are happening here, and I don't want you unduly exposed to them." He paused to collect his thoughts. He didn't want to tell her too much, but he had to tell her something. "The problems I had with my father were more widespread and complex than I had originally thought. He disapproved of our marriage. You know that, but apparently some other people did, too and still do. They're friends of my father's who control part of Pemberley. But it's more than just our marriage they disapprove of—they disapprove of me. They don't believe I have the drive and determination that my father possessed when it comes to running the company as CEO. But don't worry; everything is going to be all right. I can't tell you more than I've already told you, because I know nothing further at this point. When this is over, you'll to come to London. It shouldn't take long. We'll be together very soon. I love you so much, Elizabeth…never forget that."

"I understand why your father disapproved of our marriage, but why would anyone else?"

"It's not so much the marriage as the rift that it caused between my father and me. Some others think I should have chosen a wife with a similar background—someone in the same social circle. In the end, it doesn't matter, because I don't care what anyone thinks. Elizabeth, I have to go. We're ready to leave. I'll call you when I can. I love you."

"I love you, too. Call me and keep me informed. I'm worried."

"Don't worry, Elizabeth. All will be well."

After talking to her husband, Elizabeth didn't feel reassured at all, even though she knew he was trying to comfort her.

More people than his father disapproved? What did he mean by that? Something was very wrong. She would have to wait until he called again. She shrugged her shoulders and chewed her lower lip. She would go to Longbourn for the weekend. Her strength was always renewed at Longbourn, especially in the cove.

Having returned from the family estate in Derbyshire, Fitzwilliam stood in his father's study at Darcy House contemplating all that had happened. He would arrange to meet his closest advisors and cousins as soon as the will is read, but first, he had to talk with his brother about the events of late and what their father had told them. Hopefully, it would mean as much to David as it did to him. Deep in thought, he didn't notice the knock on the door.

"Fitzwilliam, are you there?" his brother asked as he pushed the door open and stepped inside.

"Oh, sorry. I've been thinking about Father—his last words to us and other things."

"Is that what you wanted to see me about?"

"Yes, partly." Fitzwilliam glanced from the rose he'd carefully placed in a crystal vase and set on his desk to his family's coat of arms, hanging on the wall. The dove on the shield held a fern and a sprig of two rosebuds and a single rose in its beak. The rose and the white dove had always had a special meaning in his family's history, symbolizing faith, hope, and love, and sometime in the Middle Ages, those symbols had been incorporated into the D'Arcy Coat of Arms. He took a deep breath and turned to his brother. "David, did anyone give that rose to Father whilst he was in the hospital?"

"No, not that I know of." David looked at his brother strangely. "Why do you ask?"

"Oh, nothing really. It just reminds me of Mother and her rose garden at Pemberley. What was it she used to say? 'Where a Rose is tended, a thistle cannot flourish' or something like that. It was a quote from one of her favorite novels, **The Secret Garden**, I do believe. Also, did you notice the white doves that flew over the gravesite? One of them dropped a rose in Father's grave. Roses are not in season this time of year. Don't you think it strange?"

"Not particularly. It was a freak accident, and the rose could have come from anywhere. Perhaps from one of the many flower arrangements. It was simply coincidental. That's all," David said with a shrug.

Fitzwilliam shook his head. "Well, I think it's a strange happenstance that we find a rose in the hospital room floor, and then that bird drops one in Father's grave just as the casket is being lowered."

"So? Do you think that rose has some meaning attached to it?"

"I don't know. All I know is that it makes me feel peaceful, and I'm going to have this one pressed and framed. I'll place it between Mum and Dad's pictures over my desk. I just wondered about the rose and the quote from the book. That's all."

David looked from the rose to his parents' portraits. "Surely you didn't call me in here to discuss a rose and some novel."

Fitzwilliam glanced at his brother as he ran his fingers through his hair. "No, I didn't. I had something else in mind as well." He turned and caught his brother's gaze. "David, what did you think of Father's last words to us? I think he really did love us."

David shook his head and came across the room to the drinks cabinet where he took out a decanter of brandy. Pouring out two measures, he surveyed the room as if to collect his thoughts. Finally their eyes locked. "Fitzwilliam, you're the sentimental one, not me," he said, sipping his drink while he composed himself. "I'm sorry it took his deathbed before Father could confess what he should have lived, but, if I have to be frank with you, all I can say is that I feel nothing. I'm not sad. I'm not glad. It's as if there is a big gaping hole where my heart should be. I feel absolutely nothing... except... freedom." He smiled. "Think about it. We're now free... free to marry whomever we choose, free to claim our inheritance without any strings attached. Free! That's what I feel."

Fitzwilliam was taken aback. "But David, you seemed upset when we last saw him alive. I saw you."

David snorted. "Don't mistake me. If I shed a tear or two, it was for what should have been and now can never be. That's what you saw, Brother." He finished his drink and set his glass down firmly. Then, he turned and left the room, closing the door with a resounding click.

Fitzwilliam stood rooted to the floor, staring at the door. He understood David perfectly. Fitzwilliam knew he had loved his father, but he didn't feel the sense of loss that he knew he should feel, either. The loss he felt was one of regret—and that he felt keenly. Regret over the reserve that had distanced them from one another and the fact that his father had never understood him, nor had he understood his father. Yet his father's last words had meant that he was right. His father had loved his children the only way he knew how, and in that knowledge, Fitzwilliam took comfort.

He also understood what David meant about being free. They were indeed free— one burden had been lifted. They were now free to live as they chose without the looming threat of their father's influence in the background. Fitzwilliam breathed a sigh of relief. He had persevered. He had married Elizabeth, had his inheritance, and now he was equally determined to secure Pemberley. He glanced at the rose and downed his drink. Then he, too, left through the door his brother had exited.

Chapter Thirty-seven

... Money is power and Hilda is money...

Tension hung in the air so thick it could be cut with a knife as Hilda Vanderburgh stalked the floor of George Darcy's study, waiting for the group assembled there to take their seats. Fitzwilliam, David, Georgiana, Harvey and his two sons, William and Benson, were all present, together with Thomas Metcalfe, lead solicitor of Pemberley Group, and Gordon Blakely, Pemberley's top Public Relations man. As each person sat down, the room grew silent, waiting for Hilda to begin.

Hilda observed each member present. Not only had she been George Darcy's sister-in-law and close confidante, she had also been his chief financial advisor. And, as the executor of his will and having spent many long hours in meetings with George, Hilda knew how he felt about Fitzwilliam's obstinacy—especially his marriage to a woman George considered to be beneath his son. She nodded subtly as her eyes focused on her nephew.

Taking her chair behind George's desk, Hilda cleared her throat. "Fitzwilliam, David, Georgiana, this is the last will and testament of your father, George Andrew Darcy." Breaking the seal, she unfolded the papers and began to read, skipping over much of the formal verbiage.

"Georgiana Sophia Darcy is to be given a monetary sum of £500 million to be held in trust, ten percent of my shareholdings in Pemberley, PLC, and a position in the company to be decided upon by the Board of Directors. David Jamison Darcy is to be given a monetary sum of £2 billion to be held in trust, forty percent of my shareholdings in Pemberley, PLC, a permanent seat as Vice Chairman on the Board of Directors, as they approve, and is to preside over Darcy Enterprises as president. Fitzwilliam Alexander Darcy is to be given a monetary settlement of £4 billion to be held in trust, fifty percent of my shareholdings in Pemberley, PLC, all of the estate property of Pemberley House and its lands, and Darcy House residence in London with David Jamison Darcy and Georgiana Sophia Darcy given a lifetime right to live on said properties.

"Fitzwilliam Alexander Darcy is my choice for the positions of CEO and Chairman of the Board over the whole of Pemberley, PLC as approved by the Board of Directors *with* the stipulation that he give up his current career of teaching, dedicate himself to the running of the company, and reside in Britain for a period of not less than five years. After said period of five years, he is no longer under the restraints of the will. If he is unable or unwilling to fulfill his obligation, then £2 billion held in trust and the positions of CEO and Chairman of the Board will revert to David Jamison Darcy. Should David Jamison Darcy not be able or willing to fulfill his obligations, the money and positions will revert to Georgiana Sophia Darcy."

Adjusting her glasses and looking pointedly at Fitzwilliam, Hilda dropped her gaze and continued. "As to Mrs. Fitzwilliam Alexander Darcy, she will have no claims on Pemberley, PLC or any property associated with the Darcy family. Should a divorce occur within seven years, she is to be awarded £7 million, provided she agrees not to take any legal action against Fitzwilliam Alexander Darcy or the Darcy family estate. Should a divorce occur after the seven year period, she is to be awarded £20 million in trust from the estate, but otherwise, no allowance from the estate will be made for Mrs.

Fitzwilliam Alexander Darcy. Should the marriage produce any children, they will become legal heirs under their father, Fitzwilliam Alexander Darcy, and will inherit accordingly as his said heirs." Here Hilda paused to gauge the reaction. Seeing Fitzwilliam's jaw tightened in apparent anger with his eyes fixed on her, she smiled inwardly. "That concludes the will as to how it pertains to the Darcy heirs. The rest entails small details for servants, other relations, friends, and so forth." Hilda continued reading the minute details.

Fitzwilliam was both relieved and angered, relieved that he was in possession of his most ardent desire, Pemberley House and estate, but angered by the five year clause and the high-handed controlling manner in which Elizabeth had been treated. He didn't foresee a divorce or any marital problems, but was rather hurt that she had been referred to in such an offensive way, insinuating she had married him for his money, when he knew that couldn't have been further from the truth. The sting of his father's objection to his marriage was there for everyone present to see, and that rejection of something so intimately important to him made Fitzwilliam burn with indignation.

Once the will had been read, Hilda instructed the Darcy siblings.

"Now that the terms of the will are known, it will be up to the three of you to secure the Pemberley conglomerate. If you do not do so, then you will only inherit the material items of the will."

Hilda looked pointedly at the two brothers. "If I can be of further assistance, please feel free to call upon me. I was your father's advisor, both personally and financially, as well as one of his closest friends."

With the reading of the will concluded, people began milling about and talking. "Fitzwilliam, my sons and I plan to stand by your side throughout this entire ordeal," Harvey said, clapping his nephew gently on the shoulder.

"Yes, we do," William said. "I'll be behind you, and I'll take on as much responsibility as you're willing to give me. We've worked closely in the past, and as your lead accountant, I'm well versed in all of the financial aspects."

"I, too, am available. And since I oversee the sales and publications of Darcy & Winthrop Publishing, I can help you in that aspect," Benson said.

"Thank you both. I will need all the help I can get." Fitzwilliam embraced his two cousins warmly before turning to his uncle. "Harvey, I'll need you and Thomas to interact with some of the board members on my behalf since you know them much better than I do. I'll call everyone in a day or two for the first meeting."

"We'll be waiting," Harvey said.

At their initial meeting following the reading of the will, the Darcy brothers and Georgiana began formulating a plan to counteract those intent on taking control of the company away from the founding family. Sitting around the large conference table in the executive boardroom were Richard Winthrop, Harvey Darcy, William Darcy, Benson Darcy, Gordon Blakely, Thomas Metcalfe, and several other loyal supporters. Fitzwilliam addressed the group.

"I've called this meeting to assess the damage Pemberley has suffered and to explore our options for recovery. Thomas, can you give us the latest information?"

Thomas Metcalfe passed a copy of his preliminary report to each member while addressing those assembled. "This is how things stand as we meet. Fitzwilliam, David, because of the way you have led your personal lives, many of the directors on Pemberley's board do not have sufficient confidence that the two of you can take the company forward. According to some of them, you have not shown a serious interest in running this company. In essence, they don't believe that either of you has the same drive and strong determination of your late father. Neither of you has established a successful track record. In fact, it's quite the opposite!" Thomas glanced in David's direction. "David, your public image is that of a spoilt playboy with a dubious lifestyle that suggests you have neither the ability for financial success nor the mental maturity needed to hold a position on the board of directors. A man who is self-indulgent is rarely perceived as being dedicated to business."

Thomas then turned to Fitzwilliam. "And Fitzwilliam, the fact that you didn't remain in England in the decision making and corporate training loop seems to indicate that you have no real desire to run the business. It's not so much your marriage that has alarmed the board, but rather the fact that you were willing to give up your birthright and position within the company so easily—as if it were nothing. Had you met your wife here in Britain, dated her and married her whilst still working within the company, probably no one on the board, other than George, would have cared."

Thomas cleared his throat. "The concern of the board boils down to two things: profits and whether or not the two of you can deliver them. The board believes that neither of you have sufficient knowledge of the intricate workings of this company to deliver satisfactory profitability." Metcalfe laid down the sheet of paper he held in his hand. "Therefore, your uncle, Harry Dashwood, perceiving a leadership vacuum, has made a move to launch a proxy battle. He, Jonathan Stanley, and Jason Wesley are focusing on directorial and management positions with the intent of reorganizing them. And surely, you must be aware of the possible repercussions of that!"

Shuffling his papers, Thomas continued. "They have already asked the Pemberley Group solicitors for a list of all the shareholders, which I am bound by the by-laws to provide. They will have to persuade the existing shareholders to vote out the current company management, thus making it easier for them to take control. They will appeal directly to the shareholders to vote in favor of Dashwood's hand-picked candidates. The shareholders will receive copies of Pemberley's financial reports as well as directors' and auditors' reports for the past fiscal year. This information, coupled with the preceding years' reports, will be used to sway their vote. Should you be replaced, you will be given a two years' salary severance pay in accordance with the company's by-laws."

Metcalfe hesitated a moment to let them consider what had been said. "There is one other thing. When they started, they did not anticipate George's death. Now, with George gone, they believe their success is all but certain. Perhaps George's insistence that he handle this alone, without informing you or David, is what brought about his heart attack. I do not know. The bottom line is this. Pemberley has lost ground over the last few years. Profits are at their lowest in five years at 2.5 percent. That's a decline of 63.5 percent. The only bright side is your division, David. Darcy Enterprises earned an anemic 4.5 percent which is better than the corporate average."

Fitzwilliam slouched in his chair. His gut twisted—pained that his father would attempt to fight his uncle alone without seeking his help. Remorse crept in, but only briefly. This was not the time to grieve.

"Thomas, that's the situation, which I will admit *is* serious. Now what are we going to do about it?"

Picking up his report, Metcalfe said, "Well, if you'll examine the handouts I've given you, you'll see that I've outlined our strategy point by point. First and foremost, we have to put together a majority coalition of our own. Dashwood is forming his as we speak. He does have the time advantage since he's been undermining you for months and has begun to buy shares. But all is not lost yet.

"Look at the attached lists. The first is a list of your enemies. You'll see it has the names of many of your cousins. Look at the friends' list. They fully support you, so we needn't worry about that list. The third list contains those who are undecided. They are the most important because they own a block of shares that is sufficient to help decide this battle, albeit by a razor's edge. Dashwood is working feverishly to obtain their support. You must do the same. I've marked five of the names on that list. Make a note of them—Anderson, McPherson, Ashcroft, Bennington, and Marlow—the Gang of Five as I call them or better known as the Pemberley Five. To form a challenging coalition, you need at least three of them to support you. To form a solid majority coalition that will put you within striking distance, you will need all five. These men were not only loyal to your father, they were his friends, and all of them owed George personal favors. If you can convince them that you have what it takes, you'll be ninety percent there."

"What about the other ten percent?" David asked, jotting down notes as Thomas spoke.

"Cold hard cash and lots of it—£17 billion, more or less. Let me explain. Turn to the back page of this report and follow along as I speak. I have it charted out for a clear understanding."

As those assembled found their place, Metcalfe began. "Notice the pie chart. The total amount of Pemberley's outstanding market shares is 19.4 billion. You and those who solidly support you have forty percent of that number. The five aforementioned shareholders hold roughly nine percent. If you can garner their full support, together you will have use of forty-nine percent, leaving you short two percent or about 388 million shares. Shares sell in the vicinity of £43 per share, depending on which stock exchange we're talking about. To buy the needed remaining shares, you need roughly £17 billion, depending on your ability to secure full support from the Gang of Five. More will be required should you only gain their partial support, and that amount will vary depending the amount of support you do gain. But let us not forget the small shareholder. They count, too, and I am convinced that with the right strategy, we can pick up support there as well.

"However, if you do not secure at least three of the Pemberley Five *and* the needed monies, you're sunk. So you see, you'll have to secure loans, and that requires influence. You need Hilda Vanderburgh."

Fitzwilliam let out a resigned sigh and threw down his pencil. He and Hilda had had a strained relationship at best, but he remembered his father's words. *...Her power and influence carries a great deal of weight. Money is power and Hilda is money. If she is your enemy, she can break you. If she is your friend, nobody can touch you.*

Fitzwilliam blew out a hard breath. "Contact Hilda. Ask her to meet with me as soon as possible," he said, picking up his pencil to scribble a note. "Now, what about the other points?"

"The other points are to move decisively to clean up your public images. David, no more photographs of you with porn stars, strippers, or in drunken stupors. Fitzwilliam, give interviews and try to look serious about what you're doing, but don't give away too much information. 'No comment' is your friend. And keep your personal life low key. Let them focus on the business aspects of this ordeal. Your wife is still in America. Keep her there. If she comes, she'll be dragged right into the thick of things. She's perceived, rightly or wrongly, as having divided you from your father. If she were here, the publicity she would generate would complicate matters. The fact that she was a bone of contention between you and your late father has already caused many in the press to dislike her. They will search for anything they can find, dissecting her, exploiting her and her family, especially considering the quagmire they find themselves embroiled in. She is vulnerable. And what the media cannot find, they will make up. Many people who read trash publications actually believe everything they read. It's up to you, but I would advise you against bringing her here until this matter has been resolved."

"Fitzwilliam, Thomas is right. There are a lot of people within the family who already hold your wife in low regard because they think she's beneath us. She's upset the equilibrium. The talk would only become worse if she were here," William advised.

"I see," he drew in a deep weary breath, "I want her protected at all costs. I will not have her harmed, especially because of me. What else do you have, Thomas?"

"Last but not least, you need to hit the ground running. You will have to move quickly to announce marketing strategies and new ideas with innovative concepts. You must have a plan to present to the board, but first you need to immerse yourself in the company. That's where William, Benson, and Richard can help you. They already have a working knowledge of the company, as does David, but you and Georgiana are at a disadvantage. I have a list of documents for the three of you to read. You'll have to come up to speed very quickly. I'll arrange a series of meetings with Hilda and your loyal supporters on the board. You will need to chair the upcoming meetings from an informed perspective. You'll be questioned by the press. Answer all questions truthfully, but remember, don't give away too much information and keep your personal life off limits. Is that understood?" Metcalfe paused briefly and met Fitzwilliam's stare. "It will be tough, yes, but is there an alternative?"

"No," Fitzwilliam tore his gaze away, "there is no alternative." His determination set, he put down his pencil and looked up, surveying the room. "Gentlemen, failure is *not* an option. I'll begin tonight with the Financial and Operating Information documents covering the last five years on Pemberley as the parent company. David, you take these on Darcy Enterprises and the Technology Group," Fitzwilliam said, handing his brother a stack of documents. "Georgiana, immerse yourself in the publishing and manufacturing businesses." Handing the third stack to his sister, he turned to his cousin. "William, I want to meet with you in my office at nine o'clock sharp tomorrow morning to go over what I've read. Benson, you meet Georgiana at her convenience, and Harvey, I'll get back to you before the end of the day. I want you to take the British American Petroleum Division. William will help you. The world's energy supplies are volatile right now. It's our time to move quickly and grab the market shares. I want a teleconference with the Saudi prince in charge of Brit Am in Saudi Arabia, and I want a detailed report on what we are doing in the North Sea. Also, I want you to explore the potential for growing our activities in the former Soviet Union for future reserves. We already own fifty percent of the Russian oil company. I'd like to control all of it if not outright own it. There is the potential to make billions in the oil industry, and once we secure Pemberley, I want you to replace Dashwood on the board as Executive Director in charge of Brit Am." Turning to his left, he continued. "Oh, and Richard, you help David with Darcy Enterprises. You're to become senior vice president of that division once I have secured the corporation."

"Will do." Richard smiled. "David, I'll see you before our next meeting."

"I'll be there," David said, slapping his cousin on the back as the group adjourned.

"I'll take the challenge, Fitzwilliam, and I'll have a report on your desk as soon as possible," Harvey said.

"Fitzwilliam, that's the kind of talk I want to hear," Thomas said with a smile. "You have less than five months to succeed. I will explain about the loan your father made to your uncle about a month ago. It is of critical importance. Harvey, you and your boys stay behind and you, too, David," Metcalfe said as the others left the room.

Once the room was cleared, Thomas proceeded with a detailed account of the loan.

"He was a fool to agree to those conditions," Harvey said, astounded by his brother-in-law's arrogance.

"Yes, but when men are consumed with a burning ambition and the quest for power, rarely do they consider the possibility of losing—and he may not. In which case, the point is moot. He'll be able to repay it with very little discomfort to himself, *but* should he lose, he will be at your mercy," Metcalfe responded, looking directly at Fitzwilliam, "At your mercy to either extend the loan and let him pay it off gradually, or suffer the consequences of a quick financial death should share prices fall below what he's paying for them, as I suspect they will."

"Well, Thomas, time is of the essence," Harvey said. "We need to get to work. Is there anything else we need to know?"

Shaking his head, Metcalfe answered, "No, that is all. I'll get back to you tomorrow morning." The Darcy siblings gathered their documents to leave for their respective offices, but before Fitzwilliam and David could exit, Thomas called them aside.

"There is one other delicate matter we need to discuss," he said, concern written across his features. "I have a message from your uncle."

Fitzwilliam creased his brow. "What is it, Thomas?"

"Fitzwilliam, this fight is not for the faint of heart."

"I'm well aware of that…and your point is?"

"Harry has asked me to inform you that if you will surrender the company peacefully and both you and David resign, he will not drag your wife's name through the mud…or…" Thomas paused and glanced away.

"Or what?"

Looking back, he breathed deeply. "Otherwise he's prepared to release sensitive information about you…and her."

"Like what? Thomas, out with it."

"Like the conversations he and George had…the fact that George kept your marriage a secret and why, and… he has copies of the checks and documents your wife signed, linking you personally to the drug trial in Tennessee. He will release those to the press if you push forward with this." Metcalf glanced at David. "And David, your indiscretions will be more fully exposed. He has pictures of you with high class prostitutes and showgirls, and I'm afraid they are quite scandalous. Some of them infer that you are using cocaine. He's staging a propaganda crusade for the benefit of shifting public opinion with the object of making you both appear weak so you will scuttle and run."

Fitzwilliam's features grew dark. He threw down the folder he held in his hand and locked eyes with Metcalfe. "His intended climate of intimidation and fear will have no effect on me. I shall not back down, nor will I give in to his campaign of smear tactics. He can do as he pleases with me, slander my name if he dares, but tell him," Fitzwilliam paused, "tell him that if he harms my wife in any way, I will send him to hell."

Taken aback, Thomas nodded. "I'll relay your sentiments."

Calm and fully composed, Fitzwilliam gathered up his documents and exited the room without so much as a backward glance.

David lingered. "Tell him for me to take his best shot and aim closely because, if he misses, I'll take mine—and I won't miss." A wide smile spread across David's countenance as he shook his head and walked through the same door.

By the afternoon, news of the proxy battle had broken all over Fox and CNN international business news as well as the BBC with *The London Financial Times* and the *Wall Street Journal* reporting the news the next day.

"The Darcy brothers are in the fight of their lives over the Pemberley Conglomerate left in shambles by the death of billionaire tycoon, George Darcy. He has left the company vulnerable with his sons fighting to recover it, if they can."

The international stock markets fluctuated with the news *Pemberley, PLC in the Throes of a Hostile Takeover from Within.*

Everywhere he went Fitzwilliam was confronted with tabloids, newspapers, financial publications, or magazines, all with the glaring captions: *American Woman Threatens to Tear Darcy Family Apart. Pemberley, PLC, in Financial Straits...Did George Darcy Hide the American Marriage of his Son, Fitzwilliam, and if so, Why? Will Harry Dashwood Rescue Pemberley. Is Fitzwilliam Darcy involved in Defence of Drug Dealers? Wife Pays Legal Expenses. Who is this Woman? Son Shows Little Concern for Father or Business. What's the Story on the Financial Situation with Pemberley, PLC?*

"This is rubbish. Harry! I **will get him**!" Fitzwilliam stormed aloud. *The one thing I'm grateful for is that this rubbish is not published in the U.S. Elizabeth will never see it.*

David's flagrant lifestyle was also paraded in the tabloids where he was portrayed as the arrogant rich playboy unconcerned about his father or his business obligations. Pictures were circulated of him from as far back as five years, showing a scantily clad woman on each arm, with captions claiming that David was either drunk or high. Several ladies of questionable character had come forth, stating they had snorted cocaine with David and some claimed to have been pregnant with his child. Although Fitzwilliam knew none of it was true, perception was everything, leaving them at the mercy of those presenting the image they wanted to convey.

In spite of the negative publicity, Fitzwilliam and his team trudged on, working late into the night and sometimes around the clock. The early morning strategy planning sessions went well, so much so that finally they had a loose plan of how they would proceed. William had proven to be invaluable to Fitzwilliam, filling in the gaps of uncertainty, and Thomas had arranged a meeting between Fitzwilliam and his aunt. If the meeting went well, he would have the money he needed.

Looking at the clock on the wall, Fitzwilliam poured himself a glass of mineral water. Hilda would be here in fifteen minutes. As he sipped his drink, his mind drifted to Elizabeth. *...I'm grateful she isn't here to see that latest article in the tabloids. When will it stop? They've gone back seventy years to show a connection between illegal whiskey during prohibition and marijuana distribution, leading one to the conclusion that her entire family has been involved in vice as far back as the 1850s. Have they nothing better to do? Why can't they find a story with Lord Weddington or Westbury? The trial is over. When will they let this drop?*

Fitzwilliam felt the crush of all that was coming down upon him as if the weight of the world were upon his shoulders. His dad...the will... and now the tabloids. He couldn't deal with one more thing. It was consuming him. The bitter memories, the resentment, the regret, and the maddening thought of what was being done to his precious wife tore at his very soul. He only prayed she didn't turn on the television set. Her world had been so unlike his own, and the thought of her being torn to bits was more than he could take, especially because of him. Lost in contemplation, he almost didn't hear the knock at the door. He glanced up just in time to see his aunt step through the threshold.

"Fitzwilliam, I'm here a little early. I hope I'm not intruding on your thoughts. You had such a look of intense concentration."

"Not at all, Aunt Hilda. Won't you come in and sit down?" he said, rising from his chair to greet her.

She took the offered seat and promptly asked, "You wanted to see me. I presume you need money. Am I correct?"

He smiled. His aunt didn't miss a thing. "You're always very perceptive and to the point. Yes, I do."

"I don't believe in wasting time. Time is money, and I don't waste either. How much do you need? Ten billion? Twenty? Or is it thirty?"

He laughed. "Is it that easy? I need seventeen billion to buy—"

"I know what you need it for. I've only been waiting for you to ring me. I told you the day the will was read to ring me up. I've already held negotiations with several large bankers in case you needed more than my bank could lend. I have up to £20 billion secured with more promised if you need it. I can have the money for you in a matter of days, but there is one stipulation." She paused to look him directly in the eye. "I must be allowed my say. I was your father's financial advisor, and I intend to be yours. I want to oversee the financial aspect of this. That means I am to be invited to all the meetings. You will need my expertise. Your uncle has approached me for similar help, but I've been stalling him until I heard from you. I have no intention of helping him, but neither did I want him going elsewhere—that is, not until the last possible minute. It will throw him off center for the time being. I have the capacity to cut him off at the knees. He will not obtain a loan unless I approve it."

"You never cease to amaze me, Hilda. The next meeting is at ten o'clock tomorrow morning. I have a briefing with Thomas in twenty minutes, but we'll begin in earnest tomorrow."

"I'll be there. Now, if you don't mind, I'm a very busy woman. Until tomorrow." She extended her hand with a smile as she rose from her seat.

"Until tomorrow then," he said shaking the proffered hand. Walking her to the door, he said goodbye and placed a kiss upon her cheek. Having secured the loan, only one more task remained, and that would soon be accomplished, too… he hoped.

Gathering the rough draft of his proposal for his meeting with Uncle Harvey and his solicitor, he left his office and headed for Metcalfe's with a smile.

Although Fitzwilliam had called her a week ago, Elizabeth had not heard from him since, causing her to become concerned, so she called Pemberley's corporate office.

"Fitzwilliam Darcy's office, Mrs. Foulkes speaking."

"Mrs. Foulkes, this is Elizabeth Darcy, Fitzwilliam's wife, I would like to speak with my husband, please."

"I'm sorry, Mrs. Darcy, but Mr. Darcy is in a meeting and cannot be disturbed. May I take a message?"

"Yes, tell him to call me as soon as he can."

"I'll give him the message, Mrs. Darcy."

Fitzwilliam's afternoon meeting lasted late into the evening before they broke for dinner. When he saw the message from Mrs. Foulkes that Elizabeth had called earlier in the day, he pushed it aside, feeling there was no time for a lengthy conversation, which he knew was what she expected. He and William sent out for dinner while they continued poring over the latest Statistical Review of World Energy report for Brit Am, breaking only to eat as they worked late into the night.

It was three a.m. when he picked up the note and glanced over to his mobile. There was no time to call. Besides, he was too tired, and her class would start in ten minutes. He would call her later. She would understand that he had to have some sleep.

Two weeks had passed since he had slept in his own bed at Darcy House. Instead, he used his corporate executive flat at Pemberley to sleep and shower while his valet, Watson, kept him supplied in clean clothes, along with whatever else he needed.

Elizabeth had emailed him, but he only answered her in the most cursory way, never responding in any detail. Except for the loan, there was nothing to tell her other than to reassure her of his love. With one crisis after another, he didn't have time to compose a lengthy message. He knew he should call her, but he also knew she would want to talk for more than a few minutes, which was all he could spare. Finally, she called again. This time he pushed his work aside and took her call in his office.

"Fitzwilliam, why didn't you return my call the other day? I left a message. Didn't you get it?"

"Yes, I got it." He released a weary sigh. "Elizabeth, I've been working around the clock. I simply haven't had the time to call. I'm trying to understand the intricate workings of the company so that I can assess Pemberley's status from an informed position. In fact, I'm going over one of the operations reports right now."

"Does it consume you so much that you can't talk to me?"

"Actually, yes, it is all consuming. I have so much to do and so little time in which to do it."

"Can you not spare a few minutes for me?"

He drew in a deep measured breath. "Liz, please, I know I should've called, but I've been too busy and too exhausted. I have no news to tell you other than I'm working on things. If I don't call, you'll simply have to trust me. Have a little faith in me. You must understand my position."

"Fitzwilliam, I do have faith in you, but I need to hear your voice every once in a while to remind me I still have a husband."

"I'm sorry, darling. I'll try and do better, but you'll simply have to be patient. I love you more than anything. You know that," he reassured. "What I'm doing isn't just for me, but for us and our future son. When all this is over, we'll be together and work on conceiving that son."

"When will it be over? I want it over soon. I want us to be together again."

"I don't know, darling. I don't know." Glancing at the wall clock, he realized that time was slipping away. "Liz, I have to go. I'm already late for my next meeting. I'll ring you when I have something notable to tell you. At this point there's nothing new that I haven't already told you in my emails. You know I love you, but I've got to go. Please try and understand. Darling, I love you."

"But, Fitzwilliam…"

Click.

Chapter Thirty-eight

... I liked you better when it was just you and me—a man and a woman in love...

Everywhere the brothers went they were swamped by news reporters bombarding them with questions. Weeks had gone by and June approached. Stress from the day to day worries had begun to take its toll on Elizabeth, causing her to become severely ill with bouts of nausea. Sick and weak from her last episode in the bathroom, Elizabeth sat in front of the TV in their bedroom watching the latest news from London on CNN.

"There's Mr. Fitzwilliam Darcy now. Mr. Darcy, can we have a word with you? Is it true that Pemberley's board of directors is concerned that you are not as dedicated to the business as your late father was?"

"No comment." Fitzwilliam continued walking.

"Mr. Darcy, there are many conflicting stories in the press of late. Is there any truth to the rumors circulating that you have an American wife and that your father hid your marriage to this American woman?"

"No comment."

"Mr. Darcy, is it true that your late father threatened to disown you over the alleged American marriage? Were you living with her or was she your wife? Several of your family members are saying there is no truth to the tabloid stories while others are saying there is. Your family is yet to make an official statement either to the marriage or the rumored drug connection. Are you married, or are you not?"

Finally, Fitzwilliam turned and faced the reporter with an angry retort. *"My marital status is my own business. I have nothing further to say on the subject. Now if you would like to discuss the situation of Pemberley, I would be more than happy to answer your questions."*

"What? I can't believe this!" Elizabeth yelled at the flat screen.

The attempted interview shifted to matters pertaining to the corporate struggle, but Elizabeth paid no attention. Watching the news reporter fire question after question at her husband had caused her to become sick to her stomach once again. She barely made it to the bathroom where she fell to the floor.

After violently purging her stomach, dark thoughts plagued her mind. *...Why did that reporter say our marriage was a rumor? Why didn't Fitzwilliam refute it? And why doesn't he call me? Why does he let me watch this drivel and not give me reassurance? What is wrong? I know he said he would call when he could, but it's been a week since we last talked!*

Once she had rested, Elizabeth called him, and again, he didn't take her call. Mrs. Foulkes told her he would call later that night. Again, he was late for a meeting. As she hung up the phone, a lingering uncertainty began to intensify.

That night at midnight, London time, and six o'clock Middle Tennessee time, he called.

"Elizabeth, I'm sorry I didn't call you earlier. I've had a tough day—no, it's been a tough week. I'm utterly shattered."

"I'm sorry about your day, but I've had a rough day, too. I saw that interview with you on CNN, and it upset me greatly. Why does that man think our marriage is a rumor?"

He grimaced. "Elizabeth, I can explain everything. It's not what you think."

"Oh, and just what do I think? You go off to England, leave me here, and then you call sporadically. I'm here all alone. Jane and Charles have gone to Europe, and Robert and Tana are so heavily involved with my cousin that they barely notice I'm still alive. Liddy goes before the judge next week. She had her baby, a little girl, a week ago. She'll be going to prison as soon as she's recovered. So, things are stressful here, too. And I don't dare go down to the Cut and Curl because I don't have any answers for all the inquisitive minds wanting to know what is going on with us. They're asking me why I'm not in England with you, and I have no answers that will satisfy them. It seems everyone in town heard that awful interview, and folks are calling me at home. I dread picking up the phone. It looks suspicious, Fitzwilliam. So you tell me, what am I supposed to think?"

His head was splitting from her barrage. He didn't give a damn about Liddy's baby or what the old harpies at the Cut and Curl had to say, much less what they thought, but his wife was another matter. He knew that no matter what he had to say, she was not going to take it well, but at least he would try.

"Elizabeth, please. Let me explain. My father kept our marriage a secret here in London. He didn't want anyone to know about his personal life. He didn't approve of our marriage. You know that. Only a few people knew, mostly members of the family and a few personal friends and advisors, and they were persuaded to keep quiet as well."

He let out a heavy sigh ...*She's not going to like this...* "Liz, I must keep quiet too. Our marriage is no longer a secret. The press broke it over a month ago, although the Darcy family has not officially commented on it one way or the other. And... quite frankly, I didn't refute it because...well, I don't want the focus to be on us. It's bad enough that we've been exploited in the tabloids. I don't want it spilling over into the mainstream media, too. Consequently, I've chosen not to discuss it. My father was very vociferous on the subject and many in my family don't approve of my choice. They'll use our marriage and the fact that it drove a wedge between my father and me to fan the flames of discontent, generating more negative publicity which will, in turn, make life very unpleasant for you. I don't want to see you hurt," he softly said. "That is the *one* way they can get to me. This can't last much longer. It's the first of June. It will soon blow over, and we'll be together. I promise. Trust me, Elizabeth. On this occasion, I know what is best."

She gasped. "Trust you...I've trusted you all along, but I guess I never realized what your family really thought of me, or how much they despised me. They don't even know me. Did you know your father had done this?"

His features contorted ...*I **know** she's not going to like this...* "No, not at first...I found out later."

"And you didn't correct it? You didn't defend me? How long have you known?"

"David told me before the wedding. We discussed it, and I... Elizabeth... I thought... well... I thought maybe it was best not to tell you."

"You thought it was best. I see," she said in a whisper.

"Elizabeth, it's not what you think."

"If it's not what I think, then I'm boarding a plane and coming to London within the next few days."

"**No!** Do not do that!"

"Why not, Fitzwilliam?! What about us? Why can't I come to you?"

"Elizabeth, I know you're listening, but are you really paying attention to what I'm telling you? I don't want the media to focus on you...on us. I've got enough problems without my personal life being dragged through the mud. I can't fight a war on two fronts. Please, Elizabeth, you have to understand. There are people here within the corporate structure, some of whom are my family, who don't approve of me, and they're using my disagreements with my father against me. I can't give them more fuel to add to the fire, and your arrival here will do just that. Please, I must ask you to not go against my wishes."

"Why? I still don't understand."

He closed his eyes. "Because any negative publicity could have an adverse effect on the board members and shareholders' confidence in me, which is already on thin ice, and since I am the acting Chairman of the Board and CEO of Pemberley, my public image affects the business. The tabloids are already exploiting my disagreement with my father, which goes much deeper than our marriage. Father worked very hard to promote his public image whereas I have not. He took every opportunity for photo ops to enhance his popularity. He was known for his philanthropy. People know me simply because I exist. When I was merely a son, it didn't matter so much, but now it does. I've never courted the media—I've never cared, but now it *is* important. It's important to my very survival as CEO."

He paused and rubbed his bloodshot eyes. "Do you understand what I'm talking about? I'm talking about billions of pounds and my family's legacy. As I told you the day of the funeral, I'm in the fight of my life, and I can't afford to lose this battle. Therefore it's vitally important that I keep my personal life out of the press."

"But don't you see that I need you, too, especially now that—"

"Elizabeth, listen to me! If you come here, they will pull you to pieces. They'll do nothing but find fault with you, and what they can't find out for themselves, they'll invent just to reinforce my father's position. He was known for always being right. The media climate here is hostile. If this spills over into the mainstream media, it could have far reaching consequences. Elizabeth, I don't want that to happen. I can't deal with it right now. The spin on things is that it's me against my father's memory. Don't you understand what that means? My enemies will say my father was right and that I have married beneath myself."

Her voice quivered. "Is that what I am to you—someone beneath you... an embarrassment? I thought I was your equal."

He groaned in anguish. "No, of course not! You *are* my equal. This has come about because of the disagreements between my father and me, but you're caught up in it, and I need your cooperation. Had he given us his blessing, no one would have dared say a word, but he didn't."

"I think I'm beginning to understand. You want to keep me in the shadows so certain stockholders won't change sides."

"Yes, that is true, but you know I love you. I've told you so repeatedly. You have to understand that as my wife*,* you *must* keep a low profile."

"No, Fitzwilliam I don't understand. I don't like this one bit. What's wrong? Have you changed your mind about us? I mean when you first proposed, you didn't know *I* was connected to a drug dealer."

"No, I haven't, and it's ridiculous that you should even raise the question. Elizabeth, we're going around in circles," he said, in sheer exasperation. "But let me tell you one more time. I need the support of some of my father's friends, and if the tabloids start running some sordid story about us, regardless of its veracity, then fewer, or perhaps none of them, will want to support me, especially if it's picked up by the major media. Don't you understand what I'm trying to tell you? Public opinion counts a lot right now. It isn't right, but that's the way it is. The tabloids can make or break us.

I don't want you exposed in that fashion. I'm trying to protect you!"

"Who are you really trying to protect, me or Pemberley? I wonder if you had it to do over again, if you, as CEO of Pemberley, would seek me out—a lowly *American* college professor, and if you did, would you marry me, or... just live with me..."

"Elizabeth, don't insult me like that! It's absurd that you should even think such a thing! You know how I feel about you....about us. You must have some faith in me...in us. This is very important to me, and I thought it would be important to you, too! I can't let my family's legacy fall—not whilst I'm at the helm. I am the one on which the Darcys' future hangs. If I *do* fail, it will not be without a fight. I want to pass on to our future son that which has been passed down for nearly one thousand years—from father to son to me—"

"I don't understand why the press would care about me. It seems to me that it looks more conspicuous by my *not* being by your side. It looks as if we are not a serious couple."

"Elizabeth, haven't you heard a thing I've been saying to you?" Fitzwilliam snapped. "That is **not** how the press works. Look, I have a splitting headache. I'm under a great deal of pressure and can only concentrate on one thing at a time. This is my main priority at the moment, and you will simply have to understand. If I don't ring you as often as you would like, it's because I'm either too bloody busy or too exhausted, and most likely both. I have been up for thirty-six hours straight trying to resolve the latest crisis. I hope to get at least a few hours sleep before my next meeting. I hate to say this Elizabeth, but I really feel that you're beginning to nag, and that's something I could well do without."

"Nagging you? I'm only trying to understand, and right now I'm afraid I don't understand at all, and—"

"Elizabeth, I'm going to try explaining this to you one more time very bluntly. I am a Darcy. There is a lot of prestige and honor attached to the name. I'm stepping into my legacy, and as my wife, certain things are expected of *you*. One of those things is that you have to listen to me as your husband, and do as I say because there is a lot at stake here. I want to protect you just as much as I want to protect Pemberley. You must trust me! I don't have the time or the inclination to deal with this pressure you're putting on me. What happened to my logical maths lecturer who prided herself on her ability to think and reason?"

A hushed silence fell between them for several seconds.

"She fell in love with a classics professor." Her voice trembled. "Fitzwilliam...I liked you better when it was just you and me—a man and a woman in love, doing what we wanted, with no corporate business or family to take you away."

"Elizabeth, please! Don't do this."

The conversation continued without resolution. Finally, after a long silence with both of them emotionally shattered, Fitzwilliam spoke. "Elizabeth, it's nearly three o'clock in the morning. We've being talking for hours. I have to be at the office in five hours, and before leaving, I have to finish reading this report. It's over seventy pages long and full of technical jargon that I not only have to read, but actually understand! This conversation is getting us nowhere, and I really don't know what else to say. I love you, Elizabeth, but you must do as I say and stay where you are. I must go."

As the phone line went dead, pain like a sharp knife shot through Elizabeth's heart, causing the tears she'd been holding back to finally spill. Her husband was changing. He had always told her how much his heritage meant to him, but now she wondered if it meant more than she did. All she wanted was to be with him, for him to hold her like he used to. What had happened to her? Maybe it was time to think about it.

...Understand? Yes...yes, I believe I do, Fitzwilliam...I believe I do. I'm losing you!

Once again a wave of nausea engulfed Elizabeth as she raced to the bathroom, crying bitterly.

The next day, Fitzwilliam met with his personal advisors in his office. Twisting his signet ring as he paced the floor, frustration was evident in his gaunt features. Fatigue had set in from the long hours of grinding and demanding work, poring over document after document, but this did not concern him at the moment. It was his wife that occupied his thoughts. Their last phone call, or rather fight, had unnerved him. Should he send for her or shouldn't he? He wanted to, but... He cast a quick glance at his personal advisors seated in his office waiting for him to speak. His mind was made up.

"I'm going to send for my wife. I'll have her secretly whisked away...to Pemberley Estate. Yes, that's what'll do." Seeing the look on their faces, he pleaded, "I can't leave her there."

"**NO!**" shouted Blakely. "You can't give in. If you bring her here, the tabloids will tear her to bits. The stories have died down for now, and so far the mainstream media has not focused on your personal life to amount to much, but that will change if she enters the country and is discovered." Blakely paused. "If you think things are strained now, just wait until the press has finished with the both of you. Fitzwilliam, do you really think you can clandestinely whisk her away just like that?" He snapped his fingers. "And to a place where she knows no one? It will never do."

Fitzwilliam threw his hands up in despair. "Gordon, then what am I to do? This is tearing us apart. It can't be any worse than what we're already going through. Last night we had one of the bitterest arguments I've ever had. She's painfully unhappy, and that knowledge is killing me, yet I feel helpless to do anything about it."

Hilda shook her head. "I understand what you're saying, but you must be practical. Bringing her here would not help matters. What supporters you do have could very well withdraw their backing, not to mention the impact it would have on your upcoming meeting with the Pemberley Five. Such a move would be bound to have unwelcome consequences. If you fail to gain their support, Pemberley will fall from Darcy control. Do you want to be known as the Darcy who failed to fulfill his obligations?"

Twisting his ring as he continued to walk, he responded, "Of course not, but it's more difficult that you can imagine trying to hold on to two equally important things."

"It is, but you must think of her and any children you may have. If you love her, you'll keep her well out of this," Metcalfe said. "You know I'm telling you the truth. You have an obligation and a duty. If she can't understand that, well—"

"Thomas is right. We can't let the family legacy slip though our fingers. You're the heir and the responsibility falls on your shoulders, not mine. The coalition doesn't take me seriously, but they do respect *you*. If you show any sign of weakness or vulnerability, we very well could lose all that we've worked so hard to build," David added, crossing his arms over his chest.

Looking from one advisor to the other, Fitzwilliam sank into his chair and ran his fingers through his hair. He knew what he had to do. Glancing up, he said, "I know all of you are right. I just hope she'll see it that way. Our marriage is suffering. I only hope it will be able to survive."

One week later

As Fitzwilliam sat in his office poring over the last minute report his uncle had submitted concerning Brit Am, he caught sight out of the corner of his eye of two white doves perched on the window ledge outside his office. As he turned to get a better look, the birds took flight. An ominous feeling swept over him as he watched them leave. He glanced from the window to his family ring as he shook his head and shrugged. Taking a deep breath, he turned back to Harvey's report. He had fifteen minutes before the next meeting began, a meeting that would either make or break his chances to win control of Pemberley. He was running out of time. He had to secure their support or all would be lost. The gravity of the moment weighed heavily on him. One last cursory look out his window, and he gathered the report along with the other relevant papers and left for his meeting.

Fitzwilliam entered the boardroom and glanced around at those assembled as he took his seat. This was it…make or break. With no time left to secure any more money should he fail in his objective, he had to win over at least three of these men.

David, Georgiana, Hilda, Harvey, William, Benson, Richard, Thomas Metcalfe and Gordon Blakely were all present. Fitzwilliam closely observed the five men seated around the table while Thomas and Harvey talked.

John Jacob Anderson, a wealthy investor from Boston, Massachusetts, owned a considerable amount of Pemberley shares. A pious man of Puritan descent with old English ancestral ties, Fitzwilliam knew Anderson would not readily sanction David's behavior on moral grounds. Then there was Edward McPherson, a wealthy Scotsman whom his father had helped in his whiskey venture many years ago. Next to McPherson sat George W. Ashcroft, a Wall Street venture capitalist whom George helped launch early in his career. They had been mates at Oxford. Richard B. Bennington, a wealthy Englishman and close personal friend of his father's, was seated next to Ashcroft. And finally, there was Jonathan W. Marlow, another Englishman who owned Marlow Technologies. George had underwritten Marlow in the 80s, launching him into the international marketplace. All looked at Fitzwilliam as they gathered their copies of the agenda and waited for him to begin.

Fitzwilliam cleared his throat. "Gentlemen, I'd like to thank you for coming. I won't bore you with formalities. All of you know why I have invited you here, so let's get to the point. In short, I would like to have your support." Fitzwilliam paused for a second and shook his head. "No, I need your support. I need it in order to keep Pemberley within the Darcy family. You have always had the greatest regard for my father, and I hope you will give me the same consideration. As we begin this meeting, I am open to any questions you might have."

Marlow, speaking for the group, began. "Fitzwilliam, it's not a question of our friendship or loyalty to you or your father. It's a question of leadership. You have to give us a reason to believe that you are capable of doing the job and not simply relying on your family name. We all know full well that George wanted you to hold the position of Chairman of the Board and CEO, but we are not sure whether you could or would do the job properly. We are also very concerned about your lack of business experience. You have loyalty, honesty, integrity, and strength of character, but do you have what it takes to deliver? Can you successfully lead this company into the next decade and turn a profit for the shareholders? That's what we are not sure of. The corporation is in decline. Your open disagreements with your father, such as your marriage to an American, have hurt you, yes, but what is far worse is your apparent total disregard for your duty to not only your father and family name, but to this company. You are not well perceived by the public—in fact, from the average investor all the way up people generally have a very low opinion of you. You are seen as only caring about your own personal gratification rather than being dedicated to the company."

Fitzwilliam straightened himself in his seat. "Gentlemen, I've already said this to my staff, but I will reiterate it here. Failure is *not* an option for me! Just because I chose to pursue a teaching career doesn't mean that I didn't have any interest in the family business. It is quite the contrary, and I really regret not having been here when my father was ill. Believe me, had I known about his illness, I would have returned. As to my lack of business experience, you are correct. I do lack experience, but I can assure you that my staff and advisers do not. I've been working around the clock, reading and absorbing as much as possible, and I have the best people available to answer any questions that I might have. I believe I've come up to speed very rapidly. I also have the advantage of having one of the best financial and business advisors in the world, Hilda Vanderburgh."

His aunt smiled and nodded.

The five gentlemen mumbled among themselves before Ashcroft spoke up. "That's all well and good, but what about your plans for the future. Pemberley is falling behind in the global market. Dividends paid out last year were dismal! What do you plan to do to boost profits and increase income for the shareholders?"

Fitzwilliam took a deep breath and looked at each one in turn with a slight smile. "I'm glad you asked that. I know the return is poor. I have been studying the situation at great length, and I have a plan to revamp the corporation and reverse the downward spiral. Let us begin with our biggest asset—Brit Am."

Fitzwilliam turned in his seat and flipped a chart cover to reveal a map. "I'll give you a general idea on our proposal for our petroleum division, including our strategy for drilling in the North Sea." He paused to point to an area on the map between Britain and Norway. "We have three new oil fields in this area consisting of six platforms that should go into production by the winter of next year, increasing our output by thirty-seven percent. With these new facilities online, next year's North Sea oil production will exceed our standard output at any given time during the past ten years, bringing our production up to 1.5 million barrels of oil per day. Along with the two million cubic meters of natural gas, which are also contained there, that is a substantial increase. This is a project which I am aggressively pushing forward as our oil fields in Saudi Arabia, due both to the volatility in the Middle East and field maturity, are not doing quite as well as they once did, but the North Sea will more than make up for it.

"Also we have plans and designs for bringing both our British and American refineries more up-to-date with the latest state-of-the-art technologies to improve efficiency." Glancing up, Fitzwilliam asked, "Are there any questions so far?"

"Yes," Ashcroft said, "what about the fields in Alaska? What do you propose to do there, and tell me about your plans for the wind farms?"

"In Alaska, we will close the remaining six wells and cut our losses. William has thoroughly researched that aspect, and concluded that it's far more cost-effective to shut them down than to repair the leaks. As to the wind farms here, we're going to dump those plans and go with the farms in the United States. The U.S. government's tax shelter incentives for clean energy provide a very lucrative opportunity for energy revenues. We stand to make $20 billion if we go that route." Fitzwilliam paused momentarily to gauge the executives' reactions. Pleased in what he saw, he continued. "Now, gentlemen, that's a brief overview. Harvey and his son, William, will give you the details."

"So, Harvey," Edward McPherson interrupted with a smile as he glanced at Harvey Darcy. "You are now taking a role in Pemberley interests. Your father would be very pleased. Andrew always wanted you to take an active part in Pemberley, and I am delighted to see you on board as well. I look forward to hearing your proposal."

"Edward, I think you will not be disappointed," Harvey said with a smile.

McPherson turned back to Fitzwilliam. "Now what about the rest of the divisions? What are your plans for Darcy Enterprises and the technology sectors? In particular, I want to know about Darcy Technologies, especially the semiconductor division."

Fitzwilliam picked up his pencil and checked off an item on his list, and then looked from one to the other with confidence. "I have positive news in both of those business units. Benson Darcy has thoroughly researched our holdings in the technology sectors and has a full report. He will brief you on our plans there, especially for our semiconductor manufacturing facilities in California and Singapore, and David will give you our report on Darcy Enterprises."

"Darcy Enterprises is of special interest to me since I had a part in building it to its present state," Richard Bennington said. "Also, I want to know the health of the publishing subdivisions. So I will require a full disclosure in that field as well."

"Well, I would be glad to give you a brief overview on both." Fitzwilliam paused, knowing Darcy Enterprises was dear to the older man's heart, he treaded lightly. "Let us begin with Darcy Enterprises. Those operations will continue, but we also need to diversify. My father was beginning to explore Asia, particularly China, for some of our manufacturing needs. David was there for about a month this year, looking into those prospects. He will give you an assessment of Darcy Enterprises together with his plans for growth in that segment. Georgiana will do the same for Darcy & Winthrop Publishing, and I will fill you in on anything else you might like to know. Now gentlemen, that is a brief summary of our plans. We will discuss it in detail, beginning with David," Fitzwilliam said with a nod to his brother, but before David could begin, he was interrupted.

"Ah yes, David. That brings us to yet another cause for concern—your self-*destructive* tendencies," Anderson said, looking David directly in the eye. "What do you have to say in reply to all the apprehensions we have about your lifestyle? It would seem that not a week goes by without some outrageous newspaper report about your drunken debaucheries. Are we to expect an obituary in the near future… death as a result of AIDS?"

David's eyes narrowed ominously, but as usual, he kept his composure. Placing his report on the table, he looked from one to the other. "Gentlemen, I won't deny being guilty of some of the things you allude to. What good would it do? They are true—but it's not part of my normal day-to-day life. You should also take note that I haven't appeared in the tabloids in an unseemly fashion in over six months. Everything you've read is stale news, and *no*, I won't be making an early exit due to AIDS, although I *do* appreciate your concern for my welfare." His voice dripped sarcasm. "Judge me, if you will, by my business record, if you judge me at all. The highest profit margin in the entire corporation has come under my leadership."

As if nothing was amiss, David picked up the report he'd put together. But, as he was about to begin, Mrs. Foulkes interrupted the meeting. "Mr. Darcy, I'm very sorry to bother you, sir, but Mrs. Darcy is on the phone."

Fitzwilliam looked up from his notes in astonishment, glaring at his administrative assistant. His face darkened with a combination of shock and anger. "Tell Mrs. Darcy that I'm in a very important meeting. Betty, you know better than to interrupt us."

"Yes, sir, I do, but sir…she's crying."

Fitzwilliam let out an exasperated breath. "Excuse me, gentlemen, I have to take this call, privately."

Once Fitzwilliam was out of sight, the board members began mumbling. "What is the meaning of this, Thomas? Can't he even run his own household without his wife interrupting a business meeting?" Anderson asked.

"This is absurd! Absolutely unheard of," Marlow said.

"Does the man kowtow to a woman?" Bennington asked.

"This is incomprehensible!" exclaimed McPherson.

All five mumbled and complained while Thomas raised an eyebrow and shook his head as he glanced towards the door, but it was Hilda who made the excuses. "Gentlemen, Fitzwilliam's wife is an American, and I'm afraid she's not accustomed to her husband's status, but I assure you he can handle his personal life, and I'll be his chief advisor on the conduct of his business activities. He has my backing *and* my money. You would be wise to follow suit." She nodded.

Fitzwilliam exited the boardroom and stalked towards his office, fuming silently with every step he took. Furious with his wife when he finally reached his phone, he snapped into the receiver. "Elizabeth, what is the meaning of this. I'm in a very important meeting with my advisors and top executives. Do you realize what it looks like having to leave a crucial meeting to take a personal call from my *wife*?"

"Fitzwilliam, I need you. You haven't called me back in days. I'm worried…worried about us, and—"

"Elizabeth," he interrupted, "listen to me and pay heed. I'm stretched as thin as a man can stretch without snapping. I'm fighting for our future, and I need you to be my wife—to support me. Instead, you're pulling me down, tearing me apart. I don't know how much more of this I can take. I'll call you tonight." He hung up.

"But Fitzwilliam," she whispered into the dial tone, "I'm pregnant…" A single tear slid down her check. Still clutching the dead phone in her hand, Elizabeth made a resolution. Tired of the arguing that resulted every time she called, she determined she would not tell him she was carrying his child. She would not use a child to hold a man who no longer cared. Elizabeth stomped her foot and fell onto their bed, crying herself to sleep.

That night, her dreams were filled with what used to be before he went to London only to change into the nightmare their life had now become. She dreamed he came, but not for her, but rather to take her child away. She awoke in a cold sweat.

The meeting with the Pemberley Five at an end, the Darcy brothers had overcome a major hurdle. After much discussion and with the evident support of Hilda Vanderburgh and Harvey Darcy, the group in its entirety decided to pledge their support to the brothers, but there were many details yet to be resolved.

With Hilda's support and that of the majority of the board of directors, it was now certain that Pemberley, PLC would remain firmly under Fitzwilliam and David Darcy's control, and through the process, Fitzwilliam had gained a newfound appreciation and respect for his aunt. He now trusted her implicitly.

Chapter Thirty-nine

... I've always loved you—never forget that...

Coming out of his first official Pemberley, PLC Board of Directors meeting, Fitzwilliam was elated. Preliminary voting results from the company's emergency general meeting showed that shareholders would reelect Fitzwilliam Darcy and his brother, David, overwhelmingly. At the gathering, shareholders had lined up before microphones to express their support for the Darcy Brothers. Second quarter earnings were projected to be up, and third quarter profits looked promising. The vote was an overpowering vote of confidence. The opposition was crushed.

"We've made it! It's finally over," Georgiana exclaimed as she hugged her brothers.

"Yes, we made it. I'm officially CEO and Chairman of the Board. David is Vice Chairman and President of Darcy Enterprises, and *you*, little Sister, are President of Darcy & Winthrop Publishing of London. We still have a lot to do, but the battle is over. Next week we'll meet again and decide on further offices, but for the time being, let's go to dinner and celebrate. Tonight, I will sleep in my own bed at Darcy House. How about you, David?" he asked, turning to his brother. "Are you coming home tonight, or do you have a hot date with whomever it is that's been ringing you?"

"No." David grinned. "I don't have a date, and believe it or not, I have no plans for any excursions in the near future. But I am staying here for the rest of the week. Father left me a set of journals which I haven't had time to read. I think after dinner, I will burrow away with a good bottle of wine and read."

Fitzwilliam laughed as they rounded the corner to his office. "You do that. Hilda and I have some business to discuss, and then I will meet you at Ledbury's at seven. Finally, I have some good news to share with Elizabeth. I can't wait tell her."

"Congratulations, Fitzwilliam," Hilda said catching up with them. "Your position is secure. Next week, you can begin reorganizing the London offices. What do you plan to do with your uncle? His loan is due in a few weeks."

"I've given that a lot of thought. Because of Samantha, I plan to allow him whatever allotted time he needs to repay, but I will insist he resign all of his offices, including his board position. If he, Stanley, and Wesley refuse, they will be voted out and fired. They are finished with Pemberley," he flatly stated. "That goes for my cousins, too. They'll receive their severance salary as per the by-laws, but I cannot and will not allow them to stay. It's a promise I made to myself... and my father," he murmured. "Come, Hilda, I need to talk with you. David," he said turning to his brother, "I will see you later, and Georgiana, I'll collect you in thirty minutes. We'll return to Darcy House to prepare for dinner."

"I'll be waiting," Georgiana said, continuing down the hall to her office.

Entering Fitzwilliam's office, Hilda took a seat while he walked over to the drinks cabinet and took out a decanter of port. Pouring two glasses, he handed one to his aunt. "Hilda, I can't tell you how relieved I am that this is finally over. I'll ring Elizabeth tonight and tell her the good news. I know she'll be relieved, too. Things have been tough for her, and now she can finally come home. I've missed her so much."

Hilda eyed her nephew closely. "Fitzwilliam, you and Mrs. Darcy are not getting along, are you?"

He snorted. "That's an understatement." Taking a seat behind his desk, he continued. "I've been thinking a lot about us. I know what you and the others have said, but I should never have left her in Tennessee. Our relationship has suffered greatly over this."

"You could not have brought her here. I fear you would not have been able to persuade the majority of the board if she had accompanied you."

"I know, Aunt, I know," Fitzwilliam said as he ran his hand over his face. "There was so much working against us wasn't there?"

"Yes, I'm afraid there was." Hilda sighed. "Her family is very different from yours. Your father was highly respected throughout all of Britain and not only for his business skills. Your father knew how to dress his public image. It makes a strong contrast against your wife's family. You did the right thing by leaving her in Tennessee."

"Yes, Elizabeth and I are from two different worlds. I do understand that, but she didn't. However, now that this is over, I plan to put it all behind us as quickly as possible. I will introduce her to society, and God help the man or woman who harms her in any way."

Sipping her wine, Hilda responded, "Your father has set the stage for her not to be accepted, and you very well may have a difficult time receiving invitations to social functions because of it. Your wife is tainted by negative publicity, and it **will** affect you."

"Oh, I'm very well aware that it was my father that has caused this. I'm also well aware of how things work with the public perception of my image, the press, and what it all means, but I'll **not** have my wife disrespected. I have the money and the means to do something about it, and you can be assured that I will do just that. No one will dare to say anything publicly. I cannot control what they might think or even what they say outside of my presence, but it had better not be said in front of me or her."

"That's all well and good, but what are you going to do about your wife?"

"What do you mean what am I going to do? I am going to send for her and bring her to London."

Hilda eyes narrowed. "Has it occurred to you that she may not want to come? I could not have helped but to noticed how you were arguing. You had better be sure she feels as you do."

"Aunt," he chortled, "I know my wife. She may not understand what I've been through or all it has involved, but she will come. She is my wife, and we love each other. I'm going to ring her tonight and make the arrangements. I want you and a team of advisors to go to Tennessee. Tie up all loose ends and bring her home. I'll send a letter explaining everything. She'll come. She loves me. That's the one thing I'm sure of."

Hilda smiled. "I will do as you say. As it was with your father, your best interest is my primary concern." She lifted her glass and arched a brow.

While they were talking, Mrs. Foulkes interrupted them. "Mr. Darcy, Mr. Metcalfe has just called. He needs to see you as soon as possible."

"Tell him I'll be right there, Betty." Turning to Hilda, he said, "Excuse me, Aunt. This will only take a minute."

"Don't bother with me. I need to return to my office. I'll see you at dinner," she said as he left the office.

Finally alone in her nephew's office, Hilda seized the opportunity she'd been waiting for. Slipping over to his desk, she carefully opened his middle drawer, being cautious so as not to disturb the contents. After one quick glance at the partially closed door, she silently lifted several sheets of his personal stationary with his signature in place from the drawer. With the stationary safely secured in her legal binder, she left his office with a smile.

Later that evening before dinner, Hilda met with her team of advisors.

"Jones, I want you to draw up divorce arrangement papers for Fitzwilliam and his wife. Make a settlement for £7 million contingent on her not pursuing any other monetary claims against him. I want no loopholes. Should she refuse the payment, make the contract such that she cannot come back later demanding money."

"I will do as you say, Ms. Vanderburgh, but you cannot force her to agree. If she does not choose to do so, it will all be useless."

"Leave it to me, Jones. She will agree." Hilda nodded. "The grandson of an earl should not be married to someone of lesser society, and I plan to do something about it."

At midnight, London time, Fitzwilliam called Elizabeth. "Darling, it's over. I've secured the company. It's official. I'm now in complete control." He leaned back on his bed, resting comfortably against the soft pillows. "I am firmly CEO and Chairman with no threat hanging over us. I'm sending for you next week. My Aunt Hilda will come along with two advisors."

She hesitated for several seconds. "I'm not sure I will be coming to London. Too much has occurred between us. I'm not so sure I would be happy there."

Rising up from his bed, he declared, "Elizabeth, what are you saying?! You can't mean that. You're my wife. Your place is here with me."

"Is it? I'm no longer sure anymore. If you come for me personally, I'll think on it."

"I can't leave, Liz. I have a very important board meeting that I cannot reschedule. It's critical that I remain in London all this week and the next. I have meetings scheduled. For me to leave on an extended visit to America would undermine the hard earned authority I've won." Pausing briefly, he realized she needed reassurance. "You mean everything to me. Have I not told you that?"

"Not lately."

"Elizabeth, I know this has been very hard on you. It's been hard on the both of us, but nothing has changed. Hold on to what we have. You're my world. I love you, Liz, and I need you. I've always loved you—never forget that. Please, come to London. Your place is by my side."

"And what if I don't?"

He couldn't believe what he was hearing. "Oh, you'll come. It's been a long time for both of us, and we need each other. You need me as much as I need you. You'll come."

"You're very confident in yourself, as per usual, and I suppose you're still accustomed to getting your way. It seems you always get your way, be it in business or with me."

"Have we just entered a time warp? I believe we've had this conversation before."

"Yes, yes we have...a long time ago. You always go after what you want, and you're used to getting it. I remember it well. I just wonder if you, as CEO, would pursue a math professor now."

"And you think that I wouldn't?"

"I have no idea. I hardly know you anymore. You've changed."

He heard her choke back tears. Rubbing his brow, he took a deep breath. "Elizabeth, please, that's not fair. Yes, it's true. I've changed, but in essentials, I'm still the same man—the man who loves you—the man who needs you. Come home, Elizabeth. Please…I need you. I want you."

"I don't know. I'll think about it."

"There is nothing to think about. You're my wife, and as my wife your place is here with me. Hilda will be in Tennessee as soon as I can arrange it. I'm going to send a letter with her. It'll explain everything. I communicate better in writing than over the phone. When you are here, I will make it up to you. I will not be able to take off and spend time with you at first, but I will make everything up to you. We'll take a long holiday. Perhaps to Greece or the Virgin Islands. I promise. Have everything ready to go and close the house down in one week. I'll be expecting you."

"It's too little, too late, Fitzwilliam."

"I don't believe that, and neither do you. Have you forgotten what's it's like to be loved—to be held. We need each other, and we love each other." Feeling the weariness finally catching up with him, he said, "I've got to go now and get some much needed rest. I'll see you next week, darling. I love you."

"I love you, too… I really do."

"That's my girl. Goodnight, love."

"Goodnight."

Once they were off the phone, Elizabeth made a pot of tea to sit and think on all that had occurred over the past few months. Being the wife of Dr. Darcy, university professor, had been one thing. They had been so close with their lives together being one of contentment, but what would it be like as the wife of Fitzwilliam A. Darcy, CEO of Pemberley, PLC? It scared her to think about it. She feared she would be very lonely, and now that she was pregnant, she no longer had herself to think about.

An instinctive need to protect her unborn child was beginning to take form in her heart. She would meet with his aunt before deciding anything for certain, and she would also read the letter he promised to send. But in the end, her decision would be made based on logic and what was best for her and her little one.

Chapter Forty

... I have gone from hurt to bitterness and finally to nothingness...

L ater that night after the celebration dinner, David returned to his flat and placed a decanter of port wine on his bedside cabinet. He made himself comfortable as he piled up pillows behind him and opened the first volume of his father's journals. Through the classically laid pages of his father's leather-bound journal, he was transported back in time to Pemberley when his father had been a young adult. David had to laugh aloud as his father described how he and Harvey were so rambunctious that their mother constantly complained to their father. *"Andrew, if you don't rein them in, these boys will be the death of me yet."* David sighed. He could not remember either of his grandparents. Andrew and Estelle Darcy had died when he was an infant.

Turning the page, he continued reading. He read of laughter, of boyhood pranks played on Harvey by his father and their sister, Samantha, and about his father catching Samantha in the hayloft with her boyfriend. George beat the poor chap to a blood-spattered pulp, having intervened just in time to save his sister's virtue.

David sipped his port as he turned the pages, learning how close George and Harvey had been and how both had always been protective of their sister. *Strange... it sounds like Fitzwilliam and me with Georgiana. If I'd caught her when she was sixteen in a hayloft with some creep, I would have beaten him to a bloody pulp, too.*

Reading on, halfway through the first volume, David began to notice a change. Harvey had brought his girlfriend home for a family dinner. David turned the page in anticipation. Was it his Aunt Susan? No! Shocked, he had to reread the passage again. Harvey had brought the beautiful Anne Winthrop home to meet his family. *...My mother! My uncle went out with my mother. I don't believe this.*

Continuing, he read his father's words. *"When Anne walked through the door, my heart leapt into my throat. I have never seen a more beautiful or captivating woman. I engaged her in conversation whilst Harvey and father discussed his plans for the future. Anne is as intelligent as she is beautiful. She loves gardening, especially roses, and she loves Renaissance literature. Her favorite poet is Sir Philip Sydney, and she loves Voltaire. Of all the French philosophers, trust her to like him best. Her favorite is La Henriade. I found that strange, as it is also a favorite of mine. Harvey has made a very fortunate choice. I hope he understands that, for had I met her first, I would do everything in my power to make her my wife. Is there such a thing as love at first sight? There must be, for I find myself in love with her."*

David read on, turning page after page. By now dawn was drawing nigh, yet he couldn't bring himself to stop. His Uncle Harvey had been madly in love with his mother while his father had sat back quietly brooding over her—wanting her—silently loving her. He had even composed poetry for her, speaking words to himself in the privacy of his room that he dared not voice anywhere else.

David inhaled sharply at the next lines. *"Let it be said that I am a fool. I love her when I know I shouldn't. She is engaged to my brother, and it's tearing me apart to watch them when they think I cannot see. This poem is for you, Anne, but you will never read it. Tonight I'll burn it over a candle whilst I tell the quiet of my room that I*

M.K. Baxley

love you. It's an agonizing pain, knowing that I love you, but you can never be mine. Anne... Anne... Anne...You don't even know I exist."

David was greatly surprised by his father's words and his reaction to his mother.

...My father writing poetry! Who would have imagined that? I've never read anything quite as beautiful or sentimental. Father, you should have been a poet.

As dawn approached, David decided that since he had worked relentlessly over the past few months, he deserved the day off—and tomorrow, too, if he wanted it. He'd become so engrossed in his father's story that he knew he would not be able to put it down until he had discovered all there was to know.

He read on, learning that even though his father had gone out with many women and was then keeping a lover, he was hopelessly in love with Anne, but out of respect for his brother, he would never show it. Then one day the unthinkable occurred. After three years of being virtually inseparable, Harvey broke off his engagement just before he graduated and then went on a summer holiday to Italy and the South of France. Anne was devastated, whereas glimmers of hope flickered in George's heart.

David shook his head, greatly disturbed by what he was reading. His grandparents had been so bitterly upset by their younger son's behavior that they had asked George to console Anne, which he gladly did. His heart soared at the chance to take her to dinner, the theatre, dancing, a concert, or anywhere she would go with him. Soon they were a couple, and the usually reserved George Darcy wore a smile everywhere they were seen. Anne's affections had transferred from the younger brother to the older, or so it seemed.

On the day Anne accepted his proposal, George wrote, *"It is the happiest day of my life. Anne is the center of my world."* But when Harvey returned in desperation to reclaim Anne, the two brothers came to blows. The resulting confrontation was so heated that Andrew and two servants had difficulty separating them. The close bond that had existed between the brothers was shattered—replaced with raw hatred. Harvey pleaded with Anne to return to him, but she flatly refused. George and Anne were married within the month.

Overwhelmed by what he had read, David closed the book and fell back against the soft pillows, utterly exhausted and emotionally spent. Intending to close his eyes briefly, he soon fell into a restless sleep, tossing and turning. He slept for hours before being awakened by the raucous clamor of the alarm clock on his bedside cabinet. Reaching over to silence the noise, he rubbed his weary eyes. *...I'll take a shower and go out for breakfast. Then I'll phone in until further notice. I must carry on reading until I finish these.*

Returning to his flat from breakfast, David again settled himself in the center of his rumpled bed. He'd left word with the maid service that he was not to be disturbed. With a pot of freshly made coffee and a cup in his hand, he opened volume two and began reading. The wedding night had been a disaster. Anne had pushed George away, crying, leaving him to wonder if she might be a virgin. When he questioned her, she told him that was not the case. However, she did reassure him that there had been no one other than his brother. But this did nothing to console him. Instead, it left him feeling vulnerable.

Three days passed before she consented to consummate their marriage, and though he was as gentle and loving as he could be, he knew he had failed to touch her heart. As he lay there holding her close, he realized that he had made a terrible mistake.

It broke his heart. She didn't love him—and yet she had married him. Had it been to spite his brother? That was a disquieting thought. It was one thing to lose his brother over Anne, but not to have her love in return pricked his conscience. While David read his father's words, his heart ached as he began to understand his father's sorrow. *"If I am to survive this, I have to build up my defenses. I've allowed her to get inside of me. I've given her a piece of my soul, and she treats it as if it were nothing. I've got to get away from the pain she drives into the heart of me."*

They'd spent that year in London, socializing as George began taking over his father's responsibilities while Estelle and Andrew retired to Pemberley. Everyone who saw George and Anne together thought they were the perfect couple, and people often commented as much. They appeared to be very much in love, but that was not the case. They lived in separate bedrooms, barely speaking. And Harvey was still not speaking to George and would have nothing to do with Pemberley, PLC. Instead, he chose a career in medicine. The hatred between the brothers intensified.

Then came New Year's Eve, and George and Anne were to host the most magnificent ball of the evening. The champagne flowed freely, and everyone present was having an excellent time. One passage in particular arrested David's attention as he softly read aloud.

"That night Anne had more to drink than usual, making her especially loving and inviting. It was the first time she actually seduced me. At last, I thought there was yet hope for our marriage, but then, at the height of one of our most passionate moments, she cried out my brother's name. At first I was stunned as we climaxed together. She kissed me wildly, and then she called me Harvey—not once, but repeatedly. Stricken with grief, I pushed her away. Getting up from the bed, I told her how much she sickened me as I took my clothes and retreated to the adjoining room. Days passed before I would even look at her, although she did try to apologize on numerous occasions."

David winced at the lines that followed. *"Something within me died that night. People tell me that love is the greatest of all the emotions—that it is beautiful. I am here to tell them that is not true. It's a lie. Love wounds. It scars and leaves its mark. It's distressing how I have let it work its way inside of me, eating and gnawing away at my heart. It hurts—and not just in the conscious thoughts, either, but deep down inside of me, like a shard of glass working its way into my soul, cutting and slicing, slowly killing me. I toss and turn all night long. Sleep evades me. The pain is unbearable, but at least the pain tells me I'm still alive, and I can deal with that. I am not afraid of pain. God help **me** for I am **not** a weak man."*

David swept the book away and sat up straight, shouting out loud, "Mother, how could you? How could you marry a man you didn't love? A man whom you knew was in love with you? You came between Father and Uncle Harvey and you destroyed their relationship, not to mention what you did to Father. Had you done that to me, I would have hated you. Like my father before me, I am no fool. No woman will ever do that to me. *No* woman."

Unable to stop, David picked up the book and continued reading. Two months after New Years, Anne called to tell George she was pregnant. Her joy was so intense, that he couldn't help but forgive her, and once again, they were back together. Anne was making an effort to save their marriage now that she was pregnant. The months that followed were to be among the happiest days of his father's life as they went about preparing for Fitzwilliam's birth. They decorated the nurseries both at Darcy House and Pemberley, laughing, cuddling, and making love almost daily. George wrote, *"Perhaps we will make it. Anne is happy. I am happy. All is well."*

Fitzwilliam was born four weeks early, three days after George's birthday, frightening everyone, and though small, he was pronounced healthy. Estelle was elated and Andrew couldn't have been prouder, but the happiest person of all was George when he held his newborn son for the first time. George recorded it as being the *second* happiest day of his life, but as David read on, he saw the clouds once again begin to loom over their marriage.

After Fitzwilliam's birth, Anne withdrew again, protesting that all her time was taken up by her tiny son, whom she doted on. George pleaded with Anne to stay with him in London, but she refused, claiming the country air suited her better than London's dreary fogs.

Time passed and George's father had begun to notice that something was wrong and felt it was time he stepped in. David read on.

"My father rang me Thursday afternoon and told me I should come home immediately and that it would be wise to take my wife back to London. I have tried repeatedly to get Anne to come to London with me. We have argued over it many times. I come home every weekend, and every Monday it is the same. She refuses to accompany me. Now I know why. My father has informed me that my brother is spending far too much time with my wife, and that he and Harvey have had quite a row about it. I left for Pemberley as soon as we hung up, intending to stay for a week, thinking I would play with my son and try once more to convince Anne to return to London with me.

"When I walked into the drawing room, anticipating the joy of holding Fitzwilliam, I was greeted with the sight of my brother holding my son whilst my wife looked upon my brother lovingly. I became furious as I stalked across the room, ripping my son from Harvey's arms and handing him to Anne. Once again Harvey and I found ourselves in a fierce fight. This time it took four men to separate us, but not before the room had been destroyed.

"All weekend long Anne tried to console me, begging and pleading with me, telling me it was not what it seemed, until I finally relented. She knows my weaknesses, and she knew how to exploit them. After my anger had abated, I found myself again in her bed making love much of Saturday night and into Sunday morning. In that respect, it was a good weekend, but by Sunday, I was so ashamed of my behavior, that I left for London on Monday without Anne and my son. She begged me to allow her to accompany me, but I remained firm. I left her crying under the shade of the portico. Why I didn't allow her to come, I cannot say. I suppose I wanted to be alone, or perhaps my pride still stung from seeing my brother holding my son as if he were his own. Though he and Anne deny it, I know what I saw. Harvey has Anne's heart. Must he also have my son? Once again my heart hardened at the thought of Anne giving her body to me whilst her heart belongs to my brother. I will not allow her to take me hostage again, eating away at my soul, leaving me to darkness. Some fools think of love as blissful happiness. I laugh at the irony. The loneliness of unrequited love is slowly killing me."

David got up and poured himself another cup of coffee. This story was not what he had expected. It was his mother, not his father, who had entered into a loveless marriage. Returning, he picked up the book and continued to read. Two months had passed.

"I received a call from Anne today, telling me she's pregnant again. She begged me to come home and bring her back to London, but I declined, telling her it is a little too late for that. When I had wanted her with me, she had refused. Now it was I who refused her. She cried all the harder, but I was unmoved. I remember well what I said to her, for I shall never forget it. It was meant to deliberately hurt her, just as she had hurt me. I asked her whose bastard was it, my brother's or the stable boy's. I took perverse pleasure in her pain when she burst into tears. I laughed and hung up on

her."

David threw the volume aside, cursing as he picked up his coffee. Sipping the lukewarm drink until it was gone, he set the cup aside and glanced over at the abandoned journal. *...Well, that's how I came into being. Disturbing at it is, I might as well read about it.* He picked it up and turned the page.

"By the weekend, I relented to my mother's pleas and went home to Pemberley and to my wife. When I walked through the door, Anne flew into my arms, grabbing me and holding me tight. Part of me wanted to fold her into my arms and hold and kiss her, but instead, I peeled her off of me and pushed her aside, telling her not to touch me. I cannot stand the way she thinks she can worm her way back into my life with another child. I was cold and indifferent. Not even the look of pain in her eyes moved me. I wanted—no needed a second child—a son, and yet I don't want this child. God help me. I don't!"

David looked up from the book furious. "You bastard! That was *me* she was carrying—*me*—your son! Couldn't you see she was reaching out for you? " David raged out loud. "I've got to get some lunch and a couple of packets of cigarettes, and some whiskey. I can't take this."

Getting up from the bed, he went downstairs to the company cafeteria for lunch and then down the street to the local off-license for what he needed. Returning to his flat, he poured himself a stiff drink and put the cigarettes on the bedside cabinet. Once again, he piled up his pillows and picked up Volume Three. Reading about his birth upset him all the more. He, too, had been premature, but his birth had not been the joyous occasion his brother's had been, although his father had been proud nonetheless. However, it was his mother's reaction that most caught his attention and probably explained the close bond between them. He was the joy of her life.

His father had left a few days after she had come home from the hospital. Anne had insisted on having both her boys in bed with her, telling Grams that if she could not have her husband, then at least she had her sons. She had not nursed Fitzwilliam, but she did nurse David. Estelle later related the story to George, hoping to soften his heart towards his wife, but he had remained unmoved.

David slammed the book shut and threw it across the room. "Damn you! *Damn* both of you!" he screamed.

Downing his glass of whiskey, he lit up a cigarette, silently incensed. "How could the two of you do this? Mother, how could you marry the brother of the man you loved? Why didn't you marry Uncle Harvey? Why did you destroy my father? And *you*, Father? How could you have treated her like that? It's obvious she wanted to love you and make the marriage work. You cheated us! Couldn't you have forgiven her? Not even for our sakes—for your children? How hard could it have been?"

No sooner had the words slipped from his mouth, than David knew the answer. He and his father were alike—cut from the same cloth. He would have been no different. Reading his father's journal was like seeing into his own dark soul.

After finishing his third cigarette, he walked over to where the book lay and picked it up. Sitting back down in the chair beside his bed, he began reading anew. His grandmother died within a year of his birth, and his grandfather passed the following year. Things only disintegrated further between George and Anne, and when David was two, his father took a mistress, thus permanently breaking away from his wife. David read of the last bitter confrontation between his uncle and father, but this time, they did not resort to physical violence. David knew from recent events that it would be another twenty-six years before they spoke to each other again.

David closed the third volume and picked up the fourth, placing it in his lap. He dreaded learning how Georgiana and his younger brother had come about. Surely it couldn't have been pleasant. Opening the book, he began to read. It was Christmas Eve and his father was coming for the holiday, his first time home since August when they had celebrated his and Fitzwilliam's birthday. Anne and George slept in separate bedrooms, and although they were always polite and civil, they only spoke to each other out of necessity.

"It is so good to be home with my boys. How I have missed them. I picked them both up and swung them around as they giggled and laughed. Fitzwilliam is now nine, and my baby boy is five. I have an American quarter horse for Fitzwilliam and a pony for David. Tomorrow we shall all go riding. Fitzwilliam has insisted that his mother be allowed to join us, so yes, she shall come. Anne looks particularly lovely tonight. I've missed her, but I'll be damned if I will tell her.

"Anne...Anne... my precious Anne. I've tried to fill the hole you've left in my heart with strong drink and a succession of women, but nothing can take your place. All they have done is to fill a transient need—that is all. Oh what I would have given if only you had loved me. I'm sure you would be willing to live in harmony, but if I cannot have your heart, I don't want your body. I feel so helpless. It hurts deep down inside of me.

"Sometime during the night, I dreamt that Anne was in my bed, and that I was making love to her. It was the sweetest, most pleasant dream I'd had in a long time, but when I awoke the next morning, I realized it hadn't been a dream. There Anne lay in my arms with all the evidence that we had made love during the night. Apparently I'd had a little too much Christmas cheer, and I'd found my way into her bed. I apologized profusely, and although she begged me to stay, my pride would not allow it. Slipping out of bed, I returned to my room, consumed with guilt."

George left a note at the end of the entry. *"Two months later, I received another phone call. Anne is once again pregnant. This time I was somewhat kinder. I only told her I hoped she had the little girl she wanted."*

David read on. He had smoked the first packet of cigarettes and now he opened the second. Taking a puff, he began the next entry. *"My youngest son won't speak to me or even look at me, but I can't blame him. David has never liked me. Fitzwilliam is the one who runs to greet me when I come home, followed by his mother. Yes, she always greets me with a hug as if she really means it. She says she loves me, but I don't really care. She laughs whilst her eyes plead silently until she finally asks, 'Can we talk now? I love you, George. I need you.' It's always the same. I tell her not now—someday maybe—but not now. This last weekend was particularly bad. I finally told her I'd had enough! So disgusted was I with her pleadings that I packed my things and walked out before the evening meal, returning to London to spend the weekend with my mistress. If Anne truly cares for me, then that is **her** misfortune. I no longer give a damn. I have gone from hurt to bitterness and finally to nothingness."*

David threw back his head. He dropped the book and cried out loud, "Why, Father? Why didn't you give her a chance? Again, I know the answer, it's because you're just like me." He sighed and picked up the book. The next passage was particularly painful because it rekindled David's memory.

"There is one event that I'd just as soon forget. Yesterday was my fortieth birthday, and Anne did something she has never done before. She drove into London with my sons. I was still in bed when she arrived, and I'll never forget the look on her face when she opened the door to my room, for I was not alone. I thought she was going to faint, or worse, lose the baby when she doubled over as if in pain. I quickly got out of bed and ran to her, naked as I was, but she bolted like a startled deer, and then I caught sight of my ten-year-old son staring at me from the corner of the room. Oh God,

what have I done? The look on my child's face shook me to my very core, and to know that I was the person responsible for having put that look there. Will Fitzwilliam every forgive me? Perhaps I should divorce Anne and let her go. Perhaps we'd both be happier.

"Our daughter was born two weeks later. Anne named her after me. I am extremely touched. She is so beautiful and looks just like her mother, whereas the boys take after me."

Reading to the end of the fourth book, David closed it gently and placed it aside. One more volume, and he would be through. He decided he would go out for dinner and buy more cigarettes. Cecilia had called him on and off over the last three months, and he had taken a great delight in their talks, but for once, he hoped she wouldn't call—not tonight. He didn't feel like talking to anyone—not even to her—especially *not* to her.

Settling back in his bed after dinner, he poured himself another drink and opened the last book. The things recorded there he remembered well. His father had begun the habit of coming home every weekend to spend time with his children. Fitzwilliam was always glad to see him, while David was indifferent, and Georgiana was afraid of him. David read his father's account of those times with pain. George grieved the loss of his family. Georgiana's fear of him tugged at his heartstrings so much that he actually took the summer off to spend time with her. It was the last summer their mother was alive.

For the first time, George seriously attempted a reconciliation with his wife and had even given up his mistress, though not for Anne, but for the sake of his children. There was one stipulation, however, to which Anne agreed. George would share her bed.

After reading that passage, David lay the book down. It was time for yet another cigarette. Damn! Rummaging through the packet, he discovered there were only two left. Another sip of whiskey and one more cigarette, and he'd get back to reading.

Stubbing out the cigarette, David picked up the book, reading about the times he remembered well. George had spent a lot of time fishing and riding with them, and they even swam together down in the cove. That Christmas had been an especially good time—the happiest David had ever had, an old fashioned Victorian Christmas complete with snow and candles and the most beautiful tree he and ever seen. But the best of all was that David remembered his mother had been happy that year for the first time in his memory. However, it was not to last.

By late spring, Anne had become pregnant again, only this time she was older, and there were complications. A lump had been discovered in her right breast. The diagnosis came back as cancer, and she was advised to terminate her pregnancy immediately to begin treatment. Anne, now in her fourth month, refused. The only doctor in the U.K. at the time who specialized in this type of high-risk pregnancy was Harvey Darcy. Both Harvey and George begged Anne to terminate the pregnancy, but she was resolute, telling them she could not in good conscience take the life of her child. She begged Harvey to save the baby even if it meant losing her. He worked feverishly, along with her oncologist, to save both mother and child, but in the end, both were lost.

Meanwhile, the relationship between Harvey and Anne deepened, and George's jealousy again took root. The day Anne died, George was in a drunken stupor, unable even to get out of bed, let alone make his way to the hospital. No one, until now, knew why he had not been there. In reality, the pain of knowing he was losing his wife was so acute that he could not bear to see her for the last time in the presence of his brother. Harvey had cast a shadow over their marriage from the very beginning, but with Anne's death, their tortured love was finally concluded.

M.K. Baxley

David closed the book and lit his last cigarette. He had been told his mother had died from complications of childbirth. Anger flushed his face. ...*Why didn't they tell us the truth!* Finishing his cigarette, he put it out in the ashtray now piled high and picked up the book to resume reading, knowing he had to finish it tonight.

He learned of the intense pain his father had felt at the loss of his mother—a pain he was forced to keep to himself. The only one George had ever been able to share his feelings with had been his father, and he, too, was dead. George Darcy felt more alone than he'd ever felt in his life. He had three children—one who loved him unconditionally, one who shied away, and one who hated him. David winced when he read that last line. Did he really hate his father? No, not really, but he had not loved him either—not until now when he finally understood him.

He continued reading the entries up to a few months before his father's death. He read how disappointed he had been in his sons and of his perceived failure as a father, yet he had been unwilling to admit weakness in any form, convinced that this would help his sons to become the men they were meant to be. George saw their strengths as well as their weaknesses, and on occasion, chose to give them a swift kick in the trousers when he felt they needed it. David chuckled at that remark because it was true.

The last pages concerned the will and a personal note addressed to him. His father had written that he had been greatly disappointed in Fitzwilliam's marriage, but if this was what his son really wanted and it would make him happy, then he would accept it and give his blessing, but first, Mrs. Darcy would have to prove herself. He would meet her in the summer and see for himself. If she proved to be as good as his son claimed and was willing to give him a grandson, then he would love her like a daughter. If she was a fraud, he hoped the will would weed her out, though he knew full well the will would hold no influence over her if she really loved his son and their marriage endured over a lifetime, because Fitzwilliam's vast estate would provide for her. It was merely his way of testing her.

Looking up from the text, David rubbed his bleary eyes and brushed away a tear. "It must be all the smoke. Cigarette smoke always gets to me. This mustn't become a habit." Glancing back at the written page, he read his father's final words. *"David, this set of journals is for you alone. I am ending them here. The ones for Pemberley will be continued until my death, which my doctor informs me is imminent. I have congestive heart failure.*

"David, you may not believe me, but now, in the twilight of my years, I have many regrets of which our relationship is but one. In spite of what you must think of me, I love you, and I loved your mother. You're too much like me for your own good. Don't repeat my mistakes. You have an obligation to duty, honor, and responsibility. Be the man you were born to be."

David shook his head and once again laid the book in his lap. ...*Father, now I understand...and I love you...Dad.* David smiled. His father signed off as he always did when composing a note to his sons.

Your father,

George A. Darcy

...*So the old man **did** have a heart.* David shut the book and then collapsed on his bed. Sleep. He was in desperate need of sleep.

Chapter Forty-one

...Pretty words pretty poison...like a snake in the grass...

Having gone home to Longbourn the previous week, Elizabeth had contemplated her future while spending time at the cabin. She had decided that unless Fitzwilliam's letter contained something truly remarkable or his aunt could give her an excellent reason to come with her, she would not be traveling to England. Her plans where to take a small vacation, perhaps to a mountain cottage in Cherokee, North Carolina or maybe to Hawaii.

She didn't tell her aunts and uncles her plans, but rather told them she was leaving town, letting them think what they would. All she knew for certain was that she needed time away to think before returning for the fall semester, if she returned at all.

Once back from the farm, she sat and waited. Finally, Hilda arrived at 223 Willow Street. Answering the knock at the door, Elizabeth welcomed her and the two men accompanying her.

"You must be Elizabeth, my nephew's wife," Hilda said, eyeing Elizabeth carefully.

"Yes, I am, and you must be his aunt, Hilda Vanderburgh." Elizabeth smiled as she cordially invited them into the house.

"Yes, I am, and this is Thurman Jones and Herbert Cornwall. They are the advisors Fitzwilliam told you about. We will be closing out his accounts and settling his contract with the university." Walking around the house, she remarked, "I see you have packed your belongings. Is the computer equipment packed as well?" she asked, glancing around the library and front parlor.

"Yes, everything is packed as per his directions. All of his things are in this room," she gestured towards the library with one hand, "while mine are upstairs."

"Do you have any questions, Mrs. Darcy, before the men begin loading the truck?"

"Yes, I have several," Elizabeth said with a smile. "Tell me about Pemberley, PLC. What are my husband's responsibilities, and what will be expected of me? Also, could you tell me about Fitzwilliam's father? I would like to understand the late Mr. Darcy. Come with me. I'll fix some tea, and we can talk."

Elizabeth led Hilda into the kitchen where the two women sat and talked while they had refreshments. As the two advisors went about supervising the hired men while they loaded the truck, Hilda detailed for Elizabeth all of the responsibilities expected of the CEO of Pemberley.

"Mrs. Darcy, your husband will be working late hours and probably spending most of his time at the office. They have three executive penthouse suites there. He and David have been living there for the last three months." Hilda waved her hand and shrugged as if this were nothing.

"You will be expected to fulfill your role, too. There will be parties to plan and host for international business colleagues, charity functions to organize, and then there is the Darcy Foundation, which you will be expected to chair. You must become active in London society, behaving as expected for your station. As Mrs. Darcy," Hilda said, bearing down on Elizabeth, "you will not have time for a career. Promoting your husband *is* your job and being your husband's wife *is* your career."

M.K. Baxley

A sharp knife cut through Elizabeth's heart as she sipped her tea. Though she felt anything but calm, her expression remained composed and placid. "Somehow, this is not quite what I envisaged. Fitzwilliam never told me about any of this." Keenly curious, she had to know. "How did the late Mrs. Darcy fare in her role?"

Hilda sat her teacup down and placed her palms on the table. "Unfortunately, my sister never adjusted to her role as Mrs. Darcy. She preferred to stay at Pemberley Estate House in Derbyshire instead of London with her husband as duty required, leaving George to shoulder the responsibilities alone. He had to take a mistress who escorted him in society. My sister was often lonely and felt neglected. She died from cancer, but some say it was cancer brought on by a broken heart."

A quiver of pain shot through Elizabeth as she struggled not to let her feelings show. Swallowing hard, she asked, "And the children? What about Mrs. Darcy's children?"

"Well, of course, my dear." Hilda paused to sip her tea. "Dear sweet Anne was ever devoted to her children, but you must know that when the children reach a certain age they are to attend boarding school for their formal education. My sister and her husband were at odds on a great many things, the children being one of many. She could have performed her role as George's wife, but she chose not to do so. Her misery was of her own making."

Elizabeth cringed. "And what of Mr. Darcy? How did he interact with the children? Did he spend time with them?"

"Poppycock! Children! Mr. Darcy did not have time for the children," Hilda said with cold civility, "but such is often the case with powerful men who shoulder so much responsibility. Important men have no time for children."

...Or wives! Elizabeth shuddered, recoiling from what she heard. It all sounded so unfeeling and sterile. Rubbing her stomach, she grimaced. *...This was not what I want for my child.* Upon hearing all his aunt had to say, Elizabeth made up her mind. She would not be going to London with Ms. Vanderburgh. However, there remained one more thing to consider.

"I believe my husband has given you a letter for me. May I see it please?"

Hilda reached into her purse and produced an envelope which Elizabeth eagerly took. After carefully removed the letter, she looked it over twice. The first half outlined all that he had done since his father's death. Most of this she already knew from his emails and the times they had actually talked about his struggles, but it was the second half that grabbed her attention—and sunk her hopes.

Elizabeth, you know how much I love you, but I have to be truthful with you. It will not be easy when you come. For that, I must prepare you. It'll be many months before things settle down into a somewhat normal routine. I will be spending sixteen to eighteen hours a day at work, probably every day, except Sunday, when we will attend church services at my family parish. As my wife, you will be expected to take an active role in the church, especially with the benevolent endeavors and acts of charity, but that will be explained when you meet the vicar and his wife.

Whilst I am working such long hours, I will stay at my executive flat. You may stay there with me if you choose, or you may prefer Darcy House, which, I'm sure, you will find much more comfortable. I'm sorry to inform you, but there will be little time for me to entertain you or even spend with you. I hate that, but that's how things must be now that I have assumed my place within the family business.

As for your teaching career, I'm afraid we will have to set that aside for the time being. I need you to take over some of the responsibilities at the Darcy Foundation. I will give you the details when you come, but basically, it is our charity and benevolence organization, specifically the AIDS Research Institution and Hospital. It's a massive undertaking and will monopolize much of your time, leaving little for a teaching career. When you arrive, I will give you a tour of Pemberley, and then we can talk more about your new responsibilities.

Elizabeth, I love you. I've told you so many times, but things have changed. I am no longer able to be carefree as I once was. Nor will I be able to take you on holiday as we had planned. I know this is not what you expected, nor is it what I wanted, but it is the reality of my life now. Therefore, it is with great pain that I must say this, but, if for any reason, you choose not to join me, I've left instructions with my aunt. She will explain everything to you. It is my deepest hope and desire that you will join me, soon. I need you and I love you.

With all my love,

Fitzwilliam A. Darcy

Fitzwilliam A. Darcy

CEO Pemberley, PLC

Elizabeth flushed. Her blood ran cold as she folded the letter and placed it back in the envelope. Her eyes narrowed. "Hilda, what does he mean by saying he's left instructions with you should I choose not to accompany you back to England?"

Hilda glanced down at her cup, gently stirring her tea. Returning her gaze to Elizabeth, she asked, "First, I must ask you what your plans are. Do you intend to return with me?"

"When you came, I still had an open mind about it, but after our frank discussion and reading this, I'm not so sure. Frankly, I can't live with his stipulations, and I won't, so you had better tell me what he's referring to in this letter." Elizabeth leaned back in her chair while she held Hilda's gaze.

"Mrs. Darcy, I must be honest with you. I was present for some of your conversations with my nephew, and we discussed this dilemma. If you cannot live with him, then you must set him free so that he can find someone who will be willing to take on the role of Mrs. Darcy and all that it entails. If you will not come with me, then I have come prepared to dissolve the marriage, setting you free to find someone who can meet your expectations." Reaching into her purse one more time, she pulled another envelope out. "I have a contract with me that will allow Fitzwilliam to obtain a quick divorce. He is prepared to offer you £7 million, but you must agree not to pursue him for any more money."

For a split second, she almost fainted as she sat there shocked speechless. Elizabeth inhaled sharply, feeling overwhelmed as she struggled to suppress her hurt and humiliation. She was devastated. Had he been living a lie with her, a daydream outside of Pemberley? Had he been truthful to himself or her about their relationship? Who was the REAL Fitzwilliam Darcy? Was it all about sex? Would he marry her simply to conquer her innocence? She had heard of foreign men marring American wives only to dump them when they returned to their own country. Or worse yet, to take them abroad to a life of misery. Was that what he was doing to her? This cold, sterile delivery was *not* what she had expected, but somehow it didn't surprise her, either.

Her hands trembled as she took the envelope and read its contents. Unable to believe what she saw, she read it again. "So he has anticipated me," she whispered against the lump in her throat. "Somehow, I'm not surprised, but I don't want the money. Our marriage was never about money. I have my own and the ability to support myself. I don't need his. And I won't have it."

She paused, suppressing the urge to cry. Even as the words flowed from her mouth with a brooding sense of finality, they refused to register in her brain, though she'd rather die than show it.

"He can have his freedom. I will let him go. But first I'll call him and give him a good piece of my mind."

Hilda sighed heavily and shook her head. "Mrs. Darcy, I would counsel against that. I'm afraid he is in a series of meetings... critical meeting. You will never get through to him, and if you did, it would only make him angry should you interrupt another meeting. If you value your peace of mind, I strongly advise you to let him go."

Elizabeth tensed. "I see," she said with mortification as she remembered the last time she had interrupted a meeting. "I wouldn't wish to disturb his tranquility or upset his priorities then. I suppose we've said quite enough to each other already, and frankly, I can't take it anymore. I'll write him a letter."

"What will you do, Mrs. Darcy?"

"Don't worry about me," Elizabeth said with feigned confidence. "I have a long over due vacation to take." Maintaining her composure, Elizabeth signed the papers, refused the money, and penned her husband a short, but *sweet*, farewell letter meant to drive her point home.

After Hilda left, Elizabeth became violently ill. Sick and weak from the stress of the previous weeks, the arguments with her husband, and now this, it finally hit her full force. Had he loved her so little that he couldn't even bother to leave his precious company to deliver his news himself? Instead, he had sent his aunt, his advisors—and the shameful offer of money. This outcome was not what she had expected or hoped for. In her heart, she had held onto the hope that he still loved her as he had when he'd last kissed her. Now that that hope had been shattered, bitter anger and disappointment began to settle in as she cried uncontrollably, feeling isolated and alone.

...How could you do this to me, Fitzwilliam? How could you! Did our relationship mean so little...was it a passing dalliance? On one hand you tell me you love me, but with the other you have stipulations—demands. You used me, didn't you? Oh, God! I've been a fool! The shame of being cast aside. I cannot stand the thought of it! First Liddy and her child and now me and mine. ... My child! Oh my God! Her head shot up as she remembered her dreams. *...He'll take my child ...*

Bewildered and struggling with an overwhelming sense of despair, she threw herself onto her bed and cried herself to sleep. Completely exhausted, Elizabeth slept through the afternoon and into the early evening.

That night, after eating what she could, and after deliberate thought, she called an old friend.

"Celia."

"Lizzy?"

Chapter Forty-two

Love … it dissipated into nothingness, seemingly overnight…

July – Charleston

"Lizzy, honey, what's wrong?"

"Celia, I am in trouble, and I need a place to go. Can you help me?"

"Do you even have to ask? Where are you? Do you need me to come and get you, or can you come to me?"

"I'm in Walnut Grove, but I'm sick and weak. Fitzwilliam and I have separated. It's permanent."

"Oh, no, Lizzy, I was afraid of that. Where's Jane? Is she with you?"

"No, Jane and Charles are still on their honeymoon," Elizabeth paused. "Celia, I don't want Jane to know a thing about this. Charles and Fitzwilliam are best friends, and I don't want Jane to be caught in the middle. I'll explain it all when I see you."

"Oh, Lizzy, what happened?"

"I'm still confused about that myself, but if I rest a bit, I think I can make it to you, and then I'll tell you everything. There are some accounts that I need to close before I leave, and I want to change my cell phone number. Then I will try and drive to Charleston."

"No, stay where you are. I'll come to you. I need two days to clear my calendar. Is that enough time?"

"Yes, I'll call you tomorrow with my new number. Then, when you arrive in town, you can call me."

"I'll be there as soon as I can."

The next day, Elizabeth began the process of erasing her trail. She had the money that she believed to be Fitzwilliam's transferred to his bank account in England and closed her personal accounts. She discontinued her phone service, effective that day, had the utilities and cable scheduled for termination, and had her cell phone number changed. She then submitted her resignation to the university. Although she didn't want Jane to know, she did confide in Robert and Tana, telling them she was leaving for an extended period of time.

Before Cecilia came, there was one other thing Elizabeth did—she cut her hair. She couldn't explain why she felt a need to do so, but the desire to cut it overwhelmed her. Her long hair had been the one thing he'd loved most of all, and the memory of him spending hours brushing and playing with it proved too painful, so perhaps the act of cutting it would sever him from her life. Regardless, shoulder length hair was much easier to manage, and the new style flattered her as it hung in soft curls about her face.

Just as she'd promised, Cecilia came two days later, bringing with her a driver and a hired nurse, just in case Elizabeth needed assistance. Cecilia was shocked with what she found. Not only had Elizabeth cut her hair, but she was pale and very sick. The nurse advised that she be seen by a doctor as soon as possible.

Once they arrived on Battery Street, Cecilia had all of Elizabeth's things taken to what would be her room at the townhouse—the room on the southeast corner of the second floor overlooking Charleston Harbor. Soon, after everything was settled, she had Elizabeth taken to St. Mary's Hospital, where the attending physician, Dr. John Adams, diagnosed her with severe dehydration and admitted her for twenty-four hours' observation. She was given IV fluids, along with some medication to bring her nausea under control. Within the hour, it was confirmed that she was indeed pregnant and expecting twins with a due date of January 29th. As Elizabeth listened to the heartbeats and watched two tiny fetuses swimming and turning somersaults on the big ultrasound screen, a warm feeling filled her heart. They were hers…her babies…her children to love and care for.

The next day, Dr. Adams entered Elizabeth's room with her chart in hand. Flipping through the pages, he scribbled a few notes as he approached her bedside. "Ah, I see you were taking the pill, but apparently no one told you to use extra protection when taking an antibiotic. Birth control pills have a higher failure rate when antibiotics are introduced. That's probably why the pill failed in your case," he said, looking up with a smile. "Nevertheless, you certainly look much better than when I saw you yesterday."

"Yes, and I feel better, too."

"Well, Mrs. Darcy, everything looks good," he said as he scribbled out a prescription. "I'm releasing you today, but I want to monitor your progress until you deliver. Make an appointment with my office as soon as possible. I to want see you in a month." He handed her his card, along with a prescription for prenatal vitamins.

"Thank you. I'll do that today."

"Okay, everything else looks fine. We'll see you in one month," he said with a smile as he reached and shook her hand.

Once she was settled into the Lawton Townhouse, Cecilia and Elizabeth went for a walk in The Battery, the park across the street. A nice breeze was blowing in from the ocean, and the smell of fish and saltwater along with the piercing cries of seagulls filled the air. While they strolled along under the shade of the live oaks draped in thick blankets of Spanish moss, Elizabeth thought of her needs.

"Celia, how is my trust fund doing? Is there enough money for me to live off the interest until I am able to work again?"

"Umm, yes, I'm sure there is. My group invested that money in mutual funds, and they are doing quite well, tracking along the same percentages as last year, but I will not hear of you taking one penny out of it. I have more than enough money to take care of you, and I don't mind one bit. You just worry about those babies you're carrying. You're under my protection now."

"No, you mistake me." She snapped a twig from a tree as they passed by the first cannon. "I need access to *this* year's interest, not the principal or last year's earnings. I'll need money to live on until I can become established. I'm contemplating leaving the country as soon as I can."

Cecilia's head shot up. "Lizzy, where will you go? You can't leave!"

"Oh, yes I can. And if you think I won't, then you don't know me very well. If I decide to go, I'm moving to Belmopan, Belize. I will take a teaching position there, and when the children are old enough, and I feel it's safe to return, I'll come back to Charleston and teach. That was my choice in the first place."

Inhaling sharply, Cecilia quizzed, "But, Lizzy, you wanted to manage the farm. What was all of that talk about duty and responsibility?"

"Oh, I still feel that way, only I can't do it anymore. I've given my Aunt Tana power of attorney to take care of things. I can't go back." She bit her lower lip and gave her friend a quick glance. "Charleston will be my home when it's all said and done. I have no desire to return to Walnut Grove. I want to start over with a new life. Going out of the country is only a diversion. When my husband remarries and there is little to no chance he will find out about the children, then it'll be safe to return."

"Lizzy, you don't really have to leave the country. You *know* I will help you. The culture in Belize is so different. It'll be hard."

"No, Celia, I'll be fine. I speak Spanish fluently, and besides, Belmopan is mostly an English speaking city. It's very small, and I already know many people there. Mom and Dad supported the Southern Baptist Medical Compound in one of the outlying villages, and our estate still does. They will take me in until I've situated myself, and didn't you tell me my trust fund paid three hundred thousand dollars last year or thereabouts?" she asked. "That is a fortune in the Belizean economy. I'll do just fine."

"It can be arranged for you to have a monthly income off the interest. I'll take care of it tomorrow, but stay here with me until you are well enough to go—only, I don't want you to go." Attempting to lighten the mood, Cecilia giggled. "Besides, maybe you can talk some sense into me and help me keep Cameron Taylor at bay."

Elizabeth grimaced. "Oh, please don't tell me you're getting back together with him. You can do so much better."

"I'm afraid that's what he wants, and yes, I am seeing him, but I promise you I am not sleeping with him—much to his dismay, I might add. Although I may just marry him someday if someone better doesn't come along."

"Do you mean to tell me you won't crawl between the sheets with the most eligible bachelor in all of South Carolina?" Elizabeth mocked. "Most women would think there is no one better to be found."

"Never!" Cecilia burst out laughing. "I don't care what most women think. He may be handsome and rich, but I couldn't care less." She sighed. "Still, I have to marry someday. I wish I had the option to either stay single, or, at the very least, marry a man I deeply loved, but then, I don't suppose such a man exists, not for me anyway," Cecilia said, looking up into the treetops. Turning back to her friend, she smiled. "Besides, you know how I really feel about love. It's not important."

Elizabeth stiffened. "I married for love," she whispered softly. "As I look back on it, I agree. It's overrated."

Wrinkling her brow, Cecilia asked, "Do you think you can tell me what happened? If I can't help you, I can at least offer you a shoulder to cry on."

"Yes," Elizabeth sighed, "this is as good a time as any, I suppose."

Elizabeth began her tale, starting with when the English gentlemen came to the Cumberland Plateau almost a year ago. Elizabeth explained how everything had been wonderful until that phone call in the early morning hours. She explained about Pemberley, PLC and how the London group disapproved of her marriage, culminating with her husband's emotional withdrawal as things unfolded in London and their many arguments that followed.

"You know that I wanted to join him in London to be by his side, but he refused, claiming the tabloids might expose me to ridicule, thereby jeopardizing Pemberley." She glanced sideways at her friend. "Fitzwilliam was concerned about his public image. I never realized to what extent his father disapproved of our marriage until all of this happened. He seldom called unless I called first."

"Lizzy, as I told you then, he *is* correct about the media. If they had chosen to vilify you, they would have been unmerciful. And with Liddy's trial and all that came out in court, it would've been just as he told you." Tilting her head, Cecilia looked Elizabeth straight in the eye. "As far as Liddy goes, that girl was very lucky. She could have been sent to prison for a very long time, and you would have been tarred and feathered just the same as her. The British press is brutal—much more so than ours. That's the way it is, Lizzy."

"Well, it very well may be. I don't care. It was my choice to make—not his. I think it would have been a lot easier than being left here all alone. Where was he when I needed him? I wonder if he would've called me at all had I not called him. I don't think it was me he was concerned about, but rather his public image. Had I gone to London with his aunt, our lives wouldn't have been what they were before all of this happened. He wanted to change me, and I couldn't do that, so he left me. After the way we had argued, I wasn't surprised. You see, I wanted him to come for me personally. If he had come, then I would've known that he still cared, but instead, he sent his aunt, whom, I might add, was kind enough to explain to me how things really were. When I refused to go with her, I thought—no, actually I had hoped—she would return to London and convince him to come for me. But instead, Fitzwilliam had anticipated me, already having divorce papers and terms settled with his aunt. That's when I decided to leave for good. Aside from losing his love, for a *company* no less, being abandoned is possibly the worst thing I could've imagined. I don't want people's pity, and I *know* that is exactly what I would've received from both my family and the community. If I weren't pregnant, it wouldn't have been so bad."

"Oh, I'm so sorry, Lizzy. It must be tough living in a small farming community where everybody knows everyone and their business."

"Yes, and what they don't know, they make up."

Cecilia laughed. "Well, here in the city, nobody cares."

Cecilia looked at her old friend wondering how much to reveal about a certain gentleman who occupied more of her thoughts than she cared to admit. She pinched off a leaf from a hedge. Twisting it in her fingers, she decided that telling Elizabeth a small part wouldn't hurt.

"Lizzy, I must tell you that I know something of the Darcy brothers, well, at least David Darcy. I sell them my South American coffee each year. David is a shrewd businessman whom I've dealt with personally, and I also know of their problems. In fact, I consider David to be a friend. We've talked over the past few months, but I confess that I don't know them as well as you do, and I've never met his brother. David only mentioned him in passing. He never even mentioned his name, and until I called you about Liddy's trial, I had no idea he was your husband or the heir to the Pemberley conglomerate. You never talked about it."

"I never thought it was important. To me, he was simply Dr. Darcy, professor of Classical Studies." Elizabeth turned her gaze to Cecilia. "You didn't mention me to David, did you?"

"Lizzy, it's my business to be shrewd. When I picked up that there was trouble in paradise, I held my tongue. Besides, like I said, he never mentioned his brother except once in passing. We never talked about our personal lives."

"And he's not likely to, either." Elizabeth chuckled. "Celia, David's a nice man, but be careful about becoming too involved with him. I understand he's quite a lady killer, and he'll never commit—ever."

Cecilia laughed. "Well, that makes two of us. Lizzy, you know I don't have a problem with that. I don't commit either, and besides, I'm not looking for love. You're the sentimental one—not me. Now why don't you show me those divorce papers you told me about? I want to read over them."

Taking a seat on a nearby park bench, Elizabeth pulled the papers out of her purse. "Here, tell me what you think."

Cecilia took the papers and carefully read each one. "Have you read this letter?"

Tears streamed down her face. "Yes, of course I've read it. And he put it so nicely, didn't he—written with cold civility and all on corporate stationary!"

"He has some nerve. How dare he! I can't believe the cold-hearted bastard said this to you! And they call me cold-hearted!" She rolled her eyes. "Lizzy, he owes you, especially now. Say the word, and I'll go after him. They're vulnerable right now because they've had to borrow heavily, and I can tell you that in an American court of law this divorce settlement won't hold up. We'll sue him for half of everything he's worth. He owes you quite a bit. You're carrying his children."

"No, I don't want anything from him. He offered me the equivalent of fourteen million dollars, and I refused it. I don't want his money. Besides, that would only affirm his family's perception of me. They think I married him for his money. But they can think what they will."

"Lizzy," Cecilia frowned, "are you never going to tell Fitzwilliam about the children...not even later?" she asked, handing the papers back to Elizabeth.

Elizabeth placed them back in her purse as both rose from the bench and made their way toward the house. "No, I will never tell him. That is why I'm leaving the country after the babies are born. He forfeited the right to know when he left me all alone back in April. These are *my* children, and I'll take care of them by myself. Besides, if he were to discover I'm pregnant, he would either try to take the children away from me, or, if I'm *lucky*, allow me to have joint custody. Either way, the children would be exposed to a way of life I wouldn't approve of, and I cannot and will not allow that to happen."

"Lizzy, I will not let him hurt you or the children. I've never been one to believe in love for this very reason. It leaves you vulnerable. All women are to men is something to screw. They use you, they dump you, and then they walk off. Men can ruin your life if you allow them to. I ought to know. I saw plenty of it from my own daddy," she said. "And because of it, I will never allow myself to be at a disadvantage with a man. Mark my words, Lizzy. No man will ever do this to me, and I thought I had warned you and Jane, too."

"Yes, you did, but I remember my mother and father. They had a loving relationship all of their lives, so I *know* it does exist. And Fitzwilliam is the father of my children. For that reason alone I choose to remember the good, even if he is not the man I thought he was."

Cecilia shook her head. She knew Elizabeth spoke out of anger. "Lizzy, someday you will have to face him. As much as I am an advocate for women victimized by men, I am here to tell you that keeping the children from him is not right. You'll see that in time."

"Don't bet on it!"

"You will, darling, but if he dares to try and take them from you, he'll have a fight on his hands."

Elizabeth smiled and put her arm around her friend as they crossed the street and strolled into the Lawton Townhouse courtyard.

Chapter Forty-three

…what good does it do for a man to amass untold wealth and yet lose that which is most precious to him…

July London

Mrs. Foulkes stepped into Fitzwilliam's office and handed him a message from his aunt. Hilda had just arrived from the U.S. about an hour ago and was headed directly to the Pemberley Complex. A big smile crossed his face as he read the note and thought of Elizabeth. *…It seems like ages ago since we last held one another. I can't wait to see her…to feel her body against mine.*

Within the hour, Hilda walked through the door—alone. The look on her face alarmed him. "Where's my wife, Hilda?"

Sorrowfully, Hilda answered, "Fitzwilliam, she has decided not to join you."

"What do you mean!?" He swallowed hard. "Explain!"

Laying the contract, along with Elizabeth's letter on his desk, Hilda told him Elizabeth had refused to come with her to England, and that she no longer felt the same about him. Hilda explained that Elizabeth had given it much thought before deciding she was not suited to be his wife or to live in England.

Looking over the letter and the divorce statement, Fitzwilliam fell back into his chair, devastated.

"Fitzwilliam, you will forgive me in time, but I knew this was coming when I observed how much you were arguing. And when I talked with your wife, she made it very clear that she had no intentions of coming with me. Since I suspected this would be the case, for your protection, I took the liberty and had papers drafted in preparation. She was very agreeable to signing them. Mrs. Darcy says you have changed, and that the two of you have drifted apart."

Glaring at his aunt in utter shock, he could not believe what he had just heard. "Hilda, it was not your place to make a decision for me—especially a personal and very important one like this. What the bloody hell makes you think you have the right to make decisions for me? How dare you! I will get Elizabeth on the phone and get this straightened out."

"Fitzwilliam, the woman does not want to be your wife! She has given you a handwritten letter. Is that not her handwriting?!"

Looking over the signature on the document and the letter, he concluded it was indeed Elizabeth's signature and handwriting. Livid with rage at his aunt's intrusive interference, his glare bore straight into her. "Get out Hilda! I will talk to my wife myself. I should have gone after her personally—Pemberley be hanged!"

"I was only protecting your interests. It's what I do. You're worth a lot of money!"

"Money?" he shot back. "Do you think I care about money?! She's worth a lot more to me than mere money!"

"That's exactly why I felt the need to protect you. The woman has affected your good sense!"

Pausing to regain his composure, he carefully selected his words. Eyes ablaze, he turned on Hilda. "No one...not you...not my dead father...or anyone else directs the course of my life. Do you understand me, Hilda?"

Staring at him with her head held high, she met his wrath. "I have a duty to *you* whether you like it or not. It is my place, in your father's stead, to look after you, even if you are too naïve to realize it."

"**GET OUT!**"

"Fitzwilliam—"

"I said *get out*...get out *now!*"

Hilda slowly backed out the door and left his office with the feeling of having done her duty to the Darcy family. Even if her nephew didn't understand now, he would in time. She felt sure of it.

Fitzwilliam called Elizabeth's mobile, only to find it disconnected. He called Longbourn and found Elizabeth was not there. Her uncle had assumed she had left for England. He called Robert, who told him Elizabeth had informed them she was leaving town, but had refused to tell them where she was going. Her only words were that they were divorcing, and she needed time to think. Other than that, Robert had no idea what was going on.

After interrupting Jane and Charles's belated honeymoon, Fitzwilliam learned that the Bingleys had no idea of anything other than his troubles with Pemberley. Jane had not spoken with Elizabeth in months. Fitzwilliam ran his hand through his hair in frustration. *...Oh God! What has she done! Does that woman know what she is doing!*

Mrs. Foulkes, having overheard the argument taking place in Mr. Darcy's office, sent for David who noticed Hilda in a huff on her way out as he turned the corner and entered his brother's office. While waiting for his brother to conclude his calls, David observed the disheveled office. Papers were strewn across his desk and his brother looked panicked. When Fitzwilliam slammed the phone down in its cradle, David had had enough.

"Fitzwilliam, what the bloody hell is wrong with you!?"

"David, Elizabeth has left me! I can't believe she has done this! What the hell is wrong with her? I know we have been arguing and that she felt slighted because I didn't ring her every day, but this is ridiculous." Fitzwilliam nervously rose from his desk.

"Calm down and tell me what happened."

In exasperation, he looked his brother directly in the eye. "I sent Hilda to Tennessee to close out my affairs, and apparently she took it upon herself to close out my marriage as one of them. Here, look at this!" he demanded as he threw the letter at David while he paced back and forth. His eyes shined with unshed tears while he twisted his wedding band.

David picked up the letter and read it out loud.

Fitzwilliam,

By the time you read this, I will have resigned my position at the university. I shall not be going back. I will soon be leaving for an extended vacation to evaluate my circumstances. I no longer know what it is that I want from life. It's time to discover who Elizabeth Bennett really is, for I no longer know.

Do what you wish with the papers I've signed. I trust you will seek a speedy divorce, but there is one other thing I'd like to say. I am deeply insulted you would even think you could buy me off! Keep your money. I don't want it.

Elizabeth R. Bennett

David handed the letter back. "Fitzwilliam, what the bloody hell is she talking about?"

"This," he said, handing him the document.

David glanced over the contract.

"Hilda said Elizabeth was adamant about not returning with her. Since she had witnessed our numerous arguments, she anticipated Elizabeth was going to leave me, so she had this contract drawn up just in case it was needed. Hilda said she was protecting my interests. What must Elizabeth have thought?"

"Have you called her?"

"Oh, yes, numerous times. But she has disconnected her mobile number, and her family has no idea where she is. Elizabeth has simply vanished."

Fitzwilliam began to pace again. "We've been fighting a great deal of late, but I thought we had sorted it out. Though, when I think about it, the last time I talked with her she didn't actually *say* she would come to England. In fact, she said she would think about it." Fitzwilliam looked up to the ceiling and whispered brokenly, "I guess this is her answer."

His mind quickly shifted from Elizabeth to himself. "Well, if she wants to leave me then let her! I've had enough!"

He picked up a paperweight and flung it at the wall, putting a hole where the object made contact.

"Fitzwilliam, calm down! We'll find her and get this straightened out. If you two talk, I'm sure you can work this out."

"David, there is only so much I can take. Between Elizabeth and Pemberley, I've reached my breaking point. I can't handle any more stress. If she wants to go, then let her, damn it! To hell with her!"

"You don't mean that."

"Don't I? I've been to hell and back. I've done my duty, kept my word, sacrificed everything, but she didn't understand nor did she support me. Father was right. She didn't understand... Oh, God, David, she *didn't* understand." He dropped into his chair and cradled his head in his hands, crying out in anguish.

David crossed the distance between them and grasped his brother's shoulder, giving it a supportive squeeze. Then he quietly left, clicking the door shut, leaving his brother alone to grieve.

Later that afternoon, Georgiana approached David for answers. Employees were complaining about Mr. Darcy's foul mood. He had made two secretaries cry, and threatened to fire a filing clerk when she accidentally handed him the wrong file.

"David, you must tell me what is wrong with Fitzwilliam. He has the entire office staff on tenterhooks. What is wrong with him? We have been through so much. I know this has to do with Elizabeth. There is a rumor circulating that she's left him."

"It's no rumor, Georgie" David shook his head. "She has indeed left him. In all my life I have never seen him this angry or upset. Normally our brother is cool and under control, even in our most difficult of circumstances he was confident, but this has clearly shaken him."

"I don't believe this. Something is terribly wrong. Elizabeth loves Fitzwilliam! We have to find her and figure out what happened."

"Georgiana, I think she made it very clear. I read her letter, and she signed an agreement allowing Fitzwilliam to pursue a divorce. We have to get our brother through this, not give him false hope. I don't think you understand women."

"How dare you, David! I'm a woman, and I understand my gender very well, thank you very much, especially a woman in love. And I *know* Elizabeth loves him!"

Shaking her finger in his face, she asked, "What do you know of women? You pick them up like shoppers select meat at the market. You wouldn't know anything about what a woman feels or thinks. You only think of yourself. You're so commitment phobic."

David leaned into his sister's face. "That's enough, Georgiana. I'm not the villain here, and I resent you taking this out on me."

"I'm sorry, David, but something happened, and you're too dense to see it. I know Elizabeth and Fitzwilliam were fighting. Perhaps he doesn't understand women any better than you do! So don't talk to me about real women. I shall take care of this *myself*."

As she turned on her heel to leave, he grabbed her arm. "Just what do you think you are going to do, little Sister?"

"I will go to America and hire an investigator to find her. It's what you should've thought of, Brother," Georgiana fumed, jerking herself free from his grasp.

"Georgiana, calm down. Don't do that. We'll do this together. I will hire a team on both sides of the Atlantic, but you have to consider that she may not want our brother."

"If that is true, then let Elizabeth tell me to my face! Keep me informed as to your progress, but I intend to see her. Know that!"

Georgiana pivoted around and marched to her office. In an effort to calm down, she settled in front of her computer and decided to check her email. An instant smile crossed her face. There was a message from Joseph Bennett. He had been corresponding with her for the last six months.

To: GDarcy@Pemberley.co.uk

From: J. Bennett

Subject: My final email

Dear Georgiana,

This will be my last message to you as I'm being deployed tomorrow and will be out of reach for many months. This will be my last mission. My service obligation expires in twenty-one months. I can hardly wait. I do not intend to remain in the Corps. I'm tired—weary from all I have seen. I've done my duty to my country. Now I want to come home, which brings me to another thought.

I want you to know how much your emails and letters have meant to me. At first, I didn't think I would care for a correspondent beyond my own family circle, and then you came along. With each correspondence, I found myself eagerly anticipating a word from you—even more so than from my family. I think we have gotten to know each other quite well over the last six months. More importantly, we share the same deeply held faith in God and love for the countryside. I'm sure your home in Derbyshire is beautiful, and I look forward to seeing it someday.

Georgiana, I'm not very good with words. I never have been, but from what we have discussed, I want you to know that you give me one more reason to come home beyond my love for my family and Longbourn. Somehow I know that I will survive. Georgiana,

M.K. Baxley

I have come to love you, and if you feel the same, wait for me.

Tell my family I love them.

Semper Fi

Capt. J. E. Bennett

There it was—his last email for a long time to come. She could read between the lines and knew he was in grave danger. Georgiana knew Joseph had been developing feelings for her. She also knew he was not used to expressing them, but the fact that he had expressed them in his email, changed her day from one of despair to one of hope. She would wait for him, but there was one thing that bothered her—Elizabeth. She was glad Joseph had no idea of what had happened between her brother and his sister. He didn't need the extra worry. They would find Elizabeth. Georgiana was sure of it.

Chapter Forty-four

...Ah...but the woman only has the power I choose to give her...

Several days later, the full ramifications of what had occurred finally hit Fitzwilliam. The weekend had arrived, and he had locked himself in his bedroom, refusing to eat or see anyone. He drank heavily. When he would not respond to his valet's pleading, Watson sent for the only one person who could get through to Mr. Darcy—his brother.

David had to force his way into Fitzwilliam's room. "All right, Brother, out with it. It's not like you to feel sorry for yourself."

"I don't want to talk about it," he said, lying prostrate on his bed, clearly in need of a shave, a shower and something to eat to offset the whiskey he'd been drinking.

David paced the floor in front of his brother's bed, his hands clasped behind his back. "You have to talk about it. Your behavior is causing Georgiana to worry herself sick. I'm worried, too. Don't shut us out. We're a family that looks out for one another."

Fitzwilliam released a sigh and looked his brother directly in the eye, speaking philosophically. "David, what good does it do for a man to amass untold wealth and yet lose that which is most precious to him? I've accumulated everything I wanted, but I lost the one thing that meant the most to me—my wife. How on earth am I to live without her?"

The words choked in his throat. His eyes were red and swollen. "I was only trying to protect her, but I couldn't make her see that. Elizabeth wanted to join me here in London, but I knew what the tabloids were capable of doing. It would have been horrible for her, but she didn't see it that way. She didn't understand.

"The publicity that would have resulted might have cost us Pemberley, and I suppose I was thinking of that as well. Still, I should have done more. I failed her, David." He ran his hands though his hair, choking back tears.

"I suppose that, if I had called her every night no matter how tired I was or whatever matter of pressing business I was trying to accomplish and flattered her with pretty words, Elizabeth might not have left me. But no, I expected her to understand simply because I asked her to. I see now it wasn't enough. The rose and Mother's words keep reverberating in my mind. I've been thinking about it all afternoon. The rose had a meaning...a warning. 'Where a rose is tended, a thistle cannot grow.' And what did Longfellow's nursery rhyme say? 'Take care of your garden and keep out the weeds.'"

Twisting his wedding band, he looked up towards the ceiling. "I guess I let my garden grow up in thistles and weeds didn't I?"

Leaning against the wall, David only shook his head while he watched and listened.

"We should have weathered the storm together as husband and wife. Elizabeth was probably right about that. The victory of retaining Pemberley feels hollow now." He cut his eyes across to his brother. "The price I've paid is high, David—too high. If I had known the cost would be so high, I'm not so sure I would have paid it. My mistake was my determination, the drive to win at any cost. And look what it has cost me...my wife."

Finally, David settled on the bed next to his brother and took a deep breath. "I don't know. You were doing the best you could, given the circumstances. Some of the responsibility lies with her. Fitzwilliam, you did what you had to do."

David glanced at his brother. "Father was right about one thing. We are Darcys, and Darcy men do what they have to, and our women have to understand that. I think it was unreasonable of Elizabeth not to have had more faith in your judgment. After all, you are a man of your word. Surely she knows that?"

Shaking his head, Fitzwilliam wrinkled his brow. "I don't know what she knows. You would think after living together for four months, we would have known each other a little better. I'm beginning to think we rushed into marriage before we should have, and that is my fault."

"Fitzwilliam, I have no experience in affairs of the heart, so I am of no use to you there, but I do know one thing. You cannot wallow in self pity. You have to go on."

"No, I can't." Fitzwilliam's voice resonated with a sad, bitter hollowness. "And in time, I will get better. I'm sure of that." Pausing, he caught his brother's gaze. "David, it hurts. I feel like she has ripped my heart out while it was still beating." Sitting up slightly, he cringed from the physical pain of a hangover. "I don't know why they call it heartbreak. It feels like every part of my body is broken."

"Come downstairs and eat, or maybe I can have something sent up, and we can eat here together. I'll stay with you."

"Have them send something up. I don't feel like going downstairs." Easing himself back down, Fitzwilliam smirked, "Father had his revenge from the grave, didn't he?"

"No," David softly spoke, "it's not like that at all. Father loved you. He loved all of us. I've read his journals, and I understand him much better now. It's not at all what we thought. Someday we'll discuss it." David sighed and looked at his brother. "I know one thing from Father's life, at least. If you let them, women have the power to destroy you. We must both be careful."

Fitzwilliam glanced up at his brother and tilted his head as if straining to comprehend his brother's words. He opened his mouth to speak, but shook his head and fell silent.

With a quizzical brow, David asked, "I have to ask you. You don't think Elizabeth could be pregnant, do you? I mean women act strangely when they are expecting. Remember how Lord Rothwell's wife behaved last year? It nearly broke up their marriage with her calling constantly, always wanting to know where he was, who he was with, and what he was doing. She couldn't let him out of her sight. It was as if she wanted him there with her no matter what. She even called him when he was in the House of Lords during an important debate. Much like Elizabeth has done."

Fitzwilliam shook his head. "No, David, she wasn't. I know that for certain. We used birth control. If she were pregnant, she would have told me. Of that much I can be certain. Elizabeth wouldn't do that to me. She knows how much I wanted a child." Pausing for a moment to think, he muttered beneath his breath, "No, Elizabeth would never do that."

"Well, it was just a thought."

Getting up to open the curtains, David's thoughts turned to Cecilia whom he hadn't heard from in several days. *...Cecilia Lawton. I know I care deeply for her, but I can't let her have that power over me... the power that women are apparently able to wield over Darcy men. We tend to love deeply. Strength of character, men of principle, and powerful in the business world, yet weak when it comes to a woman's love. Ah...but the woman only has the power I choose to give her. I must remember that...*

Chapter Forty-five

... worry was ever-present in David's mind where his brother was concerned ...

Late September

Fitzwilliam went through the motions of living but inside, he was dead. He spent his waking hours in excess of work and drink. On the weekends, he stayed drunk. His mind continually relived his arguments with Elizabeth as he tried to come to terms with what had happened.

Another weekend arrived, and like the others that preceded it, he was drinking heavily, languishing in self pity and despair. Stone faced, Fitzwilliam sat and poured another drink—thoughts and memories coursing through his brain.

...How did I end up like this? Why did I give so much of myself to her, that she had such power over me? Why? As he emptied the bottle and drank the last drink, his anger rose. *...Damn her.* He flung the bottle, followed by the glass into the fireplace and sank into unconsciousness as he slid out of his chair into the floor.

When Watson found Fitzwilliam the next morning, he immediately sent for David. Together they lifted him up. "Watson, help me get him to bed, and when he wakes, call me. I'll help you clean him up. I don't know who he thinks he's fooling, but it isn't me." David looked at his brother—incensed that he would let himself go in such a self degrading manner.

"Yes, sir, we'll take care of him. I never thought I would see Mr. Darcy come to this." Watson shook his head.

Fitzwilliam slept into the afternoon while Watson kept watch over him, reading the paper and waiting for some sign of life. When Fitzwilliam finally began to stir, Watson sent for David.

Upon entering his brother's room, David seethed with renewed anger. The room reeked from the smell of stale whiskey.

"Watson, open these windows to let some fresh air in," David said, clearly disgusted. "Fitzwilliam, you need a shower and a shave. You look awful, and if you don't get into the shower on your own accord, I'm going to personally put you in there. Get up!"

"Bugger off, David, I can barely move. Leave me alone."

"No, you're getting up! Now come on, you're getting into the shower or I'm going to put you in there myself. Do you understand me?"

Fitzwilliam looked at his brother in disbelief.

"Do I have to undress and wash you myself? Come on. Get out of bed!"

David flung back the covers. It was clear he meant business.

As Fitzwilliam rose up, he dipped his head and rubbed his brow. "No, I'll take care of myself."

Moving very slowly, he struggled to push himself from the bed.

Watching his brother labor to stand clumsily to his feet, David cursed under his breath before grabbing his brother's arm and helping him to the shower. Returning to the bedroom, David helped Watson clean up the room before taking a seat and waiting for Fitzwilliam to stumble back into his chamber.

"Feel better?" David asked when his brother emerged.

"Some, but my head is splitting, and I think I'm going to be sick," he said, dropping down in the chair next to his brother.

"Yeah, I don't doubt that, so I had this sent up for you."

Reaching over to the table beside them, he poured his brother a cup of tea and handed it to him.

"Sip it slowly and then eat a little. You should feel better soon. Now, we're going to talk. Fitzwilliam, I know the breakup with Elizabeth has been a painful shock to you, but you have to get a hold of yourself. You have to go on. I'm here for you. Together we will get through this, but you have to take the initiative."

"I don't need sympathy or help, David. I will recover after I've come to terms with what has happened."

"I'm not here to offer you sympathy, Brother, but help is another thing, because you definitely *do* need help, and yes, I know you will recover, but I don't want you to be alone. We're going out today. It'll do you good to get out of this house—out of this room. We'll go to White's this afternoon and Pemberley tomorrow. We'll spend time riding. Pack your things. We're leaving in the morning. I've already spoken to Richard and William, and they have agreed to cover for us."

"David, I don't want to go anywhere," Fitzwilliam said, still holding his head.

"Oh, I beg to differ. You don't have a choice in this matter. If you don't go, I'll ring Uncle Harvey. Now, do you want him to see you like this?"

"No, of course not!"

"Very well then, I'll have Watson pack two bags. I'll even let you drive my Lamborghini. It'll do you a world of good to feel the power of a beautiful machine under your control."

They spent the afternoon and evening at White's, playing cards and catching up with old friends and acquaintances. The next day they left for Derbyshire, with Fitzwilliam driving David's car for the first time as he put the Murciélago to the test, laughing like he hadn't laughed in months. They spent two weeks at Pemberley, riding, playing billiards, swimming in the cove, and doing the things they had done as boys. Gradually, Fitzwilliam came back to life. David had always had the ability to bring him out of whatever dark mood had overtaken him, and this time was no exception. By the time they returned to London, David had even gotten his brother to joke and kid around again. However, worry was ever-present in David's mind where his brother was concerned. He had one more thing to do before leaving on his annual business trip to Charleston. He had to secure his brother's wellbeing in his absence.

Chapter Forty-six

... I was her hero and she was my lady...

Mid October

Darcy House

The five cousins, Fitzwilliam, David, William, Benson, and Richard Winthrop, their mother's nephew, had been close all of their lives. All five held a tight bond to one another and could be counted on in times of trouble. It was with that thought in mind that David decided the time had come to call upon the counsel of his cousins. Gathering together in the library, David addressed the group.

"Thank you for coming on such short notice," David said as he retrieved a decanter of port wine and poured four glasses, handing one to each cousin.

"It sounded urgent when you called. What's the matter? Not another problem with Pemberley, I hope." Richard spoke for the group.

"No, it's nothing like that, but I'll come to the point. I'm going out of town next week, and I'm worried about Fitzwilliam. I want you to keep a close eye on him. When I come back, I'll be here for a short time then I'll have to leave again, and, except for the Christmas break, I'll be gone from November until March. Although I believe I have helped him through the worst of it, my brother still tends to drink too much, and he doesn't need to spend time alone, especially in the evenings."

"We've all heard his wife has left him and that he hasn't taken it very well at all. What do you suggest we do?" William asked, clearly concerned.

Sipping his wine, David answered, "Have your father invite him to spend time with your family. Take him to White's or Bilbray's—anywhere you can think of to get him out of the house in the evenings. I don't want him to slip into another drunken stupor. His mind has to be kept off his wife. He's not ready to be introduced to another woman, but you might take him to a few parties, to dinner, or maybe even some clubs."

Benson spoke next. "It surprises me that Fitzwilliam is the one of us to be so afflicted. I wouldn't have thought the breakup of his marriage would have affected him like this. I understand being upset, but for him to fall apart really astounds me. Somehow I thought he was stronger than that."

David looked upon his younger cousin and shook his head. "No, I've always known he was vulnerable. We used to have philosophical discussions late into the night about our respective feelings on marriage and life. Unlike mine, his feelings run deep, and therefore, any woman he ever fell in love with would also possess the power to wound him, which is exactly what has happened."

David raked his hands through his thick dark curls as he turned to face the others. "We'll be at Pemberley the week of Christmas through the New Year. I'm asking you to come if you can. We need to be together like we used to when we were boys. The Christmas season is going to be very difficult for him, and I believe it will help him. I don't want to let him down. I'm counting on your support."

"David, I have no firm plans for the holidays. I'll speak with Rhonda. If she agrees, she and I will come to Pemberley. We can probably come right after Christmas. I'm sure her parents will watch the boys," Richard offered as he walked over to the table for another glass of wine. "I'll make it a priority to see Fitzwilliam as much as I'm able whilst you're out of town. But William and Benson will have to fill in the gaps when I must be away myself."

"David, don't worry. We'll take care of Fitzwilliam," Benson said, reaching for the wine decanter to refill both his and Richard's glasses.

"There are several parties we are always invited to in November and December," William said, giving David a reassuring look. "I'll be free, since I'm not seeing anyone at the moment. I'll make sure he attends. I'll also make sure that we go out as much as possible. Father would love to have Fitzwilliam 'round. He and Mother have been very worried about him, as we all have."

Richard looked at the others thoughtfully. "I know his wife was not believed to be pregnant, but from what I heard of their telephone interactions, she reminds me very much of Rhonda when she was pregnant with our first child. You don't think she could have been, do you?"

"No, Richard, she's not. I talked with Fitzwilliam about that, and he assures me it was impossible, but if she were, that would definitely complicate things," David answered.

Richard shrugged, placing a hand on David's shoulder for reassurance while he and the Darcy cousins continued to talk a little longer before taking their leave. David felt somewhat better leaving Fitzwilliam in the care of his cousins and thanked them all for their encouragement and support.

After seeing his cousins off, he turned and left to find his brother. *...Fitzwilliam, you've got to conquer this. You must! And I've got to find Elizabeth. Where the bloody hell is she?*

Several days later, Harvey decided it was time to pay his nephews a visit, so he called to make the arrangements. When he entered Darcy House, Harvey was shown to Fitzwilliam's study where he found his nephews waiting.

"Uncle, what brings you here on such urgent sounding business? May I offer you something to drink?" Fitzwilliam asked with a quizzical look.

"I'll have a whiskey if you have it. Brandy if you don't."

"Scotch it is then." Fitzwilliam poured three measures while they all took a seat. "Now, to what do we owe the honor of your visit?"

Harvey smiled. "Fitzwilliam, I've come to talk—to see how you are doing and to invite you and Georgiana to dinner next week whilst David is out of town. I also want you to drop by when you can over the Christmas holidays. Make our home your home. Susan and I would really love to see you."

"Thank you, Uncle. I'll speak with Georgiana and get back to you. And I'll see about Christmas," Fitzwilliam said with a soft sigh, "but to tell the truth, I hadn't thought much about it. I'm not in the mood for celebrating."

Harvey looked at his nephew thoughtfully. "Fitzwilliam, it's not good for you to immerse yourself in work as you do or to spend time alone. Listen to me, Fitzwilliam. I do have some idea of what you are going through. You're not the only man to have loved and lost. I know something about that, too."

There was a long silence between the two brothers and their uncle. David was the first one to speak. "I suppose you are talking about our mother."

"So," Harvey said with a gentle smile, "you've read the journals."

David nodded.

"What is he talking about, David?"

"Simply this," David glanced between his uncle and his brother, "Uncle Harvey was engaged to Mother before she married Father."

"What!"

Harvey rose from his seat and walked over to the fireplace. "It's true, Fitzwilliam." He hesitated for a moment. "I was once in love with your mother… and she with me." Harvey sipped his drink as Fitzwilliam stared.

David cleared his throat. "Why don't you tell us about it? After reading Father's account, I'd like to hear yours."

Harvey smiled and nodded. "I've been waiting for this moment. I knew it would come. Well, I told your father I would answer any questions you have." He sighed as he returned to his seat. "What would you like to know?"

Fitzwilliam rubbed his chin and stared in at his uncle. "You? You were in love with my mother and engaged to her? Well that explains a lot," he drawled sarcastically. "Is that why Mother and Father had a strained relationship and you and Father didn't get along?"

For a moment, Harvey said nothing as Fitzwilliam looked on. Then, he finally spoke. "Yes, it is, but it's a long and complicated story. Would you like for me to tell you about it?"

Shaking his head in disgust, Fitzwilliam said, "No! I don't think I want to know the sordid details. I have enough problems of my own."

David reached over and gently clapped his brother's shoulder. "When you are ready, you can borrow the journals Father left me. They're slightly different from the ones that are to be ensconced at Pemberley. These are more personal and have more details."

Fitzwilliam cut David a sharp look, but before he could answer, his uncle interrupted. "Fitzwilliam, we need to talk about you…and your wife. It's the main reason for my visit."

"*No*—we don't." Fitzwilliam bore down. "I can handle my own life. There is no reason to worry about me."

"Ah…on the contrary," Harvey said, warmly. "I believe there is. You're drinking far too much and burying yourself in your work. You cannot sleep at night unless you're drunk. You're drowning in your sorrows."

Fitzwilliam's eyes averted his uncle's stare as he fidgeted with his wedding band. After several uncomfortable moments, he softly spoke. "It hurts—it really hurts. I don't even know why she left me. Oh, I know what she said, but I still don't understand it. I thought she loved me, but she told me that being the wife of a CEO was not what she wanted," Fitzwilliam said, fighting the tears that threatened to fall. He took another large sip of whiskey, downing his glass.

David had come to know this as his brother's usual habit for calming his nerves and numbing the pain. He shook his head. Looking from Fitzwilliam to his uncle, he determined now was the time for answers. "Uncle, Fitzwilliam may not be interested in yours and Father's love triangle, but I am. Now why don't you tell me your side of the story? I want to know the truth—all of it."

Looking David straight in the eye, Harvey replied, "I see you come straight to the point. Well, you get that from your father. You're very much like him in that way, but in other ways, you're like your mother, too. You do know that she loved you, don't you?"

"Yes, and I loved her," David said "We all did. Carry on."

"Fitzwilliam," Harvey said as he turned to his older nephew, "do you wish to hear this? If not, I can speak with your brother at a later date."

"Oh, what the bloody hell! I might as well hear it."

"Well, I'll tell you what you want to know then." Harvey halted briefly as he cleared his throat and leaned back in his chair. In a hushed tone, he began. "I met your mother at a Cambridge dance I attended with a friend. As you know, I was at Oxford whilst she was at Cambridge. Roger, that was his name, was there to see a friend of your mother's, and I was along for moral support." Harvey smiled as if reliving a fond memory. "When we were introduced, I think I fell in love right there on the spot, for I was taken by your mother from the first time I laid eyes on her. We sat and talked for most of the night." He chuckled softly. "We never even danced. That's how taken I was with her. I was absolutely mesmerized, so before I left, I asked her out for the next weekend.

"After that first date, we were inseparable. People did not live together back then without the benefit of marriage, but we spent as much time with one another as possible. We read books together, critiquing them as we went. We listened to music. She liked the Beatles whilst I liked the Stones. I remember how happy we were. We were so very young and carefree and very much in love in those days. So, when we were in our second year, I asked Anne to be my wife, and she accepted me. That was the happiest I ever remember being. I still ache for that lost love, and yes, I know I shouldn't."

Releasing an exasperated sigh, he shook his head and took another sip of whiskey as he looked between the brothers. "Your mother was sensitive and charming with a sharp intellect and a keen sense of humor. We connected on such a deep level that speaking was virtually unnecessary at times. We could look at one another and tell what the other was thinking. I would start a sentence, and she would finish it. That's how deep our connection was. I was her hero, and she was my lady. It was as if we were one." He briefly closed his eyes. "I loved Anne very much."

David briefly cut his eyes away. A tinge of sorrow echoed in his voice. "Yes, I recall my father writing similar words. So tell me, if you loved her so much, why didn't you marry her?"

"Because I was a selfish fool, that's why." Harvey's eyes shimmered as he sipped his drink. "By the end of our last year, I was beginning to rethink my position. I told your mother that I wanted some time to be free and enjoy a single man's life before I married. I listened to the counsel of foolish friends and broke off our engagement. They convinced me to leave with them on an extended holiday and explore life after graduation. We partied every night, living lavishly, first in Italy, and then in the South of France. My picture appeared in the papers with women of questionable character much like yours have, David. I'm afraid I wasn't very circumspect. You have come by that honestly."

David rolled his eyes. "Things run in cycles, I suppose."

"Yes, I suppose they do at that." Harvey nodded. "Of course, your mother saw the pictures, read the papers, and I'm sure was very hurt by it all, even though we were no longer committed to each other. George, who had met Anne through me, came along behind me, picking up the pieces. They began to date and before long, became engaged." He paused, fighting back obvious pain as a tear slipped from his eye. "When I found out about their engagement, I returned to England immediately, but it was too late. I begged Anne for a second chance, but she refused, telling me she would not break your father's heart as I had broken hers. Consequently, she married George, and I was left with a misery of my own making. I suppose it was poetic justice, because I didn't realize how much I loved her—wanted her—until I had lost her. You see, I had erroneously assumed that your mother would always be there, waiting when I decided it was time for us to marry. I never stopped loving her. I simply wanted a little freedom to experience life before marriage. That foolish mistake cost me dearly, and I lost the love of my life to my brother—your father." Harvey turned to face his older nephew. "So you see, Fitzwilliam, I do know what it is like to have loved and lost."

Wiping his eyes, Fitzwilliam replied, "Uncle, I do feel for you, but it's hardly the same—"

"No, it's not. My loss was final, but yours is not, at least, not yet. Fitzwilliam, your wife is out there somewhere. I know what separated you. It was Pemberley. I know of your arguments. And I also know how much she begged you to let her come to London and why you did not let her come." Leaning toward his nephew, Harvey said, "You still wear your wedding ring. *She* still holds your heart. *You* still love her."

Fitzwilliam glanced at the rose, now hanging between his parents' portraits and shook his head. "It's not that simple. She left me of her own volition. I didn't leave her."

"Fitzwilliam," Harvey smiled kindly, "I have regretted to this very day letting my foolish Darcy pride destroy my chance to have the woman I loved. I am confident that, had I married her, Anne would be alive today. She wanted a large family, and since I had no objections, there would have been many children," he said. "Oh, do not mistake me. I love your Aunt Susan, and she knows about my relationship with your mother. We almost separated over it many times whilst your mother was alive. Somehow, though, we managed to reach an understanding and stay together, but the kind of love I shared with your mother only comes once in a lifetime. It's a deep soul connection, and I know from looking at you that you've loved to that same degree. All Darcy men are capable of it if they will only allow themselves the opportunity." Harvey looked pointedly at David. "I have little doubt that, to the best of his ability, my brother also loved your mother, but from what I've heard, the specter of me was always between them… if only in his mind."

"Yes, that is true. Father did love her, and because they could never *connect*, as you call it, it destroyed them both. He loved her every bit as deeply as you did," David said sharply with a biting edge.

Harvey fought to suppress his emotions. "Yes, I know he did. We both loved the same woman deeply. She was a beautifully spirited woman with a beautiful mind, and she didn't deserve the life she had. I loved her until the day she died," Harvey said. "David, you know your father and I fought bitterly over your mother, but what you don't know, as I'm sure Anne never told him, is that I begged her to run away with me both before and after Fitzwilliam was born. But she wouldn't. The last violent encounter between your father and I was when he came home to Pemberley and interrupted your mother as she was telling me her resolve was set, and that we would not speak of us being together again, even though she would always love me in a special way. Before your father walked in, she was in the process of telling me that she had grown to love and respect him, and for the sake of her son, she would remain with my brother. George, of course, misunderstood what he saw and assumed that we were having an affair, but I never touched your mother in that way after our engagement was broken."

"My mother…torn between the two of you. What a disaster the three of you created." David rolled his eyes and shook his head.

Harvey cast a quick glance at David as he rose from his seat. "It is as it was. *Fait accompli*. Choices were made long ago, and I have to live with them." He turned to his left. "Fitzwilliam, nothing is final until it's final. Ring me next week for dinner and do spend time with us. Take it one day at a time. Things will get better. If it does become final between you and your wife, then life does goes on. You are a Darcy. There is pride associated with our name, both proper and improper. We're all here to help you get through this. You know I love you, and so does Susan." Uncle Harvey finished his Scotch and set his glass aside as moved towards the door, but David stopped him.

"Uncle, there is one final thing I have to know. Why didn't my father tell us the real reason for Mother's death? Why was her cancer kept from us?"

Harvey drew in a deep breath and released it slowly. David could tell this was not going to be easy for him. "We didn't tell you because your mother didn't want you to know. She was afraid you would be bitter because she had chosen to risk her life for your brother. Had she not done that, her oncologist probably could have saved her life."

David winced. "Yes, I can see that. At the time, I thought my whole world had died with her. I would have felt betrayed if I had known it was a choice." David turned to Fitzwilliam. "Did you know?"

"No, I didn't. Her secret was well kept. This is just as much a shock to me as it is to you," Fitzwilliam said, staring at his uncle in disbelief. "And I'm afraid I would have felt betrayed, too."

Harvey walked back and placed his hand on Fitzwilliam's shoulder. "Someday we'll all talk again, but for now, I must go. It's past tea time, and Susan is waiting. Fitzwilliam, do ring me. I care as if you were my own son. George would want it that way. In the end, we made our peace, so do ring us."

"Thank you. I appreciate your concern, and I will call 'round."

They both saw their uncle to the door and then returned to the study to talk.

"Fitzwilliam, if you were to find Elizabeth, would you want to reconcile? Would you take her back?" David asked as he paced back and forth, casting a meaningful glance from his brother to their mother's portrait.

"I can't honestly answer that. I would want to see her, but primarily to ask her why—why she did this to me, to us. Trust has been broken," he said. "I just don't know. Right now I'm trying to get over her. All I know for sure is that I don't think I can ever trust or love anyone ever again after her. I don't want to ever take the chance of going through this again." Fitzwilliam glanced wearily at David. "Someday, I intend to read those journals. It's just that right now is not the time. I can't take any more pain. It seems to be a family affair," he smirked. "Now, if you'll excuse me, I have something to attend to." Fitzwilliam turned and left the room.

Later in his room, David contemplated what he would do once Elizabeth was found. ...*I will speak with her first. I will not allow her to hurt him again. She will answer to me before I let Fitzwilliam know where she is.*

Chapter Forty-seven

... You're out of your league, darlin'...

With the third week of October approaching, David prepared for his annual appointment with Cecilia Lawton. Shuffling through the Lawton Coffee account Rita had placed on his desk, he was torn between personally attending the negotiations himself or spending time with his brother and sending his cousin Richard in his place.

He rubbed his hand across his face as he mulled over the decision. Besides his brother, something else disturbed him—Cecilia. In light of his father's and uncle's experience and Fitzwilliam's broken heart, he wondered if he was going to be the next Darcy to make a mistake about a woman. Something was wrong with their relationship, and he wanted to discover what it was. Her calls had abruptly stopped after weeks of hearing from her on a regular basis, leaving him puzzled as to why.

How had he allowed himself to become emotionally involved against his better judgment? He laughed ironically. He knew why he'd let down his guard. It was like the running of the deer in the heat of the hunt. The thrill of the chase had challenged his ego and stimulated his mind. But after weeks of calling him regularly, why had she stopped? Perhaps she had decided to marry that dreadful creep and had not chosen to tell him. Whatever her reason, it bothered him. He wondered if Cecilia was simply living up to her reputation, and he had become another one of her victims—another notch on her bedpost. He couldn't be sure, but he intended to find out. He picked up the phone and made the call to his personal assistant to finalize his travel arrangements. He would leave tomorrow.

Arriving in Charleston late the previous afternoon, David had once again booked a suite at the Lawton Hotel. He had contemplated calling Cecilia for a dinner date, but then decided against it. Standing in front of the mirror while attempting to knot his tie for the third time, he scolded himself. *...Damn it, Darcy! How on earth did you get yourself into this predicament? You've let a five foot seven-inch, violet-eyed blonde get under your skin. You used to love 'em and leave 'em, and now you've managed to fool around and fall in love. ...That's why you're here. You had to see her even though she hasn't returned any of your calls. ...What's your game, Cecilia? What **do** you want? It's time to put an end to this game.*

He shrugged his shoulders as he left for the short walk to the Lawton Executive Complex. It was a beautiful autumn afternoon—perfect for musing He sighed as he walked. *Damn it, Lawton...What are you doing to me? If only I could be assured of your loyalty...your love...your trust...if only...*

Cecilia dreaded the afternoon. She had thought long and hard about the Darcy coffee account. For the past three years, she had sold her premium coffee to Darcy Enterprises, giving them better terms than any of her other clients. She wondered why she had allowed David to secure such a deal when she never gave anyone an inch, let alone a mile, but then she realized she knew the answer to that. She liked him. In fact, she liked him a lot.

M.K. Baxley

It wasn't the same as it was with her other lovers. Darcy was different, but she couldn't pinpoint exactly why or how. She knew there was a danger that her resolve could slip, and that could cost her. But then Elizabeth had called, and once again her defensive walls had gone up. She was no fool. She knew what David was about. Had she not seen the same thing in her father? But still, the way he made her feel when they made love. She shuddered. No one had ever come so close to touching her heart as he had.

She sighed. What should she do about the Darcy account, and, in particular, one David Darcy? She drummed her fingers over the Darcy Enterprises account folder. Should she drop them as a customer, or make him pay the price everyone else paid? It was a difficult decision since he would be here within the hour.

Finally, Cecilia decided that she would let the Darcys keep the coffee account. *He wants me...I know it. If I play it right, I can get anything I want out of him... and information is what I need! I want to know what type of man could hurt such a tender-hearted woman the way Fitzwilliam has hurt Elizabeth.*

Her resolve set, she would use every weapon she possessed and play her Scarlett O'Hara card. After all, it had worked with Rhett, hadn't it? And besides, David Darcy was an English version of Rhett Butler if she'd ever seen one. She chuckled softly. "I can turn David's head with a smile. Men willingly believe what they wish."

Dwelling on that thought, she quickly went to her computer and searched the Internet where she found a condensed family history, Fitzwilliam's academic credentials, his achievements, all of the tabloid stories concerning his marriage to Elizabeth, and a brief description of his involvement in the struggle to maintain control of Pemberley, PLC. There was also something else—the discord that had existed between him and his father. The information she found indicated that Mr. Darcy and his son had been estranged at the time of his death, but more than the marriage had caused the rift between father and son. The article indicated that father and son had been opponents in a fierce battle of wills. Mr. Darcy had been distressed that his son had shown no desire or inclination to assume the responsibilities of the family corporation.

Cecilia thought that his relationship with his father seemed to be similar to her own, except for the fact that she and her father got along. If she were a betting woman, she'd be willing to wager that Mr. Darcy didn't know his son—probably neither of them. The family was definitely not close.

Since she was not satisfied with the results of her search, she decided she would have her firm investigate both brothers. She could not let David know what she really thought of his family—she would play him. The concept bothered her, but not as much as what his brother had done to Elizabeth. A knock at the door interrupted her thoughts.

"Ms. Lawton, Mr. Darcy of Darcy Enterprises is here for his 1:30 appointment."

"Send him in, Ashley." Cecilia took a deep breath and waited for him to enter. Her defenses were up and her mask firmly in place. She knew him well enough to know he'd ask about the phone calls. David was shrewd. She'd have to make it good, or he would see straight through her. She'd have be spontaneous, but she figured a few tears and a few tender moments would be all it would take until he swallowed her every word like sweet wine going down his throat.

David strolled through the door and paused, his gaze catching Cecilia's and holding it. He was going to have an answer before the negotiations started.

"It's good to see you, at last. Actually, it's good to have any contact with you. Why have you been avoiding me, Lawton?"

She rose abruptly to greet him. "What are you talking about? I haven't been avoiding you," she said, confusion creasing her brow.

Stalking closer, he commanded, "Lawton, don't give me that. You know *damn* well what I'm talking about. Why haven't you returned any of my calls?" Throwing down his note binder, his gaze never faltered, his stare demanding an answer.

Taken aback, she stammered slightly. "David, I... I haven't been avoiding you. I have been very busy. An old friend needed my help. Her husband abandoned her and her children. She's like a sister to me, so I'm afraid I've spent all of my time looking after her and her babies. You know how I am when it comes to helpless women and children."

David's chest tightened, his eyes searching hers for the truth. He ached to draw her into his arms and hold her, but he managed to hold his feelings in check. "I left you four messages. You could have at least picked up the phone and talked to me for five minutes."

Tears welled in Cecilia's eyes as she shook her head. Closing the gap between them, she encircled her arms around his waist and laid her head on his shoulder. "David, I'm so sorry. Yes, I should have called, but I did send you an email. I know you got it because you responded. Please forgive me."

Exasperated, but unable to resist, he gave in. "All right. We'll talk about it later." His arms slowly crept around her shoulders. He wanted to believe her, but for some reason he instinctively knew she was lying, and yet, he couldn't help himself as he bent down to catch her lips. Kissing her, he could feel that something had changed. It was a subtle, almost imperceptible change, but there nonetheless. She was lying to him, and he knew it, but there was business to attend to. Later he would decide what, if anything, he would do about it.

Taking a seat across from her, they began their bargaining. After ninety minutes of renegotiating, they reached an agreement he felt he could accept. Due to bad weather conditions, it was a little more expensive than last year, but it was not unreasonable. David agreed to pay her price plus the usual percentage he'd paid in the past.

Their business concluded, Cecilia pushed her chair back and looked him straight in the eye. "David, there is one caveat. I need an escort to a formal function I'm hosting tonight. It's a dinner for the United Daughters of the Confederacy. Daniel was to escort me, but I would really prefer for you to take me."

Studying at her for several seconds, he tried to assess her true motive. He knew he should turn her down, but in all honesty, he just couldn't. He felt like challenging her on his suspicions, but instead he cautiously queried. "Cecilia, why do I have the impression that you want something other than the obvious?" He watched her carefully as she replied.

"Well, of course I do, David. You know how important the preservation of history is to me, especially the history of the Confederacy. Some of the most important people in the South will be here tonight. I need a date who understands how to move in society, and here you are. Besides, you're much more handsome than Daniel. Help me on this one, and I will forever be in your gratitude."

Knowing it wasn't wise, he surrendered against his better judgment. "All right, Cecilia."

"Good! I'll pick you up at six. The dinner is at seven in the Blue Room of the Lawton Hotel. Still staying at the Planter's Inn?"

Her smile was engaging, but her flinty gaze betrayed her. He studied her closely before he answered. "No, I booked a room at the Lawton. I'll pick you up. If you are staying at your penthouse, I'll collect you at six-thirty."

"The suite it is then."

As David left the building, his mind began to wander. He knew she was lying to him. She didn't ring him because she didn't want to—he just didn't know why. If this was a game, He was no longer interested.

Mulling over the implications of the evening and the fact that he had allowed her to so easily pull him in, he realized he was once again unable to resist. ...*What am I thinking? I can't leave her alone. Damn it, Darcy! If you think about it, she scares the hell out of you! You—the President of Darcy Enterprises and heir to one of the most powerful dynasties in the world has let a woman get to you...pandering to her every whim... even when you know she's using you.*

Cecilia smiled to herself as David left her office. She hated being deceptive, and the thought of it pricked her conscience, but she needed information. She had to keep a clear head. Cecilia knew it was a dangerous game she was playing as she thought about the Magnolia Festival and how he had made her feel. She also knew that with very little provocation, she could fall for him and fall hard. This man was not like the others. He was dangerous.

Picking up the phone, she called the head waiter at the Lawton Hotel to finalize the arrangements for the evening. "Maddox, be sure to have our finest wine set aside for my personal table tonight... and a bottle of Crown Royal."

"As you wish, Ms. Lawton."

At the appointed time, Cecilia's maid let David in and escorted him to the den where he took a seat and waited. When Cecilia entered the room, his chest tightened as he stared, mesmerized by the sight of her. From her slender shoulders left bare by the elegant, black silk strapless evening gown to the luscious length of smooth thigh playing hide-n-seek with the split in the white skirt, he was held him spellbound. His eyes finally came to rest on the ample breasts he knew so intimately, fighting the restraint imposed by the gown. She was beautiful. He held no doubts that she was the most stunning woman he'd ever known.

Cecilia smiled and greeted her maid. "Thank you, Sandy. You may leave for the evening. I won't need you tonight."

"Thank you, ma'am," Sandy said as she quickly grabbed her coat and purse and exited the suite.

"Oh, I forgot. David, will you please help me with this choker?" Her eyes sparkled and danced as she handed him the necklace.

"No problem at all," David replied, stepping closer to comply.

While fastening the necklace, his eyes slowly traced the delicate curve of her neck, following it down to the swell of her breasts. He swallowed hard. He could feel the heat beginning to rise as it crawled up the back of his neck. His lips begged to retrace the line his eyes had followed. The scent of her perfume, the heat of her body, her closeness, all caused his mind to falter. He quickly fastened the necklace and cleared his throat as he stepped away. Suddenly the room had become very hot.

"You look very nice tonight, David."

Cecilia had that look he'd come to know so very well. This was going to be a *very* long evening. "So do you," he murmured. He could tell by the glint in her eye that she was well aware of his condition, and that she was enjoying his torment.

She attended to a few more details, selecting music for later in the evening, arranging scented candles on the tables, and placing a floral arrangement on the coffee table. He laughed to himself. He knew exactly what she was doing. After she had completed her last minute preparations, she was ready to go.

Amelia Wilkes, the current president of the United Daughters of the Confederacy, South Carolina Chapter, stood in the corner, whispering to her friends when Miss Lawton was announced. Amelia turned and looked up sharply, scrutiny burning in her steel gray eyes as they all detected the man by Cecilia's side. A long animosity existed between the two women, going as far back as childhood. Many of the blue bloods considered Miss Lawton the most beautiful and wealthiest young heiress in Charleston, and because of Cecilia's money and position in Charleston's society, the standing matrons favored her over the other younger women within their circles. The thought of it incensed Amelia.

"Amy, who is that gentleman with Cecilia?" Cassandra Norwood asked. "I thought she was datin' Cameron."

"Cecilia faithful? Come now," Amelia mocked.

Hyacinth Delafonte eyed the couple curiously while stepping a little closer to get a better view. "I've seen him with her before. Who is he?"

"I don't know, but he sure is a hottie!" Lucinda Armachor giggled.

Cutting a sharp look to her friends before returning a steadying gaze to the dashing Englishmen, Amelia offered, "It's that *Brit* she's been datin'—the one from the Magnolia Ball."

"Yes, that's where I saw him," Hyacinth said. "They made quite a scene with Cameron. Now I remember."

"Oh, I just love a man with a British accent," Cassandra drawled with her deep Savannah inflections.

Amelia rolled her eyes.

"Well," Cassandra raised a brow, "you have to admit he *is* good-lookin' with those dark curls and deep brown eyes, not to mention that regal nose…hmm. He can pick this Georgia peach anytime."

"I don't understand it," Lucinda asserted. "Cecilia attracts men like bees to a honey pot. She's no prettier than we are. I wonder what he sees in her."

"Oh, hush, Lucy," Amelia whispered, her thoughts more pleasurably occupied as she slowly eyed the Englishman, taking in his every detail from the sole of his black Italian wingtips to his dark tousled locks. *Mmm…mmm.* She breathed deeply. He was tall, dark and handsome—lean and trim, every woman's dream. Except for the dark hair, he was just like Cameron, distinguished and handsome.

Amelia narrowed her eyes. It galled her that Cameron preferred Cecilia over her, but if she had something to say about it, she would thwart Cecilia's plans yet.

Amelia closed her eyes and shook her head. "Yes," she murmured, "I suppose he is good lookin'. I too wonder what he sees in Cecilia—that little whore. He couldn't possibly care anything about her," Amelia replied, contemplating her next move with a noticeable scowl on her pretty little face. Amelia desired anyone Cecilia was interested in. It was the nature of the beast that existed between them.

"I see you're still jealous, Amy darlin'," Hyacinth simpered with a devilish grin. "You shouldn't be. You beat her in the last election for presidency of the UDC." The women snickered and laughed knowingly.

"Yes, but she has something I want," Amelia sneered in contempt.

"What's that?" Cassandra asked.

"A man!" Amelia arched a brow as she turned to walk in the direction of Cecilia and her date. Even though Cecilia was Amelia's arch rival and greatest adversary, except for one time during their sophomore year in college where a certain boyfriend was involved, she had never been able to defeat Cecilia in anything. In fact, the only other thing she had ever beaten her in since then was the election for the presidency of the United Daughters of the Confederacy, and there was speculation as to whether that had been an honest election.

As Amelia reached them, a wide grin spread across her features. Cecilia stepped to the left and then to the right, trying to avoid her. Amelia tossed her head and laughed as she moved directly in front of the couple, forcing Cecilia's recognition.

"Cecilia, darlin' aren't you gonna introduce me?"

Amelia curled her lips with glee.

Cecilia smiled, knowing the game only too well. "Forgive me for forgetting my manners," she said, turning to David. "David, this is an *old* acquaintance of mine, Amelia Wilkes." She wanted to say nemesis, but she held her tongue. "Amelia, darling, this is Mr. David Darcy of—"

"Pemberley in Derbyshire, England," David completed with a slight bow, taking Amelia's offered hand while studying her keenly.

Cecilia glanced between the two, fully aware of what was taking place.

"Such a lovely accent, Mr. Darcy. It is so very good to finally meet the mystery man who swept me away last April. Such a shame the dance did not last longer, don't you agree?"

"Ah, yes, I remember it well." David met her stare with a smile.

Shifting her eyes from David, Amelia returned her attention to Cecilia. "I see you wasted no time replacin' Cameron as soon as his back is turned. What a pity his intended cannot be faithful." Amelia glanced at David, flashing a smile meant to kill.

Cecilia had had enough. Her eyes narrowed. "Amelia Wilkes, I know exactly the game you play, and I'm not playing. So why don't you eat shit and die! You're out of your league, darlin'."

Glancing from the two women to the gathering crowd, David quickly took control of the situation before another scene could occur. "If you would excuse us, Miss Wilkes, I believe they are about to begin. Cecilia, it's time to go." Putting his hand to the small of her back, he escorted Cecilia to the table marked for them.

Helping her to her seat, he said, "It seems I'm always having to rescue you." As he took his own chair, he inquired, "Now, why don't you tell me what that was all about? Who is she?"

Cecilia hotly retorted, "She's an old shrew who just happens to be jealous of me and wants whatever she thinks I have, or I should say whomever she thinks I have, which at the moment, just happens to be you." She raised an eyebrow. "So you had better watch your step unless you prefer her to me."

"I thought as much." ...*jealously between two women*... "So what's the story behind her, Cameron, and you? Are the two of you back together?"

Cecilia picked up the bottle of wine and poured a glass for herself and then one for David. "No, Cameron and I are **not** back together." Her eyes flashed white hot. "I don't remember if I told you what happened between us, but let's just say that a long time ago he *did* prefer her to me. She's hated me since grade school, and the feeling's mutual." Cecilia cut her eyes away for a split second, still seething. "She takes every opportunity she can to goad me, and now I see she wants you like she did Cameron before you." She smiled dryly. "That little remark was meant to embarrass me by attempting to make me look like some sort of faithless wench in your eyes. Surely I don't have to teach *you* about women."

"No, I've begun to learn quite a lot about women lately. Probably the most salient thing I've learnt is that they are not to be trusted." Their eyes locked. "Now, I'd like to know about Cameron and *why* she made that remark, and more importantly, I want to know the *truth* about us—I want to know the real reason why you didn't return my phone calls." He lifted his glass and slowly sipped his wine.

"Okay, David." She broke eye contact and released her breath. "We'll start with Cameron. He was supposed to be escorting me tonight, but he was called away on a business emergency a few days ago. Daniel agreed to stand in for him, but then you showed up. And since I had much rather spend my time with you, I asked you instead."

Taking a sip of wine, she continued. "David, you're not that naïve," she chided. "She's jealous of me, and I might add, Cameron is jealous of you."

"Me? Why?"

"Why do you think?" She slowly savored her wine. "It's because of me—because I prefer you to him, and David…I'm glad he's out of town."

A rush of heat shot through David, not only because of her words, but also because of the soft sensual look in her luminous eyes, but he composed himself and attempted to appear casual. He raised his glass to his lips and took another long slow sip before pressing on. "That's all very well and good, but you still haven't answered my last question. Come on, Cecilia. Tell me the truth! Why did you **not** return my calls, and I don't want to hear any story about a 'poor friend'. I want the *truth*." Putting his wine glass down, he crossed his arms over his chest and leaned back in his chair and waited.

She toyed with a foil wrapped candy in her fingers. "David, I have been very busy. That *is* the truth, and I am seriously involved with a friend who needs me very much. Remember when we talked right after you and your brother secured Pemberley?"

He nodded.

"We talked for hours about the Central American palm oil from Honduras that you were so eager to secure for Darcy Enterprises. Well, two days later I learned that I would be negotiating that very same contract. I'm a wholesale distributor whereas you are both a wholesaler *and* a retailer. At times that makes us competitors, such as then. I thought it unwise to talk, especially since I had signed a clause forbidding me from collaborating with others bidding on the same contract. I mentioned that in the email I sent you in late July. Don't you remember?"

David shifted in his chair. "Yes, I do recall that email, but I didn't see it as a conflict of interest. Nor did I realize until much later that you were vying for exclusive rights to the entire crop. Anyway, I won that contract in early October, so why didn't you ring me then?"

"Because of the friend I told you about." She leaned forward as she inched her hand close to his. "I've spent all of my spare time and energy getting her situated, and I knew I would see you in a few weeks. David, I'm very sorry for the miscommunication. I thought you understood. By the way," she smiled, raising her glass in a toast. "Congratulations on winning."

Returning her smile, he shook his head. "Thank you. You aren't upset that I beat you, are you?" He flashed a sexy smile. Relieved by her explanation and choosing to believe her, he felt his reservations had been allayed, especially since her eyes glimmered and radiated with sincerity.

"No, David," she laughed, "I'm not. I contracted for the Belizean crop. It's not premium, but it's good just the same."

Silence reigned for a moment while both unfolded their napkins and prepared to dine. Cutting her eyes across at David as she picked up her knife and fork and began to cut her meat, she casually said, "David, I want you to watch Amelia. She's trying to worm her way into your life and into your bed."

It was obvious to David that their little exchange had affected her. If she was jealous, there was no need to be. In an attempt to reassure her, he responded, "Don't worry, Cecilia. I only have eyes for *you*," he teased, but meant every word. He picked up his knife and fork. "I know nothing of your past squabbles, but I do know that it's in very poor taste to behave in public as Miss Wilkes has done, particularly at the ball last April, so forget about it, and let's enjoy the evening." Giving Cecilia a quick glance, he added, "And you have nothing to worry about. Miss Wilkes doesn't hold a candle to you no matter how well connected she may be."

"Thank you, David. That is very kind of you." Giving him a smile, they settled into their meal, forgetting all about Amelia.

The purpose of the dinner was to raise money for the restoration and upkeep of Southern battlefields and Confederate cemeteries. Soft music from the Old South played in the background while several speeches were given. David had always enjoyed Charleston cuisine, and tonight was no exception. While they ate, Cecilia made sure his wineglass was never empty, and when the meal was concluded, she made sure he had a glass of Crown Royal as well.

After the fundraiser came to an end, they socialized with some of Charleston's finest families where Cecilia introduced him to those of her peer group. David rather liked the open, genteel manners of Charleston's Southern society, and before the evening was over, he felt relaxed and at home. He even left a donation for the UDC.

When the event was finally over, he escorted Cecilia to the lobby, feeling rather tranquil. Walking to the lift, David momentarily looked toward the glass wall of the front entrance. A quiet rain had begun to fall and the low rumble of thunder could be heard in the distance. A flash of sheet lightning lit up the darkened sky. Looking back at Cecilia, an ominous feeling swept over him.

Chapter Forty-eight

...tell me that you want me...tell me that you love me...

Stumbling unsteadily from the lift, David's mind whirled in mayhem from drink and the woman beside him. Although he wanted to stay and make love to her, taking her until he filled his need, he knew he shouldn't. It was surreal. He was in love with her, but like his father before him, he wanted her heart as well as her body.

Arriving at her door, he stopped and smiled down at her. "I had a lovely time, Cecilia, and I thank you for the evening. I enjoyed it." His hands slowly reached for her waist as he dipped his head to give her a chaste kiss, but when their lips met, it was like fire—a rush of heat—hot and burning, intense and consuming. Her arms automatically curled around his neck, her fingers sinking deep into his thick curls, pulling him into her as she deepened the kiss.

A low guttural groan escaped his throat. His arms instinctively tightened, pulling her closer. His body ached as her lush figure sank deeper into his embrace. He could almost feel the way her body gripped him when they made love. Her breasts beckoned him. Her kiss lured him. It would take a supreme act of willpower to break away...willpower he was rapidly losing.

Breaking the kiss, Cecilia coaxed him. "David, you need to come in for a few minutes, perhaps for some coffee. I think you've had a little too much to drink. You can barely walk."

Swallowing hard, he stammered while her fingers continued to play and her eyes called. His mind drifted to a childhood nursery rhyme. *'Come inside,' said the spider to the fly'.*

"No," he said, "I don't think so. I... I need to return... to my room." His eyes closed in physical agony as she reached up and nuzzled his neck, softly caressing him with her kiss. He moaned. His mind screamed for him to leave, but his body was quickly telling him otherwise. Again he whispered, "No, I can't."

Releasing him, Cecilia stepped back and grabbing him by his tie, she pulled him inside. "Oh, yes, you can!"

Once inside, she slipped off her shoes and put on soft romantic music. She lit a few candles before helping him out of his jacket. A loud thunderclap shattered the quiet as he peered into her dark luminous eyes. "What happened to coffee, Cecilia?" he asked, futilely trying to raise his defenses.

Calling him with that soft sensual bedroom look, she said, "We'll have it in the morning."

That was it. His resolve completely snapped. The attraction was too strong, his need too great, and before he knew what was happening, she had removed his tie and unbuttoned his shirt, while he unzipped her dress, dropping it to the floor. His mind and heart were filled with longing and desire as he kissed her. They groped one another, fumbling their way to the bedroom, leaving a trail of clothes in their wake. Outside a storm ragged, the winds howled, and thunder cracked as lightning flashed.

Tearing back the bedcovers, he pressed her onto the bed, covering her with his body. Hot with desire and numb from the drink, he completely let go of all restraints.

M.K. Baxley

They tumbled and rolled, tangling the bedcovers until he firmly settled on top of her, taking control of their lovemaking. A violent thunderstorm tore through the South Carolina night, lighting up the bedroom with a white flash and a loud thunderclap.

Peering deep into her eyes, his voice rasped, "Cecilia... tell me that you want me."

...*Tell me that you love me*...

"I...I want you, David. I *want* you."

Entering her easily with one hard, swift thrust, he dipped his head into the curve of her neck.

"David, love me. Love me," she cried out.

Sensing her orgasm was close, he completely let go. "Cecilia, I ..." he whispered breathlessly in her ear as he collapsed on top of her, completely spent. They laid there for what seemed like an eternity.

Calm enough to breathe normally, he cupped her face in his hands, kissing her with light feathery kisses as he swept her hair from her face and gazed into her violet blue eyes. He contemplated telling her what was in his heart, but the words stuck in his throat. The time wasn't right. Instead, he rolled over and pulled her into his arms as he gently guided her face onto the curve of his shoulder, giving her one last kiss.

"David... stay with me tonight. Don't leave me... please." She trembled in his embrace, clinging to him.

The rhythm of his heart kept time with the steady downpour beating against the windowpane. He tightened his arms around her and gave her a tender kiss. "I'm not going anywhere. Not tonight, love...not tonight." He snuggled closer, gently caressing her face with his lips, his mind awash with emotions.

As they lay there holding one another, Cecilia stroked the side of David's face with one soft hand, brushing his damp curls from his forehead.

"David, we've been in each other's company several times now, and I'm afraid I know little to nothing about you. Tell me about yourself," she said, looking up at him with adoration.

"What would you like to know?" he asked softly, her head resting on his shoulder while he played in her hair.

"Tell me about your family—your brother, your sister, and any others? What do they do? What are they like?" she asked while her fingers combed through the thick tuft of hair on his chest, still damp from their lovemaking.

"Well, Fitzwilliam is my only brother, and I have one sister. Georgiana is six years younger than I, and Fitzwilliam is four years older," he said. "For the first time, I would say we're a family. I'm very close with my brother and sister, and things couldn't be better with Pemberley." Brushing his lips against her hair, he inhaled deeply as a smile graced his lips.

"How is that coming along since we last talked?" she asked, gently stroking the line that followed from his navel southward.

"We're recovering. If things continue as they are, we'll be able to pay off our loans in five years."

She smiled, nuzzling his throat with a kiss, intent on seducing him into loosen his tongue while her fingertips played on his firm abdomen. "Tell me about Fitzwilliam. I was not aware he took a part in the family enterprises until recently. In fact, I didn't even know he existed until all of this happened."

David breathed deeply. "Well, heading up the family corporation is not what he originally wanted to do. He was forced into it by our father's death. Father preferred him as CEO as opposed to me." David paused and cleared his throat. "He's the eldest and therefore the heir, and he's the sensible one. Father believed me to be too unsettled and ah …well, not morally fit." David stammered as if feeling awkward.

"So your brother is more discreet than you?" she asked, twirling her finger around a wayward lock.

"No, I wouldn't say that. His desire is to be married with a family, whereas mine wasn't, and his behavior has been considered more honorable than mine." He smiled, gently bending down to kiss the tip of her nose.

"So he's single then?" she continued, playing in his curls.

"Yes… I mean, no, not exactly. He and his wife are separated. Cecilia, why are you asking me all of these questions? Right now I can think of things far more interesting than Fitzwilliam." Evidenced by his arousal nudging against her side, his desire had once again begun to build. Snuggling closer, he cupped her face and caught her lips.

She closed her eyes and deepened the kiss before breaking away. The temptation was great, but she had to press on. "I'm simply trying to figure out two of the most powerful men in the global economy, that's all." Her hand slid over his chest and down his abdomen to play. A gentle roll of thunder sounded off in the distance as the rain pelted against the window.

"Well, if you must know, Fitzwilliam loved his wife very much. She hurt him dreadfully when she left, but I don't see this as any concern of ours. He's recovering well enough and hopefully will soon be over her and ready to go back into society. In fact, my cousins and I have planned to see to it that he's entertained throughout the Christmas season with parties, dinners, and night life. But of what importance is this to you, or to us? His personal life has nothing to do with his business life, and he's quite able to keep them separate," David said hoarsely, turning towards her, his body once again in full blaze.

Cecilia knew he was tired of discussing his family, but she needed to strike while the iron was hot. Calmly, and with precision tuned skill, she continued. "And what of the business then? Everyone cuts corners on international trade laws if they can." Her fingers ever so lightly traced the line of his jaw as her lips followed. Feeling his hard swallow catch in his throat, Cecilia sensed David's concentration teetering on the edge.

Releasing a deep breath, he answered, "Neither my brother nor I would ever take such a chance. I know in many countries it is quite common to bribe heads of state, but we have never done it, nor will we ever. It's illegal under British law."

Fully aroused, David reached for her. "No more talk, Cecilia. Ride me." Pulling her on top of him, they made love for a second time. She sensed his deep feelings for her and for a brief moment she wavered, but just for a moment.

Fully satiated, he fell into a deep, contented sleep while she held him in her arms as the rain poured and dripped from the eaves, gentle like the steady breathing of the man in her arms.

Her attempts to gain information having failed, Cecilia would follow through with her plans to have the Darcys and Pemberley, PLC investigated through her attorneys. Now convinced that David had a strong attraction to her, she would use it for all it was worth, though the thought of it pricked her conscience even more than before.

She creased her brow and gazed at his sleeping form. What was it—these burgeoning feelings, feelings that gripped her inner being? Feelings she couldn't comprehend… feelings she struggled to understand as she thought about the man lying next to her. It wasn't his passionate lovemaking that was so devastating to her emotions, although that was certainly helpful, but rather it was his tenderness, his kindness—something she'd never known from her other lovers. She felt safe and warm, an odd sense of belonging while cradled in his arms.

The rain had dissipated into a gentle patter against her window, and the wind had settled into a low moan. As she contemplated these new feelings, her thoughts drifted to the man sleeping in her arms. ...*It is possible the two of you could fall in love... and that would not be good, considering the course you've taken... he could get hurt... even worse ...**you** could get hurt.*

She gave him a tender kiss and snuggled a little closer, resting her head over his heart, listening to its steady beat. His arm instinctively reached for her, pulling her even closer and murmuring something she couldn't quite make out. In his arms she drifted off, listening to the sound of the falling rain.

The next morning, Cecilia was the first to awaken. Turning to face him, she propped up on one elbow and closely observed the man sleeping beside her. He looked peaceful... so serene as his chest steadily rose and fell in his sleep. Gently brushing an errant spiral of hair from his brow, she placed a tender kiss where the stray strand had been and sighed in contentment.

With a smile, she wiggled out of his arms and tumbled out of bed. She showered and dressed, leaving him to rest while she went to the kitchen and made coffee along with her father's recipe. She knew David would have a hangover—perhaps even feel deathly ill.

Several minutes later, David was just beginning to wake up. As she approached the bed with the drink in hand, she lifted his head up from the pillow and put the glass to his mouth. "Here, darling, drink this. It'll make you feel better. Daddy swore by it."

Stirring out of his sleep, he asked, "What is this? It smells awful!" Making a terrible face, he drank it down.

"It's Daddy's recipe for the morning after. You'll feel better in about twenty minutes."

"I highly doubt that. What happened last night, and how did I get here?"

"You don't remember?"

"Not much. We didn't... did we?" he asked, looking at her with a helpless grimace.

She smiled. "That bad, huh? Well, if you don't remember, then I'll tell you—yes, we did—twice as a matter of fact. Oh and... ah... you're a very good lover."

"Ohhhh... I think I'm going to get sick."

"Well, it wasn't that bad. I think you rather enjoyed it."

"It's not that."

She laughed. "You'll feel better soon, and then maybe I can refresh your memory."

True to her word, David recovered. After a shower and two cups of coffee, he returned to his room to freshen up and change clothes. She had invited him back for brunch and tea, and they made plans to see each other again in November. She agreed to show him her Sea Island Cotton Plantation, the historical sites of Charleston, and finally her family home, Carlton House—the home of the Carolina Gold Research Institute and Development Foundation. They laughed and talked about much of nothing while passing the afternoon away, making love once more before he left for London.

Reflecting over their progress, David couldn't be more pleased with the way this trip had gone—both for business and his personal life. ...*Progress is being made, Darcy. Progress! You have one week to make her yours—one week to win her love. Make good on it, Darcy... make good on it...*

Cecilia Lawton was a challenge—one he was determined to win!

Chapter Forty-nine

… I could love him if it were a different time…

During the flight back to London, David's thoughts were filled with Cecilia. He leaned back in his seat, relaxing as his mind wonder. Just as he was about to drift off into a comfortable dream-filled sleep, the sudden intrusion of his air phone snapped him from his dreams of the lady he'd left behind.

"Mr. Darcy, this is Herman Biggs. I received your message and want to update you."

"Yes, tell me how the investigation is coming along."

"Well, so far, we have no leads, and although this is not unusual, it is irritating, I know," he said. "Mrs. Darcy must have someone helping her cover her tracks, but don't worry. We'll find her."

"Irritating doesn't even touch it! I want to know where she is!"

"Like I said, don't worry. We'll find her. We have a few more avenues to pursue. She can't stay hidden forever. When we get something, we will let you know, but until then, you will begin to get monthly updates from us. If you need anything further, feel free to ring me, otherwise look for my report. I'll send it though the post."

"Thanks for the update, Biggs. Keep looking, I want Mrs. Darcy found. Do whatever it takes, and spare no expense. Find her, Biggs."

"Will do, Mr. Darcy."

David cursed. Where the bloody hell was she! It had been a little over three months since he had hired Biggs, and still there was nothing. It was as if she had vanished from the face of the earth. Except for the week between Christmas and the New Year, he would be out of the country until March. He had hoped there would be *some* news by now. He released an exasperated breath. *…Make no mistake, Elizabeth Darcy, you will be found!*

That evening after David left, Cecilia returned to the townhouse. Walking through the door, Elizabeth greeted her. "Hmm, you look good! How did the fundraiser go last night?"

"Wonderful! Just wonderful. I don't know when I've enjoyed myself more," she mused, placing her coat on the rack and sending her purse upstairs with the maid.

Elizabeth chuckled, rubbing her stomach as she and Cecilia turned to walk toward the sunroom. "Well, I daresay David Darcy is a lot more fun than Cameron Taylor, but really, Celia, you should try to find a nice man. If you must marry, at least marry someone who will be faithful, which we both know Cameron will never be. And David? He's a playboy. I wouldn't waste my time with him either. Besides, his future is in England, not here," Elizabeth advised as she and Cecilia took a seat.

Cecilia tossed her head. "Lizzy, it's not what you think. I know perfectly well what David is and that we could never have a future together, but he is a lot of fun, and I enjoy his company. Which brings me to my next point. He's coming back in November to spend a week, so I will need you to move to the plantation house on James Island when the time comes." Cecilia sighed. "Like I said, David may be fun, but he's also dangerous. I've come to know he is fiercely loyal to his brother. Should he discover you, it would not be good for either of us."

Elizabeth cringed. She, better than anyone, understood the bond that existed between the two brothers. "Thanks for the warning. I don't want to face him or my husband."

Leaning back against a cushion, she chewed her lower lip. "Hopefully, when he is remarried, I will feel more at ease and able to handle it," she lied as her hand protectively went to her protruding belly. Cutting her eyes across at Cecilia, she softly spoke, "And yes, Celia, I know."

"You know what, darling?" Cecilia watched her sympathetically.

Elizabeth glanced over to the large picture window and peered out. "I know that someday I will have to tell him about the children. I know it cannot be hidden forever, but I'll cross that river when I come to it." Her voice trailed off into sadness.

Cecilia reached over and took her friend's hand reassuringly. "We'll get you through this, and in time, all will be better."

Elizabeth looked down, unable to meet Cecilia's warm smile. "Perhaps it will. I don't know."

"Of course, it will. Just you wait and see. Now let's eat and get to your class. I'm so excited about being your birthing coach. Just think, I get to experience the joys of childbirth without any of the trouble. I can't wait until those babies are here." Cecilia patted her friend's hand as they rose to leave for the dining room.

Now in her seventh month, Elizabeth spent as much time as possible outside, often going to the park across the street to read or walking down King Street to shop in one of the many stores. Overall, her life was as content as it could be, given the circumstances. Many an hour was spent under the shade of the towering live oaks in White Point Gardens where Elizabeth had begun to read and talk to the children, having now named them since she knew she was having a boy and a girl.

Although separated from her husband, Elizabeth felt compelled to maintain his family tradition of naming sons after their ancestors. Therefore, the boy would be Fitzwilliam Alexander Bennet Darcy—Alex for short, and the girl would be Emmaline Cecilia Bennet Darcy, but she would be called Emily.

Resigned to her lot in life, Elizabeth's days were filled with reading and sewing as she and Cecilia stitched the entire layette for her babies. Creating the designs occupied her mind and brought her a feeling of accomplishment. However, the hours of darkness brought something else. In the loneliness of the night, she ached for the touch of her husband's hand upon hers, for his warmth when he hugged her, and most of all, for the assurance of his love. She remembered all of their talks about life, books they'd read, the music they liked, and their exploration of their family histories. She recollected her last birthday, their three days in the snow, their quiet evenings at home working on school related projects, and most of all, their nights of passionate lovemaking. Those were perhaps the hardest memories of all. Her body ached for his touch, for the feel of his skin against hers, and the feel of his lips when he kissed her. He had promised to love her always, and yet, he hadn't. He had left her.

She pulled out his letter and reread it, crying as she looked from the only picture she had kept of him to his letter. He had broken her heart. Then she felt the children quicken and knew for their sakes she had to move on.

Cecilia finally received a disappointing report on the Darcy brothers. As she sat at her desk in her executive suite at Lawton Complex, she read over the details. It appeared that Fitzwilliam Darcy had an impeccable character—no moral, legal, or ethical indiscretions. The only item of note was a two-year love affair with a Miss Stella Fitzgerald while he attended Oxford. That was nothing so different from any other college student, and it seemed to not have been repeated, therefore it wasn't a pattern.

Pemberley, PLC was also clean. There were only a few minor questionable activities, but nothing more than she or her father had done—there was nothing illegal.

David, on the other hand, had an extensive sheet of misdeeds. As she read through his long history, she had to laugh. There were several pictures of him in very compromising positions with scantily clad women hanging on him. Shuffling through them, there was one photograph which caused her to pause. It was a tabloid picture of him with Sandra Hamilton, a popular porn star and exotic dancer, accompanied by an article of a supposed engagement between them which was hotly denied by both him and his father. Knowing him as she did, she laughed at the absurdity of such a notion, especially when she considered his position in society. She laughed again as she resumed perusing the photographs one by one. His hands were always in places where they should not have been. Cecilia smiled, shaking her head. ...*So he is a playboy just as Lizzy told me—a real scoundrel even. He's your kind of man...an alpha if I've ever seen one. Hmm...no wonder you like him, Celia. He lives life on the wild side, not so very different from you.*

She shrugged her shoulders and filed the report in her personal file folder. She hadn't learned much more than she had from her own search—just a few more details. Rising from her desk, she walked over to the large picture window of her second-story office overlooking downtown Charleston, deep in thought as she chewed on the tip of her pencil eraser. What she read should have distressed her, but instead, it intrigued her. He hadn't been the playboy with her. He had been sensitive, even loving. Strangely, she found herself more attracted to him than ever. While staring out her window, she anticipated seeing him again as she daydreamed of their last encounter.

Fitzwilliam buried himself in his work with little time to think of anything else. During the day he fared well, but at night, it was a different story. In the loneliness of his room, all he could do was think of Elizabeth and the times they had experienced together.

He knew he was growing dependent on alcohol, but it was the only way he could block the thoughts and memories that caused his body to ache… desiring her… wanting her—and not having her. Desire and need ate away at him. This was insane. He knew he had to defeat this demon, and that of the bottle, too. But even as those thoughts echoed through his mind, he picked up his brandy decanter and poured one more drink while staring at her photograph beside the letter she had written him. He was sinking into despair, yet he felt helpless to stop it. Surely the dull ache in his heart would subside in time. Once he had overcome his past, he would live again. But what about the future?

He sighed heavily. Having thought upon it, he decided he would never marry again, but that did not mean he wouldn't have female comfort for his needs. No, in time, he would take care of it like other rich men, finding a pretty woman to escort in society and take care of him at night, much as his father had done in his desperate times during his marriage—and particularly after the death of his mother.

In Fitzwilliam's way of thinking, sex was a need while love was optional. He was vastly different from the man he used to be. Honor, duty, integrity—the code he'd lived by much of his life had left a bitter taste in his mouth.

Chapter Fifty

... no one will cry at my funeral, will they...

Corporate Reorganization

By the first of November, Pemberley, PLC was back on track. The three members who had led the insurrection were ousted, along with all who had supported them, even down to the faithless Darcy cousins. Fitzwilliam had not only purged them, he'd cut them off from the family, revoking any allowances they received from the estate. They were on their own, having to find employment elsewhere. He also made sure that would not be easily done. He went for blood, setting an example for those who remained. Now that he had control of sufficient shares of stock, the board of directors and those who worked for him would fear and respect him. Whether they liked him or not, he didn't care.

After effectively cleansing the London office, he called a special meeting with some of his top executive officers to discuss the restructuring of the U.S. and Canadian headquarters. He had replaced Dashwood, Stanley, and Wesley with his cousins William, Benson, and Richard. Now it was time to reorganize abroad. As the group assembled around the boardroom table, Fitzwilliam called the meeting to order.

"Gentlemen, I've called you together to advise you of my plans and our next move. I am reorganizing the U.S. offices in New York and L.A. Ottawa has already been taken care of. Stephen Darcy left yesterday to replace Sean Ashton as President of Darcy & Winthrop Publishing in Canada. Both the U.S. and Canadian restructuring is to be a complete surprise to those who work there. Therefore, as I have already directed Stephen, I require total secrecy. These changes I'm about to disclose will take effect immediately after the New Year with a target date of January tenth to be completed. As with Sean Ashton, I want Edward Darcy and Charles Wilson to think they have survived." Fitzwilliam tapped his pencil on the table while he looked from one to the other of those assembled there.

"William, as my Financial Director, I want you to also take control of the New York office as President of American Affairs, replacing Wilson. When you arrive, you are to inform him that he no longer works for us. Give him this letter which will explain his termination along with a severance settlement," Fitzwilliam said, handing a package to his cousin.

"Once there, I want you to do a systematic audit and investigation of the office. Fire anyone who took part in this attempted takeover or whom you believe to be incompetent. If you want the position on a permanent basis, it's yours. Wilson is to vacate the penthouse in sixty days, and then it too, is to be yours. Until then, use the corporate quarters at the Darcy Executive Suite. Do you have any questions?"

"Not at this time. I'll review the situation and get back with you at a later date if I do," William answered, as he studied the papers in his hand.

"Benson," Fitzwilliam said as he turned to his younger cousin, "you're being promoted. As Technical Director for the Pemberley Board, I want you to go to the L.A. office and do the same in your new position as President of Darcy Technologies. You will replace our cousin, Edward. Here is his letter of explanation," Fitzwilliam said, handing a package to Benson. "He gets no severance package beyond that which I legally have to provide. He's a Darcy—he should have known better. There's a high cost to pay when blood betrays blood. As with your brother, if you want the position permanently, it's yours. The same living accommodations apply to you, except Edward has only thirty days to vacate the Los Angeles suite.

"Once the two of you have secured the offices and everything has returned to normal, you may split your time and residence between Britain and the U.S. Let me know in six months if you plan to take the positions on a permanent basis."

Glancing around the room, Fitzwilliam concluded. "I think that about does it. Unless there are any further questions, this meeting is adjourned."

Everyone remained silent.

Fitzwilliam nodded and dismissed them. "Now let's go to lunch. I'll meet up with you at White's in about half an hour."

As the others were leaving, David pulled his brother aside. "Fitzwilliam, may I have a private word with you?"

"Sure, give me a minute to give this paperwork to Betty, and I'll be right back."

Taking the papers in his hand to the desk just outside the boardroom, he gave them to his personal assistant to be filed and then returned to speak with his brother.

"What is it, David?"

David sat on the edge of the table and looked his brother squarely in the eye. "Fitzwilliam, don't you think you're being a bit excessive with this entire restructuring? I understand firing them, but cutting them off from the family completely? You seem intent on causing as much pain as you possibly can. You enjoy watching them twist in the wind. Edward, Ashton, and Wilson were only minor players, barely involved, and yet you toy with them, letting them think they survived. And what about Henry and Edmund? You served their heads on a silver platter in the last board meeting. Edmund lost everything he had. He and his wife and children are now living with his parents whilst Henry is living with his wife's family, barely surviving. I don't like it, Fitzwilliam."

"Edmund and Henry Darcy," Fitzwilliam breathed out. "When we were young, they were like brothers to us. But they grew up and away from the Darcy heritage. It's been a long time since they held any feelings of loyalty or allegiance to us. They are Darcys in name only. They hate us, and you know it. They have accused us of seeking special privileges, when in reality they wished for what we had even though they benefited from the family legacy and were quite well off."

"Yes, but does the end justify our means?"

Fitzwilliam released an exasperated sigh as he took a seat on the table beside his brother. Stroking his family ring, Fitzwilliam glanced up and looked his brother in the eye. "David, in some respects you have as much of a classical education as I do. You know from history that *all* of the enemy must be destroyed in order for the empire to continue and prosper. It was even true amongst our own family. There comes a time when family loyalties are put to a test." Fitzwilliam paused and locked eyes with his brother. "Have you not learnt anything from our family history? I'm sure you remember *The Wars of the Roses* and Richard Darcy's attempt to wrest control of Pemberley lands from Thomas, his brother, the rightful heir. Thomas had to cut him down on the battlefield—his own brother. And have you forgotten our forefather Henry Darcy and the *Wars of the Three Kingdoms*? I don't know about you, but I have learnt from history, and I don't intend to repeat its mistakes. From this point on, I will demand total loyalty."

Fitzwilliam glanced at the portrait of Fitzwilliam A. Darcy I that hung over the

Chairman's seat. Looking back at David he nodded with a light sigh "When you have two forces vying for control, only one can succeed. The opposition must be eliminated, and all that is affiliated with it must go. In order to prosper, we must be willing to get our hands dirty and eliminate anyone who stands in our way. Maybe you should refresh yourself with Machiavellian principles. If I can't have their respect out of friendship, I'll have it out of fear." Fitzwilliam's words were as cold as his eyes.

"I told you I would go for blood and you agreed. If this were the 16th century, I'd have their heads on London Bridge. I want the people who work for me to be loyal, and I don't care what I have to do to obtain their allegiance."

David frowned, clearly uncomfortable with his brother's answers. "Yes, I did agree in principle, but this is excessive." David glanced away and then back. "What about Uncle Harry? You have been excessively cruel to him. I thought we agreed to allow him to gradually pay back the money Father had lent him. He's on the brink of bankruptcy. You have ruined him!"

"Father is *dead*. That loan belongs to me now!"

"But we agreed to extend the olive branch for Aunt Samantha's sake and yet you didn't."

"That was before Elizabeth left me. After that, everything changed." Fitzwilliam's words rang with a twinge of sorrow. "She was my grounding force, my reason for living. It was her and our plans for our children that drove me, motivated me. When I lost her, I lost all care and concern for life. All that's left is a job to do, and *that* is what motivates me now." Fitzwilliam paused and cocked his head as he narrowed his eyes. "Did you really think I would show them mercy? The board of directors, *especially* Dashwood, cost me my wife. I told you I would get them—*every single one of them,* right down to the last *cousin!*"

"Yes, but Fitzwilliam, this is a scorched earth policy. We will be viewed as ruthless. Does that not bother you!?"

"Not in the least, Brother," Fitzwilliam shot back. "I've never cared much for what others thought, and I care even less now. I never wanted this job, but now that it is mine, I will do it. Do you think they would not have done the same to us had circumstances been different and they had been successful? Still waters run deep, David. They should not have underestimated me. It's a world of mice and men." Fitzwilliam spoke in a hardened voice. "Which are we?"

"Fitzwilliam," David shook his head, "we are more than the wars of our fathers. This is *not* the medieval world. You've done things I wouldn't do."

"Then I guess no one will cry at my funeral, will they?" He glanced away and then drew back, catching his brother's gaze. "David, I'm operating on gut instinct—trust me!" Fitzwilliam said, slapping his brother on the back as they rose from the table and made their way out of the boardroom.

David glanced at the portraits of Darcy men about the boardroom as he walked out shaking his head. ...*There's nothing like a wake of blood to see where you've been is there, Brother? We're just like our predecessors.*

Welcome to Charleston
The City of Hospitality

Beaufort above, Lawton Townhouse below

Chapter Fifty-one

... She was putty in his hands ...

The flight to Charleston gave David much needed time to reflect and read. First of all, he took Fitzwilliam's advice and picked up a copy of **The Prince.** He remembered it from his studies, and if he recalled correctly, many powerful men of Europe had taken this advice to heart, including some in his own family.

The theory in principle was a good one, but in practice, it was heartless and bloody. He also knew what his brother alluded to concerning their family in the Middle Ages. It had been brother against brother and cousin against cousin, but this wasn't the Middle Ages. David thought for once, he might have to be the tempering force in his family. He'd have to wait and see.

After hours of reading, his thoughts inevitably turned to Cecilia Lawton. David wondered if she'd seen the December issue of *GQ Magazine* where he was on the cover, or if she would even notice it. He'd been featured in a full length article as one of the most eligible bachelors and well dressed international businessmen in the U.K. The interview had been one of the things he'd agreed to do in order to clean up his image, but the article was secretly dedicated to Cecilia. Although the dedication was privately held in his heart, there were enough subtle hints that he hoped she would notice.

Pemberley Two touched down in Charleston in the mid-afternoon. Cecilia waited in the terminal, and when he came through customs with his luggage, she greeted him, looking even better than the last time he'd seen her.

"David, don't you look good, just like on the cover of *Gentleman's Quarterly*," she said reaching up to give him a quick kiss as they walked.

"You saw that, did you?"

"How could I miss it?! It was displayed in every checkout line I went through last week. Naturally I had to buy a copy, if for no other reason than to read about what the hottest bachelor of the year had to say. After all, *every girl's crazy 'bout a sharp dressed man*, and I'm to spend a whole week with him." She gave him an affectionate squeeze as they moved through the airport towards the door.

"So now you're quoting ZZ Top, are you?"

"Well, it's true, and besides, that's what the journalist said, not me." She laughed. "But seriously, David, you really are sexy, you know."

"Cecilia, you're such a flirt. Tell me truthfully, what did you think of the interview?"

"Well, if I didn't know better, I'd say you have softened towards marriage, although I realize that's *not* what you said. It was rather implied as some sort of tease, I'm sure, for all of us hopeful girls who swoon when you walk by."

Glancing down he mused ... *So she did get it...almost...*

"Hah!" Amused, he continued as they walked through the airport door to the outside. "Cecilia, what are your plans for the week?"

With a quick glance, she replied, "We're staying at the Lawton Townhouse for part of the week. I want to show you as much of Charleston as I can, and I want you to see Carlton Plantation, my family home, and then Lawton Hall, my Sea Island Cotton plantation on St. Helena Island."

"I look forward to it. Anything else?"

"Yes. I'd like for you to learn a little bit about our culture and history, especially Charleston, so tomorrow I'm going to take you through the Downtown Historical District and to the Old Market Place. It's been in operation for nearly three hundred years. People still bring their wares to sell each day, and fishermen bring their morning's catch. My staff buys produce and fish there almost daily. In fact, we're having She Crab Chowder tonight from today's catch. You're going to get enough Charleston food to last a lifetime." She giggled as they walked through the parking garage to where her car waited.

Rummaging through her purse, she pulled out the keys and tossed them to him.

Catching them in mid-air, he quickly opened the boot.

"It sounds like fun. What are we doing tonight?" he asked light-heartedly while loading his things into her car.

"We're going to have a quiet dinner at home and rest. Tomorrow will be a busy day, so I thought we would watch a movie. I've chosen *Gone with the Wind*. Is that all right with you? It's fitting for what we'll be doing tomorrow."

"I'm easy, and it's been a while since I've seen it, so frankly, my dear, I don't give a damn!" He winked as he slammed the boot shut.

"You tease!" She tapped his arm playfully at the sound of his rich laughter.

"Now, what about James Island? Will I get a chance to see your home there as well?"

"No," she shifted nervously, "not this time. My friend that I told you about is staying there. She's not been feeling well lately. I don't want to disturb her, but next time, we'll make a point of it."

Changing the subject, she said, "David, you know where I live, so why don't you drive?"

"All right, I don't mind if I do," he said as he walked around and opened her car door.

Walking into the townhouse, Cecilia addressed a servant, while handing him the keys, "John, take Mr. Darcy's things up to the room that adjoins mine, and put the car in the garage."

Strolling down the hall, they entered a room with large windows on two sides. "Well, David, we're here. This is the sunroom—my favorite. Over there from that window, there's a nice view of Charleston Harbor. Make yourself at home. I'm going into the kitchen to see how dinner is coming along. When I come back, I'll give you a short tour of the house."

"Take your time," he said.

After Cecilia left, David moved to the far window and looked out over the harbor at the sailboats and large freighters slowly moving over the ocean. The moon was rising out of the east, casting a tranquil shadow over the still waters as the rising tide slapped against the barrier. A slight smile crossed his face. *...I've one week to accomplish my goal... one week...and it begins tonight.*

Engrossed in his thoughts, David didn't notice Cecilia entering the room until she spoke. "Dinner is almost ready. Let me give you the tour before we eat."

Turning, he smiled. "Let's go."

Leading him down the hall and to the right, she opened the first door they came to. "This is my office. I do most of my work for the Charleston Historical Society here, and those are my collection of history books and journals." She gestured to the oak bookcases that lined the four walls.

David walked into the room, studying it carefully, getting a feel for the lady who owned it. Strolling over to one of the bookcases, he pulled out a copy of **A Defense of Virginia and the South** by Robert L. Dabney. Opening the book, he read a few paragraphs and smiled… *interesting.*

"Come on, and I'll show you the library."

Placing the book back in its place, he turned to follow her.

Walking down to the next room, she opened another door. "This is the family library where we have an extensive collection of classical works dating back three hundred years. Every generation has contributed to it."

Glancing around, David was reminded of his own family's library at Darcy House and Pemberley. His family also had contributed books to their libraries throughout the generations. Walking over to the closest shelf, he ran his fingers over the selections. There were leather bound copies of Henry Fielding, Daniel Defoe, Edward Gibbon, and Plutarch.

Placing her hand on his shoulder, she nudged. "Now, if you'll follow me, we'll see the front parlor and family room. They overlook the park across the street. You saw the parlor when you were here last, but not the family room." She led him through a wide opening leading into a beautifully decorated room.

As they walked into the room, he noticed two sofas facing one another with a small table in between sitting in a little ways from a large bay window. A pair of wingback chairs faced one another across a chess table. Persian rugs, heavy silk curtains, lamps, vases, and various tables graced the room—all from the antebellum period. Impressed by her taste, he smiled.

Continuing to glance about, he spied a substantial fireplace covering one entire wall decorated with a large family portrait hanging above it, probably from the 1800s. The woman resembled Cecilia—blonde with the same violet-blue eyes. He strolled over and stood in front of the painting.

"Who is that woman?" he asked, pointing to the work of art above the mantelpiece.

"That is Cecilia Sabina Lawton, my ancestral grandmother from the Civil War Era." She glanced between David and the portrait. "You see the resemblance, don't you?"

"Yes, she looks very much like you." He tore his eyes away and looked at Cecilia. "Your home is very beautiful, very tastefully decorated."

"Thank you," she said with a smile. "Downstairs there's a bathroom and the servants' quarters, and I'll show you where the breakfast room and kitchen are located. After that, we'll eat and tour the upstairs later."

After dinner and touring the second and third levels, they retired to the entertainment room where they planned to watch *Gone with the Wind,* and maybe, if time allowed, *Scarlett.* Lying on the chaise lounge, David held her close as he slipped his hand under her sweater and cupped her breast, gently caressing and stroking. While he supported her against his body, Cecilia rested her head on his shoulder just under his chin, comfortable and content.

Turning in his arms, she nestled closer and breathed in his spicy masculine scent. God help her. He was getting to her. Unable to resist, she reached up and guided his mouth to hers. The gentle caress of his hand, the closeness of his body, and the comfortable coziness of him being with her was more than she'd expected. Somehow this felt natural and right. He snuggled her closer. Cecilia looked up at him and briefly stared. She was right. David was very much like Rhett—confident, sure of himself, and just as handsome. She softly shook her head and returned to the film.

Once the movie ended, they both realized the hour had grown late and decided to forgo *Scarlett* until tomorrow. As they walked up the stairs, Cecilia turned to David.

"I've given you the room next to mine. The two rooms are separated by a common dressing room and sitting area. When you're ready, meet me in my room, and we'll shower together."

David squeezed her waist. "You know, I've never showered with anyone before."

She chuckled. "Really? Well, you're in for a new experience, then, aren't you? Next time we'll take a bubble bath. I bet you haven't done that either."

"I'm always up to new experiences."

"I bet!"

As they reached the landing, she put her arm around his waist and led him into the family wing. "Well, this is it. This is my room and yours is one door down. Meet me when you're ready." Without even realizing it, she found herself kissing him. Breaking away, he smiled and tapped her nose, then left for his room.

Ten minutes later David entered her room dressed in nothing but a robe and carrying a bottle of champagne with two long stemmed flutes and a bag.

"What's that?"

"It's for you. I bought it in London." He handed her the bag. "The candle is Sensual Orchid. When I smelled it, I thought of you. The CD is Santana's *Abraxas*. It's a favorite of mine."

"David, this is so sweet of you. Sensual Orchid is one of my favorite scents." She smiled. "Come. I've prepared something for you, too."

There by the bed on a round side-table set a bowl of strawberries, a bowl of chocolate fondue, and a bottle of wine with two wine glasses. She took David's champagne and flutes and set them with the wine.

"When I left you in the sunroom, I arranged for this surprise to be set up while we watched the movie."

She walked over to the entertainment cabinet and placed the candle next to the sound system. After putting the CD in, she lit the candle.

As David inspected the wine, Cecilia said. "Let's have the champagne tonight. We'll have the wine another time."

A small smile curled his lips. Setting the wine down, he opened the bottle of champagne and poured two glasses.

Lifting the flute to his lips, David took a small sip. "Drop your robe."

Her breath caught in her lungs. The intense look in his dark eyes sent quivers coursing through her body. She set her glass aside. Slowly, she untied her robe and slipped it off her shoulders, dropping it to floor. His eyes caressed her body as the silky cotton fell. After a long slow drink, he set his glass next to hers. Untying his own robe, he let it fall into a puddle beside hers.

Reaching over, he tenderly caressed her face with the tips of his fingers before cupping it in his hands. Leaning in slowly, he kissed her sensuously on the jaw.

She swallowed hard and closed her eyes as his lips made their way to hers, gently teasing her mouth open with his tongue. As he kissed her, his fingers slid into her hair while his thumbs softly caressed her temples.

Her arms slipped around his waist and traveled up his back, caressing him as she stepped into his form, slowly surrendering as his tongue slipped in and out of her mouth, making her body shudder.

Reluctantly breaking the kiss, she breathed deeply to recover her composure. "Let's take a seat on the bed and listen to the music," she whispered softly. "I've set it to auto replay. After a song or two, we'll shower."

Sitting across from him on the bed, Cecilia took a strawberry and dipped it in chocolate. "Here, have one."

As she fed him, he turned and licked her finger, taking it into his mouth and suckling it.

Picking up a strawberry, he returned the gesture, accidentally smearing chocolate on her mouth. He smiled. "Here, let me get that." Taking his finger, he wiped the chocolate from her mouth and teased her lips.

She turned and suckled his finger. "You remembered."

"Lawton, I remember everything about you. That night you had me in such a state that, to coin a Southern phrase, 'You turned me every which way, but loose.'"

"Ah," she laughed, "but as I recall *I* did turn you loose."

He chuckled as he took another strawberry. "I remember it quite well. I wanted you so badly, I physically hurt. But it is a good thing the evening ended as it did, or I may not have taken notice of you on a deeper level," he said with a soft smile. "I want you to know that no one has ever done that to me before."

"I can imagine not, and it almost killed me to do it. I wanted you that night, too. It took every ounce of willpower I had to turn you away."

"It worked out for the best, though, and here we are."

"Yes, here we are." She dipped another strawberry and put it to his mouth, and then took a sip of champagne. They continued to relax, sipping champagne and eating strawberries while they listened to the music.

"David, this is a side of you I would have never guessed existed, but since our dinner at the Woodlands and now this, well, I must say I am pleasantly impressed." She arched one eyebrow as she raised her glass.

"Let it never be said that a Darcy wasn't a gentleman."

David set his glass down and took hers, placing it with his. "Umm... you smell good...jasmine and orange blossom...my favorite." He slowly brushed his nose against her cheek. Taking her mouth in a slow sensual kiss, David reached back and pulled her closer, slipping his tongue inside her mouth, dueling with hers and suckling her lips. Kissing his way down her neck, David gave her a playful bite as the tips of his fingers glided down her shoulder to her breast, lightly fondling it in a gentle caress.

His warm breath against her skin caused Cecilia to tremble violently. The scent of the candle, the mood set by the music, and the bubbles of the champagne all created an atmosphere she'd never shared with anyone. He could open the door to her soul with a simple kiss. She was confused. She was supposed to be the one seducing him and yet she was falling prey to his every whim. She was putty in his hands.

Breathing heavily, she broke the kiss. "David, let's shower first, then we'll go to bed."

His lips curved. "Whatever you would like."

She took him by the hand and led him to the shower where she turned on the water. When the temperature was right, she guided him inside, and they both allowed the water to wash over them.

Taking the shampoo from the shelf, David said, "Let me wash your hair." Squeezing a small amount into his hand, he began to lather her hair, gently massaging her scalp. "Umm, this is not so difficult." After a moment, David backed Cecilia into the stream of water and said, "Close your eyes, love. Can't let the soap get in your beautiful eyes."

He placed a generous amount shower gel on a bath sponge and began to slowly wash her back, working his way down her bottom, her thighs, her calves, and feet. While kneeling down, he turned her around and began working his way back up. Dropping the sponge, David put some gel on his hands and began to massage between her thighs before returning to her breasts where he gently stroked, washing and caressing them.

Staring at Cecilia intently as she closed her eyes, he returned down her body, his hand finding its way to her center and his finger to the heart of her desire. She moaned in pleasure, falling into him. Cecilia shuddered violently, flushed with intense pleasure before breaking away. She could feel the heat of his gaze, but she couldn't meet his stare—not yet.

He tipped her chin and asked with a boyish grin, "Are you all right?"

Finally composed, she returned his smile. "Yes, but now it's your turn. Turnabout *is* fair play." She raised an eyebrow and took the gel. When she came to his erection, she dropped the sponge and took him in her hands, stroking and watching him. He moaned, and she couldn't tell if it was in pleasure or pain.

"Oh God, Cecilia, stop—stop now!"

"Why, David?" she teased.

"Because if you don't, I'm going to explode, and that's not how I want to come."

"How do you want to come?"

"Inside of you!"

David quickly turned around and pushed her against the tiles as he lifted her up, letting her long legs wrap around his waist. David kissed her hard and deep, unleashing his passion until he gave her all that he had. As a wave of pleasure swept over them, they both slid down the wall into a puddle on the shower floor while the water splashed over their bodies.

Breathlessly, Cecilia gasped, "I thought you weren't experienced in the shower."

"I'm a quick study, and you're a good teacher."

"No," she chuckled, "you're the good teacher. This was my first time, too."

He laughed. "Well, at least we have our first in something. Let me help you up."

Cecilia smiled. ...*We have our firsts in many things, David Darcy. There's never been anyone quite like you.*

As they stepped out of the shower, Cecilia grabbed a towel and handed it to him. "Dry me off, and then I'll dry you."

He smiled and took the towel. When finished, they made their way back to the bedroom where she turned down the bed and gently guided him to her under the covers. Thinking they would probably sleep after their intense love making in the shower, she reached to give him a goodnight kiss, but when their lips met, she knew sleep was not on his mind.

"David, don't you ever get enough?"

"No, do you?"

"No."

Gathering her into his arms, they made love over and over again until exhaustion overcame them. While laying there in one another's arms, Cecilia thought about the article in *GQ Magazine.*

When asked about a serious relationship, he had said, *"I'm an alpha male with a strong sexual appetite, but should I ever commit, I would be faithful. I don't believe in infidelity, nor would I accept it in a partner."*

"So, Mr. Darcy, would you commit?"

"Should the right one come along, I just might."

"What do you look for in a woman, Mr Darcy?"

"What would I look for in a woman? Hmm...well, she has to be strong, independent, and able to handle herself under pressure, but she must still need a man. She would have to complement me where I am weak and allow me to be strong where I am strong. We would have to complement one another in that respect—like alpha and omega—the beginning and the end. And she would have to understand me well enough to know when to let me have my space and to know when not. And it would be the same for me with her. I'm aggressive in business as well as my personal life. When I see what I want, I pursue it."

"What physical attributes do you look for in a woman?"

"Oh, I don't know. I've been known to prefer leggy blondes with violet-blue eyes."

Cecilia reflected on that last thought. Was he talking about her? She wondered. He knew what a girl wanted and how to deliver it. He was thoughtful, kind, and patient, a gentle and tender lover, and he was confident and strong—even cocky at times. He made her feel good like a real woman... loved and cherished.

She snuggled a little closer and kissed his neck. Satiated and content, holding him close, she drifted off to sleep while breathing in his unique male scent—a scent that was soothing and relaxing. One that reminded her of recently baled fresh cut alfalfa hay in the South Carolina summertime at Carlton.

White Point Gardens and Battery Ramsey

The Battery

Chapter Fifty-two

... flirting with disaster...

When the alarm sounded at seven a.m., both David and Cecilia wondered how they would make it through the day she had planned for them. Rising out of bed, they showered and dressed. After descending the stairs, she led him to the breakfast room where the kitchen staff had prepared breakfast with toast and dark roast coffee, which both felt they desperately needed.

Looking over breakfast, David asked, "What is this?"

"Shrimp and grits. Have you never tried it?" Amused by his look, she laughed.

"No, I don't believe I have."

"Well then, you must try it."

David took a bite and smiled. "Umm...unusual, but not bad."

After they finished eating, she explained their plans for the day. "We will start by viewing the park across the street, and then we will take a turn up King Street. There are several shops there I want you to see. After we've done that, we will go to Queen Street where we'll eat lunch. Then we're going to Meeting, Broad, and Church Streets where I'll tell you a little more history and then we'll tour the old churches and cemeteries. Next, we'll go to Market Street where the Old Market Place is located. And finally, we'll visit the Old Customs Building on East Bay. So, as you can see, we have a very busy day."

"Well then, let's get to it." He smiled.

"All right," she replied as she reached over and took his hand, leading him through the house and out the door.

Entering the park, Cecilia began narrating as they walked along. "This park was known as White Point Gardens, established in 1837, and it still goes by that name, but it became Battery Ramsey when the War of Northern Aggression began. This was one of the strategic points from where the first shots were fired. It's better known now as simply Battery Park, or as we say in Charleston: The Battery."

Lacing her fingers with his, she began again. "On December 20, 1860, the South Carolina General Assembly voted to secede from the Union. They asserted that one of the causes for this action was the election to the presidency of a man 'whose opinions and purposes were hostile to slavery,' but there were other numerous causes as well, such as the unfair tariffs levied against the South—South Carolina in specific," she said. "It was obvious that the government was sucking the wealth out of the South, using it for projects in the North, and it seemed that the South was powerless to do anything about it due to the more populous northern states having control of the House of Representatives. I'll tell you more when we come to the places where it all happened, but for now, we'll stick to what happened here at White Point Gardens."

She stopped to pick up some litter and drop it in the trashcan as they walked by. "It would be less than a month after the secession before the first shot would be fired. South Carolina had been stationing battery posts all along the coastline and on a few strategic Sea Islands for months. Then, on January 9, 1861, cadets from the Citadel fired on the Union ship *Star of the West* as it tried to enter Charleston Harbor."

Pointing to a small mass in the distance, she said, "That island on the horizon became the flash point on April 12, 1861, when shore batteries under the command of CSA Brigadier General Pierre G. T. Beauregard opened fire upon the Union-held Fort Sumter in Charleston Harbor.

"Negotiations with Major Robert Anderson, the garrison commander, had begun on April 9, 1861 and lasted until the 12th. General Beauregard had demanded the surrender of the Union garrison at Fort Sumter. Major Anderson refused. So, at 4:30 in the morning, with a single mortar round fired from Fort Johnson, the American Civil War was underway. The beginning of a long dreaded and equally anticipated war exploded over Fort Sumter with a forty-three guns and mortar bombardment launched from Fort Moultrie, Fort Johnson, the Floating Battery of Charleston Harbor, and Cummings Point. According to the diary of a famous Charlestonian woman, Mary Chesnut, the shelling from the shore batteries ringing the harbor awakened Charleston's residents, and they rushed out into the predawn darkness, watching with shouts of jubilee, having a grand time as the shells arced over the water and burst inside Fort Sumter, lighting up the darkened sky."

David looked out into the harbor at the small island dotting the horizon. "It must have been something to see."

Cecilia softly spoke. "I've been told it was much like a celebration of fireworks. My ancestral grandmother, Cecilia Sebina Lawton, watched it from the third story piazza of our townhouse. That event was the official marking of the beginning of the bloodiest war this nation had ever fought up until WW II. Brother fought against brother and father against son." Cecilia shook her head and wiped a tear away.

Strolling along to where the big cannons sat, she paused for a moment, placing her hand on one of them. "Officers and cadets from the Citadel were assigned to various Confederate batteries during the assault on Fort Sumter. My grandfather, four generations back, Cecilia's husband, Wallace Lawton, was a Citadel cadet at the time and had been stationed with the shore batteries here in White Point Gardens. He wrote in his journal that after a thirty-four-hour bombardment, Major Robert Anderson finally surrendered the fort on the morning of April 14, 1861. All of Charleston came out in the streets, dancing and celebrating, not realizing they were celebrating their own demise."

As David glanced at Cecilia, he couldn't help but think how this was very real to her, as if she'd been the one on the veranda witnessing the event rather than the one retelling a historical account.

Looking out over the harbor, David shook his head. With the live oaks hanging heavy with Spanish moss and the gentle breezes blowing in off the ocean, the tranquility here belied the park's history. He took Cecilia's hand in his and gently pressed it as they walked.

"I thought the military institutions closed during the war. Is that not true?"

"Some think they closed down, but no, that's not true. The Citadel and the Arsenal Academy in Columbia, South Carolina continued to operate *as* academies, but the cadets were made a part of the South Carolina Military Department, forming the Battalion of State Cadets. They aided the Confederate Army by training recruits, manufacturing ammunition, protecting arms depots, and guarding Union prisoners.

"They carried on in that capacity until December of 1864. That was when the State Cadets joined Confederate forces at Tullifinny Creek in an attempt to stop the Union troops advancing on Charleston from General William Tecumseh Sherman's army, but on February 17, 1865, Charleston fell and the Mayor of Charleston surrendered control of the city to General Alexander Schimmelfennig on the 18th, while Sherman went on to take Columbia. It happened at nine o'clock on a Saturday morning. It was heartbreaking, and Charlestonians were in shock as Union troops moved into the city and took control."

Cecilia shook her head. "Sherman's March from Atlanta to Savannah, and finally to South Carolina—bloody and sickening." She repressed a sob. "The bloom of the South was picked. A whole generation of our men was decimated, lying dead in battlefields across the South and at Gettysburg. It would not be until the 20th century that we would recover. The war and events that followed were spoken of for years as the recent unpleasantness by the genteel ladies of Charleston. They could not bear to speak the words 'Civil War'."

"Unpleasantness indeed!" David breathed out. "It sounds a lot like the movie we watched last night."

"Yes, but the book details so much more. It's a very comprehensive history of a bygone era. Margaret Mitchell captured it well. She thoroughly researched both Charleston and Savannah, Georgia when she wrote her book. The shanty town scene is an actual historical event that happened north of Charleston just as Mitchell outlined it in her book. Read it some time. Much of it is based on the actual history of Charleston and Savannah."

"I will." He squeezed her hand as they walked.

Reaching the edge of the park, she turned to him. "This is all I have to show you here. I'll tell you more when we reach some of the other sites. Now, let's head to King Street."

Leaving the park, they strolled across Battery and up King Street where she showed him the various shops. Many of which had been established before the Civil War and still sold some of the same type of goods as they had back then.

"Over there," she pointed to the King Street Tailor Shop, "is where historical period fashions are recreated for the various reenactment functions during the season, which will officially begin on December 12th. They measure you and sew authentic clothing for the costume balls held during that time. You can also get a bespoke suit made there. It's the only kind my father ever wore."

"How many functions do you have that would warrant period style clothing?"

"We have two that I attend, sometimes as hostess. One is the Antebellum Christmas Ball and the other is the Camellia Ball. However, next year the Magnolia Ball will also be a reenactment, celebrated on the 20th of April in commemoration of the firing on Fort Sumter. It's going to be a grand event. The Charleston Historical Society is sponsoring it."

"You know, I rather enjoyed myself last April, and I normally don't at those types of functions. In fact, I almost didn't come, but I'm glad I did."

"I'm glad you did, too. It was one of the best times I've had in a long time," she said in a near whisper.

David circled his arm around her waist and gently hugged her.

Strolling up the street, Cecilia showed him the bookstores and the historical artifacts and antique shops, explaining their significance. "These shops sell histories, journals, and antiques from the Civil War period, but occasionally there will be something from further back. There are all kinds of interesting things in there. If you remember from attending the historical society meeting with me, you know we comb the South looking for old journals from the 1600s through the 1900s to publish and sell in these shops. This helps to preserve the truth of what actually happened during that period in our history," she said. "One thing I learned from my father is that the truth is not always found in a history book. If you want to know what really happened, look at period writings and journals instead of relying on someone else's slant."

Walking across the street, they entered Ben Silver's. "David, you're going to like this store. Ben Silver's the embodiment of elegant haberdashery. At one time, stores like this were on every town square in America, but now I'm told they can only be found on London's Savile Row. This is a step back in time."

Looking around, David could see she was exactly right. Perusing through the selections, he found many things that could be found in the finest shops in London. There were fine shirtings, blazers, and suits, and on the hand-carved shelves, authentic English-made shoes were displayed. Smoking jackets, dressing gowns and evening wear of every style conceivable hung discreetly near the storefront window. He walked towards the back and found elegant socks, fine cufflinks, and leather braces lining the shelves. Anything he could want was here. He smiled. "Should I ever have a need for something whilst in Charleston, I now at least know where to come."

"Yes, this was one of the few places my father would shop—that and the tailor shop I told you about. Daddy liked fine accessories, and that's what he wore. My favorite shop for lady's things is Bits of Lace, but I won't bore you with that. Let's get something to eat before we continue. Come on." She grabbed his hand. "We're going to the café on Queen Street."

Once they reached the café, they sat under the pergola eating their sandwiches and sipping tea—his hot, hers cold. After lunch, they walked up Meeting Street to a bank building where she explained the beginnings of the Confederacy.

"On this very site where the bank now stands was the location of the South Carolina Institute Hall where it all began with the election of Abraham Lincoln. South Carolina had warned that if the Republicans won, South Carolina would use its Constitutional right and withdraw from the Union. Therefore, on November 10, 1860, following the election, the General Assembly called for a Convention of the People of South Carolina to draft a secession ordinance.

"They met first on the 17th of December, 1860, in the First Baptist Church of Colombia, but there was an epidemic of smallpox in the capital at that time, so the convention was adjourned to Charleston where they met here at Institute Hall on the 19th."

David ran his fingers over the brass marker on the bank's brick wall as she talked.

"The movement to secede from the Union was driven by the Lowcountry Planters—primarily those from Beaufort and Georgetown as they controlled the South Carolina General Assembly. They drew up the Ordinance of Session and the planters, aided by the fiery rhetoric of Robert Barnwell Rhett and the Charleston Mercury, persuaded the Charleston merchant class to vote for secession. So, the next day, on December 20th, 1860, they met in St. Andrew's Hall on Broad Street to adopt the resolution on a roll call ballot. The vote was 169 to 0. Before it was all said and done, eleven Southern States would eventually withdraw from the Union and come together to form the Confederate States of America." She once more took David's hand and said, "Let's walk on."

They went down Meeting Street to Broad and stood in front of a large parking lot. "This is the location of St. Andrew's Hall where the infamous vote was cast. The original building was destroyed almost a year later, as was the South Carolina Institute Hall along with five hundred beautiful homes, churches, and public buildings. They were all destroyed on the 12th of December by one of the worse fires in our history. The horrible event was known as the fire of 1861. It was a pity, too, because St. Andrew's Hall was also home to the St. Cecilia Society and the heart of the social life for upper class Charlestonians in its day." She sighed and looked at David. "St Cecilia was a members-only club and hosted the most exclusive and elegant balls of the season. Even today, its historical records remain sealed to non-members."

"Was your family a member?"

"What do you think?"

He smiled. "Of course they were, and that's interesting, but don't you think it rather strange that the city burned, these locations in particular, nearly a year later?"

"Yes, I do—almost like an omen and a warning of things to come. That, coupled with the almost daily cannon bombardment from the Union forces, nearly destroyed our city." She shook her head as she reached for his hand. "Come on; we're going to Church Street next. Our most famous cemetery is located there, along with the churchyard cemetery of my family."

As they walked from Broad Street to Church, she continued. "The seeds of the Civil War were planted by John C. Calhoun, who is considered our most famous town father. During the first half of the 19th century, he was a leading southern politician and political philosopher from South Carolina."

"I've read about him. He had a varying career, I do believe."

"Yes, he did. He served as vice president under Presidents John Quincy Adams and Andrew Jackson, although he resigned the vice presidency two years into the Jackson term." She leaned into David as they walked. "He was disappointed with Jackson on the issue of slavery and states' rights, so he decided he could be of more use to South Carolina in the U.S. Senate."

Turning onto Church Street, they walked on to the historical churches and cemeteries. Pointing to St. Phillips Churchyard, Cecilia commented, "That is Calhoun's tomb over there. It's the largest monument. You can't miss it. The leading fathers of South Carolina are also buried in that cemetery. And over there," she pointed to the opposite side of the street, "is the Lawton family church. My grandmother, four generations back, is buried there along with her husband, Wallace, and their six children. You saw her portrait in the library. I'm named after her. Let's walk over." Stepping out onto the street, they walked over to an old parish cemetery covered in leaves.

"You look just like her, you know. She was a strikingly beautiful woman, but looked rather young in that painting."

"She was young—barely seventeen when she married Wallace. They were married two days before the firing on Fort Sumter, and yes, I know cadets were not allowed to marry. But he was one month away from graduation, and they wanted to marry before he went to war, therefore it was done in secret. Things were changing rapidly, and there was no assurance of tomorrow. She had to grow up hard and fast like I've had to. I'm well named as we are quite alike."

"I'm sure you are. She sounds like a lovely lady who could take control, much like someone else I know," he said. "Continue on. I want to hear the rest of it."

Cecilia went on to tell how Wallace had taken his young wife to her family's plantation in the countryside of Savannah for safekeeping while he went to war and how he later had to come and rescue her from Sherman's advancing army. All of her family had been killed or died while the plantation home was burned to the ground as it fell in Sherman's path. Cecilia and her young daughter were the only ones of the family to survive and that had only been because of faithful slaves who had hidden them in the swamps.

"The Union Army burned everything. They took our food, leaving us to starve, burning what they could not eat. They killed all of the livestock, horses, and mules, leaving them to rot where they dropped. There was massive starvation and malnutrition. No one was spared in Sherman's wake, from the planter to the cracker, the poorest of them all. They were all affected and burned out. The intent was to teach the South, particularly South Carolina, a lesson. Cecilia recorded in her journal how they walked for mile after mile with their nostrils filled with the stench of the dead and dying, animals and people alike. It was a horrible time, and it only got worse after the war.

"People with money were in short supply, and jobs were scarce. Some planters, particularly the rice planters, did pay their ex-slaves a regular wage for their labor and kept them on. We were eventually able to return to Carlton and hired many of our former slaves, too. Samuel had foreseen the collapse of our economy and had our gold safely stored away in a bank in England under the care of some of our English relatives."

Brushing her fingertips over her ancestor's gravestone, she sighed. "Samuel died in 1861, consequently he did not see the destruction, but Cecilia and Wallace did. They witnessed a way of life that had existed for nearly two centuries in South Carolina destroyed—swept away, seemingly overnight. Hence Margaret Mitchell's title, '**Gone with the Wind.**' It's called the death of the Old South. Some say it was a good thing. I don't know. I'm not defending the Old South. I'm only telling you what happened.

"However, one thing was for certain. Coping with the new social and economic order was not easy for anyone, black or white, and South Carolina's response to the results of the war did not please Washington, so we soon found ourselves in the throes of Reconstruction."

The entire time he listened, David couldn't help but admire the Lawton family. They were survivors just like the Darcys. Her story was not unlike some recorded in his own family journals—tales of how his family had survived through the Middle Ages, into the Renaissance, and to the present day. He couldn't resist giving Cecilia a gentle hug.

Standing under the tall oaks, she pointed to five small graves. "Cecilia's five young children died during Reconstruction due to disease and poor nutrition. They were all less than ten years old. Most were less than five. Only one son survived, and through him, one son up to my father, who tragically lost his only son. The Lawtons have never been able to have more than one son since the war, and in my case, child, to survive to adulthood." She paused for a moment and picked up a leaf, shredding it to bits.

"Wallace Lawton became a broken man, as he could not accept the death of the Old South. His father, mother, and all of his brothers died during the war, leaving his family, my line, to be the last of the Lawtons." She repressed a sob.

"It was Cecilia who pulled her family through. Her husband surrendered to drunkenness and gambling, neglecting his family, but when he died, she controlled everything through her son. No small endeavor, I might add, since society and the laws of that time were against women. It was a man's world, but we owe our very survival to her, and now it's down to me. Now *I* am the last of the Lawtons, and since I'm not a son, there will be no more after me."

David hugged her and released a sigh. "Someday you'll marry and have several sons."

"Perhaps." She shrugged. "That's what's expected of me. People say it's my duty and obligation."

As Cecilia talked, David walked over to a small bleached out headstone and read the caption as he ran his fingers over it in reverence. "Cecilia, whose buried here? It's different from the rest."

Cecilia joined him, placing her hand on the white stone as she read out loud.

"Chloe and Peter Chaplin...much beloved and much missed," she whispered. "This is the resting place of two former slaves that were more like family than anything else. They were dear friends. Without them, we would not have survived. Chloe was Cecilia's handmaid and close confidant, and Peter was Wallace's overseer and close friend. Peter stayed by us and convinced many of the other slaves to remain as well. Together they worked Carlton Plantation, planting and harvesting the rice. It was because of Peter that we were finally able to get back on our feet. One of his great-great grandsons is my overseer for the Carolina Gold Research Institute and Development Foundation and sits on the board of directors. He also manages all my affairs concerning the plantation. You'll meet him and his wife, Ruby, my housekeeper, when we go to Carlton Plantation tomorrow. Another one of Peter's great-great grandsons works for me at Lawton Hall. He lives there with his wife and grandson and oversees the Sea Island Cotton Foundation and sits on the foundations' board of directors. You'll meet him, too, when we go to Lawton Hall. They are known to me as Uncle Willis and Aunt Tully of Lawton Hall, and Uncle Reuben and Aunt Ruby of Carlton Plantation."

Cecilia hesitated, and then looked up. "David, in spite of what you've been told of our history, not everyone was cruel. I'd like to think that we were not. Even before they were freed, we treated our slaves well and even paid them. It was a small amount, paid at the end of the harvest. We also gave them a few pigs and a plot of land, and they were given time to work the land and raise their own food. They sold what they wanted to and were allowed to keep the money. Like I said, after the war, we kept as many on as we could, provided they wanted to stay, that is, and paid them a regular wage as best as we could."

David stepped back. "I'm glad to hear it, because my family abhorred slavery, and I have to agree with them. I had one ancestral uncle who was involved in some way with having slavery abolished in the British Virgin Isles, but I don't remember the details. However, I plan on finding out when I return home for Christmas."

He halted briefly. "I have another question. I thought it was illegal to bury a person of African descent in a white cemetery."

She gave him a pointed look. "With enough money, you can do anything you want to."

"Ah, I see."

When they left the churchyard cemetery, she took him to The Old Market Place.

"Over there," she pointed, "is the fish market I was telling you about. An experienced shopper can pick the best crabs. They must be she-crabs as the males have a strong taste which I find unpleasant. You did enjoy the She Crab Chowder, didn't you?"

"Yes, very much." He chuckled as she gave him a hug.

As she talked, David watched her and marveled as he realized he was seeing her and the people of Charleston in a different light. He smiled as she tugged at his hand leading him across the street.

"Now, let's enter the market. I want you to find something for your sister."

As they entered, David perused all the things the various vendors had to sell. There were handmade quilts, tatted lace, crocheted doilies, linens, and wood carvings as well as fruits and vegetables. He found an assortment of beautiful hair ornaments crafted from abalone shell and selected a few hair clips from among them along with a pair of hand carved bone hair sticks that he thought Georgiana would like.

Leaving the old marketplace they walked on, finally coming to the Old Custom and Exchange House on East Bay Street. The Exchange House was the center of commerce in its day, serving as both a jail and a business terminal. As they walked up the steps, she explained how business was conducted in the 19th century.

"Cotton and rice factors were an essential part of an agrarian society in antebellum times. They bought, sold, and stored cotton, rice, and other goods for planters as well as performing many different services, including placing the planter's children in boarding schools and advising their clients concerning market conditions and the wisdom of selling or withholding their crops given the current market stability, and they would also issue a line of credit against the planter's crops."

"How did it work?"

"Well, in the case of cotton, the factor would come to the field warehouse and assess the cotton for quality. Then he would find a buyer for the best price and have the cotton moved to his warehouses in Charleston where the export fees would be assessed. After they were paid, it would be shipped to a merchant in the North who would then ship it overseas. This was a very risky business because unless a planter was diversified, he could lose his entire annual income if the shipment were to be lost at sea. You see, he wasn't paid in full until the cotton was delivered. The same process held true for the rice planter."

"That's very similar to the Old Commodities Exchange in London during the same time period."

"I don't doubt that." She laughed. "Our social structure was modeled after the English. I mean we were English, after all."

David smiled, putting his arm around her. "I'll have to look it up, but I think we had a mercantile in Liverpool for both cotton and rice, and perhaps sugar."

"I wouldn't doubt that either. Your family is probably older than mine. I can only trace mine to Devonshire in the 1650s to the third Earl of Devon. One of his descendants was a member of the Lords Proprietor in 1670. We were among those that settled Charles Towne."

"Interesting, ours goes back to 1066 and there are numerous lords and marquises within the family lineage with several settling in the British Virgin Isles and Barbados."

After viewing the Exchange they made their way back to the townhouse. Strolling along Charleston Harbor's sea wall, David could not remember when he'd had a more pleasant or relaxing time. Cecilia had an air about her that spoke of class and sophistication, and it was easy for him to infer that her roots were every bit as noble as his. In fact, he wasn't even sure he knew as much about his own family as she did hers, for he, unlike his brother, had never taken the trouble to read the many journals ensconced in the family library.

Descending the steps of the barrier wall and crossing E. Battery Street to the townhouse, Cecilia asked, "David, is there anything special you would like to do tonight?"

"Let's watch the sequel to *Gone with the Wind*. I don't believe I've ever seen it."

"All right, but I have to warn you. It's not as good as *Gone with the Wind*. You can tell Margaret Mitchell did not write the book, but it does finish the story," she said. "Though, David, I highly recommend that you obtain the books and read them for yourself because so much was left out, especially from *Gone with the Wind*."

"I'll do that. I never thought I would enjoy a chick flick, but this is a fascinating story. I want to go back to some of those little shops and buy some books. I don't often read for pleasure, but Fitzwilliam reads all the time, and so did Elizabeth. He's been out of sorts lately, so I think I'll buy him a book, too."

She looked at him curiously. "Elizabeth? I've never heard you speak of her."

"She was Fitzwilliam's wife."

"Was?"

"Yes," he sighed, "she left him, and I've been very worried about him. He's not been the same since they separated. She left him without cause or reason. He was devastated. I have hired investigators to find her, but so far they've been unsuccessful in locating her."

"Are you sure she didn't have a reason? I mean it's highly unusual for a woman to just up and leave, don't you think?"

"No, I know she had no reason. I don't know the particulars, but I do know they fought bitterly whilst they were separated during our struggle. It seemed that she wanted him to spend more time talking to her on the phone than he had to spend. She couldn't understand the pressure he was under." David shrugged. "He was doing the best he could both by her and his responsibilities to our family. Apparently she wasn't concerned about what he was going through or his feelings. Her only concern was for herself."

"Well, David, sometimes things are not as they seem. I'm sure she must have loved him."

"If she loved him, then why did she leave? No, had she loved him, she would've understood and waited for him, but instead she ran at the first sign of trouble." Turning to Cecilia, he asked, "What was he supposed to do? Abandon everything for her?!"

"No, David, but a man is supposed to see to it that his wife is secure in their marriage. He should have made every effort to see that she was assured of her importance to him—that she mattered first in his life. It sounds to me like he took her for granted."

David bristled. "You don't even know Elizabeth. How could you say such a thing? I don't know what more Fitzwilliam could have done!"

"I don't know Fitzwilliam, either," Cecilia responded defensively, "but I do know there are two sides to every story. I'm just telling you how I see it from a woman's perspective."

"Well, I'm telling you my brother is an honorable man. In fact, he is the best of men, and whilst he might be the forgiving type, I certainly am *not*. If she were my wife, I don't think I could ever forgive her for her lack of faith and trust, nor would I have her back. My temper is resentful at best. When my opinion is formed, it's rarely changed, and Elizabeth Darcy has lost my good opinion forever."

Shocked, Cecilia reeled from his vehemence. As they silently walked across the courtyard and into the house, she shuddered. *...I'm flirting with disaster. I have got to be careful!*

Lawton Family Cemetery 19th Century

Lawton Family Cemetery 18th Century

A Sea Island Garden

Carolina Gold Rice

Chapter Fifty-three

… They were simply a man and a woman falling in love…

As they entered the house, the scent of something delicious greeted them. "What's for dinner? It smells scrumptious," David said as he gently tapped Cecilia's bum and then rubbed it.

"That's just like a man. Are you ruled by your belly?"

"Not quite," he said as they walked towards the stairs.

"Well, we're having beef a la mode, Hoppin John with Carolina rice, spinach and mushroom casserole, homemade bread, and blackberry cobbler. You'll like it." She reached up and tapped his lips as they climbed the stairs arm in arm.

"I'm sure I will. You have excellent cooks."

When they reached the landing, she turned and said, "I'm going to change and freshen up. Meet me in my room in twenty minutes, and we'll go downstairs together."

With dinner finished, they once again went to the entertainment room to watch the second film. Curled up together on the chaise lounge, he held her as he had the night before while they watched *Scarlett*. Snuggled close, David couldn't help but think how right it felt to be here with her, and for once, there was no place he'd rather be. When the movie ended, David contemplated how much Cecilia resembled the heroine and how his own personality mirrored that of Rhett Butler's.

"What a difficult time they had! Do you suppose it's always like that?"

"Oh, I don't know. When two head strong people come together, there's usually trouble if there is not a deep commitment and devotion to one another, but what would I know about it? My parents were like Scarlett and Rhett, but unfortunately, their marriage didn't end as happily as it does in the movies. I suppose it never does. Now let's get ready for bed. Tomorrow will be another busy day. We're going to my home, Carlton Plantation."

"I'm looking forward to seeing your childhood home. Maybe someday I can show you my home, Pemberley, in Derbyshire. It's in the North of England."

"I'd love that," she said as they took the stairs to her room.

That night they once again made love into the wee hours of the morning. When both were sated, they held one another until sleep overtook them.

Up again at seven a.m., they made their way downstairs to the breakfast room where the kitchen staff had prepared Spanish omelets with mushroom sauce, raspberry crepes, and coffee.

Finishing the last of his crepes, David said, "This was very good. You must give my compliments to your cook." Wiping his mouth, he put his napkin aside. "Now what's first on our schedule for today?"

Cecilia pushed her chair back and rose from the table. "I've decided we'll leave straight for Carlton. There's a lot to see there, and I want to arrive before lunch. John has the car loaded. Let's get going."

After finishing their preparations, they headed twenty-five miles northwest, up Hwy 61, the Ashley River Road, into the heart of Lowcountry. The trip from

M.K. Baxley

Charleston to Carlton Plantation was beautiful. Winding roads lined with Carolina Pines and live oaks draped in Spanish moss created an enjoyable drive as they exited the city. The cabbage palmetto palm, South Carolina's state tree, grew wild everywhere, and the clear blue sky was gorgeous cast against the deep green of the conifer trees in the open countryside.

When they finally came upon the massive lands of Carlton Plantation, David observed the landscape as they turned onto Lawton River Road. Cypress knees peeked through the murky water in the marshes where an occasional turtle dropped into the river from a snagged log, and willow oaks hung over the riverbank. Alligators sunned themselves on the sunny banks while gulls flew overhead and cranes waded in the swamp waters.

"Well, this is it. This is the beginning of Carlton Plantation, one of only two rice plantations still in operation in South Carolina. About a mile and a half more, and the first glimpse of the house will come into view. What do you think so far?"

"It's huge. Far bigger than I expected, and it's beautiful. What's the name of the other rice plantation and who owns it?"

"The other plantation is Whispering Winds, and it's owned by my godfather, Daniel Russell. It's located down in Beaufort County."

They followed a winding road lined with huge trees draped in grey-green tendrils as it snaked its way around to the entrance of the massive house of Carlton Plantation.

"Carlton House is designed in the antebellum architectural style of the 1820s when it was originally built. It replaced the original house built in 1710. Very stately, don't you think?"

"Yes, yes it is and the grounds are magnificent." David glanced around. There were ancient magnolias, wisterias, mimosas, crape myrtles, pecan trees, and gardens of fragrant gardenias and jasmine, along with azaleas, which at this time of year were not in bloom, although the camellias, hibiscus, roses, and chrysanthemums were.

Turning to Cecilia, David asked. "How did it come by the name of Carlton House—not after the Prince Regent, surely?"

"No," she laughed, "John Francis Carlton was the original landowner, but it passed to his grandson, Franklin Lawton, in 1735 when Carlton's only son died at sea. The Carlton rice plantation and the Lawton indigo dye plantation bordered one another, and subsequently, they combined when Franklin took possession of his inheritance."

"I see." David nodded.

As they pulled around to the front entrance, Cecilia gestured with her hand. "Well, this is it. We'll put our things in the master suite, have lunch, and then we'll go to the stables and have two horses saddled, if you'd like. I'm assuming you do ride since you are an English gentleman," she said, giving him a mischievous look as she popped the hatch and exited the car.

"I ride, probably as well as you do," he chuckled, "provided it's an English saddle."

"Is there any other?" She arched one eyebrow."

As they took their things up the steps, an older black man looked up and greeted them as he came through the door. "Miss Cecilia," he said with a broad smile. "What a pleasure to have you home."

"Uncle Reuben!" Cecilia stepped forward and gave the old man a warm hug and a kiss. "How are you and how is everything going?"

The old man laughed. "Things couldn't be better. With the rice harvest complete, we will soon be preparing the fields for spring, and I was about to go and see about your mare up at Blue Willow Farms."

"Good. When you return, I want to talk with you, and give Solomon and Miss

Evelyn my best regards."

"I'll do that, and you best get in the house and see Ruby. She and Tuwanda have been up since dawn cookin' up a storm. She's been askin' about you ever since you called, tellin' her you were comin' up."

"Well, before you go, I'd like to introduce a friend and business associate, David Darcy from Derbyshire, England. David, this is my overseer and manager of Carlton Plantation, Reuben Chaplin. Reuben sits on the board of the Carolina Gold Research Institute and Development Foundation," she said with a smile.

Reuben stepped forward. "I'm always pleased to meet any of Miss Lawton's associates."

As David took the proffered hand, he responded, "It's a pleasure to meet you, Mr. Chaplin. Miss Lawton has spoken very highly of you, and I'm honored to finally make your acquaintance."

"Likewise, Mr. Darcy," he said, "but I best get on. As much as I'd like to, I can't stay and talk. I should have been there by now, so if you all will excuse me, I'll be on my way."

As Reuben left, Cecilia and David entered the house where a stout, older woman greeted them in the foyer. "Lord have mercy, Miss Cecilia. I heard Reuben out front and thought it might be you. Now you come right in here to your old Aunt Ruby, and let me have a good look at you," she said as she pulled Cecilia into a hug. "You ain't been getting none too much to eat I can see, but I'll remedy that." Ruby turned and said, "Now, who do you have here." She eyed David carefully. "He sure is a handsome beau."

Cecilia laughed. "Ruby, this is my good friend, David Darcy from England."

David, amused by the woman's curious stare, stepped forward. "I'm very pleased to meet you, Mrs. Chaplin," he said as he took the housekeeper's hand in his.

"Well, any friend of Miss Cecilia's is a friend of mine. You just call me Aunt Ruby. Everyone else does, so don't you go being any different," she said with a twinkle in her eye, giving David her approval.

Ruby gestured for a servant to come and take their luggage as she gave him instructions on where to place it. Then she turned back to Cecilia. "I best head back to the kitchen and get your lunch served up. Tuwanda's got a hardy stew with homemade bread all made ready for lunch, and we're havin' a roasted lamb's leg with squash casserole, Carolina Gold rice, corn pie, fried okra, purple hull peas, and peach iced tea, for supper, and don't you think Aunt Ruby forgot dessert. No, ma'am. I personally fixed your favorite—cherry pie. Now, I best get to the kitchen and see about things. You go on and get yourselves ready. Aunt Ruby will have lunch quick as a flash." With that, Ruby slipped through a doorway and disappeared.

As the housekeeper left, David chuckled to himself and looked around. He was impressed by all that he saw of the house. A massive staircase, splitting into two sections leading to separate wings of the house, occupied the center of the large entryway. It was much more formal than the townhouse or the Lawton Hotel and rivaled Pemberley House in its style and elegance.

As he canvassed the house, Cecilia tapped his shoulder. "David, let's wash up and eat."

After lunch, they walked to the stable and saddled their horses, then set out to see the plantation.

"I'll take you to the rice fields first and then to the wooded area," Cecilia said. "The rice fields are in the lowlands, and it's marshy towards the river, so we can't get too close."

She kicked her horse in the side, and they were off, clearing the first fence and out into open pasture. Cecilia took him as close to the river as they dared. When they came to a stop, David looked out over the fields. "How many acres of rice do you grow?"

"Only a thousand at the present, but I plan to change that. Carolina Gold is considered the world's best rice. It's a research project my father started in conjunction with the University of South Carolina."

"Tell me about it. It sounds interesting."

She glanced at him thoughtfully as the horses trotted along the edge of the fields. "It's a culmination of twenty years of work. South Carolina was once famed for its rice and cotton production. In fact, we produced the best in the world of both the Carolina Gold Rice and our Sea Island Extra Long Staple Cotton. As I told you, between the war and reconstruction, our agricultural economy was virtually destroyed. Many of the rice plantations that had survived no longer had the money to pay for help, and those that did, were wiped out by hurricanes, disease, and pestilence. By 1913, it became unprofitable to continue."

As he gazed out over the fields, David could tell this was very much a part of who Cecilia Lawton was.

She turned to David with a smile. "It grieved my father to see the barren wastelands of what was once a booming part of our economy and history, so he embarked on a project to return South Carolina to its former glory," she said, looking out into the distance. "Scattered here and there, various old families, ours included, still had the heirloom seed rice. So, he and several others, Whispering Winds among them, formed the Carolina Gold Research Institute and Development Foundation for the sole purpose of the development and restoration of Carolina Gold, and thus the project began. It's my goal to return all six thousand acres of our plantation back into a thriving agricultural estate. I have a unique product which is in high demand, and I have every bit of the drive and determination my father had to see this project succeed."

"Does Daniel have any children? I don't recall hearing you mention whether he did or not."

"No, he and Miss Ellen were never blessed in that way. Whispering Winds will pass to Robert's children when Daniel passes on."

"I see." David nodded. "Now, tell me the history of the rice. It's not native to America. Where did it come from?"

She laughed. "I'm glad you asked. It came from West Africa along with the slaves. In fact, they not only brought it with them, but they taught us how to grow it. They had been growing it on the coast of West Africa for hundreds of years. And until the slaves taught them, the English had been unsuccessful in their attempts at rice farming. Africans have taught the Europeans much, of which the cultivation of rice is but one small thing. When we get back to the house, I'll give you some of our booklets and newsletters to take with you, if you're interested. I think there's a book or two, as well. You ought to read **Black Rice** by Judith Carney. Ms. Carney did an excellent job researching the history of rice cultivation in both Africa and America."

"I'd love that."

Cecilia patted her mare's neck. "The only thing I'm not proud of is that our wealth was built upon the backs of slaves." She sighed. "It's getting up in the afternoon, so let's go from here."

Taking him back from the river to open pasture, they gave the horses a good run. Before heading back to the house, she showed him the wooded area, the pasture lands where the cows and horses were grazing, and the open hay fields of alfalfa bordered by a tributary stream that flowed through the broad expanse into the Ashley River. Cecilia laughed and talked as they walked back from the stables. It was clear to David that she loved Carlton Plantation as much as he loved Pemberley.

While they walked, Cecilia slipped her arm around his waist. "This place is beautiful this time of year, but miserable in the summer. There's no breeze coming in off the ocean like there is in town. That's why planters kept a townhouse for the family to escape to during the summertime—that and to flee the malaria-ridden swamps."

Strolling along, he slid his hand into the back pocket of her jeans. "I can see why you love Carlton. It's very beautiful…and peaceful. The grounds have a natural beauty all of their own with the moss hanging down from the trees as it does, and the velvet green swamp water. It looks like a lush carpet. Very beautiful."

"Yes, it is." She gave him an affectionate squeeze. "You see things as I do. I'm glad you like it," she said, smiling as they walked up the steps to the front door.

After dinner, Cecilia approached David. "Now let me give you a tour of the house."

"I was wondering when you would mention it. I really would like to see it."

She smiled and reached for his hand. "Follow me, and we'll start with the downstairs."

Cecilia was obviously proud of her home as she showed it to him, beginning with the drawing rooms. "This is the room where my mother entertained friends and guests with teas and formal parties. It's the largest of our three drawing rooms."

David glanced around the room. It was furnished similarly to the townhouse, except it was more elegant with higher ceilings and large bay windows on two sides that overlooked the wraparound porch. A large ornate fireplace covered the back wall.

Across from the first drawing room was a massive library. Stepping into the room, Cecilia said, "This room is not only the main library of all our homes, but it was my father's research study." She walked to the back corner and opened a door. "In this small room is where all of our technical papers and documentation for the plantation are kept."

David followed and peered into the neatly organized study. Four walls of bookcases filled with scientific periodicals, the plantation's history journals and research materials dominated the room.

"David, here are the books, newsletters, and progress reports and field documentation I told you about." She picked up a stack of papers and then went to the bookcase and pulled out three books, handing everything to him, **Black Rice** among them.

"Thanks, I'll be sure and read these when I'm on my way to the Asia." He smiled as he took the materials from her hand.

Exiting the study, he looked around the library. His lips curled into an impetuous smile. There were floor-to-ceiling oak cases filled with books on three sides only broken by equally tall windows interspersed between them. A large round table with two chairs sat in front of the far window. This must have been where Mr. Lawton worked on his project, David thought. As it was in the first drawing room, a large fireplace occupied one wall. Sofas and tables with lamps sat back from the bookcases. A wingback chair with a smoking stand was strategically placed in front of the fireplace. And a sheepskin rug with a worn spot lay in front of the hearth.

Cecilia smiled. "I see you eyeing the rug. My father kept his coonhound in the house. That's where Bessie slept while Daddy read, sipping his whiskey and smoking his pipe."

David grinned, glancing from the rug to Cecilia. "What breed of hound did he have?"

"A Treeing Walker, of course, also known as an American Foxhound—a descendant of *your* foxhound."

David's lips curled. "Your father had good taste then."

"Yes, he did. Come on. Let's finish the tour."

She took him to the smaller drawing room and then to the dining rooms he'd seen earlier—one large and formal and the other smaller and modest. They were separated by a large double fireplace between them. Impressed with what he saw, David complimented her on the fireplace. Walking through the dining rooms, they entered the kitchen, which in itself was the size of the smaller dining room. Off to the side of the kitchen, jutted another room.

As they walked into the room, she said, "This room is used as a breakfast room now, but it was once the kitchen staff's room where they slept and ate. We'll be eating breakfast in this room tomorrow morning. We only have a few rooms left to go, and then we will tour the upstairs."

She took him to the ballroom, the game room, the master study, the bathrooms, and the third drawing room where her family once spent much of their time before her mother's death. David gave her a pleased smile. All of the rooms were richly furnished, but not overly done.

Walking up the staircase, she began with the east wing where the guest quarters were located. Then they proceeded to the west wing which was kept for the family. There were several bathrooms in each wing, along with the bedrooms, and sitting rooms, but in the family wing there was a nursery connected to a study and a library that had once been the children's schoolroom long ago. The schoolroom opened onto a large piazza used for a sitting and reading area for the children in the autumn and spring of the year, but it had not been used for that purpose since the 1850s. Wallace Lawton's only surviving child, John, had had the room converted into an upstairs library in the early 20th century. They ended their tour on the upstairs piazza outside the library, overlooking the beautiful moonlit gardens where the sweet scent of night-blooming jasmine and the sounds of the nighttime filled the air, creating a peaceful mood. David took Cecilia's hand in his as they looked out into the evening.

"Cecilia, it is a beautiful home. Do you spend much time here?"

"No, I haven't lived here since I was eight. It's too lonely for just me alone. It was meant for a family, and the last family to occupy the house as it should be was my ancestor, Samuel Lawton, in the days before the war," she said with a tinge of sadness. "There seemed to be some sort of a curse on us after that. From Wallace to me, only one child has survived to adulthood."

A shadow of concern crept over David. "Tell me about your family, Cecilia. What happened to your mother?"

Despondency overcame Cecilia's features. Leaning against the rails, she softly spoke. "My mother was a Savannah, Georgia socialite and only child. The Bouchards, my mother's family, were from old money, but very little of it remained after the war. So, consequently, Mother wasn't in my father's class. People said she was a social climber, and many of the blue bloods never accepted her. Even my grandparents didn't like her. They died when I was very young, but I think their dislike was because my mother's family wasn't of English descent. They were French. My parents didn't have the same religious background, either. You see, my father was Episcopalian, and Mother was Catholic. They couldn't agree on anything from church to family life—and that was the beginning of their many problems. But then it could have just as easily have been my mother's attitude. She had a duty and a responsibility, and she spurned it."

"What do you mean?" David asked.

"Well, it's simple." Cecilia tilted her head and sighed. "Mother was vain and selfish and had a fiery temper, but Daddy could be quick tempered, too. However, it did take a bit to set him off. After I was born, Mother didn't want any more children, and of course, Daddy did. He wanted a son, but she said childbirth had ruined her figure. They fought bitterly about it until she finally locked him out of her room." Cecilia lowered her lashes. "One night, after he had been drinking, he kicked the door in. When she became pregnant with my brother, he accused her of infidelity while she accused him of raping her. I heard the whole argument."

David cringed at her words. They reminded him of himself when he was a boy, and of the many arguments he'd overheard as a child. He placed his hand on her shoulder.

She glanced up, blinking back tears and shaking her head. "My mother was about eight months along when they had another terrible fight. I overheard the entire argument that day, too. Mother told him that the brat was his, and he knew it. He slapped her out of anger and hurt." Cecilia stopped and wiped a tear. "She left the house in a fury, saddling a horse to ride out, but she didn't get the cinch tight enough, and the saddle slipped, throwing her off. My father found her an hour later when she didn't return to the house and rushed her to the hospital where my brother was stillborn later that night. They never spoke to each other again. Mother died a year later in a boating accident when she was out with her lover, but no one knows about that except for her lover, me, and Daniel. And I only know because I heard my father tell my godfather about it. My parents' lives are one of the reasons I have such a glowing outlook on domestic felicity. My mother never loved my father."

David frowned. "Who was her lover?"

"Gregory Garrison—one of my father's best friends."

"Then…was it possible that…I mean—"

"No, I know where you're going, and the answer is no. The child was my father's. My mother's affair had just begun when she was killed. My father had shut her out, so she turned to someone else."

"I'm sorry, Cecilia, that's awful." He pulled her into a hug and held her close. Cecilia's words brought back memories of his own childhood. He could see his mother crying, but he had no memory as to why.

"Yes, it was," she agreed. "My father realized he would never have a son, therefore he trained me to be his heir. From that time on, we were inseparable. I went to card games, the race track, and later I even took care of him when he'd had too much to drink. I attended all the social functions with him and learned to take pride in who I was and what it all meant. His mistresses treated me like a daughter, but I treated them like mistresses. They were not my mother, and I resented them with their simpering and fawning…except for one."

David looked at her with a frown. "One?"

"Yes, one." Cecilia smiled. "My father's second mistress, Anna Carrington. She was the closest any ever came to replacing my mother. I do believe Annie loved me, and I loved her very much. She was kind and good, and she loved my daddy, but he didn't return her love. It was heartbreaking to watch what Annie went through. She wanted to marry him and have a family. She would have given him the son he wanted, but no, Daddy wouldn't have it, and Annie couldn't live forever in-between. So she left us with a broken heart, and with her, she took a little piece of mine, too." Cecilia choked back a sob. "I later heard she married a business tycoon over in Tupelo, Mississippi. I hope she's happy."

M.K. Baxley

Looking up through tear laden lashes, Cecilia said, "I know what they say about me, and if it's true, I learned it from the best of the best. I even learned to drink and smoke from Daddy. I also learned by his example that love breaks your heart. When you care, you open yourself up to hurt. I've seen it firsthand…" Her expression was placid and her voice void of any emotion as it trailed off into a whisper.

Then, for the first time, as he stared deep into her beautiful sad eyes, David Darcy saw what he'd never imagined seeing—vulnerability. Cecilia Lawton was vulnerable. And she'd been hurt. Could she love him? He now believed it was possible—even probable. He drew a deep breath and asked, "Cecilia, can you tell me how your father died?"

"Well," she sighed, "after the death of my mother, he threw caution to the wind, living reckless and wild, and it finally took its toll on him. He died from a heart attack, or more like it—a broken heart, at the age of fifty-two. But don't think he didn't love me, for I know he did. I was all he had."

David couldn't help feeling sorry for her and her father, too. *....James Lawton must have loved his wife very much, but she didn't return his love. It must have destroyed him… just like my father.*

A sudden desire to protect Cecilia from all the hurt and pain of the world overcame him. In his mind's eye he saw a little girl standing in the shadows, much as he had done when he was a boy. David instinctively wanted to reach out to her—to love her— to be her family. He came very close to telling her how he felt, but he knew now was not the time. Instead, he settled for pulling her into his embrace, holding her tenderly while gently stroking her back and softly kissing her forehead.

"Cecilia, my parents didn't have a very happy marriage either, but I never knew why until my father died. Like your father, he married a woman who didn't love him— not at first, at least, although she did come to love him later. Until my father's death, I believed him to be cold and indifferent to her, and therefore cold and indifferent to his children—especially me. But before he died, he told me that he loved me, and that he'd left me a set of journals. Those journals broke my heart as I learnt the truth of what really happened."

Cecilia tilted her head gave him a puzzled look.

David continued, telling her everything he knew about his parents' history. When he concluded, he stepped back to lean against the rail.

"She broke my father's heart, and by the time she had fallen in love with him, he wanted nothing to do with her. But, that's not the worst part. When they finally did decide to try and make the marriage work, my mother had become pregnant again only to discover that she had cancer. Needless to say, neither she nor my brother survived. I was devastated. I loved her very much and she loved me. I blamed my father for all her sadness only to discover it was both of them. Had it not been for Fitzwilliam, I don't know what I would have done. My brother pulled me through. That's why we're so close."

Cecilia stepped into the shelter of David's body and held him close, her head resting on his shoulder. While holding her, David thought of something else that had been bothering him since the Magnolia Festival.

"Cecilia, tell me about Cameron. Who was he and, if you don't mind my asking, what did he mean to you?"

Releasing a long breath, she pushed back and looked directly into David's eyes. "David, it was a long time ago, but no, I don't mind telling you. You already know that I dated him." She peered out into the night sky and took a deep breath. "Cameron Taylor is the son of a well-respected businessman here in Charleston. They own an international shipping company that dates back almost to the beginning of Charleston when it was Charles Towne. We sort of grew up together, with his father and mine being close friends."

"I know you said you don't love him now, but did you ever love him?"

"No, I didn't. I now know that for certain. At the time, though, I thought I did." she paused. "David, it's very difficult to say this, but…well…Cameron was my first… the first boy to ever kiss me… the first man to ever..." Her voice faded into a whisper as she momentary looked off to the side before drawing her eyes back to him. "I was sixteen, and he was seventeen when we began to date. Our families were thrilled and wanted us to marry in time, and I probably would have, except for the fact that I caught him with someone else, and I don't think I have to tell you who that was."

"You cared though, didn't you? I remember you telling me you were considering marrying him even now."

"David, it was an infatuation only. I know it's unbelievable," she softly laughed, "but I really was shy in high school and didn't date much, so when he began to pay attention to me, I was naturally flattered." She stopped and shook her head. "I was young. I admired him…he was handsome and confident—captain of the high school football team and later quarterback for the University of South Carolina, and all the girls wanted him, but he wanted me. It made me feel important to be seen with him, and Amelia Wilkes, my childhood nemesis, hated me all the more for it, but I didn't care. I had Cameron, and he loved me, or so he said." She gave a cynical laugh and took a deep breath. "He took me everywhere and made me feel good. I thought that he cherished me. He would gaze into my eyes and speak pretty words—sweet little lies... sweet little nothings." Glancing at David, her eyes glistened. "He told me I was beautiful…that he wanted me, and he made me *feel* beautiful." She laughed, but there was no mirth in her laughter. "We dated for two years before I gave in to his constant pleadings."

Another tear slipped from her eye. She wiped it away. "David…women are not like men. They don't give away their innocence easily. It's a precious gift a woman can only give once, and if she gives it to the wrong man, then what's the point of saving anything else." She locked eyes with David and stared. "He told me that he loved me, that he wanted to marry me. That's primarily why I gave in to him. I thought we'd marry when we finished college. I thought that I was in love with him, but about a year after we'd begun sleeping together, I caught him with Amelia, and all plans were off." She smirked. "I remember it clearly as if it were yesterday. It was a turning point in my life. After that incident, I hardened as the cold reality of life hit me in the face like a bucket of ice water. From that moment on, I knew I'd never be the same again. Something died that Sunday afternoon when I caught them down by the creek near an old grist mill, supposedly *our* special place." Cecilia drew in a sharp breath. "David, I gave myself to him after he repeatedly told me that he loved me. He even wrote poetry for me, declaring undying love and devotion. His courtship was so intense that I had convinced myself that I loved him, too, but he took what I gave him and trampled it as if it were nothing."

She blinked back a tear. "Daddy would have killed him if he'd known what he'd done."

"Oh, love, I can't imagine what that was like. What did you do?"

"Nothing." She shrugged nonchalantly. "What was there to do? I just stood there, watching them until they noticed me. I felt nothing as I gazed upon their naked bodies. All I remember about that day is that I needed to get away—get away from him, from her, from everyone concerned, because you see, Cameron doesn't know this, but it was no accident that I found them there that day. I'd received an anonymous call, telling me to meet him." She sarcastically laughed. "An anonymous call from none other than one of Amelia's friends, Lucinda Armachor. But I'm nobody's fool, and I would be damned if I'd stick around and let Amelia and her cluster of catty bitches rub it in."

She propped against the rail and folded her arms over her chest. "That's when I petitioned my father to allow me to join two of my friends in Boston. Daddy agreed and I was accepted into Harvard. In August, I left. After that, I didn't see or speak to Cameron Taylor again until about a year ago when he came back into my life, and we started dating." She halted briefly and cocked her head to one side. "I know you think it's crazy, but I have to marry, and I am considering him. I've gotten past the initial hurt he caused, and I mean…it only makes sense. He and I are connected in all the right ways. We belong to all the same clubs and organizations. We share a similar heritage. We move in the same social circles, and it would combine Lawton & Co. with Taylor Shipping. It would be a very lucrative merger, combining our wealth and social status, and I have to be cognizant of that. But I… I don't want to." She glanced at the stars, and then turned to David. "I don't love him. I don't even like him." She looked David straight in the eye. "David, I don't even know what love is. But I know enough to know that love and sex aren't the same thing. Yet, at the same time, it's difficult for me to feel anything when it comes to what others call love. That's why I thought I could enter into a loveless marriage, one of convenience, and not be affected by it. My reasoning has been that if I don't feel anything, well, no one can hurt me, but now…I don't know. I've changed."

David drew her into his arms, shaking his head. What she had shared with him tore at his conscience, and it wounded him to see the look of pain reflected in her beautiful eyes. It had never occurred to him how a woman might feel about losing *her* virtue. For a man, it was a milestone, a rite of passage, but apparently, for a woman, it was a loss if the man did not value what she had given him. David winced at the thought and held her a little tighter. He'd done a lot of things in his life, but lying to a woman wasn't one of them. He had never taken a woman's virtue under false pretenses.

Later that night as they lay in bed, David smiled. She'd changed, and he suspected he knew why. Although neither had intended it nor wanted it, it had happened just the same. He was no longer David Darcy, president of Darcy Enterprises, and she was no longer Cecilia Lawton, president of Lawton & Co. They were simply a man and a woman falling in love. He could see it in her eyes, feeling it in her touch, and he knew she struggled as he had struggled.

While he lay there holding her next to his heart, David Darcy determined that he would marry Cecilia Lawton, and together they would have a family. The Lawton line would live on through him. He also knew he had both the ability and the money to expand the Lawton dynasty, and he intended to do just that.

Settling back against the softness of the pillows with the woman he loved in his arms, England grew farther and farther away, while South Carolina began to claim a place in his heart.

Chapter Fifty-four

... Could those eyes be for her...?

The sound of a crowing rooster in the distance woke Cecilia bright and early. She stretched out lazily, glancing over to the man beside her as a warm smile crossed her features. *David.* She reached and gently prodded him.

"David...David, we have a busy day. Aunt Ruby is fixing pancakes with wildflower honey. We need to get up."

"Umm...what do you have planned, love?" he asked as he turned to greet her.

"Well, it's going to be warm today, in the mid-eighties, so I thought we'd go down by the creek for a picnic. Aunt Ruby is having the kitchen staff prepare fried chicken with coleslaw and homemade biscuits, and then I have to meet with Uncle Reuben about my thoroughbred mare."

"Mid eighties? Love, that's not warm—it's hot."

She laughed softly. "Compared to England I guess it is, but for South Carolina, it's warm."

"Well, it sounds like fun. But what about your mare? What's wrong with her?"

"Nothing," Cecilia shrugged. "I'm having her bred to one of Solomon Abercrombie's stallions. She's a lead mare and very spirited, and I'd like to explore her potential."

"Umm...Abercrombie, yes I remember him. His horses are among the best on the American track."

"That's right. Solomon owns Blue Willow Farms, and though I have no intentions of racing, I still enjoy a fast ride."

"Well, that makes two of us, love." He smiled and caressed her face as he reached for her.

After breakfast, they took the picnic basket and set out for the creek that ran through the heart of her property. As they walked along, David said, "You know, I think Mrs. Chaplin likes me."

"Oh and why do you think that?" Cecilia cut him a mischievous grin.

"Umm, I don't know. It could be the fact that she was very attentive to me at breakfast, making sure that I had enough to eat, and that it was all to my satisfaction. She also never allowed my coffee cup to go empty until I told her I'd had enough."

"Yes, I believe she does like you." Cecilia sighed on a soft laugh. "She mentioned it several times as she packed the basket, telling me to be sure you got the chicken breast. It appears that you mentioned you prefer white meat to dark."

David only smiled as they reached the slope above the creek bank.

"Here, let's spread the blanket out on this grassy spot. When everything is set, let's play."

"Play?" he said with a naughty smile.

"Get your mind out of the gutter, Darcy. Yes, play! I haven't ripped and romped in years, and this was my favorite spot when I was a child, so let's play."

She pointed to an old gnarled willow oak, drooped in moss, bent low and hanging over the creek. "You see that tree?"

"Yes, what about it?"

"I used to climb it. Come," she said, "I bet I can climb higher than you."

"We'll see about that," he said as they both raced for the tree.

Cecilia quickly scaled it and nestled into the tallest fork, but he was fast behind her, settling into the crook of the tree, trapping her body with his. "Now what are you going to do, Lawton? I have you were I want you."

She curled her arms around his neck and pulled him into a deep kiss, then nipped his lips. "I'm going to kiss and run," she said as she slipped out of his embrace and scurried down the tree. He was quick to follow.

"What are you doing, now?" he asked.

"It's a warm day, and I'm going into the creek. Join me."

David shook his head with a smile as they both took off their shoes and socks and waded into the stream where she reached down for a handful of water and splashed him before turning to run. Just as she made it to the center of the brook, she slipped on a moss covered rock, but he was there and caught her before she could fall. They frolicked and played like a couple of children, soaking each other and laughing like two young lovers. He tickled her until she squirmed and wiggled into his arms, and soon they were kissing. She sighed gently. This was more fun than she'd had in years. Breaking the kiss, she ran from the water while he gave close chase.

"Catch me if you can," she shouted over her shoulder as she headed out into a field of tall sage grass.

"Lawton, I'm faster than you."

"We'll see about that. I have the lead."

When he caught her, she stumbled and fell, but he broke their fall. Tumbling to the ground, David supported her as she toppled on top of him, rolling and laughing, tumbling until he settled above her.

He looked deep into her eyes. Gazing back, she wondered. What did she see? Could those eyes be for her? Could he love her…did he love her? She asked herself as he bent low and tenderly kissed her. As he deepened the kiss, their passion grew. They kissed and touched, and soon they had stripped off their clothes and were making love under the midday sky of November.

Later, satisfied and contented, David rolled over and folded Cecilia into a protective embrace. "I haven't made love under the open sky since I was fifteen."

"Fifteen! You started young, didn't you?"

"Oh, I don't know about that. I'd certainly been thinking about it for a lot longer. Thus, when the opportunity presented itself, I took it."

"Well, now that you've begun, you may as well tell me all about it. Was she your first love?"

"No. Far from it. She was a girl I met while at Eton. She attended Windsor, a nearby girls' school. We would sneak out whenever we could and meet up. I would *borrow* my father's car." He grinned and chuckled. "I didn't have a driving license at that time.

"We would leave for a secluded area in the country where we'd strip naked and shag in the tall grass just like this." David plucked a piece of grass and put it between his teeth. "She was as inexperienced as I was, so you could say we taught each other."

He laughed. "I remember our first time. We were both so scared that I nearly lost it before I began, but that didn't last long. Soon we were confident and bold enough to tempt the wind. That's when I did something very unwise. I parked in a farmer's field. We must have shagged most of the night, causing me to lose track of my surroundings. I didn't notice it had begun to rain until it was too late. I don't have to tell you the rest. You can imagine what happened."

"Yep!" She grinned. "You were stuck in the mud in your daddy's car, borrowed without permission! So what did you do, call your father?"

"Are you serious? I might have been foolish, but I wasn't daft. My father would have killed me. No, I called my brother, who, after thrashing me soundly, demanded a full explanation as to what I thought I was doing."

"Hmm…how did you feel about that?"

"I didn't care. He didn't either. Not really." David shrugged. "He got the car out. We cleaned it up and snuck it back home, and then he told me to be sensible and to never do anything so foolish again. The next weekend he gave me a box of condoms and never mentioned it after that."

"I assume you were sensible, then?"

"Of course. I've been careful ever since." He turned and tapped her nose. "Now how about you? Have you ever made love in the out of doors?"

She tensed. "A few times. It was a long time ago, too."

"Cameron?"

"Yes, Cameron." She picked a seed head from the tall grass and began to shred it. "It was down by the old grist mill on his family's plantation. There was a special place there—a smooth rock that overlooked the creek. I can't especially recall it as a good time."

David's eyes were piercing and full of questions. She sighed with a soft smile. "No, David, I've already told you I did not love him." She shook her head as she shredded the last of the grass stalk. David pulled her closer and kissed her forehead.

After several minutes of suspended silence, he reached over and brushed her breast with his fingers. "Lawton, I think we should eat. Mrs. Chaplin would be upset if we let her food go to waste, and besides, with all of this exercise, I'm hungry."

"I don't see how you could be after all you ate for breakfast."

"Ha! That was hours ago. Besides, you've worked it out of me…playing, as you call it, so now it's time to eat," he said, helping her up as they retrieved their clothing.

After they ate, they packed everything away and headed back to the house where Cecilia's caretaker was waiting.

"Uncle Reuben," she said as she handed off the picnic things to a servant, "How is Lady Grey? Did the breeding go well?"

"Yes, she's bred, and you should have a fine foal come this time next year, but it has cost you a pretty penny."

"I don't care about that. All I want is a foal."

"Well, that you'll have. Solomon wants to keep her for another week just to be sure, so I'll pick her up next weekend. We can go down together. Now if you two will excuse me, I need to check on the rice fields. I have the men making repairs to the flood gates. We'll talk later. Nice to see you again, Mr. Darcy," he said with a smile as he nodded at David.

"And likewise, sir," David acknowledged.

That night after dinner, Cecilia talked late into the evening with Reuben Chaplin, discussing last year's rice production and her plans for the following spring. David sat and listened with keen interest. Then later, in the confines of their bedroom, he discussed it with Cecilia, offering his advice.

"Cecilia, from what Mr. Chaplin has said, I think it's time to take the project forward and reintroduce it as a commercially grown crop. You should also expand and plant all of your available lands. That's my opinion based on what I've heard tonight, but I'll be able to give you a more informed response once I've had a chance to read and digest the progress reports. I also need to read all the documentation on the entire project."

"You do that. I'll be anxious to hear what an outsider has to say about what we are doing."

"Give me two months to read everything over, and I'll have an assessment then."

"Thanks, David. That sounds great. Now let's prepare for bed. We've had quite a day."

"Indeed we have, and we're going to have quite a night, too."

With a wry smile, she took him by the hand and led him to the shower.

Lawton Hall Road

Sea Island Cotton

Chapter Fifty-five

… Please… please, don't leave me…

The next day, shortly after breakfast, David and Cecilia headed back to Charleston. Cecilia stopped by the townhouse to get a few things, and while there, she called Elizabeth to make sure everything was all right. Elizabeth had kept herself busy with walks in the gardens, reading, and sewing. She reassured Cecilia, telling her not to worry. If anything happened, her driver would get her to the hospital. Relieved that Elizabeth was okay, they headed eighty miles south along U.S. Hwy 17 through the heart of the countryside to Beaufort and then they took U.S. 21 to St. Helena Island.

Pulling into the drive of Lawton Hall Road, Cecilia gestured. "This is Lawton Hall—once a thriving cotton plantation. Let's take our things inside, and then I'll take you on a tour of the plantation and tell you all about the research project."

Walking up the path to the house, they were greeted by the caretaker. "Good morning, Ms. Lawton. I trust you had a pleasant drive down from Carlton."

Cecilia smiled. "Yes, we did. How have you been, Uncle Willis? It's been a while."

"Oh, I'm doin' as fine as hair on a frog's back. Here, let me have Stuart get these things for you," the old man said as he took the suitcases and handed them to a younger man standing nearby.

"Thanks, Willis. Now if you will allow me, I'd like to introduce you to a friend I've brought along. Willis, this is David Darcy from England, and David, this is Willis Chaplin, my caretaker who oversees the cotton growth and development project. He's Reuben's brother."

David stepped forward and extended his hand. "I'm very pleased to meet you, Mr. Chaplin."

Shaking the offered hand, Willis replied, "The pleasure is all mine. I'm always honored to meet any of Ms. Lawton's friends and associates." He nodded towards the boy holding the luggage. "And this is my grandson, Stuart."

"Pleased to meet you," David said as the young man nodded.

Turning back to Cecilia, Mr. Chaplin added, "Tully was elated to hear you were comin'. She's been waitin' all morning, frettin' with the house and dinner preparations, so you best go in and see her before she wears a whole in the floor pacing back and forth," he said with a laugh. "Now, if you will excuse me, I need to check on the south field. If you need me, that's where I'll be."

"Thank you, Uncle Willis. We're going to have some lunch, and then we'll tour the fields. I'll see you later."

When they entered the house, a plump black woman approached. "Oh lordy be! Miss Cecilia. Come here, child, and let Aunt Tully have a look at you."

"Aunt Tully, how are you doing?" Cecilia asked as the two women embraced.

"Oh, I've seen better days. This old rheumatism has me down every now and again, and I've got grunts and groans, but today I'm fine, especially with you here." The old woman turned, eyeing David with a gentle smile. "And who do you have here, sneaking up on this old woman?"

M.K. Baxley

Cecilia laughed. "He's a friend and business associate. Let me introduce you," she said with a smile. "Aunt Tully, this is my good friend, David Darcy from Derbyshire, England, and David, this is my dear friend, Tulia Chaplin, but we call her Aunt Tully."

David stepped forward. "It's a pleasure to meet you, Mrs. Chaplin."

As the lady took David's hand, she said, "And likewise, Mr. Darcy. It's always a joy to meet Miss Cecilia's friends—and any friend of Miss Cecilia's is a friend of old Aunt Tully's. You make yourself right at home, and be sure to call me Aunt Tully. You hear, now?"

David stood by in quiet amusement at the reaction of the old woman to his and Cecilia's presence. He did not miss the sly looks she gave, nor did he fail to comprehend their meaning. He only smiled.

Turning back to Cecilia, Aunt Tully continued. "I'll get y'all somethin' to eat, and your room is all fixed up. I even put some fresh gardenias in your grandmother's milk-glass vase for you. "

Casting a glance at the young man standing there with the luggage, the old woman reprimanded, "Stuart, what you doin' standin' there like some moon-eyed calf, lettin' the moss grow on your back? Get Miss Cecilia's things up them stairs right this minute. Do you hear your grandmamma? Now shoo."

"Yes ma'am," the boy said as he turned and quickly headed in the direction of the staircase.

As the boy disappeared, Tully returned to her company. "I'll have sandwiches and some fresh made lemonade for you lickity split. Now, I best get on about my business. Dinner don't get cooked on its own these days." The old woman gave David an approving smile before she turned and left through a wide entryway, disappearing into the next room.

After putting away their things and having a light lunch, Cecilia escorted David to the cotton fields, explaining the history behind the cotton project as they walked.

"Traditionally, Sea Island Cotton was used to make the fine laces for the aristocracy of Europe. In the Old South, all Sea Island Cotton went to England to be processed in the mills there."

Approaching the first field, David asked, "What makes it so costly and so much in demand?"

"Well, for one thing, true Sea Island Cotton can only be grown here on these Sea Islands, and today not very many of them are farmlands as they once were, but that's not the only thing. What makes it sought after is the feel and texture of the cotton. It's extra-long staple cotton, finer than the best pima and Egyptian cottons, giving the cloth a smooth, tight weave akin to the sensation of fine silk. It has an unusually high yield, which I've managed to increase over the last five years based on my father's research." Stooping to pick up some of the sandy soil, she continued while sifting it through her fingers. "These seeds taken anywhere else will not produce the same quality. It's the soil and growing conditions here on these islands that make Sea Island Cotton the most sought after cotton in the world."

Reaching over to snap off one of the few bolls left behind by the pickers, David rolled it between his fingertips, admiring its texture. "What is the history behind this cotton, and why do you have to bring it back? What happened to it?"

"I don't think anybody knows the exact origins, but it is reputed to have come from the Bahamas in 1786 where it was then developed by cross breeding. The first successful crop was grown on Hilton Head Island by William Elliot in 1790, but the best crops were grown on these Sea Islands you see around you, especially St. Helena.

"I've told you of the destruction brought on by the Union Army, well, chalk it up to them. When they came through the Sea Islands, it was their aim to extract the highest cost possible from the planters of South Carolina because they were the ones who had spearheaded the secession movement. The Yankees not only burned our homes, killed our livestock, and destroyed our food, but they stole our cotton, sending it north. When they ginned it, fools that they were, they threw away the seeds."

Walking along the outer field, she continued. "A few seeds, however, did survive, and we did plant again, but Mother Nature raged against us. A severe boll weevil infestation attacked the cotton, and by 1920, it was no longer profitable to grow. Planters attempted to revive the production in the 1930s, but by then the country was in the throes of the Great Depression. It was just too much, so they gave up until my father took the project on in the 1990s in conjunction with the University of South Carolina at Beaufort. We've been working on it ever since, and this year's crop is one of the best yet. The SI-4, SI-5, and SI-6 produced record yields and the spinning quality was superb, but SI-7 has the highest yield on record, and this year's crop promises to be even better. I haven't gotten the report back on SI-7's spinning quality, but I expect it to surpass the previous years."

"Very good. I'm glad to hear your hard work is paying off. By the way, this cotton feels exquisite, just as you say—like silk."

She chuckled. "Yes, it does. It has a lustrous shine when woven into cloth. I hope to introduce it back into the economy of South Carolina soon, but for now, I sell my cotton raw to one of the few mills in the U.S. that's still in operation. They, in turn, process it into cloth and sell it abroad to be used by designers for some of the most chic fashions available."

"I bet." He laughed. "How many acres did you say you plant?"

"Currently it's about seven hundred, but I intend to increase that next year to include the small islands off the shore of St. Helena. That should increase it to around a fifteen hundred. And I'm always looking to buy additional farmland when it becomes available."

"Very impressive." David nodded.

Strolling along, she explained how they prepared the fields for spring planting, elaborating on the differences between modern farming and the way it was done in antebellum times. By the time they began their trek back to the house, it was late afternoon.

"David, let's eat. Then we can retire to the front porch swing where we can sip iced tea and talk."

"That sounds good to me," he said, lacing his fingers in hers as they walked towards the house.

Walking through the front door, she said, "I'll show you the house later on, but there's not much to it. It's not much more than a large farm house with six bedrooms upstairs and two down. It has no formal rooms and is considered small for a plantation home, very much like Tara." She sighed. "Had they survived, it would have gone to one of Wallace's brothers, as would have the James Island Plantation, but they didn't, so it's all been passed down to me."

"It's still a nice home, even if it is small, and yes," he said looking around, "It does remind me of Tara." He circled his arm around her, hugging her as they moved towards the dining room and the aroma of a country dinner waiting for them on the table.

Each night after lovemaking and before sleep, Cecilia probed David for information concerning Fitzwilliam. And each time, David relaxed and told her a little more.

"David, what is your brother like? Is he like you?" she asked.

"No," David chuckled, "we're nothing alike. My brother has a very serious nature. He's quiet and reserved. Besides Elizabeth, I only remember him having one serious relationship, and that ended badly."

"Who was she and what happened?"

"Her name was Stella Fitzgerald. She was beautiful with long auburn hair and vivid green eyes." He softly laughed. "My brother has an affinity for long hair and green eyes. It must be the medieval history lover in him, or his fascination for Tolkien's works. His wife, Elizabeth, had incredibly long hair and beautiful green eyes, too. Fitzwilliam often said she was his vision of Lúthien from the **Silmarillion**. It's fitting, too, since Lúthien means enchantress. But that aside, I could never forget Stella for all the uproar she caused between my brother and our father. In fact, I doubt I'll ever be able to forget Stella or Elizabeth for the havoc they've heaped on my brother." David smirked, "He's a romantic—not necessarily a good thing."

Cecilia felt the blow to her spirit at the mention of Elizabeth's name, but she'd come this far. She wasn't about to stop now. Thus, she pressed on. "What happened with Miss Fitzgerald?"

"Fitzwilliam caught her in bed with another man," he stated matter-of-factly. "She thought he'd gone to Pemberley for the weekend whilst she stayed at Oxford, supposedly to study, but he came back a day early to surprise her and caught them. Obviously, the relationship was over, that is, until she returned a few months later saying she was pregnant and claimed my brother was the father," David said. "Fitzwilliam would have married her right there on the spot had Father not stepped in. He paid quite a lot of money to keep that story hushed."

"You mean your brother has an illegitimate child?"

"No, that's the thing. It wasn't his child at all. In spite of Father, my brother would have married her, but reason prevailed, and he insisted on waiting until the child was born and a blood test taken. When the results came back, it wasn't Fitzwilliam's. He never entered into another relationship again. It was clear Stella had tried to trap him."

"Oh, David, that was terrible. It must have been a nightmare."

"Yes, it was," he sighed, "but as hard as that was for him, Elizabeth's leaving devastated him far worse. For a while, I wondered if he *would* recover, but he's much better now. He's moved on, and hopefully, by spring, he'll be divorced and dating again."

"By spring," she whispered. "Hmm…it doesn't sound like he was too affected then."

"You don't understand. After Stella, it was ten years before he entered into another serious relationship—and that was with his wife. He's thirty-three. He doesn't have ten years to waste. My brother doesn't fall into casual relationships. He has to have some sort of affection before he will become intimate with a woman. Besides, Fitzwilliam needs to marry. He needs an heir."

A chill ran through Cecilia. ...*He has an heir.*

"David, I don't know. From what you have described, your brother and his wife apparently loved one another at some point. But to me, it looks like either things changed or there was a misunderstanding. Do you think they could possibly make up? I mean, if she were to be found and they had a chance to talk."

He tensed. "I have no use for Elizabeth Darcy. Should I find her, I won't allow her to see my brother. I want to talk with her to get a few things straight, but I will not allow her to hurt him again. There is no possible way that what she has done can be justified. He asked her to have faith in him—to trust him, but she couldn't do it."

Clearly angered, David pulled away.

"You don't forgive, do you?"

"**No!** *Not* something like that. *Not* betrayal."

Cecilia cringed. "David, there's a reason for everything. You shouldn't judge until you know the facts."

"Cecilia, I know enough. Now let's not waste our time talking about my brother's failed marriage. I leave for Tokyo tomorrow evening. Let's spend our remaining time together more pleasurably." He reached for her once more before falling asleep.

As David slept, Cecilia lay awake. She hated what she was doing. Her guilt increased. It was obvious that Fitzwilliam had once loved Elizabeth, but what would he do if he found out that Elizabeth had concealed her pregnancy? This was a keg of dynamite waiting for a lit match, and she knew someday it would come between her and David.

When it came time for David to go, he didn't want to leave her, and he could tell she felt the same. She took him to the airport to see him off. As he was about to walk through the gate to his private jet, he cupped her face and kissed Cecilia goodbye.

"I'll email you when I get to Tokyo, and I'll ring when I arrive in Canada."

She blinked several times, and he wondered if she wanted to say something. But she said nothing, so he slowly turned and walked away. He hadn't taken more than a few steps when he stopped short.

"**David!**"

He turned to catch her trembling gaze—tears welling in her eyes, threatening to spill.

"David...I...I love you..." Her voice trailed off.

He stiffened and drew in a quick sharp breath as a rush of emotions swept over him. Walking the few short steps back to where she stood, he touched her face, his eyes searching hers. She quivered as tears spilled out over her cheeks. He cupped her face and then wiped her checks with his thumbs. He knew what it had taken for her to say those words—the three words he had longed to hear.

"I know," was all that he could say. Overcome by the moment, knowing the plane was ready for takeoff, he lowered his head, catching her lips and kissing her deeply, wishing he had one more day. Breaking the kiss, he once again peered into her eyes.

"I'll see you when I can. I love you, too," he whispered.

She fell into his embrace, resting against his shoulder, crying softly. "Don't go. Please—please, don't leave me," she begged.

He gently stroked her back as people stopped to stare. "I must go, but I'll come back. I promise," he said as he pulled her back and dipped his head, kissing her once more. Then, releasing her, he turned and walked through the gate to the plane that awaited him. Leaving her was the hardest thing he'd ever done.

Chapter Fifty-six

... How could you think such a thing when you know that I'm in love with you...?

Cecilia strode briskly from the airport terminal, her mind greatly troubled. She'd finally fallen in love, and it had to be with him. Now what was she going to do? If David should find out she was harboring a pregnant Elizabeth, he would be furious. And what if Fitzwilliam tried to take the children? She could not let that happen. It would be the end of her relationship with David. Where originally she hadn't planned to care, she now cared deeply. She swallowed hard and bit back a sob. ... *Oh what a tangled web we weave when we first practice to deceive...*

As she drove back from the airport, her ringtone sounded. She cringed. Cameron.

"Celia, why have you not returned my calls this week? I've been trying to locate you for days. We have a dinner engagement tonight. Have you forgotten?"

"Oh, I'm so sorry, but yes I had," she breathed out. "Cameron, I'm going to have to cancel. I've had a rough week, and I'm tired."

"I imagine you are," he sneered. "Darcy's been in town, and you've taken a week off to spend with him. What are you now—*his whore*?"

"Cameron, I don't have to take this crap from you, and I'm sick of it!"

"People are talking, Celia. You made a fool of yourself at the fund raiser!"

"The only ones talking are Amelia and her catty circle," Cecilia snapped. "I've had enough. I'm through with you. I thought maybe we could come to an understanding and possibly form an alliance—a marriage of sorts, but it's not in the cards, *babe*. I'm not marrying for convenience."

"Celia, you don't have to. I've told you that I loved you, and I meant it. You once loved me. We can make it happen again. I'll pick you up in one hour. Be ready. We'll talk about it then. I want to announce an engagement by Christmas and marry by June."

"Hello! You're not listening. I'm not dating you. David and I have an understanding. I'm with him now. I love him."

The deafening silence screamed through the phone as Cameron's heavy breath echoed in her ear. Finally, he spoke. "He will never marry you, darlin'. His family is much more important than yours will ever be. He's English. He will use you and throw you away like Christmas trash. Babe, he will never love you," Cameron said, "You know he's from the English aristocracy. They don't marry people like *you*. Search yourself, Celia. You know what I'm telling you is the truth. Your future is with me. Think about it, babe."

His patronizing arrogance angered her—and also pricked her conscience. She'd never lacked self-confidence, but she knew David's world was much bigger than hers. Thinking back to the *GQ* magazine article, she sighed. He could have any woman he wanted—the daughter of an earl, a duchess—anyone.

She shook her head and softly replied, "It doesn't matter. I love him, and I will follow this for as long as it lasts. Cameron, I'm sorry, but I can't marry you."

"I'm coming over to take you out as a friend. You'll come to your senses. We need each other, Celia. You'll see that in time. In the meantime, I'll wait for you. I've waited for six years. I can wait a little longer."

"You just don't give up, do you?"

"No, I don't. I'll pick you up in an hour."

"No, you won't. I'm not going home, and I'm not attending the Christmas Ball with you, either. Ask Amelia. She'll be pleased as punch," Cecilia smirked. "I've got to go."

Sliding her phone shut, her tires screeched as she spun the car around and headed towards the Ashley River Road. Carlton House. She needed the strength of home.

Early December

Hodges Investigators had extended feelers throughout all fifty states, searching for a lead on Mrs. Fitzwilliam A. Darcy AKA Elizabeth Rose Bennet. Finally after many months, they'd struck gold. Fumbling around, trying to locate David's number, Biggs finally put a call into Pemberley's corporate office.

"David Darcy's office, Mrs. Honeycutt speaking."

"Hello. This is Herman Biggs, Private Investigator. I need to speak with Mr. David Darcy."

"I'm sorry Mr. Biggs. Mr. Darcy is not in his office at the present. May I take a message?"

"Just give me his mobile number. I'll reach him that way."

"I'm sorry, Mr. Biggs. You're not on the authorized list."

"What!? Just give me the number. I assure you, he wants to hear from me!"

"I'm sorry, but I'm not authorized to do that."

"Mrs. Honeycutt, please…All right, just have Mr. Darcy ring me at this number as soon as he can."

"I'll give him the message, but he's not expected back in town for a few days, and I'm not sure he'll be in the office before we close for the Christmas holiday."

"Just make sure he gets the message. I'm leaving for the holidays myself. He can reach my mobile. He has the number."

No sooner had Mrs. Honeycutt placed the receiver on the cradle, than she received a summons to meet Fitzwilliam's secretary in the boardroom as soon as possible. Gathering the note, she placed it with the stack of papers accumulating on David's desk.

David had emailed Cecilia every day while first in Tokyo, then Singapore, China, and finally, Hong Kong. And he called her every night from Canada. He told her more about himself, his boyhood, Fitzwilliam, Georgiana and what it was like to grow up at Pemberley. He told her he loved her and wanted to see if they could make something work. Cecilia wondered if he was thinking marriage, but if he did, he kept it to himself.

While waiting for his call, Cecilia prepared for the evening as she reflected on their last conversation. He had agreed to attend the Fort Sumter Reenactment Ball at the Magnolia Festival with her. When he came next, they would go to the King St. Tailor Shop where he would be fitted for an 1860s suit. David even had gone so far as to research it and send her the pattern he wanted for his suit, and he had been insistent on the fabric choices, but they mutually agreed on the colors. He would wear cream colored linen cotton trousers with a burgundy lightweight wool vest and a black tail coat. A cream colored lawn shirt, burgundy and black checkered patterned cross-back braces, and a black cravat would complete the look. They would be the perfect couple. Cecilia teased, telling him he reminded her of Rhett Butler with his impeccable taste.

She couldn't help but chuckle as she thought how her cream colored silk hoop skirt with voile overlay and black velvet ribbons and a burgundy silk sash would give Scarlett a run for her money. Her seamstress had even agreed to fashion her gown with burgundy Irish roses in silk ribbon embroidered along the neckline coupled with mother of pearl beading. She laughed. She couldn't remember when she'd had so much fun—even if it was over the Internet—or when she'd enjoyed late night conversations as much as she had theirs. The phone rang. She smiled as she picked up the receiver.

"How are you, love?"

"David, it's so good to hear your voice. I'm preparing for the Antebellum Christmas Ball tonight. I'm going to wear a hoop skirt I already own. I wish you could attend." She leaned back against her headboard wearing nothing but her pantaloons and chemise, settling in for a nice long talk.

"I would if I could, but even if I were in town, I don't have the proper clothes for the event. If we do a lot of this, I'm going to have to see that tailor on King Street quite often."

"Yes, you will. He still wants to double check with you on the measurements your tailor in London sent. It's ready for a fitting. We'll have to see him when you come."

"We'll do that." He chuckled. "I must admit, I'll have to become acquainted with some of the dances since I've never done this before. The waltz I know. The Virginia Reel? I haven't a clue, but I'm a quick learner, and I'm looking forward to it."

"You are indeed! I haven't forgotten the last time you were here. David, I miss you so much."

"I miss you, too, love." He released a long breath. "Cecilia, come back to England and spend Christmas at Pemberley with me and my family. I want Fitzwilliam and Georgiana to meet you. My cousins William, Benson, and Richard and his wife, Rhonda, will be there. They will all love you as much as I do."

"Oh, I wish I could," she sighed, "but I can't. I have an urgent matter of business that I have to attend to at that time. It can't be put aside."

They talked for another two hours before he yawned.

"It's getting late, love. I have a nine o'clock meeting, so I must go. I'll see you in eight days. I love you."

"I love you, too."

David arrived in Charleston, planning to stay for two days and nights. He bought Cecilia a garnet pendant for Christmas to match her ball gown for the Magnolia Ball. Cecilia gave him a pair of 18k gold cufflinks with the Great Seal of the Confederacy to wear with his suit. Sitting in her master suite, they huddled together like two excited children on Christmas morning as they opened their gifts from one another.

"David, this necklace is beautiful! And it matches my dress perfectly." Taking the pendant out of its case, she held it up to the light, watching it sparkle and shine. Tears stung her eyes. No one, other than her father, had even given her anything so lovely. She was truly touched. "Would you mind helping me with it?"

"I'm glad you like it. I'm not very experienced in picking out jewelry for women." He smiled as he took the necklace from her hand and gently brushed her hair aside to fasten it around her neck.

"Well, you did very well. It's beautiful." She smiled. "Do you like the cuff links?"

"I love them. They're handcrafted, aren't they? Where did you find them?" Tracing his fingers over the great seal, he examined them closely.

"There's a jeweler downtown who crafts custom made jewelry. I'm glad you like them." She turned away to hide a tear sliding down her cheek.

Turning back, she caught David intently examining her. "What's wrong, love?" He reached and touched her face. "Tell me what's bothering you."

The kindness she read in his eyes caused another tear to slip as she shook her head.

"David, I want you to know that I love you. It is *not* an infatuation or something that will pass. I truly love you, but I am afraid...afraid of the unknown."

"Don't be afraid," he reassured. "You mean more to me than anything, and I'm not going to leave you. I promise. I love you, and it's real." Stroking her face with the back of his fingers, he asked, "Cecilia, have I done something to upset you, something to make you doubt me? Please tell me." He studied her eyes, almost pleading.

"No, you're perfect. It's not you...not us. Oh, David, I can't tell you. Someday you will know, but today I cannot tell you." She dropped her gaze for a moment. "There is one thing I want you to know, though. No matter what you hear, no matter what I do, please believe me when I tell you that you are the only man I have ever loved—the only one I ever *will* love, but someday you're going to leave me." She sobbed.

Pulling her into his embrace, he said, "How could you think such a thing when you know I'm in love with you?"

She shook her head and continued to cry.

Tipping her chin, he tenderly looking into her eyes. "Cecilia, you're not pregnant are you? If you are, I don't want you to worry. I wouldn't leave you. I would welcome a child—our child. It would be a cause for celebration, not a cause for distress. I love you—on *that* you can depend."

She looked at him, shocked, then laid her head on his shoulder and cried all the harder. "No, I'm not pregnant. I wish it were that simple."

He released a sigh and pulled her closer. "It's all right, love. Shh...hush...It's all right. I love you, and I'm here. You can tell me when you're ready. I want you to know that whatever it is, I will stand by you. I am *not* going to leave you," he murmured, stroking her back and scattering tiny kisses in her hair as she cried on his shoulder.

She glanced up and peered into his eyes. She wanted to believe him, but her doubts plagued her.

Later that night after they had made love, she cried herself to sleep while he cradled her in his arms. David's worry was apparent, but if she told him what ate away at her, she would possibly destroy her best friend's happiness, and if she did not, she would destroy her own.

On the return flight to London, David's recent visit to Charleston preoccupied his thoughts. ...*What's wrong with her? She's not pregnant... so what could it be? I don't understand. There's nothing, or anyone, who could make me leave her. I don't understand women. Why does she not believe me?*

Days passed with growing concern gnawing at Cecilia. At times she felt almost ill from the thought of losing David. She knew what she must do, and she dreaded it. Elizabeth had become very emotional as she approached the final stretch of her pregnancy, but if Cecilia had any hope for her and David, she knew she must talk to her friend. Handing her purse to the maid as she came through the door, she left in search of Elizabeth as she had finally worked up the courage to speak with her concerning all that she had learned from David.

Cecilia found Elizabeth in the sunroom where she often sat putting the final touches on a baby gown she was embroidering. Cecilia knew she would have to tread lightly.

"Lizzy, I would like to speak to you."

"Sure, what would you like to talk about?" Elizabeth asked as she placed her handwork aside.

"Fitzwilliam," Cecilia said, hesitating. "Lizzy, are you absolutely sure that things are as you think? Is there a possibility you could have misunderstood?"

"Celia, I can't believe we're having this conversation," Elizabeth answered in shock. "You saw his letter. I told you about our phone conversations, and then there was his aunt. All of this could not *possibly* be a misunderstanding."

"You also told me that he loved you and that you loved him. Soon you're going to give birth to his children. Lizzy, you really should tell him. Perhaps the babies would make a difference. Perhaps he was simply under a great deal of stress with his family crisis. I know what it is like to have a heavy responsibility resting squarely upon my shoulders." Cecilia paced the room wringing her hands. "I think it is very possible that the pressure he was under came between you." She turned to catch Elizabeth's worried look. "That does not mean his feelings have changed, or that he would not be the husband he was. Lizzy, won't you contact him? Won't you talk to him? I can help you. I'll be by your side. Please, Lizzy."

"No, Celia, I can't. It's too late for that. I saw him on the BBC at some charity foundation ball." Elizabeth turned away and swallowed a sob. "He wasn't alone. In fact, there were women all over him, and he wasn't fighting them off. He was even dancing with them, smiling and happy. He's moved on. It's too late for us." Tears spilled.

"Lizzy, perhaps if he knew about—"

"No! Celia, he's moved on. I will not be with a man who does not love me for me. I won't live with a man who would only want me because of the children. I won't! Please, you've got to stand by me in this." Elizabeth burst into tears as Cecilia went to her and tried to comfort her.

"Shh… Lizzy, it's all right. You don't have to do anything you don't want to. Hush now. All will be well."

Cecilia bit her lower lip as she gently soothed Elizabeth, tears spilling down her cheeks. *…I'm going to lose the only man I have ever loved. I have three choices. I can tell David I have Elizabeth and let Elizabeth and Fitzwilliam work this out, or I can tell Elizabeth about David and let Elizabeth deal with things as best as she can, or I can do nothing. With any choice I make, I lose. Fitzwilliam will someday find out—as will David.* Cecilia looked down at her trembling friend and shook her head. *…Lizzy, we both lose… Lizzy…Lizzy, we often fear that which we don't understand.*

Cecilia's resolve was set. She would stand by her friend no matter what it cost her.

When David returned to England, he headed straight for Pemberley House where Georgiana and Fitzwilliam, along with his cousins, awaited him.

"David, I'm so very glad to see you. I've missed you." Georgiana kissed his cheek as she greeted him.

"And I've missed you. It's good to be home," he said. "I love you, Georgie."

"What's with you, David? Are you in love?" she teased. "You certainly act like a man in love."

"I'll tell you all about it in good time." He laughed. "But yes, in fact, I am. I need to talk with our brother, so you'll have to excuse me," he said with a smile.

"Oh, David, this is wonderful news! You're to see me immediately after speaking with Fitzwilliam. I want to hear all about it." She hugged her brother exuberantly.

Turning to his cousins, he slapped first William and then Benson and Richard on the shoulder. "How have you been?"

"Busy as usual," Benson said. "But, have we just entered an alternative universe? Did I hear you correctly when you walked in? Don't tell me some skirt has caught you!"

"Benson, you're young and your day is coming. I'll tell you about it later."

"Well, you may as well tell us all," said Rhonda Winthrop. "Anyone who can hold your attention for more than a couple of dates has to be very special. When do we meet her?"

"Soon. After my marathon trip to Eastern Europe and Asia, I'll bring her to London. She's an American girl from South Carolina. I'll tell you everything after I speak with Fitzwilliam."

William stepped forward while Richard stood back shaking his head and smiling. "Congratulations on your first love. I wish you the best of luck."

"Thanks," he shook his cousin's hand, "but now, if you will excuse me, I need to speak with my brother."

Leaving the drawing room, he walked the short distance to where he knew his brother would most likely be. Entering the library, he smiled. There he sat, reading. "Fitzwilliam, I need a word with you in your study."

Fitzwilliam glanced up, putting his book aside. "All right, let's go," he smiled. "Hmm…you look happy. It must be good news."

"Indeed it is."

As they entered the study, Fitzwilliam settled behind his desk while David shut the door and took a seat across from him.

"Now, what is this all about?"

Grinning, David said, "I've met someone whom I'm planning to marry."

"You? You're joking?" Fitzwilliam gaped.

"No, I'm not joking. I'm deeply in love. She's amazing, and you will love her when you get to know her."

"Who is she? When did you meet her? And how long have you known her?"

David chuckled. "I've known her for two years now, but more closely in the last year—specifically since November. She's a South Carolina Belle and the sole owner of Lawton & Co. I've been going to Charleston every chance I can get and attending society functions with her for a few months now. She's also the one who rang me last spring and summer. You remember—the one you kept asking about."

Fitzwilliam stiffened. "David, let me get this straight. You're in love with Cecilia Lawton of Charleston, South Carolina?" He paused and took a deep breath. "Is she not the one you told me about last year? What did you call her? 'A cold, hard bitch?' And now you're telling me you want to marry her!? I knew you were seeing her, but marry her? You aren't serious, are you?"

"That's the one, and yes, I'm very serious. When I told you those things, I thought they were true, but since then, I've come to know her better."

"I would hope so! From our previous conversation, I had a different opinion."

"No, Fitzwilliam. You've got it wrong. She's not like that. She's a warm and beautiful woman. I love her, and there's no feeling in the world that can describe what it feels like to make love to someone you're in love with. Fitzwilliam, please, reserve judgment until you've gotten to know her. I stood by you when you wanted to marry Elizabeth."

Fitzwilliam winced. "And we all know how that turned out." He sighed as he passed his hand over his face. "David, I don't want to see you hurt. Think it through before you commit. It might be better to simply have an affair. If you must marry, why don't you stay within our own sphere? Cecilia Lawton is *nouveau riche*. She's beneath you."

David leapt from his seat. He shook his head violently. "Fitzwilliam, you don't know what you're talking about, and I can't believe you're saying this! I respect her too much to demean her by reducing our relationship to a meaningless affair, and I *do* know what I'm doing. Last time I checked, I was over twenty-one and responsible for my own decisions." He stared, incensed by his brother's attitude. "And since when did you give a damn about connections and social class?"

"Since Elizabeth, that's when! If I had it to do over again, I wouldn't be pulled in so easily. I should not have married her." He raked his fingers through his hair, pain etching lines in his face that hadn't been there before the ordeal with Elizabeth had begun. "I didn't know her well enough."

"Well, let me tell you something, Brother. Southern society is no different from ours. Cecilia is from the first circles; she descends from the Lord Proprietors of 1670 and is *not* new money, as if that matters to me!" Nostrils flaring, David looked at his brother with contempt. "In many ways, I find their society superior to ours. The people are warm and open. At least they're not pretentious. Good God, Fitzwilliam, what's gotten into you? Do we even know each other anymore?"

Fitzwilliam's face crumpled in grief. "David, forgive me. I know I'm callous. I'm sorry." Rising from his desk, he walked over to his brother and embraced him. "Sometimes bitterness overtakes me. But I'll be all right in time, and more than anything, I want to see you and Georgiana happy, so perhaps you're correct, and Miss Lawton is the lady for you. If she is, then I want you to be happy." He smiled faintly. "Now, I suppose you want to talk with me about the family jewelry?"

"Yes, I do, and I'm really sorry for you. Don't give up," David said, clapping his brother on the back. "I know how important family is to you. You'll love again. You're too good of a man not to."

"No," Fitzwilliam smirked as his shoulders slumped. "You're wrong. Perhaps I'll develop some of your old habits, but I will never love again, nor will I ever remarry." Bitterness dripped from his words as he walked back around his desk and took his seat.

"No, you won't." David shook his head. "You're a better man than that."

Fitzwilliam took in a deep breath. He knew David was right, but the pain of a broken heart had a way of altering a man. He rubbed his wrinkled brow, trying to suppress a headache as he changed the subject back to the jewelry.

It was decided that when Cecilia came with David to Pemberley, she would have her pick of the family heirlooms. The more the brothers talked, the more Fitzwilliam realized his brother was indeed in love, but he would still reserve judgment. He no longer trusted things to be as they appeared. Perhaps she was David's equal in some ways as he claimed, but Fitzwilliam could not so easily accept things anymore. When they had finished their discussion, Fitzwilliam noticed his brother lingered.

"Is there something else on your mind?"

"Yes, as a matter of fact, there is. I want to see our family business journals and ledgers from 1800 through 1852. I'm going to take them with me on my Eastern European trip."

Fitzwilliam studied him. "They're in the library annex. May I ask why the interest?"

"I know," David laughed. "I've never taken an interest in history before—let alone our personal family history, but let's just say I want to know about our involvement in the commodities market with the Southern United States during that time period."

"Well, I can tell you that in a brief précis. Darcy & Sons were heavily invested in the importation of cotton, rice, and sugar from Charleston, Mobile, and New Orleans. But Alexander saw the war coming, and after our losses in the panic of 1837, he sold the Liverpool operation to W. C. Weakly & Sons, taking a handsome profit and divesting Darcy & Sons from all Southern interests."

"Alexander was an abolitionist, wasn't he?"

"Yes, our family abhorred slavery and eventually supported the efforts to abolish it in the West Indies. And in 1853, Alexander sold the Lancashire mills to Matthews & Pettigrew, washing our hands completely."

"I thought I remembered it that way, but I wasn't sure. Our family never owned slaves, did they?"

"No, not really. Fitzwilliam's uncle, Bartholomew Darcy, was one of the few landowners in Barbados who actually freed his slaves and paid them—well before 1834 when they were set free by an act of Parliament. Anything else?"

"No, that about covers it," David chuckled softly. "I'll check the journals for the details. I'll see you at the church service."

As David left Fitzwilliam's study, he found Georgiana loitering in the hall, waiting for him. She quickly pulled him away, leading him to a smaller study that had belonged to their mother.

"We have an hour before Fitzwilliam wants to leave for the Christmas Eve service, so you must tell me all. Who is she? Does she love you? Are you going to ask her to marry you?"

Looking upon his sister with fondness, he laughed to himself. So much for the journals. He'd get them later. "Slow down, Georgiana, and I'll tell you everything. Well, maybe not *everything,* but most of it. As I said, she is an American from Charleston, South Carolina, and in some ways, she reminds me of you. She has long blonde hair to her waist and big beautiful blue eyes like yours," he said, tapping Georgiana's nose with the tip his finger, "except hers have a violet hue. She's the most beautiful woman I've ever met in every way. She's a businesswoman, loves history, and works very hard for the preservation of Southern culture and history. In fact, I feel as if I have been in an American history class just from knowing her," he said with a smile.

"I've been seeing her whenever possible for a year now, but the most important thing is that we love each other, and yes, I'm planning to ask her to marry me." He paused, looking at his sister thoughtfully. "Georgie, for the first time in my life, I'm in love, and it's the most wonderful feeling in the entire world."

Georgiana knew this was real. She had never seen her brother like this. His face glowed with happiness, and he laughed with genuine mirth. "David, seeing you so happy is the best Christmas present you've ever given me. I love you, and I'm very happy for you. Now, let's ready ourselves for the church service. I'll ride with you so we can talk further." She hugged him as they exited the study. "I have one brother at least to rejoice over this Christmas."

That night, after everyone had retired for the evening, Fitzwilliam slipped down to the library and poured himself a brandy. He sat in an overstuffed chair by the window and gazed out into the midnight sky. It was Christmas Eve, and the moon shone brilliantly over the rolling hills. He picked up the book he'd placed on the side cabinet beside his chair and removed a well worn photograph and a letter he always kept with him. The picture depicted a woman sitting on a white stallion wearing jeans and a flannel shirt. She was smiling. Her long dark hair blew in the gentle breeze. As a tear slid down his cheek, his mind wandered. *...So long—so long ago, and I can still remember the way you taste. Why, Elizabeth? Why? I loved you so much. ...I can't seem to get you off my mind no matter what I do. You're forever burned into my soul. I can't work enough or drink enough to extinguish your memory. ...The hardest thing about loving you is trying to forget you were ever mine.*

He finished his drink and returned to a cold bed.

Across the pond, another aimless soul couldn't sleep. It was Christmas Eve, and the babies were restless. Sitting in a chair in her room by the window, she stared out over the moonlit surf as she took a dog-eared photograph and a letter from the book she'd been reading. While she stared at a picture of a man sitting on a black horse, wearing jeans and a flannel shirt, smiling as the wind tousled his dark curls, a tear streaked down her cheek.

...Fitzwilliam, you were always the perfect gentleman, moral and upright with an intelligence that captured my heart from the beginning. What happened to us? Where did our love go? I loved you so much, Fitzwilliam. Why? Why didn't you come for me? You told me you would cherish me always—that I would have no cause to repine. I shall never get over you. You took possession of me, body and soul. My only hope is that it will become easier in the years to come. She soothed her belly, gently rubbing it as she settled the children inside of her before returning to bed.

The babies were due January 29th, but Elizabeth went into labor late in the night of January 22nd. Fitzwilliam Alexander Bennet Darcy and Emmaline Cecilia Bennet Darcy were born the following morning at seven o'clock and seven thirty, respectively—on Elizabeth and Fitzwilliam's first wedding anniversary. Cecilia stayed with her throughout the long, difficult night, and though it should have been a morning of rejoicing, Elizabeth wept bitterly for the one whose absence overwhelmed her—and for the void that would never be filled.

Chapter Fifty-seven

... There comes a time when a man's had enough...

Traveling between Charleston, Asia, Canada, and Eastern Europe, David hadn't been to his office in three months. When he finally reached his desk, he discovered papers stacked high. Going through the pile, he noticed several messages and three manila envelopes. He wrinkled his brow as he quickly snatched them up and scanned through the messages before opening the envelopes. As he read through the enclosed reports, his chest tightened. Scanning the last one, he dropped them and picked up the photographs. He swallowed hard and blinked in disbelief.

"Oh, no," he shook his head. "This can't be. Cecilia? This can't be!" Falling back into his chair, he clenched the pictures in his hand, shaking as he flipped through them one by one, his heart aching as he went.

The first photo was of an obviously very pregnant Elizabeth with shorter hair. She sat reading on a park bench in White Point Gardens. Next, he observed her walking down King Street, Battery, and finally into the Lawton Townhouse. There was another of Cecilia, carrying a small infant into the house, followed by Elizabeth with a second one. Twins? The final picture showed Elizabeth with a double stroller in the park. *...Cecilia, you lied to me! I can't believe this. I trusted you, and you lied! Oh God, Cecilia, what have you done?*

Bolting from his office, he approached Mrs. Honeycutt. "Rita, why didn't you call me when these messages from Herman Biggs came in? Or better yet, why didn't you just give Biggs my mobile number? These messages were vitality important."

"I didn't realize they were important to you, and you set the policy yourself. I'm never to give your personal number to anyone unless you have approved it," she said in alarm. "Mr. Biggs is not on the authorized list."

David rolled his eyes. "You follow directions very well. I should've made sure he had the number."

David turned and rushed from his office to his brother's, bursting through the door.

"Fitzwilliam, I must have a word with you—this is important. NOW!"

"David, what's wrong?" Fitzwilliam asked as he set aside the account he was reading.

"Look!" David dropped the pictures along with the reports on his brother's desk.

"What is this?" Fitzwilliam asked, looking at the stack before him.

"She was discovered when she applied for her passport renewal."

Fitzwilliam glanced up as David spoke. "Elizabeth?"

Snatching up the pictures, he went through them one by one, his hands trembling as his eyes scanned each photograph. Fitzwilliam shook his head in shock and disbelief, as he read the reports. Realization began to wash over him. *...Pregnant! A son and a daughter! She plans to leave the country!* A mixture of angry disbelief and pain flooded him. "She was pregnant and didn't have the decency to tell me? A son and a daughter born on... January 23rd." His voice faded into a whisper. "How could she do this to me? I don't believe it!" Raking his fingers through his disheveled curls, he tumbled back in his chair. "What should I do?"

"Bloody hell! Fitzwilliam, do I have to tell you! We're going to Charleston—today. She's staying with Cecilia—the woman I was going to marry! Oh God! I was going to propose this weekend. But now…" He shook his head. "She kept this from me! All this time. She knew all about you and what you were going through. She could've at least told Elizabeth."

"You don't know that she didn't." With great effort, Fitzwilliam composed himself. "Whilst Elizabeth may want to be free of me, *those* are my children, and I will have a part in their lives. *I will!* She knew how much I wanted a child. She's the one who balked at the idea—her career had to come first." Fitzwilliam looked up. "She wants to leave the country, does she? The bloody hell she will! I won't have it! Those are *my* children, and I want them! I won't allow her to leave the country—not with my children." He shook his head. "No, she's not going *anywhere*. I will assess the situation and do whatever is necessary to stop her. Call the airport. I'll be ready to go within the hour." Fitzwilliam rose from his chair, now in complete control.

"Fitzwilliam, before we leave, I've got to let Georgiana know what we've found and where we're going. She'll want to come with us, but I'm going to persuade her to remain behind. We'll need someone here to make arrangements just in case we don't return alone. There's no way in hell I'm not going with you!"

David made the call to Watson, telling him to pack two bags with everything they would need for one week's time. Next, he made arrangements for their assistants to cover for them while they were gone.

"We'll get there in the late afternoon, local time. We have the advantage of the time zones working in our favor. I'll have Mrs. Foulkes make reservations at the Planter's Inn. Although the Lawton is closer, we won't be staying there." Pausing, he attempted to release the giant hand squeezing his chest. "I'll get a car, and we'll surprise them. I called earlier, so I know Cecilia is staying at her townhouse this week. We shouldn't have any problem getting in since I'm a regular there. What are you going to do?" David asked.

"I don't know. I will take it as it comes, but one thing is for damned sure. I want to finally hear her say the words herself. If she wants a divorce, she will have to ask me personally," he said as he shuffled papers. "You can be assured that I'll not walk away from my children. I know that for certain. My son is my heir. And my daughter, let's just suffice to say they will know who they are."

"You never filed for divorce then, did you?"

Fitzwilliam dropped his gaze and looked away.

David rolled his eyes. "I assumed you hadn't. Fitzwilliam, you have to end this one way or another. You can't go on forever living in-between. If you decide that you and Elizabeth can't make it, get a solicitor specializing in divorce law and end this now," he pressed. "I, for one, have had enough of lying women, but the children are another matter. The one thing I've learnt is that family is important."

Fitzwilliam grabbed his briefcase, and both men headed out the door and towards the lift. As they entered, Fitzwilliam hit the button for the ground floor. "David, it's not so easy to tear yourself in two when you've been one—it hurts." He glanced at his brother. "I ought to know. I've been trying to do just that for a year now. As far as Elizabeth goes, I no longer know what I want. I loved her. She was—is—the other half of me. I'm incomplete without her, but that woman has hurt me more than I could've ever conceived possible. But don't concern yourself. I'll do whatever is necessary when the time comes. I have no choice but to survive, and I will survive for my children's sake, if for nothing else," he said as they stepped out of the lift.

Watson met them at the airport with their luggage and they were quickly on their way. The plane touched down in Charleston in the afternoon. After hurrying through customs, David swiftly secured the rental car and they were off to the hotel. Wasting no time checking in, they were soon back in the car and on their way to No. 2 S. Battery Street.

The late afternoon sun streaked lazily into the sunroom of the Lawton Townhouse, warming Elizabeth and Cecilia as they fed and fussed over two tiny infants. Rising from the couch, Elizabeth crossed the room with Emily held in the crook of her arm.

"Here, Celia, you take Emily and burp her. Alex is stirring. I'll change and feed him," Elizabeth said. "What would you like to do tonight?" she asked, glancing over at Cecilia as she picked up Alex. "The Clemson Theatre Group is presenting *A Midsummer Night's Dream.* Are you interested? It starts at seven."

"I don't know. I'm expecting an important call around five. How about we just go to dinner down by the beach and then take the babies for a walk in the mall. You could use some new clothes. You've really lost a lot of weight, and your clothes are beginning to hang on you. You know what Mrs. Parker from the La Leche League told you."

"Yes, I know. If I don't start eating, my milk will dry up." Lifting Alex to her breast, she sighed, "but I'm not hungry. You are right about the clothes, though, so let's do that, and I promise I'll eat tonight even if I have to force myself." Elizabeth laughed, and then abruptly stopped, the smile draining from her face. "Celia, are you expecting company?"

Noticing Elizabeth's startled look, Cecilia turned to face the French door. Her jaw dropped.

"Ma'am, the gentlemen would not wait to be announced, but since it is Mr. Darcy, I thought it would be all right."

Shocked almost speechless, Cecilia managed to say, "It's quite all right, Jennings. Let them enter."

Entering the room, Fitzwilliam's eyes went immediately to Elizabeth while David's sought out Cecilia.

"Surprised to see me?" David's eyes locked with hers, his fierce gaze contrasting with his icy expression.

She tore her eyes away and pulled in her lower lip, nipping it. Returning to meet his piercing stare, she said, "So now you know."

"Yes, I know." He nodded in agreement. "I will have a word with you in your study—privately." David glared, his tightly controlled rage barely concealed under his cool demeanor.

"I don't think so. I'm not leaving Elizabeth." Cecilia rose from her chair.

"It's all right, Celia, please leave us. Fitzwilliam and I need to talk." Elizabeth spoke with a measure of control that Cecilia sensed was more contrived than real.

"Are you sure? I can get a servant, if you like."

"No, that will not be necessary."

Cecilia walked over to place Emily in her crib, and then slowly followed David out of the room.

As the door clicked behind them, Fitzwilliam finally spoke. "Hello, Elizabeth, it's been a while," he said in a cool tone.

Elizabeth breathed deeply and pulled her child closer. "Yes, yes, it has," she said softly as she turned away.

Fitzwilliam paced in front of her, twisting his family ring as he studied her closely. Noticing her altered appearance, for a moment, he almost faltered. Her beautiful hair was gone, and her complexion was pale. Fatigue stretched over her tired gaunt features, etched with worry.

M.K. Baxley

He walked over to the window and stared out blankly at the ocean. Turning to his wife nursing his son, he noticed a tear had slipped from her eye as she looked away. The urge to gather her in his arms and kiss her senseless was incredible, but he refused to be the fool again. Those were his children, and she knew he wanted them. She knew, and yet she'd hidden them from him. Inhaling sharply, he looked her directly in the eye as she turned to face him.

"There is one question I want to ask you, Elizabeth Darcy—well, actually, two. The first is…why? Why did you do this to us, and the second is…" pausing to swallow past the pain in his chest, he zeroed in, "were you never going to tell me I was a father?"

With a defiant notch of her chin, she responded. "Fitzwilliam, first of all, I did nothing more than what you wanted, and second, I felt the need to protect my children."

That lit his fuse.

"What I wanted! To protect *your* children! What I wanted was a life for us *together*! And I thought you wanted the same. Oh, and madam, unless there is some universal secret I am unaware of, it takes *two* to have children, so they are *my* children, too! And make no mistake, love, I plan to have them."

He stopped and pulled up short. "How could you, Elizabeth? How could you do this? I've been through hell because of you. Tell me what you want. If you want a divorce, I want to hear you say it, because at this point, madam, I will gladly give it to you, but the children are another matter entirely. They will be with me at least part of the time, if not *all* of the time! And I'm not letting you leave the country with *my* children, so don't even think about it!"

She shot back. "First of all, Fitzwilliam, I did *not* leave you; you left **me**! I think your letter explained it very well, or have you forgotten? And, yes, I did have to protect them, protect them from the likes of you, and what I can only presume your family to be like. I want my children to be raised in an environment where their lives, their tender feelings, are cherished and they are allowed to grow and develop into *normal* young adults, not reared in some cold, sterile, unfeeling environment like you and David were brought up in. I don't want my children to *be* like you and David!"

His rage flew at her. "Elizabeth, what the bloody hell are you talking about? I didn't leave you. I sent my aunt to bring you to England. I'd just come through one of the worst times of my life, and I needed you, but you told Hilda that you no longer wanted to be with me, that you no longer wanted to be married to me. The letter I wrote to you expressed my love and need for you. I tried to explain all that I had been through, but *you*, you wrote me a letter that ripped my world apart. How could you? I loved you!"

She shook her head and glared.

"And furthermore, as for the children, you are again wrong—wrong about me, my family, and my resolve. I want nothing more for them than their happiness and wellbeing. They are Darcys, and therefore, are entitled to their family heritage. *He*," Fitzwilliam said, pointing to his son, "is my heir and will one day have all that I own, and you have no idea what all *that* entails. It is far more than mere money, so if you want a fight, love, you shall have one! For I will have possession of *my* children."

Her son wiggled and squirmed until the blanket slipped, exposing him tugging at her breast. Elizabeth quickly moved to cover herself.

Fitzwilliam smirked and rolled his eyes. "Dispense with the feigned modesty, my dear. I've seen it all before."

"How dare you! How dare talk to me like that! I—"

"Oh, I *would*—I would dare and more." He cut her off. "Because, if you think I will just walk away and let you take my children to God knows where, as if they were nothing to me, you'd better think again, Mrs. Darcy."

"Never in my life as anyone ever spoken to me in such a manner. I don't have to sit here and listen to this." She wrapped her child up and rose to her feet.

"Sit down, Elizabeth. You're not going anywhere. I want answers, and I want them now!"

Elizabeth glared as she sat back down and pulled the blanket more securely over her shoulder. "Okay, Fitzwilliam, you want answers?" she said "Well, I'll give you a good piece of my mind to chew on. If you loved me as you say you did, why didn't you call me? No, you couldn't be bothered. Instead, I had to call *you*, begging you to let me come to London, but you wouldn't. Then, when Pemberley was secured, why didn't you come for me? Again, I know the answer. You couldn't spare a few days for me, the woman you claimed to have loved. Instead you sent an envoy to clean up for you, and one of the things they cleaned up was *me*! If I was so damned important to you, why did you let me go through the hell of not knowing, all alone, so ill with morning sickness that I practically lived in the bathroom?"

Rising from her seat still clutching her son to her breast, she shouted, "Where the hell were *you* when I needed you! I don't give a damn about your precious family. There was *no* excuse to have kept me in some backwoods hollow as I'm sure you and your family think my home to be. I was your family, *too*! But, you were ashamed of me!"

The piercing wail of the baby interrupted her bitter barrage. She inhaled deeply, looking up as she tapped her foot and rocked from side to side, comforting the crying child. "Oh and let's not forget that horrible interview when that CNN reporter questioned you about our marriage. How incredibly safe your answers were! Do you have any concept of how I must have felt listening to that drivel, or how it made me look in the community?! Did you even once think of *me*?"

Feeling the sting of her words, Fitzwilliam squeezed his eyes shut, thoroughly frustrated. "Elizabeth, why didn't you tell me you were pregnant?! It would have changed everything."

"Would it?" her brow shot up. "Who was it you wanted, me or the child? No," she said in bitterness, "I would never use a child to bind a man to me who no longer wanted me!"

Stunned by her angry words, he now realized she hadn't understood anything he had tried to tell her over the months they'd been separated. It had never occurred to him that she would feel this way. Had he not reassured her of his love? Had she not promised to wait for him? Moving towards the window, he turned to face her. He opened his mouth to speak, but she was not through.

"Furthermore, Fitzwilliam, when your aunt came with your letter and that divorce contract, what was I supposed to think? She told me what was expected of me as your wife, and if I couldn't fulfill my duty, then I would have a life of misery as your mother had suffered. At that moment in time I hated you as much as I had ever loved you! You had changed, and I no longer recognized you! As far as I was concerned, you had emotionally abandoned me."

Elizabeth paused to draw breath and then looked him directly in the eye. "I knew— I knew only too well where your thoughts and loyalties lay when it came to me and the Darcy legacy. If you were forced to choose between me and your family, it wouldn't be me. I should have seen it when you told me all about your family heritage, but then you cleverly hid it until it was too late, didn't you? Your loyalty to the Darcy legacy meant more to you than me. After all, you are a Darcy—your father's son, and now you want *mine*." She stopped long enough to comfort the wailing child. Looking up, she nodded. "I didn't need your aunt to confirm what I already suspected, but confirm it she did. You've become your father!"

Fitzwilliam bristled. Leaning heavily on his hand planted against the window frame, he glanced over his shoulder before turning back to gaze out the window. While she sat holding their screaming son, his mind whirled. How much he would tell? He didn't know, but he couldn't bear Elizabeth thinking the words she'd spewed forth were true. Releasing his grasp, he walked towards her.

"Elizabeth," he began, pacing back and forth in front of her, "regardless of what you believe about me, I am not my father, and I deeply resent the allegation." Fitzwilliam took a deep breath, gathering his thoughts. "First of all, if you will recall, you know I was willing to marry you even if I had to give up my inheritance to do so. I told you as much, and you should know from the time we spent together that I never exaggerate my word. I would have done it even if I hadn't had my own money to fall back on. With nothing more than the income of our professions we could've lived quite well. I would have worked to support you and our family to the best of my ability. However, Pemberley House and grounds does mean a great deal to me. If there was a way I could have both *you* and my home, I intended to do it, although if I had been forced to choose, as you say, I would've chosen you. I know you don't believe that, but it's the absolute truth, and if you need confirmation, I can refer you to my brother. I confided in him all that I've just told you," Fitzwilliam said. "Elizabeth, I loved you enough to give up everything I had for you."

She blinked in disbelief.

"I told you once before that I didn't grow up in a family like yours. When my mother died, my father withdrew, and any love that I was shown died with her. She was the only good thing my brother and I had when we were growing up. Unfortunately, Georgiana was too young to remember or know her as David and I did, so she doesn't have those memories."

He sighed deeply as he walked the floor. "Do you remember when we talked, I mean really talked for the first time? You wanted to critique *A Rose for Emily*, and I didn't. Do you remember that conversation?"

She nodded.

"Well, the reason I didn't want to discuss the story was because it hit too close to home. Emily's father was a reflection of my own, and though the story is not quite the same, it was too close for comfort."

He glanced between his daughter's crib and his wife holding his son, trying to form his thoughts into words. Where to begin and how much to tell? He released a deep breath.

"My mother and father's marriage was, unfortunately, very unhappy. Neither David nor I knew the reason why. Thus, we were both left to speculate, and we consequently blamed our father, because as children, we saw things through the eyes of a child. It would not be until my father died and left his personal journals to my brother that either of us would learn the truth, but I'm not going to go into that here. The important thing to say is that, as a result of what I saw in my parents' lives, I withdrew into a world of books, the grounds of Pemberley and later my studies whilst David found other diversions, namely girls. We both coped as best we could.

"I chose to ignore what I saw around me. I told myself I would make a better life— be a better man. Subsequently, from about the age of nine or ten, I set myself to that purpose. I would be very careful in whom I chose for a wife, because I intended to cherish her always. She would never know the pain my mother had known. I would have a family—children to love the way I had always wanted to be loved. I vowed that I would *not* become my father." Stopping in front of Elizabeth, he looked down at his son and then back at his wife.

"Because of our family life and my relationship with my father, I didn't want to be the CEO of Pemberley, PLC. I'd had duty and responsibility drummed into me since birth, and I hated it, or so I thought—that is, until it was my turn to take up the helm." Fitzwilliam paused, attempting to gauge Elizabeth's reaction. Her eyes were filled with uncertainty. He sighed and shook his head.

"However, when I realized that six hundred years of blood, sweat, and tears were about to crumble right before my very eyes and that it would happen on my watch, I could not allow that to occur if it were within my power to stop it. As I thought about what the Darcys have lived for...died for since the time of the Norman kings, all of my father's teachings came screaming back to me in full force." He hesitated, watching her closely. "Elizabeth, I am a Darcy. It is a heavy responsibility, but I was born to fulfill that role, as my son is."

He stopped and took deep breath. From the scathing look his wife gave him, he felt as if his integrity were on trial, but he'd be *damned* if he would apologize for being the man he'd been reared to be. He took another deep breath. She would hear him out whether she understood him or not.

"Elizabeth, I am a man of principle—a man of honor and duty. I once told you there comes a time when a man has to take a stand. If I had done anything less—been anything less—you would not have respected me, because I wouldn't have been able to respect myself. And if I had not risen to the occasion and done what I had to do, you would not have been able to live with me because I wouldn't have been able to live with myself. Since you never understood that, you never understood me."

He shook his head. His emotions were in turmoil as he nervously twisted his wedding band, but looking from his son to his daughter, he decided he would try once more, for them, if for nothing else. "Do you remember our wedding vows, Mrs. Darcy?" he asked. "I never forgot them. Before God and a church full of people I pledged to you that I would be your shelter and your light, to be a safe haven from life's storms. And that's exactly what I was attempting to do. One love, one life, one lifetime." He halted briefly. "Those vows meant something to me, and I took them seriously. Elizabeth, I've told you before, and I'll say it again. I was only trying to protect you as I promised your parents I would that day in the cemetery at Longbourn Church."

He turned and looked her directly in the eye. "What you never understood was, that had the sharks gone after you, *I* would have jumped in the water to save you. That's the kind of man I am and how much I loved you. My concentrations and loyalties would have been divided. I would not have been able to save both you and Pemberley, and in the end, it would have destroyed us both. That's why I needed you to stay where you were and wait for me, but you couldn't do that and so our marriage was destroyed anyway."

He hesitated to give her time to absorb all that he had said before he continued, but upon further reflection, he decided he'd said enough. He would leave her to think about what he'd already told her. He had a lot to consider himself.

"I'll call 'round tomorrow," he said. "We both have a lot to think about—our future—their future."

Fitzwilliam glanced meaningfully at the children and then walked over to his daughter where he reached into the crib and gently caressed her head as she grunted and wiggled under his touch. The child reached up and curled her tiny fingers around one of his, grasping it with surprising strength. Pain gripped his heart at the feel of her tiny hand encircling his finger. He desperately wanted to pick her up, to hold her, caress her, but a warning look from Elizabeth checked his desire. With one last touch, he gently eased his finger from her little hand and turned and strode towards the door. Now that he'd seen his children and his daughter had held his finger, there was no way he would let them go. He'd been through hell, but he'd walk there again, barefoot over broken glass if he had to…for them…and their mother.

As he prepared to leave, he turned back. "I'm filing papers today to prevent you from leaving the country. Even if you were to leave, make no mistake, madam, I would track you down. We will face this one way or the other, Elizabeth Darcy…one way or the other. Do I make myself clear?" His eyes bore down on her, absolute sincerity ringing in his voice.

"You needn't worry." Sarcasm dripped. "I'll be here."

As he was about to exit the room, he stopped and turned. "I'm filing the paperwork just the same."

"I see you don't trust me." She raised an eyebrow.

A smirk curled his lips, "Frankly, my dear, no, I do *not*!" He cocked his head. "Elizabeth, a marriage is like a rose garden. It has to be tended for the rose to grow and flourish. Left to its own accord, it's soon taken over by thistles and weeds. And love, along with the sunshine, comes the rain." He halted for a moment and caught his wife's gaze. "Mrs. Darcy, if we are to make it, and that's a very *big **if***, we have a lot to work through. The question is do we want to make it? You think about that—about what you want, but keep this in mind. There comes a time when a man's had enough. And love, I've had enough heartache to last a lifetime."

With that parting shot, he opened the door and walked through it without so much as a backwards glance.

Chapter Fifty-eight

... Trust is a difficult thing...

David's mind was in turmoil as they walked the long hallway to Cecilia's study. His temper was in check, but his emotions were not. Everything had become crystal clear—clear as to why she had abruptly stopped calling last July—clear as to who her mystery friend was—clear that she'd planned the whole thing from the dinner engagement in October to the present. She had played him for a fool. He couldn't believe he'd been so deceived. He had trusted her, and she had betrayed him.

Entering the room, Cecilia immediately rounded her desk and sank gracefully behind it. David followed, closing the door behind them with a sharp snap. He drew in a deep breath and leaned against the thick slab with his arms folded across his chest.

He nodded. "Now I finally know the truth—the truth about why you didn't ring me last summer." He paused and tilted his head. "Let us see. Yes, your calls abruptly stopped at just about the time Elizabeth disappeared. And then there was your mystery *friend*—Elizabeth."

Pushing away from the door he strolled over to her desk.

"How could you do this? You knew—all this time—and *you* knew. You knew I was looking for Elizabeth, that I wanted to know where she was, and you knew what was going on with my brother. We had discussed Fitzwilliam and his marriage and what he was going through in great detail. You had the information I sought, and yet you kept it from me. You also knew enough about me and my family to understand that my brother would want to know he was a father. Why? Why did you do this?"

Cecilia's brow rose in an aloof manner as she met David's intimidating stare, answering him in what he considered to be her boardroom tone. "First of all, David, I have known Elizabeth and her family far longer than I have known anything of the Darcys. Our families go back for many generations. Our ancestral grandfathers were business partners in the early 1800s, and I spent my summers at Longbourn after my mother's death. Secondly, when Elizabeth called last year, she was sick and frightened. When I brought her here, I had to admit her to the hospital. She needed to escape from whatever it was that had happened to her, and if I hadn't been there, there might not have been any children."

Cecilia dropped her gaze. "It was her wish to stay hidden, so my hands were tied." She glanced up and looked David directly in the eye. "My loyalty lies with Elizabeth first and foremost, as yours does with your brother."

His jaw tightened. "Then where does that leave us? I thought as my wife, your loyalty would lie with me."

"Wife?" She blinked in disbelief. "I wasn't aware we were married, or even engaged, for that matter."

"Oh, come now, Cecilia. You must have known where my intentions might lie. I mean, we had an understanding, and you knew I loved you."

"David, you presume too much! We've never discussed marriage. In fact, you've told me repeatedly that you're not the marrying kind. If you intended marriage, you should've told me. I do believe it is customary in England, as it is in America, to ask first rather than assume!"

He pivoted sharply. "Yes, I suppose I should've asked—but thank God I didn't! If I cannot be your first loyalty, then I am nothing at all. Deception of every sort is repulsive to me, and you have certainly deceived me, Lawton. We could've worked this out if you had only come to me."

Glaring, his features grew darker. Pain shot through him at the thought of what she had done. It was time to cut through the chase.

"Tell me, Cecilia, what was all that pillow talk about?"

She turned away, biting her lower lip. Tears welled, threatening to spill as she shook her head. Her eyes once again found his, but she remained silent.

"You used me, didn't you?" he asked as he paced back and forth, cutting his eyes in her direction. "You used your beauty and feminine charms to draw me in—to obtain information concerning my brother. And for what? To protect Elizabeth from my brother—the man who loved her?" He looked away, and then drew back. "I was trying to find her, and you knew where she was all along, yet you pretended to not even know her." Stopping in front of Cecilia's desk, he placed both hands on the fine oak finish as he leaned into her. "How long did you think you could get away with such duplicity?"

He waited for her response, but she only stared, unshed tears glistening in her eyes. His patience wore thin.

"Answer me, damn it!"

Flinching, Cecilia held his furious gaze and drew in a quick sharp breath, trembling violently as tears burned her eyes. "In the beginning, I will admit that I was trying to get information about your brother. I wanted to know why he'd left his wife, breaking her heart."

"Breaking *her* heart!" He pushed away from her desk and straightened to his full height. "Don't even go there," he cried in disgust. "Elizabeth broke his heart! I witnessed him going through the hell she sent him to!"

"David, please, let me finish," Cecilia pleaded, her eyes begging him for understanding.

"Oh, by all means, carry on. Let's hear it!"

Cecilia whispered as she shook her head. "I felt terrible about using you—I really did, but it was done for my dearest friend. Then something happened that I did not anticipate. I fell in love with you. I hadn't planned it. I hadn't even wanted it, but it happened all the same." Chewing on her lip, she blinked back her tears. "I was confused by what you told me. I didn't know what to think. I wanted to go to Elizabeth and tell her the truth about us, and I wanted to tell you. But I was afraid that once your brother found out where she was, he would try to take her children away from her, and I couldn't let that happen."

Tears streaked her cheeks as her voice shook. "You must believe me when I tell you that I was caught in the middle between the man I loved and the woman who has been a lifelong friend. Truly, to deceive is not honorable, but when the truth holds a bitter reality, deception is pardonable. I never used anything you said against you or your brother, but I could not tell you about Elizabeth."

He glared at her from across the room as her explanations fell on deaf ears. All he could see or understand was how she had betrayed him. Memories of how he had held her their last night together, comforting her as she cried, tried to intrude. He squashed them, refusing to feel what those memories would invoke. Sucking in a furious breath, he laid in to her.

"So you used your body to draw me in—to weaken me and loosen my tongue, and it worked. Oh yes!" he ground out. "It worked! The oldest trick in the book, and I fell for it. I trusted you! You're good, Lawton—*damned* good!" He clenched his jaw and shook his head. "True to your reputation, you used me! And true to mine, I fell for a beautiful face. You used my weakness against me. I must congratulate you, love."

Tears burned his eyes. His heart broke at the thought of being deceived by the one woman he'd dared to love. Never in his dreams could he have imagined a woman would play him. Him! David Darcy—the shrewd, calculating man who played and never lost, the man who took what he wanted and discarded it when he was finished. Angry at her, but more angry at himself, he turned to face her.

"I told you she left him! She left him with a signed divorce statement and a letter! It was Elizabeth's word over mine, and that meant more to you than I did. You could have told me. *You should have told me*!"

She shook her head as the tears began to fall.

He glared at her in revulsion. "How does it feel, Cecilia? How does it feel to be a Mata Hari, no better than a harlot? Or to use your own words, a whore! Payment made for services rendered."

Her eyes widened as her temper finally snapped, letting him know the gloves were off. "David, I don't give a *damn* about what you think of me! I've told you the truth, and if you don't believe me, then you know where the door is, and don't let it hit you in the ass when you walk through it!"

David stood, staring her down. The words she'd spoken from their first intimate encounter echoed inside of him. *...But one thing must be made crystal clear, Darcy. Just because I screw you, it does not mean that I love you or that I ever will. Understand that and we'll get along just fine.*

He nodded in recognition. She had used him, true to her reputation.

"You're the best, aren't you, Lawton?" David laughed sarcastically. "Yes, you fake it with the best of them, with such elegance, such grace, such refined style—charm honed to a skill, and what a skill you possess! You fucking little hypocrite!"

Shaking with anger, she erupted. "Has it come to this? Has your love turned to hate, so fickle that you change your feelings as often as you change your socks? You haven't heard a word I've said, have you?" Furious tears streamed down her face as she leaned forward and bore down on him. "You think I don't know? Well, I do my homework, too, and I know all about your reputation, David Darcy, so don't you dare speak to me about my faults because you live in a glass house. In the beginning, you were using me just as much as I was using you, and you *damn* well know it!

"Don't think I was fooled by your charms. I know full well I was nothing more to you than your next lay, a score you finally made, nothing more than one of the sluts you're accustomed to dating. You men are all alike. It's a man's world, and it always has been. You think you can do as you damned well please and throw women away when you're through with them. I learned that truth only too well under my father's tutelage!"

"And have I not learnt anything from my father about the deceit of women? He taught me well! Only I chose not to see what was right there in front of me. I knew you were lying back in October, but I chose to believe you when all my instincts declared otherwise. You're all just alike. **YOU BITCH!**"

"How dare you, you *bastard*!" She hissed. "I'm not some naïve little country girl still wet behind the ears, clinging to her nanny, and I'm not going to sit here and take your insults, so don't hand me that bullshit of how I've used you. I've bought all of it I'm going to buy! I haven't done anything that you haven't done. You have nothing on me. We're two of a kind, two peas in a pod. My loyalty to Elizabeth is every bit as deep as yours is to your brother, so if you can't see past your pride, you *arrogant* prick, then you can take a one way ticket straight to hell! **GET OUT!**"

Silence screamed between them. There was plenty he wanted to say…wanted to deny…wanted to explain. But not one word would make a difference. He drew back and arched a brow with a sarcastic smile.

"Touché, Miss Lawton." He shook his head with a humorless laugh. "May we both be happy with the choices we've made!"

"Yes," she bit back, "your temper is resentful, and your good opinion, when lost, is lost forever," she scornfully quoted him.

With tears stinging his eyes, he said, "I made my first mistake when I thought you cared—no I take that back. I made my first mistake when I had dinner with you over a year ago. Goodbye, Cecilia." He turned and walked towards the door.

She rose from her desk. Confusion and desperation erupted amid her fury.

"David, there's one more thing you need to know. If it comes down to a fight between your brother and my friend, I will be your enemy. If he takes her to court, I will hire the best attorneys this country has to offer, and I will *win*!"

David slowly turned back. "I'll see you in hell first!"

With that, he opened the door and walked out, slamming it shut behind him. The sound of smashing glass against the door punctuated his departure. Their relationship ended as it had begun—with a final flash of her temper and the smashing of what was most likely the antique vase sitting on her desk.

As Fitzwilliam walked down the long hallway towards the front door, his attention was alerted to the sound of breaking glass. He stopped and turned to see David fast approaching.

"Fitzwilliam, let's go. I want to get out of here as quickly as possible. I've had quite enough."

Without saying a word the two brothers exited the house. When they stepped out into brilliant sunshine, Fitzwilliam stopped short. A white dove flew by, soiling his jacket as it passed. He paused briefly and watched as it headed for the old magnolia at the corner of East and South Battery Streets. Fitzwilliam glanced back at his brother as he removed a handkerchief from his pocket. The day did not match his mood, and by the look on his brother's face, neither did it reflect David's.

Finally calming down, Cecilia sat in her office thinking about what had just happened. Tears of anger streamed down her face. She had known this day would come, and whatever the outcome, she would live with it, knowing she had protected her friend. If she had it to do all over again, she would do it all the same. A harsh sob escaped her throat, betraying her anguish.

…So, he intended to propose. Well, if he loves me like he said…? And if he doesn't? I'm better off without him! One man like Daddy was enough! I've shed all the tears I'm going to…Cameron… Cameron was right.

Shaking, she rose to her feet and left her study to go in search of Elizabeth. When she entered the sunroom, she saw Elizabeth sitting alone, both children sleeping peacefully in their cribs.

"Lizzy, are you all right?"

"Yes, I'm all right, just a little shell-shocked."

"Do you want to talk about it? Shall I call for tea?"

"Yes, please do. I need to talk. I have been avoiding thinking of the future. And now I have to face it."

Cecilia motioned for the servant standing outside the glass wall, making her request for tea and whatever scones there were left in the kitchen from breakfast. They sat for hours talking about what had happened. Elizabeth told Cecilia all Fitzwilliam had said, and Cecilia, in turn, related everything about her and David from the beginning nearly three years ago to what had just happened in her study.

"Celia, I'm sorry." Elizabeth moved next to her, hugging her friend close as Cecilia dabbed her eyes with a tissue.

"It's not what you think, Lizzy. David loved me. I know he did, but he'll never forgive me. I understand him well enough to know that."

Drying her eyes, she squared her shoulders. "Lizzy, what are you going to do about Fitzwilliam and the babies?"

"I don't know. For the longest time I have missed him—wanted him. Now I just don't know. I can't go through this again, and I don't trust his family. We will talk again tomorrow. We do have to decide what we are going to do. I suppose I have to at least give him visitation rights, and he'll probably press for joint custody. This is not how I wanted things to be!" She sighed heavily and shook her head.

"Celia, I'm beginning to think Fitzwilliam's family conspired from the beginning to separate us. I knew his father didn't approve of our marriage. Apparently, neither did his aunt, and who knows who else. His aunt deceived us both. I'm certain of it. Even though neither of us trusts the other, I know Fitzwilliam told me the truth today, which doesn't match with what his aunt told me or his letter. Something doesn't add up."

"No, Lizzy, it doesn't, but building trust takes time, which it appears the two of you didn't have enough of."

"Yes, I know we shouldn't have rushed into marriage. Yet, it's not entirely his fault. We really did love one another. I wanted him as much as he wanted me." She turned to her friend. "What about you, Celia? What will you do?"

Cecilia released a long breath. "Nothing. What can I do?" she shrugged her shoulders and shook her head. "I should never have used him. It was wrong. Still, he was just as much at fault as I was. He was more than willing to use me. We used each other in the beginning. I don't know what I want anymore."

Elizabeth took Cecilia's hand in hers, patting it softly. "Promise me one thing. Promise me you'll not take Cameron Taylor up on his offer. Whatever you do, don't do that."

"I'll make no such promise. It's time I gave Cameron a second look—when I'm recovered enough, that is."

Her mind in turmoil, she compared the two men in her life. One she loved. The other she'd probably marry.

As the Darcy brothers pulled from the curb onto South Battery Street, David finally spoke. "Fitzwilliam, let's have an early dinner and retire for the night. I'm in no mood for anything more."

"Where do you suggest? This is my first time in Charleston."

"There's a little café on Queen Street I've always liked. I'll take you there. Tell me, how did your talk with Elizabeth go—better than mine, I hope?"

"Probably not. Elizabeth tells me she won't attempt to leave the country, but I intend to make sure she keeps her word. William will be in the New York office for the next several months. I'll ring him up and ask him to contact our corporate attorney to file whatever paperwork is necessary to block Elizabeth from leaving should she change her mind."

He cursed under his breath. "I didn't even get a chance to properly meet my son and daughter. I was so upset by our confrontation that I left with nothing more than acknowledging their presence, though I did caress my daughter." He smiled. "David, she grabbed my finger in a vice grip. She's a Darcy—strong and confident."

David grinned. "You don't even know her name, do you? But *she* already has *you* wrapped around her little finger. Girls are like that. Cute and cuddly when they're babies, and then…oh never mind. Tell me, what did Elizabeth say?"

Fitzwilliam laughed. His brother's reasoning on women was the only humor he could find in all that had happened. "No, I don't know either of their names. As to Elizabeth, I'll tell you everything tonight. Let's just say she's as angry with me as I am with her. She has a very negative view of me and the Darcy family."

"Are you going to reconcile or make this separation permanent?"

"I don't really know. I have a lot to think about before making any concrete decisions. Apparently, according to Elizabeth's way of thinking, I've really botched things up. It's up to her as to what we will do," he said. "All I was trying to do was the right thing. I wanted to protect her—to shield her from the storm. Now, I'm not even sure what the right thing was." He released an exasperated sigh and shook his head. "I thought from the beginning of our marriage that I had reassured her of my affections and intentions, but apparently I didn't do it well enough. She needed more than my word. About the only thing I *do* know is that I don't understand women at all."

The two brothers glanced at each other and laughed. They found the little sidewalk café, but neither was in much of a mood for conversation or the scenery of the historical district. Seated in the glass sunroom, they ate in silence, contemplating the day's events. The more Fitzwilliam thought about it, the more it ate away at him. Something wasn't right. Tonight, when he was alone with David, they would explore this, but for now, he had more pressing matters to consider. He picked up his sandwich and took a bite. When they had finished eating, Fitzwilliam called his cousin.

Before heading up to their rooms for the evening, David ordered a bottle of wine from the hotel bar. Settling in the sitting room, he poured two glasses while he and Fitzwilliam talked, discussing the events of the day.

"Fitzwilliam, are you telling me that she honestly believes you had abandoned her? That's ludicrous."

"That's what she thinks. She doesn't believe me." He shook his head.

David released a sigh as his voice and expression darkened. "Then she's a fool! There is no better man than you. You always tell the absolute truth, even if it's to your own detriment."

"Don't say that, David. I have faults enough. I was so focused on what we were going through that I took her for granted. I had put too much faith into a relationship that was still new and budding. I should have taken the time and called her regularly to reassure her, but instead, I let her watch the whole thing unfold in front of her on television—including that terrible attempt at an interview by that poor excuse of a reporter from CNN. I even accused her of nagging me when all she wanted was my reassurance. I can hardly think of it without remorse. I was doing the best I could at the time, but it never occurred to me that she was so insecure about us."

He lifted his glass and took a slow sip of wine. "Had I known she was pregnant, I would have taken the extra time and put forth the effort, regardless of how tired I was. I would have also been more determined than ever to keep her here in America for her own good and protection, but I would have been on the phone with Robert and Tana, making sure she was cared for. But that's just it. I didn't know."

"Fitzwilliam, I agree, you should have called her, but what of her? Why did she write that letter and sign those papers? Unless…?"

Nursing his wine, Fitzwilliam cut his eyes across at his brother. "Yes, I see you're catching on. What did Hilda say to her, and what was the real reason she had a divorce contract drawn up unless she intended to see to it that Elizabeth and I separated for good. I wonder why? I'll try and get to the bottom of this tomorrow."

"Well, we both know how Hilda feels about distinction in rank, and Elizabeth would not be someone she would consider her equal—let alone ours."

"I'm well aware of what Hilda thinks; she drove poor Lewis mad. That's probably why he shot himself."

"Yes, poor Uncle Lewis." David sighed. "I always liked him, but between his daughter, and his wife, I can understand why he did it." David wrinkled his brow. "But what about you? Should Elizabeth decide she doesn't want to reconcile, are you going to be upset like before? I hope there won't be a repeat of last year."

Fitzwilliam shook his head. "No. I've thought about that, too. If she does wish to make our separation permanent, I'll have to accept it, but I *will* have joint custody. I won't give on that. I've always wanted children, and I want them to know that."

"Are you going to take her to court then?"

"Only if she forces me to. I won't hurt her anymore than she has already been hurt, if I can at all help it."

"So you think she won't reconcile?"

"I don't know what to think. Whatever she decides, I'll have to live with it. But for right now, I'm at peace, whatever the outcome. If I can't convince her of the truth, then I'm determined to not give a damn. I've had enough sorrow over that woman. I cannot go on living like I have."

He sighed heavily, rubbing his brow. "Enough talk of me and my problems. What happened with Cecilia?"

"What is there to tell? We broke up."

"Well, I was afraid of that. Why don't you tell me the entire story from the beginning?"

David told him everything, leaving out nothing, including their passionate nights and the week they spent in November.

"I see now, but David, if I may offer some advice, for what it's worth, coming from a man who's botched his own love life so badly—don't judge her too harshly. Give it time. We still don't know all the extenuating circumstances."

"No, Fitzwilliam, she used me for her own purposes. I don't forgive that easily. I doubt she does either." He sighed and looked away. "Trust is a difficult thing, and it's something I rarely confer. I did it once. I won't again."

"David, don't say that—not yet."

"Brother, *you* better than anyone should know that when you let someone into the inner chambers of your soul, you give them the power to inflict a death blow. I learnt that from you and Father, and now I've experienced it for myself. She drove a stake through the heart of me. I'm done with her."

"But David, you don't know all of the facts and neither do I. Don't be hasty. Now, let's get some sleep. Tomorrow will be a very busy day."

Although exhausted from the events of the day, Fitzwilliam was unable to sleep. All he could think about was a little boy with a mop of dark hair and a little girl who held his heart as strongly as she'd held his finger. He also thought of his wife. That he still loved her, he couldn't deny, but if she proved to be difficult, he'd meet her stubbornness with a strong resolve of his own.

Chapter Fifty-nine

...We were meant to meet, fall in love, and marry...

T he next day Fitzwilliam called at No. 2 S. Battery Street. Walking into the sunroom, he found Elizabeth nursing their son. As he looked upon the scene, his chest tightened with tender emotion, but her closed expression displayed no such tenderness.

"Good morning, Elizabeth. You slept well, I hope?" he asked as he walked over to where his daughter slept.

"No, I did *not* sleep well. I have two children to care for."

"Don't you have a nanny to help you?" he frowned.

"I care for them myself. They are *my* children after all," she stated emphatically. "How did *you* sleep?"

He looked at her in bewilderment, catching the barb she'd so elegantly flung at him.

"What do you think?" he asked in a cool tone.

She said nothing as she looked at him.

He strolled over to where she was and stood in front of her. "I didn't sleep well at all," he said, contempt creeping back into his voice. "I was awake most of the night thinking about us—and them." He nodded between the two sleeping children. "What will we do? If it were just you and me, it would be less complicated."

"So, now the *family* you wanted so badly is a complication. Interesting."

"Stop it, Elizabeth! You know exactly what I meant!"

"No, Fitzwilliam, I'm afraid I don't. Why don't you enlighten me?"

"Elizabeth, please, I didn't come here to fight with you. Of course, I want my children. I don't want to divide them up like property. You should know me well enough to know that! The question is what do *you* want?"

"Tell me what *you* want, Fitzwilliam. I want to hear you say it," she spat out.

He looked at her with a piercing gaze. "You already know what I want. I've told you repeatedly. And I thought I had made it perfectly clear yesterday. I want what I've always wanted. For us to be together as a family. I want *you* and our children to come home with me to England." He sighed. *...Why does she have to complicate things?*

Elizabeth dared to meet his gaze. "Fitzwilliam, I'm still numb from all that has come between us." She shook her head, her eyes filled with regret, but the curve of her mouth was still set in a mutinous line. "I can't get past those things your aunt told me and that letter—especially the *letter*. I'm not sure that I can be a Darcy, nor am I sure I want to fit in with them."

Fitzwilliam shook his head wearily. "Elizabeth, I don't know what my aunt has told you, but be assured that before this day is over, we are going to get to the bottom of it. As to the Darcys," he heaved a heavy sigh, "there are some of them that I don't even like, but for the most part, they are like anyone else in manners and disposition. You already know my brother and sister. My Uncle Harvey, Aunt Susan, and many of my cousins are wonderful people who would love you very much."

He stopped in front of her and released a long-held breath laced with building frustration. "May I see the letter my aunt gave you? I know what I wrote, and from what you have told me, the letter you received is not the letter I sent."

She eyed him with suspicion. Finally, she shrugged her shoulders and rose from her seat.

"Well then, if you'll help me, I'll retrieve it. Meet your son. He's asleep, but he needs to be burped." She placed the receiving blanket over Fitzwilliam's shoulder and handed him the bundle.

He took the child, completely overwhelmed, never having held an infant before.

"What do I do?"

"Pat him on his back gently until he burps, and then just hold him until I return. Your daughter is over there in her crib."

"What are their names?"

"He is Fitzwilliam Alexander Bennet Darcy with one 't', and she is Emmaline Cecilia Bennet Darcy, but I call them Alex and Emily." She gave him a slight unsure smile.

...She named our son after me... with one 't'...? Why would she do that...unless she still loves me!

"Emmaline Cecilia... I presume our daughter is named after Cecilia?"

"Yes, she is. I chose to honor my friend. Without Cecilia, I'm not sure how I would have survived. She did more than offer me a place to stay. She offered me her home and her love when I needed it the most."

...So I owe Miss Lawton a debt of gratitude.

After Elizabeth left the room, he looked down at the child resting on his chest. Fitzwilliam gently patted his son's back while the baby grunted and wiggled trying to make himself comfortable. Fitzwilliam snuggled him close, brushing his soft head with his lips as he breathed in his sweet baby scent. A tear escaped his eye and slid down his cheek to rest upon a small head full of dark hair.

When Elizabeth returned to the room, father and son stood in front of the large picture window overlooking Charleston Harbor. Fitzwilliam rocked from side to side, gently humming a lullaby into the hair of the small sleeping child. He glanced up and smiled. The anger that had been a resident in his heart since last year was slowly beginning to dissipate, replaced by tenderness.

"Here, let me take Alex and put him down." She handed him the envelope as she took the child.

Taking a seat on the sofa, he slipped the letter out of its envelope and carefully unfolded it. His shock grew with each word he read.

"Elizabeth, this is my signature, but I didn't write this. The letter I wrote was hand written. Hilda set us up!" He looked at his wife in stunned disbelief as he glanced across the room at the two sleeping babies.

"I keep copies of blank letterhead with my signature affixed in my office so my administrative assistant has it readily available when I'm not there. Hilda knew this and must have taken some for her own purposes. When she came back from America and handed me the contract you signed along with your letter, she explained to me, from the long conversation she'd had with you, that you no longer wanted to be my wife. She said that she was protecting me by having you sign that divorce contract, but until it was presented to me with your signature on it, I knew nothing about it. I must tell you Hilda and I quarreled bitterly, and I threw her out of my office that day." Releasing a long breath, he attempted to regain his composure. "I didn't send her to you with the intent of ending our marriage. It's all a deception." Glancing from the letter to Elizabeth, he said, "I don't know what to say, except I didn't write this. You have to believe me."

Elizabeth dropped down on the sofa beside him, her head lowered, shoulders bent under the weight of remorse and sadness. "I believe you, but back then, I was afraid. I so desperately needed to know that you still cared. The letter your aunt gave me combined with the talk we had, tore me apart. I wanted you to come for me because it would've meant that I was still important to you. But when you didn't come and your aunt produced the divorce contract, I was devastated. I felt completely alone." Her voice trailed to a whisper as she shook her head. "I was so sick and frightened when I called Celia. I had only recently discovered I was pregnant, which was also quite a shock. Dr. Griffin neglected to tell me that antibiotics might cause the pill to fail."

Looking at her with tenderness, he spoke softly. "I did wonder how you became pregnant. You knew that I wanted a child, so I'm not sorry in the least for the doctor's oversight. I'm only sorry you had to go through this time alone. I should've been with you. Now tell me what my aunt told you. I want to know everything. Omit nothing."

She told him all his aunt had said that day as the tears began to flow freely from her eyes. "I thought you no longer cared for me—that you didn't want or need me any longer—that I would be condemned to the life your mother had led. Then, when you showed up yesterday, I thought you'd come for the children. I feared you would take them from me because you could." She looked at him and held his gaze. "Fitzwilliam, tell me that you want me, and not because of Alex and Emily, either. Tell me that you love me for me!"

"Oh, Elizabeth! I'm sorry—so very sorry you've had to go through this. I've wanted you from the first day I laid eyes upon you, and I want you now—and not because of Alex and Emily, either. They are a consequence of our love, not the reason for it. I would never have left you. Not then, not now, nor do I want to take anything from you. Yes, I want my children, but I want their mother, too."

He sat the letter aside and rose to his feet with his hands linked behind his back as he began to walk the floor. "I'm afraid I was so focused on Pemberley and the crisis at hand that I couldn't see what was happening to us." He turned and hesitated. "Liz, I am not my father, and I won't let what happened to my mother happen to you. We once loved each other very much, and… I still love you. Can we not work things out?"

Fighting back the tears, she reassured him. "Fitzwilliam, I have never stopped loving you. Yes, we can work things out. We have two very important reasons to try."

That was all he needed to hear. He pulled her into his arms, holding her tight to his chest, his cheek leaning against hers, tears flowing from his eyes, too. He whispered her name as his hand slid into her hair, cupping the back of her head, kissing her brow, her face, and then finally his lips found hers.

Elizabeth reached up and wrapped her arms around his neck, pulling him into her as she returned his kisses. Breaking apart, she continued to softly cry. He took out one of the embroidered handkerchiefs she'd given him a long time ago and handed it to her. She couldn't stop sobbing. Holding her, he vowed that nothing or no one would ever separate them again.

"Shhh, Elizabeth. Shush. It's all right; it's all right, Liz. Don't cry. I'm here with you now, and I'm not leaving. We've much to talk about—shhh."

Anger darkened his features as he held her. ...*When we return to England, there'll be hell to pay. She was sick and alone. I should have been with her when my children were born.*

Pulling back, he searched her glistening eyes. "Elizabeth, I know why women cut their hair. Tell me you didn't cut it because of me?" He paused, gazing at her with remorse. "Elizabeth, tell me I didn't do this to you?"

She began to cry anew, shaking her head.

Moaning in anguish, he pulled her against his chest. "Liz, Liz, it's all right…it's all right…we'll get through this."

Finally, as his mind settled into a rational mode, he picked up the letter from the tea table and asked, "May I keep this? I want to show it to David, and I want to make sure Hilda sees it again. She has some explaining to do."

"Yes, you may keep it if you think you need it." She looked up at him quizzically. "Fitzwilliam, are we still married?"

He softly laughed. "Yes, Elizabeth, we're still married. And you still wear your rings. We both still wear our rings. Surely, that means something." He smiled as he gazed into her eyes. "A promise made over two hundred years ago sealed our fate. We were meant to meet, fall in love, and marry. It was written in the stars, and the forces of hell could not prevail against it."

She smiled, reaching up and pulling him into another slow lingering kiss only to be interrupted by a high, demanding wail.

"I think we're being called. I'll get her. It'll be a pleasure," Fitzwilliam said.

Hearing the small delicate cry of his daughter warmed his heart. Releasing Elizabeth, he went to Emily and lifted her from her bed, taking her to her mother. As Emily began to nurse, he gazed tenderly at the sight of his daughter gently tugging at his wife's breast.

"Fitzwilliam, I think it's best if you stay with David and I stay here. I need time to think and absorb all that has happened. And then there's Cecilia. She needs me. I've never seen her this hurt," Elizabeth said, tears welling in her eyes anew. "I can't leave her."

"I understand. It'll be all right. I'm going to talk to David, but I must warn you, he can be very stubborn, and he's been deeply hurt, too. He needs time and space, but I'm sure his heart will soften in time."

"He and Cecilia are just alike then. There's no one more pig headed than she is. I'll do what I can here, but I'm afraid David will have to make the first move. As I see it, David will have to forgive her and ask for her forgiveness. He said some very cruel things."

"I can only imagine what he said," Fitzwilliam replied, shaking his head.

Elizabeth bit her lower lip, hesitating. "There's one more thing we have to discuss. Fitzwilliam, it's only been four weeks since Alex and Emily were born. I won't be released from my doctor for another two…and…I'm not ready…not yet."

He smiled, knowing what she meant. Although he would like nothing more than to have her right here and now, he understood. Resigning to her wishes, he said, "It's all right, Elizabeth. We've waited for close to a year. We can wait a little longer."

She took his hand in hers and squeezed it, whispering, "Thank you."

They talked a little longer, trying to crowd a year into those few short hours. Before long, he reluctantly took his leave with promises to return the following day.

Chapter Sixty

... When the doves have completed their purpose ...they drop a flower ...

That night at the hotel, Fitzwilliam took the letter Elizabeth had given him from his coat pocket and handed it to David, leaving him to read while he fixed them both a glass of brandy.

"What is it?" David asked, turning it over in his hand.

"Just read it and tell me what you think."

David took a seat on the sofa, intently studying the letter, shaking his head as he read. When he finished, he set it on the side cabinet.

"Fitzwilliam, where did you get this? It doesn't sound like you at all."

"That's because it wasn't me. I didn't write it, but it was given to Elizabeth as if I had."

"Hilda! She wrote that letter and—"

"Yes, she wrote it and gave it to Elizabeth, passing it off as being from me," Fitzwilliam said as he approached the sofa and handed David a brandy before taking a seat. "You're not going to believe all the twisted lies she told Elizabeth about me. The thing about it is, is that Hilda knew more of the truth about our parents than we did at the time. She portrayed me as if *I* were my father—the way we believed him to be. The audacity of that woman that she could insinuate I would be my father!"

Fitzwilliam laughed contemptuously as he sat and related to David everything that Elizabeth had told him and how greatly it had upset her. He explained that after Hilda had finished with all of her contorted truths, Elizabeth held an extremely negative opinion of not only him, but the entire Darcy family.

"Incredible, absolutely incredible. We should have followed our intuition about her. Yes, we needed Hilda, but we should never have trusted her!" David said.

"Elizabeth and I have reconciled, and we're going to put all of this behind us. This time we're going to make it work, and I'll never take her for granted again," he emphatically stated. "David, for the first time since I left her in Tennessee, I am alive again, and I will do whatever it takes to protect my family."

"What are you going to do about Hilda?"

"I can't let that go," he said with a firm resolve. "I'm going to deal with her when we get home. I can't forgive her. Her deceptions against my family are too raw!" He paused to sip his brandy. "What I did was done out of ignorance, but her actions were premeditated. There'll be hell to pay, but as to the details," he smirked, "I'll have to think about it."

"Whatever you decide, I'll back you up, and I'm sure Georgiana will too, once she hears the truth!"

"Now David, changing the subject to your concerns, tell me what you are going to do concerning Cecilia now that you know the truth about me and Elizabeth?" Fitzwilliam asked, setting his glass aside.

David leaned back on the sofa and crossed his legs. "It's not the same. She set out to deceive me, and she knew what she was doing. Cecilia used me!" he exclaimed, his anger rising once more. "I trusted her. I can understand that she thought she was helping Elizabeth, but that doesn't change the fact that she didn't trust me enough to tell me the truth. I cannot forgive her for deliberately taking advantage of me in order to obtain information about you."

He laughed derisively. "Fitzwilliam, I'm almost embarrassed to confess how much she was able to extract from me about you during our times of intimacy. That's what gets to me. She used our lovemaking to her advantage, and I thought we had the real thing."

Fitzwilliam sighed as he listened. "It may not have begun as real, but I think it was by the time it ended. Think about what you're doing. If you love her, don't let her go. I've changed my mind about her, and I now think she is right for you," Fitzwilliam replied. "Do you really think you can be happy without her? Go after her, David."

"I can't. It's water under the bridge. Too much has happened." He shook his head. "Besides, I'm not sure she would even have me after the spiteful things we said to each other. The words are out there, and they can't be recalled. Words have consequences."

Fitzwilliam sighed as he picked up his drink. He knew better than anyone what his brother was going through, and he also knew his brother was far more stubborn and prideful than he was. Finishing their drinks, both retired for the night.

While Fitzwilliam visited Elizabeth and his children, David walked the streets of Charleston, thinking about all that had happened. Remorse and regret were quickly giving way to bitterness. Taking the path Cecilia had taken him months ago, he relived their every moment, allowing for both joy and pain to wash over him—joy from the brief months of happiness her love had given him and pain from the loss that now replaced it.

He'd planned a future for them, a future of building a family and increasing her business, not only for her, but for their children. He'd even made plans to help her with her research projects by taking on as much of her business responsibilities as she felt comfortable in allowing so she would have more time to work on her projects and be a mother. He'd even gone so far as to talk with his solicitor, making preliminary arrangements to have her name placed on all that he owned once they were married. And he had planned to have half of his fortune made available to invest in Lawton & Co., thereby expanding her corporation. As he walked down King Street, he sighed heavily. It hurt to see his plans go up in flames. Everything he valued in life paled into insignificance to what he'd lost.

Fitzwilliam and Elizabeth met several more times to discuss their future. Finally, they agreed upon her moving to England with him. They also decided she would take a leave from teaching in order to spend time with their children. But, when she was ready, she would return to the classroom, though he knew he would never be able to.

With each passing day, Fitzwilliam became reacquainted with his wife and more acquainted with his children. Emily had captured his heart when she'd curled her tiny fingers around his larger one. He marveled at her perfection and innocence as he held her and softly sang lullabies. She would lie upon his chest positioning herself like a little frog. It looked terribly uncomfortable to him, but Emily slept contentedly while her father happily watched over her, listening to her rhythmic breathing as he observed the slight expressions and jumps she made while she slept. Sometimes she smiled in her sleep, and he would whisper, "Sweet dreams, my little one, sweet dreams," as he tenderly cradled her in his arms.

His son, on the other hand, proved to be the loud one. He demanded the most attention and was the most aggressive eater. Mother and son amazed him as Elizabeth tenderly held Alex while he eagerly suckled at her breast. *Like father like son,* Fitzwilliam smiled. He had never been more content than he was at that moment. The only thing missing was his childhood home, Pemberley, but before he took his family home, there was one thing that had to be done. They had to go back to the Cumberland Plateau.

He turned to his wife. "Elizabeth, we must contact your family and see them before returning to England. They are worried sick about you. I have kept in contact with Charles and Robert, so I know how worried they've been."

Rising from her seat and placing Alex in his crib, she turned and replied, "Yes, we should. I feel badly about that. Jane will be very upset, and I can only imagine what my aunts and uncles will think of me."

"They will be relieved that you are alive and well. I'm going to ring Charles tonight. We'll leave for Tennessee tomorrow, and whilst we're there, I intend to take care of one small item of business that's long overdue. The promise is met. Charles and I are having a marker made for John Bennet's grave. I'm having Georgiana order one for Edward Bennet's burial place, too."

"You didn't forget."

"No, I didn't forget. He's my ancestor, too."

"That's very thoughtful of you. I greatly appreciate it," she said with a gentle smile as she saw him to the door.

When they pulled into the driveway of the Bennett townhouse, Jane, followed by Charles, Tana, and Robert, holding a squirming toddler, came out to greet them. Jane hugged Lizzy as soon as she exited the car while Charles pumped Fitzwilliam's hand. Helping Elizabeth remove the twins from the car, Fitzwilliam proudly introduced Alex and Emily to their aunts and uncles, and Robert introduced his baby girl.

"This is our newest addition, Linda Jane Bennett." He grinned. "We agreed to adopt her once the trial was over. Cute little thing, isn't she?"

"Indeed, she is." Elizabeth smiled as she tickled her niece's toes.

Turning to Robert, she asked, "May I ask about Liddy—what is she going to do when she gets out of prison?"

"Randy and Lydia are sending her to Ole' Miss in Oxford, Mississippi. Liddy has decided to study counseling. She wants to work with young people, hopefully to help them avoid the pitfalls in life that she's experienced," Robert said. "Liddy's grown up through all of this, and I believe has become a better person. She told Tana the only unselfish thing she's ever done was to have Linda and give her to us. I can't tell you what this little girl means to me. I never thought we'd have a child after Tana's cancer, but now we have Linda, and what a joy she is!" The little girl giggled and wiggled in his arms.

"I know what you mean, Robert. I *know* what you mean," Fitzwilliam said, casting a meaningful glance at his own daughter.

While the men continued to talk, Jane gasped with shock when she finally realized what her sister had done. "Lizzy, you cut your hair…you *cut* your hair!"

Elizabeth swallowed hard. "Jane, it will grow again. I know it's a shock, but it will grow."

"It's just that you've never had short hair. Although mid-back isn't short, it is for you."

As they went into the house, Tana addressed Elizabeth. "Lizzy, your children are beautiful. It's for certain that you and Fitzwilliam make beautiful babies."

"They are cute, but I'm not sure it's because of me. I think they both favor their father."

"No, Lizzy, Emily looks just like your baby pictures. She will be beautiful, just like her mother," Tana said as she gazed at her niece and nephew's wrinkled faces while they lay sleeping in their carriers.

Once in the house, Jane fixed tea while the men went to the study for brandy, leaving the twins and Linda with the ladies.

"Lizzy, may I have a private word with you?"

"Of course, Jane. What do you want?" Lizzy looked at her sister, knowing full well what was coming.

"Excuse us, Tana, while I speak with my sister."

"Of course. I'll stay here and watch the babies. You go right ahead. They'll be fine."

Leaving Tana in the kitchen, the sisters went to the sitting room. As they entered, Jane closed the door and turned to face her sister. "Lizzy, why didn't you contact me? I've been worried sick and praying constantly, wondering if I would ever see my sister again. Why didn't you tell me what was happening to you? We have always been close. And why did Celia lie to me when I called her?"

Elizabeth hesitated as tears began to fill her eyes.

"Jane, I couldn't...I couldn't tell you, with you being married to Charles, and Charles being Fitzwilliam's best friend. I was afraid at the time. I know now that it was all wrong, but back then I felt I was doing the right thing. I didn't want to come between you and Charles by asking you to keep a secret from him, and Jane, I know it would have because I know you. I was protecting you as much as I was protecting myself. As for Celia, well, that part I really hate because she was only doing what I had asked her to do. Jane, don't hold it against her, please. It was my fault, and I feel terrible about it. Please, can you forgive me?" Elizabeth pleaded.

"Lizzy, I'm sorry you felt that way, but you're probably right. If you had asked me, I would've tried to keep your secret, and it would've caused problems. I do understand. But Lizzy, don't you *ever* do anything like this again. I've already forgiven both you and Celia, but I promise you, I will *skin you alive* if you ever pull something like this again. You and Celia both! Do you understand me, Lizzy?" Jane said with a very forgiving smile as she hugged her sister.

Elizabeth whispered her thanks to Jane as the sisters held one another her tight. With a gentle pat on the back, Jane released her. Taking her sister's hands between her own, she squeezed Elizabeth's fingers gently. "Lizzy, I have an announcement of my own," she said. "You are going to be an aunt in September."

"Jane, are you really expecting?"

Jane nodded.

Elizabeth grabbed her sister. "I'm so happy for you and Charles. Does Fitzwilliam know yet?"

About that time they heard the men laughing and Fitzwilliam congratulating Charles as they made their way toward the kitchen. Jane looked at Elizabeth and smiled.

The three couples talked for hours before deciding to go out for dinner. They relived old times, and Fitzwilliam questioned Charles about the classics department and the students. Elizabeth saw a look of sadness come over his features as Charles filled him in on all that had happened during the academic year. Elizabeth felt terrible for him. She knew his future was fixed, and it was not the one he'd wanted.

That evening, after dinner, the Darcys took the twins for a walk around the corner to see the old Harwell house. Fitzwilliam laughed and talked to Alex and Emily while he showed them the vacant house, telling them they had come into being right there in that very house. As he glanced over at their mother and smiled, he told them how happy Mum and Dad had been while living there.

Elizabeth smiled in amusement. He certainly made a good father just as she had always believed he would. *...He talks to Alex and Emily as if they were grown and can understand him. I'm so sorry that so much came between us...he missed their birth...but he'll be there next time. ...What? Am I thinking of the next birth?* She chuckled to herself.

The next day, the Darcys drove to Longbourn Farm. When they pulled into Longbourn proper, everyone poured out to greet them.

"Lizzy, Fitzwilliam, it's so good to see you." Lori pulled first Lizzy and then Fitzwilliam into a hug.

"It's good to be home, but where are Bette and Florence?" Elizabeth asked. "I thought they'd be here."

"The two of them are such rascals." Henry laughed. "They won a trip to Aruba. They won't be back for two weeks!"

"Well, I'm happy for them," Elizabeth said with a soft laugh, "but I'm sorry I won't be able to see them, especially since I have two little someones for them and you all to meet." Elizabeth reached into the car for Emily while Fitzwilliam reached for Alex. "Meet your new niece and nephew," she said, presenting the children. "This is Alex and this is Emily."

"Niños pequeño. Lizzy, your bebes are beautiful! And you look so well. And Fitzwilliam, you are looking well, too."

"Thank you, Grace. I am well. In fact, I'm better than I've been in some time," Fitzwilliam said, looking off into the distance of the farm.

Daniel had been standing off to the side when they drove in and got out of the car. After the others had greeted the Darcys, he approached his sister.

"Lizzy, I've been so worried about you that I could hardly study. Jane told me what happened, but don't ever do anything like this again." Daniel hugged his sister, his eyes glistening. He was the most tender hearted of all the Bennetts, and his look broke her heart. Elizabeth pulled her little brother into another hug, holding onto him, fighting back the tears. Fitzwilliam approached them, putting a hand on both brother and sister. Then he left them to themselves as he walked around to the back of the house.

Grace and Lori took the twins inside, leaving Elizabeth with Daniel, but before long, they followed the others into the house, walking hand in hand. Elizabeth was grateful no one mentioned her hair, but it was clear by the initial shock on their faces that they all had noticed it.

As the others went into the house, Fitzwilliam lingered and walked towards the barnyard. Although he had only spent a brief time on this farm, he knew he would miss it. He had come to realize that the Cumberland Plateau was every bit as beautiful as his home county in Northern England. He could understand why the Scots-Irish and English had settled here. If Fitzwilliam couldn't be in Derbyshire, here is where he would want to be, too. He knew his wife would miss her home. He only hoped that he could make it up to her with Pemberley.

Thinking of Pemberley, his mind drifted to the spring calving at Longbourn last March. This year's calves were playing in the barnyard. Last spring, he had enjoyed picking up the newborn calves and bringing them to the barn in the first few weeks of their lives. Had things been different, he had planned to help with the spring planting and autumn harvest, but as fate had it, his life had taken a different course.

Awakened out of his thoughts as Elizabeth approached, he turned and smiled as she wrapped her arm around him. Walking her to the back porch, he stopped long enough to reach down and rub the ears of one of the old hound dogs, lying by the steps.

Sitting at the kitchen table having tea, they told the story of what had happened. Elizabeth deliberately left out many details. They were personal, for Fitzwilliam and her only.

The next few days flew by as they rode out over the farm to the cove where they strolled through the woods, then around to the old cabin, which they wanted to see one last time. Jane and Charles made plans to see them in England at Christmas, and Fitzwilliam said they would return to the Cumberland Plateau at a future date.

There remained one final matter of business yet to be completed. Bingley and Darcy took their wives to Longbourn Cemetery to view the small stone plaque they had ordered to be placed next to John and Rebecca's headstone. It read:

Promise fulfilled January 23, 2007 with the marriages
Of
Fitzwilliam A. Darcy and Elizabeth R. Bennett
And
Charles R. Bingley and Emily J. Bennett

As the couples stood in a far corner of the Longbourn Cemetery, the coo of a mourning dove called in the distance. Darcy looked up and saw a pair of white doves perched on a low hanging laurel bough, overlooking the scene before them. White doves were no longer unusual to him. In fact, they were like old friends. He smiled and gave a gentle nod. As if in recognition, the two birds took flight and cooed once more as they passed over the staring couples, dropping a stem of flowers onto the graves of John and Rebecca.

"Look, Fitzwilliam," Elizabeth pointed, "it's that pair of albino mourning doves we saw over a year ago. One of them dropped this sprig of wild mountain laurel," she said as she stooped to pick it up.

Jane took the twig from Elizabeth's hand. "It's unusual to be sure. Mountain laurel doesn't bloom for another month. Only rarely does it bloom earlier." Jane glanced at Charles. "Whatever is bound on earth is bound in the heavens. When an oath is spoken, it is fixed." She turned to her sister and brother-in-law. "There is an old Cherokee legend in these mountains called the *Legend of the Snow White Dove*. It goes like this: When there is something left unresolved, a pair of pure white doves will appear until whatever is left undone is accomplished. When the doves have completed their purpose, the circle is said to be complete, and they drop a flower. That's what these birds have done." Jane glanced at the graves and then at the laurel in her hand. "They've completed the circle. Rest in peace, John and Rebecca."

"Strange indeed," Charles said as he looked on. "I would have never dreamt it."

"All my life I've heard of it, but it's just an old fable, isn't it? Surely there is no truth to such a thing. I don't believe in myths and superstition."

"Lizzy, you have the second sight, too. All in the female line do."

"No, Jane, you're mistaken. This is not real." Elizabeth glanced up at her husband, "What do you make of it?"

"I've seen it before," Fitzwilliam said in a calm voice as he caressed his family ring. "It happened similar to what you've seen here. A red rose, pressed and dried, hangs between my parents' portraits at Darcy House. Remind me later, and I'll tell you about it." He turned to his wife and said with a sigh, "Let's go home, Mrs. Darcy."

"Yes… let's go home."

Elizabeth nodded and glanced back at the grove of trees near the edge of the churchyard. She could have sworn she heard voices whispering in the pines as the wind rustled their branches. It was the sound of a man and a woman softly speaking mixed with gentle inflections of laughter. She shook her head. It couldn't be real. It must be her imagination. She turned back to Fitzwilliam and got into the car.

Sitting there next to her husband, a strange euphoric feeling swept over her. Perhaps she was wrong and maybe Aunt Cordy was right. As she left Tennessee for Charleston and her new life in England, another thought occurred to her. Maybe… just maybe Divine Providence or Fate somehow did rule her destiny. She turned and looked back at the churchyard one last time. With a soft smile and a hushed voice, she said her goodbyes to her childhood home—to John and Rebecca—and the only life she'd ever known.

In one week's time, the Darcys boarded Pemberley One for the U.K. With Elizabeth and the twins secured in the master suit, Fitzwilliam took a seat next to David. From the look on his brother's face, David knew he wanted to talk, but his feelings were still too raw. Nevertheless, he decided would endure the conversation.

Fitzwilliam cleared his throat. "David, if you feel anything close to what I think you do, don't let it go. Go after her. If you don't, you'll regret it for the rest of your life. Think of our uncle."

"I can't forgive her," he said with a sigh. "She used me—lied to me, and *that* is unforgivable."

"But she loves you," Fitzwilliam pressed.

"She'll get over it."

"No, David, I don't think she will."

"Then *that* is her misfortune," David bit back, letting his brother know this conversation was over.

Fitzwilliam sighed and shook his head. "Don't let the infamous Darcy pride cost you what it has cost so many of us. Don't hold her to a standard not even *you* can meet. You know what you have to do."

David nodded and then returned to his reading, but his mind was frozen. The words on the page seemed to sit there, unabsorbed as Cecilia's words echoed through his thoughts.

*…There is one thing I want you to know. No matter what you hear…no matter what I do…you're the only man I have ever loved—the only one I ever **will** love—but someday you're going to leave me.*

Looking up from the pages, he shook his head and rubbed his brow, trying to dispel those thoughts. He sighed. *…Though I love her, she can't be trusted. A marriage has to be built on trust…love it not enough…not for me.*

Chapter Sixty-one

… She finally understood the man who loved her…

Getting through customs and the airport with two small screaming babies and all the baggage the Darcys brought with them was no small endeavor. Weary and hungry by the time they reached Darcy House, Elizabeth thought only of lunch and a comfortable bed, but when the estate came into view, she quickly revived and sat up straight.

The grounds were enclosed by a large rock wall covered in English Ivy, giving wonder at what might lay beyond it. As the massive iron gates opened, what she saw whisked away anything she might've imagined. A well-manicured lawn flanked both sides of a yellow brick drive leading to the house. In front of the home, a Greek statue of Aphrodite, balancing an urn on her shoulder, rose up out of a massive stone fountain, spilling water into the pool below. Gardens of spring flowers in beautiful hues of reds, yellows, purples, and blues contrasted vividly against the vibrant green lawn. And to the right of the driveway climbed a maze of topiary hedges clipped in the fashion of exotic animals.

Then there was the house! Constructed of white stone, it was box-shaped with two large wings extending forward. Large white columns spread across the breadth of the portico. Its beauty and size rendered her speechless. On the first level, ornate stained glass windows adorned the alabaster stone while small balconies dotted the large windows on the second level. Surely, Elizabeth thought, they must lead to bedrooms. And on the third, there was yet another row of windows, albeit not as elaborate as the previous floors, but beautiful all the same.

"Fitzwilliam, it's so big and magnificent!" Elizabeth exclaimed.

He laughed. "It's over two hundred and fifty years old and has been kept up all these years. Do you like it?"

"Yes!" was all she could say.

"Well, I'm glad you do, because it belongs to you, love—you and me, that is. Don't be intimidated. I'll show you around after we've eaten and rested."

"I'll never get used to such a large house. It's so imposing. How will I ever take care of it?!"

"Love, that's what we hire servants for, and yes, you will get used to it. Just you wait and see."

As the car rolled to a stop, servants came out and quickly took control of unloading the car.

Entering the house, Elizabeth stood rooted to the floor as she looked around. If she'd thought the outside was something, the inside was *really* something! The high vaulted ceilings were painted in a tapestry of murals—cherubs, Greek gods, and mortal men and women sitting at a banquet table. Marble floors in black and white contrasted against the rich colors of the walls and furnishings. A massive staircase ascended to the second floor with a large balcony overlooking the entryway below. It might have been a scene from Twelve Oaks out of **Gone with the Wind**, she thought, or perhaps from one of the famous antebellum mansions in the Deep South. To be sure, Elizabeth had seen grand houses, but none so luxurious as this! It was magnificent—and it belonged to her.

Elizabeth had had no idea of the magnitude of her husband's wealth. Nor had she understood him until this moment. No wonder his family thought of her as commonplace, unequal to them. Compared to him, in terms of wealth and status, she was. If she'd only known before what she did now, she would've understood the thin line he walked. The love she felt for him increased at that moment—the moment she finally understood the man who loved her.

Georgiana and two servants quickly came around the corner. Kissing his sister's cheek, Fitzwilliam greeted her. "Georgiana, meet Alex and Emily."

Georgiana's eyes widened as she released a squeal of delight, hugging Elizabeth in welcome. Releasing Elizabeth, she gently approached the children and carefully peeled back the thin blankets. A smile graced her features as she gave each child a gentle squeeze and kissed their little heads.

Glancing at her older brother, she said, "Oh! I'm so glad you're all home. I've been worried sick about you, and to think I now have two adorable babies to love. I've fixed the nursery to your specifications and have placed two cribs in the master suite as you requested. I only did the basics, so when you're fully recovered from the flight, we'll go shopping and really fix things up. I'm so excited to finally have children in this house!"

Fitzwilliam looked upon his sister with a bemused smile and laughed. "You may change your mind when they're fully awake, announcing their presence. They can be quite loud, especially Alex in the middle of the night."

Turning to catch her other brother, she hugged him. "David, I'm so glad to see you, too. I've missed you both."

David smiled and kissed his sister's cheek. "I'm glad you finally noticed me, Georgie," he teased with a wink. "I've missed you, too. And Fitzwilliam is right. The babies are indeed loud."

"Yes, your brothers are quite right. They *can* be a handful." Elizabeth laughed.

"I highly doubt it," Georgiana said, taking Alex from Elizabeth. "It will make us all feel alive again and offer some diversion to this otherwise dull and stuffy house." Cradling Alex in her arms, Georgiana gently rocked back and forth.

"Let's give the children to their nannies. They need to be settled in the nursery," Fitzwilliam instructed. "They've been fed and changed, so they won't need anything for a while. We need to eat something, and Elizabeth needs to rest."

After handing the sleeping children to the two caregivers, Georgiana led the way to the small informal dining room where a light lunch was laid out. Once they'd eaten, David excused himself to his room while Fitzwilliam took Elizabeth by the hand.

"Let me show you to our rooms. You can freshen up there and then rest if you would like. Love, you look very tired." he said stroking the side of her face. "I will give you a personal tour of the house later, and then I'll also introduce you to the staff. I have some business with David and Georgiana. When it's concluded, I'll join you."

Leading her to a wide staircase, they took the stairs, veering to the right and then to the left where they entered the family wing. He stopped five doors down in front of a large oak door. Opening it, he glanced over his shoulder as if trying to gauge her reaction.

She smiled to reassure him. She knew he wanted her to be pleased, but he needn't have worried, for she was more than pleased.

"These are our rooms," he softly spoke as they went inside. "It is the master suite of the house."

As Elizabeth walked into the room, her breath caught. It was larger than any bedroom she had ever seen before. The entire room was done in a rich cherry wood. A magnificently crafted king size four-poster bed with a canopy and bed curtains dominated the room. Matching night tables with reading lamps flanked the bed. The coverlet was a rich deep-blue silk satin with several pillows, and a large chandelier hung from the ceiling. Two writing desks, where she could just imagine Fitzwilliam and herself working—she on her test papers and he on his corporate contracts—stood on either side of a large double door that led to a comfortable balcony sitting area. A section of bookcases holding a treasure trove of novels and histories bordered a door that led to...where? She didn't know, but her curiosity urged her to find out later.

Walking about the room, her lips curled pleasantly as she saw a sofa and chaise lounge that invited one to loll about lazily on its cushions before a fireplace that appeared to be still capable of hosting a blazing fire. And there was a black and white Alpaca rug in front of the hearth. Finally, her eyes rested upon two rocking chairs with matching cribs beside the bed. She glanced at her husband and smiled.

"Are you pleased, Elizabeth?" Fitzwilliam cautiously asked.

"Very much," she said. "Fitzwilliam, I'm pleased to be home with you and our family. The room is beautiful. Everything looks very comfortable and cozy. I'm looking forward to us being together again." She reached up with one hand and gently caressed his face.

He bent down and found her lips as he tenderly pulled her into his arms. Breaking the kiss, he whispered, "Come, I need to show you the rest of our rooms."

Elizabeth's eyes widened. "The rest of our rooms?"

"Yes," he laughed, "come, and I'll show you."

Leading her by the hand, they approached a great archway to the right of the bed with a curtain made of glass beads. This led to a sizeable dressing room with two large open walk-in closets situated across from one another. Through the dressing room, another door led to a huge, ornate bathroom. Elizabeth stared, impressed, since she had never seen one so luxurious before. Her eyes swept over the room. She saw a sunken bathtub, an oversized walk-in shower, and marble counters with gold fixtures and cherry cabinets.

"Fitzwilliam, this bathroom is as big as some of our bedrooms at Longbourn, and my closet is so large I will never be able to fill it. I have never seen anything like this!"

He chuckled softly. "You'll get used to the bathroom, and I'm sure you'll rather like it. We can relax in the hot tub later. As for the closet, yes, you will fill it. I want you to buy a whole new wardrobe when you feel up to shopping. I'll accompany you and show you all that London has to offer. Now come, I have one more set of rooms to show you."

"More rooms! You've got to be kidding?"

"No, I'm not joking." He laughed, lifting her chin to tap her lips.

Taking her by the hand, they walked back into the master suite and towards the door flanked by the large bookcases she had noticed earlier. He spoke softly as he put his hand to the latch. "Through this door is a small sitting room that connects the mistress's quarters to mine. Once upon a time, it was the room of the mistress of this house, but with the occasional exception of my mother, it hasn't been used for that purpose in nearly two hundred years, and I don't plan for you to break the long standing tradition." He smiled as they walked into the rooms.

Her eyes twinkled. "No, neither do I."

Elizabeth glanced around. The sitting room and mistress's quarters were as grand as the other rooms. She took a deep breath as her husband once again took her hand in his.

"On the other side of the mistress's quarters is where the nursery is located, but whilst the children are still young, they'll be with us during the night so we can care for them ourselves. During the day, the nannies will attend them in the nursery, unless you wish to do so yourself."

"Yes, I do want them with us at night, but help during the day will be very much appreciated."

"Very good," he said. "Now, let's view the nursery. Then our tour of our chambers will be complete. I'll show you the rest of the house at another time. Come, let's go in. Maggie and Clara are there with the children. I'll introduce you."

Fitzwilliam opened the door and stepped aside as Elizabeth entered. They found the nannies comfortably situated in large overstuffed chairs having tea and talking. Once the introductions were complete, he turned to Elizabeth and gestured with his hand. "Well, what do you think?"

"Oh, Fitzwilliam, it's beautiful. It's as I have always pictured a children's nursery to be. A large common room with beautiful white French Provincial furnishings and painted murals."

He smiled. "It's as my mother left it. Everything is still fairly new. It was rarely used by us as we spent most of our young years at Pemberley. Take a look around."

Elizabeth beamed. "All right," she said as moved around the room carefully inspecting every aspect. There were bins and shelves for toys along one wall. Along another was a French Versailles combination chest and changer positioned between two grand armoires with wire doors. Turning about, she walked over to the spindle cribs and ran her hand over the smooth finish as she gazed upon her sleeping infants. Off to her left, she saw a child's oval tea table with six tiny chairs. Walking over, she reached down and felt of the elegant cutwork tablecloth embroidered with pink and blue roses. The Peter Rabbit dishes she had chosen would look lovely on this table. She smiled. Completing the room were gliding rockers and a dining table where Elizabeth presumed the children would take their meals. There were even two larger beds for the nannies to spend the night.

Against the back wall she spied two doors separated by several floor to ceiling bookcases filled with children's books and collectibles. Elizabeth glanced up at her husband. "And I suppose those doors lead to the dormitories."

"Yes, they are the boys' and girls' wings. They, too, are furnished in French Provincial," he said as he led her to the first door.

Opening it, they stepped inside.

"This set of rooms is in pink and white with a fairy princess flare. The other rooms are done in oak with a Lothlorien theme. David and I preferred that. We had our rooms decorated in that design both here and at Pemberley. When the time comes, we will redo them to our specific tastes, but for now we will leave them as they are."

"It's all very lovely—like a storybook." Her eyes sparkled with pleasure. "I can't wait to make them personal. The common room is beautiful, too. Mother Goose is very traditional."

"I'm glad it meets with your approval. But if you decide otherwise, you can change anything you like."

She looked up and smiled once more. After surveying the boys' dormitory, they left the nursery and returned to the master suite.

As they entered, Fitzwilliam enclosed his wife in his arms. "Elizabeth, I've missed you. This year has been hell for me, but for right now, if you'll excuse me, I have something important I need to do. Go ahead and freshen up. I'll be back to join you later. Dinner is at seven, so you'll have enough time to rest. Oh, I almost forgot. If you need her, your maid, Sally, will help you unpack and put away your things."

"Thank you. I am very tired, so I think I will shower and rest. And I would appreciate Sally's help."

"Good. I'll send her up. You rest, and I'll return shortly," Fitzwilliam said as he went to leave.

"Fitzwilliam?"

"Yes," he said, pausing at the door.

"This year has not been easy for me either." She hesitated. "I have missed you, too, and sometimes, especially at night, the ache was unbearable. Tonight…I want you as my husband." Crossing the room, she moved into his arms and reached up to kiss him.

"Liz…Liz, you don't know how much I've longed to hear those words come from your lips. Tonight I'll make it up to you."

"We'll make it up to each other," she murmured, taking him in a deep lingering kiss before relinquishing him to his errands.

Fitzwilliam would waste no time in forming his tactics for cutting ties with his aunt. He needed to consult with David and then Georgiana before devising a strategy with the intent and purpose of dissolving all relationships, both business and personal, with Hilda. Settling behind his desk, he picked up his pen and addressed his brother who had just arrived and taken a seat.

"David, I want us to contact Pemberley Group tomorrow and set up a meeting as soon as possible. We need to find another banking partner and set the plans into motion to break all ties with Vanderburgh Banking. When everything is in place and irrevocable, we'll meet with Hilda."

"Are you sure…absolutely sure this is what you want to do. Once it is done, you cannot undo it."

"David, I have never been more certain of anything in my life. Hilda has been a thorn in my side for years with her attempts to order my life. First she dictated to Father how much education she thought I needed, and then she used her power and money to try and force me into marrying her step-daughter. If she'd had her way, I would've never been allowed to get my D.Phil. Not to mention all that I witnessed in her attempts to force her will on Father. If I hadn't known better, I might have thought she wanted to become the next Mrs. Darcy and run the company herself. And now her deception and betrayal with Elizabeth! I was a fool to have trusted her, and it has cost me dearly. It's a mistake I'll never make again."

"Well, she did help us when we really needed it, and she is family."

"I don't care how much she helped us. The help doesn't justify the harm. Besides, I haven't overlooked familiar ties before. I won't this time either." He looked his brother dead in the eye. "If it had not been for you, I don't know what would have happened to my wife and children."

"I understand," David nodded, "and you're very welcome. I'm glad it has turned out so well for you."

Fitzwilliam released a sigh. He could hear the hurt in his brother's voice. "David, I know you and Cecilia quarreled over Elizabeth and me, but now that you know the facts, I think you should seriously consider what it is you want. As I've said before, if you truly love her, go after her. We can wait on meeting with Pemberley Group. Go back to South Carolina tomorrow. Don't let her slip away. You will always regret it if you do."

"I can handle myself. Don't worry about me."

As David stood to leave, Fitzwilliam replied, "Well, then, there's nothing else to say. We'll discuss our plans in detail tomorrow. Send Georgiana in on your way out."

After briefing Georgiana of their tentative plans, Fitzwilliam left his study and returned upstairs where he found Elizabeth sound asleep. He smiled tenderly as he watched her sleeping, curled up in a ball on his bed where she belonged.

Turning, he went to freshen up. After he showered, he joined her on the bed where he gathered her into a tight embrace and fell asleep. Several hours later the nannies gently knocked on the door. Fitzwilliam slowly awakened, bidding them to enter.

"Elizabeth," he softly said, shaking her. "Elizabeth, wake up. We need to take care of the children, and there is only so much I can do."

"Oh, yes, I must have been asleep for a long time. Bring them here. If you will help me, I can probably feed them both at once. Alex won't wait, and poor Emily seems very hungry, too."

Taking the two fussing infants one at a time, he helped her place one at each breast while she leaned back against the soft pillows. Once they were situated, he lay down beside her and propped up on one elbow. It was a new and amazing experience, watching his children. Alex pulled and tugged in an almost angry fashion as he grunted and squirmed while Emily gently nursed in a leisurely manner.

"Alex is quite aggressive, isn't he?"

"And painful, too! He is neither gentle, nor respectful of me, and I can tell he's going to be strong-willed. We'll have a difficult time with him if we're not careful. I don't know of any Bennetts who are as determined as he promises to be," she teased.

"Don't you now?" Fitzwilliam smiled. "I know of at least one. Alex comes by it honestly. He reminds me of myself and David. We'll handle him just fine." He nodded. "Our daughter, on the other hand, is going to be a beauty. I dread her coming out. I'll have to screen her suitors closely."

Elizabeth rolled her eyes in amusement. "Well, just remember that you were once a young suitor, too."

A serious note entered his voice as he watched his nursing daughter. "That's the problem. I know what young men are about, and now that I have a daughter, it's different."

Elizabeth laughed and shook her head.

After the children were fed, their nannies returned for them, and the Darcys dressed for dinner. When dinner was finished, it was late, so they all retired for the night. Clara and Maggie had brought the twins to the master suite where they were waiting when the Darcys returned. Fitzwilliam took the children and dismissed the caregivers. After checking their nappies, he brought them to bed where he and Elizabeth played with them. They were wide awake, taking in everything around them, studying their parents intently as they glanced from one to the other.

"Do you suppose they can see us?" Fitzwilliam asked as he let Emily grasp his finger.

"Of course, they can, and they're beginning to smile. They're happy children, aren't they?" Elizabeth sighed as she stroked Alex's tiny face. "Mostly though, they relate to us by sound and feel. They respond to your voice. Your singing soothes them, whereas with me, it's my softness that soothes them. Soon they will be laughing and sitting up."

"Your softness soothes me too," Fitzwilliam said, casting a warm, yet intense look at his wife. "Let's see if we can get them to sleep—for at least a few hours, anyway."

As she nursed the babies, she gave them to him to be burped and rocked. Soon both children were sound asleep in their own little beds. Now, it was their time.

It had been so long since Fitzwilliam and Elizabeth had been together as man and wife that, observing her fidgeting, he could sense she was a bit nervous, so he decided to take things slowly. Walking over to the chaise lounge, he made himself comfortable.

"Elizabeth, come here, love, and just let me hold you."

She did as he asked, and they sat on the chaise, holding one another for some time with her head resting on his shoulder. He breathed in the rose scent of her hair, taking him back to when they'd first met—when he had first held her.

Finally, as he ran his hands through her tresses, he said, "I understand why you cut it, but please, won't you let your hair grow long again? It was one of the first things I noticed about you. You had the most incredibility long hair that I had ever seen. It was beautiful." He paused, tenderly gazing at her.

"Yes, I will let it grow. My hair has always been long, and I intend for it to be so again."

He caressed her arm with a gentle stroke, snuggling her to his chest. "Elizabeth, you are so beautiful…so very beautiful."

She sighed gently and murmured, "I don't feel very beautiful. I'm still fat, and the babies make me so tired. I feel old at times."

He looked at her lovingly. "Elizabeth, at twenty-seven, you're still young, and no, you're not fat. In fact, I rather like how your body has changed since giving birth to our children. I love you just the way you are, and that, my lovely Elizabeth, will never change." Pulling her into his lap, he said, "I have missed you, my darling wife."

She looked up with shimmering eyes as he took her face in his hands. Whispering her name, he began to kiss her unhurriedly. As their kiss deepened, a groan rumbled in his chest. He'd almost forgotten what it felt like to hold her in his arms, to kiss her, to make love to her. His body tightened, wanting her in every possible way.

While they kissed, his hand traveled the length of her body until he reached the hem of her gown. Slipping beneath the fabric, he began caressing her thighs, traveling to her hips, waist, and abdomen. He felt her quiver and tremble as his hand slowly edged closer to its destination. As he stroked her silken hair, she parted her legs to allow him access. He drew in a ragged breath, delighted at how she writhed under his touch. As his fingers caressed her, a soft moan of pleasure escaped from her throat. He kissed her once again, deeply and ardently—his tongue teasing… tasting… ravishing… devouring her mouth.

Elizabeth repositioned herself in his lap so that she straddled him. Edging closer, she pressed hard into his erection, rocking back and forth. She released a slight whimper as she sunk both hands into his hair, pulling him to her and covering his mouth with hers. Breaking the kiss, she arched her back and allowed him access to her throat which he aggressively took, kissing, nipping and suckling, scraping his teeth over her delicate skin while his hand continued to travel the curve of her body until it reached her derriere where he pressed her into him and arched against her.

As they moved against one another, his mouth found the spot behind her ear that used to drive her wild with desire. Settling on that spot, he forcefully sought it with his tongue and lips, kissing and suckling, nibbling her earlobe every now and then. Moving down her shoulder to her engorged breasts, he freed them from the slits in her nursing gown and caressed them, lightly stroking his thumb over her swollen nipple before bending down and gently flicking it with his tongue. He knew her breasts were tender, so he was careful, although he found the taste of her dripping milk to be sweet and exotic.

By now, his passion had grown to an almost painful state, but she still wasn't to the point where he wanted her, so he continued to caress her body, stroking her every curve. Feeling her hot dampness as his fingers slid inside of her, he paused and quickly withdrew. She was fully aroused and ready for him, and he was more than ready for her. Gathering her in his arms, he picked her up and carried her to their bed where he ripped back the coverlet and gently laid her down. Removing the remainder of their clothes, he climbed in beside her.

"Elizabeth, Elizabeth…my Elizabeth, how I've missed you!"

She tried to answer, but he covered her mouth with his, silencing her.

Elizabeth pressed the softness of her enlarged breasts against his chest while whispering in his ear in-between kisses. "I love you, Fitzwilliam… I love you."

He rolled her over in one smooth, quick motion, settling on top of her. Cupping her face in his hands, he looked deep into her beautiful eyes. "Liz, I have wanted you and needed you for so long. I love you, Liz."

"Fitzwilliam, please…please don't make me wait."

Tenderly he caressed her cheekbones with his thumbs before gently sliding his hands under her back and gathering her in his arms. While he held her close to his body, she raised her legs, encircling him, clinging to him in a lover's embrace.

Linked as one, they moved in an effortless, rhythmic motion, one with the other. Fitzwilliam felt her tremble beneath him, and it took all of his concentration to hold back as he fought to remain in control. Finally, feeling her fingernails dig into his back as her muscles forcefully tightened and contracted, his resolve broke, and he followed her over the edge, letting go.

Collapsing on top of her, still rocking gently and savoring the feelings of the moment, he began to kiss her again. As he broke the kiss, he pulled back. "I didn't hurt you, did I?"

"No, no, I'm fine. In fact, I'm wonderful. I'm not fragile…I won't break."

"I love you, Liz, and I have missed you in more ways than I can tell you. Welcome home, Mrs. Darcy," he said, showering her face with tiny endearing kisses as he rolled over, taking her with him and cradling her against his body.

She laid her head upon his shoulder while she stroked his face, whisking his damp curls away from his forehead. "I love you, Fitzwilliam. Hold me close and don't ever let me go. Promise me you will never, never leave me again—ever."

Her words broke his heart as a tear fell from her eye onto his shoulder. He gently wiped it away.

"Please, don't cry, Liz. We're together now, and I have no intentions of ever leaving you again. If for any reason we do have to be apart, I'll come for you personally, and I *will* ring you every day. I promise."

Elizabeth reached up with one small hand and cupped his face, bringing his lips to hers. Fitzwilliam responded in like and once again they found pleasure in one another's arms. Resting for about an hour, they repeated it, only to be interrupted by a small cry in the corner of the room.

"Well, I guess we have to put this on hold. Duty calls," Elizabeth said, softly laughing as he moaned and climbed out of bed to change the babies and bring them to her.

She smiled as he placed the twins between them and slipped beneath the covers. The children nursed contentedly while they all four drifted off to a peaceful sleep.

Early the next morning, Fitzwilliam awoke first. He propped up on one elbow and watched his sleeping family. How things had changed from a year ago! He had his wife back and two children along with her. He now had a purpose beyond Pemberley, and he knew he must take care of them properly, never forgetting what they meant to him. No one would ever hurt them again. They would be first in my life with their needs and wellbeing always met.

Elizabeth awoke, noticing Fitzwilliam staring at her. "What are you thinking?" Elizabeth asked.

"I was thinking about you and the twins, and how different things are from a year and a half ago. I think I have a made pretty good return on my investment, don't you?"

"I think you invested wisely, darling." She sleepily smiled. "Fitzwilliam, they've nursed much of the night. I think we can turn them over to Clara and Maggie now. Let's shower, get dressed, and have breakfast. I'm starving. Georgiana and I are going shopping later. I've decided that I will change the nursery. I'm thinking Peter Rabbit. What do you think? I bought Peter Rabbit dishes, and Cecilia and I made several quilts and blankets with that theme. It was what I did while I waited."

"I like Peter Rabbit. I'll commission for the murals to be changed. You can design it yourself. How would that be?"

"I would love it!"

He chuckled and shook his head. "My little domestic mathematician—the best one I've ever known." He nuzzled her nose with his as he nipped at her lips.

"I'd better be the *only* one you know." Giving him a saucy grin, she kissed the tip of his nose.

"Believe me, madam, I can only handle one, and that is you. Now, you and Georgiana have fun today. I'll be going into the office. I have business matters that I can't put off. I'll see you this evening." With a kiss, he headed for the shower.

Chapter Sixty-two

...I want them to see that I love her...

After meeting with Pemberley Group's team of solicitors, the brothers met in the Fitzwilliam's corporate office to hash out the details of their proposal.

"David, what do you think of J.C. Hanover as our new banking partner? It's either them or Chase Manhattan."

"Umm, well, the animosity that exists between Jack and Hilda is well known, therefore choosing Hanover would make a statement as well as firing a shot over the bow. As for Chase, I don't like that option at all. Although they are well establish in London, it's an American owned bank. Therefore, it's my opinion that Hanover is the better option on many fronts. However, if you choose them, Hilda will know this is personal...and final. So, let's discuss the perils as well as the particulars. We have to be cunning, and she cannot know what we're planning."

"You're absolutely correct. It's time to play hardball, and I know Hilda is a master player."

The two brothers set about developing their plan. They spent the better part of forty-five minutes thrashing the matter out. When they had finally reached a consensus, David reiterated. "If you are absolutely sure this is what you want to do, then let's go forward. Make it swift, and make it deadly. But... you must be sure. Hilda's clout is considerable, and as you say, our actions will be irrevocable all the way around, therefore, the consequences could be immense. There is no room for a mistake."

"Oh, I'm sure—absolutely sure. And I am well aware of the risk we take. Hilda is a force to be reckoned with, but I assure you, she has met her match in both cunning and skill."

David sighed. "She is our aunt, Mum's only remaining sister, and you know, in spite of her cruelties, Mother loved her."

"Yes, I know, and it grieves me to do what we are about to do, but I cannot forgive her for what she has done to me." He passed his hand over his face and released a sigh. "Now, let's put this aside and have a good weekend. Since Thomas is on holiday, there is nothing more we can do for now. We'll take care of business when he returns. Besides, it'll give me a little more time to pull things together before I meet with Jack Hanover," Fitzwilliam said while shuffling papers into a portfolio.

"Well, if there is nothing else, I'll return to my office and finish up on Jacob's report. I'm about to finalize the contract on the new manufacturing facility in Singapore," David said as he rose to leave.

Glancing up Fitzwilliam added, "By the way, I'm just curious, have you called Cecilia yet?"

David stopped short and shot his brother a look meant to kill. "No! And I'm not about to. I've told you it's over between us. It should have never been in the first place, so drop it."

"Little Brother," Fitzwilliam sighed, "you're making a mistake—a big mistake."

"And it's mine to make. Like I said—drop it. I've told you, this is a topic I refuse to discuss with you or anyone else."

"Okay, David." He shrugged. "It's Friday. I'm going home early. If I don't see you later, have a good weekend."

David nodded and left.

As the door closed behind his brother, Fitzwilliam sat back in his chair and shook his head. The warning David had flashed in his eyes let Fitzwilliam know he'd overstepped his bounds, even for two brothers who shared everything—everything except that very private spot David kept for himself alone.

Fitzwilliam smiled, humming a lively tune when he came through the front door of Darcy House. Now that he and Elizabeth were back together and in a place where there was actually something to do on the weekends, he wanted to take her out. Feeling the need to have time for themselves apart from the children, he'd made reservations for dinner at a fine restaurant in Knightsbridge. Tomorrow he would take her shopping and sightseeing in London.

Making his way to the library, he found Elizabeth reading while the twins squirmed on a pallet in front of the fireplace. He took a seat beside her and slipped his arm around her shoulder. "Elizabeth, I want you to dress in something elegant for the evening. We are going out tonight. I'm taking you to Petrus," he said with a smile. "It's a very exclusive French restaurant, one that I think you'll enjoy."

She glanced up in surprise. "That sounds wonderful! I love French cuisine, especially escargot, and I haven't had any since graduate school." She stopped to think for a moment. "It's been so long since I was actually out. I'm looking forward to the evening."

He chuckled softly. "Order whatever you like. If you like escargot, then you shall have it. We're going out tonight, but that's not all we're going to do. Next week I plan to take you to the Embassy. It's a private club where David and I are members. Liz, my love, I'm going to properly date you as I would have when we first met had there been someplace to go and something to do."

She hesitated for a moment and tilted her head. "Well...I suppose we did miss out when we were dating, though I never really noticed. Hmm...I guess it's true. There's not much to do or see in Walnut Grove, is there? But somehow I never felt cheated. Being with you was always enough for me back then. However," she said with a twinkle in her eye, "I don't mind you taking me places and dating me now, if that's what you really want to do."

"It's exactly what I want to do. This is *my* world, and I'm going to show it to you. We're going to make up for what we've missed. Tonight I'm taking you to dinner, and tomorrow I'm taking you shopping on Bond Street and Oxford. We're going to buy you some appropriate things for London society, so make arrangements. We'll eat out, and if you would like, we can take Alex and Emily."

"I've already been to Bond Street with Georgiana, and I bought a lot of things. However, if you want to take me, I'd love to go again, but I don't think it's such a good idea to take Alex and Emily out for an all day trip. They're still too young, and I don't think we would enjoy ourselves with two fussy babies," she replied. "When they're a little older, we can take them."

"You're probably right, but I thought you might want them along, especially since you're nursing."

"I can take care of that, and we can come back after a few hours to check on them."

"All right, if you feel comfortable with those arrangements, then it's fine with me. Now, as for shopping, I'm going to do more than show you. I want to buy you several things." He tipped her chin and pecked her lips.

"But, Fitzwilliam, I've already spent £5000 on clothes!"

"And you can spend another five thousand. Liz, I've already told you not to be concerned about the money. I can afford it!" He moved closer, pulling her into his embrace." I want you to have your heart's desires. Besides, you're going to need an appropriate up-to-date wardrobe for some of the places I want to take you."

Smiling, she gingerly gave him a quick kiss. "Well, if that's what you want to do, then let's go shopping. Now then, come with me to my dressing room and help me pick out a dress for dinner." Rising from the sofa, they picked up the children and headed towards the stairs.

After settling the twins in their cribs, they moved to the dressing room. "How about this one?" He picked out a short white cocktail dress with thin shoulder straps tying in the back and a slight draped ruffle down the front and held it up to her.

"Perfect!" she exclaimed, taking the dress.

After dressing for the evening, Fitzwilliam had the car brought around, and Singleton drove them to the restaurant. As the Darcys exited the car, the paparazzi stepped forward, snapping pictures. Their sudden appearance startled Elizabeth, but Fitzwilliam had expected it. He waved, greeting them with a smile and then gently placed his hand to the small of Elizabeth's back, guiding her into the restaurant. Fitzwilliam was going to do something he had never done before. He was going to court the media. He knew curiosity about his wife ran rampant in all of London, and he deliberately intended for Elizabeth to be seen in the best possible light. He would be in control, comfortable and at ease with the press just like his father.

"Fitzwilliam, what was that all about?" Elizabeth asked, pausing in the lobby.

"That, my love, is what's to be expected in the short term when we come out into society. Greet them with a friendly smile, and all will be well. We'll be in the news for a little while to come, but it will pass soon enough when the novelty of your appearance as my wife is no longer a topic for public gossip. Besides, I want to show them how beautiful you are." Glancing down at her with a wide smile, he guided her through the door.

Following the hostess to their table, curious eyes turned towards the Darcys. Elizabeth seemed unaware of the inquisitive stares as they were seated, but Fitzwilliam was very much aware of the commotion they created amongst the other diners.

During the course of the evening, several members of London's elite stopped by the Darcys' table to greet Mr. and Mrs. Darcy. Everyone was cordial and polite with a genuine interest in knowing the woman who had been the point of contention in the very public split between George Darcy and his son.

Fitzwilliam sat back and watched with delight. Much to the surprise of many, Mrs. Darcy was not only beautiful, but pleasantly at ease with them, possessing a quick wit and a charming allure. Elizabeth held up her part of the conversation comfortably, showing herself to be well informed on many subjects and uncommonly intelligent. Many commented on the sound of her voice, finding her genteel southern accent to be pleasing. They treated her with respect, not only because she was the wife of one of their own, but because she carried herself with a refined deportment—as one who deserved respect on her own merit.

She, in turn, treated them with the same warmth and kindness as she would anyone whom she'd just met. They genuinely liked her and it showed. Fitzwilliam hoped it was also evident to all who saw them that he loved his wife very much and that his love was returned.

Later that night as they undressed for bed, Fitzwilliam was anxious to discuss the evening. Since Elizabeth had accused him of trying to hide her away when he first found her after their year-long separation, he wanted to reassure her with more than mere words. This evening was to be the beginning of his well laid plan to present her to the public.

"Elizabeth, how did you like your first evening out in London?"

"I enjoyed it very much. Everyone seemed very pleasant and not at all like I had expected, but I did get the impression that it was a little stifling to you," she said as she sat before her dressing table and took down her hair.

"I have to confess, I never did like being on public display, but I want all of London to know that I am exceedingly proud of my wife and that I love you. And I want *you* to know that I'm not ashamed of you as you once thought." He took her hand in his, stroking her fingers.

She rose from her vanity and wrapped her arms around his waist. "Fitzwilliam, I know now that my thoughts during our separation were a collection of misjudgments."

"That's true," he said, tightening his embrace, "but I still want you to know with more than just words. As I said, I plan to take you out into London society and show you as much as I can of what there is to see whilst we have the time."

She snuggled into his arms, allowing him easier access for a kiss. Since the children were asleep, they took full advantage of the moment they had before other priorities claimed their time.

The next day while taking his coffee in their sitting room, Fitzwilliam perused the morning paper. He and Elizabeth were on the front page of the society section of the *Times* with a picture featuring him wearing a wide smile and Elizabeth appearing very composed and beautiful. The society pages featured a well written Cinderella story about a man who chose to marry the woman he loved in spite of his father's disapproval.

Fitzwilliam had given the interview the day before, detailing how they had met and fallen in love. As evident from the story, London had been curious about the mystery woman who had captured the heart of one of the most eligible and richest men in the United Kingdom, and his intention was to make her the darling of the press in order to dispel the negative image they had previously created because of her middle-class American status, not to mention her cousin's tarnished reputation. Overall, Fitzwilliam was pleased with the story. The first step in the right direction had been taken.

After breakfast, Elizabeth and Fitzwilliam made arrangements for their shopping trip. She left instructions for the nannies as well as breast milk for Alex and Emily. With all the arrangements settled, Fitzwilliam and Elizabeth left for Bond Street.

Their first stop was a salon specializing in the care of long hair where he bought her a full line of products. Watching her pick up and put down a Mason Pearson brush with natural bristles twice, Fitzwilliam smiled. Knowing she wanted it, but was probably reluctant because of the price, he quietly instructed the sales person to add it to the purchase along with a handmade sheep's horn comb to go with it.

Going from one shop to the next, he bought her more dresses, casual wear, formal wear, shoes, accessories, and lingerie than she thought she would ever need. Some of the things she considered either excessively expensive or too provocative, bordering on immodest, but he insisted, assuring her that women in London society would be wearing this and less. She simply smiled and shook her head as he paid for the purchases. Before it was all said and done, they had gone to so many boutiques that Fitzwilliam had lost count, and when the expenses were counted up, it came to over £30,000. Fitzwilliam only smiled at her shocked expression.

They ate lunch at a sidewalk café and then stopped by the house to check on the twins and drop off the packages. Next they set out to tour *The Victoria and Albert Museum* with a promise from Fitzwilliam to take her to the National Art Gallery where one of the greatest art collections in all of Europe was housed. They made plans to see Westminster Abby, the castles, the Tower of London, and as many of the museums and galleries as time would permit.

Of course, the paparazzi appeared, snapping pictures and asking questions, and each time they asked, Fitzwilliam gave them a brief interview. Appearing relaxed, he showed how very fond and protective he was of his wife as he casually wrapped an arm around her.

Speaking with Elizabeth, the press formed a very positive impression and warm regard for her. Her friendly smile and sparkling green eyes were hard to resist. Fitzwilliam hoped their curiosity would soon be satisfied and the media would move on to the next story so that he and Elizabeth could soon enjoy a normal life.

When Sunday arrived, Fitzwilliam insisted they all attend church services as he wanted Alex and Emily to grow up in the Anglican Church. Elizabeth agreed since her father had felt similarly about taking his children to the small Southern Baptist Church near Longbourn when they were young.

Sitting in church, cradling his baby daughter against his chest, Fitzwilliam couldn't have been more content with his life and family. While all heads were bowed for the closing prayer, he gave thanks that he'd found the woman he'd always dreamed of and had the family he'd always wanted.

Chapter Sixty-three

…every place of refuge had its price…

Cecilia entered her cold, dark house and slowly trudged up the stairs to her lonely room. With Elizabeth and the children gone, the house seemed so big…and empty. And for the first time in her life, she was lonely. Yes, she'd been alone before, especially after her father's death—but never lonely. With a heavy sigh, Cecilia contemplated paying a visit to her godfather. Though she saw him at the office every day, she hadn't been to No. 33 ½ Legare St. in months. No, she shook her head. She couldn't go there. It would be too humiliating to let Daniel see her like this. He would know. He always knew. So, no, a visit to Daniel was out.

Cecilia left out a long breath. Since that awful confrontation with David, all she could do was sit in the quiet of her room each night, reliving their times together while listening to the CD he'd given her. The candle, now long spent, she'd replaced. Cecilia moved to her closet and hung her purse on the doorknob. Turning, she walked over to light the new candle. Before changing her clothes, she once again slipped the CD into the sound system.

Gently drawing back the bedcovers, she smoothed the sheets, softly caressing David's pillow. Breathing in the sweet scent of Sensual Orchard, she could almost feel his presence in her room—in her bed once more.

What had been the difference between David and the other men she'd known? Mulling it over, she sighed. It was manhood. While most men never learned the secret, David, like her father, understood what it meant to be a man. He was strong and confident, secure in who he was, and he made her feel like a woman. That's why she'd fallen for him…and why the pain of losing him was so acute.

She'd never known what it was like to be loved until she met him. He had given her a sexual experience she knew she would never have again—a connection so deep that it came straight from the heart. No one would ever replace him. No one would even come close. No, she shook her head. She'd never allow another man that close again. No one would ever be given the power to break her heart like David had.

Walking over to the side-table, she opened a fresh bottle of peach brandy and poured herself a stiff drink. Another night, another bottle of brandy. This couldn't go on. This was not like her.

…Celia, get a grip. Face it…he's gone. You knew it wouldn't last…it was too good to be true. Cameron was right. Cameron…he's called you twice. You need to return his call.

Picking up the phone, she punched in his number. "Cameron, it's Celia. I need to talk. Can you come over? I'm at the townhouse."

"What's wrong, baby? You sound down. Did he leave you?"

"How very perceptive of you," she smirked. "Let's just say it didn't work out. Too many cultural differences, I suppose," she lied. Hell would freeze over before she confessed anything to him.

"I'll be there in thirty minutes. You need to get out. I have a standing table down at The Wharf. Do you feel like seafood tonight?"

She laughed. "When have I ever *not* felt like seafood? I'll be ready—and Cameron—don't be late."

"Celia babe, I'm never late."

True to his word, Cameron arrived at her door on time with flowers and a bottle of champagne. Cecilia invited him in while her maid took the flowers and put the champagne in the refrigerator. As Sandy was about to place the flowers in a vase, Cecilia stopped her.

"No, not that vase. I want you to pack it away. Use Grandmother Lawton's crystal vase in the drawing room."

"Sure, Ms. Lawton." Sandy frowned. "It's an awfully pretty vase to be packed away, though. Are you sure?"

"I've never been more certain of anything in my life. Pack it away."

She couldn't bear to see Cameron's flowers in David's vase. That night at The Woodlands had been special. Thinking back upon it, she realized that was the night she had begun to fall for him.

Looking at his watch, Cameron prompted, "Celia, are you almost ready? It's nearly six thirty. We need to eat, and we have a lot to discuss."

"I'll get my purse."

Once at The Wharf, Cameron wasted no time in coming to the point. "Celia, now that the Brit is out of the way, it's time for you and I to come to an understandin' and discuss our future, the blendin' of our corporate assets, and of course, children," he said with a confident smile. "You know your father wanted us to marry, and there is nothing that would make my daddy happier. Mother has always loved you…and you know *I* have loved you since we were children in grade school."

Cecilia smiled as she lifted her glass to her lips. *…So this is how it is…we negotiate a contract. Well, if that's how it's going to be, then I might as well negotiate the best deal I can get.*

"Cameron, I'm not ready for a formal arrangement, but if you're willing to take what I have to offer, I believe we can come to an informal understanding."

He nodded for her to continue.

"First and foremost, you have to give up Amelia. I won't have you sleeping with her when you're supposed to be with me. Second of all, don't push me into marriage until I say I'm ready. And when we're married, you *will* remain faithful. If you don't, I want a clause written into the prenuptial where I can obtain a speedy divorce with no hassles. Lastly, I will maintain full control over all Lawton assets, including the cotton and rice foundations." She sat her drink down and crossed her arms over her chest.

He smiled. "I'll accept your terms as long as the sons you give me are set to inherit Lawton. Other than that, we'll have our attorneys draw up prenuptials to which we both can agree. As for Amelia, I'll give her up…on one condition." Pausing for a sip of wine, he looked Cecilia directly in the eye. "Invite me back into your bed. Spend the weekend with me at Magnolia Place. My parents are in town for the season. We'll be alone."

Breathing deeply, she picked up her napkin and unfolded it, placing it neatly in her lap. She cut her eyes across at him and then to the waiter who'd just approached with their meal. This was not what she wanted. The thought was revolting, but she knew she couldn't keep him at bay forever. A decision had to be made. She'd spent enough time with David to know he wouldn't be coming back riding on a white steed to rescue her. When the waiter finished serving their food, she picked up her wine glass and made a toast.

"To us. Pick me up on Friday after work. I'll be ready." Setting her glass aside, she picked up her fork and began to play with her salad.

The entire drive back from the restaurant, Cecilia's stomach churned. For the first time in her life she felt cheap. She'd just agreed to sleep with, and eventually marry, a man she could barely stand, let alone love. He said he loved her, but she didn't believe him for a moment. She knew the real reasons for his interest were the merger of Lawton and Taylor Shipping, as well as the merger of two of Charleston's oldest families. And he had cleverly side-stepped the issue of faithfulness. She inwardly laughed. He would cheat in a New York minute, and she knew it.

When they reached her door, she invited him in. They had the champagne he'd brought while he babbled on about kids, houses, and wealth. She couldn't really remember what all he'd said. Inwardly, she silently cried. The only thing that reverberated through her mind was David's laughter...his smiles...his kiss...his touch. Snapping out of her fog, she realized Cameron was leaving.

"I'll pick you up tomorrow at six for dinner, and then on Friday we'll go to the plantation. We'll ride down to the creek by the old grist mill and sit on the rock overlooking the water like we used to. I'll even bring my sketch book and a bottle of wine. You bring cheese and grapes." He laughed. "I still have that collection of poetry I wrote for you when we were teenagers. I'll bring that, too, and we can read it and reminisce. It's gonna be like old times... Just you and me babe. Wait and see."

She smiled. *...No...it'll never be like it used to be. I don't love you. I never have. And the old grist mill? It still holds the taint of another woman. You still don't get it...*

Seeing her smile, he pulled her into his arms, talking to her in between peppered kisses. "I'll make it up to you, baby. All I ask for is two sons...two sons. You can have anything you want—a house full of kids if that's what you want or no more than two—provided they're sons." Tightening his grip, he continued to kiss her. Finally breaking away, he said, "We have a lot to talk about...a lot to settle. I love you, babe. I'll pick you up tomorrow. Be ready," he said, making his way out the door for his car.

Watching him go, Cecilia reflected. She had no brother, no sister, no cousins. Duty and responsibility—the thought of it made her sick. She knew she was settling for one of the most pompous asses in Charleston, but her options had just run out. Suppressing a sob, she lingered against the doorframe, staring out into the nothingness. David wasn't coming back. Whenever she closed her eyes, she could still see that look... the look of hurt, pain, anger, and betrayal. *...David...he was going to marry me...and I lost him...I've lost him for good.* She shook her head as the tears fell. Every place of refuge had its price, and she had just paid it. She hung her head and cried.

Getting into his Canary yellow Vette, Cameron sped away to his townhouse on Tradd St. He smiled. He finally had what he wanted—the prettiest woman in Charleston. With her connections, business was sure to improve. He'd have access to the Carolina Gold *and* the Sea Island Cotton. His wealth would increase substantially. Two of the oldest families in South Carolina would finally be uniting. He grinned. *...I can't wait till this weekend. I still remember what it was like when she wrapped those long legs around me. Celia always was the best piece of ass I've ever had. I wonder if she's still as tight as she used to be. Umm... perhaps we can catch the NCAA playoffs Sunday afternoon. South Carolina's playin' against Alabama in the finals.*

Chapter Sixty-four

...Oh God, what have I done...?

David exhaled in frustration as he tossed the file in his hand on his the side cabinet and fell down in the chair beside his bed. Eyeing the Thai Silk account, he shook his head. Corporate accounts and business were the last things he had on his mind. He reaching into his pocket and pulled out a packet of cigarettes and took one out. Tapping it on the cabinet, he inhaled sharply and leaned back in his chair.

If he'd thought it had been bad before, it was much worse this time. The sight of happy couples walking arm in arm wherever he went grieved him, and searing pain shot through him every time a leggy blonde walked by. But that was during the day. During the night was another story entirely.

At night, David was barely able to sleep. His body ached, and his mind was flooded with thoughts and memories of Cecilia. He remembered the times they'd talked late into the night planning their costumes for the Magnolia Ball, the silly little things they'd shared about their respective day, and perhaps the worst and most bittersweet of all were the memories of their passionate nights spent in each other's arms.

He clenched his jaw. Unable to resist, last week he had looked her up online and had seen her picture with her latest man in *The Post and Courier*. David smirked contemptuously. Cecilia had wasted no time in moving on, and with *him*, a man David knew she did not love.

He took out a lighter and lit his cigarette. Taking a long slow drag, he reflected on recent events. Although he was a man who never did without, he hadn't been with anyone since he'd known he was in love with Cecilia. It had been three months now since he had slept with a woman. He was not his brother. He could not remain celibate indefinitely, though he doubted he'd ever love again.

He eyed the glass on the side cabinet. Another bottle of brandy, another night ...alone. He couldn't go on like this! He had to get her off my mind. What was he to do? Sandra! He had to see Sandra. She had been his favorite girlfriend before Cecilia. Perhaps they could reconnect.

David quickly grabbed his mobile and searched the directory for her number. Since he hadn't called her in over a year, he wasn't sure where she would be at this hour or if she would be working or not. All he knew was that if someone could replace Cecilia, even for one night, it was Sandra. In looks they were very similar. He had to see her.

"David...how good of you to ring," she said rather flatly.

"Sandra, I need to see you. Can you meet me tonight?"

"You come right to the point, don't you?"

David creased his brow. Sandra's response had a biting edge. Surely she wouldn't refuse him?

"It's been a long time since we've seen each other, and I really would like to see you again."

A full three seconds of silence stood between them before she answered, leaving David even more confused.

"Sure, David." She hesitated. "I'm working till midnight, but after that, I'm free."

Relieved, he asked, "Where are you working?"

"The Pink Palace. Do you want to pick me up or meet me at my flat?"

"I'll meet you at your flat. I'll see you around one. Will that do?"

"I'll see you then. You still have the key?"

"Yes, I'll let myself in and wait for you."

Sliding his mobile shut, he poured himself a brandy while he contemplated Sandra. Her tone was cool and clipped. For a moment, he had feared she would refuse him. He wondered if it was just his imagination or something else.

She knew their understanding. That had never been a problem. He could be with her and go on his way without so much as a second thought. She had never made any demands and there were no expectations. Puzzled by her tone, he dismissed it as nothing. Finishing his brandy, he put out his cigarette and left for Sandra's flat.

Sandra arrived a little after one and found David reclined on the sofa in the living room, waiting for her.

"David, it's so good to see you again. I haven't seen you in…what, a year?"

"It's been a long time, love, but I'm here tonight. How have you been?"

"Lonely. I've missed our times together. You're one of the best lovers I've ever had, and… well, I've missed you."

David arched an eyebrow, startled by her confession and not quite sure how to answer.

"I've been very busy, love. I haven't had time to visit old friends."

"Yes, I'm sure you have."

David pulled in a deep breath. *There it is. That cool tone again. What's wrong with her?*

Walking over to the small cabinet beside her sofa, she threw her wrap over a nearby chair and turned. "Well, let's have some wine and make up for lost time. I'm looking forward to being with you again. This time we'll work extra hard to be discreet, so there'll be no more problems." She poured two glasses of port and handed him one before taking her seat beside him. He pulled her close and held her as they sipped their wine in silence. Relaxed, he once again dismissed his reservations. Apparently, she thought he hadn't called because of the tabloids. He'd let her think whatever she wanted. It was better than the truth.

"David, what's wrong. You're not yourself. You've barely said two words to me. Something's bothering you."

"Why do you say that? I'm a little tired. That's all."

"Precisely. You were never tired when we were together. In fact, it was quite the opposite. I sense the presence of another woman."

Shocked at her perception, David jolted. He'd thought Sandra beautiful and talented, but perceptive was not an attribute he would have ascribed to her. "No one is here besides us, and there is nothing wrong with me…nothing at all."

"It's me you're talking to, David. I know you fairly well. If you're not crawling all over me, something is wrong. We haven't made love in a year, and you aren't interested."

"Sandra," he sat up straight, "I've never made love to you, and tonight, I feel like it even less. If you're looking for love, I don't have it in me. Intimacy is something I can *try* to share, but if I disappoint you, I'm sorry."

"It's because of her, isn't it?" Sandra persisted. "The *American*."

"Sandra, what on earth are you talking about?"

"The one I read about in society pages. The wealthy corporate executive from America. The story was picked up by *The Sunday Times*. It's reported that you've been seen traveling to South Carolina to see some woman. The papers say that you are quite serious about her." She shifted to face him. "Are you in love? Is that the reason you came to see me? Are you running from her?"

"She has nothing to do with it. I don't love her. I don't love anybody. I told you once before love is an emotion I don't feel—not for her, not for you, not for anyone," he lied.

"Oh, but I believe you do. Perhaps you're unaware of it, but you're more affected by her than you think."

David attempted to respond, but Sandra held up her hand to silence him.

"David, I know our relationship has only been about sex. I meet your needs and you meet mine, but tonight you're distracted. You're in love with her, and I know it," Sandra whimpered.

Stunned, David looked at her in confused disbelief. "You're wrong. I've told you I don't love her. So let's drop it!"

Sandra set her glass down and began to tremble, crying softly.

...Oh God, a crying woman! I can't handle a crying woman. A twinge of pity pierced his heart as he set his wine glass aside and wrapped her in his arms. He wished it could have been her he loved, but it wasn't. In a storm of emotions, he lied again.

"You're mistaken, Sandra."

"No, I don't think I am. She or someone else is here tonight. It's not me you desire. I'm only a diversion—someone to help you forget what you don't want to remember."

"You're wrong, Sandra. I'm not in love," he breathed deeply, "but you're right about one thing. I...*we* do need a diversion."

Hearing his words, she turned in his arms and embraced him, kissing him in a way she had never kissed him before. David sensed her desperation—desperate for whatever he was willing to give her.

Knowing she had feelings for him disturbed him greatly. It had been a mistake to come here. But since he was here, he couldn't leave her so distraught. A year ago, he wouldn't have cared, but not today. Somewhere along the way he'd become a different man—a man torn by her emotional state and by his guilt in knowing that he could not return her feelings. All of it only increased the pain he had sought to escape in her arms.

For the second time in his life, he was taking a woman to bed for her sake—not his. He would give Sandra what he knew she wanted and needed—some tenderness, but he could never return to her flat again. One thing he'd sworn he would never do was to deliberately hurt someone, especially the way Cecilia had hurt him. Sandra deserved better than that. After he knew she was satisfied, he lay there holding her until she fell asleep.

Once he was sure she was asleep, David got up and dressed. As he reached for his pen to leave her a note, he saw the December issue of *Gentleman Quarterly* lying on her dresser. Eying it carefully, he picked it up and thumbed through it until he reached the article. Sandra had written a note in the margin. She had thought the article was meant for her. Pain gripped him as a slow guttural moan escaped his throat. *...Oh God, what have I done? I never meant for her to love me. No matter what I do, I will hurt her, but at least I will hurt her less by leaving.* He glanced back at her sleeping form and shook his head. Then he took out his pen and wrote her a quick note, leaving it, along with the key and £2000, her usual fee, on her dresser. After one quick look at Sandra's sleeping form, he turned and quietly left, closing the door behind him for good.

Chapter Sixty-five

...He's throwing his happiness away with both hands...

At long last David and Fitzwilliam finally met with Thomas Metcalfe, lead solicitor of Pemberley Group, to begin the process of separating Pemberley, PLC from Vanderburgh Banking. Wrangling back and forth over the contents of the brief Fitzwilliam and David had put together, Fitzwilliam finally said, "Thomas, I want all ties to Vanderburgh Banking severed. That's not negotiable, and I don't care how you do it—just do it."

Scanning over the rough proposal once more, Metcalfe replied, "Fitzwilliam, that's a difficult process. Vanderburgh Banking is deeply entrenched in Pemberley. Your family has been heavily involved with them for generations. You do realize that this will be a heavy financial loss for them? And not only that, but to replace them with J.C. Hanover? That act alone will be viewed as a deliberate affront."

"As I intend it to be!"

Metcalfe let out an exasperated breath. "I don't understand your reasoning, and I think it ill advised, but if this is what you want, I will arrange it. I'll have a contractual separation draft on your desk by the middle of next week. If you approve the preliminary version, the final document can be ready by Friday of the following week. I'll also have the necessary paperwork for the formal agreement with Hanover drawn up by then as well. But you had better be bloody damned sure this is what you want because once it begins, it cannot be reversed."

"Good!" Fitzwilliam exclaimed.

"Thomas, we are bloody damned sure, or we wouldn't be sitting here in your office, taking up your time and wasting ours," David interjected.

"Yes, I rather imagine you are at that. Well, I'll meet with the others and get on with it."

"Very good. Now I have one other thing of great importance we need to discuss." Fitzwilliam turned to David. "Unless you wish to stay for this, I'll see you in my office in ten minutes."

"No, I'd rather not. I'll meet you when you're through here," David said as he rose to leave.

When they were alone, Fitzwilliam pulled out a piece of paper from his binder. "Thomas, Hilda stole some sheets of my personal business stationary with my signature attached and used one of them. I want you to make note of that and file a copy of this letter with it," Fitzwilliam said as he handed Metcalfe a copy of the letter Hilda had written to Elizabeth.

Thomas glanced up from his paperwork as he took the letter. "Is that why you want this separation?"

"Precisely." He gave a curt nod. "As to the letter, I will swear out an affidavit stating that I did not write it, and should other such letters appear with my signature on them, I want legal action taken."

As Metcalfe scanned the letter, he looked up in shocked disbelief. "Good God, Fitzwilliam, what on earth were you thinking to have left signed letterhead lying about.

This is serious business! You've got to get that stationary back and change your security practices. Get that stationary out of your office, and have Mrs. Foulkes keep it under lock and key. Do you realize the ramifications of this? That stationary could be used for anything, though I highly doubt Hilda is stupid enough to commit a crime with it, but get it back just the same! For now, I'll make a legal record of this and file it, but get that stationary back!"

"I intend to, Thomas, believe me, I intend to. And I do know how serious this is. I can't believe I was so foolish. Nevertheless, take care of it for me."

Metcalfe arched a brow and slowly shook his head.

With their business concluded, Fitzwilliam left Metcalfe's office and headed back towards the lobby where Mrs. Foulkes informed him that his uncle was waiting on line two.

"Thank you, Betty. I'll take the call in my office."

Once at this desk, he picked up the phone. "Uncle Harvey, what can I do for you?"

"Fitzwilliam, how are you?"

"Things couldn't be better."

"Good…good. Susan and I have been thinking about you since we talked last week. How are your wife and children?"

"We're all doing well. Elizabeth and the twins are adjusting, and I couldn't be happier now that I finally have my family home with me."

"Well, I'm glad to hear it. We're both very happy for you," Harvey said. "Now, this brings me to the point of my call. Susan and I would like to invite you and your wife to dinner one night this week at your convenience. We would like very much to meet her. David and Georgiana are invited as well. And William and Benson will be here, too, as well as Amanda Elliot, William's girlfriend."

"Amanda Elliot? I didn't realize William was dating Amanda."

"Oh yes, they have been seeing each other for a few months now, at least whenever he's been in town, but I believe she has also been with him in New York." Uncle Harvey laughed. "Perhaps, in the not too distant future, he'll have an announcement of his own to make."

"Well, it could be. Last December I did notice how he seemed to stare at her from across the ballroom. I guess he finally found the courage to speak with her."

"Yes, I would say he did, and I think they've been doing a little more than talking." Harvey chuckled. "He has the same Darcy reserve that most of us have, but I do believe he has overcome it just a bit. Anyway, what do you say about dinner?"

"I'll speak with Elizabeth tonight and get back with you tomorrow."

"Very well then, we'll look forward to hearing from you."

Fitzwilliam hung up the phone and shook his head, smiling. David, who had just entered his brother's office, noticed. "What's so amusing?"

"That was Uncle Harvey on the phone inviting us to dinner one night this week." Fitzwilliam tilted his head with a wide smile. "David, did you know William was dating Amanda Elliot?"

"Yes, I did. He's quite taken with her."

"So I'm finding out. Anyway, back to the dinner invitation, are you free? I'll have to speak with Elizabeth to set a date."

"Yes, any night or time will do for me. I don't go out much anymore," David murmured. His eyes filled with sadness for a split second before composing himself. "Fitzwilliam, I need that proposal for the Thai silk contract I was working on. You did look over it, didn't you?"

"Yes, I studied it, and I'm in complete agreement with your suggestions, but David, you don't have to personally handle that. Delegate the job to your assistant. Bruce could use the experience."

"No, I'll handle it myself. I'm working late tonight, and I'm staying here at my flat, so don't expect me home for dinner. I'll have something sent in. In fact," he hesitated, "I'll be staying here and working for the next several weeks." David smiled, taking the file Fitzwilliam handed him.

Staring at his brother, Fitzwilliam said, "David, if you need to talk, I can stay here with you tonight. Elizabeth will understand."

"No, I'm fine. I just need to finish this proposal."

"David, you're not fine. I've been there. Remember? Take some time off and go back to South Carolina. Bruce can handle the contract. Go back to Charleston before it's too late."

"It's already too late," he flatly stated. "She's seeing another man."

"But she doesn't love him. Elizabeth's told me all about their sordid story. Don't you see she's settling? Cecilia doesn't have your options. From what Elizabeth has told me, she has to marry. If not *you*, then somebody! If you let her slip through your fingers, then you're harder than I thought. Don't be a fool, David. Don't live up to the family tradition! David—"

"Enough, Fitzwilliam! I'll handle my own affairs. You take care of yours!" David snapped.

"But that's the point! You're not handling them!"

"I said *enough*!" David glared. A long uncomfortable silence reigned between the brothers until David finally broke it. "I'll finish this tonight and have it back to you by tomorrow morning." Pausing, he drew a deep breath. "I know you care, but you don't understand. I'm not like you. I must have time and space. I need to be alone." Slapping the folder against his palm, he nodded and then turned and left.

Fitzwilliam sighed. As much as he wanted to help his brother, there was nothing he could do. He fell back in his chair and raked his fingers through his hair...*He's throwing his happiness away with both hands and about to make the worst mistake of his life...but he won't listen to a thing I have to say. Perhaps he'll listen to Harvey.*

Chapter Sixty-six

...You don't understand. She betrayed me...

D inner with the senior Darcys was to be at seven o'clock. Still plagued with many reservations concerning her husband's family, Elizabeth was thankful Georgiana and David were free to attend. Unsure of what to expect, she consulted Georgiana. As they sat in the master suite having tea, she broached the subject that had bothered her for several days.

"Georgiana, I was wondering... could you tell me a little of what your aunt and uncle are like? Are they friendly?" Elizabeth asked as she sipped her tea.

Smiling, Georgiana reassured her. "Elizabeth, I know why you're concerned, but you needn't be. My aunt and uncle are some of the finest people I've ever known. You will like them, and they will like you. They have always been kind to us—especially to my brothers. Our cousins, William and Benson, are very down to earth, not at all like some of our other relatives who can be arrogant and rude." She took Elizabeth's hand and gave it a gentle squeeze. "Relax, Elizabeth. They will love you, if for no other reason than the fact that my brother is so smitten by you, and you are the mother of their great-niece and nephew."

"All right," she breathed a breath of relief. "I'll try and not be so nervous. Now, will you please help me pick out something to wear? I do want to make a good first impression."

Setting their tea cups aside, both rose from the tea table and walked over to the closet. Georgiana pulled a dress from the rack. "Elizabeth, how about this violet semiformal? I think the color is flattering."

"Yes, I like that one. And I can wear my amethyst pendant and earrings that your brother gave me for my birthday. I think it'll do nicely."

They arrived at the Darcys at six o'clock to give his aunt and uncle time to become acquainted with Elizabeth before dinner. As they entered the house, Fitzwilliam made the introduction.

"Uncle Harvey, Aunt Susan, this is my wife, Elizabeth Darcy."

Susan was the first to embrace Elizabeth. "We're pleased to finally meet you, my dear. I've heard nothing but good things about you from David and Georgiana. I hope you will feel at home in our house."

"Thank you, Mrs. Darcy. I am very pleased to finally meet you and Mr. Darcy as well. Georgiana tells me you are very close with my husband and his brother."

"Yes, we are, but you must call us Susan and Harvey. We are family, so there's no need for formalities."

Harvey stepped forward. "Oh yes, my dear! You mustn't be formal with us. That will never do. I've watched these boys grow up. They're like sons to me," Harvey smiled warmly. "Now, Elizabeth, I want you to meet our sons, William and Benson, and William's date, Amanda Elliot."

After they'd been introduced, Elizabeth said, "I'm very pleased to meet you all. Fitzwilliam has often spoken of you. I'm also honored to meet you, Miss Elliot." She shook hands with each brother as well as with Amanda.

The two Darcy cousins smiled, but said nothing, their demeanor curious, but reserved. Reacting to the cool reception, Elizabeth stiffened slightly but returned their smiles, choosing to ignore their aloofness. Fitzwilliam placed his hand on Elizabeth's back to show his support for his wife.

Breaking the awkward moment, Amanda spoke. "It is an honor to meet you, Mrs. Darcy, and do call me Amanda. Miss Elliot seems so stuffy."

"Yes, I will and you must call me Elizabeth, or Lizzy, as my family does."

"That will be lovely. I shall call you Lizzy, and you should call me Mandy. All of my close friends, except Wills, call me by that name. He can be so stuffy at times. He insists on calling me Amanda no matter how much I ask him to call me Mandy." Amanda cut William a wide mischievous grin which he returned as he gently encircled her waist with his arm.

"Mandy it is, then." Elizabeth gave her an affectionate smile.

David and Georgiana exchanged small talk with their aunt and uncle as the entire party moved towards the main drawing room. Dinner passed with much conversation and light laughter. As the evening wore on, Elizabeth relaxed with her husband's family, very relieved they were nothing like she had anticipated. She also liked Mandy very much. Observing the interaction between Mandy and William, she concluded that they were much more than just dating. In fact, she could tell they loved each other. She wouldn't be surprised in the least if she and Fitzwilliam would be attending a wedding in the foreseeable future.

After dinner, the ladies and gentlemen separated for conversation and drinks. Uncle Harvey led the men to his private library for wine and cigars. Very pleased by the interaction between Fitzwilliam and his wife, Harvey relaxed. He had watched them closely all evening and had determined that they not only loved each other, but that George had missed a blessing.

Satisfied with the evening, Harvey pulled his nephew aside for a private word. "Fitzwilliam, I like your wife very much. I can see why you were drawn to her. She's not only beautiful, but has grace and style, too, and I might add, she appears to genuinely care for you. She complements you. She's outgoing and friendly where you are cautious and reserved."

"Thank you very much." Fitzwilliam laughed softly. "Elizabeth is all of those things and more. And I would say that we do complement each other perfectly. I only wish my dad could see how happy we are. I'm sorry he'll never know Alex and Emily. He would have loved them, and he would have loved Elizabeth too, if he'd only given her a chance."

Harvey sighed with a slight smile. "Fitzwilliam, I, too, grieve for the fact that your father never met your wife or his grandchildren, and I do feel sorry that your children will never know either set of their grandparents, but I want you to know that your father would have accepted Elizabeth. He told me so before he died."

"Thanks for telling me, but I already knew that. I read his last entry in his journal. His words were a bittersweet revelation—and painful."

"I'm sure they were, but you'll have to move on and relay to your children their Darcy family history and heritage. It's what my brother had wanted to do in the later years of his life. He wanted grandchildren, and he wanted to pass along our history and heritage."

Fitzwilliam glanced from his glass to his uncle. "Yes, I know he did, and I've already thought about these things. Elizabeth and I are both proud of our family histories. It is our intent that our children know who they are." Shifting uneasily and not wanting to reopen an old wound, Fitzwilliam changed the subject. "Now, Uncle, Elizabeth and I would like to invite you and Aunt Susan to come for dinner on Monday of next week. I want you to meet our son and daughter."

"We would be honored to come and meet the children, and since I have no grandchildren of my own as of yet," he said as he eyed William with a wide smile, "I would like very much to know my niece and nephew. Perhaps, I can be a grandfather to them since Elizabeth's and your parents are no longer here."

"It would please us very much. Thank you. We'll look forward to Monday at seven then."

When he left Fitzwilliam, Harvey took the opportunity to speak to David. He knew from talking with Fitzwilliam that David was about to follow in the family tradition of self-imposed unhappiness, but not if he could help it. Although Fitzwilliam had warned him of David's stubbornness, Harvey was determined to speak with him.

"David, why the despondent look? You've been out of sorts all evening. It wouldn't have to do with a certain young lady in South Carolina, would it?"

David shook his head, giving a sarcastic laugh. "Uncle, how did you know about that? Fitzwilliam, I suppose."

"Let us just say that I keep a close watch on my nephews. I understand that the lady means a great deal to you." Harvey raised his glass and took a sip while studying his nephew.

"*Meant* a great deal," David scoffed, his words betraying what he really felt. "I had planned to ask her to marry me, but the relationship is over."

Harvey caught David's gaze and held it. "Is it really? What have I told you about love?"

David's jaw clenched. "You don't understand. She betrayed me. And I just can't forgive her." His voice was cold and aloof as his eyes shifted away from his uncle's knowing gaze.

Harvey took a long slow drink of wine, his eyes never leaving his nephew. "Then another one bites the dust," he said as he arched one brow.

"What do you mean by that?" David retorted.

Harvey drew a deep breath. "Simply put. Another one falls...You, David. You will follow in the long tradition of Darcy men who have let their pride stand in the way of happiness, and you'll be in good company, too, standing alongside Great-great Uncle Charles, Great Uncle Edgar, my father's brother, Randall, me, and now *you*. One victim falls with each generation." Harvey finished his wine and set his glass down. "Think about it, Nephew." He raised a brow and nodded, and then turned and exited the room.

David stared at his uncle's glass. Empty—empty like his life. ...*Why won't they leave me alone, damn it?*

As soon as it was appropriate, Fitzwilliam strolled across the library floor and approached William and Benson. "I noticed that you were rather standoffish towards my wife when we first arrived, and I think I know why."

Both brothers momentarily dropped their gazes. Benson remained silent as William spoke for the two of them. "Fitzwilliam, we truly are glad you're happy, but after what she put you through, well, we're just a little surprised that you have so easily taken her back."

"William's right," Benson interjected, "I would never have done it. If a woman were to ever burn me like you were burnt, she'd not get a second chance."

Fitzwilliam sighed. "It's not what you're thinking. Whilst it is true that we had a very rough go of it last year, I want you to know that all of that is behind us now. We're together as a couple and as a family. Let me tell you everything from the start to the present."

Fitzwilliam related the entire story to his cousins and insisted that his wife was to receive the full measure of respect due her.

William spoke up. "Don't trouble yourself over us. We only want your happiness. And now that you've explained what happened, of course, she will always be treated with the utmost respect she is due as your wife. We always knew you loved her. It was the pain she caused you that concerned us, but now we understand. I suppose if you can forgive, then so can I."

"Count me in as well," Benson expressed with a broad smile.

"Thank you, I appreciate your concern," Fitzwilliam clapped their shoulders, "but it isn't necessary anymore."

After Benson left to join David, Fitzwilliam changed the subject. "William, tell me about Amanda. Are you two becoming serious?"

"I suppose you could say that. I intend to ask her to marry me in the very near future." He raised his glass to his lips. "We met at the Yuletide Ball we attended last December. I think you remember."

"I remember you staring at her. Did you actually talk to her?"

William chuckled. "Yes, I did. In fact, I even danced with her. It must have been after you left for the evening."

Fitzwilliam shook his head and smiled. "I'm afraid I wasn't good company that night."

"No, I must say you weren't." William laughed and shook his head. "Anyway, we saw each other for much of the Christmas season. She was the reason I hesitated about the position in New York. However, I think it'll work out just fine. I called her regularly until finally inviting her to come and stay with me there. We've been together ever since." He grinned. "I'm not the type of man to trifle with a woman, and since I love her, I'm going to propose rather soon. If she'll agree to it, we'll live primarily in New York with a second residence here in London."

"William, I couldn't be happier for the two of you."

Fitzwilliam shook his cousin's hand in sincere congratulations. Then they returned to the drawing room where they rejoined the rest of the party for the remainder of the evening.

Once at home in the privacy of their bedchamber with the children sound asleep, Fitzwilliam and Elizabeth finally had the opportunity to review the evening. As Elizabeth sat at her dressing table, Fitzwilliam sat behind her, brushing her hair while he recounted his conversation with his cousins.

Elizabeth turned slightly to catch his attention. "I wasn't worried about their opinions of me. They weren't rude. I understood that they were only cautious and reserved, much as David was when he first met me long ago, and I can imagine that they were concerned for you," she said. "It's evident that they care for your wellbeing. I don't mind being scrutinized as long as no harm is intended, and I don't believe it was. We'll all get along fine, so don't worry. Besides, I can see that William's girlfriend and I are on our way to becoming fast friends."

"Well then did you enjoy yourself this evening?"

"Yes, I did, actually. I really liked your aunt and uncle. They do have very pleasing manners just as Georgiana said, and your aunt has invited me to a garden party next Tuesday. I'm very much looking forward to it, and I'm looking forward to spending time with Mandy." Glancing at Fitzwilliam's reflection in her mirror, she continued. "I hope your cousin realizes what a jewel he has in her."

"I'm quite sure he does, and if all goes well, we will be attending a wedding in the near future."

"Oh, I hope you're right. I really like her. We have a lunch and shopping date next week. She'll be returning to New York soon, but we plan to spend several days together before she leaves."

Studying her husband, Elizabeth finally came to the point. "Fitzwilliam, are they living together?"

He only smiled.

"Well, are they?" Elizabeth asked, turning around and placing her hands on his knees.

He grinned, setting the brush aside. "He didn't tell me that exactly. All I know is that he loves her."

Rising from his seat, he took Elizabeth's hand. "Let's go to bed. It's been a long day. Tomorrow you and Georgiana need to discuss the upcoming Middleton Ball. If you don't have a suitable dress, you'll need to get one, and we need to look at my mother's jewelry to see if you can find something appropriate to wear, or, if you would rather, I can buy something special just for you. Let me know what you prefer by Friday."

He pulled her into his waiting embrace, effectively ending all conversation and taking advantage of the opportunity to love each other before Alex and Emily wailed for their parents' attention.

Chapter Sixty-seven

...look beyond the pretty face to the heart of a woman...

The night of the Middleton Ball, Elizabeth fretted over her hair, her dress, and her jewelry. Knowing her worry went deeper than her appearance, Fitzwilliam folded her in his arms.

"Elizabeth, you are a beautiful and elegant woman. No one who has seen you could ever deny that. Yes, there may be those there who are predisposed to find fault, but they are of no consequence. Others will see you as I see you—a very warm and beautiful woman. Besides," he smiled, "Amanda and William will be there. Just be yourself, and you'll be fine."

"I'm not so sure," Elizabeth hesitated, "but I'll do as you say and be myself. However, it is a relief to know Mandy will be there. At least I will have somebody to talk to."

As his eyes took in her form dressed in the deep fuchsia pink silk-satin evening gown, he couldn't help but smile and shake his head. The halter style flattered her bust, showing just enough cleavage to be alluring, and the skirt fell in elegant folds, clinging to her every curve, complementing her hourglass figure.

"No," he whispered, "you'll have far more than Mandy to talk to. Of that I am sure. Elizabeth, you are absolutely stunning. Every man's head will turn when you are announced."

"Don't be silly. They won't even notice me among so many guests."

"Oh, they will notice you, my love. The fact that you are my wife will cause them to take notice. But it will be more than that. Trust me. You will be the most beautiful woman there."

"I don't know." She dropped her gaze and shook her head. "I'm as nervous as a cat on a hot tin roof."

He smiled and hugged her close. He knew the significance of this ball better than she did. The most important members of Parliament, the nobility, and possibly even some of the Royals would be there. But he wouldn't tell her that. There was no need to increase her anxiety. He shook his head as he held her close. She'd do just fine, for she possessed the uncanny ability to rise to the occasion, and this time wouldn't be any different. However, there were a few details that required his attention.

Feeling the tension ease from her body, he pulled back and stepped away. Walking over to his bureau, he opened the door and took out a small box. "Liz, come here. I have something for you."

"What is it?"

"Come and see."

Elizabeth crossed the short distance and took the box from his hand. When she opened it, she gasped. "Oh, these are beautiful! They match the hair sticks you bought me for Christmas when we became engaged." Elizabeth lifted the piece from the box. It was a diamond necklace with a teardrop ruby framed in tiny diamonds with a bracelet, earrings, and a ruby ring to match, all set in platinum. She brushed her fingers over the deep fuchsia stone. "This ruby must be at least fifteen carats. You really shouldn't have. You mother's pearls are suitable and very lovely."

"Yes, I should have. The more I thought about it, the more I wanted you to have your own jewels for tonight—not my mother's, so I had Garrard's make these for you. It's the finest ruby they had, and it is twenty-five carats. When I saw the dress you chose, I knew these would complement it perfectly. Here, let me help you with it." He took the choker from her hand and fastened it around her neck."

Stepping back, he beamed. "You look lovely, Liz. Truly lovely. And," he said as he brushed a lock of hair from her brow, "yes, they do match your hair sticks. The set looks lovely grouped together. Now let's talk about your announcement. The ladies are announced as they descend the stairs to the ballroom. You will give a card to the servant at the top of the stairs before descending. As you walk down, he will read the information. When you step onto the floor, I'll be waiting to escort you. We'll walk over and pay our compliments to our host and hostess. At this point we will either dance or mingle with the others," he said. "I'll write the announcement for you, so you needn't worry about that."

"I'm not worried," Elizabeth insisted, "so let's address the card and go." She smiled as he hastily put pen to paper, and then they grabbed their coats to leave.

The hum of conversation buzzed throughout the ballroom until Elizabeth Darcy handed her card to the servant. Silence fell over the crowded room, and heads turned as Fitzwilliam Darcy's wife descended the elegant spiral staircase. Her striking beauty held them spellbound while cameras flashed like twinkling stars as the reporters grabbed the opportunity to capture the moment. Fitzwilliam only smiled as he listened to the quiet murmurings while Elizabeth carefully made her way down the winding stairs. Lady Westcott and Lady Crawford came by to give their approval. There was even an approving comment from the Duke of Westchester who said Darcy had the prettiest wife at the ball. Another commented that from the foolish grin Darcy wore, marriage must agree with him. Fitzwilliam only chuckled as he shook their hands.

While Fitzwilliam waited for his wife, two men in particular took careful notice. Artimus Dashwood, Fitzwilliam's first cousin and son of Samantha Darcy Dashwood, stood at the wine table with Stuart Hampton, the twelfth Earl of Westbury—a tall, handsome, fair-haired man who had always disliked the Darcys, especially Fitzwilliam. A long standing grudge between the two rivals dated back many years and ran very deep.

"Westbury, is that Darcy's wife?" Dashwood asked with a curious look towards the lady descending the stairs.

"It must be, although she's not at all what I would have expected him to choose. I've never seen a more beautiful creature. Look how she smiles and laughs. Not his type at all. I'll have to get to know her."

"You're not thinking of flirting with my cousin's wife, are you?" Dashwood glanced at his companion with a raised eyebrow.

"If I can have my way, I will do more than flirt. Just listen to that adorable accent. Why should she waste her charms on Darcy?" A rakish grin spread over his features.

"Westbury, you had better watch yourself. You've had too much to drink. Fitzwilliam is not the kind to share his wife with anyone—especially you! I believe he actually loves her," Dashwood warned as Lord Westbury's intentions became clear.

"Relax, I just want to have a little fun, and if I embarrass Darcy, so much the better," he smirked. "When it comes to women, they have always preferred me to him." Both took a sip of champagne. "You do remember Stella, don't you?"

"If you want to embarrass him, you'll have no disagreement with me. In fact, I wish you luck. He's no favorite of mine—especially after the way he treated my father, but I don't exactly recall Stella. Who was she?"

"She was his first love." Westbury grinned. "It was about twelve years ago. They were quite an item at the time, except she secretly preferred me to him. He walked in on us one day, and Stella never forgave me," he sneered. "She fully expected to marry him, but *he* never forgave *her*. She lost him, and I lost her." Westbury raised his glass to his lips as his eyes followed Elizabeth Darcy.

Dashwood was momentarily taken aback. "So you were shagging his lady, and now you wish to repeat history? Westbury, you are *indeed* a piece of work."

A large smile crossed both men's lips as they watched and listened.

Oblivious to the conspiracies around them, Fitzwilliam, after they had paid their respects to Lord and Lady Middleton, escorted his wife to the dance floor for the first dance. He danced next with Amanda, while William led Elizabeth in a waltz. Afterwards, they mingled with the other guests where he introduced his wife proudly. He was amused at how Elizabeth easily discerned who greeted her with sincerity and respect and who relied on false flattery to garner information for gossip. Through it all, she handled everyone with the grace and style he knew she possessed, and she moved with ease amongst his peers as if she had been born one of them.

After a lengthy conversation with Lord Rothwell, William and Fitzwilliam joined the ladies at the refreshment table where they were soon approached by Lord Westbury and Artimus Dashwood. "Fitzwilliam, won't you introduce us to your lovely wife?" Lord Westbury greeted, smiling at Elizabeth.

Fitzwilliam eyed both gentlemen closely. Of all people, he didn't want his wife to meet this pair. Weighing the dictums of society against his instinct, he reluctantly relented.

"Yes, of course. Elizabeth, this is Stuart Hampton, the twelfth Earl of Westbury, and my cousin Artimus Dashwood." With a hand gesture between the two, he continued. "Gentlemen, my wife, Elizabeth Darcy."

"Mrs. Darcy, it is such a pleasure to meet you. We have heard much of you, and I must say none of it has been exaggerated," said Lord Westbury.

The gentlemen each bowed and gently kissed Elizabeth's hand while Fitzwilliam seethed in quiet anger at the audacity of his cousin and Lord Westbury. Both men met the anger in Fitzwilliam's gaze with a challenge of their own.

Fitzwilliam keenly observed the quick glance Elizabeth shot between the two gentlemen and himself. Realizing she had caught the quiet tension between them, he nodded with a gentle smile.

Her lips curled softly as she responded, "It is indeed a pleasure to meet you, Lord Westbury, and you as well, Mr. Dashwood. I'm always glad to meet my husband's family, and I can see the family resemblance," she said with a smile. "You're as handsome as my husband."

"Darcy, may I have the next dance with your wife?" Westbury asked.

Noticing the way Stuart's eyes caressed his wife's body, Darcy replied, "Westbury, I don't think that would be a good idea. Since this is Elizabeth's first time out in society, I thought I would keep her with family."

A wide grin spread across Dashwood's face. "Well, then, you won't mind if I dance with her, will you, Darcy?"

"Artimus, I don't think he has *you* in mind as family." William's eyes flashed in warning.

"Stay out of it, William, unless our cousin cannot speak for himself."

Rolling his eyes, Fitzwilliam responded, "No, Artimus, I don't think she'd like to dance with either of you." The last thing he wanted was to cause a scene, especially with so many cameras about.

"Come now, Darcy, surely your wife would like to dance?"

Feeling the heat in the room becoming uncomfortable, Fitzwilliam was beginning to regret this ball. He was on the verge of telling them both in no uncertain terms that neither of them would be dancing with his wife when he heard Elizabeth speak.

"Lord Westbury, I hate to disappoint you, but I have reserved the night for someone very special—my husband." She raised an eyebrow, giving a sweet but firm smile.

"I see," Westbury said. "Darcy always seems to inspire that sentimental devotion in women." Turning to Fitzwilliam, he aimed a finely honed parting shot. "Have you seen Stella lately? I hear she's suffered a most unfortunate turn in events since you abandoned her. The little girl is what? Eleven years old now." He tipped his head towards Elizabeth. "At least you married this one. I bid you and your lovely bride a good evening," he smirked with biting sarcasm before departing with Artimus almost bursting with laughter as he tried to contain himself.

Incensed and feeling like a caged animal, Fitzwilliam violently exhaled as he cast a fleeting look between his wife's shocked expression and William's clenched fists.

"Fitzwilliam, one of these days we are going to have to settle things with those two."

"Maybe so, but not here. That would give him the satisfaction he's looking for."

"Fitzwilliam, what was that all about, and what did he mean by 'at least you married this one?' Am I to presume that you have an eleven year-old daughter?" She studied him intently with questioning eyes.

"*No*, you are *not* to assume any such thing. It is a ghost from the past, but you do have a right to an explanation, and I will tell you everything tonight when we're alone." He released a tensed breath and smiled. "For the time being, let's not let those two ruin our evening. I'd love to dance with you. William, would you and Amanda care to join us?"

William answered as he took Amanda's hand, "I think it's a good idea."

Fitzwilliam and William led the ladies in several waltzes before stopping for conversation with numerous lords and Members of Parliament. While speaking with Lord Wellesley, he watched Elizabeth conversing with Lady Crawford and smiled. He was exceedingly proud of his wife. Not only did she have the self-confidence to rise to the challenge of whatever came her way, but she also possessed the keen ability to discern a person's character. He knew she would understand when he told her about Stella.

Shortly after midnight, the ball ended and the Darcys paid their regards to their hosts once more before departing for home. Silence weighed heavily during the short drive to Darcy House. Fitzwilliam's anger had cooled by now, although it hadn't completely abated.

By the time they reached their bedchamber, both Elizabeth and Fitzwilliam were exhausted. They changed their clothes, attended to the children, and settled down on the bed.

He took a long, steadying breath. "Elizabeth, we need to talk."

"Yes, we do. Why don't you begin?"

Raking his fingers through his tousled curls, he briefly closed his eyes. It was so long ago. He shook his head and stated more than asked. "Where do I begin?"

"What about the child, Fitzwilliam. Do you have a child with this woman?" Her eyes widened. "Tell me you didn't abandon them?"

Pain shot through him as he released a deep moan. "Elizabeth, I'm hurt that you would even think me capable of that, but to answer your question, no, I didn't. I swear to you that I have no other children besides the ones I share with you."

"Fitzwilliam, the man I know and love would never do such a thing, but I know nothing of the man you were in your youth. So tell me about Stella. Who is she, and what did she mean to you?"

He momentarily looked to the side. "Elizabeth, I'm the man I've always been. I've matured, but in essentials, I've not changed. My character, my sense of personal honor, of duty and responsibility, are as they've always been. The only difference is…I grew up." He held her gaze. "It began when I was an undergraduate at Oxford. Believe it or not, I was once into the party scene and nearly as bad as David. But what the hell. I was young and impulsive, and once the hormones turn on in a young man, well, I think you have some idea of what it must be like. Men don't have to have an emotional tie to derive pleasure from the 'act'. In fact, with most men, even me in the beginning, it's preferable if we don't. Less complicated, if you understand what I'm telling you."

"Like the guys I dated at MIT."

"Exactly. And when you told me about your experiences, I thought of myself. You would probably have dismissed me if you'd met me when I was twenty because back then sexual attraction was everything to me, and I don't think I could have settled for a platonic relationship as I was willing to when I met you."

"I understand." She nodded.

He breathed deeply and shook his head. "But underneath it all I really wasn't like that, and after a while, it began to eat away at me. I wanted a steady relationship—one rooted in affection, not lust. That's when I met her—Stella Fitzgerald." He hesitated, delving into his memory, remembering the pretty little redhead with the shapely backside. Taking his wife's hand, he gently brushed her fingers with his. "Stella was somewhat like you. Very pretty with long waist-length thick red hair, vivid green eyes, and a freckled face. She was lively and witty and fun to be with. You know the type," he softly said, "a bubbly personality that draws you in. So, when I met her through a mutual friend, I was captivated by all of those things. The attraction was immediate and strong on both our parts, but I was too naïve to fully understand what Stella was about or her true motivations. It never occurred to me that she would use me or that a woman would stoop to such measures to obtain what she wanted." Pausing for a moment, he glanced away and exhaled loudly.

Elizabeth shook her head and motioned for him to continue.

With a nod, he took a deep breath. "Stella and I dated through the latter part of my undergraduate years. Six months after we began the relationship, we moved in together. The first twelve months were great," he said with a slight smile. "I thought I was in love. We were quite close, and I even considered marrying her. But then we began to quarrel. She wanted to party, and I wanted to study. I needed to do well in my finals as I intended to go on and do a doctor of philosophy, but she had lost all interest in university. Instead, she preferred the nightlife. She wanted to be seen at clubs and private parties where only I could take her because of my connections. To her, it was important to hobnob with celebrities and the nobility. It was then that I knew I'd made a mistake. You see, I'd never taken the trouble to get to know her before hopping into bed. I assumed she'd like the same things as I did since we were both reading Greats." He laughed ceremoniously. "However, I soon discovered the truth. We had nothing in common beyond the physical attraction, but I was too deeply involved to get out by the time I realized it."

He briefly closed his eyes and shook his head. "Because I had considered marrying her, I had allowed her access to the very generous allowance I received from my father, but even that was not enough when she had to have clothing from the most exclusive shops in London. As you can imagine, it wasn't long until I found myself overdrawn, with a call in from my father demanding an explanation. That, perhaps, was the most humiliating experience of my life. You can't imagine how upsetting that was for me, knowing as you do about the friction that existed between me and my dad. And yet, I still hung on because I'm the kind that commits. But whatever love I thought I might have had for her was gone by the last year of our relationship. I didn't love her, and I knew it."

"So why didn't you just break it off?"

"Liz, it's not that easy. We were living together."

"Did she love you?"

"Love me?" he smirked. "No, she didn't love me."

Elizabeth shook her head and sighed. "Tell me what happened. How did you get out of it, and where does this child come into play."

He laughed a humorless laugh. "It was by a stroke of luck, or perhaps someone was watching over me. I don't know." Darcy took her hand in his and gently brushed his fingers over her wedding band. "I discovered in a most painful way that the entire time we were together, which was a little over two years, she had been sleeping with Lord Westbury who was attending Oxford at the same time I was. She never loved me. She used me for who I was and what I could give her. I felt like a fool, especially since I had been forewarned." Fitzwilliam released Elizabeth's hand and briefly looked away.

"Forewarned?" Elizabeth frowned.

"Yes, forewarned. My cousin, William, who was at Oxford with me at the time, had seen things I didn't see. He never liked Stella and had warned me that something was going on behind my back. He had followed her and knew she was meeting Westbury, but I refused to believe that anything was happening, until one day, I unexpectedly came home to our flat and found the two of them in bed," he said with a cynical smile. "You should have seen the smug look of triumph on Westbury's face when he saw me.

"Anyway, I didn't see Stella again until three months later when she approached me, claiming to be pregnant and demanding I marry her and provide for my child. At first, I was going to marry her, but after a talk with my father, I kept my reserve and insisted that she prove my paternity. If the child was mine, I told her we would marry, because even back then, I was a man of honor, but I would wait until the child was born and a blood test taken to decide what I would do. As it turned out, the baby, a little girl, wasn't mine, but my father did pay Stella a handsome sum for her silence, and she left with the child. I never saw her again."

"Oh, Fitzwilliam, that must have been terrible for you."

"Terrible? Yes, it was. The entire ordeal, not to mention my father's many lectures, disillusioned me. I vowed I would never again put myself in a position to be trapped by some woman I didn't love. I had to be sure it was the real thing. Elizabeth, there's no way I'd ever let a child of mine suffer. That's why I was alone until I met you. I haven't been with that many women." He paused and softly smiled. "In fact, ours is the only other relationship I've ever had—the first since Stella, and I intend for ours to be my last. At twenty-two, my brain could become easily disengaged by a pretty face and a shapely body, but at thirty-two, my reasoning was much more finely tuned to look beyond the pretty face to the heart of a woman. When I met you, your looks drew me to you. I will admit that, but your heart keeps me here. Elizabeth, I don't have the experience you think I have with—"

Interrupting with a wave of her hand, she said, "You've explained enough. The rest is in the past. The things that are important to me are you and our family—right here and right now."

Releasing a relieved sigh, Fitzwilliam gazed at his wife. "And that's one of the many reasons why I love you."

"I know," she said, smiling tenderly.

He reached over and gently brushed her lips with his.

"I caught on right away to what Lord Westbury was doing. My only concern was for the possibility of a child. Had it been yours, then I felt I had a right to know about it."

"Liz, he's been my enemy for years. It began at Eton when we were boys, but I won't go into that now. All I will say is that ever since then, he's taken every opportunity to goad me and cause me pain. Why do you think he slept with Stella? It was to hurt me. I want you to stay away from him."

Tilting her head, she frowned. "I have no desire for his company."

"Good. I'm relieved to hear it."

He took her hand in his. "Now, whilst we have this opportunity, I need to tell you about my family—all of them. Many of my cousins are not very nice. Dashwood is but one among many."

They talked for most of the night, in between sessions of caring for their children. He told her about family disagreements and which members were on good terms and which were not. When he was through, he glanced between the clock and his wife, yawning heavily, weariness finally taking its toll. "Now you know everything there is to know. Let's try and get some rest whilst we can." He pulled her into an embrace as they lay down, quickly falling asleep.

Chapter Sixty-eight

...a measure of mercy...

As he walked the long corridor to Fitzwilliam's study, David couldn't help but think of all that had happened in the past weeks. His uncle's counsel and his brother's words resonated in his mind. He knew it was hopeless to try and push Cecilia from his thoughts. It hadn't worked before, so what made him think he could do it now? But just as he was contemplating what he might do, his pride rose to the surface. He shook his head as he remembered his uncle's words *...every generation has a victim.* No, he would not go back. He would find a way to put her out of his mind. If he were to take the fall for his generation...then so be it! *...I'll not be the object of a woman's whims. I'll not be trifled with. If she lied to me once... she'll do it again.* Finally reaching his destination, he opened the door. Georgiana was already present.

"Fitzwilliam, I can't believe Aunt Hilda did this to you. It was horrible and unforgivable," Georgiana said.

David stepped inside and closed the door. "Hilda was loyal to the old way of thinking. She honestly thought she was doing the right thing. She hasn't realized that times have changed and people no longer think as they once did. Still," David shrugged, "that doesn't excuse the harm she's caused."

"Yes, but her day of reckoning is upon her. Are we all in agreement? David? Georgiana?" Fitzwilliam asked, glancing between the two.

"Yes."

"Yes."

"I have the documents in hand. Let's go," Fitzwilliam said.

When her secretary announced that all three Darcys were waiting in the lobby, Hilda was more than a little surprised. She was terrified. As they entered her office, Hilda paused, taking in a long breath. "Georgiana, David, Fitzwilliam, how good to see you." Her eyes narrowed as she looked from one to the other. "Now, to what do I owe the honor of this visit?" She pushed back in her chair and waited.

"I don't think you will find it such an honor when you read this," Fitzwilliam said, dropping a folder onto Hilda's desk along with the letter she'd written to Elizabeth. "What do you have to say about this? You've seen it before, but the first time I saw it was when my wife presented it to me in South Carolina." He bore down on her with eyes as cold as ice.

Calmly, Hilda opened the folder for a cursory look before glancing up to meet her nephew's intense gaze. Opening her mouth to speak, she found herself interrupted before she could even begin.

"Did you think I would never find out? Did you really think you could get away with this?" he snapped. "You lied to me... and my wife! You saw that we were having disagreements, and you exploited our situation for your own purposes, didn't you?" His lips curled into a steely smile.

Hilda blinked twice and swallowed hard. "Fitzwilliam, everything I did was for your welfare. I have always only cared for your wellbeing and that of this family."

"Cared about me?" he shot back. "Have you any idea what you did to me?! If you cared, you would have seen to it that my wife returned with you instead of telling her those twisted half-truths about me and my family." His blood boiled, incensed at her audacity. "How dare you, madam!"

She met his icy stare with one of her own. "What I did, I did for your own good—for the good of this family. All I have ever thought of was the welfare of my sister's children. I wanted to preserve our family status and see to it that the Darcy name remains held in the highest esteem as your father would have wanted. The grandson of an earl should *not* be married to an American—a low class woman!"

His temper erupted. "An American of low class? What my father wanted? Is that what you think?" He gazed at her in astonishment. "How dare you insult my wife! And furthermore, what about what *I* wanted? What about the welfare of *my* children! I am a man, Hilda—not a child who needs you or anyone else to look after him!"

"I was trying to save you. Fitzwilliam, I—"

"Save me from what? Those are my children, and she is my wife! You wished to save me by destroying them!" He stalked the floor in front of her desk. "Don't you see that they are an extension of me? My blood—my family!" Fitzwilliam took a deep breath, steadying himself. "Listen to me, madam, and listen carefully, for I'll only say it once—if you ever approach any member of my family again, I will have you before a magistrate. What you did was illegal. It was theft and forgery. Do I make myself clear, Hilda?"

She glared at him, causing him to chuckle in amusement. "Oh, and Aunt, there is one other small detail I need to mention. We are dissolving all business associations with Vanderburgh Banking, and henceforth, we are severing all family ties with you. You are never to set foot in my house, my office complex, or in any business or residence under my control. From this day forth, we are no longer connected. We're through!"

She gasped. "You can't be serious, Fitzwilliam! We are family! You cannot do this. It will mean billions. My financial status will collapse. I will be ruined," she breathed out in disbelief.

"Oh, the bloody hell I can't! Watch me."

"What about all I have done for you—the money I secured for Pemberley?"

"It is already in the process of being repaid—every single penny!"

"Fitzwilliam, you will regret this," she hissed.

"No, I don't think so," he laughed sarcastically. "What you did is unpardonable! Not only was the pain you caused me and Elizabeth inexcusable, but you jeopardized the well-being of my son and daughter, and for *that*, madam, I can never forgive you."

As he was about to leave, he turned back. "Oh, and before I forget, Hilda, hand over the remaining pieces of stationery you took from my office. I've filed a legal affidavit reporting them stolen. If they turn up in a suspicious manner, things could get very ugly, very quickly. You wouldn't like that, now would you?"

Swallowing hard, she reached in her desk to pull out the remaining sheets of letterhead. Neither said a word until the Darcys were at the door about to leave.

"Georgiana, David, are you in agreement with this?" Hilda asked.

Georgiana Darcy had remained silent up to this point, but she held her tongue no longer. "Aunt Hilda, your actions clearly indicated that you cared nothing for Fitzwilliam or for any of us. How can you claim to care about Fitzwilliam and inflict the pain on all of us that you did? It wasn't you there picking up the pieces when he was in agony. David and I were. That's not love and concern. That's cruelty." When she finished speaking, she stood by Fitzwilliam's side.

David spoke next. "The pity is that you don't even realize the serious damage you've done and what you've lost. Your financial loss is nothing compared to what your forgery and lies almost cost Fitzwilliam. Your loss is great indeed, but his would have been greater."

"How dare you!" She stared defiantly at all three Darcys. "You will regret this, Fitzwilliam. This will not stand. I will not allow it. I will use every weapon within my means. You will beg me for forgiveness before I am through with you!"

Fitzwilliam marveled at her daring. That she thought she held any power or control over him, he found astonishing. It was apparent he would have to make things crystal clear. Handing the binder he held in his hand to Georgiana, he walked in a slow, deliberate stride back to Hilda's desk. Placing both hands on its sleek surface, he leaned into her.

"Let us get a few things clear here, madam. You don't have any choice in the matter. I choose whom I *will* and *will not* do business with," he said in warning. "It could be worse for you. Do you understand what I'm telling you?" His eyes locked with hers. "Hilda, think of it this way, I'm extending you a measure of mercy, which is more than I've done for some, and more than you did for my wife! Consider yourself blessed. Your loss is only financial! At least I'm not prosecuting you for theft and malfeasance of my interests. Considering that I have the power to break you, madam, I would say you've made out quite well. Wouldn't you agree?" A triumphant grin spread over his face.

"Besides," David responded, "you can't stop this. It's done. And Fitzwilliam is right. Read the separation agreement. Your greatest nemesis, J.C. Hanover, International, has become our new banking partner." He paused to allow his words to have their full effect. Seeing Hilda's breath catch as the blood drained from her face, he spoke with an air of finality. "And you know they'd like nothing more than to bring Vanderburgh Banking to its knees. The Pemberley account is the only thing that has stood between you and them for years, and now they have it, and *you*, madam, are in trouble." David looked upon his aunt with a mixture of pity and sorrow.

With that, the two brothers bowed slightly, and all three left, with their aunt's demands for them to return ringing in their ears.

Chapter Sixty-nine

… Lawton, you'll be the death of me yet …

That afternoon as David sat in his office sipping a cup of coffee and poring over the latest report on the Alpaca wool he'd purchased from Peru, Mrs. Honeycutt interrupted.

"Mr. Darcy, there's a Mr. Taylor here from Charleston, South Carolina to see you. I've told him he doesn't have an appointment, but he insists you will see him."

Shocked, but also curious, David answered, "Send him in, Rita."

Strolling into the office with a conceited confidence and condescending smile, Cameron said, "Good afternoon, Darcy. I was in the area, so I thought I might come by and pay you a visit."

David wasn't fooled. Taylor had come for one reason, and one reason alone, but he thought he might as well play along to confirm his suspicion. "Have a seat." David gestured to the office chair closest to his desk.

"There's no need for that. I won't be stayin'," Cameron replied as he walked over to David's bookcase feigning an interest in the contents.

"You're a long way from home, Taylor. May I ask what brings you to London?"

"Hmm, nothin' much. I just thought you might like to congratulate me on my recent engagement."

"Oh? What engagement would that be?" David's eyebrow shot up along with the tension in his neck and shoulders.

Cameron laughed. "Hasn't that sweet little sister-in-law of yours told you?" he asked with a contemptuous grin. "Hmm, I guess Celia has been far too busy to call. I mean, with the preparations and all, maybe she didn't feel it was worth her trouble. I guess I'll have to be the one to break it to you then. Celia and I will be announcin' our engagement tomorrow night at the Magnolia Ball, and since Celia was an *old* friend of yours, I thought you'd want to congratulate me—I mean us." He grinned in triumph.

David stiffened, barely containing his emotions. Cameron's words cut him like a knife, but he'd be damned if he'd let it show. Composing himself, he coolly replied, "Tell me, Taylor, you came all this way to inform me of this? Why?" He folded his arms across his chest and leaned back in his seat.

Cameron smirked. "Don't flatter yourself, Darcy. I didn't come just to see you. You were a side trip. I was in Liverpool on business, and since you'd once *admired* my fiancée, I thought I'd stop by on my way back to South Carolina to let you know our happy news. Celia is beside herself with joy."

With his eyes fixed on the arrogant bastard before him, David drew an unsteady breath. The thought of this arse married to *his* Cecilia turned his stomach and made his blood run cold. "Taylor, I want to know one thing," David said, watching Cameron carefully. "Do you love her?"

"Love her?" Cameron's lips curled in a scornful sneer. "It's not about love, Darcy. I thought a man of your means and knowledge of the world would understand how things work. It's about money and power. Celia and I understand each other. You see Darcy, I was her first—the first man to ever touch her—the first man to, well you get my point. We hold a special bond—a bond she'll never have with anyone else but me.

Celia is *mine*, Darcy. I claimed her years ago." Cameron strutted in front of David's desk, casting him a look of pure condescension—a look of a man who'd won as he stared at David and shook his head with a prideful grin.

"But since you asked, of course we love each other, but it's much more than *that*. We belong to two of the oldest families in South Carolina. We can trace our ancestries back to the aristocracy of England—to The Lords Proprietors. Ours will be a marriage of wealth, power, and—"

"Is that what marriage is to you—money, power, connections…bloodlines and pedigrees? You sicken me, Taylor."

"What, Darcy? No congratulations?" Cameron snickered.

His contempt growing by the second for the sorry excuse of a man before him, David snarled. "You've said what you came to say. Now get out. Get out before I throw you out." David rose from his desk in a slow burn.

Cameron threw up his hands in feigned surprise. "All right, Darcy, I'm leaving, but I don't know why you're so upset. She was never anything more to you than a good piece of ass anyway."

David was suddenly at Cameron's throat, shoving him up against the wall. Opening the door, he hurled him through it. "Rita, if this worthless excuse of a man isn't in the lift in sixty seconds, call security."

"Don't worry, Darcy," Cameron said with a smug smile as he straightened his jacket. "I'm leavin'. I just wanted you to know, the *best* man won."

David's jaw hardened as he clenched his fist, ready to spring like a lethal cat, when his brother stepped into the waiting area, catching David mid-stride.

"Whoa, David! What's going on here?"

"Let me go, Fitzwilliam, let me go! That bastard! I'll fucking kill him!" David shouted, fury flashing in his dark eyes.

As Cameron walked away laughing, Fitzwilliam held David firm. "That's enough, David. I could hear you all the way down the hall. Why don't we go back into your office, and you can tell me what this is all about."

Storming back into his office, David slammed the door and paced as he told his brother everything that had just happened.

Listening carefully, Fitzwilliam responded, "So, if what Taylor's said is true, what are you going to do about it?"

"I don't know." He violently shook his head. "How could she accept that pompous arse when she knows why he's marrying her?" David raked his fingers through his dark disheveled curls, and suddenly it struck him. He could lose Cecilia for good. Fear gripped him—fear for himself and fear for her.

"David," Fitzwilliam said, "Elizabeth and I have talked about this extensively. Cecilia thinks she has to marry, and since you left her, she may feel she has no other choice. Taylor's family is equal to hers in social standing. I can't see her making a choice for anyone less than someone she views as her equal. That's why she's doing it. She doesn't believe she has any other choice."

Fitzwilliam rose from his seat and approached the door. Just as he was about to exit, he turned and said, "Does she, Brother? Does she have another choice?" Studying his brother's heated stare, he added, "As Father would say, be the man you were meant to be." With that, Fitzwilliam opened the door and walked through it, leaving David alone with his thoughts.

David released an exasperated breath and ran his hand over his face. He thought back to his night with Cecilia at The Woodlands, back to the look of her beautiful smile when he'd told her the vase was for her, back to how those luminous eyes sparkled in the candlelight, and finally, back to the night at Carlton when he'd first seen pain reflected in her violet-blue eyes—eyes that had so captured him from the beginning.

He winced, remembering their argument—the terrible words he'd said, the horrible names he'd called her. The words reverberated in his mind, and the thought that he had caused her pain, crushed him.

...Oh, God, what have I done? I can't let her do it. Taylor doesn't love her, and I do. I can't let her go through with it. Damn it! I've got to get to her by tomorrow night.

Picking up his interoffice phone, he called his secretary. "Rita, ring the airport and have Pemberley Two made ready for a Trans Atlantic flight. I'm leaving for Charleston tonight."

Next he called home and spoke to his valet. "Watson, pack two bags, one for each of us with enough clothes for one week. You and I are leaving for South Carolina in three hours. Be sure to pack my re-enactment suit—and practice knotting an 1860s cravat."

David could hear the roar of laughter through the phone. "Yes, sir! It will be a pleasure, sir!"

They arrived at the airport in two hours, only to be informed that no planes were permitted to take off from Heathrow until further notice. British Home Office Security MI5 had issued a severe alert for a terrorist threat, indicating an attack was highly likely. After a five-hour delay and many calls to his friends in Parliament, they were finally in the air but were told they had to land in New York until further notice as all incoming flights into the U.S. were also affected due to the high alert worldwide. As they waited for the all clear, David paced the floor looking at his watch. Time was running out. It was three a.m.

Anxiety gripped him. *...What else can go wrong!* Desperate to get to Charleston, David approached airline security. "When will we be allowed to take off? I have to be in Charleston right away. In fact, I should have been there yesterday."

"Sir, nobody is leaving LaGuardia anytime soon. If it's as you say, I'd suggest you take a rental car," the port authority guard replied. "At this point, it'll be faster."

"You're kidding! It's at least a twelve hour drive!"

"Then I'd suggest you get a move on. Time's a wasting." The hefty agent smiled while spinning his keys on his finger.

After securing a BMW and leaving instructions with his pilot to follow him to Charleston as soon as he was allowed, David and Watson tore out of New York for the long drive south, putting the pedal to the metal with hard rock music blaring, keeping time with the speedometer.

On the south side of Richmond, Virginia, a loud pop sounded as the car veered to the right almost spinning out of control. Guiding the Beamer into the emergency lane, David flung the door open, getting out of the car to inspect the front tire.

"A flat! Damn it! I'm never going to make it. I wish I had my Lamborghini," he said as he kicked the tire and let loose a string of curse words under his breath.

Watson calmly opened his door and slid out. Surveying the damage, he unbuttoned his cuffs and rolled up his sleeves. "Don't worry, sir, I'll have us back on the road in no time flat—no pun intended. And sir, at the speed we're already traveling in this vehicle, I'm glad the Murciélago is in London," he said, giving David a cheeky grin.

"Yes, well, it's a moot point." David glanced over at his valet with a half crooked smile. "I suppose the jack and the spare are in the boot."

"I would assume so, sir."

"I'll see what I can find," David said, sprinting around to the back of the car.

M.K. Baxley

Thirty minutes later and a little dirtier, they were back on the road. Speeding down I-95 at over ninety miles an hour, Watson finally spoke up. "Sir, you're going to get a speeding ticket or worse, if you continue at this speed. The sign back there read 70 mph. I suggest you slow down to 75. We'll get there, sir."

David cast Watson an incredulous look and rolled his eyes. "Watson, if they pull us over, I'll simply pay the *damn* ticket and get on with it." But he did ease up on the accelerator, causing Watson to smile.

They drove on through the early morning and late into the afternoon, taking turns behind the wheel and stopping only for gas and to grab a quick bite to eat. Not long after taking the exit from I-95 to I-26, a tractor trailer jackknifed, backing up traffic for miles. After two hours in grid-lock traffic, David took the nearest exit with the navigation system recalculating the route that took them into Charleston on the back country roads. Finally arriving at five o'clock, David was exhausted.

Time was of the essence, and there wasn't a moment to spare. Securing a room at the Lawton with less than one hour before the ball began, David took a quick shower. Watson hurriedly helped him dress, knotted his cravat, and smoothed his re-enactment suit. With the preparations complete, David flew from the room for the lift, followed closely behind by Watson. They arrived just as the door closed.

"Damn it! We'll have to take the stairs. The ball begins in fifteen minutes, and the engagement will be announced before the first dance. Come, Watson, there's not a moment to spare."

David raced down three flights of stairs faster than he'd moved since his rugby days. Was it the Blue Room or the Green? He couldn't remember. Just as he was about to decide, he heard the orchestra strike the warm up. *...it's the Green!* Making a mad dash, he entered the room, and there stood Cecilia next to Cameron on the platform, with Cecilia's godfather preparing to speak.

Cecilia's eyes instantly locked with his as he took a few steps and stopped. Summoning every ounce of strength he possessed, David stood tall and erect, his calm demeanor not revealing that his confidence was rapidly deserting him. Uncertain of how she would receive him and aware of the spectacle he knew he was creating, he glanced around the room. *...I'm not too late. Thank God! I'm not too late.*

As he walked towards Cecilia, a deathly silence fell upon the room. His pulse quickened. He could feel the hair on the back of his neck standing on end. All eyes were riveted on him. For a split second, both he and Cecilia were frozen in place, gazing at one another.

Cecilia's eyes pierced him, searching questioningly. Swallowing hard against the lump in his throat, some force from deep within propelled him forward. Slowly moving towards her, he saw her take one tiny step in his direction. When he reached the middle of the room, David halted, once more swallowing hard and blurted out, "Cecilia, you have a choice."

She stood still for what seemed an eternity, staring, her eyes glistening with tears. David's heart lodged in his throat as the room appeared to close in around him.

"Sir." Watson tugged at David's sleeve. "Speak."

David turned to catch his valet's encouraging nod. Turning back, he looked her directly in the eye. Having rehearsed his speech a thousand times since crossing the state line, all he could say was, "Cecilia, I'm the one—the one who loves you. Marry me!"

She stood silent, rooted in place. Suddenly, a big smile spread across her face as she ripped off her engagement ring and pressed it into Cameron's hand. "Yes!" she whispered, and then rushed down the steps and into David's arms as they fell together.

Grabbing her, David swung her around and kissed her as the room erupted into a loud round of applause and cheers. But he was oblivious to everything except the woman in his arms. Holding her in his embrace, the crowd faded away into a clutter of noise and shadow, peace finally washing over him while weeks of pain and numbness dissipated.

Cameron was about to lunge in a fit of rage when a large hand clenched his shoulder. "Don't do it, son. Let her be. She's made her choice." Daniel Russell stood firm, holding him back.

Cameron turned and jeered at the older man. Jerking himself free, he stalked from the room followed by his mother and Amelia.

Before following his son, Sheldon Taylor turned to Daniel. "Cecilia has gone too far this time, Russell. If she thinks she can embarrass my son publicly in front of all of Charleston and get away with it, she'd better think again," he ground out. "Nobody shames my family and gets away with it. She and that Englishman will pay for this!"

"Sheldon, I would counsel you to be prudent. The Darcys are far more powerful than you know, and Cecilia has friends in high places who will come to her aid, so I wouldn't make idle threats. Cut your losses and leave, if you know what's best for you."

"I'll leave, but only because Cameron has chosen to do so. Lawton doesn't own this town, and Darcy's an upstart here. This is Charleston—not London." With that parting shot, Sheldon Taylor turned and joined his family.

When the room quieted from all of the commotion, Daniel took the podium. "Ladies and gentlemen, I am proud to announce the engagement of my goddaughter, Miss Cecilia Emmaline Lawton, to Mr. David Darcy of London, England." The old man smiled, and once again, the room erupted in applause. When it died down, Daniel continued. "Let the first dance begin. David, Cecilia, this year's Belles and Beaus," he said as he gestured towards the couples, "please lead the way."

The orchestra struck the chord and David and Cecilia led with the Viennese Waltz. He held her close while directing her to a small alcove near the back of the ballroom. Once securely out of sight, he fought to steady his nerves. It was important to state his case—to swallow his pride and tell her how he felt.

"Lawton, I've missed you. Heaven knows I tried to forget you, but I couldn't. I love you, Cecilia." He hesitated a minute, gathering his courage as he gazed into those amethyst eyes, eyes that had held him captive almost from the beginning. "Cecilia, I've been a fool. The things I said, the things I did! Can you ever forgive me?"

She smiled. "When you're in love, there is no need to say you're sorry. You being here tonight tells me everything I need to know. I love you, David. That's all that needs to be said."

Tightening his arms around her, he covered her mouth with his. He knew she'd forgiven him because she'd accepted his proposal, but there was nothing that compared to hearing her say it and knowing she still loved him in spite of all he'd said and done. Breaking the kiss, he brushed her cheek with his fingers, gliding down her throat to her necklace. He gently lifted it. "You wore my necklace. Why? Did you believe I would come?"

Shaking her head, she replied, "I had no expectations that you would come. I thought I knew you well enough to believe I'd lost you forever, but I once told you that no matter what, I'd always love you. That's why I wore the necklace." She sighed. "Though, I do wish to know, what made you come?"

"You know me too well. You're right about my damnable pride. If I hadn't been able to put that aside, I would have lived with the regret for the rest of my life—but it was Cameron. Cameron made me come. While he was in England on business, the pompous arse made a special trip to London to tell me the news of your engagement." David shook his head. "I knew you didn't love him, and worse, I knew he didn't love you. His arrogance, his conceit, was more than I could stomach, but it served its purpose by jarring me to my senses."

He stroked the side of her face, brushing away a stray strand of hair. "When I was thinking of only me, it was easy to deny what I felt, but the thought of you being married to him shocked me into reality. I couldn't bear to see you in a loveless marriage, not when I loved you, not when I needed you. If I'd lost you for good, I don't know how I would've survived it." He smiled tenderly. "Cecilia Lawton... a long time ago you took the best of me. As an old song from the 70s put it, finish what you've begun and take the rest." He bent low and kissed her.

Pulling back, Cecilia's lips curled into a mischievous grin. "Bread?"

He nodded.

She shook her head and laughed. "David Darcy, you're a real scoundrel. Do you know that? Coming in here and sweeping me off my feet."

The twinkle in her violet eyes encouraged him. "Ah, but I'm a reformed scoundrel—though I think you rather like scoundrels, Miss Lawton," he said with a mischievous grin of his own as he leaned down to brush her lips again.

"Only when they're handsome, Mr. Darcy—only when they're handsome," she whispered against his lips.

"Lawton, you'll be the death of me yet," he said, just before their lips met again in a deep lingering kiss.

Breaking the kiss, she murmured, "Then we'll die happy," and kissed him again.

Releasing him, she took his hand in hers, gently caressing the cufflinks. "You wore them."

"Yes. They were a present from a very special lady. I will treasure them always."

Smiling, she reached up and touched his face.

"Cecilia, I'd rather stay here all night and snog like a couple of teenagers, but we must return before we're missed."

She sighed. "I suppose so, but for once, I'd like to do what I want instead of what's expected." They kissed once more before breaking their embrace.

Returning to the ballroom, David caught sight of Watson and laughed. His valet had managed to find a beautiful redhead serving wine at the refreshment table. David flashed him a smile and Watson returned a thumbs-up. As David and Cecilia stood by the serving table, Charlestonians came forth, one-by-one.

"Congratulations, Darcy." Solomon Abercrombie clapped David's shoulder before offering his hand. "Apparently you are the right stud," he winked. "Now that you are to be one of us, we'll have to talk about that horse of yours, and Smith here wants to see your English Setter."

Asa Smith stepped forward, pumping David's hand. "That's right, Darcy. Both my pointers and my setters could use some fresh blood. I'm looking forward to seein' your English bird dogs in action, especially that stud you told me about. As I told you before, I'm lookin' for a good stud dog for my champion setter. You'll have to come huntin' with me." He smiled, raising an eyebrow as he tipped his head to Cecilia.

"Sir, all in good time... all in good time." David laughed while Cecilia rolled her eyes.

As Asa and Solomon left, Robert and Elaine Russell approached. "Cecilia, I'm so happy for you, darlin'. And he's such a handsome beau, too!" Elaine said, taking Cecilia's hands and kissing her cheek.

"Congratulations, Darcy. I always knew you were a smart man. You've walked away with the most beautiful Belle of the Ball." Robert gave a hearty laugh. "I wish the two of you all the happiness in the world," he said, extending his hand.

"Thank you, Mr. Russell. I'm sure we will be very happy. In fact, I know it!"

All but a few came by to offer their congratulations, and as Robert Russell had told him long ago, those few didn't count anyway. If they wanted to scowl and look down their self-righteous noses, David didn't care. The only thing that mattered to him was that he was at peace, and that he had the woman he loved. Mingling and mixing into the early hours of the morning, David couldn't think of any place he'd rather be than here in South Carolina, here with Cecilia, the only woman he had ever loved, the only one he would ever love—his future bride.

Chapter Seventy

...I moved heaven and earth to get to you...

When the ball ended, David and Cecilia were among the last to leave. On the way up to the eighth floor, David said, "I'm glad this is over. I had a wonderful time, but I'm tired. You don't know what I've been through. I moved heaven and earth to get to you." He looked down into her sleepy eyes. "Let's just go to bed. We can talk more tomorrow."

Yawning, she leaned into his tall frame. "It's already tomorrow, but I know what you mean. I'm emotionally exhausted as well as physically drained. I just want to sleep in your arms. We'll talk when we wake up, and you can tell me all about it." She chuckled. "Wake up? Will I wake up and discover it was all a sweet dream?"

"No, love, it's no dream, or if it is, it's one that comes true. We're together never to be parted again."

Entering her suite, they undressed and fell asleep almost instantly, holding one another in a lover's embrace.

When they awoke, Cecilia had David's things brought up to her suite and ordered room service. They showered together, making love, kissing, caressing, and talking. Before they dressed, he pulled her onto the bed where they sat facing each other.

"Do you think you can clear your calendar for two weeks and come to London with me? I want to show you my home, and I want you to meet my family and friends. Then we can come back to Charleston and marry. I don't want to wait any longer. We've been through enough, and we've waited entirely too long already."

"We'll go by the office on Monday, and I'll see what I can do about my calendar. I'd love to come to London, and we'll talk about a wedding while we're there. I agree that we've waited long enough. Would one month be soon enough?"

David only smiled and nodded. One month would seem like an eternity to him, but it would have to do. He wanted her to have a wedding, and a wedding would take time to plan.

As they sat looking at one another, Cecilia laced her hand with his. "David, I'm curious; when did you first fall in love with me?"

He sighed in contentment. "I don't know exactly when I started to love you, it's been so long now, but I think it must have begun back when we spent our first night together nearly two years ago. Although the night you threw the vase at me gave me pause to think."

She grimaced, and he chuckled.

"I didn't know what I was feeling at the time, but I knew it was different with you. I found myself making excuses to come to Charleston. I know I tried to resist being drawn to you, but it proved useless," he said. "Did you ever wonder why I cut our time short when I came to see you that January?"

"Yes, I did, and I was quite upset when you left."

"You were?" he shook his head with a smile. "I would have never guessed it. I simply thought it was in keeping with your disconcerting ways and impenetrable manner." He smiled and shook his head. "I left because my emotions were in turmoil. Had I not left, there was a good chance I would have been in danger of declaring feelings I wasn't ready to admit to yet. I was attracted to you, and it bothered me. I fought it for months. As to when I knew for certain that I loved you, it was when I came for the Magnolia Festival a year ago. I never wanted to be in love with anyone, but you pulled me in before I knew what was happening." He pressed her hands between his.

Tossing her head, she laughed. "My story is similar. I had resolved never to allow my true feelings to be known. It was a defense I constructed for the label people gave me."

"Cold, hard bitch?"

"Yes," she nodded, "cold, hard bitch."

"You're anything but. One simply has to get past the wall you've raised to find the woman within—a beautiful woman who is as good as she is beautiful."

Cecilia laughed. "My closest friends have said that, but you're the one who scaled the wall, *Prince Charming.*" She smiled.

"And I found my *princess.*"

She laughed. "I don't know about that, but I do know that you were so gentle with me, and no one had ever been so loving or kind. I was taken aback by it. I responded to your tender affection, and I wanted more of it. It caused me to look deeper. Like you, I was not looking for love. In fact, I didn't think I needed it until that week in November when I knew I loved you."

Abruptly changing the subject, she frowned. "David, you do want children, don't you? It's important to me. I want to have a son." Her eyes searched his.

He chuckled. "Yes, I do. Very much. I've thought about it, and I want to see your family continue. The thought of you being the last of the Lawtons bothered me from the first time you told me about it. I know we can't produce a Lawton heir, but we can start a new branch on the family tree, uniting your family with mine. We'll have sons, and daughters, too, and we'll teach them to value their heritage."

"I'm so glad you feel that way. You don't know what it means to me to hear you say those things."

"I haven't always felt that way. Before you, children and family heritage held little to no appeal to me, but you have taught me that our roots are important, and a knowledge of the past is essential for the preservation of the future."

"David, where should we raise our family? Where do you want to live?"

He laughed. "Hmm…Well, I've thought about that, too. I'd like for us to live at Carlton House at least some of the time. I'd like to use the old school room for the purpose it was intended. Even though our children will bear my name, they will still be Lawtons. I want them reared in your family tradition."

She squeezed his hands. "Nothing would make me happier, David. The house has been empty for far too long, and the thought of children—our children, playing in those hallowed halls is more than I could ever hope for."

David smiled as he reached for her and pulled her to himself. "There'll be time enough to talk about living arrangements later. Right now, I need you." Toppling back, he caught her in his arms and rolled them over, settling on top of her and making love.

Once contented and relaxed, he cradled her close to his body, her head resting against his shoulder. "Marriage is going to be one bloody hell of a love affair, Miss Lawton."

"Yes, indeed it is, Mr. Darcy…indeed it is." She rose up on one elbow and gazed into his eyes. "And we are going to be the happiest couple in the entire world." As she bent down, capturing his lips, David was once again lost in Cecilia Lawton's kiss just as he'd been from the very first time she had kissed him.

Chapter Seventy-one

...a gentleman's gentleman...

As Cecilia fell back into her chair, she took a deep breath, her head still spinning from the change of events. Two days earlier, she'd been engaged to a man she could barely stand, and now she was engaged to the man she thought she'd lost forever, the only man whom she knew she would ever love. Sighing, she picked up her appointment book. It had taken all morning, but finally, the last appointments were attended to.

That left only one more detail—Daniel. She hadn't seen her godfather since Saturday night, but from the relieved smile that had graced his face, she knew he was pleased, especially after that scathing talking to he'd given her when she'd told him about her engagement to Cameron. She laughed to herself. *...Apparently he likes David. Well, we'll see. I need him to cover for me. I'd better call him.*

After attending to one more minor detail, she picked up the phone and called. When all was said and done, Daniel had agreed to oversee her operations for the next two months, giving her the time she needed to be with David. With the business considerations taken care of, Daniel moved the conversation onto a personal level.

"Celia, I've been watching you and young Darcy from afar. I've always known there was an attraction between the two of you. I've even talked with him about it." Daniel heard her gasp and chuckled. "Oh, don't sound so surprised. After all, your happiness is one of my main concerns. I recognized right from the start that Darcy was worthy of you, and I want you to know that I could not be more pleased with your decision, even if it does have most of the old women from here to Georgetown burning up the phone lines, talkin' about it." He laughed into the phone.

"They'll most likely still be talking about me this time next year. I've done it again, haven't I?"

"The old biddies will get over it, so don't give them another thought. They don't amount to a hill of beans anyway. Besides, I do believe Darcy would have gotten along well with James. That little stunt he pulled Saturday night reminds me of your father. I could see James doing the same kind of thing, or for that matter, it just as well could have been me when I was Darcy's age. But, just because I approve of him, doesn't mean I don't want to grill him, so send him down to my office."

Cecilia released a nervous laugh. "Daniel! I'm over twenty-one and out of school. You don't have to scrutinize my dates, let alone my fiancé. I'm quite capable of deciding my future."

"Oh? Are you now?" he teasingly reprimanded. "You came very close to making one of the worst blunders of your life. I want to speak with Darcy, and I'm not joking, Celia. It's my responsibility to look after you." His firm voice declared he wouldn't be moved, and she knew it.

"Why didn't you talk with Cameron when we became engaged?"

"Who says I didn't? That arrogant ass! I've known him since he was in diapers, and I've never liked him or Sheldon, either one." Daniel paused for a moment. "Cecilia, let me be very serious with you. You suspected it was Lucinda who called you that fateful afternoon, and in fact, it was, but don't forget—Lucinda is my niece. She acted at my directive."

"You! Daniel, how could you do that to me, and why haven't you told me this before now?"

"Because I saw no reason to. Also, I knew I had to show you instead of tellin' you, or you would not have believed me, so it had to be as it was. And do not think your father didn't know about it. James knew, and it was all I could do to keep him from going over to Sheldon's and having it out with both him *and* Cameron. But reason prevailed, and we separated the two of you. That is why your father was so agreeable to sending you away. Didn't you ever wonder about that?"

"Yes, I suppose I did, but I thought that perhaps he wanted me to explore life, and besides, I was with Ron Bennett's daughters."

"*No*, it wasn't that. Being with the Bennett girls certainly helped, but James wanted you away from Cameron."

"He cared, didn't he?"

"Yes, Celia, he cared, and so do I. That's why I promised your father that I would take care of you. I've watched over you all these years, and of late, I've grieved over you. If Darcy is half the man I believe him to be, it will be a pleasure to turn you over to him and let him worry with you for a change. This old man needs a rest."

"I love you, Daniel."

"I love you, too, dumplin'." Daniel chuckled. "Now, I want to see if Darcy is the man I think he is. Send him down."

Cecilia rolled her eyes and laughed. "Dumplin'! Daniel, I'm warning you, behave yourself."

Cecilia placed the phone in its cradle and glanced up, still smiling as David came through the door with a cup of coffee. "Darling, I hate to do this to you, but Daniel wants to speak with you. Seems he takes his role as my godfather very seriously. His office is on this floor. It's to the right of the elevator. His name is on the door," Cecilia said with a smile.

David laughed. "Is this a joke?"

Cecilia lifted a brow and tilted her head with a smile. "It's no joke, darling. He's for real."

Startled, David asked, "Do I have to ask permission or is this for a blessing only?"

"Hell no, you don't have to ask permission! He made a promise to my father, and I'm afraid he takes it very seriously. This is his way of fulfilling it, but don't be surprised if he also has a little fun at your expense." She laughed, slightly embarrassed. However, after the argument they'd had over Cameron and the little talk he'd just given her, she knew Daniel was deadly serious.

David drew in a measured breath, shaking his head as he shrugged his shoulders and set his coffee on her desk. "All right, for you, I'll do this." He turned and exited.

Cecilia rose from her desk and went to the door, watching David head in the direction of Daniel's office.

David released a deep breath as he walked towards his destination. This turn of events had been totally unexpected. He knew he hadn't experienced what Fitzwilliam had, but he certainly felt like he'd been through the wringer, and now he was about to jump into a bloody inquisition. He knew he must really be in love to put himself through this!

When David reached Daniel's office, he felt somewhat intimidated, but he was resolved to follow through with whatever it took to make everybody involved happy. If he had to ask for her hand, he would.

Daniel was scribbling something on a legal pad when David appeared at the door, but he glanced up and signaled David to have a seat before returning to his work.

"That was quite a spectacle you created Saturday night, Darcy." Daniel continued to write. "Do you always make such a grand entrance to a ball?" Daniel asked in a dignified manner as he finally raised his eyes.

"Sir, I do apologise for creating a scene, but I was des—"

"Desperate. Yes, I had that much figured out, but Darcy, come now, why did you have to make such a display?"

Studying the man before him, David thought Daniel was beginning to enjoy putting him through torture.

"Sir, I believe the answer is obvious! I'm in love with Miss Lawton, and you were about to announce her engagement to someone else!" David paused. "If I must ask for your consent, your blessing, or whatever you deem necessary, then consider this an application. I love Cecilia. I want to marry her, and I've never been more certain of anything in my entire life!" David spat out, jumping up.

At this, Daniel broke into a big smile and laughed. "Darcy, come down from your high horse and resume your seat. I was only testing your resolve. You have my permission, blessing, and anything else I can give you. A marriage in a month's time is a hurried up affair, but I know Celia, and I suppose you, too, can't wait to marry. If that's what the two of you want, then go to it," he said with a smile. "She isn't gettin' any younger and neither are you." Daniel laughed once more. "But on a more serious note though, make her happy, Darcy, make her happy, because she deserves it."

David let out the deep breath he'd been holding, and smiled, looking directly at Daniel Russell. "On that, sir, we can agree. I will spend the rest of my life doing just that. Her happiness is my greatest concern. You can be assured of that. She means everything to me."

"I'm greatly relieved to hear it, and Darcy, I've always known since I first noticed you looking at my goddaughter that you were the one to make her happy. That's why I pointed you in her direction. Of course, I had to let nature take its course, but I was confident in which direction this would go, though you almost blew it. But, if Celia can forgive you, then so can I."

Startled, David observed the old man closely. "Sir, how did you know when we didn't know ourselves?"

"Because I'm older and wiser than you, and I've been around the block a few times. That's why." Daniel chuckled in amusement. "I noted the attraction, and furthermore I recognized that you are a good man. I also knew that Celia's heart is not easily touched, and that *you* cannot resist a challenge attached to a pretty woman. She, on the other hand, needs a strong man, and you are definitely that. She won't be happy with a man she can dominate, or a man she doesn't respect. Remember that, Darcy. She needs a man who is her equal, and you are certainly her equal in so many ways."

"I like you, Russell." David reached over and shook his hand.

Daniel smiled as he rose to his feet and went to his liquor cabinet where he took out two glasses. "Now, have a whiskey with me before you go back to your sweetheart. You two should be planning your honeymoon. I'll be covering for her for the next two months." He poured two glasses of Gentleman Jack and handed one to David. The two men conversed for another thirty minutes before David left to find Cecilia.

When David returned to his fiancée's office, he looked rather grave.

"Well? What did he say?" Cecilia asked, more than just a little concerned.

David broke into a big smile. "We have his blessing. He said, and I quote, 'Go to it.' I rather like him, even though he had me very anxious for a short time. Let's find someplace to eat, and I'll tell you all about it over lunch."

Cecilia shuffled a few more papers, left some instructions for her personal assistant, and then they headed in the direction of the stairwell. But before leaving, she stopped by Daniel's office to give him a hug and a kiss. Soon after, they headed down the stairs and out the door to Cecilia's car, making their way to their favorite café on Queen Street.

When they arrived, they took an outdoor table under the pergola now covered in sapphire blue, sweet-scented, wisteria blossoms. Ordering their sandwiches and iced tea, they settled in to talk. "Cecilia, were you aware that Daniel set us up?" David asked before taking a sip of tea.

"What do you mean?" She frowned, startled at his words.

"Just what I said. He set us up. You remember our first night together? It was by his design."

"How do you know that? Did he say so?"

"No, he only told me that he pushed us together and let nature take its course. I figured it out from there. Remember the day we were negotiating the coffee contract? Remember his phone call?"

"Yes, yes I do. Why that—"

"Lawton," David held up his hand, "have a little respect for your elders. It didn't turn out so bad, now did it? But had I known back then what he'd done, I wouldn't have liked it. However, now that it's done, I'm rather glad he interfered. Look at us, Cecilia. We owe our happiness to a well meaning man's interference. He loves you, and so do I."

"Well, since you put it that way, I suppose I can forgive him just this once, but I'll wring his leathery neck if he ever does anything like that again." She lifted her glass to her lips.

"You'll do no such thing. I like him, even if he does drink foul tasting whiskey."

Cecilia burst out laughing, coughing tea into her napkin. "Oh, so you don't like Gentleman Jack, do you?"

"It's the worst tasting stuff I've ever had."

Amused, she replied, "It was Daddy and Daniel's favorite. The two of them used to shoot it straight. I see you have a lot to learn about Southern gentlemen."

"You're kidding, aren't you?"

"No, not in the least, and if you are going to be here with us, you'll have to acquire the taste. It's what most of the men drink."

"What am I marrying into?" he whispered as he rolled his eyes.

"You'll get used to it. After a while, it's not so bad." Cecilia glanced up to see the waiter approaching their table. "Well, here comes our sandwiches."

While they ate, David suddenly fell back in his chair, uttering a low curse. "Damn! I forgot all about Watson. I haven't seen him since Saturday night. I need to ring him. He probably thinks I've dropped off the face of the earth!"

Cecilia laughed. "David, I'm sure he's all right. The last time I saw him he was in the very capable hands of one of my maids, Jenny O'Donnell, but you go ahead and call him if it pleases you."

"I have to, Cecilia. I need him to get my things ready for the return flight tomorrow. He'll need access to your suite in order to pack."

"Go ahead and give him a call then and tell him we'll meet him at your room, and then he can come up with us—but don't expect him to be alone. Jenny gets around." Cecilia winked.

"I see," David said with a crooked grin as he pulled out his mobile.

After several rings, a very sheepish Watson answered the phone. David couldn't help but hear a woman's giggles in the background. Once business was concluded, David admonished Watson. "Now off you go, and Watson…"

"Yes, sir."

"You're a gentleman's gentleman. Remember that. I expect you to be at least as good as me."

"Yes, sir." Watson chuckled.

Sliding his mobile shut, David looked at Cecilia and grinned while she rolled her eyes.

"This must be the third British invasion. First the Redcoats, then the Beatles, and now you and Watson."

David laughed aloud. "Never let it be said that a Brit doesn't know how to handle a woman." He touched his glass to hers. "Cheers, Ms. Lawton." They finished lunch and headed back to the Lawton Hotel.

Chapter Seventy-two

... You're insatiable...

T he next day, David, Cecilia, and Watson boarded Pemberley Two, headed for London. Shortly after takeoff with Watson secured in the front sitting room, David and Cecilia comfortably situated themselves in the bedroom of his Lear jet for privacy.

They discussed their plans as David held Cecilia close, her head resting on his shoulder. "I'm going to put an announcement in *The Sunday Times* soon after we arrive. When we return to Charleston, will you do the same there, and do you think we could be married in your family church?"

"I think it can be arranged. I'll place the announcement and speak with the parish rector. I'm sure Bishop Lowndes would be pleased to marry us, but I don't want a society wedding. I will not be put on public display. I only want our closest friends and family there. I have no family of my own, but of course, I consider Daniel Russell and the Chaplins to be family."

"I'm relieved about the wedding since I don't like public displays either, but you are wrong about one thing. You'll soon have more family than you can imagine. I have several cousins, aunts, and uncles who will love you. When we're in England, we'll have a formal dinner to announce our engagement to my family."

"That sounds good to me. I'm looking forward to meeting them." Cecilia snuggled closer with her head resting on David's chest just under his chin. "I still can't believe this is real. We are getting married, and you want to live in Charleston. I wouldn't have thought you would ever leave England."

David kissed the top of her head. "You can't leave Charleston, but I can leave England. Since Pemberley Estate and Darcy House belong to Fitzwilliam, I have nothing holding me there. You have your business, your father's research and historical work, and four homes in South Carolina, so it just makes sense that Charleston should be our home. My personal preference would be to live at Carlton House in the winter, but what would you say about spending the summer at James Island? Then, perhaps, we can use the townhouse whenever we need to be in town. What do you think?"

"Oh, I would love that. James Island is beautiful in the summertime. I only lived in town because it was convenient."

David looked at her with a warm smile. "I'm glad we agree on that then, for I want our children to learn to ride and grow up in the country. I believe it gives one a greater appreciation for the land. I want to stock the libraries with works of literature, history, and philosophy. I want our children to have the same education Fitzwilliam, Georgiana, and I had. We can do some of the teaching ourselves, if you would like, and we can hire tutors as needed until they're old enough to attend the prep school you attended. With your MBA from Harvard and my undergraduate degree from Oxford, we would do well," he said, glancing down at her with a smile. "If you disagree with any of this, tell me. I want you to be happy with whatever we do."

Cecilia propped herself up on her elbow and looked at him intently. "So far I agree with you on everything, but you had better inspect *our* libraries before you buy any books. They may not be in as much need as you think. And I do want our children to have a classical education. It's been years, but I can read and write Greek and Latin, and I speak Spanish and French fluently. I've read all of the classics, and I'm familiar with more than just Southern history. I was educated in the classics at a Jesuit school. My father saw to that."

David eyes twinkled. "I thought as much. There's a lot more to you than one notices upon first acquaintance. And you're right; I'll have to inspect *our* libraries. In fact, I haven't even been interested in such things for many years. It was always Fitzwilliam who took an interest in books, but now I have a reason to have that interest myself."

David shifted about on the bed for a comfortable spot. "I'm going to bring my cars, personal horses, and shooting dogs with me when we return, and I want to acquire a set of hounds. Asa Smith wants to introduce me to coon hunting. I've looked into it, and it looks interesting. He says that Walkers and Redbones are the best breeds for that. He tells me they fox hunt here, too."

She looked at him and laughed. "Yes, that's right," she said. "They'll make a Southern gentleman out of you yet! As for hounds, they're not hard to find. As soon as we're settled in, I'll take you to some of the best breeders in the South. We'll get you a set of whatever you want and a bloodhound for me."

"I'll hold you to it, Lawton. From what I've seen, a farm is not complete without some kind of hound. We'll get a pair of each and a bloodhound for you. I want to breed them, and after talking with Solomon, I think I'll explore horse breeding, too."

He hugged her and gave her a gentle kiss. "Now, I'd like to select your engagement ring and our wedding bands whilst we're in London. Would you like to come with me, or do you want me to surprise you?"

"I think I'll come along."

"Very well, we'll go together then. Also, I'm entitled to some of my family's estate jewelry, and I want to choose several pieces for you. I thought you might like to have one of the family wedding sets. There are many precious gems as well as diamonds and pearls."

"I will look, and we can choose together. There are several heirloom pieces in my family as well that were worn mostly during the season."

"That's when these pieces were worn. My mother would wear them when she was in London attending some social function or other."

He paused for a moment, turning and looking her directly in the eye with a more serious countenance. "I want you to know that I plan to retire from Darcy Enterprises to work for you, but I will remain on the board of directors for Fitzwilliam's sake, and I'll still retain a joint controlling interest of the company. I'm also going to put your name on everything I own and control concerning Pemberley, PLC."

"David, I'm honored that you would consider that, but it isn't necessary."

"On the contrary; it's very necessary. In case something should happen to me, I want you to carry on in my stead. It would also secure my interests in Pemberley for any children we should have. I trust you in this."

"I can see the logic behind it, and I suppose we will need to talk about Lawton, too. I don't plan to have a prenuptial for the same reason. I trust you."

David laughed as she gave him a hug. "I have dreams for your company, Cecilia. I want to build a legacy for our children, and I'm willing to invest half of my cash inheritance into Lawton. I would like to see you go into the international markets more heavily than you already are. That's my field of expertise with Darcy Enterprises. I believe you need to expand your import/export business and contract to have your cotton processed yourself instead of selling it raw. We'll have to go overseas to have that done, and then we can market the cloth to top designers. With your shrewd business sense and expertise, along with my import/export knowledge, we can go far towards expanding your family business. What do you think?"

"I'm listening, and I'm very interested. Tell me more."

He smiled and nodded. "I've been studying your rice and cotton foundations. We need to accelerate those projects. There is a big demand for the cotton cloth. You need to plant all the available land you have. I know it's still in the developmental stages, but you already have the best cotton on the market. You need to go with it now. Don't wait. As for the Carolina Gold, I've researched the markets there, too. In its day, it was the world's leading rice. It can be again."

She wrinkled her brow. "I'm encouraged about the rice, as I've thoroughly researched it myself, but do you really think we can compete with the Egyptian and Pima cottons?"

"Yes, I do. Months ago, I mentioned it to a couple of my associates in London who contacted some of the top designers in New York, Paris, and Milan, and they will take all we can sell them."

She reached up and brushed a lock of hair from his brow. "Then, it will be your project. We're planting fifteen hundred acres this year, and I'm buying all the land I can as it becomes available. If you think you can market the cotton, then go for it."

He tightened his embrace. "There's one other thing. I know you haven't gone public with the company, and I also know what a headache it is to do so, but you might want to consider it. You'd make an excellent CEO, and you know I'll be there to help you every step of the way if you ever decide to take Lawton in that direction."

She dropped her lashes, tapping her fingers on her lower lip. "I have been thinking about it for several years now. Daddy didn't want to take that step because he would lose control by giving power to the stockholders, but the benefit is that I wouldn't have to work as hard. I believe Daddy's heavy drinking and his pouring himself into Lawton shortened his life. I'll think about it, and then we'll talk. I want you to learn everything you can about Lawton, and we'll discuss this again."

"*After* our honeymoon."

"Yes." She chuckled and nodded in agreement.

Smiling, she reached to take his hand. "David, I couldn't be more please at how well we complement one another. I know how good you are in the business world, and now that you're willing to work for me, I get an international business partner as well as a husband. I am indeed fortunate."

"And I get a shrewd businesswoman as well as a wife who is GIB."

"GIB?"

"Good in bed," he said with a mischievous grin.

"So that's important in the bargain, hmm?"

"Very—perhaps the most important." he teased, pulling her on top of him.

"Sometimes I think you can't get enough. You're insatiable."

"It's been five months, Lawton."

"Didn't you see anyone while you were in London?"

"Lawton, I won't ask you about Cameron if you don't ask me about London."

"You're incorrigible!"

"Do I hear any complaints?"

"None!"

Chapter Seventy-three

... you complete me in every way...

As the limo pulled through the great iron gate of Darcy House, Cecilia's eyes widened. Although she'd been to London many times with her father, and then later on her own, she'd never taken the tour of the beautiful estate homes, nor could she have imagined the splendor of an 18th century English townhouse such as the one set before her. Unlike Southern mansions, this one was landscaped with ornately sculptured hedges and a water fountain in the center of the drive. Pleasing statues decorated a neatly manicured lawn. All of it spoke not only of the wealth of the family that owned it, but also of their discriminating taste.

To Cecilia, it looked like the perfect place for children to play yard games, hiding in and amongst the gardens and maze of hedgerows. Elizabeth had told her of the majesty of her new home, but there were no words to describe what Cecilia saw. She glanced at David and smiled. He could marry anyone—the daughter of an earl, a duke, a marquis. And yet he had chosen her! Her heart warmed and filled to overflowing for the man beside her.

David carefully took her hand in his and gave it a gentle squeeze. "What do you think?"

"It's beautiful. Different from what I'm used to, but beautiful. Elizabeth is indeed a lucky woman to have fallen in love with *Prince Charming* and I with his charming brother—a prince of my own."

David heartily laughed. "Somehow that's not what I expected you to say. We are far from being royalty. This is nothing compared to the Queen's castles." Seeing a man standing on the portico, he gestured. "Higgins has come to meet us. He'll get someone to unload our luggage, and I'll give you a tour of my family's home," he said as a servant followed by two others approached the limo.

When the car rolled to a stop, David exited, followed by Cecilia. After giving instructions, David turned back to Cecilia. "Let's go in. My brother and Elizabeth should be there to greet us."

When they stepped into the spacious entryway, Elizabeth flew down the stairs into Cecilia's embrace, hugging her old friend dearly. "Celia, I am so very glad to see you and to know that we'll soon be sisters. I couldn't be happier for you."

"I'm so glad to see you, too, and I can't wait to see how Alex and Emily have grown. How are they treating their daddy?"

"Fitzwilliam is a natural. He's quite good at changing nappies," Elizabeth said, glancing at her husband with a teasing smile as he made his way from the library.

"Nappies?" Cecilia raised a brow.

"Diapers," Elizabeth giggled. "That's what they call them over here. You have a lot to learn."

"David, just you wait. Your turn is coming," Fitzwilliam said with a confident smile.

"Well, to let you know how much I've changed, I'm kind of looking forward to it."

Just as they had finished greeting one another, Georgiana entered the room with Alex followed by Clara with Emily. "David! I'm so glad to see you," she said, passing Alex off to his father before pulling David into a tight embrace.

Hugging her back with an affectionate kiss to the cheek, he replied, "Georgiana, I want you to meet my fiancée, Cecilia Lawton, from Charleston, South Carolina. Cecilia, this is my sister, Georgiana."

Georgiana quickly extended her hand. "Cecilia, it's so good to meet the woman who has tamed my wayward brother. It's about time he settled down. My brother's been smitten with you for some time now. You should have seen the way he pined away in that semi-dreamy state for the last year. I knew there had to be a woman behind it." She laughed.

"Georgiana! I've done no such thing!"

"Oh, yes, you have." She gave him a cheeky look. "Just because I'm six years younger than you doesn't mean that I don't have a keen eye when it comes to analyzing my brothers. Observing the two of you has educated me in matters of the heart," she giggled, glancing between her two brothers' red faces.

"Well, it's a pleasure to finally meet you, Georgiana. I have heard so much about you that I feel I already know you," Cecilia said, smiling with genuine affection.

Turning to David, Cecilia raised an eyebrow. "Hmm… I think we have some more exploring to do. Pining away, huh?"

David rolled his eyes and laughed.

Lifting Alex from Fitzwilliam's arms and taking Cecilia's hand, Elizabeth suggested, "Come, ladies, let's call for tea and take this conversation to the drawing-room. I believe Fitzwilliam and David need to talk." Elizabeth took Georgiana and Cecilia with her for refreshments while the brothers left for a private conversation.

As they entered the study, both walked over to the drinks cabinet. Fitzwilliam poured two glasses of wine and selected two cigars. They took seats in the wing-backed chairs in front of the fireplace and lit their cigars while they settled in for a long talk.

"Fitzwilliam, what do you say to spending a week at Pemberley? Elizabeth's never seen the estate, and I want Cecilia to see it before we have to return to Charleston."

"I'm glad you brought that up, because now that the two of you are here, we're planning to have the children christened at Pemberley Chapel. I called the vicar at Lambton as soon as I knew you were coming to set the christening for Saturday. It's long overdue. Elizabeth wants you and Cecilia to be the godparents."

"I know Cecilia would be as honored as I am. She talks frequently about the children. I believe she really grew to love them whilst they were in Charleston."

"Then it's settled," Fitzwilliam said as he took a sip of his wine. "I understand you want to host an engagement dinner. Do you want to hold the dinner in London or Derbyshire? The family can make it at either place."

"I'd prefer Pemberley. We'll invite some of the neighbors as well."

"Good, I'll have Elizabeth and Georgiana arrange it."

"Fitzwilliam, before I forget, I want to mention that I have discussed with Cecilia the matter of our family heirloom wedding sets. Cecilia and I would like to choose one together. Have you given one to Elizabeth yet?"

"No, we can take care of that when we go to Pemberley, but I do suggest you get Cecilia one of her own as well as the heirloom set."

"Yes, I intend to. Tomorrow, when we will go to Garrard's, I'm going to buy her a ring and an engagement present."

With a lull in the conservation, David contemplated what he was about to say.

Although he'd thought it through, he knew it would not be easy to tell his brother his plans, but tell him he must.

"Fitzwilliam, there is one other thing that I need to tell you." He took a puff of his cigar and hesitated. "I'll be leaving Darcy Enterprises to join in partnership with Cecilia. My resignation will be effective in one month, when we marry."

Fitzwilliam winced. "I thought you might be leaving. I'm not entirely surprised, but I hate to lose you. You're good at what you do and will be sorely missed—and not just in business, either." Fitzwilliam looked into his brother's eyes. "David, if there is anything we can do to help you and Cecilia, just ask."

Knowing his concern, David reassured him. "I will, but I want you to know you're not losing a brother. We'll visit each other often. I want very much for our families, especially our children, to know one another. Cecilia told me she used to spend her summers with the Bennetts, and I want our children to do the same. Perhaps we can alternate spending Christmas and holidays between Charleston and Pemberley." David swallowed against the lump in his throat while suppressing the burning sensation in his eyes. "Fitzwilliam, you're gaining a new family—mine, and I want us to keep that close connection."

"Yes, we will." Fitzwilliam took a long draw on his cigar and lowered his gaze. "I have always wanted us to remain close, especially with our immediate families. I feel life is taking us in different directions, and it saddens me to think that you won't be here when I will want to see you on a whim. You'll be an ocean away. I'm going to miss you."

David quickly added. "Yes, but I'll only be a phone call away, and if you should ever need me, I'll come. And I know you would do the same for me."

"I do know that, but I'll feel the loss just the same."

Both brothers remained quiet for a moment, and then David spoke. "Fitzwilliam, I'm taking my inheritance to invest in Cecilia's company. I've learned a lot working with our business, and I plan to use that knowledge to expand Cecilia's interests, but I won't undercut my family."

Fitzwilliam glanced up. "I'm not worried about that. Even if we do cross markets, there's enough for both of us. Although, there is one thing. I want you to remain on the board of directors. I need you."

"I have no intention of giving up that position. I'm marrying—not divorcing my family."

"I know, David, I know—and thanks."

The following day, David and Cecilia left for the offices of *The Times*. He intended to place a simple announcement in the upcoming Sunday edition, but before he could leave the building, the editor-in-chief called him back.

Once *The Times* editor realized who was placing the announcement and its significance, he insisted on pictures and an interview. David, knowing he must relent, granted the interview along with a series of pictures of him and Cecilia for the front page of the society section. David was his usual confident self, and Cecilia had to laugh at the interest one simple announcement appeared to create.

After leaving *The Times* building, he and Cecilia made their way to Garrard's of Mayfair to choose an engagement ring. The very same sales associate that had helped his brother was available to help them as well.

"What are you looking for in a ring, Mr. Darcy?"

Deferring to his fiancée, he said, "Cecilia, do you want gold or platinum?"

"Hmm…I'd like yellow gold and a single round diamond no larger than a carat or perhaps two."

"Nonsense! Rhett bought Scarlett the largest diamond he could find. I'll have the same." He looked the clerk directly in the eye and said, "Bring us all you have in two carats and larger."

Cecilia blinked twice and nodded to the associate. "Let me see what you have, then."

"Miss, would you like to see our colored diamonds. They're all the rage this year. We offer black, blue, red, pink, and yellow."

"No, I'm a traditional American girl. I prefer white diamonds."

The sales associate smiled and went to the back, returning with several trays of engagement rings of two to five carats, all flawless with no inclusions. Cecilia immediately spied an 18k gold elegant engagement ring with an eternal cut five carat diamond. It was surrounded by a circlet of fourteen interlocking sapphires mounted in platinum upon a diamond heart shaped, split-shank channel setting. Completing the collection was a choice of either a matching 18k gold wedding band with a full circle of channel-set round diamonds, or a similar band of sapphires and diamonds. With either band, it was a striking combination with an equally impressive price tag of over £450,000. David smiled as he glanced between the rings and Cecilia's captivated look.

"Cecilia, are you sure this is the one? You haven't looked at them all yet."

"Yes, I'm sure. I love this one! Sapphires are my favorite gemstones. I also want the matching diamond wedding band and one plain band, the one with interspersed diamonds. I'll wear it when we're just around the house. The other one will be for work and formal occasions." She smiled, giving his hand a gentle squeeze before leaving him to investigate something that had caught her eye in another showcase.

When Cecilia was out of hearing, he whispered to the sales associate, "All right, we'll take that set with the additional band she indicated, and add the band with the sapphires, too. I've decided we'll take them both, and I'll take a plain gold band for me. Also, I want the ring and all the bands engraved to read *Lawton & Darcy, Ltd.*"

The clerk smiled. "I'll take your measurements, and we'll have them ready for you in three days. Will there be anything else?"

"Not at this time, thank you." He moved to join Cecilia at the precious gems case where the associate met them to take their measurements.

Three days later, when David returned for the rings, he also bought a heart shaped locket he had seen previously. It was gold with a small diamond set in the center. Etchings bursting forth from the diamond gave it the appearance of a solitary star. The rest of the locket's face was covered in filigree. This he would present to her with their wedding picture enclosed after they were married. The inscription *Yours... Forevermore... David* was to be engraved on the left side. He also purchased a sapphire and diamond necklace with matching earrings and a bracelet.

Later that evening while sitting on the divan in front of the fireplace, David gently stroked the delicate box he held in his hand. "Cecilia, come here, love. I have something for you."

Turning from the mirror perched over the dressing table he'd had brought to his room for her use, she put down her brush and rose to join him. "What's this?" she asked as she took a seat next to him.

With a smile, he opened the small case. "I picked up our rings today." He took her engagement ring from the box and placed it upon her finger. Then he reached over to the side cabinet and produced a jewel case and another small box. "And I want you to have this as an engagement present."

M.K. Baxley

Setting the boxes in her lap, Cecilia held her hand up to the light of the chandelier. "Oh, David," she whispered, "it's beautiful!" Light from the diamond and sapphires danced and sparkled about the room.

Reaching down for the smaller package, she slipped the case from the box and opened it. David carefully removed the bands and showed her the inscription: *Lawton & Darcy Ltd.* She gazed at him in awe. Suppressing a sob, she said, "I'm deeply touched by the way you view our union."

David reached over and tipped her chin so that their eyes met. "I view our marriage as a partnership—a true melding of minds. After all, you've always said 'we're two of a kind'" He laughed. "Even my father said so. Now open the next one," he coaxed.

Opening the box with the sapphires and diamonds, she gasped at their sparkle. Her eyes filled with tears. "Oh David, you shouldn't have. The ring was enough, but these are truly beautiful..." Her voice trailed into a whisper.

"It's a lovely ring for a lovely bride, and when I saw the sapphires, I couldn't resist. They were meant for you," he said in a soft hushed tone. "I love you, Lawton." Cupping her face in his hands, he brought her lips to his while her arms instinctively encircled him. When he released her, she was crying.

"Why the tears, my love? This is to be the happiest time of our lives," he said, tenderly brushing a tear away with his thumb.

"I'm crying because I am happy—very happy. I never thought I could be so happy. I don't deserve you." She smiled through her tears.

With a tender chuckle, he kissed her forehead, pulling her into his arms. "Yes, you do. If anything, it's I who doesn't deserve you. I didn't even know there was anything missing from my life until I found you, and now I don't know how I would go on without you. Cecilia, you complete me in every way. We were meant to be together." He paused as he brushed a strand of hair out of her beautiful eyes while he gently caressed her face. "You and I were born for one another—created from conception to be together. I love you, and that'll never change. I'm not the man I once was, nor are you the woman you once were, but we are the man and woman we should be. Lawton, never say you don't deserve to be happy. I'll hear none of that," he said as he lowered his head to give her a gentle kiss.

Releasing her lips, they held each other, savoring this tender moment. Neither said another word, for there was nothing left to be said.

While Georgiana sat in her room sipping a cup of Earl Grey, she thought about her brothers. They were happier and more content than she could remember ever seeing either of them, but it was David who pleased her more. Even though she knew how David had treated women, and didn't approve, she also knew he was a good man deep inside, and that, when he found the right woman, he would become the man she had believed him to be. And now that David had found Cecilia, she had transformed him and brought out the best in him. Georgiana couldn't have been more pleased.

Then there was Fitzwilliam and Elizabeth. They had a rapport with one another that astounded her. The former lecturer from Tennessee kept her brother on his toes with her wit, humor, and love for him. And both were totally dedicated to their children. She had never thought she would ever see her brother changing nappies or burping babies and allowing them to spit up on his impeccable bespoke suits. But there he was, and perfectly content with doing it. Georgiana Darcy smiled as she thought of all of this, but she also thought of another man whom she had not heard from in nearly a year.

Each night before bed, she would put on her favorite music, light a few candles, and take out his letters. Gently untying the lavender ribbon that held them bound, she went through them one by one. As she came to the final email, she sighed and held it to her heart. He'd all but said he wanted to marry her. He'd asked her to wait for him and wait she would. Watching her brothers' happiness only made her long that much more for her own. She knew it would mean giving up her home and all that she'd ever known here in England, but it didn't matter. From what she'd witnessed her brothers go through, she knew that life wasn't worth living if it couldn't be shared with someone you loved.

While she lay there on her bed, he appeared before her in her mind's eye, standing on a grassy knoll, gazing down at her with clear blue eyes. She could see the curve of his smile, his sandy blonde hair cut a little longer than most Marines, and his strong muscular build. She sighed deeply as she remembered how he had made her feel when he'd pulled her into his arms and kissed her that first time. It hadn't been her first kiss, but it had been the first time someone's kiss had sent shivers through the heart of her womanhood, causing her to long for what she knew her brothers shared with their loves.

Folding his letters, she tied them back with the lavender ribbon and neatly tucked them under her pillow. She blew out the candles, set the sound system to auto-repeat, took off her slippers, and then climbed into bed. Sliding under the covers, she pulled her pillow into an embrace and said a silent prayer. As she closed her eyes in sleep, she whispered against her pillow, "Joseph, don't be a hero. Come back to me."

The next day David found Fitzwilliam in the library reading the morning paper with Elizabeth resting in the chair next to him as the children squirmed on a blanket in front of the fireplace.

"I've prepared the guest list for my engagement dinner and have the invitations almost ready to post. It will be a party of thirty-six," he chuckled softly. "It's amazing how few friends one really has—and most of these are our family. But I only want to share my joy with those who are dear to me, and I'm afraid that isn't many."

"Well, though a small party, thirty-six is still quite a lot. What day did you choose?'

"Next Friday. We need to return to Charleston on the following Tuesday."

"Friday is good. The christening is this Saturday, so we will have a full week in between. I will let Mrs. Reynolds know, and the ladies can begin the planning for both events this week. We'll leave for Pemberley on Friday. I'm anxious for Elizabeth to see her future home, and I'm sure you wish to show it to Cecilia. Have you two made plans for the wedding and honeymoon yet?"

"We've made tentative plans, but nothing is fixed as of yet."

"I still owe Elizabeth a honeymoon. Ours was interrupted by Father's death and the subsequent problems which followed," Fitzwilliam said, folding the paper as he glanced at his wife. "Elizabeth, you and I need to plan as well. Perhaps we can go to the Caribbean after David's and Cecilia's wedding. That's what I had originally planned. We own a resort villa in the British Virgin Islands," he said, softly smiling.

"The Virgin Islands! I love the sun and the ocean, but what about the children?"

"We can take them and a few servants with us. It's not what I'd hoped we would do a year ago, but things have changed, so we have to change, too."

"Not exactly romantic, but I think we can find a way."

"So it would seem, Mrs. Darcy," he murmured, catching her meaning.

David chuckled. "I think I'll find something else to do in another part of the house, or maybe I'll see if I can find Cecilia." He gave his brother a wink and exited the library, closing the door behind him with a resounding click.

Fitzwilliam rose and locked the door before gathering his wife into his arms.

Chapter Seventy-four

... Welcome to Pemberley, Mrs. Darcy...

The trip to Pemberley proved to be much more of an undertaking than either of the Darcy brothers had anticipated. Traveling with two babies was indeed a chore.

"Fitzwilliam, are you sure you need all of this?" David glanced quizzically at his brother's packed Jag.

"Yes, this and more, and I probably need a bigger car, too. Mrs. Reynolds had the nursery cleaned and made ready, but we still need many things that aren't there, and we're not even taking the half of it." Fitzwilliam grinned. "We're going into Lambton later today to buy the rest of what is needed. It's my plan to move to Pemberley when we come back from our honeymoon."

While readjusting a few boxes, David asked, "How are you going to handle Pemberley, PLC from Derbyshire? Have you thought this through?"

"Of course I have. My intentions are to open an office in Lambton. I'll split my time between Lambton and London. I'm also going to purchase a helicopter for the back and forth trips. That should solve the travel problems. I want to be in Derbyshire most of the year." Grunting as he wedged Elizabeth's needlework bag in between two suitcases, he looked up at his brother. "I want to go home, David—to Pemberley, and I want to *be* at home with my family."

David sighed as he took the car seats a servant had just brought. "I understand, and the helicopter is an excellent idea. So you'll be at Pemberley by autumn then?"

"Yes, that's the plan. I want my children to know the beauty of growing up in the countryside like we did. We'll come to London in the late autumn and winter when they're older for cultural and educational purposes. We'll tour Europe and the Americas, too. However, for Christmas, I intend to be at home, and I want to invite my family and friends to join us." He grinned as he took the first car seat from David to secure in the back of the car.

"Then I take it you'll no longer be pursuing your dream of teaching at university even part-time."

"It's still a part of my dreams, but for now, I've too many responsibilities, and you're not going be here to take up the slack. So no, I guess I won't, but then I'll at least have these two here to teach, and I think I'll rather enjoy that. I've already introduced them to the *Brothers Grimm*."

David shook his head and laughed. "Indeed you have. I guess children are never too young for fairy tales. How about Eton? Are you going to send your son off when the time comes? You know it's been a family tradition for centuries," David asked, handing him another bag for the boot.

"I don't know, but I doubt it. I want to instruct them myself, and Elizabeth is capable of doing much of it, too. So it may be just the two of us with tutors to fill in as needed. Elizabeth is going back to work next year, so I suppose when the time comes, I'll be doing the largest share of the task, or at least overseeing it. It'll all depend on how I can arrange my schedule. In a few years, I plan to hire a governess to begin the elementary phases."

"I'm glad to hear it. Cecilia and I are thinking along the same lines," David said, handing his brother one last small package. "Speaking of future plans, I need to make the preparations to have my dogs, cars, and horses shipped to America. Do you think we can arrange it whilst in Derbyshire? I want it taken care of before I leave for Charleston."

"I don't see why not. I'll have my new estate manager, Jenson Millbrook, attend to the details. But I hate to see that Lamborghini go. It drives like a dream. Won't you consider leaving it?" Fitzwilliam asked, casting a fleeting glance at David's car being loaded by a servant.

"Not on your life! I'm having it, my jag, and the Romeo changed over to the American model. They're going with me."

Fitzwilliam laughed. "You and that car. I'll have to buy one of my own."

"You do that, but put your order in now. It takes a year to have one built."

"Umm...I'll certainly consider it," Fitzwilliam replied.

Turning to survey the cars one more time, he continued. "Georgiana will ride with us, as I think your Merciélago is a bit cramped."

David laughed. "Two's company and three's a crowd, especially in a coupé."

Fitzwilliam returned his laugh. "I'll get the kids and ladies, and we'll see you there."

Once they exited the city, the drive north was peaceful and picturesque. Elizabeth absorbed all that she saw—the rolling hills, the pasture lands, the grazing sheep and cattle, the horses running across open fields, and the beautiful late spring flowers all gave evidence of the beauty of the English countryside.

When they crossed over the stone bridge and followed the long drive that led to Pemberley House, Elizabeth was mesmerized. The Elizabethan manor, built and landscaped in the style of an Italian palazzo, was surrounded by a scenic park with beautiful flowerbeds and fountains, pits and statues. A large lake bordered by Spanish chestnuts and low-growing evergreens covered much of the back of the property. Multitudes of ducks, geese, and graceful swans glided across the smooth blue waters, creating a lovely scene she might have seen in one of her childhood picture books. Her breath caught as she took in the vastness of the estate.

As they entered through the stone gate, Fitzwilliam explained the particulars concerning the land. The park encompassed seventeen acres with a Victorian garden that included a sunken parterre edged in stone, various flowering shrubs, herbs of all kinds, stately trees, and an elaborate rose garden which had been his mother's favorite. With her love for roses, Elizabeth knew it would soon become hers, too. He also told her the garden was enclosed by a medieval deer park with herds of red and fallow deer. There were pasture lands where horses, cows, and sheep grazed. She couldn't wait to see it all.

And off to the left, he directed her attention, was the orangery. The orangery! *That* she was anxious to see as well. Fitzwilliam explained how his grandmother had imported tropical plants, fruit trees, flowering shrubs, orchids, and all manner of exotic plants from all over the world. Holding her breath like a small child entering a fantasyland, she mused. *...And this is to be my home, and my children will play and grow up here. This is really beyond belief!*

"Elizabeth, do you like it?" her husband asked, beaming. "Are you pleased?"

"Are you kidding? I love it," she said with a smile. "It's more beautiful than I could have ever dreamed, and the pictures you showed me do not do it justice. The grounds are so green—like a field of emeralds—and the flowers so bright. It's like a Thomas Kinkade painting. I bet it's beautiful in wintertime, too, when covered in snow."

"Yes, it is." He chuckled. "I'm glad you like it. It's to be our home by autumn. I want our children to roam these woods and hills like David and I did as boys," he said, glancing at his sleeping son and daughter.

When they pulled up to the front entrance with David's car right behind, two servants came to greet them followed by a short, thin, older woman. Fitzwilliam and David stepped out of their cars simultaneously and greeted her in unison, "Mrs. Reynolds!"

"Welcome home, Master Fitzwilliam and Master David," she said as she pulled them into a warm embrace. "It's very good to see you and your ladies." Peeping inside the car, she exclaimed, "Oh, and what do we have here? These must be the darling children Mrs. Anderson told me about," said the housekeeper, taking a few steps to observe the two children yawning as they woke up.

Gesturing to Elizabeth as she exited the car, Fitzwilliam said, "Mrs. Reynolds, I'd like you to meet my wife, Elizabeth." Helping Elizabeth remove the children, he soon turned to display two tiny bundles. "And this is my son, Alexander, and my daughter, Emmaline."

"It's so good to finally meet you, Mrs. Darcy and the lovely children, too." Mrs. Reynolds greeted Elizabeth with an affectionate hug as she peered under the blankets at two little faces looking around in wonder.

"The pleasure is all mine, Mrs. Reynolds," Elizabeth said.

David stepped forward with Cecilia. "Mrs. Reynolds, allow me to introduce my fiancée, Miss Cecilia Lawton of Charleston, South Carolina."

Mrs. Reynolds turned to greet them. "Miss Lawton, it's a pleasure. I'm very glad to see my boy finally settling down, and I know he's happy. It's written all over his face," said the housekeeper with genuine warmth.

"Indeed I am, Dorothy. I'm the luckiest man I know."

"And Miss Georgiana, too!" She greeted the younger woman as she stepped forward. "It's so *good* to have you home—all of you."

"I'm glad to be home, Mrs. Reynolds," Georgiana said, giving the older woman a hug and a kiss.

"Now let's go into the house and get you situated." Mrs. Reynolds gave final orders to the servants concerning the luggage and all the other things to be brought into the house.

Walking down the corridor, Mrs. Reynolds continued. "Mrs. Darcy, I have prepared the nursery as you instructed, and I have two nursemaids in case you need them."

"Thank you, Mrs. Reynolds. We'll settle in, and then Fitzwilliam and I will go into Lambton to buy the personal things we need."

While the servants took their baggage to their rooms, David and Fitzwilliam gave the ladies a tour of the house, which was more massive than any either Cecilia or Elizabeth had ever seen. Fitzwilliam explained that it was partly Elizabethan with 18th and 19th century additions. It contained ninety-four rooms in total, all elaborately decorated in four centuries of period interiors.

After concluding the main floor, Fitzwilliam led them up the staircase to begin the tour of the family rooms. When they reached the picture gallery, Fitzwilliam pointed out the portrait of the original Mr. and Mrs. Fitzwilliam Darcy.

"Look, Elizabeth. That is the man whose life I told you about. Do you notice a resemblance?"

Elizabeth stood before the portraits, transfixed by the images. "Yes, you and David strongly favor him. It's as if he was your father, and the lady is a beautiful woman."

Fitzwilliam chuckled. "Look at her closely. Examine her eyes and hair color. You resemble her. It's evident there's a relation."

"Yes, Elizabeth, there is. Who is she?" Cecilia asked, glancing between the portrait and Elizabeth.

"She was the niece of my ancestral grandfather, John Thomas Bennet, from the late 1700s. I apparently carry her name just as Fitzwilliam carries her husband's."

"Hmm...well, all of the Darcy men are very handsome, especially that one. Who is he?" Cecilia asked.

"That one? That is Edward Darcy and those around him are his brothers. Alexander and his wife and children are to his left with Charles and his family to his right and George with his is next to Charles," David answered.

"That woman looks vaguely familiar," Cecilia said pointing to the portrait next to Edward Darcy, "but I can't place her."

"Hmm," Elizabeth said. "They were all very handsome, and their wives were beautiful."

"Yes, they were." Placing his arm around his wife, Fitzwilliam responded, "Elizabeth, I intend to have your portrait, along with those of all our children, added to the family collection, but let's move along for now. I have more that I want you to see." Guiding her down the corridor, he continued. "Over there are David, Georgiana, and me along with my mother and father." Turning to his brother, he said, "David and Cecilia's portrait and any children they have will be added to this gallery, isn't that right?" Fitzwilliam smiled fondly. David only laughed and nodded in agreement.

Walking a little further, they came the oldest part of the gallery. "This is the other section I wanted you to see." Placing his hand on Elizabeth's shoulder, he pointed to a selection of paintings. "There are the pictures of our Medieval ancestors—Thomas, Richard, George, William, Henry and their wives and children—the ones I told you about when we first discussed our family histories. The rest are a little further down. We'll explore those portraits at another time once you've had a chance to read about them in the library annex."

"I'm looking forward to it. You never did tell me about The Hundred Years' War," Elizabeth said.

"All in good time, my love, all in good time."

Once they finished with the gallery, the brothers took Cecilia and Elizabeth to the music room, the saloon, guest wings, studies, and finally, concluding the tour with the family rooms, they each settled into their own quarters.

When they were unpacked and settled, David and Cecilia took a stroll in the garden while Elizabeth and Fitzwilliam went to do the needed shopping. After lunch, both couples decided to ride out over the estate. David and Cecilia had already left in one direction while Fitzwilliam and Elizabeth prepared to go in another.

Saddling her mount, Elizabeth said, "I never imagined Pemberley being so vast. How much land do you own?"

Chuckling as he checked her cinch, he answered, "*We* own about six thousand acres. Much of it is pastureland and woods. Although it has been a long time since my family made their living from agriculture, we have kept a lot of it for pleasure. Even though we raise and sell cattle, sheep, and horses, it's more of a hobby now. We have about five hundred head of cattle, two hundred head of sheep, and around fifty horses." Glancing over at her while placing the bit in her mare's mouth, he replied, "I've acquired some chickens and a dairy cow for you and the children. I have several hunting hounds and shooting dogs, but I'm afraid there are no Black and Tans in the group." ...*yet*

"If I can find the time, I'm going to play around with the farming aspect. That short time I spent helping your uncle was one of the best times I've had since I lived here as a boy. I find farming rather relaxing." He smiled. "Mr. Tillman, the manager of that aspect of Pemberley, is very old and wishes to retire, so I'll have to find someone else by autumn." Rubbing his stallion's mane, he continued. "I'd like to replant the orchard, and if you would like, you can have a garden and berry patches much as you did at Longbourn. We'll hire some additional help for you, and if you want, you can preserve food, dry herbs, and bake as you did all the years you were growing up at Longbourn. In fact," his lips curled, "I think I would rather like it if you did. You have a lot of wonderful memories from those years, and I would like for our children to have memories like that, too."

"I'd love that very much. It would remind me of home." She smiled.

Mounting their horses, they headed out across the field in a full run.

Pulling his mount in the direction of a wooded copse, he shouted, "Do you think you can jump that fence?"

"If the horse can, I can."

"I assure you the horse can." He kicked his charger in the side with Elizabeth following, and they easily jumped over the dry-stone wall, heading out into the open pasture.

When they came to where he intended, he slowed, continuing on into the heart of the cove at a gentle gait. Pointing in the direction of an opened area, he said, "See there. It's Pemberley's cove. There's a waterfall and stream coming down from the hills, forming that natural pool. David and I spent many hours here swimming and playing. The stream cuts across the estate, flowing into one of the lakes. This is what I was telling you about when we toured the one at Longbourn."

"Yes, it's very similar to the cove at Longbourn, and every bit as beautiful. We should have a picnic here someday, just the two of us. We never did go skinny dipping, you know," she said with a sly smile.

The thought of her naked here in his special place was too much. Watching her eye him closely, he knew she was very much aware of his state.

"It doesn't take much, does it, Fitzwilliam?" she asked, cocking one brow.

"No, it doesn't," he replied. With a soft sigh, he dismounted and tied his horse to a nearby low branch. Then he reached up to help her down before he tied her horse as well.

"I hadn't exactly planned this, but now that I think about it, I believe we will become well acquainted with the area," he said, unfolding a blanket he had brought with him and spreading it out on the thick moss-covered ground. When the blanket was in place, he reached for her and began to unbutton her blouse while she unbuttoned his shirt. With their clothes discarded, he took her hand and gently guided her to sit down, folding her into his arms.

"You don't know how often I have dreamt of you—of us—in this very place," he murmured.

Her emerald eyes flashed. "Take me," she said. "Fitzwilliam, if you want me, take me."

Gathering her even closer, he whispered with tenderness, "I love you, Liz." Closing his eyes, he bent down and touched his mouth to hers in an embrace that was meant to be warm and loving. But, as soon as their lips touched, his restraint broke as she kissed him back with an ardent desire that instantly set him ablaze.

With the sound of the crashing falls and the birds calling in the distances, he made passionate love to his wife in the wilds of the outdoors. When their breathing returned to normal, he rolled over, taking her with him, holding her close to his chest. They lay there perfectly satisfied, having done what he had wanted to do since the first time he had seen her in the cove at Longbourn.

"Welcome to Pemberley, Mrs. Darcy," he said with a contented smile.

Reaching over to brush a damp curl out of his eyes, she caressed his face. "It's a pleasure to be here, Mr. Darcy."

After lying in one another's arms a little longer, they finally dressed to return. A chill had settled in and the temperature had dropped since they'd left the house, but neither of them felt cold.

"Do you think we've been missed?" Elizabeth asked.

"I'm afraid so. We should be there by now for tea, but frankly, darling, I don't care. This means more to me than proper protocol. Tea can wait!"

"Do you think David and Cecilia will suspect something?" she asked as she picked bits of moss and debris from their hair.

"So what if they do? We're married, and I plan many more such encounters in several of my childhood haunts. I've wanted to do this since that day you showed me the cove at Longbourn." He cut his eyes across at her with a bemused smile. "If you hadn't been a virgin, well, who knows what might have happened back then. Besides," he said, giving her a mischievous grin, "don't be surprised if David and Cecilia are late themselves."

Catching his meaning, she smiled.

"Oh!"

As they were about to mount their horses, she turned and asked, "Fitzwilliam, did you really want to do this before we were married? It was cold then, or have you forgotten?"

"Yes, it was cold, but I distinctly remember starting a blazing fire in the cabin. We almost went too far. It took all the willpower I had not to take you right then and there," he laughed, "for I almost thought you might've let me."

"Well, you never tried, so we'll never know." She grinned.

"No, I suppose not."

He smiled, looking at her in amusement. Even though he knew things might have turned out differently had he pushed it, he wouldn't have changed a thing, even if he could.

Chapter Seventy-five

… Good night, Mum and Dad…

Returning from Pemberley Chapel, Fitzwilliam glanced back at his two sleeping children. He couldn't have been more pleased with the morning's event. Alex and Emily's christening service had been beautiful and touching. The local parish had decorated the church in pink, white, and pale blue carnations mingled with baby's breath. Candles were lit throughout the church, completing the atmosphere, and the children had been surprisingly cooperative. They hadn't cried once, not even when the vicar sprinkled them with rose water. Yes, it had been beautiful. He glanced over at his wife and smiled as the car pulled around the manor to the back entrance. *…We've come a long way, Elizabeth, a long way indeed. Perhaps in a couple of years we can do this all over again.*

Later in the afternoon, David and Fitzwilliam relaxed in the study while Georgiana visited a neighbor and Cecilia and Elizabeth played with the children in the drawing room. As they sat together, Fitzwilliam brought up the subject of the family heirlooms. "I think it's time we entered the library annex and open the safe. Cecilia needs to choose her jewelry, and I want Elizabeth to take what she would like. I also want to get old Fitzwilliam's original journals. I'm curious about a great many things concerning him."

"Sounds good to me. Cecilia has expressed an interest in viewing that room, and I wouldn't mind seeing it again myself. However, I have something I want to discuss with you before we go there. If you recall, the last Christmas Mother was alive, you, Father, and I went to Garrard's to select a ring for Mum. Do you remember?"

"Yes, I do." Fitzwilliam laughed. "Because we couldn't agree, Dad ordered two rings to be made—one from each of us. I chose a tsavorite garnet with a sapphire cluster set in gold and you chose a sapphire with diamonds set in platinum. Father bought her the ruby they had on display. It cost him over £200,000, as I recall. He said someday the sapphire should be given to your wife, and the tsavorite was to be given to mine."

"That's right. The rings were replicas of the Princess of Wales' engagement ring," David said with a smile. "Today, I want to claim the sapphire ring for Cecilia. It will go perfectly with what I've already bought her."

"Yes, it will indeed. Let's go and get the ladies. I think they will be pleased."

Entering the drawing room, David found Cecilia and Elizabeth and escorted them to the library after the children had been given to the care of their nannies. Fitzwilliam removed a book and took a key from his pocket. He unlocked the door and swung the bookcase open to reveal a hidden room. Turning on the lights, they entered the library annex, a room lined from wall to wall and floor to ceiling with bookcases filled with family histories and shelves still available for future volumes.

When they stepped into the room, Cecilia gazed at the treasures revealed within. The room was welcoming, simply furnished and immaculately clean. Walking around, she brushed her fingers over the leather bound volumes. They were ancient, yet perfectly preserved with nameplates below to indicate the owner and dates. Every journal from five hundred and fifty years ago to the present was neatly filed, with a place reserved for Fitzwilliam's when his time came.

M.K. Baxley

Fitzwilliam moved to a different bookshelf and removed yet another book where a second key fit securely into a lock. The door swung open and an old combination safe was revealed. Turning the lock, he opened the safe and pulled three large boxes and a slim leather volume from its confines, handing them to David.

"Set them on that table and open the appraisal registry. You'll need to sign for the pieces you take," Fitzwilliam said, motioning towards the round table in the center of the room. "Oh and here, David, these are Mother's rings." Fitzwilliam handed three black velvet cases to his brother. "Cecilia, one of those is for you. David will show you which one."

Cecilia wrinkled her brow as David set two aside and held out one marked with his name. She took it from him and opened the box. Her breath caught. Inside was a brilliant oval sapphire with a circlet of diamonds set in platinum mounted upon a diamond channel set band.

"David, it's gorgeous, but…"

"It was my mother's," he beamed, "and now it's yours. The sapphire is fourteen carats with sixteen small diamonds. The other two are identical to it and belong to Elizabeth. I'll tell you the story behind the rings later. This ring matches the sapphires I bought you. You can wear them to our next reenactment ball," he said with a broad smile.

Cecilia lifted the ring from the soft velvet and held it up to the light. "I've never seen anything more beautiful. I will treasure it always." She reached forward and gave him a hug.

Fitzwilliam picked up the boxes with his name inscribed and opened them for Elizabeth. Her eyes widened and went directly to the green garnet. With trepidation, she reverently took the ring from the case. Green and blue shards of light sparkled and danced about the room. It was like Cecilia's except it was a tsavorite surrounded by sapphires mounted upon a diamond channel set gold band. "Fitzwilliam," she breathed out, "it's magnificent. You picked this out when you were…how old?"

"Fourteen. I fell in love with the design when I first saw the ruby version, and knew the tsavorite with diamonds and sapphires would be stunning. Since none of us could agree upon the stone selections, Father bought the ruby, which was what he wanted all along, and had the other two made for us to give to Mum. I had no idea back then, but it was as if I had selected it for you. The green matches your eyes, and the blue complements your coloring. I want you to wear it to our next ball. I'll have a matching tsavorite and sapphire ensemble crafted for you. The ruby is yours also. It matches the ruby set I bought you for the Middleton Ball. You can alternate the rings."

"Oh, Fitzwilliam!" She placed the garnet back in its case and then removed the ruby. "These are the most beautiful rings I have ever seen. I can only say thank you." She reached up to give him a hug and whispered in his ear, "I'll properly thank you tonight. I love you."

He pulled back and gave her a mischievous grin. "I'll be sure and hold you to it, Mrs. Darcy. Now," he said, turning to his brother, "let's explore the rest of the jewels."

David and Fitzwilliam went about arranging the chests chronologically. The boxes, like the bookshelves, were labeled. From each generation of the Mistresses of Pemberley, there was a collection of jewelry. The brothers began opening each box. There were diamonds of every color, rubies, emeralds, sapphires, garnets, blue and gold topaz, pearls, and opals—all of them of exquisite quality the likes of which are rarely seen in a private collection. Most had been custom made.

As the women examined the jewels, Fitzwilliam directed, "Cecilia, you're to choose a set from this collection to add to your own family heirlooms."

"I'm overwhelmed. I've never seen anything like this. David, with everything you've given me, it is simply too much," she said as she turned to her fiancé. "Help me. I don't know what to choose."

David chuckled. "Well, you already have sapphires, so what is your next favorite?"

"I suppose it would be rubies."

"How about this?" he asked, picking up an antique diamond choker with a large oval ruby surrounded by diamonds. "It comes with wedding rings, a bracelet, and earrings to match the necklace. The set dates from the late Regency period. Let me check its value." Picking up the appraisal volume, David thumbed through the pages until he located the rubies. Running his finger down the page, he glanced up and smiled. "It says here that the ruby is thirty-one carats, and there are over a hundred and ten carats in total diamond weight. It and all that goes with it, is valued at £1,000,000. It's quite lovely, actually."

"Yes, it is *lovely*, but Elizabeth wouldn't you want them?" she asked, turning to her friend.

Elizabeth's eyes widened. With a faint smile, she replied, "No, Celia, you take them. I already own a ruby set that Fitzwilliam bought me a few weeks ago, and with the ruby ring, my set is more than complete, so you take those." Elizabeth picked up a deep red garnet set, looking at it closely. Placing it back, she took a black and white diamond necklace with a large oval white diamond in a circlet of black diamonds and held them to the light. "I'll take these." She nodded. "They're more modern and suit my taste very well. There is nothing more elegant than black and white," she said placing the bracelet around her wrist.

"Well, if you prefer the black diamonds, then I'll take the rubies," Cecilia said, turning to David's brother. "Thank you so much, Fitzwilliam."

"Don't thank me. These are David's as part of a long held family tradition. Elizabeth has access to all that's here, but she has the right to give what she has chosen to whichever of her children she wishes. Mother gave a sapphire set to Georgiana before she died. They're in a separate box, and Georgiana will also get to choose from among these when she marries."

"They are all very lovely," Cecilia said, placing the jewels she'd chosen in David's hand.

"David, if you will sign the registry stating that you've taken the rubies and the sapphire ring, it'll be all taken care of," Fitzwilliam said.

While David signed, Cecilia turned to the volumes on the shelf. "If you don't mind, I'd like to look at these journals. The history lover in me can't resist."

"Be my guest." Fitzwilliam smiled while returning the boxes and the appraisal book to the safe.

As Cecilia perused the volumes, she settled upon a tome from the antebellum period which particularly caught her interest. Wondering what the Darcys had experienced in a period of history so pivotal to that of her own, she pulled it from the shelf and thumbed through the contents while the brothers talked. Reading a passage from 1847, something very curious leapt forth from the page. "David, look at this," she said, handing the book to him.

He took the book from her hand and read the indicated segment. "Yes, what of it? It's an account of Edward Jamison Darcy's wedding to an American," he said, handing it back with a creased brow.

"She's not just *any* American. She's Jacynthia Elizabeth Read, the eldest daughter of John W. Read of George Town, South Carolina and Martha Lawton Read of Carlton House. I thought I recognized that picture in the gallery. It was her—the lost Lawton."

"How do you know that? It doesn't state who her parents were."

"No, it doesn't, but I know it just the same. She is the lost daughter of Martha Lawton Read, the only sister of my great grandfather, five generations back. There was a scandal involving her. She was considered a disgrace by our family. Her story is recorded in our family annals. It's not recorded who she ran away with, but now I have discovered the truth."

"Tell us about it," Fitzwilliam said as they all took seats.

As they all settled in to hear the story, Cecilia began. "Jacynthia's mother, Martha Lawton, was born in 1800 and was the only daughter of Francis Lawton of Carlton House. She married into the Read family of George Town in 1816 and had four sons and three daughters. Jacynthia, the eldest of their three daughters, was born in 1828. She was considered the most beautiful belle in Charleston the year of her coming out in 1845. I recall hearing many stories of her raven hair and deep ocean-blue eyes. She was so sought after that her father used her as a bargaining chip. You see, John wanted, or rather needed, a merger with the Weston family of Savannah, Georgia, and so, when Jacynthia was eighteen, she became engaged to Benton Weston. But legend has it that she fell in love with a young Englishman who came to Charleston to conduct business on behalf of his father." Cecilia cut her eyes across at David.

"There was a terrible fight at the St. Cecilia Ball between Weston and the Englishman, and Weston challenged him to a duel. Witnesses said that while they were pacing Weston turned and shot the Englishman in the back, and when he did, the Englishman's brothers pivoted sharply and shot Weston dead. The Englishman lived and when he recovered and was able to travel, Jacynthia eloped with him on a ship bound for Liverpool. She was never heard from again, and her name was never spoken among any of the Reads or Lawtons after that."

"Cecilia, that's terrible. I realize women had no rights back then, but to shun her, well, I think it's awful. They never even went to the trouble of finding her, did they?"

"Elizabeth, you have to understand how things were back then. Charlestonians were very strict about their code of honor, and Jacynth—that's what she was called— had disgraced her family. Feelings ran so deep that her father removed her portraits from the family galley and destroyed all of them, save one, which her mother hid at Carlton House. My father discovered it in the attic along with a few diaries when he became the proprietor. He had the portrait restored to its rightful place of honor. The diaries are published and are in my family library." Cecilia shrugged. "Lizzy, it's just the way things were."

"Yes, I know." Elizabeth shook her head. "It also happened in my family, but it's still not right."

"Well, it didn't matter what was right or wrong. It was simply the way it was." Cecilia folded her hands in her lap and glanced between David and Fitzwilliam. "But I find it ironic that a Darcy was involved. As I recall from your gallery, Edward was a very handsome man. You Darcy men certainly have a way with poor little ole Southern women."

David burst out laughing. "Poor little ole Southern women indeed! Edward nearly lost his life. I would say it's more the other way around. Poor Darcy men who become lost in a pretty belle's smile."

"Or the victim of Cupid's arrow," Elizabeth teased, squeezing her husband's thigh.

Fitzwilliam grasped his wife's hand and laced his fingers with hers. "Cute, Elizabeth, cute." He grinned, turning to David. "So, Elizabeth's not the only one with ties into our family. This is quite a coincidence, isn't it? None of it is recorded in any of our journals, unless they're in Edward's. Stephen Darcy has those. He's descended from that line. All I know is that their love was considered one of the great loves of our family. In fact, Jacynthia is a treasured family name on that branch of the family tree."

"That's true. Stephen's sister is named Jacynthia Elizabeth," David responded. "She's named for her two ancestral grandmothers."

"Well," Cecilia said, "there is one more interesting aspect. If I remember correctly, there was a John Nathaniel Bennet involved, too. He had been Benton Weston's second in the duel. Bennet was in Charleston attending the Citadel and was secretly courting Jacynthia's younger sister, Molly Dove, known to us as Cousin Dovie. When her father found out, it was a little bit of a scandal, too, since she was only fifteen. But it was short lived, and they were later married and settled in Kentucky. That branch of the family operates one of the largest distilleries in America, so you see, my family is tied to Elizabeth's, too."

Fitzwilliam wrinkled his brow. "Elizabeth, are they the ones you told me about from Fugie?"

"Yes, the very ones. Nat was John Newton's son and John Bennet's grandson. His branch of the family is the one that ran the illegal moonshine through the Southeast during the prohibition years."

Cecilia grinned and turned to David with a wink. "That makes us all related in one fashion or another, and all with an affinity to live life on the wild side."

"Wild side indeed! I'm simply glad the circle has come 'round to us. It's now complete," David said, taking Cecilia's hand in his as he turned to his brother. "Fitzwilliam, may Cecilia and I have access to this library whilst we're here? I'd like to explore our history a little more, especially that of the Industrial Revolution and the 19th century." He glanced at Cecilia. "History has suddenly become an interest of mine. I suppose you could say I'd like to know where I've come from so I can know where I'm going."

"David, you don't have to ask. You know that. Here," Fitzwilliam reached into his pocket, "take the key and come whenever you wish. I'm going to take these original journals to our room where Elizabeth and I can study them. Take whatever you like, but be sure to sign for them so I know where they are."

"Thanks. We'll take good care of everything."

Fitzwilliam and Elizabeth left with their set of journals while David and Cecilia lingered.

Time passed quickly, and Friday was upon them before they knew it. As the guests began to arrive for the dinner party, Elizabeth and Georgiana surveyed their work.

"Elizabeth, it looks beautiful. The fresh cut flowers were just the right touch for the china, and look how the crystal reflects the color of the peonies! My mother would be so pleased."

"The decorations are beautiful, aren't they? I thought the peonies would be a nice touch since they match the china pattern and the elegant lace of the tablecloth. I'm going to love the orangery. I can have fresh cut flowers all year round."

Georgiana laughed. "Yes, you will, and I'm glad to see it finally being put to use."

While they admired their work, Mrs. Reynolds approached. "Mrs. Darcy, the first of the guests has arrived."

"Thank you, Dorothy," Elizabeth said as she turned to her sister-in-law. "Come, Georgiana. Since I am meeting many of them for the first time, I need you with me."

As the guests arrived, Georgiana and her brothers greeted each one and made the introductions to Elizabeth and Cecilia. They all mingled in the drawing room to talk and become acquainted until they were called to dinner. When everyone had found their seats, Fitzwilliam rose to begin the dinner with a toast to the guests of honor.

"Ladies and gentlemen, may I have your attention. As we are all gathered together here tonight, I wish to announce the engagement of my brother, David Jamison, to Miss Cecilia Lawton of Charleston, South Carolina. May they find as much happiness in the married state as my wife and I have found," he said, tipping his head to David. "God bless you, Brother." He lifted his glass. "To David and Cecilia."

Everyone did likewise repeating the toast in unison. After dinner, the gentlemen separated from the ladies for brandy and cigars while the ladies congregated around Cecilia, taking the time to become genuinely acquainted with the woman who had captured the heart of the man they all thought would never marry.

Harvey Darcy had been watching his nephews from the distance with a contented smile. He couldn't help from thinking how much they both had grown and come into their own over the past few years, especially David. He chuckled softly as he saw his nephews approaching.

"Pleasant evening, isn't it?" Fitzwilliam said as he lit his cigar.

"Umm, yes, indeed it is," Harvey answered before turning to David. "Let me congratulate you on finally finding a suitable woman whom I believe *you* are truly worthy of."

"I caught that, Uncle," David said, taking a puff of his cigar, "but yes, you are right. She is the best thing that has ever happened to me."

"Boys, you've handled your responsibilities well and have managed to have time for a life, too. You are to be congratulated. I only wished my brother could be here to see it."

"I'd like to think he, and Mother, too, can see us. For some strange reason, I've never felt alone. I've felt their presence as if they are with me. I think they *are* proud of us," Fitzwilliam said, turning to David with a warm smile.

"I'm very proud of the both of you, too," Harvey said. "You've done your duty, been true to yourselves, and kept the family honor. That's all any father could ask, and I knew my brother well enough to know it's all he would ask. Wherever he is tonight, he *is* proud of you."

At about that moment there was a rustling sound in the trees as a warm and gentle breeze swept by. Fitzwilliam glanced up into the evening sky, catching a glimpse of two white doves fluttering away from the lone Spanish oak that towered over the courtyard. He shook his head and smiled. "Good night, Mum and Dad."

Finishing their cigars, they walked inside to join the others.

Chapter Seventy-six

...a white dove perched on a low hanging branch with a sprig of pink almond in its beak...

Cecilia walked into her bedroom and closed the door as she leaned back against it. The wedding announcement was posted, the church had been decorated, and preparations were underway for the reception in the Lawton Hotel Dining Hall. Mr. Lee of the King Street Tailor Shop and Ella Sinclair, her personal seamstress, were to be commended for creating two well stitched sets of wedding clothes in record time. With all of the planning behind her, she released a weary breath. How she and David had managed to get through the last two weeks with some semblance of sanity still left was beyond her.

The British press had swarmed through Charleston like a cloud of bees, and at first, Cecilia questioned if they would ever be free from the media's scrutiny, but of course, she knew ultimately they would.

Pushing away from the door, she walked to her closet and rummaged through her wardrobe, choosing a strapless sundress for the evening. Satisfied, she crossed the room to her vanity and took a seat and stared at her reflection as she propped her head in the palms of her hands. Tomorrow would be her wedding day, the happiest day in her life. She would become Mrs. David Darcy. A giggle escaped her throat.

Casting a glance at her wedding gown hanging on the dress-form, Cecilia smiled. Ella had created the most beautiful dress she had ever seen—not ornate, but a simple, elegant, halter style, gently flaring from the waist and continuing to the floor with a slight train.

Reaching over, she picked up her white bonnet and brushed her fingers over the mixture of various shades of blue silk flowers. It had once been her grandmother's, but Ella's alterations had made it Cecilia's own. Hearing soft footsteps alerting her to someone's presence, Cecilia turned and smiled as she rose to open the door just as she heard the knock.

"Lizzy! You caught me."

Walking into the room, Elizabeth beamed. "You look beautiful. Happiness becomes you, and your dress and bonnet are gorgeous—just like you. Tana showed me the bouquet she designed. She did a beautiful job. The blue and white roses coupled with baby's breath blends so well with your dress and bonnet."

"Yes, it's lovely and... I'm...oh, Lizzy, I'm so happy." Cecilia smiled, tears filling her eyes.

Elizabeth closed the few steps between them and embraced her childhood friend. "No one deserves happiness more than you do, Celia. Jane and I have always said so." Elizabeth spoke softly, "We knew it would take a very special man to capture your heart. David is very fortunate, and according to my husband, he knows it."

"He and I are both fortunate, not only to have found each other but to have had the good sense to put our pride aside and forgive each other. We're so proud and stubborn, but we're equally determined to make a happy home. It's going to be one interesting marriage as we learn how to become one."

"Indeed it is, and when children come along, it will be even more interesting." Elizabeth grinned. "I can't wait to see the two of you with children. They will be spirited and beautiful."

"Well, that may not be too long in coming. We've decided not to wait. I came off the pill when we got back together," Cecilia sheepishly replied. "I always envied the happiness I saw in your family when we were growing up, so don't be surprised if I have several children. You have no idea how lonely it was being an only child."

Elizabeth's eyes widened. "Celia, I had no idea you felt that way. I always thought you looked upon children as a duty to your family lineage. How does David feel about all of this?"

"You might be surprised, but he doesn't care one way or the other. Of course he *wants* children, but he says it's up to me to decide how large our family becomes. As to how I feel about children—well, that changed when I fell in love. I never wanted children at all. Oh, I knew I needed to have them, but as far as really desiring them, I didn't... not until David."

Giving her friend another squeeze, Elizabeth said, "I'm so proud of you both. Now, come along. Jane, Kat, and Mary Beth are waiting in the sitting room. Amanda, Georgiana, and Rhonda are there, too. Oh, and I have something to tell you." Elizabeth's eyes sparkled. "Amanda and William recently became engaged, so there'll be another wedding soon. She's three months pregnant, but don't say anything unless she mentions it. It's supposed to be a secret." Elizabeth grinned.

Cecilia's hand flew to her mouth. "Wonderful! I really like Mandy, and she and William are so good together. I hope we can all be close. I know it would make David happy. He holds a tight bond with his cousins. And don't worry. I won't breathe a word!"

"I'm certain we'll all be as close as the brothers and cousins are. Now come, let's go. They're waiting."

Elizabeth took Cecilia's hand and the two walked into the sitting room where refreshments and friends awaited them. Settling in for a long evening of conversation and fun, the girls sat cross-legged in a circle around a Japanese style table set with a buffet of finger foods and wine.

Daniel Russell sat at the bar flanked on his left by Harvey Darcy, a man with whom he was rapidly forming a fast friendship, and on his right, was another man he was coming to admire—David's brother, Fitzwilliam Darcy. Past Fitzwilliam were the younger Darcy cousins and Richard Winthrop, and on the other side of Harvey sat Asa Smith and Solomon Abercrombie, both eagerly excited to be engaged in conversation with anyone who shared their love for horses or the hunt. Harvey appeared to share both. Daniel chuckled as he sipped his whiskey and silently listened.

"Say, Darcy, we are both pleased as a plump tick on a dog to have your nephew joinin' our society. I'm lookin' forward to viewin' that Arabian stallion of his," said Abercrombie. "I'm hopin' to convince him to join me in breedin' race horses. That bloodline of his will be a gold mine at the American track."

"And I am most anxious to see that English Setter and those pointers of his. I plan to have him down to Leafy Oak this fall for grouse and dove huntin'. I wanna see his dogs in action. Say, Darcy, why don't you join us? We've got some mighty fine huntin' here."

Harvey smiled. "I don't mind if I do, Smith. I'll see if my sons, William and Benson would like to come along, and perhaps my other nephew, Fitzwilliam and his cousin Richard, will want to participate. They love to shoot, too. Perhaps all of us can join you—where did you say?"

"Leafy Oak, my plantation estate down in Jasper County. We have some of the best bird huntin' around. Hell, come for two weeks, and we'll hunt duck, geese, and wild turkey, too." Smith let out a belly laugh.

Extending his hand, Harvey replied, "I'm looking forward to it. Susan, Elizabeth, and Amanda can visit with Cecilia, and we'll make a time of it." Turning to Daniel, he asked, "How about you, Russell, do you shoot?"

"I wouldn't miss it. Count me in, Asa." Daniel lifted his drink in acknowledgment. It had been years since he'd been hunting, and now with Cecilia about to be married, he intended to settle into retirement, doing the things he'd once enjoyed. He hadn't told her yet, but as soon as Darcy had a firm understanding of the business, Daniel intended to retire to a life of leisure, splitting his time between his estate in Beaufort County and his townhouse in Charleston. Since the death of his wife, Ellen, he'd spent very little time at Whispering Winds, but now, he could relax and go home. He smiled. ...*I deserve a rest, James, yes, a rest.*

Turning to his right, he caught Fitzwilliam nervously glancing from his watch to the lounge entrance. "What's the matter, Darcy, worried about your brother?" Daniel chuckled.

"Not worried—just wondering what's taking him so long. I think I'll go and check to see if he needs anything," Fitzwilliam said, excusing himself.

"You go and do that," Daniel said, amused. "It's not every day a man gets married. His insides are probably tied up in knots."

Fitzwilliam looked back with a laugh as he left the lounge.

David paced the bedroom of his penthouse suite, glancing between his image in the floor-length mirror and the picture window. Watson was in the dressing room ironing his shirt and making his morning dress ready for tomorrow. David had never been nervous about anything, but then, he'd never married before, either. He walked over to the window and looked out, gazing down at the assembled press below. ...*Damn it... it's my wedding. Can't they leave me alone? No, I know better than to have even hoped it. They'll be at the church tomorrow, too. I'm glad I only have to do this once. I'm beginning to think we should have eloped.*

"David?"

"Fitzwilliam!" David exclaimed, turning to face his brother. "I'm sorry. I didn't hear you come in. How long have you been there?"

"Long enough to see that you're a nervous wreck. What's wrong?"

"Come." David motioned for his brother to join him at the window. "It's been one bloody hell of a week. The London tabloid press is here in force, stalking our every move. Cecilia and I have had very little privacy. They've followed me everywhere, to the tailor shop, to dinner. Everywhere we go the press is there."

"So? Did you honestly think they wouldn't?"

"No, I knew they'd come. But what I didn't expect was the nasty stories printed about us." He frowned. "The latest front cover of the *Sun Sentinel* says I've walked away from my family. You don't think I've abandoned you, do you?"

Fitzwilliam clapped his brother's shoulder. "Do you even have to ask? No, David, I don't, but you know how they are. Both of us have gone against the status quo and this is part of the price we pay. Because we are Darcys, we will always be scrutinized. It can't be helped, but this chapter will close when the next story comes along."

David momentarily closed his eyes and released an exasperated sigh. Fitzwilliam had a way of calming him when he was tightly wound. He opened his eyes and saw the reassuring look from his brother.

David smiled and relaxed. "I guess it's nothing compared to the hell they put you through a year ago, is it?"

"No, and it will pass. No one bats an eyelash at Elizabeth or me now. They've moved on to *you* and Cecilia. That's just how they are. Tomorrow you'll be yesterday's news," Fitzwilliam teased. "Here, let me get you a brandy. Let's sit and talk before going down to join the others."

Fitzwilliam poured two glasses, inquiring of Watson if he'd like to join them.

"No, sir, if you don't mind, there's a certain lady waiting for me at the bar," Watson said with a wry grin.

David lit up. "Watson, are you seeing that redhead you met last month?"

"Ah, no, sir. It's the brunette—Lindsey. She works the front desk."

David's smile broadened. "Playing the field, eh?"

"Well, you know, sir, a gentleman gets around. If you'll excuse me, your clothes are ready, and if you don't mind, I'll be on my way. I don't want to keep the lady waiting." Watson winked, strutting towards the door.

David flashed a smile. "A true gentleman's gentleman."

Fitzwilliam laughed. "Off you go, Watson. We'll see you in the lounge."

Watson dipped his head and grabbed his coat, slinging it over his shoulder as he left.

Once they were alone, the brothers pulled up chairs, settling around the table in the sitting room, sipping their drinks.

"So, David, tell me what you have planned for a honeymoon. I don't think you'd decided the last time we talked."

"No, I hadn't," David laughed, "but since you are taking the house in Tortola, I'm going to take our home in Greece. We'll be in short walking distance to the village, and we'll have the beachfront home for the month. It'll give us much needed time to relax and forget about everything—especially the press."

"I hear you, Brother, and that sounds good to me. You two need the time. Cecilia told Elizabeth you're overseeing plans to renovate her estate home."

"Yes, we're converting the upstairs library back to its former purpose. It'll still be a library, but it will be set up as a schoolroom and children's library. Cecilia also wants the nursery to be converted into a combination nursery/playroom with a common room and servants' quarters like it once was. I'll be doing that, too."

"So, are you planning to begin a family soon?"

"Whatever she wants, it doesn't matter to me." He shrugged. "I never cared much for children, but with her, that's all changed. We'll have as many as she wants," David said with a grin. "The number doesn't really matter. She wants sons, but I would like a little girl to spoil."

"You cheeky devil. Come on. Let's finish our drinks and go downstairs. Your guests are waiting. Uncle Harvey has been entertaining two very interesting gentlemen—a Mr. Abercrombie and a Mr. Smith. They have a shooting party planned for us in the autumn. It seems you've interested them both in that horse the Saudi King gave you, and of course, your shooting dogs." Fitzwilliam downed his drink while David groaned.

The next morning dawned bright and beautiful. A streak of early morning light shone through the crack in the drapes, waking Cecilia. Rushing to the window, she threw back the curtains and lifted the sash, breathing deeply the crisp spring air. She whispered, "This is my wedding day... my last day as Cecilia Lawton of Carlton. This afternoon I'll be Cecilia Darcy of... Carlton!"

She turned and fell back in the oversized chair by the window and smiled. Sandy would be here soon with Elizabeth and Jane to help her prepare. She felt overwhelmed and very thankful it was David she'd meet at the church this morning and not Cameron. As soon as she was ready, they would be on their way to the church.

As he stood inside the vestibule waiting for Cecilia, Daniel Russell sighed. He'd barely made it through the crowded press, and Cecilia and the Darcys had had to have a special escort in order to make it through the paparazzi mob. He shook his head to clear the image of the pandemonium outside and focus on the events inside. The fruit of his efforts was about to be realized.

Leaning against the large glass wall, he mused. Years ago he'd made a promise to an old friend. *....James, this is the day—the day for us to celebrate, the culmination of our friendship. Cecilia is marrying today, and you would be proud of her if you could see her. You would like Darcy. He's a man after your own heart, and he will take exceedingly good care of our Celia. ...Yes...I can promise you that.*

Looking over the small church sanctuary filled to capacity with David's English relatives, the Bennetts from Longbourn, the Chaplins from St Helena and Carlton, and Cecilia's friends, Daniel nodded with a gentle smile. They were all here and waiting. Looking a little closer, he observed David standing next to his brother. Fitzwilliam had to gently brace his arm twice as they stood waiting at the front. It seemed, one would say, that young Darcy was nervous from the way he kept glancing over his shoulder and fidgeting. Again Daniel smiled and shook his head. As his mind wandered, his thoughts were interrupted by the rushing footsteps of someone approaching. He turned to catch the sight of his goddaughter.

"Daniel?" Cecilia asked, "Are you all right? It's time."

"Celia, I've never been better, and you, my dear, have never *looked* lovelier. Let's go. Darcy looks fit to be tied."

Cecilia smiled and drew in a deep breath. "Yes, let's go. I'm as nervous as a long tailed cat in a room full of rocking chairs. I can only imagine what David is feeling." She slipped her hand in the crook of Daniel's arm. As they entered the sanctuary, the Wedding March began.

Glancing down at his goddaughter, Daniel's heart warmed. Cecilia looked absolutely beautiful in her mixture of blue and white. Looking towards the front, he thought what a striking contrast she was to David dressed in black and grey with a single white blue-tipped rose in his lapel.

Was a grown man supposed to cry? No, he thought, and yet he wanted to. This was the little girl he and James had taught to ride when she was four, the little girl who threw her arms around his neck when he and Ellen came to visit. The young lady who had cried on his shoulder the day her father died, and now the young woman he was giving to an English gentleman whom he'd slyly picked for her three years ago. His only regret was that James was not here to walk her down the aisle himself, but then, just as that thought entered his consciousness, Daniel noticed a single white dove outside the sanctuary window. It sat perched on a low hanging branch with a sprig of pink flowering almond in its beak as it gazed in the windowpane. Daniel smiled and tipped his head in recognition. The bird nodded as if to smile and then dropped the sprig and took flight. Daniel turned and glanced at the lovely bride by his side and softly chuckled to himself.

Arriving at the altar, Daniel released Cecilia to her bridegroom, and the wedding ceremony proceeded. When the vows were spoken and the bishop pronounced them man and wife, no one could doubt their happiness, for the glow on their faces said it all. When David kissed Cecilia, Daniel silently said a prayer of thanksgiving. His duty to her was complete. A promise made… a promise kept.

Chapter Seventy-seven

...If I make it home, I'm going to marry her...

As the new Mr. and Mrs. Darcy stepped out into the bright sunshine under showers of birdseed and well wishers' cheers, the paparazzi pressed in, snapping pictures. Pushing their way through the crowd, David and Cecilia made it to the limo waiting to take them to the reception. They would spend an hour or two there before heading off to the airport for an undisclosed honeymoon destination. Georgiana smiled as she stood and waved goodbye—her heart swelling with joy. Both of her brothers were now married.

As she watched David and her new sister drive away, Georgiana's mind again drifted to a young Marine somewhere in the world, wondering where he was and what he was doing at that exact moment. Reaching into her purse, she caressed his bundle of letters she always kept close. As long as they were with her, so was he.

Suddenly she felt an urgency to pray as if he were in danger. Quickly she stopped and lifted him up in prayer. She wondered if that was God speaking to her as this was not the first time this strange phenomenon had occurred, and regardless of the time or place, whenever the strange feeling hit, she would pray. Then, just as suddenly as it had come, the feeling was gone. She shrugged and cleared her mind.

"Georgiana. Georgiana!"

"Benson!" she turned to see her cousin's smiling face.

"Sorry to have frightened you. You seemed lost in thought."

"Oh, it's nothing. Just daydreaming, I suppose."

"Shall I walk you to the car, or would you like to walk back to the hotel since it's such a beautiful day?"

"Well, since you asked, I think I'd rather walk. It's not too far, and you're right. It is a lovely day," she said with a smile. "What did you think of the wedding?"

Benson laughed, placing Georgiana's hand on the crook of his arm. "I'm still in shock. I never thought he'd settle down, but I must admit, he couldn't have picked a woman more suited to him." Benson sighed. "David is married. Fitzwilliam is married. William is getting married. That just leaves me and you, Georgie." As they walked down the steps of the church, he told his father that he and Georgiana would walk to the reception.

"Well, what about you and Cynthia? She's a nice girl and very pretty, too. And I dare say, I think she might like you." Georgiana squeezed his arm.

"Yes, I know she does, but I don't know," Benson said, as they leisurely walked side-by-side down Church Street. "I've never had David's attitude about marriage, but I can't say I'm eager for a ring on my finger, either. As far as Cynthia goes, well... she's let me know in no uncertain terms that she *is* the marrying kind and that I needn't expect her to live anywhere in between."

"Umm... Benson, how did you feel about that?" Georgiana and Cynthia had been friends for years, and she knew very well how Cynthia felt about marriage and sex. She also knew that Cynthia cared deeply for her cousin.

He shook his head. "I'm not ready for marriage, and yet, I respect her. I'll have to see. I'm twenty-seven. I have a successful job, plenty of money. I just don't know.

We've been dating off and on for six months, and honestly, I can't see myself married to anyone else *but* her."

"Then you have your answer, Cousin. No one says you have to announce an engagement anytime soon. Just date."

"Georgiana," Benson chuckled, "you don't understand. A man needs more from a relationship than just good company. That's why we haven't had a steady commitment."

"I'm not as naive as you think. I do know that if what you've just told me is how you really feel, then I would suggest that you tell Cynthia, and see what she thinks." She studied him for a moment. "Benson, perhaps you are ready for marriage. I mean, what's the point? If the two of you love each other, then why would you want to wait? She's out of school and settled into her career. You're one of the richest men in Britain. Figure out what you want and tell her."

He looked down at his cousin just as they turned the corner onto Broad Street. "When did you grow up to be so smart? You're absolutely right. I've played the field for years with David, but now I don't want to be with anyone else but her, so maybe it is time we talked about the future. I'll ring her tomorrow morning and see her as soon as we're back in London."

They walked in silence until the hotel came in sight. Glancing at his cousin, he asked, "What about you? Are there any prospects in your life?"

She tightened her grip on his arm. "Yes, there is someone. I met him a year and a half ago at Fitzwilliam's wedding."

"Elizabeth's brother?"

"Yes, Elizabeth's brother. We've been corresponding, but I haven't heard from him since he went on special assignment. I reread his letters every night, and I pray for his safe return."

"David told me about the way the two of you looked at each other." He glanced at his cousin. "Georgie, I don't want to see you get hurt. Are you sure about this? I mean, he's a Marine. Not only is his job dangerous, but they are notorious for wild living—drinking and partying."

She smacked his arm and laughed. "Like you and David! I'd say he's just like any other man then, so why is it different if he's interested in me? Why am I different?"

"Well, you're...you're my cousin, and—"

"I'm no different from Cynthia. That's the trouble with brothers and cousins. You have one standard for me and another for your girlfriends."

"Point taken, and it gives me a different perspective on Cynthia. I'll think about it." Turning the curve into the Lawton parking lot, he said, "Well, we're here. After the reception, let's take the horse drawn carriage tour of the city. I'd like to see the attractions and talk a little more."

She looked up and smiled. "I'd like that very much."

They walked inside and headed towards the dining hall where David and Cecilia were waiting along with William and Mandy and Elizabeth and Fitzwilliam.

Afghanistan

The day broke cold and miserable over the mountains as a cruel wind whipped through the camp. A small group of Marines huddled around a fire, smoking cigarettes and rubbing their hands together, trying to get warm.

"Bennett, you were careless last night. You're gonna get your damn head blown off. What's wrong with you lately?"

M.K. Baxley

"I don't know what your problem is, Bailey. I figure we're even now. Last week, I picked that rag-head bastard off of you just as he was about to slit your throat. You, me, and Butler—we're a team. That's what we do—cover each other's asses."

"Yeah, that's what's worrying me. We've been cutting it awfully close lately. I'm afraid one of us, maybe all of us, ain't gonna make it back this time. The further we go up into these God forsaken mountains, the more dangerous it gets. It's not like it was in Iraq when we were taking out insurgents. These guys are better trained and more determined—and deadly. One of us is gonna get killed."

Butler cut his eyes across at his companion as he took another drag off his cigarette. "Shut up, Bailey! I don't want to hear that talk. I have a wife and a baby at home. I'm going to make it outa here."

"We've been out here for six friggin' months, Butler, and we're no closer to finding their central command than the first day we arrived. We've lost two lieutenants and a half a dozen enlisted men. It's so damned cold it would freeze the wart off a well digger's ass in Utah. You can see your breath with every word uttered. Even the horses struggle with this bitter cold. When is this gonna end?"

"It'll end when we get our man. He's up there. It's our job to find him...and find him we will. Now, if you'll excuse me, I'm taking my coffee back to my tent. I've got some things to look over before we head out today. Have the horses saddled. We're going out in an hour," Bennett said as he put out his cigarette and grabbed a cup of coffee. Coffee. It wasn't good, but at least it was hot.

Once in the confines of his tent, he pulled out the reconnaissance maps they'd gotten from last night's spy planes. Poring over the maps, he jabbed his finger at one particular mountain range. *...He's there—there in those caves or those clefts in the rocks. I know he is. We've just got to find him.*

As Joseph sat studying the map, his mind drifted to last night. It had been close—too close. Had it not been for Bailey, he wouldn't be sitting here today studying this map at all. Returning to camp from a scouting expedition, he'd wandered a little further than he should have. Georgiana Darcy had been on his mind. While he'd been lost in his thoughts, an Afghan scout had crept up behind him and had been about to fire when Bailey appeared out of nowhere putting a forty-five round right between the young man's eyes. The cracking sound of the revolver had shaken Joseph to the core.

When he'd recovered his wits enough to get up off the ground, he'd walked to where the body lay and rolled the young man over. What he saw sickened him. It had been a boy—a boy no more than fourteen or maybe fifteen—younger than his baby brother. That was the thing that stuck in his craw. These people would use children to fight, and if he didn't fight back, these children would kill him just as dead as if they'd been men. Sometimes, children as young as ten had attacked his group. He thanked God he'd never had to kill a child, but others had. This was war.

He shook his head. That was why he hadn't wanted to become involved with Georgiana. She'd almost gotten him killed last night. Bailey didn't know about her. No one knew. But Bailey did know he wasn't his usual sharp self. Bennett let out a rough breath as he took another sip of coffee. He had to get a grip. He had to push Georgiana Darcy deep down inside of himself, or there would be no future for them. Still, before he went out today, he would pull out her letters and reread them. He smiled. *...She must be praying for me. Somebody is—somebody was last night.*

After he'd read the last letter, he bundled them together and tucked them safely away in his breast pocket, and then folded the map and put it back in his map-sack. Today they would scout the eastern side of this mountain range, looking for one more piece to the puzzle...one more clue.

Chapter Seventy-eight

...The only woman I want to carouse with is you ...

As soon as they could escape the reception hall and paparazzi mob, David and Cecilia were in the air headed for Greece. The reaction David received when he announced their destination had been priceless, giving him more memories to record in the journal he'd begun shortly after they'd become engaged.

Cecilia had never been to Greece, so David was elated that he could show her something for the first time—something common to him, but new to her. Seeing the look of wonder in her deep violet-blue eyes when he pointed out and explained some little ruin that seemed insignificant to him, and yet, was one she'd never heard of, thrilled him. They toured the islands, visiting any tourist shops they could find. He was amused as she dragged him from one shop to another, adding to her extensive collection of history volumes for their home library.

After a week of touring the ancient ruins of Athens, they retired to the small villa owned by Pemberley, PLC, complete with a pool and easy access to the beach. They were close enough to walk to the marketplace to shop and explore the unique treasures of the local villagers. The rest of their time they spent relaxing on the beach or swimming in the ocean, content and happy. In the evenings, they relaxed by the pool where they laughed and talked late into the night about their future and Lawton & Co.

Taking long walks, hand in hand, along the beach, they played like two young lovers. David could not remember a time when he'd felt more carefree nor could he imagine ever being without Cecilia. They were quickly becoming one soul...one mind...one body—soul-mates.

The month passed all too quickly. Soon they would have to return to ordinary life.

"Are you ready to go home, love?" David asked one evening as they sat on the beach watching the sun set.

"Well, I have enjoyed our time together very much, but I think that I am ready to go. I want to settle into our life at home and get back to work. We do have a lot to do, and I know you're anxious to begin the changes to Carlton House."

"It does need to begin straightaway, and I want to become familiar with the company. I meant everything I said about expanding into the international markets." He gave her a tender kiss and then helped her to her feet. "Let's go home, Mrs. Darcy." They walked along the beach one more time with the ocean lapping at their feet before returning to the villa.

The first order of business upon settling into St. James House was to pick up the wedding pictures. While Cecilia unpacked, David went to the studio. Standing at the counter flipping through the album, a pleased smile curled his lips. They were more than he had hoped for—memories for a lifetime. Their wedding day had been a blur to him and now, looking through the album, he could actually "see" his wedding. But most precious to him was the locket he now held in his hand. He opened it to look at the picture the photographer had inserted into the gold casing. It showed the two of them sharing their first kiss as man and wife at the altar. It seemed so appropriate to the inscription he'd had engraved on the other side. He knew she would love it.

"Thank you, Mr. Phillips. You did an excellent job with the wedding pictures."

"Thank *you,* Mr. Darcy. It was a true pleasure to photograph your wedding. You are a lovely couple, and I wish you both all the happiness possible."

"Thank you again. I believe we shall be happy…in fact, very happy." David beamed as he collected the packages and headed for home. When he arrived, he went straight to the garden room where, as he had suspected, she was resting.

"Cecilia, love, I have our pictures. Would you like to see them?"

"Of course! Bring them here, and let's look at them together."

Handing her the album along with the box, he stood back to watch her reaction.

"What's this?"

"It's for you. Open it," he said with a smile.

She opened the box and removed the locket. Opening the heart-shaped pendant, she looked at their wedding picture as she ran her finger over the inscription. *Yours… Forevermore… David.*

"Darling, you never cease to amaze me. This is lovely. I will cherish it always." In tears, she rose to her feet and hugged him. "Help me put it on."

David took the locket from her hand, and as he put it around her neck and fastened it, he remembered the first time he had helped her with a necklace. *…She still has the same effect on me.* Turning around, she kissed and hugged him again.

"You are so kind to me. I don't deserve it."

"Oh, yes, you do. You deserve it and so much more, and I am never wrong," he said teasingly before lifting her into his arms and taking her upstairs. They would look at the pictures later.

They hadn't been home a week before Cecilia began to feel sick and listless. Worried when her condition didn't improve, David insisted that she see a doctor. She was reluctant at first, but he finally won the argument, and she agreed to make the appointment with her personal physician.

After a thorough examination and a battery of tests had been done, Cecilia waited in her doctor's office to speak with him. He sat down across from her and opened a folder.

"Mrs. Darcy, the only thing wrong with you is that you're going to have a baby," said Dr. McKinley with a gleeful smile.

"You're kidding!" Her hand flew to her mouth. "I've only been off the pill for two months. I would not have expected it this soon," Cecilia said, overcome with a mixture of surprise and joy.

"Well, the test says you are. Make an appointment with your OBGYN. He can run further tests and tell you exactly when you are due, but I suspect sometime in February."

"Thank you, Dr. McKinley." Cecilia hugged first the doctor and then the nurse before she left his office, overjoyed with the news. *…I can't wait to tell David! He will be so surprised and as happy as I am. Neither of us expected this so soon.*

After dinner as the couple watched the evening news, Cecilia turned to David and asked, "Which do you think we should restore first, the nursery here or at Carlton House?"

Looking at her curiously, he replied. "I hardly think that should be our first priority. There's plenty of time to get to those rooms, and there are more pressing things to do…unless?" He paused, comprehension finally dawning. He stared at her in astonishment. "I thought you said it would take six months to a year."

She rolled her eyes and laughed at his expression, so much like a little boy in a state of wonder. "Well, that was my understanding, but apparently not, because I definitely am, and *he* is due sometime in February."

As the reality of what she had just told him fully sank in, David jumped up and took her in his arms as he swung her around, kissing her face all over until he found her lips.

"We are going to have a baby! This is wonderful news! I must ring my brother and Elizabeth, and of course, Georgiana will be thrilled, and we must tell Bingley." Pure joy spread across his face. "We will fix *all* the nurseries. I was working on the plans for Carlton House. Now I must add this to it, and of course, the townhouse will have to be redecorated. We'll have to stay in town this year. I want you close to medical care and—"

She cut him off. "David, I'm not the first woman to have a baby."

"Yes, but it is *our* first baby, and I want everything to be perfect."

"It will be, darling, but you're right, there is much to do and plan. Go ahead with the plans for Carlton House, but let me help you with the nursery. We'll move there after the baby is born. We really need to get things settled with the company, because I want to stay home for at least six months after he is born. I may work from home for a while after that. It all depends on how I feel and how he does."

David laughed at Cecilia's enthusiasm. "Cecilia, are you aware that you have called the child *he* three times now? It could be a *she.*"

"David, this is a boy. I know it is. You'll just have to trust me on this one. Besides, Georgiana has told me that Darcy men produce more boys than girls, so this little one is a boy." She laughed, but she was certain she was right. This child felt like a boy, so for now, it would be.

As she thought about the child, her mind shifted back to Lawton and her corporate responsibilities. For the first time in seven years, they didn't seem nearly as important.

"David, you'll have to assume all of the responsibility at Lawton for a while, and you'll have to help me now until this sickness stops. Right now all I can think about is our child." She walked over to the sofa and sat down, fatigue once again setting in. David followed and took a seat beside her, linking his fingers with hers as he took her hand in his.

"That's exactly what I want to discuss with you. I have been going over the books and framework of the company. The business is well structured. Your father was an excellent businessman, but I know we can do better by bringing Lawton & Co. further into the global economy.

"I'm going to begin bringing home documents to read at night. I'm going through everything with a fine toothed comb until I understand Lawton as well as I do Darcy Enterprises and Pemberley. I'll take much of the responsibilities and give you a break," he said, reassuring her.

"I always knew you were a dedicated and good businessman. I saw it the first time we met. Treat the company as if it's your own, because it is. With this child it will pass from the Lawtons to the Darcys," she said with a sigh as she gently patted his knee.

"Cecilia, it will always be Lawton, even if your son bears my name."

"I know. I'm just glad that I will have a son or, if I am wrong, a daughter." She smiled.

"Well, Darcy men do produce more sons than daughters, just as Georgiana told you, or so they have for well over five hundred years. You'll probably get your wish, if not with this one, then with the next." He looked into her eyes as he raised her hand and kissed it.

M.K. Baxley

David spent many long hours with Daniel and the Lawton Group attorneys, coming up to speed rapidly on the intricate workings of the company. He brought home the documents he'd promised, and what he did not bring home, he viewed online through the company intranet. Sitting on the sofa in the library, he pored over them, item by item, as Cecilia either sat with him, working on a piece of handwork for the baby, or laid her head in his lap, resting while he worked. As he read, he would question her about one thing or another, absorbing the information as he went.

One evening after dinner, he approached Cecilia with his plans and strategies as they retired to the library. Sitting down together, he handed her a folder. "Love, look these over and tell me what you think."

Opening the folder, she removed the contents and scanned them one by one. "Darling, this looks good. Your venture to explore the Asian markets as well as the European is really paying off. You've found a market for the cotton. Dorian Stahl? *The* Dorian Stahl—the top designer in Paris?"

"Yes," David grinned, "he's a friend of a personal friend of mine, Alex Abrahams, who does consulting work in advertising with all the top designers. Dorian mentioned to my friend some years back about his search for premium cotton cloth, so when I got in touch with Abrahams and asked him to see what he could find out from amongst his connections, he contacted Dorian who was very enthusiastic. He, along with an Italian designer in Milan, is offering to buy this year's crop once it's produced into cloth.

"Another associate, Harry Blackburn, made contact with two top New York designers. If we can double next year's production, they also want the cotton. Apparently the distinctive properties of true Sea Island Cotton are renowned even to this very day."

She stared up at him, a smile creeping over her features. "You really do have connections, don't you?"

"I told you I did. That's who I've been on the phone with all week. Read on."

Returning to the papers in hand, she continued. When the last report was reviewed, she placed them back in the folder and set it aside.

"David, you never cease to amaze me. I love the plan to create silk cotton blends. That will give a beautiful drape to the cloth, and our linen cotton blends will be the best in the world. I'm astounded by the intricate detail you've put together for the designs of the cloth—even the patterns you've chosen are unique, and I must add, very beautiful. You really do know how to put things together. I want to go with everything you've proposed. You're as much a part of Lawton now as I am." She smiled.

"Well, Mrs. Darcy, prepare yourself. I'm interviewing an administrative assistant for my office this week. I'm also going to hire two, possibly three, more assistants for marketing and sales which I intend to personally train. I want an aggressive team. I want a special group assembled for the Carolina Gold project. Next year, we are going to launch that endeavor. Reuben, Daniel, and I have discussed it, and we will be planting 3000 acres next year at each plantation. Reuben wants to use aerial planting as opposed to the way you've done it before. I agree, so I have given him the go ahead, and I've already made plans to release the seed rice to the South Carolina Agricultural Cooperative for inspection. I've been assured by the committee that they will accept it, and the seed rice will be available for sale to others who wish to grow it. Carolina Gold should be in American supermarkets in two years and European markets in four—tops."

"Uncle Reuben has really taken a shine to you, hasn't he?"

David only smiled.

"Well, David, I couldn't be more pleased. Take both the cotton and rice into your own hands, and do what you feel is best," she said with a soft smile. "You are aware that one of us will have to travel to Belize and Colombia very soon for the palm oil and coffee?"

"I've already scheduled the trip. I think you should stay here and let me go. My Spanish is decent, and I think Carlos Sanchez rather likes me." He chuckled, putting his arm over her shoulder.

"Then you go. I'm still tired, and the morning sickness hasn't abated yet," she said, placing her hand over her flat abdomen, anticipating the small bulge that would soon form.

David gently placed his hand over hers, patting it and then gently stroked her stomach. "Cecilia, do you think you will feel like attending William and Mandy's wedding in Yorkshire in two weeks? Elizabeth and Fitzwilliam will be there."

"Yes, I wouldn't miss it. I came to know Mandy quite well—especially at my bachelorette party. I think with very little effort we can become good friends," she said, snuggling into his embrace as his arms tightened around her. "Enough about business. It's time for bed, Mrs. Darcy." He took her by the hand and led her to their bedroom.

September came quickly with business concerns becoming pressing as David hung up the phone with his Asian contact. A thirteen-hour time difference made conducting business by phone difficult. He wanted to negotiate a contract in Indonesia, but after his recent conversation with Mr. Chung, he knew this could be problematic. Since he would not have the Lawton or Darcy name linked to a sweat shop, he would have to observe the operation in action. The standards had to be above average with premium wages and excellent working conditions for the Indonesian economy. Therefore, he would have to travel to Asia soon to make arrangements concerning the Sea Island Cotton.

Falling back in his chair, David rubbed his forehead. The trip had been put off twice because of Cecilia's health, but now that she was well enough to return to the office, he didn't have a legitimate excuse to postpone it any longer. Still, he didn't want to leave her alone. Suddenly a thought occurred to him. They had a trip planned in a few days. A smile crossed his features with the thought of the solution to his concerns. He'd speak with Cecilia and see what she thought. Rising from his desk in the study, he went to find his wife.

"Cecilia, when we go to the Cumberland Plateau next week, I'm going to ask Georgiana if she will come back with us to stay with you whilst I'm in Indonesia. I can't delay it any longer. The cotton harvest begins in October. It needs to be ginned and processed to ship by the middle of November. That's not much time. I have got to go soon if we're to carry through with our plans for this year. If I don't go in person, the deal will fall through."

"I can stay by myself. I've been alone since Daddy died. I'm a big girl, David."

"I know you are. That's not the point." He cast a concerned look. "You're carrying my child, so of course, I will worry. You and our child are my responsibility, and I take that responsibility very seriously," he said, releasing a tense breath as he settled down beside her.

"You are a good husband," she said with a bemused smile. "I would love to have Georgiana come regardless of the reason. I've not been able to get to know her as well as I would like. Her visit will give me the chance."

Cradling her face in his hands, he touched his forehead to hers. "Thank you. That's one less worry. Come, let's go to bed. I'm exhausted and we've got an eight o'clock appointment with the architect concerning our plans for Carlton House. Also, I need to ring Asa Smith and let him know I can't make the shooting trip he's planned for next week. Daniel will be attending, and Uncle Harvey, William and Benson are coming, but with Elizabeth in her condition, Fitzwilliam can't make it either. We'll take a raincheck." Rising from the sofa, he extended his hand and helped her to her feet.

"I'm glad you are not going. I'm going to miss you terribly while you're away on the business trips you have to make. I don't know if I could stand it with you gone on a two week hunting excursion, too. Remember that I know Asa and Solomon. They like to drink and carouse. Now mind you, I don't think they would cheat on Miss Evelyn or Miss Louise, but I don't want *my* husband carousing," she teased, squeezing him around his waist as hey walked towards the stairs.

He chuckled. "You'll never have to worry about that. The only woman I want to carouse with is *you*, Mrs. Darcy. And you must bear in mind that Harvey will be there with his sons. I seriously doubt they'll be doing anything other than shooting."

"Well, if you really want to hunt, take a weekend in late October. Ducks and geese are plentiful at that time. They come in droves to glean the last vestiges of rice left behind from the combines."

"We'll see when October arrives," he said as he placed a kiss upon her forehead. "I don't have any waterfowl dogs. I suppose I'll have to acquire a pair of Black Labradors."

"In time, darling…in time," she said, smiling. Taking the stairs, they soon retired for the night.

Chapter Seventy-nine

...memories for a lifetime...

After David and Cecilia had headed for Greece, Fitzwilliam had quickly readied his family for their flight to the British Virgin Islands. Having arranged for Georgiana to return with Harvey, everything had been taken care of. The plane had taken off from Charleston in the late afternoon, making one stop in the Florida Keys to buy Elizabeth a wardrobe of swimwear from an exclusive boutique owned by a long-time family friend in Key Largo.

Once they arrived in Tortola, he quickly had the servants settle everything in and unpack. He had one thing in mind—the lagoon. Having already changed into his swimsuit while Elizabeth settled the twins in for their afternoon nap, he approached her in their room. "Elizabeth, change into your blue swimsuit, and hurry. I have something I want you to see," he said with a glint in his eye. "Meet me on the veranda when you're ready."

When Elizabeth appeared in the turquoise blue, French bikini, he sat his lime twist aside and dropped the magazine he was reading. Exhaling slowly, he eyed her from head to toe. "Mrs. Darcy, you are drop...dead...gorgeous. Fran was right. That cut is perfect for you."

She smiled. "Fitzwilliam, you flatter me."

"No, Liz, darling. I'm telling you the absolute truth. You're beautiful," he murmured as he picked up the beach blanket and reached for her hand. "Let's go."

Quietly walking on a jungle path illuminated by beams of light breaking through the tall towering trees, the only sounds they heard were the fluttering of birds overhead and an animal screeching in the distance. When they reached their destination, Fitzwilliam stepped aside and smiled, allowing Elizabeth to cross the threshold into the heart of the lagoon. As she entered the clearing, Elizabeth gasped. Before her was a clear blue pool surrounded by mahoganies with hanging vines and philodendrons, a plethora of enormous elephant ears and large ferns, white cedars and kapok trees, and colorful flowering shrubs and multiple varieties of fruit trees.

"Fitzwilliam, it's a scene out of a tropical paradise!"

He softly laughed. "Liz, this *is* a tropical paradise."

"And we own this?" she turned and asked in disbelief.

"Yes, darling. It was a wedding gift to my grandmother from my grandfather. She christened it Eden. He acquired it when he bought the Blue Dolphin Hotel chain on the islands. We own the offshore drilling companies, too, so when a company representative comes on business, he stays here with his family."

She looked up at him in wonder, amazed at the vast wealth her husband possessed. Turning back to the sight before her, she said, "I've never seen anything like this. The waterfall tumbling down from that cliff and the white sandy beach are breathtaking. And the water is so blue. It's beautiful cast against the emerald green, and just look at all of those colorful flowers. Hibiscus, gardenias, and I don't even know what all else. Look," she said, pointing across the pool, "those are orchids and bromeliads in those trees, and those are coconut palms with real coconuts." She gestured with her hand. "And are these banana trees? They're unusual."

"Yes," he chuckled, "they're tropical pink bananas, native to the Caribbean and Central America, and they taste much better than the ordinary ones you find in the supermarket. There are papayas, breadfruit, jack fruit, and star fruit here, too, just to name a few. This lagoon is a tropical rainforest, filled with exotic animals and fauna. It's known as the land of turtle doves and love birds, and if we're lucky, we may catch a glimpse of the red-legged tortoise," he said, pulling her into a hug. "Before we leave, we'll gather some of the fruit and take it back. But for now," Fitzwilliam said as he flicked the blanket open, "put your things down and let's go swimming."

"It is safe, isn't it?" she asked with a slight smile.

"Liz, if it weren't safe, I wouldn't have brought you here," he reassured. "Now come on; let's go."

Placing her bag on the blanket, they waded out into the pool where both dived into the clear blue water. "Fitzwilliam, this water's salty. I thought it would be fresh," she said, ducking her head to wash back her hair from her face.

"It's brackish. The water coming down from the mountain is fresh, but the water in the pool is mingled with saltwater from the ocean. Often dolphins will venture in through the channel and play. The last time David and I were here with a party of friends, a school of three came and actually allowed us to approach and play with them. Maybe they will come again. The water is clear, so you're likely to see some brightly colored fish. Look. There's a school now!" he exclaimed.

"Oh, they're beautiful. Did you bring the camera?"

"You don't think I would forget it, do you? I intend to have several pictures of you here—in the falls, under the falls, in the gardenia bushes, and anywhere else I can think of…and Elizabeth, I want pictures just for me." He grinned.

She laughed, shaking her head with a sly smile. "You mean *me* in the raw, don't you?"

"I see you catch on quickly," he said, reaching over to stroke her face with the back of his fingers before tracing the curve of her neck and untying her strings. Removing her suit, he tossed it ashore.

"It works both ways, love. Remove your trunks. If mine go…yours go, too." She arched an eyebrow.

Grinning broadly, the trunks soon joined the bikini. Taking her hand in his, they both dived under water and swam, playing with the school of colorful fish which wove in and out from between their legs, nipping Fitzwilliam. Coming up for air, they laughed.

"Fitzwilliam, did those fish bite you?"

"It was interesting, but it only tickled." He grinned.

"Just as long as they don't hurt you. After all, it's my job to nibble and caress, not theirs."

He chortled. "You cheeky imp! I'll make you think nibble." He splashed her, and once again they went underwater, swimming through the rushes. Surfacing for air several times and diving back again, they explored the coral, the shells, and anything else that took their fancy as they frolicked and played for nearly an hour.

Finally, Fitzwilliam said, "Let's lay in the sun and rest. We'll soon have to return to the villa to check on the twins, and I want to take some pictures."

Giving him a saucy look, she took his extended hand as they waded through the water and walked to shore. Stretching out under the afternoon sunshine, Elizabeth couldn't resist running her fingers over the firm planes of his chest and down his torso. Finding her destination, she caressed and stroked while their arousal grew. It wasn't long until she straddled his hips, taking him inside of her. Gently rocking back and forth, she cupped his face in her hands and kissed him while his hands instinctively went to her breasts, fondling and massaging. Their soft sighs, whispered in the quiet of the lagoon, could be heard on a gentle breeze.

Before they dressed and returned to the villa, he took pictures of her standing against the rocks of the falls with water cascading over her and in the gardenia bushes with the leaves covering her appropriately while sweetly scented blossoms framed her face. She looked as if she were Mother Eve in the Garden of Eden, but instead of fig leaves, she was adorned with palm leaves, luscious fruit, and beautiful topical flowers. Fitzwilliam snapped photograph after photograph. Never had there been a more beautiful woman than his Liz. Putting the camera aside, they once again made love on a grassy mound under the yellow hibiscus.

Returning to the house with a blanket full of fruit and exhausted from their excursion, Elizabeth attended to the twins before lying down for a nap. Fitzwilliam took out his journal to record the events of their first day in their tropical heaven. Jotting down the last entry, he set it aside and transferred today's pictures to his laptop, cataloging each one. Smiling, he put everything away and sat back with a coconut-lime twist while he watched his sleeping wife and children. Life couldn't be better. He took out some work he'd brought along for down time and looked over the last proposal David had prepared before leaving Pemberley. Contented, he worked while his family slept.

Each day they enjoyed the sun and the ocean while playing with the children, being careful not to overdo it in the sun with the babies. In the warmth of the afternoon, while the children and their nannies napped, Fitzwilliam and Elizabeth would walk to the blue lagoon to swim, making love as the mood struck, which it often did. Sometimes they made love partially submerged at the water's edge while the waves lapped at their feet and legs. Then other times they found a thick carpet of grass under a flowering bush. Whatever the case or occasion, they enjoyed themselves and their time together at every opportunity, creating memories for a lifetime.

Before returning home, Fitzwilliam promised to take her to the international marketplace on Tortola, only to 'look,' as Elizabeth put it. He chuckled at the thought of his wife merely looking. Even though he had billions, she still felt the need to economize. It seemed that she could not escape her mother's teachings concerning financial prudence, though there was no real need for it.

Fitzwilliam had many things to record in his journal that would one day join the others in the Pemberley library annex. He had been keeping one off and on for years, but of late, the recordings were much happier ones.

Chapter Eighty

Shortly after their return to London, Fitzwilliam noticed that Elizabeth had begun to act strangely. She seemed to be extremely sensitive to smells and would often run to the bathroom, purging her stomach, and she scarcely touched her food. Often he would find her asleep in the middle of the morning. He was clearly worried. One afternoon he approached her in their bedroom.

"Love, what's wrong. You don't seem to have any energy, and you aren't eating. Are you ill? Do you need to see a doctor?"

"Oh Fitzwilliam, I hope you won't be upset with me, but I think I'm pregnant. I haven't had a period since Alex and Emily's birth, so I don't know for sure. I was under the impression that if I nursed regularly, I wouldn't ovulate, but I fear I may have been misinformed," she said, twisting her fingers nervously, her eyes filled with apprehension.

"Elizabeth! You don't mean it! This is wonderful!" He closed the distance between them and gathered her into his arms. "Nothing would make me happier. If you are, this time you're not leaving my sight. I want to share everything there is to experience."

"Everything? Including the morning sickness? You've got to be kidding!" she said, looking at him with amusement, very relieved at his acceptance.

"Everything. I'll hold your hand and do whatever I can. When will you know?" he asked cradling her head against his chest.

Glancing up, she responded, "Well, the early pregnancy test says that I am, but I won't know for sure until I see a doctor. I'll make an appointment on Monday, but Fitzwilliam, if I am *not*, then we'll have to take some precautions. Do you realize that if I am, this baby will be only thirteen months younger than the twins? I just got my figure back! This is what happened to my parents with me and Joseph."

He chuckled softly while holding her in his arms. "If you're not, I'll start using a condom. But if you are, then I guess you're *Fertile Fanny*, and I'm *virile* and *potent*."

She playfully smacked his arm. "That's not funny, not in the least."

After seeing the doctor, Elizabeth received confirmation that she was indeed pregnant and due in late February. David had called with the news of Cecilia's pregnancy. Fitzwilliam laughed and joked with his brother about the legendary *strength* of the Darcy men. Fitzwilliam was not only happy about the pregnancy, but very determined to be there every step of the way. This was one experience he intended to enjoy to the fullest.

Elizabeth's only concern was that she hoped it wasn't twins again. He laughed and squeezed her close, telling her that if it was, they'd survive.

Chapter Eighty-one

...I could give her anything and yet...

After William and Amanda's wedding, Fitzwilliam pushed to get his family moved to Pemberley by August. He and Elizabeth wanted to go back to the Cumberland Plateau for the birth of Charles and Jane's baby, now confirmed to be a girl.

After several weeks of hard work, the Lambton office was finally opened, and the move complete. As things settled into a routine, Fitzwilliam came home from work early one day and found Elizabeth in her study. With a broad smile, he approached her. "Elizabeth, I have a surprise for you. I have been planning this for a long time. Come along, and I'll show you."

Rising from her desk, she followed him out the door and along the graveled pathway towards the stable. As they approached the entranceway, she could hear the whimper of puppies. When they came to a certain stall, he opened the door and stood back to gauge her reaction. There they were—two Black and Tan hound puppies snuggling together on a heaping pile of straw, whimpering and sniffing. She ran to them, immediately scooped both up at once and raising them to her face as she kissed them and breathed in the sweet scent of puppies mixed with straw.

"Oh, Fitzwilliam! You remembered... you remembered! I love them so much. May I please take them to the house? I'll keep them in the kitchen until they are housebroken or as you would say, *house-trained.* I want to train them myself, as I now have the time, and they must go with us to Tennessee!" she said, reaching up with her one free hand to caress his face and place a kiss on his cheek.

He chuckled and pulled her close as he kissed her forehead. Her expression was priceless. He could deny her nothing he thought to himself as he looked fondly upon his wife with two hound puppies, squirming, sniffing and licking her blouse while Elizabeth cuddled them, spreading little kisses from one to the other.

"Yes, Mrs. Darcy, you may bring them to the house, and I think it can be arranged for them to go with us. We really are a family now, complete with two tiddlers, two dogs, and a baby on the way. The travel arrangements keep getting more and more complicated."

Elizabeth caught his playful look. "Thank you so much for being so thoughtful. You are truly the best of men. I can't believe you remembered when I had forgotten," she said with a broad smile. "I intend to train them to track like I did Old Dan and Lady Beth. They will be loyal protectors of all I hold dear." She stepped up on her tiptoes to touch her lips to his while holding the puppies to her heart.

"I'm sure they will, and I'm glad you like them. Now, what will you name them?" he asked with a smile while his hand stroked the soft heads of the two little bundles.

"They will be called Gentleman Jack and Lady Jillian—otherwise known as Jack and Jill, after my uncle's bloodhounds." She gazed lovingly on the two precious pups snuggled in her arms.

Fitzwilliam put his arm around her waist as they walked back to the house. "Now, Elizabeth, there is one other thing I want to give you."

She glanced up. "What more could you possibly give me? You've given me everything."

He looked down and chuckled. "Not quite everything, not yet," he said. "I want to build a replica of the cabin at Longbourn. I was thinking of putting it on that rise of ground just above the falls in Pemberley's cove. What do you think?"

"Oh, I would love that, but could we make it a little bigger? I'd like to develop and expand the loft into a second floor for the children, and I would like to have a modern kitchen. You can include a wood-burning cook stove if you like, but I want running water and a bathroom."

"Whatever you want, love. We'll draw the plans together, and then I'll contact my building firm. We'll have it ready by next summer. It'll be our little getaway when I can't be too far from home."

"Fitzwilliam, I do love you so."

"I know." He looked at her tenderly, watching the sparkle in her eyes ...*I am a lucky man. I could give her anything and yet... she prefers the simple things.*

Chapter Eighty-two

...Their words nearly brought him to tears...

T he week before Jane's baby was due, Fitzwilliam and Elizabeth, accompanied by Georgiana, returned to Walnut Grove. Struggling with the load of two infants, two puppies, and all the paraphernalia that went with them, Fitzwilliam began to wonder if their trip had been such a good idea after all. He felt overwhelmed at times, but when his little girl smiled with her arms extended toward him, all else was forgotten. He couldn't resist lifting her up and showering her face with soft butterfly kisses, causing her to release peals of laughter and giggles as she squirmed and wiggled within his arms.

"Darcy, you sure have changed! I never thought I would see you labored down with domestic duties, and now you've got another baby on the way. It's most becoming of you, but I guess you're relieved it's only one this time." Bingley laughed as he helped his old friend unload the rental car and bring all their belongings into the house.

Fitzwilliam chuckled. "I have to admit that I am happy Elizabeth's pregnant, but you're right, I'm glad it's not twins. These two have me on my toes constantly, not to mention what it's like for their mother. But don't worry, Bingley. Your day is coming and coming sooner than you think," he said with a knowing smile as he walked up the sidewalk with the last load in one arm and his baby daughter in the other while Elizabeth, Georgiana, and Jane followed behind, chatting away with Alex and two puppies in tow.

Once everything was taken into the house and the children settled down for a nap, the ladies regrouped in the kitchen to talk while the men went to the front porch.

"Robert and Tana said to give you their regards. Linda has an earache, so they won't see us until tomorrow," Bingley reported. "And David called. He will be here after the baby is born. They can't stay long. It seems he has an important business trip to attend to."

"Yes, he has to travel for a month. Georgiana is going back to stay with Cecilia whilst David is away. I think they have plans to sightsee and Georgiana is going to help Cecilia with sewing for the baby."

"Sewing? When did Georgiana start sewing?"

"When she met Elizabeth and Cecilia," Fitzwilliam laughed. "Georgiana has developed quite an assortment of diverse interests since Father's death. I think Elizabeth and Cecilia have been good for her," Fitzwilliam said as the two gentlemen settled into the wicker chairs beneath the veranda to relax with a cigar and a glass of wine. They talked for nearly an hour before being called in for dinner.

Sometime during the night, Jane went into labor. Charles caused quite a stir trying to get his wife to the hospital. Baby Rebecca Jane was born the next day at eleven a.m. Elizabeth and Fitzwilliam were there for the happy occasion. Bette and Johnny, Sam and Florence, and Robert and Tana all met them at the hospital. David and Cecilia left Charleston the next morning, arriving in the early afternoon.

The Darcy brothers shook their heads in amusement watching Charles, beside himself with delight, passing out cigars to any and all. Jane was her usual serene, genteel self while Elizabeth, Cecilia, and Georgiana declared that Rebecca Jane Bennet Bingley was a beautiful angel, just like her mother.

M.K. Baxley

Fitzwilliam was truly happy for his friend, but he couldn't help feeling a little empty for having been cheated out of the birthing experience. David noticed it and came to console him.

"Feeling out of sorts, Brother?"

"Does it show?"

"Not to anyone else but me. I know you, remember?" David smiled softly. "Fitzwilliam, don't look back. You can't change what happened. The only thing you can do is look forward."

"Elizabeth has told me the very same thing." He sighed as he turned and caught his brother's gaze. "But you're probably right. They have a saying in these mountains. It goes something like this—*don't cry over spilt milk* or *there is no use in closing the barn door after the horse is out.* I suppose those fit here, but I can't help regretting what I've missed. Bingley was there for his firstborn, and you'll have that experience, too, but I will not. *What's gone is gone.* That's another saying I have learnt from the people here. However, I will be there this next time." He grinned. "Nothing could keep me from it. As Cecilia would say—*Come hell or high water,* I *will* be there." He softly laughed while giving his brother a slap on the back.

Since David had to return to Charleston for his flight to Indonesia on Monday, he, Cecilia, and Georgiana left for the return trip to South Carolina two days after Rebecca's birth. At David's insistence, Cecilia was now working half-days. This pregnancy had proven to be more difficult than she had anticipated, leaving her exhausted at the end of every day. Nevertheless, she spent many hours with Georgiana, conversing and forming a closer bond of friendship.

Although happy to have Georgiana with her, Cecilia longed for her husband, and the nights of sleeping alone were hard, especially the first week. Because of the time differences and their work schedules, he only called her for a few minutes, but she knew to expect an email every day, and every day she was not disappointed. He kept her informed of his progress, and more importantly, he reassured her of his love and concern for her and their child.

In his absence, Cecilia had one special project she was overseeing along with training three top assistants. She was having Lawton & Co. restructured to Lawton & Darcy, LLC, thus beginning the steps to take the company public. At first David balked about the name change, but she explained that, as they were now a partnership, the name change was essential since, in the next generation, it would pass to a Darcy... her son.

Elizabeth and Fitzwilliam stayed on until the christening as they were to be the godparents for baby Rebecca. They stayed in the Bennett townhouse so Elizabeth could help Jane while Charles was away at the university. Tana and Robert were there as often as they could be, and Florence and Bette, along with Johnny and Sam Henry stopped by every day after work. Even Randy and Lydia came by to visit.

While Elizabeth spent her time with Jane, Fitzwilliam used his time to visit old friends at the university and reminisce over his courtship with his wife. They had met and fallen in love here while he was doing what he had always wanted to do. Reflecting back, he felt a sense of pride in what he had been able to accomplish within the short time he had taught at the university. He had always believed that, as a professor, his obligations and responsibilities lay with his students. This conviction was reinforced when a group of his former Latin students stopped him while he was in Morton Hall to express their gratitude for his work. Many had decided to go on to higher levels of study purely because of the desire to learn he had instilled in them. Some were even applying for admission to Leeds, Oxford, and Cambridge. Remembering how hard they had worked, he promised to help them with a letter of recommendation. Of all the things his students shared with him, what touched him most was when they told him that his example as a good and honest man had made a significant impact on their lives. Their words nearly brought him to tears.

As he walked across campus to the Bennett townhouse, Fitzwilliam thought about the past few years of his life. In such a short time, so much had changed. The years were bittersweet, and except for his separation from his wife, he wouldn't have changed them for the world. Here he had met and married Elizabeth Bennett, the love of his life, and he had found the lost branch of his family and fulfilled an ancestor's promise. Yes, his experience in the Cumberland Plateau had been a turning point—one that made him glad, but at the same time, he felt torn between the two worlds in which he had lived—academic and business. He knew his destiny was in England. This had been his one chance to pursue a life he had longed for. He would never teach again, and the thought tore at his heart.

Chapter Eighty-three

...I will ride over the stream and rest under the tree...

The cool winds of early November whipped through the Derbyshire hills as Fitzwilliam rode through the deer park, surveying the moorlands. The fallow and red deer were plentiful to the point of being overpopulated and were damaging the woodlands, crops, and gardens. The herd needed thinning. With the move of Pemberley, PLC from London to Lambton completed and his family settled into Pemberley House, he would host a shooting party. Turning his horse back to the great house, he noted the darkening sky. The cool chill meant that rain was coming. No, not just rain—a storm.

Trotting into the stable yard, he threw his leg over the back of his stallion and dismounted, releasing his horse to the care of a stable boy. He reached down and ruffled the ears of Elizabeth's Black and Tans as he instructed the youth, "Hansen, rub him down well, and put a blanket over him. It looks like the temperature might plummet to freezing. Then give him some sweet feed, and check his left front hoof. I think that shoe might be loose." Fitzwilliam turned to leave with Elizabeth's hounds in close step, following him to the house.

Briskly walking in the direction of the back entrance to the manor, he contemplated the progress he'd made since taking control of Pemberley. His cousin, Richard, having replaced David, was doing an exceptional job in the wholesale contract division. And after much coaxing, he'd finally convinced Stephen Darcy to replace the retiring Henry Edwards on the board of directors. With these changes in place, the board was now rock solid in his camp. He had secured the future of the corporation for his son as well as for any future sons. Future sons, he smiled to himself. The doctor had confirmed only yesterday that he and Elizabeth were to have another boy in late February. Even as the clouds darkened around him, sunshine reigned in his heart.

To make things even more complete, he'd heard from David just the other day. He and Cecilia were to have a son, too, due February 22nd, five days before Elizabeth's due date. Another smile curved his features. It would be a contest to see who was born first, James Samuel Lawton Darcy of South Carolina or George Andrew Bennet Darcy of Derbyshire. Either way, it was a joyous occasion for both brothers. Quickly bounding up the steps of the courtyard leading to the Great Hall, he entered the house along with the dogs and went in search of his wife just as the heavens opened up, releasing a torrential downpour. Thunder clapped in the distance, and lightning streaked across the sky as clouds thick as pea soup rolled in.

Finding Elizabeth in the library crocheting baby booties while Alex and Emily scooted across the floor, he couldn't help but smile. The sight of her hair fighting the confines of the clip holding it in place and his children playing at her feet warmed his heart. He sat down beside her and gave her a kiss on the cheek and then gently patted her well rounded belly. "I've really enjoyed these last few months watching you and little George grow."

Elizabeth gave him a sharp look of feigned horror. "Watching me grow indeed! If I didn't know better, I'd say it was twins again. I'm bigger than before."

He chuckled as the dogs curled at his feet. "I'm rather glad it's *not* twins," he said, glancing at their two young children guiding themselves along a table. "Those two are a handful now that they're beginning to walk. But seriously, Elizabeth, you are a woman in full bloom—a beautiful, expectant mother." Alex had made his way over to his father and raised his arms to be lifted up. A gurgling laughter escaped his throat as he reached to pat his mother's stomach just like his father had done, causing Fitzwilliam to laugh even harder. He playfully poked Elizabeth's belly with his index finger and looked at Alex. "You see this, Alex? I did that, and I'm proud of it. You're going to have a brother soon."

Elizabeth rolled her eyes and laughed. "You're teaching him awfully young about the birds and bees, aren't you?"

"What? I'm only telling him he's soon to have a brother." Fitzwilliam grinned.

Elizabeth raised an eyebrow and poked him back. "Yeah, right! I've never seen anybody act so foolish about a baby coming along. Every day, you're making plans for your sons and playing with my stomach."

Fitzwilliam threw back his head and roared with laughter. "I'm totally fascinated by it—the shape of it, the feel of it, and especially the way he kicks. I even have his ultra sound picture framed on my desk at work. And yes, I'm making plans. I'm going to enjoy every day as if it were my last. Carpe diem—seize the day! Yesterday's gone, and tomorrow may never come. I'm going to live life to the fullest, and that includes watching little George grow."

"You're impossible!" she laughed and shook her head. "Now, you've got something else on your mind. I can tell by that boyish look, so out with it."

He heartily laughed. Giving his son a kiss, he said, "Alex, you mustn't underestimate the power of women. They are very perceptive and quick to learn how to read you like a book." Alex gurgled again as Emily made her way to them, lifting her leg in an effort to climb up and join the party. Helping her up, Fitzwilliam settled her in his lap next to Alex before he turned to his wife. "Liz, you know me too well. How would you like to have company for a week or possibly two? I'd like to host a shooting party. I'll invite my cousins, William, Benson, and Richard, and Charles and David as well as our uncles. Also, I'd like to invite some of David's new friends. They've been taking him shooting, and I'm sure he'd like to return the favor."

"Oh, I'd love to see my aunts and Jane and Rhonda, and Susan and Cecilia, oh and Mandy, too. Will Cynthia come along now that she and Benson are engaged?"

"I'm sure she will. She and Georgiana are close friends, and since she's joining the family in June, I would expect she would want to become acquainted with the other Darcy women."

"Oh good. I'd love to get to know her. Invite whomever you please. It'll be fun. Let's see, Linda is eighteen months, the twins are almost ten, and Rebecca Jane is two, Mandy's due in December, and Cecilia and I in February. We'll have a house filled with pregnant women and lactating mothers."

Fitzwilliam shook his head and chuckled. "I'll be sure and keep the men outside safe from the gaggle of geese."

"You'll do no such thing! When you're not hunting, you'll be right here with us. Gaggle of geese indeed! I'll make you think gaggle of geese!" She slapped him playfully. "Now tell me, how are the plans for the cabin coming along?"

"Well, Patterson had the CAD drawings modified last week. I should have them on my desk by tomorrow afternoon. With the changes you made to the loft and the ones I made to the family room, we'll need to look them over one more time, and then they can start the construction the following week. It should be completed by mid-spring, if the weather cooperates. Perhaps we can use it in April, and just maybe there will be a touch of winter, and we'll have snow on the ground. Regardless, it'll still be cold. I plan on cutting the wood myself for the stove. It'll be good for me."

"Very good then. Now, let's give the kids to the nannies and prepare for dinner. It's almost ready. Come on. Let's go. And let those dogs outside. They're smelly." She picked up Alex as he scooped Emily into his arms and headed in the direction of their bedroom with one small detour towards the outside entrance of the Great Hall where the pups were gracefully expelled.

That night as the family lay in bed, a violent storm tore through the lake country. Howling winds and rain beat against the windows. Thunder cracked and lightning lit up the sky. Rising from her bed, Georgiana crossed the room to take a seat on her window bench, peering out into the night. The pelting against the glass became more furious with hail striking the windowpanes like a thousand angry fists. As she sat there, an ominous feeling swept over her. Something was wrong. *...He's in trouble... I feel it.*

Quickly she murmured a prayer, asking for God's protection, but the feeling did not abate as it had done in the past. It only intensified. Worry gripped her as she breathed another prayer. This had never happened before. Shooting to her feet, she quickly moved to her bedside table and lit a candle. She would stay up all night if she had to. Joseph needed her. She swallowed hard as her body trembled. She broke out in a cold sweat, perspiration beading on her forehead. Wherever he was, whatever he was doing, Joseph was in trouble. Death was looming. She knew it...she felt it...she could taste it—fear.

Chapter Eighty-four

Honor…Courage…Commitment…
Core values of the United States Marine Corps.

In a mountainous area of Afghanistan, Brigadier General William B. Haines paced back and forth, smoking one cigarette after another. The General had just received the call from the Pentagon. The mission was a go. The General breathed deeply, taking a long drag off of his cigarette before stubbing it out and lighting another one.

He'd been planning this offensive since the 2001 Al-Qaeda attack on the World Trade Center. His job had been to assemble Mountain Fox, a special operations strike team able to hit with lightning speed and deadly accuracy. The General had surveyed the academies carefully, selecting the finest they had to offer for his junior officer corps. He had also drafted the top men from all branches of the Special Forces, and had personally supervised their training under the instruction of Colonel Jeremiah Burnside, a man noted for his expertise in covert operations, who answered directly to him, General Haines.

The four hand-picked men from the academies were Marine Captains Joseph E. Bennett and Michael D. Butler, and Navy Lt. Jebediah A. Johnson, known as Jeb, all from the Naval Academy, and Captain William E. Bailey from West Point. They were four of the finest men General Haines had ever trained. Each was skilled with a knife at close range and a dead shot with a pistol as well as highly proficient in martial arts and survival tactics. Each had command of sixteen men. Mountain Fox was the best of the best in the Special Operations Forces of the United States Military.

They had found and brought to justice Saddam Hussein and then later had brought about the death of Abu Musab al-Zarqawi. Now they were going after the deadliest terrorist of them all, a Saudi militant known as The Sheik. To the best of the General's knowledge, there had never been a more capable or well trained team than the one he had created. They were perfect—highly qualified and deadly—and this was their most important assignment.

They would soon meet for one last debriefing before today's predawn assault. They would go in one hour before sunrise with the backup of the 5th Army Special Forces out of Fort Campbell, Kentucky and the Marine Expeditionary Unit from Camp Pendleton, San Diego, California. They would be reinforced with an artillery battery, reconnaissance, an infantry battalion, and a helicopter squadron with Combat Services Support coming in to care for the wounded. And General Haines was sure there would be wounded—many of them.

As the General contemplated this mission, he began to flash back to his own days in Viet Nam, remembering another mission. He'd led a group of Green Berets to take a Viet Cong command post, but the mission had not gone well. The losses had been heavy, and they did not carry the day. His best friend had died in his arms that day because he, then Major Haines, had miscalculated the enemy's resolve. In his mind, the past weighed heavily against the present as the General contemplated today's mission. It was crucial—vitally important that *this* mission succeed.

With these thoughts crowding his mind, he put out his cigarette and headed for the debriefing room at a rapid pace. Once in the war room, the General stepped in front of the aerial map and picked up his wand.

M.K. Baxley

"Gentleman," he said, "Code name Red Death is a go. Now," the General looked around at each man in the room, "we've been over these plans before, but let's go over this again. Bennett," he called out, "your men go in first through the center, followed by Bailey on the left and Butler on the right. Take out the sentries when you enter and then signal back. I will call in air support at that time. They will keep the enemy's ground forces occupied, clearing the way for you to move forward. You will have Apaches and Black Hawks for cover with Super Stallions available to airlift out the wounded." He paced back and forth, slapping his hand with the baton he held. "Taken by surprise, the enemy should not have a chance to assemble for SAM assaults, but in case they try," he pointed at the man in the back of the room, "Johnson, your job is to see that they don't. Got that, Johnson?" Johnson nodded. "Bennett, Butler, Bailey," the General struck a spot on the map, "when the air strikes begin, move in with your men to this point. The Sheik is in there." The General tapped. "We want him alive, but if you can't take him alive, then bring out the body. I am sending you three in with your men because you are the best of the best. And failure is not acceptable. Colonel Burnside and I will be watching over you via satellite surveillance." The General paused and surveyed the room one last time. He nodded and cleared his throat. "Good luck, men, and remember, you are the Elite Force Mountain Fox—America's best."

The General bowed his head and said a prayer before dismissing them.

Joseph lit up a cigarette and rested while trying to prepare himself for what he hoped would be his last mission in this bloody war. The mental anguish was intense while his mind drifted, as it usually did, to Georgiana Darcy. It had been over a year since he had last written to her. He had not wanted to become emotionally attached for many reasons, and yet he had done just that. He had implied that he wanted to marry her. If it were not for this damned mission, he would have told her more, but he could not offer her hope for a future…not yet. Joseph had to live through this operation and make it back home alive. Distractions, even those as pleasant as Georgiana, could be deadly. He'd almost lost his life once before while thinking of her. He had to get his head focused on the assignment. He couldn't afford any more mistakes.

Joseph stubbed out his cigarette and looked around at his men and the other force commanders. Who would be there tomorrow? Jeb Johnson had pulled out his harmonica and was playing *The Green Fields of France*, a sad lonesome tune about a soldier killed and buried in France during the First World War. Bailey was keeping to himself as he always did, and Butler was listening to something a second lieutenant was telling him while the other men were smoking and quietly talking among themselves. Yes, he wondered who would live and who would die.

Bennett lit another cigarette as he thought of what was coming. He remembered the first time he'd killed a man and how sick it had made him feel. He had erroneously thought that killing was killing, but taking the life of a man was not the same as slaughtering hogs back on the farm. He could be covered in pig's blood and think nothing of it. Take a shower and that was that. A man's blood was different. You could wash and wash and still not be clean. He knew he was changing—had changed. It was either him or them, and it sure as hell wasn't going to be him.

Pulling a long draw on his cigarette, Joseph wondered if he was decent enough for Georgiana, or any woman for that matter. When had he stopped feeling? Would he ever feel anything again? No, he'd had it with the guts and glory. If he ever did marry and have a son, he didn't want him to be where he was, losing a piece of his soul with each shot fired…each man killed. War wasn't fun and games. War was killing people and destroying things. It was real—not a fantasy or a video game. And yet, as he thought about it, freedom wasn't free. It came at a price, bought and paid for in blood—the blood of his friends and maybe even his own.

"Bennett, you awake?" Butler asked as he took a seat beside his friend and lit up a cigarette.

"Yeah, I'm awake."

"This is it. We've got to get through this one," he breathed out heavily. "If I make it out, I'm going home. I have a little girl I've only seen pictures of. She isn't even a year old yet. I wonder what she and her mother are doing tonight," he said. "You know, I never imagined it would be like this when we were at Annapolis. Did you, Bennett?"

"No, I never did. I hope we make it out alive, too. I have a lady I would like to see again."

"Yeah? You, Bennett? You never said anything about a lady. Well, if you still pray, maybe you had better say one before we go in. This is not like last time. I don't have a good feeling at all about this one. The losses will be heavy. It's just a feeling, but I can't seem to shake it," Captain Butler said as he gazed off into the night.

"Don't talk like that, Butler! We're *going* to make it. You'll see that little girl. You have to have some faith!" Captain Bennett spoke with more confidence than he felt.

Sitting off by himself, Bailey shook his head and smiled. He'd overheard the conversation between Butler and Bennett, and the news of Bennett's girlfriend was surprising to him as well, although he'd suspected it from that bundle of letters Bennett carried and his carelessness of late. Bailey knew that his buddies were both nervous, and he understood why. They had something to live for. Bailey, on the other hand, didn't.

He had been at the top of his graduating class at West Point, but unlike Butler and Bennett, he was a loner. He didn't have a wife or a girlfriend either, for that matter. His mother had died from cancer a few years back, and he'd never known his father.

Bailey took a draw off his cigarette and smiled to himself. The three captains had become family over the past five and a half years with Butler and Bennett always regaling him with tales of growing up on a farm. Butler had lived on a dairy farm in Wisconsin with his parents and two brothers and a sister while Bennett had been raised in the mountains of Tennessee with four sisters and a brother. Bailey felt that he somehow shared in his comrade's lives through their stories of home, which always brought him comfort, and he never tired of hearing them. Bailey smiled again as he glanced down at his watch. He slowly stood and shook the dirt from his fatigues before joining his friends.

Butler and Bennett were silently finishing their cigarettes when Captain Bailey approached. "Time to go guys. Bennett, you go in first. Butler and I will follow. Good luck." Bailey nodded to his comrades.

"Thanks, Bailey. Let's say a prayer for the mission," Captain Butler said.

Captain Bennett dropped his cigarette and stamped it. Then he called his men together and said one final prayer. Looking up, he eyed each man one by one. "Okay, men, lock and load…it's time to rock and roll."

As they moved into position, Jim Morrison's song *The End* played through Bennett's mind. All thoughts of Georgiana Darcy were carefully blocked. His mind was clear and focused. He—they—were on a mission.

All three teams crept in as silent as the grave, finding the enemy asleep at their post. It would be easy. They quietly took them out. Bennett, Bailey, and Butler had worked together and they knew their jobs well. And, all three had made a pact that if they came out of this alive, this would be it… *the end*. They only had to live through this *one* damned day.

The signal was given. Choppers hovered in the air, firing at will. All hell was breaking loose. Rockets launched. Men screamed as they jumped and died. Johnson and his men were on the move to the SAM site while the three captains with their men moved quickly to point A, killing anyone who rose up in their way. They entered the tent after their men had secured the grounds, and there he sat as if expecting them. The Sheik's lips curved into a sickly sweet smile as he welcomed them with a gesture of his hand, but there was no hospitality in his voice. Hatred like the flames of hell burned in his dark eyes. All three stared in horror when they saw what he held in his hand, but it was Bailey who moved to take him, and then...an explosion... darkness... and finally... nothing.

Bennett groaned in agony. His face burned, and he couldn't move his left arm. He gasped against the pain and bit back a moan as he slowly twisted his head to his left. Bailey was dead. The Sheik was dead. Butler lay sprawled and bleeding in the dirt, moaning while their men were scattered about.

"Bailey," Bennett ground out. Bailey had laid down his life for his friends. The words of Jesus rambled through Bennett's thoughts. *...Greater love hath no man than this... that a man lay down his life for his friends. Georgiana...* was Bennett's last thought as everything went black.

Taken at Parris Island the summer of 2009
Uncommon Valor was a Common Virtue
Memorial Monument to the Marines who fought the
Battle of Iwo Jima
(February 19–March 26, 1945)

Some people wonder all their lives if they've made a difference. The
Marines don't have that problem.
-Ronald Reagan

Chapter Eighty-five

...the great Confederate general who was wounded at the Battle of Chancellorsville...

"**N**Ooooooooo!**" Georgiana Darcy jerked awake from a restless sleep, her throat burning on a silent harsh scream. It was a dream—a horrible dream! She had seen something terrifying, but she couldn't remember the details. She shivered against the cold sweat soaking her, inexplicably frightened.

She cast a quick glance at the clock. Three o'clock in Derbyshire meant somewhere between five a.m. and six-thirty in the Middle East. How long had she been asleep? It had been one a.m. the last time she'd looked.

Quickly scrambling out of bed, she grabbed her robe and pulled it on over her shoulders. Running to the television, she turned on the BBC and saw the news flash. "Oh… my… God," she said in a hushed tone. Frozen in place, tears welled and spilled over her lashes. Snapping out of her trance, she hurriedly slipped into her slippers and ran three doors down to her brother's chamber.

"Fitzwilliam, Elizabeth, come quickly! Quickly! *NOW*!" She banged on the door with both fists.

"What is it, Georgiana?" Fitzwilliam asked, coming to the door half-dressed.

"Get dressed and let me in. Turn on the set. Something has happened in Afghanistan!"

Elizabeth made her way out of bed, picking up her gown from the floor and pulling it over her head. Then she slipped into her dressing gown while Fitzwilliam grabbed a robe. Georgiana entered and they turned on the television.

"This is Al Stokes reporting live with U.S. Army troops on the ground stationed out of Fort Campbell, Kentucky and the Marine Expeditionary Unit from Camp Pendleton. The American lead team went in this morning just before dawn, local time, in an attempt to capture a top Al-Qaeda leader. The mission is a success, but many have been injured or killed. The Al-Qaeda leader was killed. One Marine captain is dead with two others critically wounded. The Americans, as well as the enemy, have taken heavy losses."

As they watched the news coverage for over an hour, Elizabeth cried and Georgiana was visibly shaking. The only one who remained calm was Fitzwilliam.

Georgiana finally said through her tears, "This must be the mission that Joseph told me about. It was supposed to be his last. They didn't mention it as a Special Forces team so it might not be him, but we have to find out."

"Georgiana, if it was Joseph's team, they would *never* tell us. They can't. It's top secret," Elizabeth said in a trembling voice as she looked at her sister-in-law with a very shocked expression on her face.

"I'll contact the Red Cross and see what I can find out. The military will contact your brother's family if anything has happened to him, and since you're his sister, we should be able to find out something," Fitzwilliam said.

"Wait, perhaps I have an email from someone. Joseph told me he'd made arrangements for me to be contacted should anything happen. Joseph and I have been communicating, so he has my email address. I'll explain everything later," Georgiana said, realizing Elizabeth knew nothing about their relationship. Running to the computer in her brother's room, she hastily brought up her email account.

"Here it is! It's from a General Haines. I'll print it out. It says Joseph has been wounded, but he is alive and in serious condition. He is on his way to Frankfurt, Germany. We must go to him. And Elizabeth," she hesitated, "I'll explain everything in transit, but know this, I love your brother very much…and…he asked me to wait for him. I'll give you all the details, but for now, we've got to move quickly."

Georgiana rushed out the door for her room. As soon as things could be arranged, they were aboard Pemberley One headed for Germany.

Entering the ICU lobby of the U.S. Army hospital in Frankfurt, Fitzwilliam and Elizabeth found her family and David and Cecilia already assembled, waiting for them. Elizabeth's aunt and uncle were there, as were Mary Beth and André, Kat, Daniel, Jane and Charles. Even Lydia and Randy were there, but some of the family had remained behind to care for the farms.

"Have any of you been in to see him?" Elizabeth asked as she hugged each one.

"Yes, I have," Robert answered. "You'll have to prepare yourself, Lizzy. He doesn't look good. God, I can't believe what happened. By all rights, he should be dead." He squeezed his eyes shut and shook his head. "General Haines told me that apparently one of his officers sacrificed his life for his men."

At the sound of Robert's words, Georgiana winced, nearly collapsing, as David lunged to support her. Elizabeth reached over and grabbed her hand. "It's all right, Georgiana. At least he's alive."

Turning her anxious, but steady, gaze back to her uncle, she asked, "Can we see him?"

"Yes, but they only allow five people in at a time. Some of us have already been, and the next group has just come out, so you and Cecilia and the rest are next."

Elizabeth looked up at Fitzwilliam who reached for her hand, squeezing it. He drew in a deep breath. "Let's go."

Cautiously entering the room, Elizabeth almost fainted. Fitzwilliam steadied her, holding her close to keep her from collapsing. Beside him, David supported Georgiana. Fitzwilliam winced. He had never seen anyone so seriously injured. Joseph's face was badly swollen and covered in bandages and his left arm was in traction. He seemed to recognize them, but he could not see them. He lifted his right arm to hug first his sister and then Georgiana, telling them not to worry. Georgiana hugged him close and cried.

He stroked her hair as she hugged his neck. "Don't cry, Georgie. Don't cry. All will be well. I will ride over the stream and rest under the shade of the tree."

Elizabeth gasped in horror as her hand flew to her mouth. She bit back a sob and cried out, "Oh dear God! He's quoting Thomas Jackson."

Georgiana glanced up through tear stained eyes. "Who?"

"Thomas J. 'Stonewall' Jackson," Cecilia solemnly said, "the great Confederate general who was wounded at the Battle of Chancellorsville fought near Spotsylvania Courthouse in Virginia. Those are very the words he said just before he died. He was delirious."

David suddenly appeared at Georgiana's side, guiding her to a chair. After seeing that she was comfortably seated, he took a seat beside her. Fitzwilliam helped Elizabeth to the sofa where Cecilia soon joined them, offering consolation and reassurance as Elizabeth wept uncontrollably.

"Elizabeth, listen to me, honey…Listen to me." Cecilia slipped her arm around her friend's shoulder. "He's going to be all right. Jackson died from pneumonia, not from his wounds. We have antibiotics today to fight infections. Joseph *will* make it. You have to have faith. Now is the time for prayer—not despair."

"Cecilia's right, darling. He will make it," Fitzwilliam reassured, enclosing her in his arms, but one quick glance at the heavily bandaged man made him wonder.

The door to the room opened and ICU nurse approached them. "I'm sorry, but you will have to leave now. It's time for the doctor to examine him," she explained. "He will probably administer something to make him sleep. He needs rest and time."

Fitzwilliam gathered Elizabeth while David and Cecilia helped Georgiana. Once they'd returned to the waiting room, they began to discuss the evening's plans.

"They want one of us to stay by his bedside twenty-four/seven. We'll do it in six hour shifts. I'll volunteer for the first shift. Mary Beth, will you take the second?" Robert asked.

"Yes, I will. I brought along some of his favorite works—Solzhenitsyn and Tolstoy. I'll read to him."

"I'll take the midnight shift," Elizabeth said, "and I'll pick up and read where you leave off."

"Elizabeth, do you think that wise, considering your condition?" Fitzwilliam asked.

"Fitzwilliam, I have to. Night is always the most critical time. I must be with him. You don't understand. We are very close. All through our childhood, we were inseparable. I can't let him be alone during the night. If he should die, I want to be with him."

"All right, but I insist on being close by."

A little more conversation and the schedules were arranged with Georgiana, Jane, Kat, and Daniel all agreeing on their turns.

When Elizabeth's turn came, a cot was brought in for her and placed beside Joseph's bed. Fitzwilliam was given a bedroom close by, in case his wife should need him.

As Elizabeth read and kept watch, Joseph drifted in and out of consciousness, talking most of the night. He would call for Lizzy as he relived their childhood experiences, laughing as he spoke. She set the book aside and moved closer to reassure him that she was there, but he paid no mind to her words. Instead, he continued drifting to another time, another place.

He began talking to Butler and Bailey. He issued orders to his men as they closed in on Saddam Hussein. He discussed strategy for tracking Zarqawi, but when he mentioned Georgiana Darcy, Elizabeth's ears perked up. She listened intently as Joseph replayed conversations between himself and Georgiana. Elizabeth heard his declaration of love for her sister-in-law, and from what she heard Joseph say, it appeared he knew Georgiana returned his love. She smiled and released a breath.

Suddenly, Joseph's mood darkened and his expression became intense. He was once again somewhere in the heat of battle. Joseph was yelling orders. Elizabeth became alarmed when her brother began screaming. "*Bailey...*

BAILEY...Noooooooooo!"

The scream was so loud that the nurse outside the glass wall heard it. She collided with Elizabeth as she rushed into the room with a sedative which she quickly plunged into his IV. Within minutes, Joseph calmed and drifted back into a peaceful sleep.

"Mrs. Darcy, are you all right? Can I get you anything?"

Visibly shaken, Elizabeth was crying and trembling when Fitzwilliam made it to her side. "Yes, bring us some water, please." Fitzwilliam told the worried nurse.

When the nurse returned with a pitcher of ice water and two glasses, Fitzwilliam asked her to fill the glasses and leave the pitcher on the bedside cabinet.

"Shush…Elizabeth… Shh…it's all right, my love…it's all right."

She continued to sob as she talked through her tears. "Fitzwilliam, it was awful…awful. He told me what happened that day. Oh, he doesn't know he told me, but he told me…He *told* me."

"Shh, Elizabeth, shush. Have some water, and you can tell me all about it."

"Yes, thank you." She nodded.

He gently helped her to the sofa where they both sat and drank the water while Elizabeth told him everything. As he silently listened, Fitzwilliam held her in his arms, rubbing her back and spreading gentle kisses in her hair. When she finally drifted off to sleep, he kept watch through the night, holding his very pregnant wife, staring at a still man who hung somewhere between life and death.

Joseph awoke from heavy sedation one week after entering the hospital. Immediately upon awakening, he questioned his family about Butler's welfare, appearing relieved when they assured him his fellow Marine would recover. However, Joseph never inquired after Bailey.

Not long after waking, depression set in. Concerned for his well being, each family member read to him in hopes of cheering him and keeping him company. When it came time for Joseph to leave the hospital, Elizabeth wanted him to come to England to recover and rest, but military regulations required that he return to a military hospital in the U.S. Being close to her due date, she knew she could not accompany him back to the States, so it was decided that Georgiana would accompany Joseph to Fort Sam Houston in San Antonio, Texas.

Chapter Eighty-six

...Life goes on like it always has...

Two Months Later

Sitting on his hospital bed at Brooke Army Medical Center, Joseph reflected on his life, and in particular, the most recent events. His body had healed, and in a few days, he would be released to return home.

Home, he thought. He was a broken man, and he knew it. His left arm was disfigured and would require many surgeries and months of physical therapy to recover any usefulness. He rose from the edge of the bed and ambled to the bathroom. While washing his hands, he looked in the mirror and turned his head, gazing at the left side of his face. Thick scars cut across his cheek and down the side of his neck. His eye was scarred over and almost swollen shut. *Grotesque...mutilated...ugly!* He angrily dried his hands and tossed the paper towel into the trash. Returning to his room, he took a seat.

Georgiana would arrive in fifteen minutes. He sighed. All morning he'd thought of her... of them and their future together—or rather, if they should have one at all. He loved her. That he did not doubt, and he knew she loved him too, or she would not be here. But what did he have to offer her now? He was broken in both body and spirit, and he would not be a charity case. His pride forbade it. She outranked him in both wealth and social standing. Could he really ask her to be a farmer's wife, married to a man permanently disfigured? No, for her own good, he needed to let her go.

Entering his room minutes later, Georgiana wore a bright yellow dress and was as cheerful as ever. "Joseph, it's such a beautiful day. I can't believe how warm San Antonio is for January," she said with a bright smile. "I called Elizabeth last night, and she told me they have snow at Pemberley. Fitzwilliam finally had his deer shooting party. Everyone was there. Next year, we'll be there, too."

Joseph only smiled. *...No, Georgiana, we won't be there next year or any year.*

She smiled back at him. "Since it's such a warm, pretty sort of day, why don't we walk out into the courtyard? It's very lovely."

He nodded and reached for her hand. Now would be as good a time as any to tell her. Once outside, they strolled along the garden paths in relative silence. She had tried to strike up a conversation numerous times, but he remained silent. Her bubbly enthusiasm was beginning to grate on his nerves, for he felt none of it. It irritated him. All he wanted was to be left alone in his misery, but he had to tell her. He would be as gentle as he could, using what little semblance of manners and respectability he had left.

"Georgiana, I am much better now. You can return home anytime, you know."

Her crestfallen expression gave evidence to the wound he knew he'd inflicted, but he continued. "I will be going back to Longbourn soon."

With a swell of emotion, she asked, "Joseph, do you want me to go?"

"Why would you want to stay?" he asked without emotion.

"Oh stop it! You know very well why I want to stay. I thought you loved me."

His jaw clenched. "Georgiana, I was a whole man then. This is what I am now!" he cried bitterly as he turned to face her.

"Joseph Bennett! You stop feeling sorry for yourself this very instant. I won't have it. Love doesn't change because looks or circumstances change," she hotly lashed back.

His anger, mingled with humiliation, rose. "I have nothing to offer you. I was going to be a career military officer when I went to Annapolis. I had hopes of making it to general, and then I accepted that *damned* assignment. It wasn't long until I wanted nothing more to do with a military career. I was to resign my commission when my initial service obligation was completed …and then I thought maybe…That is until…until this!" he said, holding his left arm up slightly and turning the left side of his face to her.

"Don't you understand that I don't care? You are still the same person, and we don't lack for money. You can go back to school and find some other career," she pleaded through teary eyes.

"I will **not** take your money," he replied fiercely.

"Then don't. I happen to know from Elizabeth that you have thirty million dollars. Don't you think that's enough for us?"

"It's nothing to what you are used to. I can't give you the life of luxury that you are accustomed to."

"Why do you think that matters? I can be happy with more or less, and what you have to offer me is certainly *not* less," she argued. "Unless…are you telling me that you don't love me anymore?" Her lower lip trembled as her voice shook with the next question. "That you no longer want to marry me?"

She waited, but there was no answer forthcoming.

"Well?"

Still, no answer.

"Joseph, I at least deserve an answer." She choked back a sob, tears threatening to fall.

Inhaling deeply, he finally responded. "Georgiana, I have nothing to offer you. Why do you want a man with so many problems? A *broken* man!"

"Because I love you!" Her voice cracked. "I know life is not easy and that you have a lot to overcome, but will you not at least allow me share your burdens?"

"Georgiana, have you really thought this through? Have you considered what you would be giving up to marry me, especially with the way things are now? I'm not going to be a career military officer. There won't be any prestige or glory. All I can offer you is a simple life as a farmer's wife. I do plan to return to school to complete a PhD. in electrical engineering, and then I will teach in the fall and winter like my father did. That's the life I will lead. Could you be satisfied with that?" he asked.

"Joseph, if I've learnt anything over the last few years, it's that there are more important things in life than money and possessions. How much does one need? I can tell you that if you can't spend your life with the person you love, then the rest is worthless. I can learn to be a farmer's wife. I love you. Isn't that enough?" she asked with a glimmer of hope sounding in her voice.

He released a long sigh, and then looked at her tenderly. Was it her declaration of love, her refusal to leave, or his own unwillingness to be without her that had changed his mind? He didn't know. Perhaps it was all three. If she could love him with all of his problems, then he couldn't let her go, not when he wanted her, not when he needed her.

"You know I never officially asked you, but… I guess we both knew I meant to. If you can put up with me, then…well…let me formally ask you. Georgiana Darcy, I love you. Will you marry me?" he said with a slight smile.

"Joseph Bennett!" she cried, "I think I will." Her tears streaked her cheeks.

He reached down to kiss her chastely, but she grabbed him, pulling him into a deeper, loving kiss, and being a man in love, he deepened the kiss, pulling her into a tight embrace with his one good arm.

He held her close. "Georgiana, this will not be easy. You do know that, don't you? I have a lot of bad memories. I did my job, and that's all I can say about it. It will take years and my faith in God to get past the faces of the men I killed," he said. "They were just men like Butler, Bailey, and me—some of them very young. And then there is the memory of Butler and Bailey. I will never forget what I saw that day. Bailey—he threw himself on that grenade. Why'd he do it?"

Joseph broke down and cried, the tears slowly trickling down his cheeks. Georgiana held him while he washed his soul in tears.

"I know this is hard, and I have no words of understanding to speak to you. I have never experienced anything like what you have, but I do know you must not look back. Joseph, you were doing your job, and I know…I know freedom isn't free. It comes at a price, but the things that are of the past are *in* the past. We must live on and look to the future," she softly said.

"You're right. I know that. It's just that nothing has turned out like I had thought it would. When I went to the Naval Academy, I had stars in my eyes. I was going to serve my country. I was going to make a difference. Even though I knew men died in war, I don't think I fully understood it, and it's quite another thing to take a man's life with your own hands," he said, staring off into the distance.

Returning his gaze to Georgiana, he continued. "There is one other thing I must tell you. You will not live in the luxury you are used to, but it's not so bad either. The farm has a good income, and I do have hired help. My aunt and uncle live at Longbourn with Grace, our housekeeper. I want them to continue there. They kept the farm going while I was gone. I owe them that much."

"Of course, they shall stay. Your aunt can teach me all that I need to know about farm life. I plan to finish my master's degree, and then I want to teach music, perhaps at the local university. With a master's degree, I think they will take me." She smiled up at Joseph.

"Yes, I'm sure they will. So, do you wish for us to wait to marry until you have finished?"

"I don't know, but I do know I want to complete my education. I can do it in a year's time, if I work hard. Do you think you can wait for me? I can fly to see you often, or you can come to London. We could still marry. I don't mind the separation, if you don't. It's just a year, and I would be with you for the Christmas holiday, but I will need to attend in the summer in order to graduate in a year's time."

"I want you to pursue your dream. We can wait. I want you to be sure this is what you want," he said as he turned to look her in the eye.

"It is what I want, and a year will pass quickly, especially if we see each other every chance we get. And whilst I'm away studying, you can continue with your physical therapy and rehabilitation. You will grow strong again. This will not defeat you. Together we're going to make it."

He smiled and bent down and kissed her again, pulling her close. Breaking the kiss, they turned and walked back into the hospital. The arrangements for his discharge and the return to Longbourn were made. General Haines spoke with the Pentagon for a special assignment and promotion to major, but Bennett's resolve was firm. He was leaving the Corps and one bad dream behind. Joseph knew he had done his duty, but at what price?

With their plans made, Joseph returned home as Master of Longbourn, and

Georgiana returned to London for the summer semester in the master's degree program at the Royal Academy of Music. He was grateful that there were men like General Haines, but as he looked closely at the General's life, he saw the high price the man had paid for duty, honor, and country. The General was a tough, rugged individual who barely knew his wife and children. After much reflection, Joseph knew he was making the right choice. A chest full of medals and the GI Bill along with the glory and prestige were not worth the cost.

Joseph went about his duties, preparing for the spring planting and keeping a close watch on the newly birthed calves. Another bobcat was heard in the area, and the red wolf had migrated out of the national park onto the plateau, creating a potential problem. Pork bellies were down in the Futures Market but the prices of corn, wheat, and barley were up. He had two hundred head of cattle to sell by the first of June, and before summer's end, he would order another stone plaque to accompany the one his brothers-in-law had placed at Longbourn Baptist Church Cemetery. The circle would soon be complete in triplet, and all was peaceful as the crickets chirped in the night and the future looked bright as life carried on like it always had in the Cumberland Plateau.

The End

Cumberland Falls Kentucky

Tennessee Farm Lands

U.S. Special Forces in the Mountains of Afghanistan

Bennett, Bailey, and Butler

Joseph and Georgiana

Derbyshire, England

Derbyshire, England

Resources

Wikipedia, Charleston, South Carolina

Wikipedia, Battle of Fort Sumter

Wikipedia, John C. Calhoun

Wikipedia, British Petroleum

Wikipedia, Saint Helena Island, South Carolina

Clyde Bresee, How Grand a Flame – A Chronicle of a Plantation Family 1813-1947, Algonquin 1992

Clement Eaton, A History of the Old South, (Prospect Heights, Ill.: Waveland Press, 1975), P. 230.

Jane Austen, Pride and Prejudice, 1813

Ben Silver of Charleston, South Carolina, Our Products, http://www.bensilver.com/fs_storefront.asp?pagegroup=about

Mr. Jesse W. Curlee, President Supima, http://www.fibre2fashion.com/face2face/supima-cotton/jesse-curlee-interview.asp

Thomas B. Chaplin, Tombee: Portrait of a Cotton Planter, Quill William Morrow, New York, 1986

The Rice Paper, internet publication, June 2004, http://www.carolinagolricefoundation.org/page7/newsletter/files/jun-2004.html

The Carolina Gold Rice Foundation
http://www.carolinagoldricefoundation.org/page5/page5.html

Historical Landscapes, http://historiclandscape.org/Low%20Country.htm

Christopher C. Boyle, Collapse of the Georgetown Rice Culture,
http://www.ego.net/us/sc/myr/history/decline.htm

Judith A. Carney, Black Rice: The African Origins of Rice Cultivation in
the Americas. Harvard University Press; New Ed edition (March 1, 2002)

South Carolina Educational TV,
http://www.itv.scetv.org/schistory/chapter17.pdf

History of Pima and ELS cotton, Joseph McGowan,
http://www.supimacotton.org/About/content.cfm?ItemNumber=593&snIte
mNumber=538

http://www.us-civilwar.com/sumter.htm

The Cotton Factorage System of the Southern States
Alfred Holt Stone
The American Historical Review, Vol. 20, No. 3 (Apr., 1915), pp. 557-565
doi:10.2307/1835857
This article consists of 9 page(s)

The Decline of Cotton Factorage after the Civil War
Harold D. Woodman
The American Historical Review, Vol. 71, No. 4 (Jul., 1966), pp. 1219-
1236
doi:10.2307/1848585
This article consists of 18 page(s).

Author's Notes

The Cumberland Plateau is a work of fiction first begun on the forum *A Happier Alternative* in March of 2007. It has undergone three drafts over a two year period to become the story it is today. The second draft was completed in July of 2008, and the final draft, the novel as it appears today, was completed in May of 2009. Any resemblance to works began or published after March 2007 are coincidental and should not be confused with this work.

Photographs throughout the novel

All photographs, except the following, were taken by the author, including those in the Lawton Family Cemetery on James Island, South Carolina.

©iStockphoto.co White Dove internal picture 01-08-08
©iStockphoto.co Baby Girl photo 05-04-07 © Tari Faris
©iStockphoto.co Field of Cotton photo 04-10-08 © David Sucsy
©iStockphoto.co Pineapple Fountain photo 07-17-06 © Alexander Fox
©iStockphoto.co Happy Bride & Marine Groom photo 08-26-08 © Lorna Piche
©iStockphoto.co peak district landscape with fields and dry stone walls 06-30-08 © David Hughes

D'Arcy Coat of Arms purchased from Family Crest online

Purchase order from iStockphoto **VTJC3ACD5887, VXJC3F438FFD**

🖉 Mule and troop movement
🖉 Bennett, Bailey, and Butler

🖉 Symbol indicates this work is in the public domain in the United States of America because it is a work of the United States Federal Government under the terms of Title 17, Chapter 1, Section 105 of the U.S. Code

Read on for a Preview

Of

Dana Darcy

Released 07 29 2010

Prologue

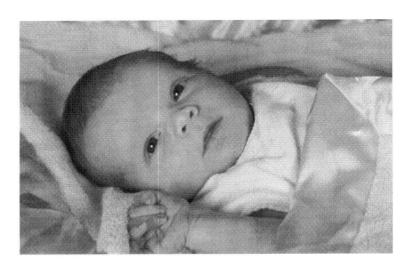

St. Thomas Hospital

London, England

It was the twenty-fifth of December, and outside the weather was cold and bitter, but inside it was warm and comfortable while a woman lay resting in a hospital maternity ward. As was the custom for this time of year, the room was decorated with festive adornments that twinkled and sparkled, and a tree stood in the corner laden with lights and colorful glass balls. The mood should have been bright in keeping with the season and the birth of a child, but that was not to be the case. After a long, difficult night of hard labor, the woman was still and somber. Except for the child she'd just given birth to, the woman was alone.

With a faint smile, the woman turned to the door as a ward sister stepped through with a little bundle wrapped in pink. Approaching the bed where the woman lay, the sister peeled back the blanket to reveal the crumpled face of a contented sleeping child.

"You have a beautiful daughter, miss. Look at this head of dark hair and those lusciously long lashes. And to be sure, I've never seen such indigo blue eyes. Why they're as blue as the bounteous ocean, and look at these slender, elegantly long fingers. She'll be the darling of her father. I'm sure of it." The nurse laughed a jolly round as she handed the bundle to the mother.

The woman took the child and laid her to her breast. On instinct, the child grunted and rooted until she began to suckle. "Yes, she is beautiful…just as beautiful as her father is handsome," said the mother.

"Well, I daresay, if he looks anything like this little daring, he's a handsome bloke indeed. Now, what should we call her? A little girl like this one needs a distinguished name. Shall it be Rebecca or Sarah, Margaret or maybe Anne, or how about Caroline or Diana? What shall it be, miss?"

"No, none of that will do for her. She is to be… Dana…Dana *Darcy* Hamilton," the mother replied as she gazed upon her suckling child.

~*~

While the child suckled her mother's breast, a being in white stood by. She held a lone red rose in her hand. As the young woman closed her eyes in sleep, the being laid the rose on the side table next to the young woman's bed and took flight; for now her vigil was complete…complete until...***Dana Darcy***.

About the Author

Mary Baxley was born in Brooklyn, New York in 1954, but spent her young formative years with her parents on her grandfather's farm in Falls Mill, Tennessee. She attended Tennessee Technological University in the heart of the Cumberland Plateau, earning a BS degree in Computer Science. Upon graduation, she worked in the aero space industry for four years before leaving her career to care for her growing family.

She currently resides in Huntsville, Alabama with her husband and three of their five children. Her daughter and third son attend the University of Alabama in Huntsville while her oldest son is serving as a Major in the U.S. Marine Corps, having completed three tours of duty in Iraq, one as a battery commander. Her second son also serves his country in the U.S. Marine Corps.

She enjoys gardening, reading, cooking, needlework and sewing. She has completed many personal designs in children's clothing, and though she lives in the city, she has often said she was more at home in the woods with a good book and a hound as her companion. She is a self described genteel classical lady from rural Tennessee.

Photo taken at Falls Mill, Tennessee, Autumn 2008